Gunty's War
By
Michael Levenson
ISBN:978-1-8382223-1-4

Published By: -

i 2 i
PUBLISHING

i2i Publishing. Manchester.
www.i2ipublishing.co.uk

In memory of my brother, Warrant Officer (Pilot) Steven Austin Levenson, who gave his life for King and Country on 17th September 1942.

Acknowledgements

My first thanks must go to Lionel Ross, the owner and publisher at i2ipublishing.co.uk, who supported the project from the outset. His feedback upon reading the initial draft chapters was positive enough to give me the confidence to attempt to turn a simple idea into a book. His sage counsel was invaluable throughout the process.

I must also express sincere thanks to my editor, Mark Cripps for helping turn this first-time author's manuscript into a fully-fledged book. A first-class editor, his patient and calm approach was perfect in helping me to fine-tune Gunty's story. I greatly appreciate his foresight and continuous encouragement.

Thanks, are also due to Dino Caruana for patiently listening to my ideas and feedback, before coming up with an excellent cover design.

My thanks also to my wife Janet and my immediate family for their support and tolerance through the writing of this book.

Finally, thanks to Lindsay Townsend, my granddaughter who has achieved her master's degree in film studies. She will be the next generation of film historians.

Prologue

Helmuth, my driver had navigated our car through the traffic of the main thoroughfare running through the Wilhelmplatz in central Berlin. We had entered the driveway of the Ministry of Propaganda, joining a line of cars waiting to disembark their passengers at the front entrance to an imposing building. Whilst we were moving forward, I had time to study my surroundings, especially the building ahead of me, which for some time, had been known as the Leopold Palace. Built in 1737, it had been the home of kings and princes, but had now become the official residence of the Third Reich's Dr Joseph Goebbels who had been appointed officially as Minister of Propaganda by Chancellor Adolph Hitler in 1933. Goebbels oversaw the press, cinema industry, radio and all the other arts. At the same time as he held this office of state, he had also retained his role as Gauleiter of Berlin. In the previous two years, he had successfully eliminated the communist power base in the city as well as crushing all political opposition to the National Socialist Party.

Since the death of President Hindenburg in 1934, Hitler had tightened his grip on Germany. Not only had he remained Chancellor, but he had outmanoeuvred his cabinet colleagues by having the Reichstag vote him into the vacant office of president, thereby, at a stroke, granting himself the full powers of a dictator. At the same time, he had gained the full support of the German military establishment and the industrialists. Hitler immediately requested that the armed forces take a personal oath of allegiance to him, allowing him the opportunity to eliminate all opposition to him and his National Socialist government.

Once Germany had become a one-party state, it wasn't long before Hitler assumed the full powers of a dictatorship, at the same time, revealing the true face of National Socialism. To the shock of many liberal minded Germans, one of the early pieces of legislation to be implemented were the infamous Nuremberg Laws, which relegated German Jews to the status of non-persons, effectively outlawing them from practising in education and medicine, as well as preventing them from belonging to any other professional body. They were also forbidden to own or partake in large business enterprises. Running parallel with those government decrees, Hitler then created a national security police force under the leadership of his two faithful disciples, Hermann Goering and Heinrich Himmler who very quickly stifled any freedom of movement or free speech amongst the people. How could all this happen so swiftly to a civilised country like Germany? A nation that had produced such great men as Goethe, Schiller, Beethoven and Thomas Mann? The answer to that question possibly lay in Germany's defeat after the First World War and the political unrest that followed. The negative impact of both these events was not helped by the great financial crash of Wall Street in 1929, which allowed a fringe party of crackpots led by Adolf Hitler to seduce an electorate, weak because of massive unemployment and humiliated by the harsh terms imposed by the victorious Allies after the war. Never was democracy surrendered so easily.

As my car inched its way slowly to the front entrance of the Leopold Palace, I wondered why I could even bother to be here, knowing how humiliated my wife Marlene and I felt. The occasion for all this pomp was the Reich Minister's Annual Artists' Ball, which all the most important figures from the various arts were required to attend, hence my invitation. Through a mixture of good luck and hard work, I had become an internationally known film actor both in Germany and the United States during the silent period of the cinema and despite my slight accent, I had survived the arrival of the talkies. I had made the decision that whilst the transition between silent and sound was taking place, I would leave the United States and seek out good quality scripts both in Britain and Germany. My train of thought was interrupted when finally, my car reached the front entrance of the palace. My eyes took in the cast iron eagles and the giant red velvet banners, upon which sat a giant black swastika encompassed by white circles, that were hanging down across the front of the building and were bathed in the glow of several searchlights, allowing the front of the palace to be lit up in all its glory.

A liveried footman opened the passenger door for me and as I stepped out of my car, I found myself joining other guests who were gradually filtering through the front doors. Despite the barrage of flashbulbs from the news photographers, I was finally able to reach the entrance.

Yet another footman greeted me with, "Good evening, sir," and as he took my invitation card, he went on to say, "Cloakrooms to your left, sir. The main gardens are straight ahead and the grand salon is at the top of the stairs." Having deposited my hat and coat at the cloak room after a short queue, I decided to move upstairs to the salon. During the process of greeting several people that I knew, I gradually climbed the grand staircase and when I was about halfway up, I found myself alongside Wilhelm Furtwangler, the great German orchestral conductor. As we exchanged greetings, I had to admit I was slightly perplexed to see him attend this social gathering, for he was publicly well known for his anti-Nazi opinions. This could be a very dangerous path to travel for not only was he the conductor of the Berlin Philharmonic Orchestra, but he was also revered throughout the world of music as one of Germany's greatest living musicians. His prestige was immensely valuable to the Nazi party which is probably why Hitler and Goebbels allowed him such a long leash. As we neared the top of the grand staircase, I had an impulse to ask him a personal question and the opportunity arose when we finally reached the first floor.

It so happened that the entrance to the salon was blocked by guests waiting to be announced by the major domo and this pause gave me the opportunity to pull him to one side by his elbow and ask him directly, "Wilhelm, forgive me, but for many months now, I have been intrigued by your association with the National Socialist government. Knowing both your private and public opinion of the Nazis and your personal courage, I wonder what brings you here to mingle with so many of them at a very public event such as this?"

"That's a quite easy question to answer, Gunther. I suppose it's what you might call a 'Mexican stand-off'. You see, whilst I remain in Germany and appear to support Hitler and his gang publicly, it suits their purpose to turn a blind eye to my protection of those musicians in the Philharmonic Orchestra who are Jewish and who, without my intervention, would automatically lose their positions. Forgive me Gunther, if I too, become personal and turn the question right back at you. Knowing that you are married to a Jewish girl, which in this glorious Third Reich of ours, is strictly forbidden, why would you wish to continue living here whilst your wife is so publicly humiliated? You are in the same position as me, in so far as you have chosen a dangerous path to follow in Berlin these days. I rather suspect that you are going to need a very long spoon to sip with these racists if you think you can have your cake and eat it! May I give you some advice, Gunther? Leave Germany as soon as you can before it is too late. You may not realise it, but you are, in fact, placing both yourself and Marlene in grave danger. Goebbels is a rabid anti-Semite and he will not tolerate your flaunting of the Nuremberg Laws for much longer before he loses patience and destroys you both. Has it even crossed your mind that the very act of us talking together is being noted by the dreaded Gestapo? I don't suppose it has, so I suggest that we part company now in the hope that one day, we will meet again in happier circumstances. Meanwhile, let's go and greet Hitler's ringmaster and become part of this dreadful circus!' With that, he turned on his heel and headed for the entrance to the grand salon.

After smoking a much-needed cigarette, I joined a group of guests at the main entrance who were waiting to be announced to the welcoming committee, which comprised the host, Reich Minister, Joseph Goebbels and his strikingly attractive wife, Magda. The minister was of medium height and slightly built, with hollow eyes, sunken cheekbones and a thin mouth. His hair was also slicked back. He gave one the impression that overall, he was not a man to be trifled with. He did have one disadvantage in that nature had inflicted a club foot upon him which he took a great deal of trouble to hide, particularly when being photographed. I also noted on this occasion that he had forsaken his usual party uniform of brown jacket and black trousers for a white dinner jacket, not only because of the glamorous occasion but also, no doubt, to impress the ladies as he had a reputation for being a womaniser amongst the Nazi elite. He was also considered one of the more intelligent and fanatical National Socialists of the Nazi hierarchy and apart from the Gauleiter of Franconia, Julius Streicher, who also happened to be the publisher of the obscene and anti-Semitic newspaper *Der Stürmer*, the most virulent of Jew haters. At that moment, my thoughts were interrupted by the major domo announcing my name and as I stepped forward, I found myself standing in front of the Reich Minister, shaking his extended hand and staring into his cold grey-brown eyes.

"Welcome, Herr Conrad. I am so glad that we have finally had the opportunity to meet. I have been a great admirer of your talent as an actor and indeed, both Frau Goebbels and I enjoyed immensely the film *Congress Dances* (a Reich film that set the gold standard for the German film industry in the early thirties, both in production values and the high standard of the German artists appearing in it). Personally, I think that there is no doubt that you are one of the standard bearers of German film culture within the Third Reich and that recently, you have been sadly underused. I think it is time that we correct that situation and officially meet at the ministry, so that we can discuss your future place in the Reich film industry."

Even as I was thanking him for his kind comments and remarking how I was looking forward to a future meeting, his attention was already focused on the next guest and I found myself standing in front of Magda Goebbels. I bowed and kissed her hand, murmuring the usual pleasantries and whilst looking up at her, I was struck by her Nordic beauty and at the same time, sensed her calculating persona. Her previous husband had been Gunther Quandt, a director and major shareholder of the car manufacturing company, BMW, and having divorced him, she had married Goebbels, bringing with her, an impressive divorce settlement. It was no secret that Hitler was very fond of her, even to the extent that when Hermann Goering, the second most powerful man in Germany, had married the actress Emmy Sonneman (Hitler had been best man), Magda Goebbels was still considered the First Lady of the Third Reich.

As I was about to take my leave of her, she held my arm and whispered, "You cannot be unaware, Herr Conrad, that you are the number one pin-up amongst German maidens and that you represent, in the Führer's eyes, the perfect species of German manhood. My husband is determined that you take your rightful place within the Third Reich film industry and has great plans for you. I would think very carefully on any generous proposals that he may make and above all, don't treat them lightly."

I gave her a charming smile and assured her that I certainly would treat any proposals that I received from the Reich Minister very seriously, but even as I turned away, I knew that my freedom of choice was narrowing and that very soon, I would have to make a final decision to my future.

As I left the line and moved further into the salon, I took a glass of champagne from a hovering waiter and briefly took in the scene before me. The salon was large with French windows that led out to a long balcony which I gradually made my way to, whilst all the while, exchanging pleasantries and greetings with other guests.

Eventually, on reaching the balcony and whilst sipping champagne and inhaling from my cigarette, I was able to take in the scene below me. It was a panoramic view of a very large garden, lit by Chinese lanterns with a lake as a centrepiece upon which, a floating platform was situated. There was an eight-piece band playing popular tunes of the time and around the lake, was a dance area populated by a dozen or more couples dancing to the rhythm of the music. To the right of the lake was a large multicoloured marquee which I assumed was a focal point for refreshment as I could clearly see guests moving in and out with food and drink. I spent some time standing there, taking in the scene and recognising many people that I had either worked with or knew as friends.

For example, I spied Marita Rokk, a very popular singer and actress, flirting outrageously with two male companions and moving my eyes further to the right, I caught sight of dear Hennie Porten, with whom I had starred in the silent film *The Mistress and her Servant* in 1925. Quite what she was doing attending tonight's ball, I did not know, as she had been a popular actress and highly regarded by the German public before 1933 but had fallen out with the Nazis for having a Jewish husband and for refusing to divorce him. Unlike her contemporary, Marlene Dietrich, who on the success of her role in *The Blue Angel* (one of the first German sound films of 1930), had left Germany for America before the National Socialists had come to power. Poor Hennie had left it too late and now that her film career was cut off, she was reduced to surviving on what little work that she could get. That example alone only fortified my belief of how fragile life could be within the Third Reich, if the individual didn't conform to the state's doctrine.

One had only to look around to see how many of Germany's talented artists had fled into exile or were conspicuous by their absence. The list seemed endless and included Franz Waxman, a prominent German composer, who had fled to America and was now composing music for the cinema in Hollywood. Elsewhere in Berlin, persecution was now so rife that there wasn't a month that went by without another exit from Germany by a talented writer, scientist or actor. The list of actors was growing monthly including Lottie Palfi, Ludwig Stossel, Conrad Veidt and Peter Lorre and these were only a few of the many that had now fled from persecution.

As I stood there, once again, lost in thought, I felt a light touch on my shoulder and turned to behold a tall, statuesque woman standing there before me, smiling radiantly. I recognised her immediately as a dear friend of mine by the name of Leni Riefenstahl, who I had known for many years when she had been a successful film actress, particularly in the genre of films about mountain climbing which were very popular in both Germany and Austria. However, it was in the field of directing that she had achieved international recognition, after having completed a documentary based on the rise of National Socialism titled, *Triumph of the Will*, a piece of propaganda portraying Hitler as the saviour of the German nation. I had to admit that it was a master class in film making, so it came as no surprise when she became one of Hitler's favourite directors. Now, despite strong opposition from Dr Goebbels, whom she had displeased by rejecting his advances, she had received Hitler's patronage to produce and direct, with all the resources of the state, a film of the forthcoming Olympic Games to be held in Berlin next year.

Leni flung her arms around me in an embrace shouting out, "Gunty! Where have you been? You naughty boy. It's been months since you've been seen around town. Most of us were beginning to get concerned about you and you will pardon me for saying so, but you do look a little peaky, darling. Come on, let's find a table and you can fill me in on what's been happening."

As we moved off together towards the table area, a good-looking man, fashionably dressed in a white dinner jacket, came striding up and I recognised him as Louis Trenker, a leading German cinema actor who had been Leni's co-star in several of her films. His greeting towards me was friendly but distant, an attitude I experienced all too frequently these days from people I had known.

"Louis, darling," Leni purred at him, "Would you mind terribly giving Gunther and I a few minutes together? It's been ages since I last saw him and I would like to spend some chat-up time with him."

Louis had agreed, saying that he had just noticed Emile Jannings, a great star of the silent period in America and somebody that I had worked with and knew quite well. He had fallen victim to the advent of sound because his voice was too guttural for American ears and because of that, he had returned to his native Germany to continue his career.

"I shall just wander over and say hello to him," Louis said, "No doubt he will keep me talking for ages about how the Führer regards him as the Third Reich's leading actor." With that, he was gone. I followed Leni through the throng of guests, occasionally giving and receiving greetings, sometimes even stopping to speak briefly to people we both knew. Eventually, we found an unoccupied table and sat down.

"So how has life been treating you, darling?" Leni asked, "Many of your friends have been genuinely concerned for your well-being. Nobody has heard or seen anything of you for the past six months. Have either you or Marlene been ill? Or are you under any political pressure? I know things can't be too easy for you, as you are married to a Jewess. I know things must be difficult. So many people I know these days, are tainted by the stigma of interrelated marriage. But don't be downhearted. These are the early years of National Socialism and many of us have had to adjust. Personally, I have been lucky, Gunty. Thanks to Dr Goebbels' influence, as you know, I was given the assignment of making a documentary about the Nuremberg rally and as you are also aware, it was received favourably both in Germany and worldwide for my positive portrayal of the Fuhrer and the rally itself. I know that there have been rumours about a relationship between myself and Dr Goebbels but right at this very moment, I will tell you the truth. Soon after completing the film, Dr Goebbels came on strong with me but unfortunately, I didn't fancy him and rejected his advances. From that moment on, he has never forgiven me and has made life difficult for me. Fortunately, the Führer took me under his protection because of my film work for the party and, despite Goebbels' objections, insisted that officially, I direct next year's Olympic Games in Berlin. You see, what I am trying to say, is that problems have a way of sorting themselves out. Not only that but a problem shared is a problem halved, so, don't forget, if I can help in any way, please don't hesitate to ask me."

"Thank you, Leni. I appreciate your support, for I realise that true friends are difficult to find in times like these. Confidentially, I have just signed a contract with the Gainsborough Film Company in Britain for a film scheduled to commence filming in January, but to complicate things, I have been informed tonight that Dr Goebbels would like to meet with me in the near future to discuss my place in the German film industry. The outcome of that meeting, I feel, will determine my future."

Leaning forward close to me, Leni spoke softly, "Please be careful, Gunty. Goebbels has great power over our lives. When you do meet, try and reach a compromise with him or else he will destroy you. Colleagues that I have known for a long time have been denied work and have either gone abroad or disappeared into labour camps. Try and be sensible, for despite all this political upheaval, I believe Germany needs the Führer's strong hand to restore the nation to its former glory and to wipe out the humiliation of the Versailles Treaty, thereby, dealing firmly with the threat of communism. Once he has achieved this, the violence will cease and the Nuremberg Laws will be amended allowing more freedom to the Jews."

"You do make it sound so simple, Leni and I do agree with you that all this racial nonsense may hopefully, blow over, and that democracy will be restored once Germany takes its rightful place in world affairs. However, at this moment in time, we are living in a dictatorship. All political parties have been abolished and their leaders have either fled the country, been imprisoned or killed. Also, there is racial and religious intolerance backed by the full force of the law. The question is: will Hitler surrender these ill-gotten gains and restore some form of democracy? I have my doubts, for I believe that there is a darker side to both Hitler and National Socialism that the German nation is not aware of."

"Not so loud, Gunty. Someone will hear you," interjected Leni. "This is the last place you should air your views. You think far too much. Just do the right thing and look after number one and enjoy the rewards. Honestly, Gunty, you must guard your tongue more. Not only for your own sake but for Marlene's as well. Promise me that you will behave yourself. After tonight, I don't know when our paths will cross again in the immediate future. Both of us may have busy schedules in front of us, so because of that, I would like you to grant me two favours."

"Okay, Leni. I'll do my best", I answered smiling, "but before I commit myself, tell me what the favours are."

"The first one", Leni said, taking both my hands and looking straight into my eyes, "is to keep any plans that you make for your future close to your chest and confide in as few people as possible. That way, fewer people will get hurt, least of all yourself and Marlene. The second favour is, that the band is just striking up Cole Porter's *You're the Tops* which I absolutely adore. The song fits the moment perfectly and I can't think of a better description of the man that I would like to dance it with. Do you accept my request, Gunther Conrad?"

"I grant the first favour willingly, Leni," I replied, as I stood up laughing and pulled her chair away from the table. "The second favour, I grant with love, for as you have already sensed, who knows when our paths will cross again." Though it was crowded, we managed to navigate around the dance floor without colliding with anybody and it was also an opportunity to exchange greetings with friends and acquaintances. However, once again, I sensed that people were more effusive towards Leni and there was a distinct coolness in their attitude towards me, a strange and unsettling feeling, but also rather sinister.

Once the dance was over, we decided to walk back to the table. It appeared Louis had arrived there before us and was in an animated conversation with two men. I immediately recognised from newspaper photographs the shorter of the two as being Hans Frank, Hitler's lawyer and the man responsible for promulgating the Nuremberg Laws, which effectively stripped Jews of all their civil liberties. However, Leni, sensing my antagonism, gripped my hand firmly and pulled me into their midst and as Louis introduced the two men to me, I had a chance to study them both. Hans Frank was of solid build with heavy features and from what I gathered of his reputation, was known as an aggressive legal manipulator without any moral scruples.

I had quickly realised, some time ago, that there were two categories of the Nazi leadership dominating Germany: one was made up of intellectual theorists and self-seeking opportunists; and the second was made up of ex-street fighters, thugs and criminals who carried out the physical implementation of the intellectuals' ideas on the defenceless population. Hans Frank obviously belonged to the former. However, the second man, who was introduced to me as Reinhardt Heydrich, had all the classic signs of a more deadly species, physically tall and slim with Satanic good looks. His smile reminded me of a jackal's and his eyes were cold and penetrating. I understood from his introduction that he was attached to the office of the Head of the Gestapo, Heinrich Himmler, as a member of his personal staff and therefore, an important cog in the internal security police. One of the benefits of being famous was that at first meeting, people intended to be in awe of your celebrity. Such was the case here and not only that, it helped me being in the company of Leni who was not only a glamorous star but was also a favourite of Adolph Hitler. Consequently, the conversation was mainly directed at Leni by a gushing Hans Frank centring on the forthcoming Olympic Games and what a great honour it was for her to have the Fuhrer's patronage. Whilst only half listening to this sycophancy going on, I took the opportunity to further study the features of Heydrich: his body language irradiated menace and stillness, which reminded me of a reptile patiently waiting for his prey.

This was brought home to me very sharply when as we started to take leave, he said directly to me, "I wish you, continuing great success with your career, Herr Conrad. I often feel a certain amount of sympathy for celebrities. It must be exhausting to maintain such a perfect image especially within their private lives, where for example, if you went against public opinion it could affect your future. Not that I am suggesting in any way that you are in that position, for I am sure that you are far too wise a man to fall into that trap." It wasn't what he said but how he said it that left me feeling vulnerable.

As we drifted away towards the marquee, both Leni and Louis Trenker, sensing my mood, had tried to jolly me along, but I was in no mood for it. After an hour of reminiscing, I decided that I had enough. It was time for me to leave. I shook Louis by the hand and kissed Leni on both cheeks and despite her protestations for me to remain, I said adieu to her. It occurred to me as I was walking away from them, that it could be an awfully long time before I saw either one of them again or that in all probability, it would be in circumstances entirely different from now.

After I had collected my hat and coat, I wandered out to the front porch to await my car and realised, in this fleeting moment, how vulnerable I had become. For despite my high profile as a public celebrity, I had become isolated and placed in quarantine by the state until I had seen the error of my ways. Though it was still reasonably early, there were quite a few other guests waiting for their transport. Amongst them, I recognised a group of men consisting of Hans Albers, a popular German entertainer and a professional friend of mine, Viet Harlan, the film director and Ernst Correll, the production head of U.F.A, the major German film studio. There was a rumour circulating that Correll was having problems with Dr Joseph Goebbels and that he was becoming increasingly isolated because of them. As I was about to make a move to join them, I heard a voice behind me calling me by name. As I turned, a gentleman had come up on me with a hand extended in greeting. He was of strong physique and in looks, not unlike the American film actor, Pat O'Brien. He certainly got to the point.

"Good evening, Herr Conrad. I am so glad that I been able to catch you before you left. My name is Carl Hanke and I work at the Ministry of Propaganda as Dr Goebbels' private secretary. I wonder if you could spare me a few minutes of your time?"

"Of course, Herr Hanke," I answered, whilst at the same time giving him the once over. He was, as I thought, a well-built man with handsome features and like all the high-ranking Nazis, had that air of power and arrogance that came when there was no opposition to challenge them. His voice suddenly interrupted my train of thought.

"Dr Goebbels is anxious to see you and wonders if you could arrange to meet him next Monday at eleven o'clock in the morning at the ministry. He wishes to offer you his apologies for the short notification and fully understands if you are unable to keep the appointment but unfortunately, he will be out of the country in the near future on an official visit to Italy. He would like you to know that he is very anxious to discuss various projects he has in mind for you and one of them, I believe, is the upcoming Berlin Film Festival, which he is anxious for you to participate in."

Cutting him off short, I quickly replied, "Of course, Herr Hanke. I'll only be so happy to attend. Please inform the minister that I look forward to our meeting. You must forgive me for leaving you so quickly as my car is just leaving the motor pool now. Please convey to the minister that I am only too anxious to enhance the prestige of the German film industry and will cooperate in any way that I can. I hope to see you next Monday, but now, I'm afraid until then, I must bid you farewell."

With that, I turned on my heel and walked towards my waiting car. Helmuth, having seen me, had already jumped out and opened the rear passenger door. As I slid into the back seat, the thought crossed my mind that I may have been a little abrupt with Herr Hanke, but I had become determined now not to give an inch to these bastards.

"You can take me home now, Helmuth. I have had enough of tonight. Incidentally, how was your evening? Did all you drivers get fed?"

"We did indeed, sir. The kitchen supplied us with sandwiches plus some leftover pastries and very tasty they were, sir."

"Well, Helmuth, if you're still hungry by the time we get back to the house, pop into the kitchen and help yourself to some food. As a matter of interest, is there any new gossip doing the rounds tonight?"

"The main buzz around, sir, is that it appears the Minister of Propaganda has fallen seriously in love with the actress, Lida Barova and that Frau Goebbels is so angry that she has gone straight to the Fuhrer, who, so the grapevine goes, is none too happy about the affair."

"You would think, Helmuth," I answered, "that after spending so many years in Hollywood, I would know better than to be addicted to such gossip. However, take my advice, Helmuth, not only keep this conversation between us but be very careful who you may talk to in the future, for you may not know you are offending! And by the way, whilst I remember, I need you to drive me to the Ministry of Propaganda on Monday morning. I must be there by eleven o'clock, but apart from that I will not be needing you over the weekend, so take the time off. Now, Helmuth, do one thing for me, just drive me home slowly with the radio on low, so that I can relax and be alone with my thoughts.

Chapter 1

Poverty Row

I would like to think that it was more than coincidental that as I closed my eyes and found myself travelling back down memory lane, the car radio was playing the opening bars of an immensely popular song of the moment. Sung by my boyhood friend, Hans Baistock, the song was titled *Auf der Reeperbahn nachts um halb eins*, which, in its own way, was a homage to the city of Hamburg and St Pauli. It was coincidental, insofar as Hamburg had been the city of my birth during the early years of the twentieth century. I was born into a middle-class family, the only child of Edmund and Lucy Conrad. My father had been a reasonably successful investment broker and I was the product of his second marriage, to my mother Lucy. When I was born, he was twenty-five years older than my mother. She was thirty years-of-age at that time and my entry into this world had been a difficult labour for her, resulting in me being delivered by forceps and my mother requiring a hysterectomy. Consequently, I was brought up by parents who were beginning to become set in their ways and were unable to connect with their son. The toys they gave me were more suitable for boys six or seven years older than I was and to make matters worse, I very seldom had any choice in selecting them.

By the time I had reached the age of seven, I was sent off to boarding school where I was able to enjoy a reasonably normal childhood despite bullying from other pupils and receiving the occasional hiding from a sadistic teacher who enjoyed prowling the dormitory at night to try and catch any boy talking after lights out. I climbed trees and made friends as part of a gang. In general, those first four years I spent at school set in place the foundation for the rest of my life, giving me the necessary sense of discipline and independence that would be so important to my dealing with the adversities in my future years. It was also during that time, that the talent for performing began to emerge from within me, awoken, I would imagine, by my first foray onto the boards in the school's Christmas play, in which I took the part of Mrs Cratchit in Charles Dickens' *A Christmas Carol,* even though I was dressed up as a woman! My performance was greeted with cheers and applause from the school and visiting parents and it was from that occasion that I learnt the first lesson of the theatre: an actor is only as good as his last performance. Still in a state of euphoria, I decided to put on my own production of a dazzling show of sketches and comedy for the enjoyment of the entire school. I would have liked to have said that it had ended as a brilliant night, but unfortunately, it didn't, as our poor audience quickly became disenchanted with a self-indulgent cast serving them up a plate of overripe ham, accompanied by much scene hugging by yours truly. They eventually expressed their ire through having to sit through this potpourri of pretentious rubbish by giving us a slow hand clap, thereby forcing us to lower the curtain to retire from the stage in utter embarrassment. Not bad for a ten-year-old! I did, however, learn another valuable lesson that night as a fledgling actor: never underestimate the intelligence of your audience.

I suppose if my life had been left as it seemed destined to be, I would have ended up completing my education at some university, but that was not to be. Several months later, after the fiasco of putting on a show, I was collected by the matron from my dormitory where I was getting ready for bed and taken by up to her dispensary, where having sat me down, she proceeded to tell me that my father had died that morning. After expressing some words of sympathy, she then returned me to my dormitory, where the boys had been forewarned. Instead of the usual hustle and bustle of bedtime, there was an eerie silence and with every boy already in bed, it wasn't long before the light was put out and I was left to grieve on my own. The bond between father and son had not been particularly strong in my case, for my father, being as old as he was, had never been able to connect with the boy of my age. Perhaps things would have improved as I grew older, who knows. There was one thing for certain. As I lay sobbing into my pillow that night, unbeknown to me, the life that I had known, had come to an end and a new chapter would begin in the morning.

That weekend, my mother came to visit me and took me out for the day. It was to be then, at the early age of ten that I became the de facto head of the family. The death of my father had not only turned my mother into a grieving widow but had also turned into a rudderless ship. She had taken me back to the local inn where she was staying and over lunch, had attempted to tell me of the circumstances of my father's death. As she attempted to explain to me what had occurred, the discourse had become very emotional and fragmented and from what I was able to understand, apparently, he had got into severe financial problems, with the result that he had been declared bankrupt by his creditors. In turn, through the stress and worry that this situation had brought upon him, he suffered a massive heart attack. Within a week, he was dead.

In the course of attempting to explain all this to me, it proved too much for my poor mother, who collapsed into floods of tears and only with the help of two female members of staff, was I able to get her up to her room where eventually, she calmed down and continued to explain the events that had occurred. When she had finished speaking, she opened her handbag, from which she pulled out a bundle of money. She proceeded to spread it on the bed. I think it came to a total of five hundred marks which I believe was all we had between us and the workhouse! I also learnt that although I would be returning to school that day I would be leaving permanently at the end of term in a few weeks' time. That would, my mother hoped, give her sufficient time in which to obtain a live-in job that would both support us and provide us with a roof over our heads. My initial reaction to this information was one of joy, as it would mean no more going back to school. If only I had the benefit of hindsight at such an early age to realise that this change would mark the end of any formal education I would ever receive. Also, I didn't realise it at the time, that the repercussions that would follow as a result of my late father's financial misfortunes, would mean that to put it bluntly, poverty was about to descend on my mother and I with a capital 'P'.

As I said goodbye to my boyhood friends, I departed school with my case and tuck box and set out on the road of life accompanied by my mother, who would, in the next few years, endeavour to help me in the process of growing up. I would certainly become older than my years. Additionally, the first and only piece of good fortune that occurred, although I didn't realise it at the time, was confirmation of the first of many positions my mother was to take up, as a live-in housekeeper to an English family by the name of Robinson-Crew, with the head of the family being a professor of English at the University of Heidelberg. During the four months that my mother worked for the professor, I learnt the English language. It appeared that I had an aptitude for languages and thanks to the tuition of the professor's wife, plus living in an English household, I became very fluent, even if I may say so myself. Also, it did not take me long to realise that my mother could not get along with people and that sooner or later, she would up-sticks and leave. That would remain a pattern for the next sixteen months until even my mother realised that she wasn't cut out to live with other people. Matters finally came to a head after the fifth employment, when she left in high dudgeon after having a series of disagreements with her employer. She whisked both of us off to Baden–Baden for a week by the sea. Even I had reservations about this move. By now, I had realised that money and my mother did not make a good partnership and sure enough, before the week was over, we had become seriously short of funds. When situations got out of control, my mother usually panicked, and this was to be no exception. Not having enough funds to remain at the boarding house, we duly found ourselves on the streets with nowhere to go. It was at that moment that I grew extremely fast in reaching maturity far beyond my years and in the process, sacrificed the natural process of growing up in my teen years. I realised then that it was just my mother and myself against the world and that if we were to survive, it would not be as mother and son but as a team, united in a bond of survival.

"Okay, Mum," I said, as I reached for her hand, "There's a café across the road. Whilst we are there, we can plan what to do next." Although the café was busy, we found a table and having placed our order, we started to explore options, which I must say weren't many, considering our lack of money.

"You know mum, why don't we just find a little place of our own to live in. You have tried live-in housekeeper jobs and they haven't proved very successful. Apart from anything else, most of the people you have worked for regard me as unnecessary baggage and something to hold over your head. Might it not be better for you to get an ordinary daytime job and be independent?"

Upon hearing the suggestion, mother briefly brightened up but soon became dejected as she started speaking, "How long do you think it will take to find a job and an apartment, Gunty? And what do you think we're going to live on whilst I am looking? Don't forget, we will also need a deposit for a flat, paid a month in advance. Just tell me where the money is coming from for that?"

''Could we not go and stay with grandma?'' I suggested. ''Perhaps she could lend you some money and you could pay her back once you have found a job?'' My mother replied, ''I don't think that idea would work. Your grandma and I don't exactly see eye-to-eye at the moment. She and your late grandfather have never really forgiven me for having married your father who they both thought, was far too old for me as well as the fact that I was his second marriage.''

''I think, Mum, that you should swallow your pride and phone gran and ask for her help. We could stay with her whilst you found a flat and a job.''

I suppose it is only the young that have the temporary ability of eternal optimism, for when I look back on that moment in time, I realise now, how distraught my mother must have been. One moment, she had a comfortable life with everything you could wish for and the next, nothing, with only the clothes that she stood up in and a young son to look after. The bitterness that she obviously felt towards my father for leaving her in such a terrible situation was already beginning to envelop her personality, leaving her very suspicious of those around her. These personality traits were to become more dominant as the years went by until eventually, it was best for her if she lived on her own.

Meanwhile, my optimism acted as a buffer between her and the outside world and in no time at all, we left the café in search of a post office, where mum phoned my gran. When my mum had finished her call, I could see, as she left the phone booth, that she had been crying, a harbinger of bad news, I thought. But in fact, it proved the opposite. It was only after that she had paid the phone attendant for the call that she told me that grandma had agreed to take us in for a short time until mum had got back on her feet. As grandma lived in Frankfurt, we went straight to the railway station, all the while keeping my fingers crossed, that we would have sufficient money to pay for the train fare. Fortunately, we did and after waiting nearly an hour, our train pulled in.

The journey itself was a long one and we didn't arrive in Frankfurt until mid-afternoon and even then, we had to wait for a bus take us to a place called Seckbach, which was situated just outside the city. This was only my second visit to my grandmother's and so it was with some anticipation that I stepped off the bus and followed my mother around the corner into a road called Seaview Avenue which had about a dozen bungalows all standing neatly in a row overlooking farmland. My mother stopped at number two and opening the gates, proceeded up the pathway to the front door and rang the bell which was promptly opened by an elderly lady with grey hair, tied back in a bun. She was of slim appearance and despite her advancing years, was physically, somewhat petite and as she embraced my mother, I noticed that she was wearing an old-fashioned long skirt down to her ankles with a white blouse and matching tunic. As she hugged me, I could not help but notice the smell of lavender on her clothes. Turning to my mother, she explained, "So, Lucy, this is Gunther, my Grandson, I presume? Hasn't he grown since last time I saw him? Come on inside then, you both look very tired after your long journey. The first thing you'll need is a nice cup of tea and a freshen up."

The inside of the bungalow consisted of four rooms separated by a passageway, with two bedrooms on the right-hand side and two rooms consisting of one front parlour and the second a back parlour leading into a kitchen on the left. It didn't take me long to settle in and after having deposited my case in the spare bedroom, I joined my mother in the back parlour, where my grandmother had prepared supper and when I entered, she was filling a large teapot up with hot water. The last time that I had seen my grandma was as a toddler when my mother had visited both her and my grandfather. The only recollection I had of him, was of a tall and severe-looking man with a big moustache and by the photographs hanging on the walls, a soldier, who had served in the Kaiser's army in various African campaigns. Judging from the few pieces of conversation that I had overheard between my father and mother, whilst my grandfather had been alive, he had been disappointed by my grandmother giving birth to my mother when he really wanted a son. Also, of course, he didn't approve of my mother marrying a divorcee considerably older than herself.

I am afraid it did not take more than two weeks for the fragile peace between my mother and grandmother to break down although fortunately, it was long enough for my mother to acquire a position as a nursing orderly in the local hospital and to rent a one room flat with a communal bathroom and toilet. My grandmother had lent my mother the first month's rent and security deposit and quickly, mother had packed the pair of us up and departed. It took me many years later to realise that whilst in my adolescence, what I had taken to be normal but sometimes embarrassing behaviour of my mother, was really, in effect, hiding a few psychiatric problems, such as poor self-worth, paranoia and possessiveness. The sad thing about it all was that though she wasn't a danger to her fellow being in any shape or form, she gradually became her own worst enemy as she aged. For me, at the tender age of twelve years old, she was my mum and as far as I was concerned, could do no wrong. We stood together against the outside world and our aim was to just survive the endless poverty. Unfortunately, it all came to an end once I reached manhood when her possessiveness overcame her and destroyed our relationship.

My years between the ages of twelve and sixteen were not only lonely, with my mother having to do shift work including nights, but also, we would run out of money by mid-week, thereby ensuring that we went without gas to cook or food to eat. I very quickly acquired the skills for survival such as raising money. For example, mother had somehow hung on to a spare blanket which we never used and every Tuesday, without fail, I would take it around to the local Jewish pawnbroker who gradually became my guardian angel. Sensing my circumstances, he would always advance me a few pfennigs even though the blanket was worthless to him. I shall never forget him until the day I die.

He would stand at the counter looking at me over his glasses as I entered the shop carrying the blanket and every single time, he would shrug his shoulders and say, "Oy vey, not again", but he would always give me a little bit more and whilst ruffling my hair, he would say, "See you again on Friday, Liebling."

That money ensured that my mother came home from work to be greeted by a few extra items of food on the table and money for the gas meter. Until I reached the age of fourteen, my life was just one long odyssey of loneliness and the only good things to come out of it was my voracious appetite for reading at the local library and my fascination with the latest wonder of the world, namely, moving pictures.

It had originally started as a novelty in amusement arcades when strips of film were shown in machines which enabled customers to view them and in no time at all, quickly transferred into theatres, where patrons were able to watch a series of short films projected onto a screen. These establishments very quickly became known as Kinemas, places that I began to frequent more and more as they became not only a magical escape route from the harsh realities of life but became my fountain of knowledge of the outside world. Sitting alone in the dark, I became acquainted with the Russian Czar, the German Kaiser, and the Emperor of Austria, France Joseph, plus I travelled the world meeting American cowboys and ducking in my seat as huge American locomotives thundered towards me through the screen. As well as all those experiences, I gradually began through the medium of the screen to become a pupil in the school of life. Watching the screen actors, I soon learnt how to conduct myself in society with all the social graces that accompanied it, especially on how to smoke a cigarette, an act which fascinated me. As films grew from one reel to three and even four to satisfy the huge demand from the public's growing appetite, coupled with my increasing dependency on the cinema to escape the misery of my daily life, also awakened within me the desire to become an actor.

Often to escape the confines of our one room flat, I would go for long walks whilst acting out film roles for myself, in my mind, particularly in playing the villain, a character which I found most exciting. Naturally, going to the cinema on a daily basis had become an expensive but necessary habit for me and to feed it, I wasn't above doing a little shoplifting, concentrating on small items such as ornate paperweights which could be hidden in my trousers to avoid detection and once away from the confines of the store would soon make my way to the nearest pawnbrokers, not the one, I may add, that I used on a regular basis for the blanket, but one that would not easily identify me. Without a doubt, had I carried on with that way of life, I would have been caught and who knows where my life's journey would have ended up.

Happily, at the tender age of fourteen, I was able to supplement our meagre weekly income. I got a job as a probationer projectionist at a local theatre going by the name of the Aeon Cinema or otherwise known locally as the 'fleapit'. Though I worked long hours, twelve o'clock midday until ten thirty in the evening, with half a day off a week, I was in heaven. Not only did I get to watch the movies for free, but I also got paid for it as well. During food breaks, I would eat a sandwich sitting at the back of the auditorium constantly watching the same movies as I sat beneath the flickering lights which were beaming out from the projection booth just above, out onto the silver screen at the other end of the auditorium. In its own way, it was an opportunity for me to attend my own masterclass in screen technique. Before long, I was able to recognise the different, individual styles between directors, the cameraman and above all, the emerging cult of the star actor. It was at that moment in my young life that I decided that I would become an actor.

What better place to start than to audition at the local music and drama academy in the hope of obtaining a scholarship. Once again, I rushed in where angels fear to tread and after paying my audition fee, duly attended the audition at the appointed time. Oh, dear me! I very quickly realised that I was heading for a disaster, for while we waited to be called onstage to perform our individual pieces, all the candidates were herded into a small room to await their call. It was while sitting there that I realised how smart and fashionable dressed everybody was whilst I was wearing my mother's cast-off raincoat to cover a worn and torn pair of trousers. By the time I was called, I was already feeling very inferior but worse was to come. As I stood centre-stage, a voice came out of the darkness of the auditorium asking me for my name.

"Good morning, Gunther. I am your head adjudicator this morning. Could you tell us a little bit about the piece that you will be doing for us?"

"Yes, sir. I would like to recite 'The quality of mercy is not strained', from William Shakespeare's *The Merchant of Venice*."

"Just as a matter of interest, Gunther, do you by any chance have a drama teacher and if so, what is her name?" the voice from the darkness asked.

"No, sir," I replied. "I'm afraid I've never been able to afford one."

"You do realise," the voice of doom said from the darkness, "You have chosen Portia's monologue from Act IV Scene 1 and that she happens to be the main female character in the play."

"I am sorry. I suppose I didn't really give that a lot of thought," I stared back into the darkness. Also, by now, I had sensed that there were at least four people sitting out there, if not more, for to add insult to injury, I could hear the subdued bursts of laughter. By now, what little confidence that I had left, had completely evaporated. But worse was to come, for out of the darkness, once again, that voice of doom descended upon me like the oracle from hell.

"Gunther, would you please remove your raincoat. We feel that it may restrict your gestures and inhibit your audition."

That for me was the final blow. For in the act of removing my raincoat, I would expose my shabby trousers, with the holes in the knees, to the full glare of the auditorium, leaving me utterly embarrassed and mortified. Once more, that disembodied voice wrapped its tentacles around my body completely and in the process destroyed what little dignity I had left.

"We are ready for you now, Gunther. Please start."

"*The quality of mercy is not strained, it droppeth as the gentle rain, upon the place beneath.*" I started but at that point, I forgot my lines and dried up, leaving me standing there like a rabbit in the headlights, metaphorically speaking. The executioner's axe hovered over me as the voice of doom commanded me.

"Could you please start again, Gunther and this time, please annunciate a little louder so that we may hear you." I never got to finish my audition piece, thank the Lord, for by this time I was a complete wreck and the voice, sensing my acute discomfort, decided to put an end to my misery.

"Sorry to interrupt you, Gunther but I think we have heard enough to deliver our appraisal. Would you come down and join us, please."

By the time I had left the stage and started to move up the auditorium, my eyes had become acclimatised to the dim lighting so that I was able to locate the four adjudicators, consisting of three men and one woman and I very quickly joined them. It did not take long for them to confirm that which I already knew. Quite simply, I was under rehearsed and appeared to be completely ignorant of any basic knowledge of stagecraft. Furthermore, judging from what they had seen, perhaps I should seriously consider another career or at the very least, if determined to follow an acting career, I should find myself a drama teacher. They ended by saying that I would be officially notified by letter as to the findings of the adjudicators. As I stumbled out of the darkness of the theatre and into the daylight, I went through a series of emotional aerial acrobatics. Despite reaching the depths of humiliation and embarrassment, I was very angry with myself and vowed that I would never ever be in that situation again. As for the judges' prediction that I would never make an actor, all I could say to that was, come hell or high water, I would prove them wrong.

By the time I had reached the age of sixteen, the world as I had known it, was changing irrevocably. Not that I was either aware of it at the time or contributing in any way to it. Both my country and the Austrian empire locked horns with Russia over the assassination of the Austrian Archduke Ferdinand in the Serbian town of Sarajevo, an event which only succeeded in dragging both Britain and France into the dispute, the results of which found the European nations at war with each other, a situation which so far, did not appear to have benefited any country involved in the conflict. Three years of war had not improved the way in which my mother and I lived. In fact, it was the opposite. The British and French had mounted a successful naval blockade against my country, resulting in the severe shortage of essential food supplies for the civilian population. Consequently, in the winter months of 1917, my mother and I, alongside our fellow countrymen, were existing on such delicacies as beetroot soup whilst huddled in front of a small open fire, fed by any small pieces of wood that I had scavenged. I also learnt from the conversations that I occasionally overheard, that there was an air of discontent creeping in against the Kaiser and his generals, particularly with regard to the mounting waste of German lives lost on the battlefields in a series of military offensives which never appeared to achieve anything. It did not help that America had now entered the war against us Germans and Austrians, thereby sewing the first signs of defeatism amongst the population.

I had left my job as a cinema projectionist, for one as a shoe salesman. It was a change in jobs that I carried out with great reluctance for I had swapped a world of make-believe which I had thoroughly enjoyed and also got paid for, for a mundane job working in a shoe shop. The reason for my decision was simple. The hours were long in the picture business and entailed working most evenings, giving me no opportunity to pursue my ambition to be an actor. I had discovered the local amateur dramatic society, who had been willing to accept me as a member but as its activities revolved around the evenings, it became necessary to change my working habits. Of course, my mother was delighted at my decision, indicating to her, a rise in the social pecking order of society. I never fully understood her reasoning, for we were just as poor as before. In fact, we were worse off financially, with my wages being slightly less than when I worked as projectionist. Fortunately for me, I had made the right decision.

I took to amateur dramatics like a duck to water and in my youthful enthusiasm, began to learn the rudiments of stagecraft and management, especially as a stagehand and it wasn't long before I became a dab hand at painting scenery, moving stage furniture around, learning the rudiments of stage lighting and even occasionally, filling in as a prompter for the cast. Eventually, I gravitated to walk on parts which required no lines and then, in time, to small acting roles. The company at that time had a female director by the name of Henrietta Gautmann, who was a formidable presence and who was both physically and mentally overpowering. She must have sensed a small spark of talent within me that needed nurturing for she took me under her wing, something for which I will be eternally grateful. It was under her tutelage that I began to understand stage movement, voice projection and intonation plus, I also began to collect a catalogue in my head of facial expression, commonly known in the film business as reaction shots. This was because the camera tended to concentrate on the eyes whereas on stage, the whole face was required to be totally expressive. I soon learnt not to overact, for my first attempts whilst rehearsing, were too often met with titters of laughter from my fellow players, followed by the booming voice of Henrietta calling out from the stalls.

"A little less ham, Gunther, darling! You are supposed to be an actor not a butcher. Remember, less is more!" Very soon, I became accepted as a peer amongst my fellow amateur thespians, and soon, it became second nature for me to enter and exit the stage and to learn instinctively how to milk a line that would draw a strong emotional reaction from the audience, such as, laughter or sadness. I also became addicted to the feeling of elation, one experienced by all actors at the end of each performances curtain call and I felt very much, part of a troupe, when as part of the cast, I lined up in front of the footlights to receive the audience's applause of appreciation. Though I was still growing, I had emotionally matured beyond my years and I was beginning to develop a sense of who I was to be. In other words, my childhood was over.

Chapter 2

An Actor's Life for Me

I could not have been in a better place than a dramatic society to learn about the facts of life. Apart from anything else, my attitude towards girls was changing. I began to experience deeper emotions towards them than I had experienced before and what was more exciting, they too, were showing a greater interest in me! It was all rather like being a kid in charge of a sweet shop. For a short period of time, it was a joyous period for me, despite my feelings of inferiority due to my impoverished circumstances. For a young man of my age, I appeared to have the best of both worlds, for whilst I was chasing young ladies in the desire that they would lose their virginity to me, the older female members of this society, whether married or not, would be busy pursuing me for mine. My life seemed to become a series of acts from a French farce with myself playing the central character, forever one step ahead of either irate husbands, fathers or my own possessive mother who certainly didn't approve of just any girl getting their hooks into me. Eventually, I received my comeuppance. I had been riding for a fall for some time. These romantic escapades that I had been indulging in had not only distracted me in the pursuit of my ambition to be an actor but had also changed me into a shallow character who fancied himself at the age of sixteen as the cock of the walk and one who tried to act like it.

That all changed one evening. At that moment, I was involved in a romantic fling with a young lady called Anna, who happened to be one of the company's youngest players. There was no doubt that she reciprocated my passion, wherever the circumstances allowed, we took every opportunity to indulge in some intimate time together, usually in the costume department. On that night, the majority, of the drama society had assembled to audition for parts in a forthcoming production of the playwright Gerhart Hauptmann, titled *The Weavers*. This was a play about the rights of workers, in this instance, the Weavers Guild and the struggle for recognition from their oppressive employers.

Just as Henrietta was about to begin casting the parts, there was a loud bang as the doors to the hall were flung open and a young man older than myself came charging through heading straight for me while shouting, "Come here, you little shit. Been sniffing around my girl, Anna, have you? Well, I'm about to give you the bloody hiding of your life."

Oh no you're not, I said to myself as I dodged the first punch coming my way. As he fell over his own feet, I raced off around the hall with him behind me, scattering chairs right, left and centre.

"Stop and face me like a man so that I can give you a good hiding!" he spluttered, out of breath. The last thing I wanted to do was to stand there allowing him the opportunity to hit me. By now, I had jumped onto the stage and was holding the chair ready to fend him off whilst I tried to explain to him in the nervous high-pitched voice, "I hope I haven't offended you, but Anna and I have only formed a platonic friendship."

"I'll give you bloody platonic friendship when I get hold of you," he roared, as he tried to climb onto the stage. "Stand still, you pansy, so I can kick your arse from here to eternity."

Having no desire for my backside to receive any such punishment, I proceeded to fling the chair at him and took off to the back of the stage and jumped down, only to see him racing towards me, whereupon I jumped back on to the stage and headed for the proscenium. Having climbed onto the stage, he wasn't far behind me but with some agility, I jumped off and headed for my fellow players. Most of the females were in a state of panic, with Anna leading them all in a display of hysteria of equal proportion. Having manoeuvred myself into a safe position behind them all, three male members of the group were able to restrain my rampaging would-be assailant, who by now, was completely out of breath and very red in the face.

Peering from around the figure of a large lady, I shouted out at him, "I am very sorry that I don't know your name, sir, but please accept my apologies if I have offended you in any way. I certainly have no desire to steal the affections of your intended."

"Do-do-don't you call me sir," he blurted out, still struggling for breath. "Trying to steal a soldier's girl whilst he was away at the front fighting the Kaiser's war, were you? Come to think of it, why aren't you in uniform? You're big enough and ugly enough or are you just shirking your duty you little sh-sh-shit," and with that, he took hold of Anna's arm while shouting at her, "I'm taking you home to your parents right now, young lady and you can forget about coming back here with this lot. As for you, Gunther Conrad, if I ever see you anywhere near her again, I shall rip your head off and stick it up your arse."

With that, he was gone, dragging Anna behind him, leaving me not only mortified but feeling about one foot tall. My fellow players were not exactly impressed by what had occurred and with an air of collective disapproval settling over my head, I gamely stuck out the rest of the evening. As for poor Anna, our paths never crossed again but I do hope from a position of being not only older but wiser that she had gone on to have a happy life.

Anna's boyfriend's last words to me had hit home, leaving me feeling guilty. After spending a restless night deciding what to do, I had made the decision to join up. The following day, during my lunch break and full of remorse, I went to enlist at my local army recruitment centre. However, much to my chagrin, the army refused to accept me as I still wasn't old enough. They told me that I should report back when I was eighteen years old. That deferment probably saved me from the possibility of either being wounded or killed, for as it turned out, Germany and her allies surrendered in August 1918, a month before my seventeenth birthday.

For those last remaining months before the armistice, I remained in a rut, leading a humdrum existence with only my ambition to be an actor to drive me on. It was at this moment that the first piece of good fortune in my life occurred. One evening, arriving early at the drama club, I discovered only Henrietta Gautmann and her husband, Irwin. It was then, whilst he was painting some flats for the scenery, that Henrietta motioned me to sit with her.

The thought went through my head that she was going to get rid of me but instead, looking at me through her glasses, she started to speak, "You know, Gunther, I have been watching you over the last few months, as you have grown in confidence as an actor, which in turn, appears to have brought out your natural and raw talent. If you are serious about becoming a professional actor, which you often tell us that you are, then you must seriously think about obtaining a drama scholarship where you will become professionally trained. As I have already said, in the past few months that I've been observing you, the potential that you are showing will not be realised if you remain an amateur. Without any doubt at all, I can see a great future for you. You plainly have the quality which makes great actors and which also, is the main ingredient for obtaining roles, not forgetting of course, one other ingredient, which is getting the lucky breaks! Don't let my comments go to your head, Gunther, for you have a long road ahead to travel, filled with many disappointments before you could possibly achieve your goal. Don't be offended if I tell you that you must exert some self-discipline upon yourself and stop chasing all those stupid girls. Finally, don't be frightened to ask me for advice, for if I can help you in any way, I will be more than happy to do so."

"Thank you, Henrietta, for your unexpected comments," I said, plainly taken aback by her remarks but at the same time, pleased in the knowledge that there was somebody out there in the big wide world who was in my corner cheering me on. I continued.

"Thank you for your encouragement, but to be honest with you, I feel I could fall at the first hurdle."

"Why so, Gunther?"

"Because, I have already tried for a scholarship at the Frankfurt Academy of Music and Drama and due to my lack of preparation and naïveté, made a complete ass of myself, an experience, that I can assure you, I would never want to go through again. The truth is, Henrietta, I need a drama coach to help me through my audition but that requires money which I do not have. To pay for it, I would have to take on a second job in the evenings and by doing that, I would have no time to spend with the drama coach, so as you can plainly see, it all becomes a rather negative, vicious circle."

"I think I could help you there, Gunther. I would be happy to coach you for a couple of nights a week, which would still leave you a few evenings free for a second job. That would help you start up a savings account to finance the scholarship, in the event of you winning one. I wouldn't charge you for your tuition but in return, I would expect one hundred percent commitment from you. I certainly won't be easy on you, for I will be expecting only the best. I can tell you now, Gunther, if this is what you really want to do, it is going to mean a lot of hard work and sacrifices and disappointments along the way, but I believe in you and will try to help you all I can."

"I really don't know what to say to you, Henrietta, other than to thank you for your support and generosity. You are one of the few people in my life that has gone out of their way to help me."

"There is nothing for you to say, Gunther. My reward will be in your succeeding and to achieve that, I will work with you every step of the way. So, don't let me down."

From that moment on, Henrietta was true to her word, mercilessly working me hard, concentrating on my weaknesses, especially, my diction and delivery. At the end of several months, she helped me select what would be my audition piece. We had decided between us that I would perform Marc Antony's soliloquy from William Shakespeare's *Julius Caesar*. First, she made me go away and read the play properly and to analyse the character of Marc Antony. Later, after listening to me delivering yet another reading of the speech, she interrupted and proceeded to give me a lengthy critique of my performance.

"Remember what I have told you so often in the past, Gunther? One of the most important tools in an actor's box is imagination. Also, his ability to convey the ring of truth into his performance is critical, something which you have plenty of, but you are not using it now with this speech; you are merely declaiming. There is no far-off commitment and what is worse, you have made it boring. Putting it bluntly, use your imagination. You are a Roman politician standing on the steps of the Senate addressing the citizens of Rome. Your friend, Julius Caesar, has been assassinated and his bloodied body lies upon those same steps. Incidentally, it is this speech by Marc Antony that so clearly illustrates Shakespeare's brilliance as a playwright. For although Marc Antony appears to be justifying his friends, Brutus, Cassius and Casca in their assassination of Caesar, he is, in fact, condemning them as traitors. Gunther, I will see you again next week and meanwhile, study the play thoroughly again and bring me back the Marc Antony I both want to see and to hear."

I spent the next few days both studying and reciting the play at every opportunity, sometimes into the wee small hours of the morning. My poor mother, who accompanied me as a prompter, must have had the patience of a saint, for having heard it so many times being recited by me, would have ended up with Shakespeare coming out of her ears. It seems that Henrietta's advice and my hard work finally paid off, for when I re-enacted Marc Antony's speech to her a week later, I was as pleased as punch when she gave me an ovation at the end of my recital.

"Well done, Gunther! Now, I'm finally beginning to see your potential. But don't think for one moment that you can rest on your laurels. There is still plenty of work to do and your audition is only three weeks off. There are two faults that I noticed today, one of which is that you are waving your arms around as if you were a puppet on a string. Restrain yourself and minimise your gestures for greater emphasis. The other important criticism that I have to make is that you are mumbling. Stop it. Improve your diction and speak clearly and do make sure that the back row of the circle can hear you. Changing the subject slightly, I notice that you are only seeing me at the beginning of each week. Does that mean, perhaps, that you have got yourself a second job?"

"Yes, I have, Henrietta. I am working every weekend in the evenings at the Carousel beer hall as a waiter. The pay is lousy, but the tips are good and the job will be handy if I can manage to get a scholarship."

"What do you mean, Gunther, if you get a scholarship? Don't be so negative. I happen to think that you stand a very good chance and if you do become an actor, you must remember to be positive, for before you succeed, you will be knocked back many, many times, so you will have to learn to pick yourself up and start all over again. You have three weeks left before you've learnt to fly, so be prepared, for that is when you will be pushed out of the nest. By the way, on a more personal note, an actor should always look his best, it helps him exude confidence in himself. Because of your circumstances, I know how difficult it has been for you to exist, so please don't take offence at what I am about to say. Your clothes look very shabby, and because I've never seen you in anything different, I must assume that you haven't anything else to wear. What you need right now is a massive boost in confidence. Please go and buy yourself a completely new outfit which I …"

"I'm sorry to interrupt you, Henrietta but I have no money to spend on clothes; all the money that I earn goes just on existing."

"I was about to say, Gunther, that I would be happy to lend you the money and you could pay me back what little you could afford each week. Don't be embarrassed but look upon it as a gesture from somebody wishing to invest in your future."

Once again, Henrietta had proved to be my guardian angel. Her offer of a loan, so that I could buy some new clothes, had come at the right time. I hadn't really given it much thought before, simply because what you can't afford, you can't have. However, the manager of the shoe shop had begun to make some comments about my appearance and that I should try and smarten myself up before I started damaging the image of the store. Somehow, I got the impression that my job could be at risk and that had begun to play on my mind. Added to that worry was the memory of my first audition and the acute embarrassment that it had caused me.

The remaining weeks passed by quickly and before I knew it, I was soon standing upon the steps of the Frankfurt Academy of Music and Drama about to enter its doors for my second try at the scholarship. This time, I was more confident, as not only was I better prepared for my audition but with Henrietta's loan, I had purchased a new suit, shirt and tie, plus a pair of new shoes. For the first time since I could remember, I now felt able to face whatever life wanted to chuck at me. Once again, I found myself striding across the now familiar stage of the Academy Theatre, pausing briefly to hand some sheet music to a pianist sitting patiently stage left, before proceeding on my way to the footlights where, I came to a stop, to stare briefly out into the darkness of the theatre.

Again, as before, a voice came out of the darkness to enquire as to my name. Having told the voice, there was a pause before it addressed me again.

"Hello, Gunther, what audition pieces are you going to perform for us today?"

"I would like to perform Marc Antony's speech from Act III, Scene II of William Shakespeare's *Julius Caesar*, followed by a ballad titled *On the Streets of Hamburg after Midnight*."

"Okay, Gunther. When you are ready, please start and good luck."

I stood there for what seemed like ages, but it wasn't, it was only a matter of seconds, but in that time, I began to feel a surge of stage fright followed by anger that I could be beaten once again before I had even started. I took a deep breath and began, driven by the same emotions that Marc Antony must have also experienced when addressing the citizens of Rome. Already in my imagination, I was no longer at an all audition but on the steps of the Roman Senate.

''Friends, Romans, countrymen, lend me your ears, I have come to bury Caesar not to praise him ...'' Looking back at that moment, I realise now with the benefit of hindsight that there was the moment, when I truly started on my journey to become a professional actor. Every tool that Henrietta had taught me, I poured into that speech. In fact, I soared so high that by the time I had finished, I had come back to earth shaking. There was a momentary silence in the auditorium, then that bodiless voice boomed out from the darkened auditorium, ''Thank you, Gunther. Could you now perform your musical piece?''

Nervously signalling to the pianist, I waited while he went into the introduction. Then, I started. I certainly wasn't any great shakes as a singer, but with the help of Henrietta, I had trained myself to speak the song musically. After one false start, I managed to complete the piece in the style of a Boulevardier, without any further hitches and to be honest, I felt that I had handled it quite well.

After a short length of silence, the disembodied voice boomed out, ''Would you please come and join us, Gunther.''

Once again, with some trepidation, I made my way up the centre aisle where the three adjudicators were sitting and once I had sat myself down, the spokesman for the panel or whatever title he used, started speaking, ''I seem to remember, Gunther, am I right in thinking that you applied for a scholarship a few years back? If so, I must tell you that at that time, I had completely dismissed any idea of you ever amounting to anything as an actor. You were so unprepared, that I even doubted whether you had the ability to become a stagehand. However, your performance today has turned my opinion right on its head. Perhaps you could tell us what you have been doing during the last few years?''

''To be honest with you,'' I explained, ''I was so angry at being humiliated by that first experience, due entirely to my own fault, I may add, that I was determined to prove you all wrong. In my quest to do so, I joined the Mercury Theatre, a local amateur dramatic society, where I had the good fortune to be mentored by the fabulous director of the society.''

''That wasn't by any chance, Gunther, a lady by the name of Henrietta Gautmann? If so, you are truly fortunate, for she is a

years ago, have now become prominent directors. I am sure that you have come across their names at drama school. One is called Raphael Lowenfeld, who so happens to be the Artistic Director of the Schiller Theatre in Berlin and the other is Otto Falkenberg, who occupies a similar position at the Kammerspiele Theatre Company in Munich. I could certainly get in touch with them and put in a good word for you. Of course, it may take some time for either one of them to get back to you. So, you will just have to be patient. Would you like me to do that, Gunther?"

"Would I! You can bet your life I would, Henrietta. That could be the opportunity that I have been waiting for and it goes without saying that I would be eternally grateful to you."

"Don't get too carried away, Gunther. They may not even bother to reply to my letters and don't forget, there are still several weeks to go before you graduate. Just keep on surviving whilst you wait for a lucky break."

I am afraid it was, not weeks, but almost a year, before I got my first professional job and that was in a small part for the local radio station. I got a boost of confidence when they offered me another small part in the next production. Then out of the blue, arriving home one evening, there was a message waiting for me, asking me to phone Henrietta as soon as possible. I wasted no time in phoning her. I gave a sigh of relief when she answered me right away.

"Hello, Gunther. I'm glad that you received my message. I expect that you thought I'd given up on you. Well, you will be pleased to know that I have just received a letter from Otto Falkenberg, saying that he would like to see you at his office at the Kammerspiele Theatre in Munich next Wednesday morning at eleven o'clock. Don't get your hopes up too high. Otto is being constantly besieged by young hopefuls trying to get their foot in the door at the Kammerspiel, but for old time's sake and because I sang your praises so highly, he has made an exception and will grant you an interview. Don't go letting me down now. Not because I've stuck my neck out for you but because I believe that you have got it in you. Don't be overawed by the occasion, just be yourself and show him what you are made of. Good luck Gunther! And I expect to hear from you as soon as you return. By the way have you got enough money to cover your expenses?"

"I can't thank you enough Henrietta for getting me this opportunity and one thing you can be sure of is that I won't let you down. As to money, thank you for your kind thought but as it happens, I do have a little saved to cover my train fare and other small incidentals. As soon as I return, I will let you know how I've got on. I would also like you to know that I shall never forget how you have supported me and that one day, I will do you proud. I will say goodbye now and will see you soon."

I hadn't realised how great the distance was between Frankfurt and Munich and to keep my appointment with Otto Falkenberg, I would have to stay overnight and find the extra money for hotel accommodation. Fortunately, I discovered that there was a mail train stopping at Frankfurt at four o'clock in the morning and would arrive in Munich by ten o'clock the same day, which was perfect for me as I could catch up on some sleep on the train and at the same time, freshen up, leaving me an hour to get to the theatre to keep my appointment. On further investigation of the train schedules to plan my return journey, I was pleased to see that there was a train leaving Munich at four o'clock in the afternoon for Frankfurt which would have me arriving home by eleven o'clock in the evening. All in all, it seemed a small price to pay for what could turn out to be a great opportunity.

The journey went as planned, although I can't say that it was comfortable. However, I was able to snatch some sleep and there was also a toilet on board where I could freshen up. My biggest worry had been the weather, so I was pleased that on arrival at Munich, it was a dry morning with no sign of rain. Had it been otherwise, it could have been a disaster, for the last thing I wanted, was to turn up from our interview looking like a drowned rat. The first thing I noticed after stepping off the train and leaving the station was a bus park and after making enquiries as to how I could get to the Kammerspiel Theatre, I was directed to a bus that would take me to the Leopold Strasser in central Munich and from there, it was just a short walk to Schabing West where the theatre was located.

True to the instructions I received, I soon arrived outside the theatre and having time to spare, took a moment to study the playbills on display. Apart from the season of Shakespearean plays due to start the following week, the theatre seemed more inclined towards showcasing the current fad of modern playwrights with avant-garde leanings. Amongst them were two that I noticed on the playbills announcing future productions, namely George Kaiser's *Gas* and Berthold Brecht's *Baal*. Whether it was because I was so young, I'm not sure but what little I knew of avant-garde theatre failed to excite me; no plots to speak of and lots of monologues about social inequality. Oh well, perhaps this might be the opportunity to learn more about that type of play.

There was no activity whatsoever in the foyer and as I stood there amidst the silence, I called out several times, "Hello." Failing to produce any reaction, I decided to enter the stalls and momentarily, standing at the back, I was able to view a group of men sitting around a long table on the dimly lit stage. As their conversation was barely audible from where I was standing, I made my way slowly down the aisle to the orchestra pit. But before I reached it, I had been noticed by the group. The conversation ceased and one of the men, who had his back towards me, turned and with his arm languidly hanging over the back of the chair spoke directly to me.

"Well, young fella, are you looking for somebody?"

"As a matter of fact, I am." I replied. "Perhaps you can help me? I am looking for Mr Otto Frankenberg."

"You're in luck, young fella, for you are looking at him. May I ask why you wish to see me."

"Yes, sir. My name is Gunther Conrad and I have an appointment to see you at eleven o'clock this morning. I have brought with me a letter of introduction from a friend of yours by the name of Henrietta Gautmann." Having handed him the letter, I waited while he read its contents. Then, he gave me an audible sigh and placed the letter back in the envelope.

"Well, Gunther, having travelled a fair distance to see me, it's only right and proper that I listen to what you have to say." Turning to the other gentleman, he excused himself before joining me.

"Follow me upstairs to my office on the mezzanine and tell me what exactly you are looking for here."

As I followed him up to the office, I had the opportunity of studying him. Physically, he was a little shorter than me, stockier built with the ruddy complexion and receding hair. Also, he wore glasses and I guessed he would be in his late forties. When we entered his office, I was struck by its disarray. There were two bookcases spilling over with books, a bust of Schiller standing in the corner, with what I took to be Otto's hat resting on Schiller's head. There was also a desk upon which were scattered many scripts and behind the desk, was a large, stained glass window looking out over the street outside. Taking yet more manuscripts off the chair and motioning me to sit down, he then walked around and sat down on the other side of the desk facing me. It took him some time whilst he looked me over before he finally spoke.

"You certainly come highly recommended, young Gunther, which is praise indeed when you consider that the person who is recommending you was considered one of the finest young actresses of her generation. Unfortunately, the theatre has only one master and frau Gautmann faced with a choice, chose to marry instead, which if I may say so, was a serious loss to the theatre. Who knows, you might have ended up with either the German equivalent of Sarah Bernhard or Ethel Barrymore. Anyway, I digress, Gunther. What quality can you bring to the Kammerspiel that will enhance its reputation? Or put another way, what is there about you that you feel makes you better than all the other young actors beating their way to the doors for the chance of fame?"

As Otto Frankenberg sat waiting for my answer, I thought to myself, I haven't come all this way just to plead. I'm afraid Herr Frankenberg will have to take me as I am.

"I don't think, sir, that at this moment, there is much difference between myself and any other young actor trying to get a break, except possibly the luck which I appear to have this moment. It was only last year that I graduated from drama school and so far, I have only obtained a few small jobs. What I need right now is the opportunity to join a theatrical company where I can start at the bottom, learn my trade professionally and try and move onto better things. That is why I am here now. The Kammerspiel is a national theatre that enjoys an excellent reputation so I couldn't think of a better place to start at the bottom of the ladder than here. Two things I can promise you: I learn well and you won't regret taking me on."

Once again, Otto Falkenberg sat quietly, scrutinising me from head to foot whilst tapping a pencil on his desktop. It seemed ages before he finally spoke.

"There's something about you, young man, that suggests good things. I would like you to come back downstairs with me so that I can have the opportunity to see how you can work a stage. I presume that you will have a repertoire of pieces to use if you are asked to do an unexpected audition should the occasion arise, which it now has.''

I quickly did a mental survey in my mind of what would be most appropriate for this moment and quickly realised that what had brought me luck in my scholarship audition could do the same today.

''If you don't mind, sir, I would like to perform Marc Antony's speech from William Shakespeare's *Julius Caesar*.''

Otto Falkenberg gave me wry smile.

''That'll be fine by me, Gunther, though the bar is set pretty low on that one, for I have heard it performed so many times by young hopefuls that I can only hope that you will be an improvement. To save time, this is what I would like you to do once we get downstairs. Wait in the wings until I call, then enter as if the play was in progress and perform Marc Anthony's monologue. What I shall also do is to supply you with a small audience consisting of anybody that I can round up from stagehands, my board colleagues and finally, my secretary and script girl, so let's get going.''

As I came down to the auditorium, I began to panic and sweat with a strong urge to throw up, so much so, that I asked Herr Falkenberg to excuse me for a few minutes while I used the men's room. I barely reached it in time before I threw up and afterwards, standing before the wash basin looking into the mirror and seeing myself looking completely washed out, I wondered whether this was what I actually wanted to do. But then, reality set in and I realised that I would be going through this ritual as an actor many times in the future. I had read somewhere that the Americans have an expression that, 'It went with the shingle', or as we Europeans would say, 'It goes with the job'. Well, if that were to be the case, I would just have to straighten up, dust myself down and start all over again.

I strode down the central aisle of the auditorium, passed two rows, which true to Herr Falkenberg's word, were now occupied by sundry members of the theatre company. Having stepped onto the stage, I stood centre stage while Herr Falkenberg introduced me to my audience.

"Ladies and gentlemen, may I introduce you to Gunther Conrad who will endeavour to impress you by his performance as an actor and convince you that he would be a worthy member for this company. Gunther would you please exit stage left and re-enter stage. You will proceed to downstage centre, where hopefully, you will transport us to ancient Rome. By the way, good luck!"

I walked to the wings in what I thought was a slow nonchalant start and briefly stood in the darkness, taking deep breaths of air in an effort to relax myself, activating what would become a lifelong habit before commencing a performance. Being partially angry with myself for getting in such a state, I escaped from the reality of my position and mentally transported myself back, once again, to the steps of the Roman Senate. Adjusting my imaginary Roman toga, I strode onto the stage and stood facing the darkened auditorium for what seemed like ages without saying a word and then raising my hands, as if to quieten the disturbed citizens of Rome, I began to address them. It seemed to me only a blink of an eye before I was finished. It appeared to me to have been a lot of emotional and physical anguish for such a small effort. However, I was somewhat gratified to receive a wave of applause, which was far more acceptable than a wave of silence.

As I stood there without any further response, watching my audience depart to all points of the theatre, leaving just Otto Falkenberg hunched in his seat staring at me, I thought to myself, I'm not standing here like an idiot and without further ado, fetched a chair from the back of the stage and sat myself down. As I crossed my legs, I lit a cigarette and casually blew the smoke out. Eventually, Herr Falkenberg rose from his seat and strode down to the footlights where he stood with his arms crossed gazing up at me, after a somewhat dramatic pause, he finally spoke.

"You certainly have fulfilled Henrietta's opinion of you, young man. You left us in no doubt that we were listening to Marc Anthony. Excellent delivery! I also left you to your own devices when you had finished so they could judge you on your self-control. Not only do you have great stage presence, but you are no shrinking violet when it comes to self-confidence, something that might have to be watched, if you are to become a good team player. You will have probably gathered by now that I am accepting you as a member of the Kammerspiel Theatre Company. You will become one of a band of talented young players, some who may go on to great careers, while others may not. As with all of them, your fate will be in the hands of the gods and ultimately, only hard work, determination and luck will determine the course of your trajectory, which will be either up or down. I would like you to join the company in a fortnight's time. The money will be a pittance and when required I will expect you to work like a slave. The theatre manager, Herr Maher, will be in touch with you shortly with formal matters regarding joining and starting. Now, before I waste any more of my valuable time, is there anything you would like to say, Herr Conrad?"

"Only to thank you, Herr Falkenberg, for the opportunity that you are giving me and to confirm that you can be rest assured that I won't let you down."

"You won't be letting me down, young man. It'll be yourself, so bear that in mind. Anyway, congratulations and welcome." With that, he was gone leaving me to exit the theatre in the state of euphoria.

I had no recollection of my journey back to Frankfurt that afternoon, such was my excitement and pride at becoming a member of the company. When I returned home, immediately, I told the two people closest to me, both of whom had two different reactions. My mother, having previously been bitterly opposed by my choice of career and the amount of money being wasted on it, now became ecstatic with the thought that perhaps now, she had a son that could possibly become famous. Whilst on the other hand, on hearing the news, Henrietta gave me a hug and with a slight moist eye, gave me her remarks.

"Well, Gunther, you have finally got your foot on the first rung of the ladder. During the next few years, I will be following your career avidly and with pride for I know eventually, you will become very famous and when you do, just remember those who were with you on your way up. God bless you, Gunther and take care of yourself.

The next twelve months sped by very quickly. I certainly had no time in which to idle. The Kammerspiel, under the guidance of Otto Falkenberg, gave no quarter. Looking back now, I realised then, that a young professional actor just starting out, could not have had a better training for his craft. I covered all aspects of theatre production, from errand boy to spear carrier, to walk-on parts and finally, junior leads. At the end of the first year, I could now look upon myself with pride as a true professional. It had not been easy, for although the theatre had recommended a boarding house to me, where at least I could sleep and bathe, it still ended up taking most of my wages. If it hadn't been for the generosity of several local café owners, who more often than not, would slip me a free bowl of soup and a sandwich, plus the fact that my fellow thespians would also close ranks around me and share what little they had, I probably would have starved to death.

It wasn't all sweetness and light and choral music, for there were some right buggers amongst the company, one in particular by the name of Frederick Pohls, who by nature, was a right asshole and one, that I would not have hesitated in administering a kick up the backside. He seemed to possess all the worst attributes of human nature, one of which was that he couldn't stand me and would take every opportunity professionally to either upstage me or feed me miscues. Offstage, he would do his best to humiliate me or attempt to muscle in on any personal relationship that I might be in. Having said all that, he was indirectly responsible for getting me a lucky break that any young actor would give his high teeth for. His character was beyond redemption and he would think nothing of berating those he considered were beneath him, particularly the stagehands and gophers. The fact that he was a bloody good actor may have gone to his head, but I doubt it. He was just by nature, that way inclined. Anyway, I am digressing.

Otto Falkenberg, decided in his wisdom, to stage a production of *Romeo and Juliet* for a two-week run and to my amazement, he had asked me to do a reading for Romeo, but guess who was in contention for the same part? None other than Freddie the freak. Now, as it so often happens in the theatre, Otto was forced into deciding between the two of us and chose Freddie to play Romeo, whilst at the same time designating me as Freddie's understudy. You can well imagine how Freddie became unbearable to both the cast and crew. By the evening of the dress rehearsal, his ego had reached unprecedented heights. In the run up to that evening's performance, he had publicly humiliated the elderly character actor portraying Friar Lawrence, much to the anger of the entire cast. To make matters worse, he had also taken it upon himself to berate several members of the stage crew and set dressers and one certainly won't dwell upon how disdainful he was of my presence. Despite the aura of tension that he had drawn around himself, he had delivered a masterly performance, unfortunately not as part of the cast but more of a great diva. It was after the curtain came down at the end of the dress rehearsal, when Freddie and several members of the cast were still on stage holding an autopsy on the evening's performance, that disaster struck.

Suddenly, a rogue counterweight from one of the stage flats came careering from stage right and sent Freddie flying into the arms of the actor playing Mercutio. When Freddie failed to get up it was very quickly established that he had been severely concussed and as a result, after an ambulance was called, he was taken off to hospital. We learned later that night that several vertebrae in his spine had been damaged and that, although he would make a good recovery, he would be out of action for several weeks. It was never established why the counterweight had behaved as it did. The incident was merely logged as being an unfortunate accident with no blame attached to any of the stage crew. The outcome for me, was only good news, for without further ado, Otto immediately promoted me to take over the part in time for opening night. With the fog of gloom being lifted, the company rallied around, so much so, that we received a standing ovation on opening night and some excellent reviews the following day, with myself being singled out for additional praise as a promising newcomer.

It was at this point that fate yet again took a hand in my life. I was totally unaware of it at the time but during the first week of the run, a prominent film producer by the name of Carl Froehlich who also happened to be a friend of Otto Falkenberg, had slipped into the theatre and had afterwards asked to go backstage to be introduced to me. It was quite flattering to have the attention of such a well-known cinema producer and although we spent a good thirty minutes discussing the play and my future aspirations, I thought nothing more of it other than it being a rather complimentary social visit which usually occurred every evening at the end of the play's performance, a rite that most actors accepted as an acknowledgement to their admirers. Therefore, I was surprised, a few days later, when Otto summoned me to his office. Immediately, I feared the worst, assuming that my performance was falling short of what was expected of me. When

I entered the office, Otto was sitting behind his desk doing his usual thing of scavenging amongst his scripts and as was his habit, took a little time before glancing up at me in acknowledgement.

"Well, Gunther, it does seem that you may have found a pot of gold at the end of the rainbow. If not, it may well be the next best thing; namely getting your foot in the door of the movie business. I can see that you are somewhat perplexed, so let me explain what this is all about. The other evening, you had a backstage visit from the producer-director, Carl Froehlich, who had originally come to watch Freddie Pohls, as Romeo. When he realised that Freddie had been replaced by his understudy, he had decided to leave but I persuaded him not to waste the evening entirely and to stay and watch your performance. In other words, cutting to the chase, especially as I don't have a lot of time to waste on this matter, he was very impressed by your performance and through me, has asked if you would consider a short-term contract to work in a film that he is about to start, a version, I believe, of Dostoyevsky's *The Brothers Karamazov*. I don't know whether you have read the book, but I suggest you do so as quickly as possible, as Froehlich has you in mind for the part of the younger brother, Alexei. This, if I may say so, Gunther, could be a great opportunity for you."

"This has rather taken the wind out of my sails, Herr Falkenberg. Of course, I am extremely flattered. But due to my inexperience, I wonder if I could take advantage of your wisdom and perhaps guide me in my best course of action."

"At this moment in time, if I were your age, I would, without any hesitation, grab the opportunity. You can be rest assured, Gunther, that I would not enforce any legal ties to keep you under contract here. I would be quite happy if you could agree to four weeks' notice of termination. The only reason for this suggestion is because there has been a very favourable reaction from the public regarding *Romeo and Juliet* and because ticket sales at the box office are exceeding expectations, much of which is due to your performance, I have decided to extend the run for a further two weeks. Now if you want my professional opinion of you since you joined the company and please don't let it go to your head, I have to say that you have the makings of a formidable stage actor. However, I feel that you will make your name in the relatively new medium of the cinema, where you will have the availability of a huge audience that no theatre could give you. Now for God's sake, go away, Gunther and decide. Remember, don't turn your back on lady luck. After all, it could be Freddie Pohls that could be sitting here now.'

Chapter 3

Silence is Golden

It took me less than an hour to make the decision to accept Carl Froehlich's offer and just over two months to implement it. The first thing that that I did on leaving Otto's office was to phone Henrietta to tell her of my good fortune. She was overjoyed at the offer I had received and told me that I should waste no time in accepting it. She also advised me, that I had now reached a point in my career where I would need the services of an agent to represent my interests, one that was highly skilled in negotiating salaries and obtaining lucrative work. If it was of any help to me, it so happened that she knew of one by the name of Oscar Korten, who had represented her in her younger days and was highly respected within the profession. Finally, she did what she always did and without any strings attached, enquiring whether I was all right for money and had sufficient funds to cover my expenses whilst moving to Berlin, or until I received my first paycheck. Her last words to me before I put the receiver down, were that we should always stay in touch.

As it transpired, in just over eight weeks, having said goodbye to my mother and my few friends, I finally found myself with case in hand, boarding the train for Berlin. The time had not been wasted, for having listened to Henrietta's advice, I had made contact, with Oscar Korten, who after some reluctance, had accepted me as a client. Having done so, he started unlocking many doors for me. First and foremost, he was responsible for getting me my first lease on an apartment. Then, he contacted Carl Froehlich, informing him that in future, I would be represented by Oscar in all contractual matters. It was at this moment that I became familiar with the peculiarities of the film world, for in a matter of weeks, Oscar had forwarded to me an advance on my salary plus a script titled *The Cabinet of Dr Caligari*, in which I was to play the character of a young man called Alan. Without any explanation, it appeared that *The Brothers Karamazov* had been quietly cancelled. It was also accompanied by instructions to report to the film producer, Eric Pommer, at the film studio, Lixie Atelier, situated at 9, Franz Joseph Strasser, in Berlin. Without a doubt, that train journey to Berlin was the most momentous moment of my life. I was young, I was fulfilling my dream of being an actor, I had money in my pockets and a part in a film. The world was mine to conquer. Now this was what I would call an adventure!

Despite the political unrest and deep divisions within German society caused by the Great War and the abdication of the Kaiser, I hadn't realised at the time, but as I stepped off the train at Berlin's, Anhalter Bahnhof Station, that with the ending of the war, the city was beginning to pulsate with life. With the loosening of censorship, it had begun to push the boundaries back on many of the social taboos of the age, at the same time, creating many new innovative styles. This was particularly noticeable in the art world, the theatre world and the new medium of the cinema, something which I would be a participant very soon. I had allowed myself just over a week in which to settle into my new life before reporting to the studio and I began to get used to my new flat, where joy of joys, for the first time, I had my own bathroom. Soon after, I hastened around to the office of my agent, Oscar Korten. I took an immediate shine to him.

Oscar was physically short and tubby with a round, jovial face, upon which was perched a pair of bifocals. His general demeanour was overflowing with energy and occasional bursts of excitability and his appearance was finished off with an unruly mop of hair which appeared to have a life of its own. Every time he gestured with his head, it would move like an avalanche over his forehead, forever causing him to brush it back with his hands. It was after completing the boring work of signing a heap of legal documents that Oscar suggested that he introduce me to Berlin's nightlife over the next few evenings. That certainly turned out to be a ground-breaking experience, for it was the commencement of turning a young naïve country boy into the beginnings of a metropolitan sophisticate.

It was in the nightclubs that I encountered my first drag acts, my first sexually liberated female singers and chorus girls and comedians, whose acts consisted entirely of political satire aimed at prominent politicians and who left no stones unturned in exposing their peccadilloes. By the end of the week, I was ready to start work and duly reported to the film studios situated at Potsdam-Babelsberg, where I was introduced to the director of the film in which I was to appear in. His name was Robert Weine and the film he was making was the script I had been handed before, *The Cabinet of Dr Caligari*, in which I was to play a character called Alan. It seemed to me that I spent an awful lot of time being photographed in profile and in what they termed reaction shots, which were supposed to express the full range of emotion. The plot had been explained to me, which seemed to be all about manipulation and somnambulism and after I had become acquainted with the film sets, which I had never seen the like of before and which I was told were part of a new form of genre known as expressionism, I was beginning to think that it was all rather weird. But what did I know? I was just a novice starting out. If it was good enough for my betters, it was good enough for me.

The other matter which took a little more time in getting used to, was the actual producing of the film itself. The first thing that I had to adjust to, was the different style of acting between theatre and cinema. I very quickly learned to tone down the heavy facial expressions and florid gestures that I had learnt to project from the stage and to adjust accordingly for the camera. Paradoxically, facial expression became the number one tool for an actor to convey a story to an audience for when it boiled down to the fact that he had no voice. On top of all this was the struggle of maintaining a romantic scene with the cacophony of background noise, which included amongst all things, the director attempting to give instruction to his actors, mixed with the sounds of the studio carpenters banging and sawing away, whilst meanwhile, the poor musicians were desperately trying to supply the mood music to enhance the actors' performances.

Despite all the challenges, I enjoyed my first experience of being in the movies, especially on meeting my first celebrity actors and being treated as an equal by them. Frequently, I had to pinch myself to ensure that it wasn't a dream, as I sat around the set with Conrad Veidt, Lilly Dagover and Werner Kraus. All of them happened to be my idols of the silver screen and it was surreal that I was now being treated as one of their peers whilst listening to the current show business gossip as we waited between scenes. I must have impressed the powers that be, for I was at the finish of the film when I was rushed into the film that I had originally been signed on for, *The Brothers Karamazov*.

By now, I was beginning to take to film acting like a duck to water or so I thought, with the arrogance of youth, for I was now entering what I thought at the time, was my weird phrase, but on reflection, would be my participation in what would be German cinema's avant-garde and expressionist period. The first film in this genre was titled, *From Morning to Midnight,* in which the plot was about a humble bank clerk robbing his employers and was mostly filmed in a highly stylised dream sequence. The second film I was involved in very soon after that, was called *Algol,* meaning 'the tragedy of power', which believe it or not, was about a being from another planet.

In my youthful ignorance, I performed in these films without any idea what they were about, relying solely on the wisdom of their directors. Amazingly, they did me no harm professionally with the public. In fact, exactly the opposite was the case and with several films now already under my belt, my confidence was beginning to know no boundaries. I was beginning to both learn and include personal mannerisms and bits of film business into my characters. I also began to feel that I had finally arrived when my photograph started appearing in film magazines and entertainment columns.

From that moment on, over the next two years, as I became well known to the public, inevitably, Oscar started to receive more offers for my services. Gradually, I became, what is known in theatre parlance as a hot property. I soon fell into a fortunate pattern of working during the day in films, acquiring along the way, leading man status, with box office successes such as *William Tell, Beloved Rogue* and my favourite at the time, *The Hands of Orlac.* Eventually, as I became a household name, in turn, this led me to receiving more offers for theatre work in the evenings. Of course, this provided me with an even greater source of revenue and before long, I had acquired all the trappings of success, enabling me to buy a car, purchase an apartment and find myself an expensive tailor and all the other outward signs that went with success and stardom.

I thought back on those marvellous times of yesteryear, meeting for morning coffee on the Kurfurstendamm, (better known as the Kur–damm) the famous Berlin thoroughfare, sharing a table with emerging greats of the German art, literature and theatre world. I can remember their names and faces even now, though most have now gone into exile. Where is Berthold Brecht? Erwin Piscatorl? Max Reinhardt and Conrad Veidt? They have all scattered to safe havens, such as France, Britain, and the New World. Looking back, if only we all knew then what we know now. But the world was our oyster, with no limit on our dreams and ambitions. As far as I was concerned, I was footloose and fancy free and at that time of my life, had no desire to marry and settle down. Indeed, as a young man of wealth and celebrity, I was really like a young boy in a sweet shop with easy accessibility to all the goodies that it contained. I had no real responsibility for anything or anybody other than myself.

Whilst I was going through the proverbial rites of passage as a young man, Berlin was beginning to rival Paris is a city that attracted the intellectual and artistic gypsies of the decade. It was certainly not unusual on any given day or night, to either take coffee in a café or attend an evening party and to be mentally stimulated by philosophers, writers, musicians and actors. By this time, I had become a devoted follower of jazz music and would spend many a night, wherever possible, at a club called Mitts, which was situated near the Tiergarten, listening to the great Eric Borcard and his jazz band. It was on these occasions that I would often swap gossip and views with my own group of friends, two of which were just beginning to make names for themselves in the film industry. One a writer, and one an actor, both who now had gone into exile and were making an international name for themselves in Britain and America and the European continent, but at that time, in the early twenties, both were just starting to make a name for themselves in Germany. The writer became known as Billy Wilder in Hollywood where he had settled, whilst the actor known as Peter Lorre has travelled from Berlin to Paris and then on, to settle in London. I truly hoped that one day, the three of us would meet up again and collaborate on a few artistically rewarding projects.

It was in the late autumn, 1926, when I was between theatre and film assignments, that I got my next important break in the form of a phone call from Oscar Korten. He told me that a very important American filmmaker had arrived in Berlin the week before. Not only that, but this important person was none other than Louis B. Mayer, who happened to be the production head of the American film studio, MGM. Apparently, from what Oscar told me, it was Mr Mayer's habit to take a two-month vacation in Europe each year, combining both business with pleasure. According to Oscar, Mayer had come to Europe with the express purpose of finding two actors who he felt had great potential and once having found them, to place them under contract to his studio. Oscar went on to say that he had already signed a contract with one, a Swedish actress by the name of Greta Louisa Gustafsson, an emerging and highly regarded stage actress who had just recently completed two Swedish films. Oscar went on to explain ecstatically that the representative of the studio's Berlin office had recently seen me in the lead role in *Hamlet* and apparently, had been so impressed by my performance, that he had advised Mr Mayer to view my film work. Consequently, on watching two of my recent movies, Mr Mayer decided on adding a Berlin stopover to his European itinerary. I had been unaware that during the last forty-eight hours, he had been in consultation with Oscar, concerning my possible availability and the type of contract he was prepared to offer. When Oscar explained the terms of the contract to me, they were very tempting, especially the clause concerning script approval. Oscar, who by this time, was clearly on a high, finished by saying that if I accepted these proposals, I could end up becoming a genuine international film star. Therefore, on reflection, there appeared to be only one answer that I could give, the answer of course, was a big YES. On Oscar's advice, I intimated that I would be only too happy to meet Mr Mayer the following afternoon at his suite at the Adlon Hotel, so that we could fully explore the contents of the proposed contract in more detail.

I suppose I have always been one to remember every detail of the momentous decisions that have changed my life. In this case, it was no different. I remember it was a Wednesday, a very dour day, with a drizzle of rain here and there with very little sun. To make matters worse, I was suffering from a monumental hangover, self-inflicted at a party the previous night. Even though the meeting had been arranged for mid-afternoon, I had left getting out of bed and pulling myself together to the very last moment. When I arrived at the Adlon Hotel, Oscar was waiting for me in the foyer. Despite his fussing about my lateness, I insisted on having a coffee and brandy to steady my equilibrium and nerves. This self-imposed delay also gave me time to run through the terms of the proposed contract. As far as I was concerned, if I had script approval and the maximum length of the contract would be no more than three years with the proviso that at the end of which, a new contract could be negotiable, I was not particularly bothered about the other clauses. I suppose, in all honesty, I simply did not have the patience or the stamina to sit there going through them. On our way up in the hotel lift to Mr Mayer's suite, Oscar attempted to coach me on how I should approach him when we finally met. According to Oscar, I was to mind my manners, and not to be too forward. I gave Oscar one of my hard stares as if to say don't push it. Fortunately, by the time the lift had stopped at the required floor, Oscar was a little less exuberant and had adapted more of an air of a skilled negotiator.

The door of the suite was opened by a gentleman whom Oscar introduced to me as Martin Friedberg, the General Manager of the Berlin office of MGM. Having got the introduction over with, the three of us proceeded to a large reception area occupied by two men who stood up as we entered. Once again, Martin Friedberg made the introductions. The first man moving towards me with his hand extended in greeting, was of medium height with a stocky build, complete with round features and a hooked nose, upon which sat a pair of glasses. His hair was beginning to show a slight tinge of grey at the temple, I was soon aware that this gentleman was Louis B. Mayer, the famous Hollywood producer. The other gentleman standing slightly to one side, I recognised at once from previous magazine photographs, as Clarence Brown, a noted Hollywood film director, who was of similar build but had a darker complexion.

Once we had sat down and gone through the motions of enquiring about the safe journey of our American visitors from across the Atlantic, and the points of interest that they had encountered on a journey across Europe, Mayer proceeded very quickly to come to the point. He talked of how the studio had recently come to the decision to build up their roster of film stars and at the same time, to tailor scripts and productions to their individual personalities, for example, selling three Lon Chaney or John Gilbert films a year to the exhibitors. Though the existing stable of stars were proving popular with the public, Mayer was looking for exciting new talent, particularly as the latest craze with the female moviegoers were romantic and sophisticated continental actors, who exuded an aura of sexual menace. In my case, not only did I fit that profile, but I had a presence that would allow me to play both hero and villain. It seemed Mayer and his colleagues felt that the studio could nurture my career with the right parts and the appropriate publicity, thereby making me a big star. I certainly did not need much persuading, as being a young man, the golden carrots being dangled in front of me outweighed any big stick hovering in the background and in any case, I was quite content for Oscar to deal with any of the boring side issues, if and when they arose. As the afternoon dragged on. I began to become bored with the proceedings and so took the opportunity of studying Mr Mayer's personality whilst everybody else was talking. He gave the impression that the studio was his personal fiefdom and that any disputes or decisions to be made be dependent on his final arbitration. Having said that, I felt that he would listen to your side of the argument and if you felt that you were right, would back you all the way. However, there was also a lurking suspicion in the back of my mind, that to win an argument, he was quite capable of employing emotions that would put any of his actors to shame.

It was during a conversation that I was having with Clarence Brown about the idea he had concerning a love story to be titled *The Torrent*, in which he thought I would be perfect playing opposite their new Swedish discovery, that the conversation was interrupted by the door to the suite being opened and closed to the sound of female voices. Within seconds, two women stood in the entrance to the reception area. They were both well laden with designer shopping bags and upon seeing us, began apologising for their intrusion. Mayer rose to his feet with the rest of us following his example. I learnt from his introduction that one of the ladies was his wife, Margaret and that her companion was called Alice, wife of Clarence Brown. It was obvious that they had been on a shopping expedition and judging by the many bags accumulated between the two of them, a successful one at that. As the conversation progressed between us, I was impressed by the no-nonsense attitude of the American women, particularly in comparison to their German counterparts. However, although they appeared sophisticated, knowledgeable, and down-to-earth in the conversation, when it was hinted that I would be going to Hollywood, both ladies complemented Mayer on his astute choice and spoke quite bluntly about my aura of sex appeal and danger, leaving me somewhat embarrassed by their enthusiasm and lack of inhibition.

The rest of the day was spent joining Mr Mayer and his party for dinner, and whilst I spent the remainder of the time flattering the ladies, Oscar took charge of the business end, such as validating the proposed contract and acknowledging the arrival dates upon which I was to present myself at the studio, all dependent, of course, on how quickly the American State Department would process my work permit and visa, not to mention as well, booking travel arrangements and leaving my affairs in order when I finally departed. It was late in the evening when finally, Oscar and I, hailed a taxi outside the hotel after bidding a temporary farewell to our hosts.

Oscar received no argument from me when he requested the taxi driver take us to the Four Seasons, a well-known late-night drinking club. I am sure that both of us were in a state of euphoria and certainly needed to bring ourselves down gently, Oscar, because he had just negotiated a big fat commission for himself and me because I was standing on the cusp of a life-changing journey which could take me to God knows where. The pair of us suffered a monumental, mother-of-all hangovers the following day, just as well, I suppose, for unbeknown to me at the time, it became an unofficial wake for the passing of the first chapter of my life.

Five days later, after that tumultuous event, I received the unexpected news that my mother had passed away in her sleep. Despite her volatile nature and our struggles to survive, we had been mother and son against the world and would forever remain so. The most rewarding experience for me was when I was able to buy her an apartment and ensure that she would never have to work again. Fate, however, decreed otherwise. The final chapter of our journey together would not end on that happy note. During the few years that she was able to enjoy the fruits of my success, she developed an aggressive form of senile dementia to the point that I eventually employed a live-in carer-companion for her. In the beginning, before the terrible disease took hold of her, she had immense pride in my success. She always made a point of attending my first nights in the theatre, where I was informed, that on my first entrance in the play, she turned to those sitting beside her and informed them that I was her son. Sadly, towards the end, it became difficult for her to remember who I was. Briefly, I suffered a mixture of guilt and deep remorse for the way that life had dealt the cards for her. I only wish that she had lived long enough to enjoy the benefits that I had achieved and eventually, would allow her to have found peace with herself. Instead, I found myself as her son and only mourner standing in the chapel as the curtain finally closed behind her coffin. I had previously spent a few private moments with her in the funeral parlour and just before I summonsed the undertakers to seal her coffin, I stroked her face which to my eyes, had never been so serene and at peace. I sincerely hoped that if there was a hereafter, that she would be finally free of her mortal demons.

Chapter 4

The Lion Roars

Within six weeks, I had arrived in New York in America after leaving from Hamburg and having crossed the Atlantic by the liner *SS Europa* in just under five days. The processing of my paperwork for my destination had been quick as I had no contractual commitments to fulfil during that time in Germany. Also, I had been lucky that the American State Department had processed my work permit and visa in no time at all. On my arrival in New York, I was met by a gentleman by the name of Eddie Strickland, whose job apparently, was to handle all the publicity for MGM stars on the studio payroll. I soon became aware that the studio functioned with precision and that Strickland did all the organising and decision making on my behalf. I had been booked into the St Regis Hotel for two nights. I would be travelling from New York to Chicago on a train known as the 20th Century Limited. After that, I had been reserved a single bedroom-drawing room on another well-known train, the Santa Fe Super Chief special, the flagship of the Atchison, Topeka and Santa Fe Railway Company. The Super Chief would be departing from Dearborn Station, Chicago and take me through Kansas City, Albuquerque, Gallup, New Mexico onto my destination, Los Angeles.

Shortly after, I would disembark at Pasadena, where the studio car would be waiting to take me to the Beverly Hills Hotel, situated in an area called Sunset Boulevard. In the meantime, just to make sure that I was well occupied whilst in New York, the front office had arranged for me to see Tallulah Bankhead's Broadway show *They Knew What They Wanted* and on the following night, I was going to see the legendary Al Jolson in *Artists and Models*. I had no sooner booked in at the St Regis when I received a telephone call from Hollywood. The person on the line introduced himself as Myron Selznick, a top Hollywood agent and brother of film producer, David O. Selznick. Selznick confirmed how, with the approval of Oscar Korten, he had arranged to represent me in Hollywood and that he looked forward to meeting me and would phone me when I arrived at the Beverly Hills Hotel, Los Angeles.

Later, I learnt that I had been somewhat hoodwinked by Myron Selznick. Far from being a top Hollywood talent agent at the time, he had, in fact, only just become one. However, my decision to stick with him paid off handsomely, for within a few short years, he rose to become the scourge of the Hollywood film studios, gouging from them large salaries for his clients. From what I experienced during my first two days in America, I couldn't help feeling impressed by the energy and get-up-and-go attitude of the American people. Nothing seemed impossible, as most service industries were available twenty-four hours a day. However, there was one fly in the ointment: America did not serve alcohol. This uncivilised situation had been brought about by a senator by the name of Volstead. In 1919, he had introduced an act prohibiting the sale of alcohol. This became known as the Volstead Act. It introduced prohibition to America. However, the act was riddled with anomalies. For instance, though it was an offence to sell it, manufacture it or transport it, it wasn't an offence to consume it.

Though I would become more familiar with New York as the years went by, I well remember on that first visit, Al Jolson throwing an after-show party at a restaurant just opened off-Broadway, called Sardi's. This venue had opened with a policy of staying open late through the night to accommodate show folk, even though they were no longer able to serve alcohol, which as you can imagine, left itself wide open for abuse. I had been invited by Jolson to accompany him to Sardi's after being introduced to him in his dressing room backstage. I had watched the evening performance of the show *Artists and Models*, and when we arrived there, the restaurant was full of theatre folk all winding down from performances in their current Broadway shows. The restaurant consisted of red leather booths on the sides, with tables in the centre and on the walls, hung pen portraits of actors and actresses who frequently visited, a tradition apparently that had just started. Despite it now becoming famous as the in-place to be, not only with the Broadway folk but also, visiting out-of-town celebrities, it didn't stop people from circumventing prohibition. As I remember on that particular night, there were, in attendance, Alfred Lunt and Lynn Fontaine, who was starring in the play *Ned McCobbs' Daughter*, John Barrymore and his sister Ethel, and Tallulah Bankhead, the most brilliant but outrageously theatrical actress that I had ever met and of course, Al Jolson. What a night that was, and a very fitting end to my first albeit, very first visit to New York.

Little did I realise that the introduction to the wonders of the American continent was only just beginning as I started out on the second leg of my adventure across the American continent by rail from Chicago to Pasadena. Like most Europeans, I was aware that the United States was a large continent, but it still came as an immense surprise to physically experience the sheer length of time and changes in climate that my train underwent as it travelled through parts of eight states, a journey that took just over two days, going from the winter temperatures of Illinois, to the heat of New Mexico and finally, the dry semi-tropical climate of California. The train itself was designed to provide first class amenities for its passengers; there was an observation car attached to the rear of the train, furnished with tables and armchairs, plus a bar, which needless to say, provided no alcohol (unless you provided your own hip flask, of course), where passengers could relax and watch the scenery roll by. The restaurant car was of equal splendour with an extensive menu, which was served on the patterned, Mimbreno Syracuse China tableware, illustrated with native American Indian drawings and if you turned the plate over, on the bottom side was carried the inscription 'Made expressly for the Santa Fe dining car service'. A high quality was maintained by the excellent standard of service from the train's six or seven stewards, most of whom were coloured. I must admit, it was the first time that I had experienced such close contact with coloured people and the impression I had of them was of a hard-working, dignified race with a great sense of humour. Looking back at that moment in time made me realise how patronising and insulated I must have both felt and looked in the real world. I had not realised then, that the black American was very much a second-class citizen in the southern states of America and I would soon experience a similar situation to that in modern day Germany.

Following through on my itinerary, after arriving at Los Angeles, I disembarked at Pasadena, where the studio had a car and studio representative waiting for me. The first thing I became aware of, on leaving the train, was the dry heat of the Californian climate and that obviously, at some stage very soon, I would need to buy a new wardrobe of lightweight clothes if I were to remain comfortable. The studio had arranged a welcoming committee of the press and studio photographers to be at the station to record my arrival, which involved me being photographed in assorted poses while stepping down from the train or sitting smiling amongst my luggage. Once I had completed a question-and-answer interview with the press, I was escorted to a studio car and driven to my destination, which turned out to be the Beverly Hills Hotel.

On arrival, I was ushered through the hotel lobby, which was designed in the Californian, Spanish hacienda style. I was then shown up to my suite. The bellboy, having deposited my luggage and shown me the amenities of the suite, then departed leaving me to switch on the ceiling fans and to learn how to adjust the window jalousies which prevented the strong sunlight from streaming through. I noticed as I was using the winder to close them that there was a swimming pool below me, where guests were either sunbathing or swimming. The pool itself was surrounded by lush vegetation and palm trees. I must say, looking through it with the eyes of a newly arrived European, it certainly gave off an aura of an exotic paradise.

Meanwhile, I'll say this for my arrival in Hollywood: I wasn't going to feel alone and at a loose end for too long, as within an hour of arriving, the phone started ringing with appointments and invitations. The first call, as promised, was from Myron Selznick, who started the conversation by welcoming me to the state of California and after further enquiries about my well-being, proceeded to give me an itinerary, covering the next seven days. The first was a social invitation for that very evening, in which he had arranged a welcoming party for me at the Biltmore Hotel in downtown Los Angeles. He assured me it was just a small reception, which would give me the opportunity to unwind with some good company, good food and some dancing afterwards. Selznick continued by saying that during the next few days, he would familiarise me with his own personal bootlegger and at the same time, would present me with a hip flask as a gift for when I dined out. He went on to say that he would advise me later about the local car dealers and realtors, as he felt it would be wiser to invest in real estate or even to rent a house rather than to stay in the hotel. As for transport, a car was essential for getting about in Los Angeles, as nobody in their right mind walked in the city! Finally, he added, on Monday, he would be taking me to the MGM studios where I would be introduced to the studio heads and be put officially on the payroll.

I had no sooner replaced the receiver at the end of that conversation when the phone rang again. This time, the caller introduced himself as Emil Jannings, an introduction that I didn't need for not only was he a noted German actor, but he was a favourite of mine, who had recently become very successful in Hollywood. It certainly was mind blowing to be speaking on the telephone to one of my film idols, especially as I had only just recently seen his latest film, *The Last Command*, where his performance completely overwhelmed me. Unfortunately, the same could not be said of his attempt at speaking English. His accent was so thick that it could be cut with a knife. But we quickly resorted to conversing in our native tongue. Emil began by saying, that on behalf of the German community, he welcomed me to Hollywood, and that he had decided to throw a party for me that weekend so that I would have the opportunity to meet many German expats who were already working in the American film industry. Overwhelmed by the generosity of his invitation, I assured him that I would be honoured to attend that Sunday night. By the time I'd finished speaking with Emil, I had arrived at the conclusion that I would soon have to employ a secretary to manage my professional and social engagements, otherwise my life would become a total mess.

Of the many phone calls that followed, the one that stood out from all of them was from Douglas Fairbanks, who along with his wife, Mary Pickford, were the reigning movie king and queen of Hollywood. I was more than flattered when he invited me to be a guest of honour at a dinner party to be held at their home, *Pickfair*, the following Friday night. His voice sounded a perfect match to his screen image, conveying enthusiasm and plenty of get up and go, so much so, that by the time I'd finished speaking with him, I had so much energy that I too was ready for anything.

True to his word, Myron had organised a small party for me that evening. However, it wasn't until he had picked me up in his car and was driving me to the Biltmore Hotel that he informed me he had included a blind date for me by the name of Trixie Montano, a young actress under contract to Paramount film studios. Not wishing for me to feel socially awkward, he had invited her to the party as my escort for the evening. I was in some trepidation as to what to expect, but I need not have worried as I was soon to find out.

On arrival at the Biltmore, Myron took me straight through to the bar area where a group of people were waiting for us. Myron first introduced me to his girlfriend, Mary, then his brother, David and his girlfriend, Irene. The rest of the party consisted of an actor by the name of William Haynes and his companion, Jimmy and finally, last but not least, a vivacious young lady who was the personification of the perfect flapper girl. She had blonde bobbed hair, a petite oval face with a pert nose and her mouth was shaped in the fashionable bee-sting look. This was my first introduction to Trixie Montano and we immediately took to each other. Even on our first formal introduction, I was fascinated by her voice, which registered low and resonated with what I would call a smoky timbre. During the evening, she told me that she had started her working life as a chorus girl in the chorus lines of various Broadway musicals, particularly the Florenz Ziegfeld extravaganzas.

After two years of getting nowhere fast and beginning to feel that she was stuck in a rut, Trixie had decided to try her luck by setting off to California to try and make a name for herself in Hollywood. After spending many months riding the tram to various studio casting departments, her persistence eventually paid off and she was able to graduate from walk-on roles, or background extras, as they were known, to small speaking roles. She was also well able to hold her own in a conversation and soon had me mesmerised to the point that I almost ignored my fellow companions for most of the evening.

David, Myron's brother, was a manager of the writers department at MGM and my impression of him was that of a very intense individual. However, I wasn't to know that in the following intervening years, David would marry his girlfriend Irene, the daughter of Louis B. Mayer and would become a major producer of many great films of the early thirties, eventually moving on to form his own independent company, culminating in his great cinematic masterpiece, *Gone with the Wind*.

As for the other two members of the party, William Haynes and Jimmy Shield, they were the life and soul of the party, keeping us all in fits of laughter with their inside stories about Hollywood. Before I had left Germany, I had seen Haynes in a film called *Little*

Annie Rooney, where he played the romantic lead to Mary Pickford's heroine. Certainly, he was nothing like his screen persona as I soon discovered as the evening went on and my suspicions were confirmed when Trixie whispered to me that he was a homosexual and that he and his companion, Jimmy Shield, were considered a couple in Tinseltown, a fact that was kept from the general public, as it would have obviously destroyed his career. Personally, I had no problem accepting them on a personal basis and theatre folk were generally known for their generosity and liberal thinking. Consequently, I had known of several homosexuals back in Berlin that I had counted upon as friends. In the end, as it turned out, with the advent of sound, Bill Haynes walked away from stardom and became a noted interior decorator amongst the Hollywood elite.

Trixie and I enjoyed each other's company so much that we decided we would like to see more of each other. On that basis, I cheekily asked her as we parted company that evening, whether she would like to be my date to the Douglas Fairbanks shindig. When she accepted enthusiastically, I immediately phoned Douglas asking if she could be included in the invitation, not realising at the time, that it could be considered a serious breach of etiquette. This was because in the social structure of Hollywood, she only was a bit player. Fortunately, he willingly agreed to Trixie being included in the invitation without any fuss, thereby saving me a considerable loss of face.

I must say that come the night, as Trixie drove me in her two-seater roadster up to the Fairbanks estate, that *Pickfair* lived up to my expectations and more. Set amongst rolling lawns, it was a large, gabled mansion, very much in the style favoured by the Hollywood community. Trixie and I were greeted at the door by a butler, who was every inch the quintessential English gentleman's gentleman, who then proceeded to announce two nervous young people into the presence of Douglas Fairbanks and Mary Pickford, plus a room full of Hollywood celebrities. Despite my years as a celebrity actor, I was still overcome with excitement at meeting them in the flesh and even more so when I was introduced to a gentleman standing beside them with a boyish smile on his face whom I instantly recognised as Charlie Chaplin. I had sensed by this time that Trixie didn't know whether to curtsy or faint, but she held her own with them all very well. I was also particularly impressed with the way she handled herself when we had all gone through to the dining room. As its centrepiece, it had a long table laid with fine tableware with the seating for twenty with Doug, as he was known to everyone and Mary, seated at each end of the table.

Whilst I had the pleasure of having Gloria Swanson seated on my right, Trixie had drawn William S. Hart, the famous cowboy star, as her table companion. Across the table from us, sat Charlie Chaplin who, during the meal, performed for us all his famous dance of the bread rolls featured in his film, *The Gold Rush*. It was turning out to be a memorable evening for both of us, especially for Trixie. It so happened as I had mentioned previously, that in the pecking order of Hollywood etiquette, it was most unusual for a contract artist or supporting actor to attend A-list social events. However, Trixie turned many heads that evening with her allure and vivacity and succeeded in turning both of us into the most sought-after couple of the evening.

I was also fortunate to spend some time with Charlie Chaplin, swapping views on the general state of Europe and especially, on Russia. Chaplin admired its communist government and its efforts to improve the quality of life for its citizens. There is no doubt, I felt then, as I do now, that he was one of the great iconic artists of the silent cinema, a new medium that was to become an art form in itself, during the early part of the twentieth century. But like many talented people, he had experienced a bad start in life experiencing extreme poverty and an unhappy childhood and as I got to know him, I realised how his tastes and opinions often clashed with the establishment opinion. However, that evening, we both discovered that we had a mutual love of tennis and consequently, he invited me to his house the following weekend for a tennis party, an invitation that became a regular feature over the next few years and more often than not, I would end up partnering him at the Beverly Hills Tennis Club in many tournaments.

If that night at the Fairbanks' party was to have been my introduction to Hollywood society, I think I must have passed it with flying colours, especially with the help of Trixie, who turned out to be the ideal partner for the occasion. Considering the group of movers and shakers who were at the party that night, she could have very easily pushed her career along by touting for moving parts and would have been thought less of by all and sundry for doing so. But instead, she created an impression by just being herself. I rather suspect that sometime soon, her agent would be receiving some very tantalising offers for her services. By the time Trixie and I finally left the Fairbanks home that night, we had somehow become kindred spirits and I had begun to fall in love with her. She aroused in me different feelings that I had hitherto not experienced with other girls in Germany and instead of loving and leaving her, as I had done before with previous women, I wanted to explore a deeper relationship.

Under ordinary circumstances I would have taken her back to my hotel with the sole purpose of taking her to bed, but somehow, we both felt intuitively that it wasn't the right moment, so Trixie, with all the naturalness in the world, deftly avoided the subject. Moreover, she suggested that if I was up for it, we go to an open all-night roadhouse (or speak-easy, as they were now known) which was frequented by the film colony and as it so happened, supplied the best under-the-counter booze and jazz in the county of Los Angeles. With the prospect of an adventure ahead of me, I required no persuasion and with Trixie driving, we were there in no time.

The roadhouse was certainly discreetly tucked away in the Holmby Hills section of Hollywood and it was only when you were nearly upon it that you saw the neon sign proclaiming Duffy's Inn. It didn't take much figuring out to see who was locally more well-known of the two of us, for when the door of the main entrance was opened by a doorman, who had all the appearances of a Japanese sumo wrestler, on seeing Trixie, he called out, "Hi Doll. Nice to see you again. Are you still working in the movies?" Even as we came past him on our way to the main clubroom, he kept up a running commentary on who had previously been in, or who was presently in. Once we had entered the clubroom, we were very quickly found a table and whilst we were waiting for our drinks order to arrive in the disguise of being dispensed from teapots, I was given an opportunity to study our surroundings.

The theme for the interior design of the inn was that of a rustic cabin, with the clubroom fitted out as a barn, more suitable, I would have thought, for a country and western hoedown rather than the great jazz that was playing from the stage in the corner. At the same time, the music was being enthusiastically received by the patrons, many of whom were crammed on the small dancefloor stomping to the sounds of Fats Waller's *Your Feet's Too Big* and for the next few hours, I felt as if I had been transported into a strange and exciting new world.

I couldn't quite get my head around the fact that I was in a country where there wasn't anything that could not be obtained twenty-four hours around the clock and at the same time, be so contradictory in its national character. It was amazing that I would have to buy spirits under the counter and serve them from a tea pot simply because the nation had blindly accepted an infringement of its civil liberties by voting in the prohibition laws. It was also equally disturbing that many of the southern states had acquiesced acceptance of apartheid, thereby making the American Negro a second-class citizen; certainly, a big leap from the sophisticated nightlife of Berlin. It was somewhat surreal to be sitting there with a background of jazz music in my ears, listening to Trixie sharing her ambitions with me, on how one day she would become the next Clare Bow, the nation's 'It' girl, whilst at the same time, producing a hip flask from her purse and covertly topping up our teapot. That my friends, is how I spent a magical evening falling in love. An evening spent dancing and drinking moonshine from a teapot, with the most enchanting girl to have entered my life. To put it simply, I was bewitched, bothered, bewildered and entirely under her spell.

I think it must have been somewhere around four o'clock in the morning when we finally arrived back outside my hotel. I must admit that I was in a somewhat inebriated state, falling over my words whilst asking her if she would be my partner to yet another showbiz party that I was going to that night. Quite frankly, I couldn't think of anybody else that I would rather take in the whole world. The things that a man will say whilst in drink! However, the thing is, I really meant them. Trixie thought the whole thing hilarious, for as she was later to recount to all those who would listen, she had gone on a blind date with a kraut actor and within forty-eight hours, he had introduced her to the Hollywood high life and with whom she had eventually begun to fall in love. After giving me a lingering embrace, she broke away from me and proceeded with great difficulty in getting me out of the roadster. She gradually proceeded to walk me into the hotel. Before leaving me at the reception desk, she told me that she would phone me later that day as to what time she was supposed to collect me, after which she proceeded to give me another embrace. I am quite sure that this vignette of eroticism had the hotel night clerk's eyes popping out of his head! And with "I'll see you later sweetheart," Trixie turned on her heel and left, leaving me entirely at the mercy of the night clerk who proceeded to point me in the right direction to my suite.

As you have already guessed, I'm sure, it took me to the early part of the afternoon to fall out of bed and another two hours to pull myself together and phone room service to send me up a hearty breakfast with gallons of coffee. Thankfully, by the time that I had showered and consumed the breakfast, Trixie, true to her word, phoned me.

"Good afternoon, Gunther and how is my favourite kraut today? I am just checking to see whether you remembered that you asked me to be your date again for tonight?"

"Speak low, speak low, my darling. My head is throbbing from the constant sound of voodoo drums whilst my heart is pounding like crazy. Of course, I remember asking you to be my date last night and I am looking forward to it with just as much enthusiasm now, as I did last night. So young lady, pour yourself into your best finery and pick me up at around six-thirty tonight. Oh, by the way, did I happened to mention where I'm taking you? Well, you will be pleased to know that the well-known actor, Mr Emil Jannings, is kindly throwing a welcoming party for me."

"Goodness me, Gunther. I do hope Mr Jannings doesn't have a good memory for faces, for it is not so long ago that I had a walk-on part in one of his films, called *The Way of all Flesh*. I sure as hell wouldn't like to humiliate us both by being shown the door when we turn up."

"Don't you worry your pretty head about that, Trixie. All you have to be is your true self and leave the rest to me. I am quite convinced that after this weekend, you will go down like a storm and that agents will be clamouring to offer you work. So, hurry up and put on your best glad rags and I will see you at six-thirty this evening."

I had only just finished putting on my tuxedo and was in the process of straightening my bow tie when the phone rang. It was the front desk downstairs informing me that Trixie had arrived. So, after grabbing a white scarf, I quickly took the elevator down to the foyer. As soon the elevator doors opened, I immediately saw her sitting on one of the lobby chairs. She looked absolutely stunning, from her fashionable bobbed hair and heavily rouged bee-stung lips, to her figure and gorgeous legs, shown off by a high fashion, roaring-twenties black dress, which in turn, was finished off by a white Boa around her neck and a small silver clutch bag. My immediate inclination was to sweep her off her feet and carry her upstairs to bed, but reality won the day, and as we were already falling behind schedule, I kissed her, grabbed her hand and made a beeline for her roadster parked outside.

"Do you know where we're supposed to go, Gunther?" She asked breathlessly as we climbed into her car.

"All I know Trixie, is that the house is situated on 2001 Sunset Boulevard."

"Jesus, Gunther, that's back the other way! It'll take at least thirty minutes to get there, so hold on to your seat!"

After a white-knuckle ride, which left me convinced that it wouldn't be amiss for Trixie to pay a visit to the opticians in the very near future, we eventually found Sunset Boulevard and took us a few more minutes to locate number 2001. Trixie swung left through the massive cast-iron gates and proceeded to drive up a lengthy driveway. After parking the roadster, we were confronted by a large house, built in the style of an early colonial Spanish hacienda. Because the house was ablaze with lights, it didn't take us long to locate the front door and after ringing the doorbell, it was soon opened by a white-jacketed Filipino manservant, with an Asian maid standing behind, waiting to take any scarves or coats. We waited briefly while the manservant left us, presumably to notify our host that we had arrived. Sure enough, he soon returned accompanied by the well-built figure of Emil Jannings and an attractive woman who was introduced to us as his wife, Gussie Holl.

Whilst Jannings was very courteous outwardly, I began to detect some of the worst aspects of the Teutonic character, picking up a somewhat overbearing, arrogant and precise attitude. His physique I may add, matched his personality, insofar as he was well-built, tall and with facial features set off by piercing blue eyes. He did, however, have one serious flaw which was that he was only able to speak English with a thick guttural accent, which made it rather difficult to understand him. It did make me wonder what would happen to his American career if the industry ever married sound to silent film (which according to rumours, the film studios were already starting experiments with). His wife, Gussie, until recently, had been both a film actress and the singer in Berlin and was both vivacious and striking in appearance. It was when she spoke in German that she exposed her sense of fun and showed capability of having an impish wit. With the pleasantries out of the way, we followed our hosts through a set of double doors into a large salon which was fairly crowded with at least two dozen or more guests, to whom my hosts soon had us introduced.

The first person I was presented to really needed no introduction, for it was none other than the screen legend, Gloria Swanson. She had recently starred in the film adaptation of *The Untamed Lady* and was attending the party with her husband, who it so happened, was also a member of the European aristocracy and went by the ridiculous title of Marquis de la Falaise de la Coudray, or Henri, for short, if you didn't want your tongue tied up in knots. With all this going on, Trixie was holding onto my hand for dear life, even more so, when the next actress we were introduced to was the number one screen vamp, Pola Negri, who was dressed head to toe in black, apparently in deep mourning for the recently passed screen heartthrob, Rudolph Valentino. She too had acquired the in-vogue and mandatory-titled husband, this one going by the daft title of Prince Serge Mdivani! - I sure as hell was at loss to know where they dug up all these titles from.

Poor Trixie was all but swooning at being confronted by all this blue blood! Mind you, Pola was no slouch herself to presenting a dramatic performance both on and off screen, as she too had recently been a big hit with the movie going public, playing Madame Du Barry to Emile Jannings' French King Louis XV in the film *Passion*. She certainly had surpassed herself off screen at Valentino's funeral where she had dramatically thrown herself over Valentino's coffin.

By the time that we had been presented to Ramon Navarro, Francis X. Bushman, May McEvoy, the renowned director, F.W. Murnau and several other notables, we were exhausted! There was to be none of the pomp and circumstance of the Fairbanks-Pickford formal dinner party of the night before, but rather a soirée of nibbles and canapés, mixed with a heavy mixture of European politics, arts and literature. This suited Trixie down to the ground, for with the absence of any formality, the atmosphere brought out the best in her and allowed her to be her natural self. She was soon laughing and joking with the best of them, swapping reminiscences on their experiences on starting at the bottom of the Hollywood ladder. I was caught between Francis X. Bushman and Ramon Navarro who were bombarding me with stories of their experiences on working on MGM's epic extravaganza, *Ben-Hur*, filmed both in Hollywood and Rome.

Jannings also told me of the wise decision that I had made in leaving Germany for Hollywood, where I could earn a considerable amount of money whilst waiting for the feeble Weimar Republic to be overthrown and the Kaiser restored to his throne, so that he could deal with the Jewish bankers and the communists who had been responsible for the treachery of 1918. Also, in the process of regaining his throne, the Kaiser could proceed to give the German people back their pride by tearing up the Treaty of Versailles. After that rather heavy conversation with Emil, Trixie and I quickly moved on, circulating amongst the other guests until we ended up in the company of Lon Chaney and his wife, Hazel Hastings. The four of us were soon swapping jokes and amusing stories about Hollywood. It just goes to prove that old adage that you should never judge a book by its cover, for although Lon was Hollywood's leading star character actor with a list of Hollywood films in which he portrayed mentally and physically deformed characters, such as *The Phantom of the Opera*, *The Hunchback of Notre Dame* and *He Who Gets Slapped*, he was, judging by our introduction to him, a light-hearted and very easy-going person off screen.

Despite the pair of us enjoying the social get-together that evening and giving me the opportunity to meet fellow actors who no doubt, I would be working with in the near future, the partying over the last three nights was beginning to catch up with me physically. The fact that I had an early appointment with the MGM bosses first thing in the morning forced me to reluctantly, say our goodbyes and leave. It was a lot quicker driving back. Trixie swung into the parking lot of the Beverley Hills Hotel where having parked up, she switched off the engine and we sat for a few minutes in the stillness of the night, listening to the orchestrated sounds of the tree frogs and their mating calls.

"Trixie, do you fancy a nightcap before setting off for home?" I asked her, breaking the silence between us.

"I think that would be a great idea, Gunty, but there is a problem."

"Pray, what is that, Trixie?" I asked, my speech slurring in reply.

"Well, sweetheart, judging by the state of us both, any further alcohol is going to make it unsafe for me to drive home. After all, I only need to get stopped by a motorcycle cop which would then probably lead to me being put in the slammer! I suppose at the risk of being called a loose woman, I could stay the night. Just as a matter of interest, Gunty, does your suite offer twin beds?"

"As a matter of fact, Trixie, the bedroom offers what you Americans call a King size double and if I may add, to alleviate any concerns that you may have, darling, on the proprietary of the situation, that I will gladly volunteer to sleep on the settee. I can also assure you that hand on heart, I have no hidden agenda. In fact, I can supply a reference to my good character if you so desire. If that meets with your approval, then let's get the hell out of this car and restart the evening! Agreed?"

"Okay, Gunty, agreed, as I don't figure you out to be a wolf! I will trust you to remain a gentleman. Tell you what, let's just see which one of us is still sober enough to win a race to the front desk for the key."

"You're on," I shouted, as I leapt out of the car and made a sprint for the hotel lobby. Unfortunately, I ran out of puff halfway across the parking lot and would you believe, as I stopped briefly to inhale some cool night air, who should come sprinting past me holding her shoes up in the air and shouting out Ra! Ra! Ra! but the indomitable Trixie who, in no time at all, had dodged around the astonished uniformed night porter, into the hotel lobby and up to the front desk, which is where I found her indulging in an animated conversation with the night manager whilst draped languidly over the desk. I rather suspect that the gentleman was well used to the goings-on of show business people in Tinseltown for he hardly batted an eyelid when Trixie ordered syrup and pancakes with side orders of sausages and bacon to be sent up to my suite. Having accomplished that, she then proceeded to dance me over to the elevator, totally hypnotising the bellboy at the sight of her gorgeous legs.

Sure enough, within thirty minutes of us entering my suite and making ourselves comfortable which also, by the way, included the pooling of our hip flasks and whatever was left over from my cachet of illicit booze, there came a knock on the door and our bellboy entered pushing a trolley containing our early morning breakfasts. By the time Trixie had finished good-naturedly vamping him, the poor lad was more than grateful to be on his way suitably rewarded with a handsome tip. The late-night snack, or early morning breakfast, was the bee's knees. In the short time that I had been in America, I had become an aficionado of the American custom of adding pancakes and syrup to their bacon and eggs, the eggs cooked sunny side up. Plus, another little touch that I had become addicted to, was the bottle of tomato sauce that accompanied the meal, identified by the Americans as ketchup. Another cultural difference that I had noticed with my American cousins was their habit of leaving the knife resting on the plate only to be used for cutting up the food before consuming it and then using the table fork for separating the food and putting it in their mouth.

On the other hand, after having watched my eating with some amusement, Trixie made the comment, "How very Fifth Avenue. Do all you guys from Europe eat like that?"

"You know, Trixie, although by heritage, we are cousins and share the same language, there is still quite a cultural difference between our two societies. For instance, you say 'ee-ther' and I say 'eye-ther'; you say 'potato' and I say 'potahto'; and finally, this one really confuses me, you say 'verhicular' and I say 'vehicle'.

After the two of us had finished laughing over that introduction to German and American pronunciations, we arose from the table and after pouring two further generous shots of bourbon, wandered out to the balcony where we stood cuddled together watching the moon over Los Angeles and soon became deep in conversation getting to know each other. I listened enthralled as Trixie told me about her childhood, growing up in the small town of Bedford Falls, Idaho and her escape from small town life to the terrifying jungle of New York City and her struggles to gain a foothold in the Broadway theatre world as a chorus girl. After a few years of learning her trade as a hoofer in stage musicals, she had decided to take off for the warmer climes of California, to try her luck in films. Eventually, having arrived at the position that she was now in, she was now accepted on the casting circuit as a supporting actress. However, her ambitions did not stop there because one day, in the distant future, films would achieve sound and that is where she would come into her own as an all-singing, all-dancing actress in Hollywood musicals.

It was only after we had wandered back in to escape the slight chill of the night-time air and after two or three drinks that I glanced at my watch realised it was already four o'clock in the morning and that somewhere in the back of my mind, I was scheduled to meet my new bosses at MGM by midday. By this time, the pair of us were feeling the effects of the alcohol that we had consumed, I considerably more so than Trixie. I think that I can honestly say that any physical desire that we may have had for each other had long since collapsed beneath the sheer excess of our non-stop partying. After a considerable amount of time spent in horseplay and giggling, don't ask me how, we managed to find a pillow and a blanket for the couch and having gently pushed Trixie into the master bedroom, I kissed her goodnight and closed the door.

Despite the room spinning at an increasing alarming rate, I just about managed to strip myself down to my underwear and collapse onto the couch whereupon with a great deal of difficulty, I was able to pull the blanket around me, giving me some degree of warmth. Only a few minutes could have passed before I felt a light shake of my shoulders and opening my eyes, I could see the silhouette of Trixie standing over me, dressed only in one of my shirts to cover her modesty. Still only half awake, I mumbled, "Trixie, are you alright?"

"No, I'm not," she answered, "I don't like sleeping in a strange bed on my own and it doesn't seem right that you should be out here sleeping on the couch, so come and join me and give me a cuddle." By the time I reached the bedroom, I had already fallen twice, trying to untangle the blanket around my ankles, much to the amusement of Trixie, who was doubled up with laughter at my inebriated clumsiness. Mind you, she wasn't in a much better state herself, whilst making every effort to remain dignified, she only succeeded in looking like a refugee from a Max

Senate comedy, especially with her efforts to protect her modesty by continuously pulling the shirt down to cover her rear end.

Anyway, to cut a long story short we began our first night as a couple, falling asleep in each other's arms and regretfully postponing our first great moment of passion for another day.

Chapter 5

The Roaring Twenties

The following morning with the help of a call from the hotel front desk and a considerable amount of effort on my part, I proceeded to prepare myself for my first experience of the MGM film studios. As soon as I had transformed from the shattered wreck that stared back at me from the bathroom mirrors into a reasonable facsimile of myself and chosen with great difficulty, a matching shirt and tie, suit and shoes, I was ready to go looking for the incumbent Trixie who was buried somewhere beneath the bedclothes. When she emerged looking as if she had been pulled through a wringer backwards, she still managed with that look of natural beauty which she had, to give off an aura of sheer sexual magnetism, leaving me in the process of feeling rather lightheaded and thinking what a waste of time it had been to have got dressed.

Common sense prevailed and whilst giving her a goodbye kiss, I whispered to her, "Stay where you are, sleeping beauty and until I return, help yourself to the hospitality of the hotel. The weather is looking fabulous out there this morning, ideal for a spot of sunbathing. Anything you want, just phone down for service."

"See you later, lover boy," Trixie mumbled as she threw her arms around my neck, "Have a great day and don't you worry because I'll still be here when you come back. It'll take me that amount of time just to pull myself together."

As I stepped out of the lift, Myron had just arrived and was striding towards the front desk when he spotted me. As he changed direction and began to approach me rapidly, he called out, "Morning, Gunther. Ready for the big day, I hope? The temperatures are already rising and I've got the top down on the car. If you don't mind me saying so but by the looks of it, you could do with some fresh air in your lungs. You look as if you been hitting the sauce too much last night?"

"I guess you're right, Myron. But a couple of cups of coffee and some fresh air will soon pull me around."

"I don't know about that one, Gunther. I rather suspect that a morning at the Turkish bath would do more to put you back on your feet. However, as we do not have enough time for that and our priority is to get you to the studio on time, I suggest that we get moving."

After a relaxing drive during which I was able to grab a few minutes of shuteye, I finally arrived, suitably refreshed at the main gates of MGM. After a brief confirmation of our appointment by the studio gate men, we were allowed through the barrier to the visitors' car park where eventually, Myron found a space to park. The walk to the front office which was situated in a large white building with broad white steps leading up to its entrance, not only revitalised me physically but also gave Myron the opportunity to fill me in on the layout of the studio. Apparently, behind the main building which housed the administrative offices was a building enveloped in glass for the purpose of exploiting the Californian sunlight. This, so Myron informed me, housed the indoor film stages where all the MGM movies were filmed. I also noticed a giant sign above the building with the logo of a lion and beneath it, in words, Metro-Goldwyn-Mayer studios. Further on from there, was a two-story white building with an outside balcony and stairs leading to it. Apparently, these were designated as the studio stars' dressing rooms, one of which, according to Myron, had already been consigned for my use.

It was whilst Myron was busy explaining the layout of the studio that I suddenly realised the contribution that Myron's father, Lewis Selznick had made to the founding of the Hollywood film industry. He was one of the first of the movie pioneers to arrive in Hollywood in 1920, to set up a movie producing studio and was the originator for turning the actors and actresses of his films into household names by intensive publicity, thereby identifying the actor by the part he played, hence the word star becoming part of movie history. Unfortunately, he had the bad habit of creating enemies within the industry by not being a team player. Consequently, with the absence of true friends for support and a few bad decisions along the way, he had only recently been made bankrupt, thereby leaving his two sons to carry the torch. I somehow sensed in Myron the need to settle old scores on behalf of his father and I was not to be proved wrong. It would be sometime in the future that both he and his brother, David, would prove to be the scourge of Hollywood, respectively as a voracious agent and a producer of formidable proportions.

At that moment, Myron's voice intruded upon my thoughts and brought me back to the present. "You know, Gunther, the battle for supremacy amongst the film studios has only just begun. William Fox, who both owns a chain of movie theatres and Fox studios and is also currently, the most powerful man in the industry, is circling MGM for a possible takeover. I think that at some time in the future with the discovery of new technical innovations within the industry that there will be an almighty battle of wills between the industry giants as to who emerges as numero uno."

"Well, while you're gazing into that crystal ball, Myron, perhaps you can foresee whether I will be signing a contract today with the winning side."

"No need to fear, Gunther. While I represent you as your agent, you will be able to swim amongst the sharks and emerge unscathed with the world as your oyster. Meanwhile, as we are nearly at the main building, I will quickly finish describing to you the main features of the studio lot. Further on down the street are various buildings containing sundry departments such as music, makeup, wardrobe, film laboratories and beyond that, the studio commissary called the Plantation Café whose piece de resistance is Mayer's famous chicken soup. Further beyond that is the studio back lot, upon which stands upon its acres, a Wild Western town, a mock-up of New York's Grand Central Station and various other sets depicting American small-time life and only until just recently, the Roman arena where they filmed the chariot race for *Ben-Hur*."

He paused briefly as the main building loomed up at us and then continued, "I am quite sure, Gunther, that by the time we have finished the morning's business and the signing of your contract, you will be taken on a guided tour of the studio otherwise known as Culver City and will be able to see it in all its glory for yourself. I can only describe my first experience of it with the feeling of being in a gigantic theatre with no audience participation, watching literally thousands of cast members and stagehands scurrying backwards and forwards, an experience I would think very similar to being part of a human anthill, something that I may add that you will very soon be part of. I am sure that you will very quickly learn your place in the pecking order of things, above all, who to trust and who not to, those to seek out who will advance your career the most and to diplomatically avoid those who won't and above all, to cultivate the friendship of the best directors and writers on the lot.''

When we finally entered the main building, Myron checked in at the reception desk and receiving directions, we then proceeded up the main stairs and along a long corridor to an open office where I was introduced to Mr Mayer's private secretary, a Miss Florence Browning. Whilst she spoke briefly into an intercom, the thought crossed my mind, that so far, whenever I had been due to meet Mr Mayer, I had been suffering from a hangover but before I had any time to read anything into that, Miss Browning had led us through an oak door into a very large office, the likes of which, I had never seen before. It was immense!

Covered in wall-to-wall white carpet upon which visitors to the inner sanctum had quite a long walk from the door, something like fifty feet I would say, to a large desk standing on a raised dais in front of which, several leather easy chairs had been placed. Behind the desk was an imposing high-backed, leather chair which had, for a backdrop, a large panoramic window, where on each of its corners were freestanding, the Stars & Stripes of America flag and the state flag of California. I noticed a door on one side of the office which I presume led into a private bathroom. Overall, the impression that I experienced was that of a medieval vassal paying tribute to his master. I suspect in all probability that was the intention of the occupier.

As we entered, there were four men standing in a group obviously awaiting our arrival, two of which I recognised instantly as Mr Mayer and Mr Brown whom I had met previously in Berlin. The other two men were introduced as Eddie Mannix, a man of burly physique with a very strong handshake and the other gentleman was Harry Rapf, who was of medium build with a non-descript appearance. However, he was easily identifiable by a very large nose. I understood that both men occupied positions of production chiefs within MGM, but the vibes that I experienced emanating from Mannix gave me the feeling that he was something more than that, possibly the studio trouble-shooter perhaps? In any case, he was somebody I would be very wary of. As for Harry Rapf, I learnt later, during my tenure at MGM, that he was in charge of the so-called 'B' unit, responsible for the studio's output of supporting features which also proved to be a fertile ground for training young actors and actresses, many of whom would go on to become great MGM stars.

It was at that moment of contemplation, that a young-looking man, almost a boy I would say, wandered in unannounced. This turned out to be Irving Thalberg, who next to Mayer, according to Myron, was the most important man at the studio and known throughout the industry as the boy wonder. Apparently, with a combination of Thalberg's ambitious drive and Mayer's ruthless headhunting of him from Paramount film studios, they had formed a partnership which resulted in the creation of MGM. I certainly couldn't feel anything but awe in his presence, knowing as I did, that at the age of twenty-seven, which incidentally was only two years older than me, he was one of the most powerful figures in the American film industry.

Apparently, the other trait that set him apart from his fellow moguls was that he was both highly articulate and intelligent and was beginning to earn a reputation for producing sophisticated films. As for me, I had not realised until much later, that I had been present at the birth of a new studio product, namely myself, which did leave me feeling rather like a prize animal being haggled over at a farmer's market. It soon became rapidly clear to me, soon afterwards, that I owed a debt of gratitude to both Clarence Brown and Irving Thalberg, for placing me in some highly prestigious films of the twenties, the consequences of which helped considerably in cementing my position as a star with the moviegoing public.

Meanwhile, I was forced to listen to a considerable amount of conferring amongst all parties present on the various paragraphs of my proposed contract. Finally, when that topic had been exhausted, the conversation came around to what film my first starring vehicle would be. At that point, Thalberg quietly injected that it had been their desire to choose as my first film, a picture called *The Torrent* and that I would appear with their new sensational Swedish discovery, Greta Garbo, as my co-star. However, that was not to be either, for I was soon to learn in the glorified stratosphere that was Hollywood, nothing was what it seemed. I discovered that despite Thalberg's objections, Mayer had vetoed the project and that I would start work in two weeks, on a film tentatively to be called, *Fifth Avenue Moll*, in which they would be trying me out in my first film with yet another exceptional, new young actress as my co-star, someone who had already developed a huge public following, for portraying vibrant flapper girls of the twenties. Her name was Joan Crawford.

Finally, the business was brought to conclusion, with the arrival of the studio legal counsel, J. Robert Rubin, for the purpose of signing the studio contract. Whilst the contracts were being laid out on Mayer's desk, a photographer entered the office and proceeded to take photographs of me signing my contract seated in Mayer's chair with Thalberg and Mayer standing on either side of me posing with avuncular joy. This little ceremony marked the birth of my Hollywood career.

I spent the rest of a very pleasant day on a guided tour of the MGM dream factory, which incidentally, because the studio was spread over so much acreage, required the use of a miniature maintenance buggy to get around. The highlight of the tour for me was a visit to a replica of a small Dutch village specially built on the MGM backlot, where I met Marion Davies and Owen Moore, who were the two stars of the film which was to be titled *The Red Mill*. I also had the surprising pleasure of being introduced to the director of the movie, Bill Goodrich. I mention pleasure, because I recognised Goodridge as the great movie comic from the early part of this century, Fatty Arbuckle, whose career had been destroyed by a sex scandal of which he had been proved innocent. Nevertheless, despite an apology from the jury of his later trial, the case had still ruined his career. Hence, my meeting him as a director at MGM under his pseudonym of William Goodridge.

It was also during my visit to the set that I had the opportunity of chatting with Marion Davies and this connection turned out to be the beginning of a lifetime friendship which endured until her death. As it happened, I was able to spend a very pleasant hour with Marion during a break in filming, most of which was spent chatting at the Plantation Café whilst having a bowl of Lewis B. Mayer's fabled chicken soup. Marion and I got along together like a house on fire and despite her bubbly personality, she proved to be no slouch in the intelligence department, constantly asking me questions about my European career and the effects of the First World War on the moral fabric of my country.

The upshot of that first meeting was an invitation to spend a weekend at Hearst Castle, which was literally a castle situated at

San Simeon on the Pacific coastline between Los Angeles and San Francisco. I did learn, later in the day from Myron, that the castle was literally named after William Randolph Hearst, the American newspaper tycoon who had transported most of the castle, piece by piece and had personally scoured Europe, purchasing rare antiques and furniture for the castle's refurbishment. Myron also filled me in on the fact that Marion and Randolph Hearst had been lovers for some time and that he had installed her as chatelaine of Hearst Castle.

Such was the size of the MGM lot, that I was more than grateful towards the end of the afternoon when I was given several scripts to read for future projects and to report back to the studio in two weeks, which would give me time to settle into the Hollywood way of life. After giving me a light schedule to follow for the forthcoming two weeks, Myron soon had me back at the hotel and after dropping me off, I went straight up to the suite ready to apologise to Trixie for being so late. However, I needn't have worried too much on that score as she had made herself very much at home, by having room service send up a lunch whilst she sunbathed on the balcony. As it happens, Trixie had just finished a small part in a movie at Paramount and fortunately for me, was now in between films, giving both of us the perfect opportunity for her to show me around Los Angeles during the next couple of weeks.

Regrettably, because of the way I was feeling, my only inclination was for a light evening and an early night. Even with youth on my side, I had been physically blown away by the sheer exhaustion of the journey from New York to Los Angeles, the overindulgence of bootleg alcohol, the uppers and downers that I had been supplied to keep me going and finally, the stress of being introduced to Hollywood society as the latest new kid on the block. All of these factors had finally taken their toll. Not knowing how Trixie would respond to not going out that evening, especially after staying in all day waiting for me to return, I proceeded to sit down beside her with the sole purpose of apologising for any lack of consideration that I may have caused her, taking a deep breath I began.

"Forgive me, Trixie," I began but before I could go any further, she interrupted me. She jumped up from the settee and striking a very in-vogue Clara Bow stance with hands on hips and legs akimbo, finishing it all off with a pugnacious and mischievous look, she made a pronouncement.

"I can't think of anything that I would want to forgive you for, yet! Unless, of course, you are trying to give me the brush off, in which case, forget it! I'm a big girl and this is Hollywood. You have treated me to a fabulous weekend, introduced me to many important people, which could very well lead me to being offered some long-term film work and finally, I have stayed in this fabulous hotel suite and been treated like royalty. To top it all, I've had a Kraut film star as my escort and incidentally, one whom I happen to think is one hell of a nice guy. Gee honey, what more would a girl want?"

"Bloody hell, Trixie! I seem to have started this conversation off rather clumsily. It's the furthest thought in my mind to even think of giving you the brush off. In fact, I want this to be the beginning of a great relationship, starting with you introducing me to the sights and sounds of Hollywood and helping me to buy a home. In truth Trixie, I am completely exhausted. Since leaving Germany, I have been constantly on the move as well as having been completely overwhelmed by the experiences that I have had since landing in America. All I want to do at this moment is to take you out for a quiet meal and for both of us to start afresh in the morning. If I am going to explore Los Angeles, there is nothing I want more than to have you by my side to help me share the experiences."

"You continentals are something else," Trixie laughingly replied. "You are so courteous and full of all that 'kiss your hand madam', nonsense that you forget that you are in America now. You must learn to be more direct. As it happens, I would like to have an early night, if only for a change of clothing and to catch up on small everyday matters and then perhaps, if you are willing, we could meet up again tomorrow and I could then take you on a personal tour and if I could suggest, perhaps we could dine downstairs in the hotel restaurant."

So, that is how we spent the rest of the day until I escorted her through the hotel lobby, where the parking valet had fetched her roadster up to the front doors. As I held the door open for her to climb into the driving seat, I was both temporarily mesmerised by the flash of thighs and amused as she reached into the glove compartment and pulled out a cloche hat and goggles which she proceeded to jam on her head and finally, whilst blowing me a kiss shouted out.

"See you tomorrow morning at eleven in the morning, Loverboy!" Then, she put her foot down and roared away from the hotel whilst sounding her klaxon horn as an accompaniment to her departure. As I turned on my heel to go back into the hotel, I had a thought that perhaps I might be rushing into a relationship that could possibly end up out of my control. Memories of my possessive mother had left an emotional wound in my psyche. But I soon dismissed it as quickly as it had arrived. After all said and done, here I was in America, young and on the verge of a great career and at the same time, mesmerised by a gorgeous, vibrant young lady. I needed to look at this situation as a classic opportunity to seize the day and enjoy life to the full.

I awoke the next morning, having taken advantage of an early night, feeling suitably refreshed and full of beans and ready to make an energetic start to the day. Punctuality was certainly one of Trixie's strong points for bang on eleven o'clock, she arrived outside the hotel. I barely had time to jump in beside her before we were off on a whirlwind tour of downtown Los Angeles which according to her was rapidly changing from its early nineteenth century, small town parochialism, to being well on its way to becoming a vibrant and cosmopolitan city. This development was all due, according to Trixie, to the invasion of the once looked down upon jobbing actors and film technicians. To prove her point, she drove me to a subdivision of Los Angeles called Burbank where Warner Bros. had built their studio. Then, further on, we saw the mighty Fox film studios which, under the guidance of its founder, William Fox, had become a major player in Hollywood and then finally, a quick drive past the huge gates of Paramount film studios, where Trixie had just recently completed a small film role.

After such an exhausting morning, she gave me a special treat by taking me to lunch at a locally popular deli eatery called Barkie's, where I had the most amazing club sandwich called a New York pastrami. We spent the remainder of the afternoon driving up to Holmby Hills, before going down along the Pacific Palisades. We finished the day off by having an early dinner at Musso and Frank's Grill, a watering hole for the Hollywood show folk, after which, we then went on to Al Levy's Tavern, where we danced the night away and finished up at my hotel suite finally consummating our love as the dawn was beginning to break. The following days were sheer heaven, either spending the time swimming or making love or during the intermissions, spending the evenings dining and dancing at local entertainment spots such as the Pig and Whistle or the Garden of Allah, a very discreet hotel with bungalows for the rich and famous.

At the beginning of the second week, I got down to spending some serious money. With Trixie's help, I bought my first American car, a Chrysler six model 426 roadster, which in turn, under Trixie's guidance, led me into acquiring my first piece of American real estate, namely the purchase of a two-bedroom bungalow at 325 Oceanfront, Santa Monica. I had fallen for its charm and made an instant decision to buy it as a freehold property rather than to rent, as I could plainly see its potential as an investment for the future rather than just a place to sleep in. Trixie proved a blessing in disguise by helping me choose the furniture and took great pains, especially with the selection of the bed. She moved in, if only, as she explained, to test the bed out. It was now obvious that we had become attached to each other and certainly, on my part, it had become serious. Even in the two weeks that we had been going out together, the press had begun to take note of the fact. Very quickly, we had become a press item for the American and international magazines, so much so, that in the end, we were forced to become very discreet on where we were seen. As a celebrity, I accepted it, as it went with the territory, but it was a lot harder on Trixie to suddenly go from an almost non-existent player in Tinseltown to having the public spotlight shining on her full-time as the girlfriend of a film star, or so I thought at the time. I would, eventually, have a change of opinion on that point of view.

At the end of two weeks and at the ungodly hour of seven o'clock in the morning, I duly reported to MGM at Culver City carrying my first script assignment, titled *Irene, Maggie and Sally*. The story was about three show girls and their adventures. I was to play a wealthy young socialite pursued by the three girls; Shakespeare it certainly was not. My co-star and love interest was to be the vivacious Joan Crawford, an up-and-coming young actress whom MGM were promoting to become a big star. She had, so far, created an impact with the American moviegoing public in her personification of the twenties flapper girl or jazz babe. I certainly was looking forward to working with her. The director was to be Edmund Goulding, who I was led to understand, was the studio's highly respected all-round workhorse, who was able to turn out many successful films, covering all genres.

Once I had passed through the main gates, I proceeded to soundstage number four where I was ushered into my allocated on-set dressing room. I spent several hours on makeup and wardrobe fitting, after which Edmund Goulding popped in with three gorgeous young actresses who were introduced to me as Sally O'Neill, Joan Crawford and Joan Bennett. The formalities over, the five of us got along famously together. I spent the early part of the afternoon standing on the side lines as the three girls went through their first scene, which was to introduce them to the film audience. Then, it was my turn to go before the cameras where I spent the remainder of the afternoon filming sixty seconds of my introduction to the young ladies. That, as it turned out, after some twelve hours of sitting around all day, was to be the total of my endeavours. Fortunately, Trixie had arrived earlier and had been sitting quietly observing the goings-on from behind the cameras so that on the final call of, "It's a wrap," we were all able to go over to Beanies, a watering hole across the road from the studio, which served the needs of the studio personnel.

This, it turned out, was to be my first experience of visiting a juke joint, a brand-new technical achievement that eventually would sweep the world. As we entered Beanie's, the first thing that I noticed was the sound of music which was surprisingly good. However, I couldn't seem to be able to see any musician's playing. Trixie, noticing my look of perplexity, took my arm whilst laughing and dragged me over to a corner of the eatery where stood a brown cabinet with a glass door through which I could see a record stack and a turntable and just below the glass door was situated a dial with both alphabet and numerals upon it. According to Trixie, for the price of a nickel, you could choose a record from the list alongside the dial and would be able to listen or dance to your chosen song. She finished my education on the subject by telling me that owing to licensing rights within the musical industry, there was a limited selection, namely blues music accompanied by artists such as Muddy Waters and Kate Smith. Very quickly, we took over several tables and chairs and armed with recently purchased alcohol from a bootlegger in the car park, plus some great burgers and fries as well as a pocketful of nickels, I settled down to enjoy with Trixie and the studio gang what would turn out to be a rapturous and merry night. So ended the first day of shooting on my first Hollywood film.

A lot of water passed under the bridge after that day. I had been lucky that my first American film had been reasonably successful with the moviegoing public and I had gone on to make many more box office successes, including *Black Shadows of the South Seas* and *The Norseman*, the latter filmed in colour and with partial sound but not dialogue. The word sound, for a brief time, referred only to sound effects, but all that came to an end when, in October 1927, Warner Bros. introduced to the public the part-talkie, *The Jazz Singer*, starring the Broadway star, Al Jolson. That signalled the beginning of the end of silent film, just when they were beginning to reach their peak as a true art form. The six words, "You ain't heard nothing yet folks!" spoken by Al Jolson, ensured the imprisonment of the camera by keeping it static and where actors stood clustered around a vase of flowers in which the microphone was hidden, speaking slowly, like automated robots, to ensure that their lines could be picked up by the hidden microphone, thereby eliminating any natural movement.

To make matters worse, Hollywood actors were put in a position where they had to prove that they could talk. Embarrassing as it sounds, as a stage-trained and a bilingual speaking actor, I was forced to attend elocution lessons conducted by a half-baked idiot to recite, "How now, brown cow." Only then, did the studio, with the approval of my elocutionist, cast me in my first hundred per cent talkie and although the public accepted my vocal cords wholeheartedly, putting it bluntly, the film only did moderately well at the box office.

As I entered 1929, I looked back at the historical events that had occurred since I had arrived in America. A young aviator by the name of Charles Lindbergh had flown the Atlantic to Europe, where a political firebrand by the name of Adolph Hitler was beginning to gain prominence in my own country. The stock market had just recently crashed and during the process, had ruined thousands of lives, thereby bringing in the great economic depression. I had never been a great believer in stocks and shares or investments and therefore, had escaped the great financial disaster. Not so lucky, was William Fox, the extremely powerful head of Fox film studios, who had only recently acquired a large chunk of shares in MGM, which had placed him in the position of being the largest player in Hollywood. However, the stock market crash and a near fatal automobile accident which had temporarily incapacitated him, contributed to him being severely financially damaged, the consequences of which, over the next two years, had allowed his competitors to topple him from his position of industrial prominence in the film industry.

MGM, alongside all the other major studios, having finally now accepted that talkies were here to stay, were beginning to run around like headless chickens in their efforts to catch up with public demand, to the extent that in the stampede to produce more talkies, they were even throwing the baby out with the bathwater. A consensus amongst them all, was that they needed to band together to find a universal sound system that they could all use and together, be able to obtain the maximum benefit. One of the first steps that they introduced collectively, was to begin to unload those silent film stars whose vocal cords were not compatible with the new medium of sound, decisions which were usually based on the moviegoing public's perceived reaction to hearing them. At the same time, they began to lure to Hollywood from Broadway, stage trained actors.

In my case, Myron had already informed me that as my present contract was up for renewal, that in view of the uncertain economic times, the studio would be happy to renew but at a reduced salary and on a short-term basis. Nevertheless, despite those terms negotiated between Myron and MGM, Mayer insisted on meeting with me in his office without my agent. Being not only curious but intrigued, I decided to keep the appointment and I was certainly glad that I did. Initially, Mayer welcomed me with open arms when I entered his office. His whole demeanour radiating a close friendship. He proceeded to sit down with me and went on to give me a lengthy spiel on how hard times were for the industry. After listening to this one-sided conversation for some time, I gently interrupted him, reminding him that I was here on a one-to-one basis to negotiate my proposed new contract on the old terms. Mayer would have none of it. He proceeded to reiterate that times were bad for the country and that the industry was haemorrhaging money in financing the changeover from silent movies to sound. Finally, he finished the conversation by informing me that if he had a son who worked for a nice man and a wonderful studio, he would tell him to be grateful and help the studio out by accepting less. After having witnessed this barnstorming monologue that would have put any actor to shame, I finally took my leave. Later, when I ran into Myron, he asked me.

"How did you get on, Gunther? Were you able to get any improvement on your proposed new contract?"

"No," I replied, "but I think I gained a father."

Frankly, I could see no point in hanging around Hollywood on those terms, merely to play in static-photographed stage plays that had already become out of fashion with the cinema going public, as well ending up becoming a prisoner of the restrictions of the sound booth. Intuitively, I felt the need to take a sabbatical from Hollywood whilst it was in its transitional stage and return to Europe, so that I could extend my artistic range in both theatre and film. Meanwhile, as I foresaw, many of my fellow silent stars were being hastily thrown into movies which also happened to be technically inadequate for sound. In other words, these stars' natural speaking voices were not even matching the screen characters that they were supposed to play.

Tragically, the vision of watching a previously great romantic star such as John Gilbert, cavorting across the screen dressed in cloak and tights mouthing the words, "I love you; I love you," in a high-pitched voice, proved too much for movie audiences, who promptly fell about the auditorium in hysterical laughter. Meanwhile, whilst I was making up my mind, the final film in my existing contracts would be in the role of master of ceremonies in their new all singing, all dancing, all speaking and all colour movie, which would showcase the musical talents of the top stars. My role in this extravaganza was to walk on and off camera while introducing the stars in various sketches and at the same time, uttering ridiculous lines. The movie was to be called *The Hollywood Review*. This venture demonstrated how desperate the studio was, as most of the stars that were involved in this monstrosity had as much musical talent as Rintintin, the reigning canine wonder. Having refused this assignment and with the studio having no alternative to offer me, we settled amicably on an immediate termination of my contract with one proviso, that as Mayer was one of the founding members of a new industrial organisation to be called the Academy of Motion Pictures and Science, he asked me if I would host the inaugural presentation. The first annual ceremony was to be held in the Blossom Room of the Hollywood Roosevelt Hotel and would be known thereafter, as the Academy Awards. Mayer made the point that as I was still part of the MGM family, he would like me to hand out the gold statuettes to the winners of the various categories. I willingly accepted though I must admit, I did not realise at the time that as a presenter, I would become part of the Academy's history and a footnote in the beginning of sound.

Meanwhile, Trixie and I had settled into the routine of a married couple without the marriage certificate, socially accepted by both the public and the Hollywood social hierarchy. Trixie as it so happened, was making the transition to sound very smoothly. She had the good luck to appear in innovative musical films where her singing and dancing had gained the affection of the cinema public. The studio had quickly recognised her potential and had placed her under a new contract guaranteeing her name above the title. Also, the scuttlebutt going around Hollywood was that Paramount was planning to put her into a series of musicals pairing her with the international dancing star by the name of Frederick Austerlitz. I should have realised at the time, as with a lot of showbiz partnerships, that as one partner's career hit a bump in the road and the other partner had soared ahead successfully, fault lines would start to appear. I knew instinctively that once I had made up my mind to pack up and leave Hollywood, that my number one concern would be my relationship with Trixie. I loved her dearly as I believed she did me and although we had never discussed our future together, I knew that the time was rapidly approaching when I must ask her, that if I decided to return to Europe, would she come with me as my wife.

When I look back on that first Academy Awards ceremony, I was struck how very low-key the affair was compared to what it would become over the years. The Blossom Room was a reasonably large suite accommodating roughly three-hundred people who were placed around tables seating ten guests per table. I would be presenting in front of them with a long table behind me, holding the appropriate number of statuettes. As it was going to be just a private affair, there was only a solitary movie cameraman to cover the highlights of the ceremony. Louis B.

Mayer gave a very articulate opening speech as to why we should have an annual ceremony to honour the achievements of the industry's artists and when he finished, I took over. I remember the Oscar for Best Actor was won by Emil Jannings, who had already returned to Germany and his award was accepted in his absence, by the actor, William Powell. Janet Gaynor received a Best Actress award for her performance in the film *Sunrise*, the Best Picture award going to the same film. After the awards had been given out, the general feeling amongst the attendees was that it was all in much ado about nothing and in all probability would not last. My guess was that it would take a few years for Hollywood to come to terms with the medium of sound but once they had freed the microphone from the static position and allowed it to freedom of fluidity, actors and scripts would adapt very quickly to the new medium. Meanwhile, the carnage would continue amongst existing stars. John Gilbert, the reigning romantic movie idol would be the first to fall and even Clara Bow, the original 'It' girl succumbed to 'mike fright' although would successfully overcome it and go on to make several successful sound movies by which time, she had decided enough was enough and retired, opting for a happy marriage instead.

Meanwhile, having finally made up my mind, I had begun to put my affairs in order, in anticipation of my departure from America. My agent was working behind the scenes to ensure that studio doors would remain open to me should I decide to return, whilst meanwhile, my agent in Europe, Oscar, had already negotiated a film for me in Germany to start in the spring of 1930. I had also decided to hold onto my property in Santa Monica and rent it out. In fact, I had already made the decision to acquire more real estate holdings with my surplus American dollars. Apart from tennis, my other indulgence during my stay in Hollywood had been the love of the sea and consequently, I had bought a small three berth schooner which I called *The Lucky Trixie*. Whenever possible, I would escape the rat race of Hollywood by sailing her, more often, than not, down to Mexico. I had found an experienced seaman by the name of Bill Taft to captain her, with Trixie and I acting as crew. We would often take friends with us, fishing and swimming along the coast of the California peninsula of Baja, finishing the days off whilst carousing in the small Mexican cantinas. It was on one such weekend that Trixie and I, just seeking our own company, took Bill in the boat sailing down to Tijuana and anchoring just off the coastline. I think Bill must have sensed that we needed some time to ourselves, for he decided to take the dinghy ashore and as he put it, to have some fun with the local señoritas. After spending the morning sunbathing on the deck, sipping a few Jack Daniels with ice, I finally decided it was time to tell Trixie that I had decided to return to Europe and with that in mind decided that it would be the perfect moment to propose to her for her hand in marriage.

"Trixie, darling, right from the first moment that we met, there was no doubt that we were meant for each other. I love you dearly and want to spend the rest of my life with you. I have finally decided in the last few days to return to Europe and broaden my career opportunities. To be honest with you, Trixie, whilst Hollywood is in the throes of dealing with its own industrial upheaval, I can't see anything but stagnation for me, so I would rather take a professional gamble by returning to my homeland and explore more innovative options. But I cannot visualise any of it being worthwhile unless I can take you back with me as my wife. I know that you are on the cusp of being a star in Hollywood, but with my support and your talent, I am sure that you would gain invaluable experience that would propel your career upwards and eventually achieve all that you wished for. I also realise that you would be making a big sacrifice in abandoning your homeland, but I honestly feel that together whilst conquering new worlds we will have a happy life together."

"Oh Gunty, this should be the happiest moment of my life and I dearly want to say yes. But I too, have been thinking things over in my mind and I think in anticipation of this moment, I have reached the conclusion that the drawbacks of leaving America would outweigh any benefits that would be gained. Apart from sacrificing my career which as you know, is about to take off, I would be going to live in a strange country where I don't speak the language. I would also be isolating myself from my family and friends and from my way of life. Even as I speak these words, Gunty, I know in my heart that it would never work. Is it not possible for you to remain in America with me as man and wife where I could support you should you fail in your desire to broaden your horizons? You know I don't even think that it is necessary for us to become married, for as you said earlier, ours is a perfect partnership which allows us the freedom of making individual choices and you know perfectly well, Gunty, that should you fail which I very much doubt, I would support you wholeheartedly."

"I understand your reaction to my sudden and unexpected proposal of marriage, Trixie. It was ungallant of me and I should have given you a little more time in which to consider. I suppose if I am honest about it, we are asking a lot of each other. We both are deeply committed to our careers and I should not expect any less from you than I would of myself. We are both Hollywood veterans and you know as well as I do that if I was to marry you and remain in Hollywood and my career was to founder, I would end up in the position of being a kept husband, a position which goes totally against my character and one, that I would never tolerate. What is more, it would place a terrible strain on our marriage. Though my pride has been somewhat injured in your rejection and that you have been forthright in your refusal, I am more than grateful that you have left me no room in which to wallow in self-pity. There is no reason why we cannot remain the best of friends for as I'm sure you know, there has been too much water gone under the bridge for either of us not to occupy a small place in our hearts for each other. If it is all right with you, my darling, I suggest we crack open a few bottles and drink to our joint futures and our continuing support for each other whilst we wait for Bill to get back and then tomorrow, we will sail back to Santa Monica."

"Gunty, I think there is still time for us to reconsider our positions and if not, we will always have our memories. I know that whatever you decide for your future in Europe, it will be successful, for you are that type of man. I do not know when your departure will be but for the next several months, I will be out of town filming on location which will make life difficult for us insofar as being together. To make it easier, I shall move out of the bungalow when we get back to town. Hopefully, we should still be able to see each other when the opportunity arises."

I knew within my heart that when we finally parted, it would be many years before I would overcome the emotional damage to my feeling of self-esteem. I was also mortified to reflect that what had been an exciting adventure in Hollywood would finish on such a dark note. I have to say that as I spent the next few days reflecting on the ending of our love affair and my decision to return to Europe, a doubt began forming in the back of my mind that perhaps Trixie, despite her love for me, right from the start, had a parallel agenda of her own running alongside our relationship. Maybe one day, I would be able to confirm that feeling, one way or the other.

The remaining weeks that I had left before my departure from Hollywood were spent tidying up my affairs and saying farewell to my friends and industrial acquaintances through a series of social gatherings. Meanwhile, on our return from Mexico, I had, metaphorically speaking, closed the door on Trixie and walked away. This, however, was not the way that Trixie chose to put an end to our love affair. In a series of discrete public relation manoeuvres, she started by a planting the breakup of our relationship in the Hollywood papers and local radio stations, implying that because of my desire to further my career in Europe, I was leaving her behind to pick up the pieces of her broken heart as well as leaving her no choice but to throw herself wholeheartedly into her film career. Naturally, the press having bombarded me daily for my side of the story and only getting a "No comment" response from me, then proceeded to embellish their own version, thereby gaining Trixie a massive wave of public sympathy, an act which was not lost on her studio bosses, who seizing the publicity bonanza announced a major new film to star her.

Trixie's final coup de grace was administered through the press, who pursued me to the gangway of the SS Ile-de-France on my day of departure for Europe with the following by-line, 'Lothario gets his comeuppance by being shown the door'. This was to be the second and final time that I was to be emotionally betrayed. The first had been by my mother who had caused me so much hurt by her possessiveness and now, for the second time around, but for entirely different reasons, by Trixie. To be honest though, I did not realise it at that time, Trixie had gifted to me the greatest lesson that I would ever learn in life; namely that never again, in any future relationship, would I allow myself to be placed unwittingly in such a subservient role. I suppose a psychiatrist and Lord knows there was enough of them in Hollywood, would say that right from an early age, I had erected in my psych a wall to prevent me from being overcome by the slings and arrows of outrageous fortune. I realise now as I matured, that although I had successfully protected myself, at the same time, I had unwittingly blinded myself to my own shortcomings and consequently, had become less of a human being. I suppose my defence mechanism kicked in when I held my final press conference on board prior to sailing. I was determined to prevent Trixie from seeing the extent of the emotional damage that she had inflicted upon me. Accordingly, I adopted a low-key reaction to the whole of the proceedings by responding in a laid-back manner, wishing Trixie all the best for the future.

Chapter 6

Love Strikes Again

The journey across the North Atlantic proved uneventful. Without a lot of thought, I had chosen the *SS Île de France* to convey me back to Europe and as it turned out, this choice had been a wise one. Though slower in speed than its other north Atlantic competitors, it was furnished in a more luxurious design ensuring that its passengers enjoyed the highest standards of service and comfort. Whilst I enjoyed the company of fellow thespians such as Douglas Fairbanks and his wife, Mary Pickford, it also gave me time to reflect on my future. I couldn't help but wonder whether I had done the right thing in leaving America and betting on my homeland to welcome me back with open arms, revitalising my career at the same time.

It was a different Germany that I returned to in 1930. Because of the stock market crash, the deutschmark had destabilised, seriously influencing the sustainability of the Weimar government to function. Unemployment had risen to a dangerous level, political unrest was being stoked up by a large communist faction and in juxtaposition, a right-wing party was growing in strength with an ever-increasing membership. They called themselves the Nationalist Socialist Party and the leader was a political firebrand by the name of Adolf Hitler, who had recently been released from prison, after serving a sentence for attempting to lead a coup against the central government of Germany. Hitler was emerging as a national politician. Like many Germans, I had many reservations about this man. Although he gave off an aura of strength and determination, he also had at his disposal, a considerable private army of uniformed members called stormtroopers, otherwise known as the SA, who under the cover of his ideological and political philosophy, had been carrying out a series of brutal attacks against his opponents. He also happened to be virulent advocate of anti-Semitism which was coupled with his desire for a greater Germany to take its rightful place amongst the other European nations. It was the latter part of his political manifesto that had struck a sympathetic chord within me as well as many others. Many of us were becoming increasingly disillusioned with massive unemployment and the humiliating terms of the 1919 Versailles Treaty imposed by the victorious allies at the League of Nations conference after the conclusion of the First World War.

I had decided to make Berlin my base of operation because it offered the best opportunities for getting theatre and film work and because of the energy that the city generated. Despite the recession and the uncertain political time, people were expressing themselves by pushing the social boundaries back, embracing greater freedom of choices and rejecting many of the old values of the past. Everywhere, clubs were offering avant-garde entertainment to suit all tastes, especially in political satire and sexual freedom. This was also where female impersonators were all the rage. In other words, social taboos were being trampled on and many boundaries extended. Because of the uncertainty of my life, my only desire was to enjoy every day as if there were no tomorrow and therefore, happily went along with the general euphoria of the times. As I had no desire to put down roots, I had rented a large apartment on the Wilhelm Strasser and immediately, reconnected with old friends. I must admit that one of the first benefits I experienced on returning to my homeland, was being able to converse in my native tongue without converting to English. Another benefit was the fact that the German intelligentsia had a far more experienced and sophisticated outlook of the times, in comparison to our American cousins, who intended to view the world from a position of isolationism.

It felt good to reconnect with old friends and acquaintances, so consequently, I decided to throw a housewarming party at my new apartment which would give me a great opportunity to further cement those relationships. Meanwhile, as far as my working life was concerned, two German films had been released over the last twelve months that had been recorded on sound discs and had been successful. The first, titled *The Blue Angel*, was released in 1930 and officially, it was the first German sound film. It starred a young actress by the name of Marlene Dietrich, who on the strength of her performance in that film, along with the film's director, Joseph von Sternberg, had become an international celebrity and had been enticed to sign a contract by the Paramount film studios in the United States and had left for Hollywood. The second film, titled *M*, was directed by Fritz Lang, a German director noted for his 1927 masterpiece *Metropolis* and starred my old friend, Peter Lorre, who portrayed a child killer being tracked down by the Berlin underworld.

On the strength of that film, both he and Lang ultimately ended up in Hollywood. It was no coincidence that most of the people involved in the making of these two films were friends of mine and were amongst the guests invited to my housewarming party which turned out to be a riotous night. As usual, more people turned up than were invited, which put the catering staff under enormous pressure in providing a continuous supply of food and drink. I had always been a lover of music and made sure that wherever I had lived, a grand piano had been installed. On this occasion, I had the good fortune to have invited the great American composer, Cole Porter, who coincidentally, happened to be in town, to spend an evening with me as my guest.

I had met Porter several times socially in New York and Los Angeles and was a great admirer of his music. So, when I heard that he was passing through Berlin as part of a European vacation, I contacted him and invited him to the party. What a night of memories that turned out to be, for as the evening progressed and without any encouragement from me, but fortified with several glasses of champagne, Cole sat down at the piano and proceeded to play throughout the course of the evening.

Meanwhile, whilst the majority of guests were joining in with the music, I was circulating from one small group of guests to another until I ended up with the circle of close friends, namely Peter Lorre, Franz Waxman, Billy Wilder, Fritz Lang and the Berlin newspaper columnist, Bella Fromm. The general discussion amongst us all was the emergence of Adolf Hitler as a national politician and the fears that because he was so obviously anti-Semitic that if he ever came to power, there would be a strong possibility of yet another pogrom against the Jews. The consensus amongst us all was that in the likelihood of him ever becoming Chancellor, they would have to emigrate. Bella Fromm on the other hand had a different view: she felt that eventually, Hitler would overreach himself and be defeated by both public opinion and the press, as well as the eventual increase in the standard of living for most working-class households.

Looking back, I think we were all very naïve and should have had greater perspective of the coming storm. But rather selfishly, being the only gentile amongst them, I did not feel that that was a problem as far as I was concerned. Little did I realise that within five years, all of them, apart from Bella Fromm, would have fled Germany and even she would join them, eventually. Franz Waxman who had cowritten and orchestrated the music score for *The Blue Angel* with the composer, Frederic Hollander, also left Germany in 1934, after receiving a severe beating in the street by Nazi thugs. He had departed swiftly for France. By the following year, he would end up in America as a composer in his own right, scoring for the film, *Bride of Frankenstein*. At the same time in 1934, Billy Wilder would also leave Germany for America via France, where he would eventually, succeed in gaining a reputation as a first-rate scriptwriter. Bella Fromm would continue to work as a political journalist for the newspaper *Berliner Zeitung* until 1934 where she was able to continue her journalistic career under an assumed name. This was only tolerated by the Nazis because she was protected by senior foreign politicians. However, even she was finally forced to leave in fear of her life.

Needing another drink, I left the group, for by this time, the discussion has gone from politics to the state of the German theatre. As I completed the replenishment of my glass from a diminishing stock of champagne, the room broke into applause at the finish of a Cole Porter favourite, *Let's do it, Let's fall in Love,* the song having been performed by a young blonde woman whom I recognised from the distance from a long time ago as having been a fellow drama student in Hamburg. As I moved towards her, I collided with another guest who turned out to be Kurt Gerron, an actor who had portrayed the clown in *The Blue Angel*. It soon transpired that the young blonde woman, whose name was Emmy Sonnemann, was Kurt's partner for the evening. As it turned out, I had fond memories of Emmy, for it was during our days as young drama students that we had become friends. I well remember one evening that I had been involved in seeing off two louts who had been threatening her and that had led to a bond between us, leaving me looking upon her as a younger sister. I had lost touch with her during my stay in America, so we had a lot of catching up to do.

Whilst Kurt slipped away for a few minutes to speak to somebody he knew, Emmy and I caught up on the past. Not that there was any explaining to do, for my early success as an actor had been well documented by the press. It appeared that it had not been quite as easy for Emmy. In fact, it had been quite a struggle for her to achieve a name for herself as an actress, especially since divorcing her husband. She was still waiting for the lucky part that would make her a star. As we were talking, I had taken the opportunity of studying her and though she wasn't strikingly beautiful, she did have a good figure, with a petite oval face topped by blonde curly hair and also, she had an air about her that commanded attention. She was also out of work and had no prospects lined up. I decided there and then to try and help her and slipped her a note with my telephone number on it, telling her to phone me within a few days because I was about to start my third German film since returning. I knew that they were still casting major female parts for that film and as I knew the producer, Eric Pommer, I would endeavour to put in a good word for her. Meanwhile, if she needed any help financially, she should not be afraid to get in touch with me. Little did I realise that the young woman standing beside me would end up marrying a gentleman who would be the second most powerful man in Germany; none other than Hermann Goering.

The first four weeks on the set for the film, *Congress Dances* had been stressful. The film was being shot at the UFA film studios in Berlin and had a lot riding on it. It was the first colour musical with a plot concerning the historical meeting of the European heads of state in Vienna after the defeat of Napoleon. The film was to be the equal of any Hollywood extravaganza, so consequently, there was a considerable amount of pressure being put upon cast and crew. However, as all of us got into the rhythm of working as a team, the atmosphere became calmer. True to my word, Emmy had been given the role of an Austrian princess and had so far, proved very talented. I was enjoying my role as a Machiavellian statesman, manipulating one politician against the other and at the same time, enjoying romantic interludes with the various princesses.

During the fifth week of filming, three days were to be set aside for the principal photography of the ballroom sequence. Two hundred extras plus principal players were assembled to stage the title of the film. This was because of the sheer size of the ball and the brilliant set with its costumes. Obviously, there was going to be no room for retakes. Such was the importance of the filming of that sequence that bleachers had been put up to accommodate chosen visitors and so it became a custom for cast members to wander off the set between filming and mingle with the visitors. It was on one of these occasions that the inexplicable happened to me.

As I was striding over to the visitors area, I noticed three women, two of which I recognised immediately. They were the prominent film actresses, Henny Porten and Renate Muller. But it was the third woman who caught my eye. Even though she was sitting down, I could see that she was tall and slim with long brunette hair down to her shoulders and styled so that it fell over her left eye. Her whole appearance generated what I would term a sultry look. In other words, she had a sexual magnetism that would make most men go weak at the knees, including me. I felt as if I had been hit by a bolt of lightning, for I was immediately attracted to her and wanted to know more about her.

After the usual greetings with Henny and Renate, I enquired as to who their companion was. It turned out that her name was Marlene Bachman and it transpired that while I had been away in America, she had become a famous model for the French fashion designer, Madeleine Vionnet and at the same time, was a fashion consultant for the German magazine *Mode und Heim*. So, at this present moment, not only was she queen of the catwalk, but she was the most sought-after model by the German and French fashion houses and had a huge fan club in both countries. Over the years, I had maintained a professional relationship with Henny Porten. Having worked with her on several films in the early twenties, a strong friendship had grown between us. The public adored her screen persona in roles that betrayed her as a woman of strength and courage, not unlike her character off screen, I may add. She happened to be visiting the set that day as she was already working on a film next door at hangar two. Fully in keeping with her image of being Mother Earth, she had taken both younger woman under her wing and was busy chaperoning them through the intricacies of Berlin's society. Renate Muller was another young actress who, whilst I had been away in America, had become famous both as a singer and film star.

Whilst we all laughed and chatted amongst ourselves, I was thinking how I could get the opportunity to ask Marlene out for a date. The moment arose when the bell sounded on set for the cast to take its place with the next shot and as I took my leave, I asked Marlene, for her phone number so that I could arrange to take her out for dinner. Giving me a throaty laugh, she said that she would think about it. However, in the next few seconds, as if to tease me, she had second thoughts, for she reached into her purse and wrote her number on a piece of paper. As she handed it to me, she gave me a beguiling smile whilst remarking that it was not a habit of hers to go out on dates with older men, especially if they were film actors, who were generally regarded as thinking too much of themselves. Having gently put me in my place, I walked back to the set leaving them laughing amongst themselves. From that moment when I first saw her, not only was I utterly bewitched, I had also fallen in love with her and in that process, I swear that she had somehow cast a spell over me to achieve that effect. It also had the effect of destroying my concentration, for knowing that she would be watching me perform, it completely unnerved me. Apart from having to do several retakes because I was fluffing my lines, I also tried the patience of the entire cast, with my lack of coordination for the ballroom dancing. The following day, I presented my co-star Lillian Harvey with a large bouquet of flowers as a sign of my contrition for any sore toes she may have suffered during a rehearsal of the film's centrepiece of the Waltz. It was late afternoon when we finally wrapped the dance sequence up and I was sufficiently mortified to publicly apologise to the crew for my unprofessional behaviour, the cause of which has long since departed from the set.

I was determined not to appear to be too obvious about my courting of Marlene, particularly after Henny Porten, sensing romance in the air, invited me to an informal get-together that she was holding at her house, whilst at the same time, casually mentioning that Marlene had also been invited and was looking forward to meeting me. It was a typical showbiz party made up with a cross-section of directors, actors, writers and agents. Yet as soon I had arrived, I noticed Marlene talking to a good-looking man who I had not seen before. They appeared to be close, and seeming to engage each other in some hearty dialogue, which made me wonder perhaps if he was her boyfriend. With an effort to appear nonchalant, I joined Henny and her husband and engaged them in some small talk. Eventually, I got around to enquiring who Marlene's companion was. Henny told me that his name was Laszlo Hartman, a noted fashion critic and whilst giving me a dramatic pause, accompanied by a mischievous smile, informed me that he preferred boys to girls. Without further ado, Henny grabbed me by the elbow and dragged me over to them. Having introduced me to Laszlo, after some obligatory small talk, she then proceeded to take him away to another group of people, leaving me alone in Marlene's company.

Left to our own devices, after a short period of uncomfortable silence, Marlene remarked on how she hadn't realised how much work went into being an actor. In reply, I made some inane comments back. I remarked that she was shorter than I realised from her photographs. She came right back at me and told me not to worry, saying that she would soon cut me down to size. Within minutes, we were talking together as if we had known each other for a long time. It seemed only natural to me to suggest to her that rather than stand in a crowded room, we should go to a dinner somewhere more intimate and she readily agreed with me. I immediately booked a table at Horchas, a fashionable Berlin restaurant frequented by the dilettante. It was on our arrival that I was made to realise how popular Marlene was, for as we were being led to our table by the maître d', the whole room stopped and stared, which was then followed by a ripple of applause. After we had been seated, the attention from the room had soon subsided, I ordered a bottle of Veuve Clicquot champagne on ice, and after the maître d' had finished being over attentive to Marlene, he had proceeded to recommend the Châteaubriand steak which would be cooked and served at the table.

During the meal, we began to relax and enjoy each other's company and I took the opportunity of studying Marlene once again. I had already been beguiled by her hair, her figure and the way she laughed, but now, I was able to take notice of her brown eyes and sensuous mouth. When she spoke, it was with a touch of cynicism and humour, as if to say, "I've seen what life could chuck at me and I'm not intimidated." As the evening wore on, she opened up to me about herself and how difficult it had been, despite coming from a well-to-do background, to fight her way to the top of the fashion industry, overcoming on the way, predatory males and avaricious hangers on. She also went on to reveal her family roots and I was surprised to learn that she came from a Jewish family, her father being Professor Hiram Bachman, who apparently, was an eminent surgeon and lecturer at the charity hospital of medicine in Berlin. I was also taken aback to learn that her mother was the renowned opera singer, Miriam Schule and that Marlene had two brothers called Hansi and Lothar, plus a younger sister, called Greta. It was obvious to me that Marlene was proud of her mother, for despite Miriam's full-time career, she had raised her family in a loving and secure environment. That evening turned out to be one of the happiest memories of my life and when I dropped Marlene off at her apartment and kissed her good night, I knew then that I had found my soulmate for life. What was even more exciting was that I sensed that perhaps Marlene felt the same way.

During the next four months, we grew very close to each other and when production finally finished on my film, I found myself accompanying Marlene, as her escort, attending fashion shows in both Paris and Berlin, meeting her friends and colleagues and escorting her to fashion awards, whilst in turn, she partnered me to film premieres and social events. It was not long before we became a hot item for both the national and trade press. Unfortunately, that is when our lives began to become a little more difficult for us when it came to our private life. Whilst it is nice to be noticed, there are times when you become a prisoner of public adulation and start objecting to it. We both became obsessed in achieving our private space but the things that most couples took for granted no longer existed for us. Eventually, I bought a small house on the Obersaltzberg in Bavaria, under an assumed name so that Marlene and I had a refuge to escape to. That little house was to give us the happiest of memories. We took long walks and went swimming in the mountain lakes and even on the odd occasion, visited the local hostelries, where we would take part in community singalongs to the sound of local bands, whilst all the while, enjoying the life of being incognito, due in no small way to the locals, who left us entirely alone to our own devices.

Meanwhile, Oscar, my agent, was making sure that I was never idle and by April 1932, I had just completed a successful run of *Hamlet* in Berlin and was just about to commence filming an aviation movie to be called *FPI doesn't respond.* Because it was an international production, it would be shot in three language versions, German, English and French. My dear friend, Hans Albers, would star in the German version and a French actor by the name of Charles Boyer would do the French version. Because I was bilingual, I would take on the same part in the English version. As I was contracted to the movie until the beginning of July and as it was being filmed at the UFA studios, it caused no disruption to our lives. However, outside forces were becoming another matter.

Hitler's National Socialist Party had gained a considerable number of seats in the Reichstag during the national elections and though it wasn't enough to form a government, I felt that given enough time, another election would soon take place. It was strange that Marlene and I were both beginning to think as one. I was beginning to have serious misgivings about the way things were shaping up in Germany. There had always been some form of anti-Semitism in the country but by and large, German Jews had assimilated well into society. Indeed, many had served with distinction in the military during the First World War. However, I was beginning to observe a more aggressive anti-Semitic behaviour amongst the population and very noticeable in surrounding shopping areas. I had seen daubing on shop windows saying, 'Jews out!' I was beginning to see, all too frequently, motorised convoys carrying brown shirted stormtroopers with banners all proclaiming, 'Down with the Communists!', 'Jews out!' and 'Germany awake!' Posters were springing up everywhere, featuring a photo of Hitler and the motto, 'One state, one people, one leader'.

I noticed some uncertainty was beginning to be noticeable in Marlene's demeanour and I also found this pattern emerging in many of our Jewish friends. So, I decided now was the time to ask her to marry me. Not only did I love her deeply, but I could not visualise the rest of my life without her. Not only that but by marrying her, I would be offering her greater protection, or so I thought at the time. Only just recently, I had accompanied Marlene to Paris where she had a photo shoot with the Eiffel Tower as the background. I had already decided to buy her an engagement ring and now appeared to be the right time. I had heard of a jewellery store on the Place Vendôme, by the name of Van Cleef and Arpels and once I had located the establishment, I was slightly overawed on entering by the glittering array of jewellery on display. Being a novice at buying engagement rings, I had no idea where to start, but after a lot of support and patience from the assistants, I finally chose a ring that I hoped would give Marlene immense pleasure and be one of her treasured possessions. It was a flawless, yellow gold engagement ring with white gold hearts and a centre diamond also set in white gold. All I needed to do now was to choose the right moment to propose.

Soon after our return from Paris, during a conversation that we were having on the general political climate, Marlene suddenly suggested that we should find time to meet her parents; she had already taken the decision to visit them. They had readily agreed and extended an invitation to lunch. They had, of course, been aware of our relationship, but it had not gone down well with her father apparently as I was not only a Gentile, but I was an actor as well. This was hardly a good start to forming a relationship with his daughter. However, I agreed with Marlene that now was the time to meet her parents. Besides, unbeknown to Marlene, it would be the perfect moment to ask her father for her hand in marriage.

The moment finally arrived when we drew up in front of the house belonging to Marlene's parents. I was suffering from a bad attack of nerves which were worse than anything that I had experienced on opening nights in the theatre. But when the front door opened, Hiram and Miriam Bachman greeted me with genuine friendliness. Hiram was of average height with a solid frame, and a shock of unmanageable grey hair. He also wore glasses which were perched on the end of his Roman nose. His wife Miriam was well built as I suppose most operatic singers tended to be and there was no mistaking that she was Marlene's mother. You could plainly see where Marlene's beauty came from, especially in those expressive eyes; even her speech pattern was similar, but despite her aura, she appeared down to earth and instantly made me feel at home. Leading us into the lounge, to my surprise, I was introduced to an array of grandparents, uncles and aunts, as well as Marlene's two younger brothers, Hansi and Lothar and her younger sister, Greta. Being thrown into this family gathering made me even more nervous.

The brothers, it turned out, had a joint ambition to have a career in aerodynamics and engineering and were studying at Heidelberg University. As for Greta, who appeared to be impressed by her sister's choice of boyfriend, she was studying hard to follow in her father's footsteps by becoming a doctor. After undergoing a collective inquisition, we all departed to a large dining room where I had a very pleasant family lunch though unfortunately, the main topic of conversation was the rise in popularity of the National Socialists and the possibility of a pogrom against the Jewish population. Hiram calmed the atmosphere by saying that the public would never stand for the persecution of a race that had contributed so much to the nation in areas like education, medicine and the arts, not to forget the Jewish ex-soldiers organisation. Why, he too, had fought in the Great War and was a holder of the Iron Cross First Class. I hadn't said very much, preferring to listen to Hiram's reasonable and balanced opinions and certainly, they went a long way in soothing any anxieties that the womenfolk may have had.

Once lunch was over, I found an excuse to be alone with Marlene's father by asking him to show me around the garden and it was while we stopped to light a cigar that I asked him as a Gentile, if he would seriously oppose a marriage between Marlene and myself. He replied that he was not happy at the idea of Marlene marrying outside her religion but in the short time he had observed us, he sensed that we were both deeply in love with each other and that it would be both bigoted and unjust to deny his daughter her happiness. I then continued to inform him that the right moment had arisen and that because I loved Marlene deeply, I wanted her to be my wife. Therefore, would he consent to my proposing to her this very afternoon. For a moment or two, he stood studying me before replying.

"It is obvious to me that you are genuine in your feelings and that Marlene feels the same way. As far as the material things in life go, it is also obvious that you are extraordinarily successful in your career and that you have the financial means to keep Marlene in the manner to which she has become accustomed. There is also a saying that 'Love conquers all' and in this instance, that may true. As difficult as it is for me to say this, Gunther, despite the difference in our religion, Marlene could not have picked a more suitable husband than you. Of course, I give my consent and blessing … all I would ask of you is that you give considerable thought to allowing any children that you may have to be brought up in their mother's religion and that you promise me that you will protect her from racial bigotry to the best of your ability. What I said earlier on regarding Hitler and the National Socialists was for the benefit of the family and what I am saying to you now is what I feel. Like most Jews, I was born with a sixth sense which was developed, I suppose, because since time began, Jews have always been persecuted and my senses tell me that we Jews in Germany are about to face another pogrom. Please put my mind at rest, that at least one of my children will be protected from this intolerance."

Having been impressed by his sincerity, I assured him, "You have no reason to doubt my integrity where Marlene is concerned, sir. I cannot say that I have been much of a political animal but since meeting Marlene, I have become more aware and I can assure you that I do not like Hitler and his policies. Please be assured that I will protect Marlene with the last breath in my body."

We concluded our chat with a firm handshake and proceeded back to the house, where on arrival, I could sense an air of expectancy hanging in the room as I entered it. All activity stopped and all eyes were upon me. Hiram broke the tension and brought the room to order by announcing that I had something important to say. Marlene flashed me an anxious look as I took her hand in mine and as I asked her to marry me, I took the engagement ring out of its box and placed it upon her finger. For a moment or two, she looked at the ring, looked at me and then as she flung her arms around me said 'Oh, you big lug. Of course, I want to be your wife! What's taken you so long to ask me?' I waited a while for the family to take in my announcement and for the womenfolk to examine the ring, then I turned to Hiram and I can remember even now saying, "Mr Bachman, will you give me permission to marry Marlene as soon as possible?" There was silence in the room and all eyes were upon Hiram, who just stood there with his hands clasped behind his back staring intently at us both. He then said, "I do!" and the whole family erupted into cheering and applause.

The rest of the day was spent with the family and I getting to know each other and finally, later in the evening, Miriam Bachman prepared a buffet of delicious food and drink with the family's small staff, which we all descended upon and proceeded to consume with great gusto. The evening finished in the early hours of the morning, with Miriam at the piano, leading us all with a singalong of popular melodies. When it was finally time to leave, Marlene and I stepped out onto the peaceful moonlit street. When we looked back, Marlene's family stood as a group in the doorway waving us goodbye. I am quite sure that none of us realised at that moment in time how precious these last few family get-togethers would become.

Marlene and I were determined to have a low-key ceremony, foregoing the traditional white wedding and despite the misgivings of her mother and father, we became husband and wife in a civil ceremony at a registry office in Berlin as soon as the necessary forms had been completed. Despite trying to keep the wedding secret, the press had got wind of it and were gathered around the entrance to the town hall when we arrived. Hans Byastock, my best man, was forced to run the gauntlet of popping cameras with me. I was also to learn later that it was even more arduous for Marlene and her matron of honour, for by the time that she had arrived, UFA studios had sent a newsreel van and a large crowd had gathered around it. In turn, this brought a small contingent of police, so that by the time we emerged from the building as man and wife, we were confronted by a jostling crowd, throwing confetti and shouting out good wishes, a whirring newsreel camera on top of a van, reporters popping their cameras everywhere and a group of poor policemen struggling to keep the crowd in order, whilst trying to keep their helmets on. In other words, it was utter bedlam.

In order to pacify Marlene's parents, we decided to have a more formal reception and no better place to hold it than in the banqueting suite at the Hotel Adlon, which was large enough to hold both Marlene's family and friends as well as mine. Because the reception was a mix of the show-business and fashion worlds, it attracted a huge media interest involving both radio and magazine. Knowing that it was a price we paid for being celebrities, Marlene and I accepted it as part of the job. Nonetheless, the reception was a great success. The meal was excellent, both Hiram and Hans delivered great speeches and the band delivered a musical entertainment that kept everybody dancing into the small hours. Unbeknown to Marlene's family, both of us had decided to include the traditional Jewish custom of the bridegroom breaking a wineglass with his foot to solemnise our marriage. When the bride and bridegroom were traditionally called to perform the first waltz, we had two wine glasses wrapped in towels placed on the floor at our feet which we then proceeded to stamp on, thereby signalling the start of a long and happy marriage. Just watching the pride on Hiram's and Miriam's faces was a reward in itself. By the time we excused ourselves and slipped away to our suite, poor Marlene was exhausted and was soon fast asleep in my arms. When we awoke the following morning, we celebrated the first day of our married life with a champagne breakfast and caught up on our first night as Mr and Mrs Conrad which we had missed the night before due to wedding fatigue. After this, we slipped away for a two-week skiing honeymoon, taking a slow journey by car to the Austrian resort of Hochgurgl, which boasted some marvellous views of the Italian Dolomites.

In the next twelve months, we were both truly blessed, living a lifestyle and achieving most of our career aspirations that most people would never experience in their lifetime. Whilst Marlene had many modelling contracts to fulfil, all centred around Berlin, I had decided that rather than being separated from each other, I would confine my work to the capital. Once more, lady luck was by my side. Noël Coward, a British playwright who had achieved international recognition, had recently written a new play for the London West End which had become a huge success. The play was titled *Hay Fever* and Coward had approved me for the leading role in the German premiere. Within a month of opening at the Berlin Opal Theatre, it had broken box office records. I was pleased, I may add, to be part of a successful theatrical production again as I had gambled from the start by signing a one-year contract which enabled me to take a sabbatical from film work.

On the social scene, we led a quiet life due to our work during the day and evening, but on the plus side, we spent most of our Sundays at Marlene's parents' home or they would come and visit us. It was on one of these occasions that Hiram enquired whether the pair of us would be interested in using our celebrity status for charity work, such as helping to raise money for new hospital equipment and visiting terminally ill patients. Marlene and I did not hesitate in becoming involved, realising that it was one way of putting back into the community that which we had been so fortunate to have received and gradually, our charity work became expanded more and more, extending to other hospitals, particularly where sick children were involved. Looking back, I now realise how good our life was then, though we had very little private life because of our career commitments and what little leisure time we had left was taken up by charity work. We still found the time to enjoy each other's company, filling precious moments with laughter and tenderness. Time simply flew by through the months of 1932 and then 1933 and it was in that year that the doorway to hell gradually started open for us and all mankind.

Hitler finally achieved his ambition of becoming Chancellor of Germany and within months of taking office, events began to take place which would consolidate and strengthen his position. Not only did he place his cronics in powerful government posts, but he used the police to round up various opposition groups such as the unions, communists and the social democrats. To make matters worse, the Reichstag was destroyed by fire in an act of arson and though a solitary individual was arrested, tried, found guilty and sent to a concentration camp, there never had been sufficient concrete evidence to say who started it. Hitler, not needing any excuse, unleashed his brown-shirts under the command of Ernst Röhm, to intimidate the population and destroy the communist street fighters. It did not take long for President Hindenburg and the army to resent Röhm's intrusion on the army's sphere of influence and coupled with Röhm's arrogance and rejection of some of Hitler's policies, he soon sealed his own fate. In June 1934, Hitler, Goering and his faithful subordinate, Heinrich Himmler leading his elite Gestapo units, proceeded to eliminate Röhm and his senior officers in what is now remembered in history as the 'Night of the Long Knives'.

Within weeks of that purge, President Hindenburg passed away enabling Hitler to become both President and Chancellor of Germany and with the acquiescence of both the army and the industrialists, an Enabling Act was passed which gave Hitler total power. By 1935, the doorway to hell was now wide open, and as a reward for their support, both the army and the industrialists went into top gear by expanding the military might of Germany. Elsewhere, whilst Hitler began to size up his smaller neighbours for conquest, the infamous Nuremberg Laws were created. Wilhelm Frick, a crackpot Nazi ideologist, was made Minister of the Interior to implement those laws and though there were many, 'Article 1' was implemented straight away. This stated: Mixed marriages between Jews and Gentiles were forbidden; Jews no longer had the right to vote; Jewish veterans were to be expelled from veteran organisations; without an Aryan certificate, all Jews would be expelled from holding positions in medicine, teaching, banking and many others, including not being able to become students at university; and finally, Jews would not be allowed to immigrate without surrendering ninety per cent of their assets.

It took a little while for the laws to take effect upon the Jewish population, but when they did, it was catastrophic. The first victim in Marlene's family was her father, who had his licence to practice surgery withdrawn. He also was no longer able to practice as a GP and was only able to hold surgeries for Jewish patients. The next victims were Marlene and her mother who, because they both enjoyed celebrity status, became immediate targets for the National Socialists. Consequently, all avenues of work in their profession ceased to exist. As for Marlene's brothers, Hansi and Lothar, they were both suspended from university, thus preventing them from achieving the qualifications they needed in their chosen profession. What amazed me was that this barbaric return to the dark ages, apart from a few isolated instances, had met with no public condemnation from the German nation.

Hitler had proved himself to be a master strategist. Taking advantage of weak opposition, he had transformed Germany to a one-party state with himself as supreme arbiter, controlling every aspect of its citizens' lives from cradle to grave. Furthermore, all the other European nations who could have stood up to him from a position of strength proceeded to do the opposite and follow a path of appeasement. It also seemed hypocritical to me that the nations of the world would nominate Germany to play host to the forthcoming 1936 Olympic Games, a country which forbade free speech, practised racial intolerance and incarcerated its citizens in concentration camps without due process of law. Because of the forthcoming Olympics and wishing to avoid international outrage, the general excesses against the Jews were not enforced for the time being and public boycotting of Jewish businesses was banned, though the general public were still discouraged from patronising these establishments. I began to feel the effects of the national ostracising and the experience of subtle pressures being applied to me.

The biggest social event of the year was going to be Hermann Goering's marriage to Emmy Sonnemann, who had been part of our circle of friends, ever since Marlene and I had been married. However, on receiving a wedding invitation from Emmy, it excluded Marlene and was accompanied by a note expressing Emmy's high regard for me but that unfortunately, the wedding invitation did not extend to Marlene, as it would be inappropriate for a Jewess to be in attendance when the Führer would be guest of honour. Naturally, I declined the invitation. My own circle of friends and colleagues was also gradually shrinking. Many were now going into voluntary exile and I began to find offers of work less forthcoming within Germany. Understandably, Marlene being concerned about her parents and family, held a family conference, where the consensus of that meeting was that it would all blow over and that the Nuremberg Laws would be rescinded.

Meanwhile, Hiram would start up a small practice in a Jewish neighbourhood and Miriam would take in private pupils. Marlene's brothers were the biggest problem, as their education had been temporarily halted at the most crucial point of their lives. At my suggestion, we would spend time in looking for alternative ways to continue their studies, even if it meant sending them abroad. There was no immediate problem with Marlene's sister, Greta, as she was seriously courting a young Jewish lad whose family had business connections in Holland. However, Marlene's parents were adamant that they would not leave Germany, especially as they had their own elderly parents to consider. From that moment on, I began to give a lot of thought to mine and Marlene's future, considering the option to leave Germany. However, I would also give serious consideration over the next few weeks into remaining in Germany as well, which I decided would be my number one priority.

Driving home that evening from the family conference, Marlene agreed with me that we would soon have to make long-term decisions with regards to our future and felt that we should look at the prospects of things getting worse, not better and that we should plan our decisions accordingly. She told me not to worry about her feelings and though she was very concerned about the safety of her family, she felt neither hurt nor humiliated, but only anger as she knew perfectly well where she stood with Adolf Hitler and his gang. Even her so-called friends could stick their prejudices and hypocrisy as far as Marlene was concerned. Even if she were invited, she would not be attending any further public occasions, as she knew that the Ministry of Propaganda was already touting tickets for sale for their Annual Artists' Ball. She preferred that I buy just one for myself as she felt it would be beneficial for just me to go, if only for me to judge the views of my fellow actors. As for herself, she would be far happier remaining at home in the company of the dogs, either reading a good book or listening to the radio.

I had already had a long telephone conversation with my friend, Hans Albers, who was in a similar position to myself. He had married a Jewish girl but because of his immense popularity in Germany, he had been discreetly advised that the authorities would look the other way if Hans and his wife no longer co-habit in Germany. The solution that they arrived at was that Trudie, his wife, would live in Switzerland and he would visit her on a regular basis. It was only by him remaining in Germany that he would be able to supply her with a steady income. Unlike myself, he did not speak English and was unknown to the rest of the world, so for them to go into exile would be a ridiculous and unnecessary sacrifice.

Chapter 7

Into Exile

After returning from the Annual Artists' Ball, which, as agreed with Marlene, I had attended alone, I stood for a few minutes in the cool night air, observing a light mist rolling off the Wannsee Lake, bringing with it, a touch of rain. For a moment or two, the only intrusive sound to be heard was Helmuth driving the car into the garage, slamming the car door as he got out and closing the garage doors from the inside. Apart from the rustle of the trees, the infrequent call of the night owl and the accompanying sound of a dog barking somewhere, drifting across the lake, silence descended once again. I turned and started to walk slowly towards the house, the sound of my shoes crunching on the gravel and reverberating throughout the drive. As I reached the front door, it opened slowly, revealing Hilder, our maid.

"Good evening, sir. I heard Helmuth drive into the garage and as I couldn't see you come through the front door, I thought that you might still be out here."

"It's okay, Hilder. I was just getting some fresh air in my lungs," I replied. As she closed the door behind me and took my coat, I enquired as to whether Marlene had retired upstairs for the night.

"Oh no, sir. Cook and I have spent most of the evening with madam in the kitchen baking a … a … I'm trying to remember the name, sir, oh, it's just come to me. I think madam called it a New York cheesecake and it certainly looks delicious. She has promised cook and me a slice tomorrow."

Laughing to myself, I followed Hilder to the kitchen and on entering, I was met with a scene of confusion. The table was covered with baking powder and pieces of dough. Cook was at the sink surrounded by dirty pots and pans. Helmuth had somehow found himself an empty surface and was endeavouring to put a sandwich together, whilst our Golden Labrador, called Chips, sat close by with his tail going nine to the dozen, salivating in anticipation of a dropped morsel. Also, I observed our two Persian cats named Bongo and Marmaluke surveying the whole scene. Bongo, in particular, had a disdainful and superior air written on his face. Last, but certainly not least, was my beautiful wife, who was standing in the centre of this orchestrated mayhem dressed in jumper and slacks with the cook's apron tied around her middle and her trademark hair, immaculately in place. She gave off an aura of someone who had just wandered into a madhouse but was far too polite to acknowledge it. She had a glass of wine in her hand and two empty bottles in the waste bin from which I suspect Margaret, the cook and Hilder had consumed their fair share! As soon as Marlene saw me enter the kitchen, she came over to me and whilst placing her arms around my neck, kissed me. Turning to the staff, she then proceeded to give them the weekend off explaining that we would look after ourselves for a change. Although I looked forward to that, it was necessary for me to remind Helmuth I would need him first thing Monday morning to drive me to the Ministry of Propaganda in Berlin. With that, Marlene wished everybody good night and finished by saying that both of us would be in the lounge having a nightcap.

Once there, Marlene removed her apron, kicked off her shoes and proceeded to sit down on the sofa with her legs curled up beneath her. Meanwhile, having managed to get through the doorway before I closed it, Chips settled himself down besides Marlene, obviously anticipating a late-night biscuit. Removing my dinner jacket, I walked over to the drinks cabinet and after depositing some ice cubes into two glasses, proceeded to pour two shots of Chivas Regal. Whilst giving Marlene one of the drinks, I gently pushed Chips to the other end of the sofa giving me the necessary room to sit beside my wife.

"You look tired, Gunty," she said gently, brushing the hair from my forehead. "You must have found the ball heavy going because you're home earlier than expected. Tell me who was there? Who was the best dressed woman? Was it Frau Goebbels? You must also tell me the all the latest gossip."

"All the ladies present at the ball tonight were lucky, as had you been there with me, none of them would have stood a chance! They would have paled into insignificance. Many of our friends were conspicuous by their absence and the few that were there, such as Henny Porten and Leni Riefenstahl, sent you their love. Despite looking worn and fragile, Henny was defiantly putting the best face on things. As you know, her husband, Wilhelm is also Jewish and he too, had decided not to go. As for Leni, the situation is completely opposite now. Due to her successful documentaries on Hitler and having been chosen by him to film the forthcoming Olympics, she is very much part of his inner circle. There were also quite a few Nazi bigwigs in attendance, basking in the glow of showbiz glamour and celebrity. I must admit if it hadn't been for Leni restraining me, more than likely, I would have given them a piece of my mind. I have forgotten to mention, by the way, that Goebbels has asked to see me at the ministry on Monday morning and it seems fairly obvious that he will either bribe or threaten me to remain in the German film industry."

Taking my hand in hers, Marlene spoke forcibly, "I can't bear to see you placed in this terrible position and with your career in jeopardy. I cannot help thinking it might be better for us to divorce, as we could still be discreetly together. I just could never be without you …"

Placing my finger on her lips and shaking my head, I interrupted her, "I don't want to hear you talk like that. This isn't about divorce or losing one's career. This is about freedom, being free to love who you choose, being free to have an opinion and being free to belong to any race or creed. I have already made up my mind on this matter and only a miracle will make me change it on Monday morning. I am a strolling player. I can act in any country, in any barn, street or park and whilst I perform for my supper, you will be by my side. So, put that in your pipe and smoke it, Mrs Marlene Conrad!"

"Gunty," Marlene leaned forward both laughing and crying at the same time, "How can I resist your charisma, your good looks and your commanding delivery of such corny lines? I haven't seen a better performance since you played Marc Anthony and talking of ham, I have some leftovers in the fridge! Would you like me to make you a sandwich before we go to bed?" I pulled her up from the sofa and holding her close to me replied, "No ham for me, madam, but I think we will go upstairs to bed for a dessert, perhaps."

Come Monday morning and the sun was out in full force, with not a cloud in the sky. Helmuth had promptly picked us up at nine o'clock. I say we, as Marlene had decided over the weekend to come with me and spend a day shopping in Berlin and as we were both going to be there, I could treat her to lunch at the Adlon Hotel. It did not take long for Helmuth to reach central Berlin and pull up on the Kur-damm, which was noted for its choice of upmarket departmental stores and shops. As she climbed out of the car, I leaned over, holding the door open and called out to her, "Try not to buy the whole damn street, sweetheart and remember, I will meet you in the bar at the Adlon, at about one thirty."

She waved and blew a kiss. In that moment, I thought that she looked as pretty as a picture, in a white dress, blue shoes and matching leather bag, with a wide-brimmed hat to set off her flowing hair. As I watched her walk away from me with her chin held high and a confident swagger that only models seem to possess, I noticed quite a few males turning their heads as she passed and thought I was one hell of a lucky guy.

Helmuth swung the car into the Wilhelm Platz where the Ministry of Propaganda was situated and drove into the visitors' car park in front of the building. Having instructed Helmuth that I should be no longer than an hour and a half, I proceeded to walk towards the entrance taking in the mandatory large cast-iron Eagles and the huge red velvet flags, carrying the symbol of the Nazi swastika. As I entered through the massive front doors, I took note of the two brown shirts on guard duty and then proceeded to a circular desk situated in the centre of a reception area behind which sat a party official. After stating that I had an appointment with the Reich Minister Dr Goebbels, they asked me to take a seat and notified me that somebody would be down shortly to escort me upstairs.

After sitting down, I took the opportunity to examine my surroundings. In front of me was a large ornate marble staircase leading up to a small landing, from which the main staircase proceeded from left and right up to the first floor. In between, fixed dead centre on the wall, was a picture of Adolf Hitler, encased in a large ornate frame. I returned my gaze to the reception area which I noticed encompassed the usual hanging flags of the Third Reich. There was also a lift with two SA stormtroopers guarding its doors. I had a feeling that they were not only there for show, but also to scrutinise the comings and goings of both visitors and staff. I also noticed the sign above the reception desk, proclaiming 'One people, one state, one Führer'. Everything so far about the building sent a clear message to me of grandiose megalomania, and what was more disturbing was that from here, a daily flow of propaganda, disguised through the media of radio, film, newspaper and literature, was gradually seducing the German nation. My thoughts were interrupted by a voice, "Herr Conrad?" I looked up and saw a plump lady, aged about thirty-five, with glasses and her hair tied in a bun. "Herr Conrad?" she repeated quizzically.

I stood up quickly. "Yes, I am so sorry. I was lost in my thoughts."

Whilst laughing, she replied, "It happens to me all the time, Herr Conrad. My name is Trudy Frost and I am one of the Reich Minister's secretaries. If you could follow me please, I will take you to his office."

I followed her to the lift and while we waited for the doors to open, she enquired if I lived in Berlin. I told her that I did not live in Berlin, as such, but in the suburb of Wannsee. My wife and I had purchased a home there set in its own grounds overlooking the lake and not only was it idyllic, but it also afforded us some privacy and quality time together. As we stepped into the lift, Miss Frost continued to chatter away. She was obviously a film fan as she commented on how much she had enjoyed several films that I had previously made, especially *Congress Dances*, which she thought was particularly wonderful for its colour and costumes.

Once the lift arrived at the second floor and the doors opened, we stepped out onto a thickly carpeted promenade which seemed to go on forever. Set into the walls were a series of picture windows, each surrounded by heavy drapes in the colour of old rose, through which he could clearly see another Berlin landmark, the Avenue of Linden Trees. As we proceeded along the promenade, I took note of the various doors situated on the right side of the promenade. For instance, one set of double doors had a plaque announcing a film theatre and several other doors carried individual titles, which I assumed were departmental heads. Finally, we arrived in front of another large pair of doors which Trudy proceeded to open and stepping to one side, she beckoned me through. I found myself standing in what I assumed to be a furnished outer office with three desks, two of which were occupied by two busy secretaries who both looked up momentarily, as we entered.

Miss Frost leaned over the unoccupied desk and pressed a button on a console, whilst at the same time picking up her phone. She then spoke into it. There was a slight pause whilst she listened, and then after putting the phone down, she turned to me and said, "The Minister will see you now, Herr Conrad. Please follow me." Once again, I followed Trudy through, yet another set of double doors situated to the right of the outer office. Having knocked, we both entered and as we did, I viewed the large room. On the right-hand side, a coffee table was surrounded by a sofa, armchairs and a panoramic window overlooking the Wilhelm Strasser, whereas on the left-hand side, there was yet another desk of large proportions (the Nazis certainly liked everything big!), behind which sat the Reich Minister himself, Dr Joseph Goebbels. Standing beside him was Carl Hanke, his private secretary, and behind them on the wall, was the mandatory portrait of Adolf Hitler, under which stood a global atlas of the world. Without looking up, he politely told me to take a seat, whilst he finished signing documents that Hanke was placing in front of him. I heard Hanke say to Goebbels that the document he had just placed in front of him was the last one and after signing it, Goebbels stood up and walked around the desk towards me with his hand extended.

"Good to meet you again, Herr Conrad. I hope you had a pleasant evening at the reception," he said, as we shook hands. "You know, of course, Herr Hanke, my private secretary. You won't mind if he remains with us whilst we have our meeting?" As I finished shaking hands with both gentlemen, I noticed that neither of them was wearing party uniforms but dressed in double-breasted suits. Goebbels continued, "I really must congratulate you on the characters you have created in both theatre and film. You have always received respect from the world press and have been an excellent ambassador for the German arts. You may not be aware of it, but the Führer is a keen supporter of the cinema and considers you not only one of the great German film actors of our time, but also a particular favourite of his."

"Thank you, Herr Minister. Please convey to the Führer my appreciation of his comments and I will endeavour to continue to live up to his expectations."

"Excellent, Herr Conrad. I know the Führer will be as pleased with your enthusiasm and I will inform him of your comments when I take lunch with him today. You know, I am sure, that the first few years have been turbulent times for the Third Reich and that the Führer has faced opposition from many quarters. However, we National Socialists have backbones of steel and have successfully stabilised the Third Reich and eliminated any enemies of the state. As Minister of Propaganda, I am determined to reorganise the Reich film industry. We need to research and introduce new technology, thereby gaining a much wider distribution of German films throughout the world. I cannot allow the American film industry to dominate European markets whilst it is in the hands of a Jewish clique, supported by its brethren on Wall Street, so that they can seduce the minds of our young, filling their heads with images of poisonous filth, particularly with Negroid jazz and dance music and with a never-ending supply of Yids such as Cantor, Jolson, Robinson and Muni. What I intend to do is to create an army of actors and technicians of pure Aryan stock to destroy the supremacy of this Jewish and Bolshevik epidemic."

I sat there with my face expressionless, completely at odds with my innermost revulsion, staring at a man who had been given absolute authority to govern by the German people, delivering the most racist claptrap I was ever likely to hear. Even more horrific was the way in which he delivered this rant, filled with vehemence and hatred. As I sat there taking all this in, he continued speaking,

"I have invited you here today, Herr Conrad, to take the opportunity of participating in several major Reich film productions, projects which will have the full backing of the state with no expense spared, employing the most up-to-date technology."

I am afraid my inquisitiveness got the better of me at that point as like most actors, when given the prospect of playing a part, they like to know what it is! Having put the question to him. Goebbels responded.

"I'm glad you asked that question, Herr Conrad. You will be honoured to know that the Fülrer himself would be pleased to see you portray Frederick the Great of Prussia and the two other roles that I personally have in mind for you, are in a film about the sinking of the Titanic in which you will play a German passenger and the other will be about the Boer War in which you will portray Ohm Kruger, who led the rebellion against the British in South Africa. I realise, of course, that you will sacrifice a few years in the process of making these films, but I can assure you that the remuneration you will receive will be extremely generous.

Furthermore, because of the magnitude of these projects, the Führer would wish to bestow upon you the title of First Artist of the State. However, there is a small fly in the ointment, so to speak, which I am sure can be easily dealt with. Putting it delicately I refer to your present marriage which is in direct conflict with the Nuremberg Laws. I refer, of course, to your Jewish wife, Marlene Bachman, the fashion model.

You must understand, Herr Conrad, that it would be both politically embarrassing and humiliating for the Führer to have such a prominent German cohabiting with a Jewess. My first inclination would be to demand that you apply for an immediate divorce and if, by chance, you refused, to inform you of the penalties that would incur both for yourself and your wife. However, because of the forthcoming Olympic Games, bringing with it both a large number of overseas visitors to Germany and also the attention of the world's press, the inevitable scandal involving an internationally known German film star would, at this time, possibly prove an embarrassment to the image of the Third Reich. I believe I have a solution that may be beneficial to you. Why not leave the matter on the table until after the Olympic Games, where six months grace would give you the opportunity to consider your options and make a calm and reasonable decision? As an example, one of your closest friends has been in the same position as yourself. I refer, of course, to Hans Albers, with whom we reached a compromise. Because of his immense popularity, we agreed that if he divorced his wife and she lived in another country, he would be allowed to visit her on a regular basis, a situation that seems to have worked out very well for them both. I do urge you to work out a similar solution, for time is of the essence. Meanwhile, please be free to liaison with Herr Hanke for any advice that you may need. I regret that I shall have to leave you now for as I mentioned earlier, I shall be taking lunch with the Führer at the chancellery. By the way, as a further thought, it would be helpful to you if you became a member of the party. That, by itself will go a long way in convincing us of your good intentions."

Both the minister and I stood up simultaneously and looking him in the eyes, I said, "Thank you for the meeting, Herr Minister. I am grateful for the time you are giving me to consider my position. As a matter of interest, I must point out that I have been offered a British film that is due to be completed either just before the start of the Olympics, or just after and that should fit in with your timescale."

Goebbels briefly gave me a hard stare before replying, "Excellent, Herr Conrad. It will allow the world the opportunity to see how the citizens of the Third Reich are free to both travel and work beyond the borders of greater Germany."

The minister, having shook hands with me, then raised his hand in a salute, exclaiming, "Heil Hitler," swung on his heel and left the room. Carl Hanke looked at me briefly, smiled and then said, after placing his hand upon my shoulder, "Come along, Herr Conrad, allow me to accompany you downstairs."

As we proceeded out of the office, Hanke, perhaps sensing my inner shock, began to talk to me in earnest, "You really must have more understanding and patience with National Socialism, Herr Conrad. The first few years have been brutal and there have been many casualties along the way. However, within twelve months, when the world has seen how much National Socialism has achieved and honour has finally been restored to the German people, I am sure the Führer will create a system where the Jewish race will be able to exist in Germany under a controlled policy. Alternatively, he may be able to create a state for them either on an island, or in the Middle East. You know, the Führer's vision of an Aryan utopia is not so original … America has been practising it for the last hundred years. It is my understanding that the southern states of America have segregation laws that forbid the Negroid population from using the same facilities as white Americans. It does seem rather stupid, Herr Conrad, that with the contributions you can make to the Third Reich, you would not want to achieve great honour and reward. By joining us, you would be fulfilling the opportunities that the Führer is offering us. We young Germans sense that the moment has finally arrived, and that the world is ours for the taking."

By the time we had reached the front doors of the ministry, Helmuth, having spotted me, proceeded to drive the car over to the front steps. Turning to Hanke, I shook his hand, thanking him for his advice and he gave me an enigmatic smile.

"I sense, Herr Conrad, that you have already made a decision on your future and I wish you luck on whatever direction you take. I fear that if our paths ever cross again, we may well be adversaries … once again, take care and goodbye."

We drove out of the Wilhelm Strasse and along the Unter den Linden towards the Adlon Hotel and as Helmuth manoeuvred the car through the traffic, I noticed that the streets and buildings were being tidied up in preparation for the invasion of the Olympic tourists. However, I also noticed the jarring note of a man washing away the words 'Juden Verboten' from the window of his bookshop. Helmuth finally dropped me off at the Adlon and after telling him to collect us later in the afternoon, I strolled into the hotel searching for Marlene. I found her in the hotel bar surrounded by shopping bags. She looked up at me as I approached and smiled, patting the chair beside her.

"Hello, darling," I said, "I hope I haven't kept you too long, though it does appear that you have been emptying the stores."

"You can stop looking so tense, Gunty! I haven't spent that much money and besides, you want me to look my best, don't you?" she replied.

Though my mind was elsewhere, I made the effort to smile at Marlene and at the same time, beckoned a passing pageboy over to our table, requesting him to deposit Marlene's shopping bags in the cloakroom, as we would be staying for lunch. I enquired, if he could ask the maître d' of the hotel's Brandenburg restaurant to reserve me a table for two as soon as possible. Within a matter of minutes, the maître d' had arrived and after announcing his name as Gustav, escorted us into the restaurant, where he seated us at a discreet booth with a semi-circle banquet seat covered in leather which was the colour of old rose. Having been given menus, we made small talk whilst we decided on our choices. Marlene ordered a Waldorf salad with fresh salmon whilst I decided on a well-done sirloin steak and a baked potato, accompanied by a side order of salad with ranch dressing. I also ordered from the Sommelier, a chilled bottle of Henken-Troken, a sparkling Rhineland wine and as an afterthought, requested an outside telephone line for my table. Whilst we waited for our meal to arrive, Marlene chatted about her shopping activities but sensing my pre-occupation elsewhere, changed the subject and asked me how the meeting with the Reich Minister went.

"I would say that it was one of the worst experiences of my life, Marlene. To say that I felt intimidated would be an understatement. To encapsulate the meeting, I was offered a choice: either I divorce you and join the party; or I will never work again within the borders of the Third Reich. Obviously, the threat was more subtle than that, but the implications were made clear. For some time now, I have been wrestling with the question as to whether we should stay, or should we go? This morning's meeting has tipped the scales firmly in going and every part of my moral fibre tells me that you and I can no longer remain in Germany under a dictatorship that has created laws that support the persecution of ethnic minorities and the total suppression of free speech."

Holding my hand and looking me in the eyes, Marlene replied softly, "I don't wish to stay anywhere where I am not wanted any more than you do and I will go wherever you go, but I am worried about my family. What future will they face after we have left? I know mama and papa will not leave my grandparents, who will never leave Germany because they are set in their ways." I tried to reassure Marlene not to worry too much and that we would make every effort for those members of her family to leave Germany if they so desired. I went on to say, "One of the advantages of my early childhood was that I learnt to become very streetwise and that later on, when I was fortunate enough to start earning large sums of money, I began to devise methods not only to keep my money, but also to invest it sensibly so that my assets grew in value. Indeed, when I went to America, I did the same thing with my dollar earnings. In view of the situation that we were now in, one of the smartest things I ever did was to turn myself into a limited company on both sides of the Atlantic. I could now liquidate my assets and move them from company to company without being personally involved. Of course, if the German tax authorities were to carry out an in-depth investigation through the state, I could easily be identified, but I believed that the forthcoming Olympic Games would give us a four-month window of opportunity."

Having finished her meal and having waited for me to finish mine, Marlene extracted her cigarette case from her purse and then proceeded to light up two cigarettes, one of which she passed to me. Having exhaled, she leaned back and gave me that famous sultry look that was a combination of sex, cynical acceptance and world weariness.

"You know, Gunty, you never cease to amaze me," she said, leaning forward with an enigmatic smile on her lips. "You have the ability, which is quite rare in an actor, to be both an artiste and a businessman. You know, now that I have grown closer to you, I have no doubts on your ability to protect me and I feel that I am the luckiest woman alive; I seem to have found my perfect soul mate. However, it is not about us, it is about the Germany that we will leave behind us and those poor souls left at the mercy of that murderous Nazi gang."

Reaching for the telephone, I dialled Oscar Korten's number and waited whilst the secretary at the other end of the line put me through.

"Hello, Oscar. It's been some time since I last spoke to you. How are you doing? I hope that are you looking after that lovely wife of yours?" I asked when finally, he came through. Having exchanged pleasantries for a few minutes, I then got down to business.

"Have Gaumont British firmed up on that offer of a film?"

"I was about to get in touch with you, Gunther," Oscar replied. "You will be pleased to know that they have green-lit the project and it will commence filming in two months. Indeed, the contract should be on my desk waiting for you to sign within a week. By the way, you will be directed by Alfred Hitchcock, the brilliant young British film director, whose latest film, *The Secret Agent,* has been received with great acclaim. Peter Lorre, by the way, who I know is a good friend of yours, has had the good fortune to have been offered a Hollywood contract on the strength of his performance in that film. I am glad that you have got this firm offer, for it appears to me that the German film studios and theatrical impresarios are holding back on offering you anything; I'm sure you know the reason why. I know that you will understand that the advice I am about to give you is not only as your agent but as a true friend. I will be completely honest and blunt with you by telling you that within a year, you will have no career whatsoever left in Germany. You must realise that you cannot remain defiant of the Nuremberg Laws by remaining married to Marlene, without expecting to be destroyed by Dr Goebbels. From what I have sensed with the German Foreign Office when dealing with your application for temporary permission to work in Britain, you have been granted a reprieve until you return from filming abroad. You know, Gunther, you don't need any advice from me over a public telephone. However, I will say this to you when you do make the right decision, remember that you have an international reputation as a great actor and if handled well by a first-class agent, you will always be in work wherever you may choose to settle. Meanwhile, I will phone you as soon as I receive the contract from Britain for you to sign and that will give us the opportunity to discuss any other business, such as finding an agent to represent you in Britain. In the meantime, take care of yourself and Marlene and I will see you soon. Goodbye for now."

I placed the phone back on its cradle, took a large gulp of wine and inhaled deeply on my cigarette. Picking the phone up again, I dialled a number for my attorneys, Baum & Baum and on getting through to the younger brother Eric, instructed him to liquidate all my German assets and transfer them to a British bank for the time being. Eric Baum then explained to me that we might just get away with this move, as the Reich Ministry of Economics would soon be placing a moratorium on capital leaving the Third Reich. Therefore, he would start transferring the majority of my liquid assets now. I had to realise that my fixed assets, such as property, would take a little longer for the obvious reasons. However, a point in my favour was that being a German of pure Aryan stock going back three generations, I might avoid severe financial penalties before fiscal legislation was approved by the Reichstag. Meanwhile, he would get in touch with me as soon as all the necessary paperwork had been completed.

After finishing with the business of the day, Eric surprised me by telling me that although we would be meeting again shortly, he wanted to say how it had always been a great pleasure to have represented a client such as myself and would I convey to Frau Conrad how honoured the firm has been to have represented her as well. He concluded the conversation by remarking, "Between you and me, although it is becoming increasingly dangerous, we would be only too happy to help her in any way that we could." As I put the phone down, I could not help but feel touched by the warmth of his voice and thinking that there was still many honourable Germans left standing, but I wondered for how long?

Whilst I had been talking on the phone, the restaurant had been filling up with diners creating an atmosphere of hustle and bustle as waiters went about their business. This atmosphere was accompanied by the general buzz of conversation from the diners but suddenly, there was an intrusion of both sound and activity from the front entrance of the restaurant created by four men, two of which I recognised. The first one was a short, rotund gentleman with a shaven head whose high-pitched braying laugh was responsible for the intrusion of the noise. I recognised him from previous newsreels as Walther Funk, an economics expert working at the Ministry of Propaganda. The other man, who was both lean and tall and younger, went by the name of Hans Fritsche, who was a well-known radio and newsreel commentator. As they proceeded to their table, accompanied by a flurry of waiters, Funk caught sight of us. He brushed aside a chair being pulled out for him and appeared to go into a tirade with Gustav, the maître d', who seemed to be trying to calm him down.

Marlene had become tense and I tried to distract her with small talk and at the same time, to catch the eye of Philip our waiter, so that I could have our bill brought to the table. By the time we had drunk our coffee and I had settled the bill, we were ready to leave. However, Marlene decided on a last visit to the powder room and as I sat and watched her with a mounting sense of trepidation, she appeared to be taking the longest way around the restaurant, almost appearing to be turning it into a lap of honour by giving it the full catwalk treatment. Her performance had the desired effect upon the diners, most of whom suspended their conversation and their meals to watch her. After a while, she reappeared, taking the same route back to our table but this time, there was a slight variation. As she passed Walther Funk's table, her shoulder bag seemed to swing out, knocking over several glasses, spilling their contents over the white tablecloth, forcing the two men to stand up and brush their trousers with their napkins. Amidst the ensuring bedlam that erupted, she stood there being sweetly sympathetic before she turned and walked back to our table with a dazzling smile on her face, leaving behind her a spluttering Funk and entourage. Unfortunately, there was still a little more of this farce to be played out. As Marlene and I crossed the foyer of the hotel to collect our car, I heard a voice calling out to me. Turning, I recognised Florence Adlon, the famous proprietor of the hotel.

"I sincerely hope that both you and Frau Conrad have had a pleasant lunch with everything up to your expectations," he began. "I wonder, however, if I could have a quiet word with you alone just for a moment, Herr Conrad." Taking the hint, Marlene swept on towards the front entrance, followed by a page boy loaded with shopping bags, leaving me behind with Adlon.

I headed him off at the pass so to speak, by starting the conversation ahead of him. "I will spare you your blushes, Herr Adlon, for I have a pretty good idea of what you would wish to say to me. But let me just inform you that neither I, nor my wife, will be returning to this hotel in the very foreseeable future for the obvious reasons. If it is any consolation to you, I am overcome with sadness that you should be placed in an undesired position and perhaps, one day, we will meet again, hopefully in different circumstances."

As we shook hands and I began to walk away, Adlon, said quietly, "I shall regretfully, despite having to turn away in denial from those that I have looked upon as both friends and customers, to continue to fulfil my duties as an innkeeper according to the laws of the land, despite my repugnance at having to carry them out. Please do not think too harshly of my weakness of character, but I'm quite convinced that one day, normalcy will be restored to our lives and that we will meet again under better circumstances. Meanwhile, Herr Conrad, may I wish you a safe journey, wherever your travels will take you."

A week later, Marlene and I attended a family gathering at Hiram and Miriam Bachman's house and in attendance, were her two brothers, Hansi and Lothar and her younger sister, Greta. I had already told them, in the greatest confidence, that Marlene and I would be leaving the country permanently in the very near future. We now attempted to persuade them to leave too. After a lengthy discussion, in which everybody had something to say, Hiram finally held his hand up for silence and spoke.

"Marlene, your mother and I have spent many months in discussing what we should do for the best and after much soul-searching, have made the decision to remain in Berlin. Your mother and I have a responsibility for your grandparents, who have expressed no desire to be uprooted from their country of birth in their twilight years and neither do your uncles and aunts. Greta has been courting and she and her boyfriend wish to get married as soon as possible, after which they will move to Holland. As for your two brothers, I would be glad of any help that Gunther could give us. I am thinking of sending the boys to Paris for a short duration, during which time, hopefully, we could get them to America on a visa that would enable them to finish their studies on aerodynamics or to obtain an apprenticeship. I am thinking that perhaps, if Gunther and I join forces together, we may be able to obtain sponsorships for both boys in the United States. Have you anything to add to that, Gunther?"

"If the boys have decided on America as their destination of choice," I answered, "then I suggest that we get in touch with an immigration lawyer who has handled work for me in the past to start processing their application forms. From past experience, I am optimistic that their visas will be granted: they are young, have excellent academic backgrounds and are seeking work in a specialised industry."

At that point, Marlene interjected by saying that she had saved a substantial amount of money from her earnings as a model but because of the Nuremberg Laws, she would not be able to take it with her when the time came for her to leave the country. She had decided that the sensible thing to do would be for her to transfer that money to her father to do with it whatever he wished. She then spent further time arguing with her father and mother trying to persuade them to leave Germany with us, but Hiram was adamant. They could survive on the income from his small general practice whilst Miriam would supplement it by giving singing lessons. As the conversation ebbed backwards and forwards, Marlene wanted to know more about Greta's forthcoming engagement. It transpired that her boyfriend's name was Philip Housman. His father was the owner of the Housman shoe empire which also extended into Holland where they had a large factory. Because young Philip had been trained in business management, it had been decided for him to go to Holland and manage their Dutch enterprise. As the evening began to draw in, it also brought an air of sadness and an unspoken sense of unease as the family realised that this may be one of the last times when they would all be together.

Six weeks later, Hansi and Lothar's visa applications had been sent to the American Embassy accompanied by a sponsorship pledge that I had obtained from Louis B. Mayer of MGM, to guarantee their stay. It had also been an extremely busy time for both Marlene and me, if not only in closing the house down at Wannsee but also with sadness on both sides, having to let the household staff go. It turned out that local party pressure was being put upon them anyway because of their working for a Jewess and that eventually, they would have been forced to leave. Nevertheless, it was still an emotional farewell. At one stage, I felt I was drowning in legal documents signing this and signing that and whatever else that was needed during my exit from Germany. To add to it all was the persistent tension that we all had to endure as I went about the process of leaving, never knowing when the government would discover what I was doing. I was also reversing the process by preparing for entry into Britain. At short notice and with the recommendation of friends, I had rented a house situated near a small town called Marlow in the county of Berkshire where we could enjoy the peace and tranquillity of the English countryside and still be close to London. I had also hired, once again with the help of friends, an English private secretary by the name of Olivia Mountback, who had excellent references and whom I immediately instructed to handle my personal and show business affairs. On that front, as well as the Hitchcock film, which I was due to start soon, I had also received a firm offer from London's Old Vic to star in Chekhov's, *Uncle Vanya* and also the possibility a four-picture deal with Alexander Korda of London Films.

As the time drew closer for our leaving, Hiram and Miriam invited us to spend the last few weeks with them, as most of our household and personal possessions had already been crated and shipped to Britain. We were down to four travelling cases consisting of day-to-day clothes. Most of the time was spent tidying up the loose ends of our affairs and bidding farewell to our friends. It became noticeable to Marlene and me, that Berlin was gradually filling up with the early arrivals of overseas tourists for the Olympic Games and because of that, there had been a considerable loosening of the draconian Nuremberg Laws. Not wishing to offend world opinion for the duration of the games, Hitler had exercised moderation in the persecution of the Jews even going so far as to grant amnesty to his political opponents. This was to become the window of opportunity for many Jews to leave Germany. As far as I was concerned, I had faced few problems in transferring my assets into an overseas company and being granted the appropriate licenses. As for Marlene, despite intense investigation from the Nazi authorities, she was able to withdraw her savings and give them to her father. Those last few weeks in Berlin were like experiencing the calm before the storm, people appeared more optimistic and light-hearted towards their neighbours with racial dogma being put aside momentary.

Our last social engagement had been organised by my friend Hans Byastock which was to be our farewell party. By now, Hans had become the biggest star in Germany and was idolised by the public to such an extent that even the Nazi party turned a blind eye to his relationship with his Jewish wife, Hansi. Hans had always been larger-than-life, a force of nature you could say, but even by his standards and considering the very thin line many Germans had to walk to survive, the party that he threw for Marlene and I was an act of sheer bravado. The invited guests were from all parts of German society, both for and against the Nazis. In fact, the minute that Marlene and I had arrived, we were accosted by Bella Fromm, the Jewish, political and society columnist for the newspaper *Berliner Zeitung* who obviously was still protected by friends in the highest political circles. Although she avoided being offensive to the Nazis in print, I wondered how much longer it would be before she either fled the country or was imprisoned. I certainly admired her courage, refusing not only to be intimidated by the Nazis but also standing up to them.

Bella was not, by any means, the only adversary of the Nazi party in attendance. We exchanged pleasantries with the conductor, Wilhelm Furtwangler and Max Reinhardt, the theatre scenic designer and director just back from Hollywood after completing the film version of *A Midsummer Night's Dream* and who had just crossed over the border from Austria to bid us farewell. There were, of course, a large number of covert supporters of the Nazis invited, one of the main reasons why it was so important to emphasise that the farewell party was merely temporary and that we would be returning very soon to Germany. Attendees also included the film director, Herbert Seplin, a great favourite of Dr Goebbels, Albert Speer, now known as Hitler's architect and Arno Brecker, the favourite sculpture of the Nazi bigwigs. I took the opportunity of studying Speer and Brecker. They were admirers of Hitler and both enjoyed his patronage. Of the two, I sensed that Speer was the most complex. He had a reputation of being an innovative architect and organiser. He appeared to be rather shy and reserved but I sensed an undercurrent of steely determination and ambition and with his wife, Margaret, standing by his side, they represented the more glamorous face of National Socialism. As to the other young man, Arno Brecker, I really did not care much for his work. I thought his sculptures tended to be oversized and invariably depicted athletes in neoclassic poses. They pleased Hitler because they represented his concept of the true Ayran race.

At some point, later that evening, political tension arose between Furtwangler and Speer. Furtwangler was telling me that he had had an offer from the New York Philharmonic Orchestra and that perhaps someday, we might meet up there. He was giving the offer some serious thought, as it was becoming increasingly difficult for serious music to both flourish and represent classical music in Germany, particularly when Mendelson, Beethoven and Paul Hindsmith were banned and all Jewish musicians were forbidden to perform or compose music. Speer interjected by disagreeing with that statement, pointing out that it was only Furtwangler's opinion and as an example, he quoted Herbert von Karazan, another great German conductor, who fully supported the Fuhrer in his political objectives. The conversation was interrupted by Hans who, in his booming voice, told everybody to leave their politics at the front door and enjoy the evening.

Both Marlene and I have fond memories of the party. Apart from everything else, just for a few hours, the outside world was excluded, as people became relaxed and spoke freely amongst themselves with Hans supplying the music and laughter. Long after the last guests had left, the four of us, Marlene, Hans, Hansi and me, finished the evening off with drinks and a marathon conversation filled with reminiscences and nostalgia. It struck me then that the only difference between us was that Hans did not take life seriously. He thought life was for living and as long as you did not interfere with outside forces, everything would be fine and dandy. We parted company embracing each other, pledging love and loyalty whilst leaving the women in tears possibly at the thought that they may be responsible for the parting, a thought that neither Hans nor I would have accepted.

I had one last visit make; for many years I had donated my time in raising money for a charity that specialised in rescuing children of all denominations, many of whom had been abused and abandoned. The money that had been raised had provided a large orphanage in Dahelm, situated on the outskirts of Berlin. It provided a full education and family support up to the age of fifteen for all its children and thereafter, supported them in career choices. It was a Protestant organisation called the Jesus Christus Church run by a Pastor by the name of Martin Niemoller, who had originally been one of the many prominent churchmen to have supported Hitler when he first came to power. However, it did not take long for him to become disillusioned with the policies of National Socialism and along with like-minded pastors, such as Dietrich Bonhoeffer and Karl Barth, had co-founded the confessional church dedicated to the resistance of discrimination against Christians and Jews. Having arranged to meet him at the Jesus Christ church, he was already waiting for us when we arrived. He was a tall and bespectacled man going bald and whose air of gentleness was at odds with his inner strength and determination. He had already become a fervent anti-Nazi and had been tried and served a short sentence for his views. He greeted us warmly and bowing his head, kissed the back of Marlene's hand and then proceeded to walk us through the church to a small room at the side of the altar which contained a desk and chairs and many, many books. I began the conversation by telling him that Marlene and I would be leaving Germany very soon and I wanted to take this opportunity of saying goodbye and to give him a monetary donation for the orphanage. I also told him that wherever Marlene and I were in the world, we would work hard to restore democracy and religious freedom in Germany. Pastor Niemoller responded softly.

"It saddens me that you are leaving Germany, Gunther. You have been an unstinting supporter of the church as well as being an important member of the German theatre. I know that you will be greatly missed but I take heart in the knowledge that you will continue to resist evil in our society. I beg of you to never lose faith in your religious beliefs and in anticipation of your visit today, I would like you to accept this small farewell gift to accompany you on your many journeys to come. I have also included a note containing part of a speech that I will be making soon."

Having finished speaking, he handed me a small brown paper parcel with a letter. I thanked him for his gift and expressed my admiration for his courage but begged him to be both cautious and mindful of his own safety. It soon became time to leave and as we drove away from the church, we had a last view of him standing at the entrance waving us goodbye.

It was ten o'clock in the morning two days later, when our car pulled up outside the grand concourse of Temple Hoff airfield. Our flight was due to leave at midday, so we had time to spare. I summoned a porter for our cases and told him to take them to the Lufthansa check-in desk. As we were making our way through the concourse, I notice the heavy volume of arrivals queueing at passport control obviously in anticipation of seeing the Olympic Games. Because Hitler wanted Germany to be on its best behaviour for the huge number of foreign visitors that would soon be arriving, I did not anticipate any trouble in checking-in for our departure and indeed that proved to be the case. While we waited for an announcement to board the Lufthansa Flight 202 for Croydon, south of London, we sat in the lounge having coffee and it was there that Marlene produced from her vanity case the package that Pastor Niemoller had given us. After Marlene had unwrapped the package, it revealed a small leather-bound bible accompanied by a letter. I watched Marlene open the envelope, take out the notepaper and read its contents. When she had finished, she sat motionless for a few seconds before handing me the note which said …

First, they came for the communists and I did not speak out, because I wasn't a communist.

Then they came for the socialists and I did not speak out, because I was not a socialist.

Then they came for the trade unionists and I did not speak out, because I was not a trade unionist.

Then came for the Jews and I did not speak out, because I was not a Jew.

Then they came for me and then, there wasn't anyone left to speak out for me.

At that moment, a message came over the Tannoy system, "Will all passengers departing for Croydon, England, please commence boarding Lufthansa Flight 202." Pulling Marlene gently towards me, I daubed her eyes gently, wiping away her tears.

"Come along sweetheart. We're off on a new adventure, a new life, and new ambitions but above all, let's never forget Pastor Niemoller's words, 'To always have the freedom to be able to speak our minds and live in a land without oppression'."

A Lufthansa representative arrived soon after and proceeded to escort us through the departure gate and onto the tarmac and as we approached our plane, our escort explained that we were boarding a four-engine Junkers G38 that carried a crew of seven and thirty-three passengers. Its three cabins were situated in the wings, each seating eleven passengers. It also had a cruising speed of one-hundred and thirty miles per hour and a wingspan of one-hundred and forty-four feet. At this moment, our estimated time of arrival was four o'clock in the afternoon. Once on board and seated, the door was closed and we were soon taxiing down the runway and as we turned away, I caught one last glimpse of the main concourse decorated with the large Nazi flags emblazoned with their black swastikas and as we paused briefly before take-off, I wondered as I held Marlene's hand when would be the next time that we would return to our beloved country.

Chapter 8

This Green and Pleasant Land

It was only as we crossed the English Channel and the white cliffs of Dover came into view that Marlene and I started to relax. Our arrival time was right on schedule thanks to good weather. As planned, it was just after four o'clock in the afternoon when we landed at Croydon airfield. Once the plane had taxied to a stop and the steward had opened the door, we all disembarked and as Marlene and I strolled over the tarmac to the reception building, we linked arms and confidently increased our step. I could not help but notice that although it was a warm summer's day, there was a slight drizzle of rain in the air, what one would say as being typical English weather. I began experiencing a feeling of calm flooding over me and in doing so, giving me a total sense of relaxation. I glanced at Marlene and she too seemed to have changed physically. She had, it seemed to me, regained the old composure of the confident young woman that I had married years ago.

"Well, Marlene, you have now stepped onto British soil. Are you ready for a new experience?" I asked her.

"I am excited," she replied. "I feel like I am starting a new chapter in my life. Even just leaving the aeroplane, I can sense a change in the atmosphere. I can smell freedom in the air."

At that moment, the press descended upon us, emerging from the reception building in a tumbling cascade of humanity. Very quickly, they formed a semi-circle in front of us consisting of reporters, photographers and one radio interviewer from the BBC. The questions came thick and fast.

"Is it true, Mr Conrad, that you have signed with London Films to make several pictures?"

"Why have you missed the Berlin Olympics?"

"What is your position on the German Jews?"

"Do you agree with Chancellor Hitler's policies?"

"Mrs Conrad, do you consider yourself a Jewish refugee?"

Fortunately, I was spared giving embarrassing answers and looking like the village idiot by the entrance of what I first thought was the local headmistress. She was tall and angular with what I would call politely, a horsey face, with a pince-nez firmly fixed to a beak of a nose, her attire consisting of a blouse, a two-piece tweed jacket and skirt, finished off by a pair of tan brogues. Oh, and I almost forgot, she was wearing a green huntsman hat with a large feather fixed to the side of it. This force of nature turned out to be our introduction to Olivia Mountebank, our permanent guardian angel and private secretary, a formidable gatekeeper to our public and private lives, daily monitor of my commitments and more importantly, a true friend and confidant. Come to think of it, she reminded me very much of the Hollywood character actress, Edna May Oliver.

Planting herself in front of Marlene and myself and facing the bank of newsmen with a look of disapproval on her face, she cried out, "Come along, gentleman, you can do better than this. I will allow you five minutes for a photo shoot, two minutes for the BBC and Mr Conrad will take four questions from the rest of you."

Exactly on the allotted time, she began to wind down the proceedings, but the newsmen were having none of it. However, they had not reckoned on Olivia's steely determination. Planting herself in front of the newsman with her hands on her hips, she bellowed out above the hubbub.

"Make way! Make way! Mr and Mrs Conrad are tired from their journey across the Channel and still have a fair distance to travel before they reach their destination. If any of you gentlemen require further in-depth interviews, please contact me so that we can arrange further appointments." She then proceeded to shepherd us through the throng of newsmen and marched us into the arrival lounge, where an airport official guided us into a VIP lounge. As Marlene and I sat composing ourselves, Olivia and airport staff processed our immigration clearance and within the hour, Olivia had collected our luggage from customs.

As luck would have it, I had authorised Olivia to buy a Humber super snipe saloon car large enough to accommodate the many pieces of our luggage. Olivia had also engaged a chauffeur, who was standing by the car as we left the airport building, supervising the loading of all the bags.

Upon seeing us, whilst touching his cap, he exclaimed, "Good afternoon, madam, good afternoon, sir. My name is John and I have been engaged as your chauffeur. I hope that I will prove satisfactory to you. May I also say, welcome to Britain."

John was a tall and well-built man, with the military bearing of an ex-soldier. I also judged him to be in his early forties and when he moved, he appeared to have a limp possibly from a war wound. His handshake was strong and firm and whilst looking him straight in the eye, I took an instant liking to him.

Once we had settled ourselves into the back of the car and Olivia had finished fussing around and tipping the porters, she then proceeded to get into the passenger seat beside John and grasping her handbag firmly, said, "I think we are ready to leave now, John. Take these two young people home."

Turning around to us and addressing us in what we now accepted as her usual forthright manner, she said, "As we must start as we mean to go on, it would be less formal for me to address you both by your first names rather than Mr or Mrs, or sir or madam. I certainly would feel more comfortable. What do you think?"

I replied immediately, agreeing wholeheartedly with her, "I totally agree with you, Olivia. Both my wife and I prefer a more informal atmosphere in our household and would rather be addressed by our first names, Gunther and Marlene."

"I think it might be better if we confine that form of address to the senior staff only, thereby avoiding any unnecessary familiarity," Olivia replied with a sniff as she offered us all mint humbugs from a white paper bag. With the car speeding along under the control of John's skilful hands on the steering wheel and Olivia's running commentary, we had soon reached Kingston upon Thames and arrived at Maidenhead not too long after that. Olivia informed us at that point, that we weren't far from home and indeed, the next signpost that came up was for Henley. Olivia informed us that this was where the famous regatta was held annually on the River Thames, a great social event on the calendar where all the young men showed off their boating prowess. Once we had crossed over the bridge at Marlow and passed the Complete Angler hotel at the water's edge, we proceeded to the top of Marlow High Street and turned left, which Olivia told us would lead to the village of Medmenham and our home.

As we drove along the winding country lanes, Olivia kept up a running commentary. For example, when we passed an entrance on our left with a barrier and guardhouse, Olivia explained that it was a royal air force station. Further on the same side of the road, we passed a vine covered public house called the Dog and Badger and just past that, on the right-hand side, was the village community centre. Sensing that we were nearly home, our excitement grew with expectations as we turned into a dirt track road which had a sign announcing Buckhurst Lane. The short road ended at the entrance to a set of imposing gates upon which a brass sign read Falcon House. Once through the gates, we travelled slowly up a circular drive, surrounded by grass borders and trees until we stopped in front of a large Georgian house, its main features being a thatched roof with red bricked exterior walls, bow shaped windows and a colonnade front door. To the left of the house was a double story garage with a ground floor area large enough to accommodate three cars. The upstairs floor, I presumed, was being used as an apartment.

Marlene broke the silence by exclaiming, "It's like a picture postcard, very much as I imagined an English country house would be. I have already fallen in love with it before I have seen inside. You certainly have chosen well Olivia and I commend you on your taste."

Olivia then proceeded to give us a thumbnail sketch of the history of Medmenham. Apparently, it had acquired a somewhat notorious reputation during the English Regency period when a certain Sir Francis Dashwood founded the Hell Fire Club at his house, Medmenham Abbey, which was just down the road from us and which had been used as the centre for debauchery and witchcraft and anything else the young Regency rakes of the time could get up to. She finished up by explaining that Marlow was a small English town consisting of family-owned shops, one cinema and even a WH Smith. Further down the road was the town of High Wycombe which boasted a departmental store and a far wider choice of shops.

As we climbed out of the car, the front door opened and a man and woman came out. The woman was well built and had a cheerful face with mischievous eyes whilst the man was tall and angular with close cropped hair. Olivia introduced them to us as Lucy, who did the cooking and her husband Bill, who doubled as both general factotum and handyman. She also added that they both lived in and had the apartment above the garage and whilst she was on the subject, Olivia remarked, John's wife came in daily to do the house cleaning and her name was Mary. After our luggage had been unloaded from the car, Olivia then led the way into the house instructing Bill and John to take the luggage upstairs to the master bedroom whilst she commenced to give us a guided tour of the ground floor. All the rooms had oak beams running through them and of course, the traditional bay windows. The downstairs area consisted of a large lounge which connected through double doors to a long dining room. On the other side of the reception hall, there was a study big enough to accommodate two desks where obviously Olivia and I would perform our weekly office routine. The next room to that, was what I would call a snug or parlour, furnished with floor-to-ceiling bookcases, some very comfortable-looking leather armchairs and a sofa, scatter rugs and coffee table plus a free-standing radio and record consul and finally, to finish it all off, a deep open fireplace. Marlene immediately fell in love with the room. Laughing joyously, she bounced onto the settee with her arms opened wide exclaiming, "I am in heaven. From now on, this will be my favourite room where I will remember all the good memories of our lives." I stood there with a smile on my face feeling a warm glow of achievement at having finally given Marlene back her confidence and realising for the first time, how little value wealth and celebrity were without the important things of life such as love, compassion and the generosity of spirit, plus keeping your feet firmly planted on the ground, of course.

Olivia led us from the snug into a sunroom with a glass ceiling leading out to a gravelled courtyard which led, in turn, to some stables behind which was tucked away a small cottage. Further on, was a large lawn and paddock and beyond that, trees where the ground sloped down to the River Thames. Once more, Olivia led us back into the house, through the kitchen which was large and held all the necessary modern equipment, plus a breakfast table and chairs, ideal for the first tea or coffee of the day. Olivia then proceeded to take us upstairs, where the first room we entered was the master bedroom which also came with an en suite bathroom. As well as having walk-in wardrobes, it also boasted a large bay window which gave us a magnificent view of the Thames. As we had entered the bedroom, John and Bill had passed us on the way back downstairs, leaving Lucy to begin unpacking our suitcases and upon seeing us enter, she asked Marlene whether she wanted her to continue to unpack.

"I would like that very much, Lucy. Furthermore, I will help you so that whilst unpacking together, we will get to know each other better. Meanwhile, Olivia can continue to show my husband the remainder of the house and later, when you and I have finished unpacking, you can show me the other rooms."

Olivia then proceeded to guide me through the other three double bedrooms plus a bathroom with all the up-to-date equipment and including a walk-in shower stall, but the pleasant surprise for me was that at the end of the passage, there was a small staircase which led up to a self-contained flat comprising of lounge, bedroom and bathroom. This turned out to be Olivia's private quarters.

Olivia must have been observing my reaction to the house for she broke the silence, "I hope that this property meets some of your expectations. It has been rather difficult to find a house that could possibly suit most of your requirements. However, I have ensured that it is let on a short lease with an option to buy at market value so at least if you don't like it, you will have time to find something more to your liking."

"Olivia, apart from my own satisfaction, I know that Marlene has fallen in love with this house and I can tell you now that there is no doubt that when the lease expires, we shall purchase it outright. You must have worked very hard not only to find this house, but also to have got it ready for our arrival. Not only am I grateful for your efforts, but I shall be forever indebted to you. Once again, please accept my thanks."

At this point, I was interrupted by Olivia exclaiming, "Tut, Tut, Gunther! Don't start getting all sentimental. I have enjoyed the challenge and I am glad that it meets with your approval but don't forget that's what you pay me for. Incidentally, you have a full day's work ahead of you. You need to call a gentleman by the name of Robin Cox who apparently, would like your approval to be your representative in Britain. I understand that there has been some agreement between yourself, your Berlin office and him. Apparently, he has a possible list of future engagements for you to cast your eyes over plus some social invitations are starting to arrive. We certainly will need to get a grip on these matters as soon as possible. Now shoo! Go and explore the grounds outside whilst I go and help Marlene finish unpacking so that Lucy can get supper ready. Incidentally, we thought perhaps, because you both have had a long day travelling, a cold plate consisting of freshly baked ham and egg pie with salad and new potatoes followed by sherry trifle would be just the ticket and before I forget, if you see Bill, could you let him know which wine you would prefer with the dinner. Finally, will you be needing John any more tonight?''

"No, I won't, Olivia," I replied. "Tell him to get off home and I will see him and Mary tomorrow. In the meantime, I shall take your advice and explore outside whilst there is some daylight left."

I strolled through the French windows of the lounge and as I lit a cigar, started walking towards the river. As I commenced my leisurely stroll, I began to look over the property. I noted the stables which would accommodate two horses and had a quick peek inside one of the cottage windows to view its interior. Walking on past the paddock and on through the trees, I came to the river and just stood on the bank watching the odd barge or rowing boat pass by as the sun finally set. In the silence, I could hear a gentle breeze echoing through the leaves of the trees. My revelry was interrupted by Marlene calling me. I turned and seeing her walking towards me through the paddock, I started back towards her.

"Hello, darling," she said as I reached her. "Olivia and I have just finished unpacking and Lucy is downstairs preparing supper. I have seen Bill and he tells me that there isn't much in the way of booze, but he has found a bottle of Chardonnay. You know, Gunty, I have to keep pinching myself. I feel that this is all a dream and that I will wake up and find myself back in Germany once again. Tell me that all this belongs to us and that we are really in Britain." Placing my arm around her shoulders, we walked slowly back towards the river's edge not speaking a word. It was almost as if the beauty and stillness of the countryside made speech superfluous. Standing on the bank of the River Thames watching the water slowly flow past us in the dusk of the evening was pure magic and I lowered my head and kissed Marlene's lips.

"At this very moment that our hearts have been planted here, we shall start a family together and we shall build our future here. Now, I'm going to stop right there before I become too mushy. On the spur of the moment, I have to inform you, Miss Marlene, that I have decided to buy a motor launch so that I can cruise up and down the river, showing off my beautiful wife. I will even buy myself a yachtsman's cap and have my own personal ensign!" At this, Marlene cracked up with laughter finally managing to say in pidgin English, "That seems more like a scene from that English novel, *The Wind in the Willows*. Are you, by any chance, Gunty, auditioning for the part of Toad of Toad Hall? Laughing, whilst giving Marlene a light tap on her lower back, I shouted out, "Come on, I'll race you back to the house."

When we arrived back, slightly out of breath, Lucy and Bill had done us proud by laying out an intimate candlelit table in the dining room. As it was only laid for two, I enquired of Olivia whether she would like to join us.

"No," she replied, "You youngsters just need your own company tonight. I'm going to have my supper with Bill and Lucy in the kitchen and hopefully, I will see you, Gunther, in the morning. With that, I wish you both good night and have a pleasant evening."

After Bill had served the main course and poured the wine, I asked him to put the dessert on the sideboard as we would help ourselves and that he and Lucy were to finish for the evening. Marlene and I would lock up so that they could have an early night.

It may well have been due to a long day's travelling and the stresses and strains of the last few months, but that simple cold plated supper would go down as one of our happiest memories and by the time we were finished, we were totally relaxed. For the first time in years, Marlene had become completely confident and laid-back. Taking complete charge of the situation, she had me helping her to gather up all the dirty dishes and carry them through to the kitchen. Finding it empty, she found an apron and putting it on, proceeded to run hot water into the kitchen sink. Having accomplished that, she flung a tea cloth at me and with a throaty laugh, told me to get drying!

Whilst she washed the dishes and glasses, when we had finished, I watched her as she wiped down the kitchen sides and generally tidied up. That was when I grabbed her in an embrace and kissed her on the neck whilst murmuring in her ear how she was my favourite German hausfrau and that I was seriously considering giving her the job of head cook and washer-upper for life. Marlene responded by putting her arms around my neck, giving me a passionate kiss and then she broke away from me and gave me that all too familiar sexy laugh.

"Well, Mr Conrad, you seem pleased to see me. I suggest that we go through to our little parlour and have a nightcap … That is, if we can scrounge anything worth drinking. I have no intention of getting up to early tomorrow and also, I seem to recollect that you said earlier this evening that we should start a family, so I think tonight should be the first of many, many attempts, my celluloid Don Juan. Meanwhile, whilst I proceed to our parlour, you will go forth and forage for alcohol and I will await you there in eager anticipation."

I did manage to find a drinks cabinet in the lounge from which I joyfully retrieved an unopened bottle of Chivas Regal. Grabbing two glasses as well, I proceeded back to our parlour where I found Marlene already curled up with her legs beneath her in one of the large armchairs. Pouring two generous shots of Chivas, I handed one to Marlene and then settled myself down on the floor beside her chair.

"You know, Gunty," she said, while stroking my hair, "I think we should be utterly selfish and spend some quality time together, not only in the house, but we should also explore the surrounding countryside and familiarise ourselves with British customs. We could even pay a visit to London and see Buckingham Palace where Edward, the English King lives."

"He's not King yet, sweetheart," I interrupted her.

"But surely, the old King died earlier this year."

"You're quite right, he did. But Edward must be crowned first before he becomes the rightful successor to the throne and to do so, he must have a coronation."

"Oh great," Marlene exclaimed, clearly excited. "Then we may be able to watch the coronation procession when it takes place. I shall have to ask Lucy to tell me how they carry out the ceremony and when it is likely to happen. I can even start planning a coronation party."

The outcome of the conversation was that I agreed with her wholeheartedly and that we should take time out and have a break before we started to reshape our future lives. We talked into the small hours of the night about many things. Marlene spoke excitingly about the pending arrival of our personal belongings and bric-a-brac from Germany so that she could start to rearrange the house and even hinted at temporarily restarting her modelling career before we started a family. I may be prejudiced but with her good looks and figure I had no doubt that she could resume her career in the British fashion world, even though she was an immigrant from Germany. It also occurred to me that it would do wonders for her self-esteem before she settled into possible motherhood. Finally, we decided to retire for the night when we realised that we had talked ourselves dry. The half empty bottle of Chivas Regal stood forlornly on the coffee table and it was only when we stood up that we both realised that it carried quite a punch.

As Marlene fell against me, she burst out laughing, "I do believe, Mr Conrad, that I am slightly drunk and that you could possibly have your wicked way with me tonight, providing, of course, that you can rise to the occasion."

"Don't you worry about that, Mrs Conrad," I said with a smile, "I have a feeling that you will soon be asleep and that the invitation you have so kindly extended to me may have to wait until tomorrow."

As it turned out, I was spot on with my assumption. By the time I had helped Marlene up the stairs and watched her remove her makeup whilst repeatedly humming the song from *The Blue Angel* called *Falling in Love Again* and then discarding her clothes as she made her way to the shower, I was left disorientated in my new surroundings.

It was to be some time before she came out of the bathroom still humming that damn song, completely naked except for a shower cap. She just about managed to reach the bed, before she was curled up and with a mumbled, "I'm waiting for you lover-boy!' she fell fast asleep. I was thinking, as I tucked Marlene into bed that she would always remember that first day when she arrived Britain and as I kissed her on the forehead, made a vow to work hard to help overthrow Hitler and his gang, no matter how long it would take.

The following morning, I was awoken by Marlene's soft voice whispering in my ear, "Wake up, sleepyhead, it's time to get up. I've brought you up a freshly made coffee. It's ten o'clock in the morning and Lucy is ready to cook you a full English breakfast. I have also spoken to Olivia, telling her that we will be taking a few days off before we settle in and that I am sure that you will spend a couple of hours with her this morning going over an agenda in our absence." Pulling the bedclothes off me and delivering a slap on my backside, she carried on by saying, "Get yourself showered and dressed and I will see you downstairs in about thirty minutes when your breakfast will be ready. Oh, by the way, I also asked John to phone around a few local garages and luckily, he has been able to find a two-seater roadster ideal for the two of us and it can be ready for collection by early afternoon. So, rise and shine, we both have a busy morning ahead of us. Whilst you are going through your business affairs with Olivia, I shall be packing two suitcases for us to take with us and issuing instructions to the staff on keeping the house running smoothly whilst we are away."

Having said that, she bent over and kissed me passionately and with a wink, sashayed out of the bedroom trailing a perfume that sure as hell had me out of bed pretty quick and straight into shower and before I knew it, I was shaved and dressed and on my way downstairs, enticed by the aroma of coffee and bacon. As I reached the main hall and started towards the dining room, I encountered Marlene talking to a red-haired lady wearing a flowered pinafore. I tried to pass around them, but Marlene grabbed my arm saying, "Darling, let me introduce you to Mary Harrison, our housekeeper. Mary this is my husband, Gunther Conrad."

"I know who you are, sir" Mary replied. "I remember seeing you years ago at the county picture house in town. The picture was called *He who gets Slapped*. Oh, I did cry, sir. You were lovely in it. I do hope you stay in Medmenham for a long time and make some more pictures, especially English- or American-speaking ones."

"I think Mary Harrison, you and I are going to get on very well together and that you will be pleased to know that I will soon be starting a new picture in London," I replied. Patting her on the shoulder, I went into the dining room where I sat down for my first full English breakfast. I was joined by Marlene who kept me company with coffee and toast and soon after that, Olivia came in with the morning papers which she placed beside me.

Whilst she poured herself a fresh cup of coffee, I apologised for getting up late.

"Better late than never," Olivia replied and went on to say, "As long as you are suitably refreshed from a good night's sleep, that's all that matters. I am also pleased to hear that both you and

Marlene are going to spend a few days away so that on your return you will be well and truly relaxed. Unfortunately, Gunther, just before you go, I will need some decisions from you on some important matters that may have to be made quickly. Also, I'll need your signature for legal documents that need to be approved." Finishing my breakfast, I took my coffee with me and joined Olivia in the office.

"Right, Olivia, give me the good news and the bad news in any order you like. Just don't give me too much paperwork."

"Well, Gunther, you will be pleased to hear that there is no bad news apart from a letter from your new business manager, Geoffrey Halifax, non-urgent I may add, but he will be needing from you sometime in the near future, your plans regarding British domiciliary and for any future extensions on your visa. He suggests that you get in touch immediately with your immigration solicitor regarding that matter plus the structuring of any British company that you might form. This information is required by the inland revenue so that you may be issued with the appropriate tax code. The most urgent matters requiring your immediate response are as follows: the BBC would like you as a guest on their programme *In Town Tonight* scheduled to be broadcast in eight days. An immediate response is required from us and if necessary, if you accept, they would be prepared to send a recording van to the house. Robin Cox would like you to contact him as soon as possible regarding an immediate answer to Lillian Bayliss of the London Old Vic to appear in her production of Chekhov's *Uncle Vanya*. We also need to check with him on the start date of the new Hitchcock film. We are now beginning to receive requests for articles from magazines, such as *Everybody's, Picturegoer, Lady*, and the *Sunday Express* would also like to do a feature as well. A lot of invitations are starting to come in and will require your attention such as invites from Alexander Korda, Emlyn Williams and Jack Buchanan and one last one, Douglas Fairbanks is in London filming and would like to meet up with you for dinner one night. Finally, last but not least, Marlow Parish Council wonder if you could open their annual summer fete next year?"

"Okay, Olivia. Let's make a start somewhere. See if you can get hold of Robin Cox for me whilst I sign some of this correspondence," I had barely signed three pieces of mail before

Olivia was handing the phone to me, silently mouthing the name, Robin Cox.

I held the receiver slightly away from my ear as a voice boomed out, "Hello, Gunther. Nice to speak to you. Both my wife Edwina and I hope that you have fully rested from your journey and send our regards to your lovely wife, Marlene. We are looking forward to seeing you both as soon as time permits. Look, old chap, I know that you have barely arrived and had a chance to settle in, but we do need to liaison on some urgent matters. Unfortunately, because you start filming at Gaumont British in two weeks, we need to schedule important meetings around that time scale and beyond. For example, I understand that you have no wish to return to Germany and would like to make your home here in this country, in which case, we will need the best legal brains to represent you. I am thinking of a legal practice by the name of Samuelson & Lester, who specialise in immigration law and corporate structures for specialised professions such as yours. I am also going to need an immediate decision from you regarding a commitment to Lillian Bayliss at the Old Vic and the four-picture deal with Alexander Korda. The Old Vic deal will only pay you peanuts but the publicity and prestige that you will receive will be enormous in kicking off your British career. More importantly, it will dovetail nicely with your daytime commitments. Regarding your proposed contract with Korda, not only will you be free to accept outside commitments as well, but you will also have security for the next three years at a very handsome salary. Finally, you need to hit the ground running when it comes to your tax affairs and I recommend an excellent business manager who specialises in handling show business clients by the name of Geoffrey Halifax and I have already asked him to get in contact with you."

He paused for breath, then continued, "I say, old chap, I'm dreadfully sorry to have dumped all this on you in one go, but there is a lot of interest being shown in you right now. Unfortunately, over the past few years, you have confined yourself to only German speaking film productions so that even with the international reputation that you built up in Hollywood during the silent period, you were beginning to be perceived as one of yesterday's stars. But from the gossip that I'm hearing in showbiz circles, there appears to be growing sympathy and professional interest in your situation. Public opinion, in general, appears to have taken a dislike to Mr Hitler and his government, particularly his views on race. There is no doubt in my mind, Gunther, that with careful guidance, you will become a very much sought-after international star."

Breaking into Robin's flow, I began by saying, "I totally agree with what you are saying, Robin and let me start by just saying that Marlene and I are both refugees from Hitler's growing tyranny and have no intention whatsoever of returning to Germany whilst Hitler remains in power. Bad things are happening there and I am convinced that things will only get worse not only for Germany but for the whole of Europe as well. Of course, I'm going to have to maximise my earnings if only because Marlene's family are still in Germany living in danger and it will take a substantial amount of money to bring them out, so I will need to take any decent job that is going. Obviously though, I have done more stage than film work, I am a little worried about accepting *Uncle Vanya* at the Old Vic. I worry whether I am ready for it just yet."

"Of course you are, Gunther," he responded. "There is very little risk involved. Lillian Bayliss is an established theatrical producer and the Old Vic has had the best and the brightest appearing on its stage. I don't think you can go far wrong with Anton Chekhov or George Bernard Shaw for showcasing your talents. Believe me when I say that I think it will open a door to a successful second stage of your career. Currently, European actors are becoming flavour of the month in Hollywood and Britain. An example of this is the case of the French actor, Charles Boyer, who has just completed his first Technicolor picture called *The Garden of Allah* and according to the trade papers, it has created a huge public response, so much so, that it has now turned him into one of the hottest box office stars on the planet. I suggest we have a meeting at my office on Tuesday week to work out a schedule for the next twelve months."

"That seems all right to me, Robin." I confirmed. " Just send the details by post to Olivia and I will look forward to seeing you Tuesday week. I will, in all probability, bring Marlene with me, so perhaps we could have lunch as well?"

"That will be fine by me, Gunther. It might be better if I cancel all other appointments for that morning as we will have a lot of catching up to do. I'm afraid I'll have to sign off now. My desk buzzer is signifying that Ivor Novello has arrived for his appointment. You probably don't know that recently, he had a successful opening in the West End of his new romantic musical, *Glamorous Nights*. By the way, let me know if you'd like some tickets. Once more, give my very best wishes to Marlene and I will look forward to seeing you both next week. Cheerio for now."

No sooner had I replaced the receiver than I had an idea. The last time that I had met Peter Lorre was in Berlin just before he moved to Paris and even when he ended up in London, we still only kept in touch by phone. The thought struck me that I should give him a ring to see how he was doing and to ask him, if perhaps, he could tell me about his experiences working with Alfred Hitchcock, especially as Peter had already made two pictures with the well-known director. Sifting through my papers, I found my telephone book and Peter's London number. After many rings and just before I was going to hang up, the phone was answered at the other end by a breathless and distinctive accent which I recognised immediately.

"Hello, Peter," I shouted down the line in response to his greeting, "It's your fellow Berliner. How are you doing, you old rascal? I know that you have recently finished a picture in Britain, so does that mean that you will be returning to Paris? Or are you now going to make your home in London, especially now that you have become a success here?"

"Gunther, you old dog. How glad I am to hear from you. Where are you speaking from? Are you still in Germany? Or have you now finally arrived in Britain?" he asked.

Having explained to him that I had only just arrived and that we would be making it our permanent home here, I then went on to enquire what his plans were likely to be for the immediate future.

"Well, Gunther, lady luck has smiled upon me in the last couple of years. The British director Alfred Hitchcock hired me for a picture in 1934 called *The Man who Knew Too Much* and although I had a tough time learning my lines phonetically because my English wasn't very good at that time, I managed to get by. Amazingly, I received excellent reviews from the British press which led to Hitchcock offering me another part in a picture that I have just finished called *The Secret Agent* and that too, has received rave reviews. Just when I thought life couldn't get any better, I received the offer of a contract to work in Hollywood for 20th Century Fox and this is where you couldn't make it up! Only in America could an Austrian Jew be paid a small fortune to play a Chinese detective by the name of Mr Moto."

It had been a long time since I'd experienced a spontaneous burst of laughter. The very thought that this brilliant film actor, whom I suspected would eventually become an iconic figure in the history of film for his betrayal of the child murderer in the film *M*, an actor who was considered one of Germany's finest classic actors, would be forced to flee his country because he was a Jew and would have to overcome so many obstacles to resume his career ending up in Hollywood being paid a huge salary to play a Chinaman, seemed to me, to be a perfect counterpoint to that malevolent dictator in Germany.

"When do you leave for America, Peter?" I asked. "You can't just slink away without having a farewell party. We can either meet up in London or you must come down to us and stay for a few days. Either way, I will leave you my phone number so that you can get in touch. One favour that you can do me right now is to tell me what it has been like working with Hitchcock. I am starting a picture with him very soon and would be interested to know what he is like working on the set with."

"That's an easy question, Gunther. Professionally, he is the number one British director with the style not unlike our own Fritz Lang. His genius lies in his use of camera and sound and here's one tip for you, Gunther. Before he starts a picture, he has already worked it out in his head so that it will be edited in his mind before the film reaches the cutting room. As an actor, you merely have to follow the flow. I must warn you that he does appear to doze off during takes and has a ribald sense of humour and enjoys practical jokes so BEWARE! I think it's a great idea that we meet up. Celia has been dying to meet you for some time. She is your number one fan you know, although goodness knows why!"

If it had been left to me, Peter and I would have been still talking until the cows came home. However, when I glanced at my watch, I realised I still had a lot to do, so reluctantly I bade a fond farewell to Peter leaving him with making the final arrangements for our get together. It was just after one o'clock in the afternoon by the time I had finished signing any remaining documents, transferring funds into our current account for everyday expenses and giving Olivia authority to run everything in our absence and even then, the phone never stopped ringing. Fortunately, Marlene came into the office like a ray of sunshine, carrying a vase of flowers that she had just picked from the garden and placed them on the windowsill bringing a smile of appreciation to Olivia's face.

"That's it, Olivia." Marlene gave one of her famous throaty laughs, at the same time, explaining, "I'm stealing Gunther away from you now for the next few days so you're on your own, baby! As for you, Gunther, I packed you a small case of clothes for while we are away. Meanwhile, when you have decided on what form of transport we are going to use, Lucy and I have gone ahead and prepared a light lunch for both of you in the kitchen."

The minute Marlene mentioned the word transport, I kicked myself because I had forgotten all about the bloody car. It must have crossed Olivia's mind at the same time for she reached for her telephone book but as she reached for the phone, there was a knock at the door and John poked his head in exclaiming.

"Excuse me, everyone, but I hope that I haven't kept you waiting. But you will be pleased to know that I have just got back from Marlow where, after a long search, I finally found a garage under the name of Wilkes & Son who, as luck would have it, have a brand-new Bentley Sendago drop-head coupe just arrived in their showroom and they can have it ready for your collection this afternoon if you so desire. I have gone over it thoroughly and it is as sweet as a nut, I understand that the price is £1,150. If you wish the sale to proceed for delivery today, please phone them now and just a small tip to consider but I think if you negotiate with them, you may possibly get a discount, if you pay cash."

Turning to Olivia, I instructed her to phone the garage and confirm that I would pick the car up this afternoon and not only that, could they fill her up with a full tank of petrol and if possible, could they please supply some road maps as well? As to payment, I told her to write a cheque from my Coutts account for the amount but not before she had attempted to negotiate a discount. Turning to John, I invited him to join the rest of us for lunch in the kitchen and soon after that, be ready to drive Marlene and myself to the car showroom to pick up the car. It was during lunch that Marlene decided that our itinerary for the trip would be both Brighton and London. Apparently, Olivia had told her about the fabulous

Regency Pavilion and the marvellous Lanes inhabited by dozens of small antique shops, fashion salons and bric-a-brac shops plus the Brighton and Hove seafront with its famous piers. Having seen Brighton, we could then drive to London and see some of the historical sites such as Buckingham Palace, the Houses of Parliament, Trafalgar Square and not forgetting Harrods, the world-renowned departmental store. I had never heard of Brighton or the Regency Pavilion and I wasn't familiar with London, but I had heard of Harrods, so I immediately knew that there was going to be some serious shopping involved. Giving a sneak look at Olivia, I am sure I detected a slight smile, suggesting to me that I had become a victim of a conspiracy, which was soon confirmed when Olivia decided it might be wiser for her to book us into the Hotel Metropole, Brighton and Langham's Hotel in London.

So, there you have it. I was going to hit the road in a new car that I had never driven before and in a foreign country I had never been to before and hoping to arrive at a destination that I had not heard of before. But then, when I looked at my beautiful Marlene and saw how happy she was, looking every inch a *Paris Match* cover-girl, very cool and very sophisticated, I didn't have the heart to scold her.

We collected the car, signed all the necessary documents and set off for Brighton. We lost our way at Hayward's Heath and ended up in a town called Lewis. Finally, driving along London Road towards the Old Stein and figuring out the complexities of a British roundabout, we finally exited right and drove along the seafront until we finally arrived at the Metropole Hotel dead on seven-thirty in the evening. I admit that even though I was physically exhausted, in this instance, I was very grateful for my celebrity status. Olivia had done her job well, for as soon as we had booked in at reception, the concierge had immediately summoned the night manager who personally escorted us up to a suite that overlooked the promenade which gave us a panoramic view of the beach and the sea.

The manager informed us that we were situated in the middle of two piers which were named the Palace Pier and the West Pier, both of which were lit up and full of people taking their evening stroll on the piers and along the promenade. I noticed that the hotel had placed a welcoming vase of roses and a basket of fresh fruit in the suite and the manager also enquired whether we would like a maid sent up to assist madam in unpacking our suitcases, an offer which Marlene declined with a smile declaring that she preferred putting our clothes away herself. However, as he was about to leave, I had an afterthought and asked him if he would kindly reserve us a discreet table in the hotel restaurant for later on that evening, a request that he acknowledged, giving us a slight bow. Having asked if there was anything else that he could do, he left.

It didn't take us long to hang our clothes up, but it took a hell of a long time for Marlene to choose something to wear for dinner. However, we got there in the end with Marlene looking absolutely stunning in a simple black cocktail dress and accessories consisting of court shoes and evening bag in the colour of gold and as I placed a string of pearls around her neck, I whispered to her, "I wonder if later this evening, perhaps we could continue what we started, but never finished last night?"

Turning around to me, putting her arms around my neck and looking directly into my eyes with the saucy smile, she replied, "If you are up to it, big boy and don't fall asleep on me, I think there is every possibility that we can conclude last night's negotiations." Having said that, she gave me a kiss on the lips and then casually, picking up her white wrap from the chair and slinging it over her shoulders, sashayed towards the door whilst giving me a sultry, backwoods look.

As I have often said before, being either a famous actor or sportsman can seriously restrict your private life when it comes to doing the ordinary things that people take for granted, such as taking your wife out for dinner. Because I had both lived and worked in Germany during the last six years, I had become identified as more of a European film star rather than an international one. Consequently, I enjoyed a less identifiable profile when travelling abroad. However, I hadn't counted on Marlene's charisma and beauty which drew peoples' gaze to her like a magnet. Such was the case tonight, for as the elevator reached the ground floor and we stepped out, within seconds, there was a slight buzz of excitement in the air and as we proceeded towards the bar, the normal volume of conversation and activity around us seemed to abate. I must admit that Marlene looked absolutely stunning which made me feel rather proud for being her husband. As for Marlene, she appeared blissfully unaware of the stir that she was creating, making an entrance into the cocktail bar that even Sarah Bernhardt would have been proud of. Because the bar area was busy, we decided that we would go straight through to the restaurant. On our arrival, the maître d' escorted us to a discreet table at the back of the room. Normally, hotel restaurants leave a lot to be desired but, in this instance, the hotel obviously had an excellent executive chef in charge of the kitchen. Consequently, both Marlene and I enjoyed a first-class meal accompanied by an equally as good selection of wines from which to make our choice.

Time passes very quickly when you are enjoying yourself and this occasion was no exception. It seemed to come naturally to the pair of us to avoid any serious conversation and to confine ourselves to light-hearted stories and anecdotes from the past interwoven from time to time by Marlene planning a new décor for the house once we had bought it. This was one of those magic moments in married couples' lives when the moment comes together to provide them with an opportunity to be lost in each other's company. Alas, the spell was interrupted by a lady standing at our table holding a pen and a piece of paper in her hand.

"Please forgive me for intruding upon you like this, Mr Conrad," the lady said, "but I have been a fan of yours for quite a few years. I have fond memories of going to the cinema to see *Vienna Express* with my husband-to-be and you were absolutely marvellous. Would it be too much to ask for you to give me your autograph? If only to prove to my girlfriends that I have actually met you in the flesh."

When I first started out as an actor, I made a vow that if I ever became famous, I would never become churlish with the fans that had made me and as aggravating that it could be at times, I had firmly kept that promise. Looking up at her, I held out my hand for the pen and paper and said to her, "I shall be only too happy to give you an autograph but you will have to give me your first name or better still a nickname." Handing me the pen and paper, she told me her name was Edith, but she was known amongst her family and friends as Edie. Writing on the piece of paper, I scribbled, *'Dear Edie, Hope you have a wonderful evening, fondest regards, Gunther Conrad'*. Giving her one of my most dazzling of smiles, I handed the pen and paper back to her. Having given me a look of adoration, she thanked me, before returning to her table. After she had gone, Marlene and I exchanged glances and smiled at each other. "I must apologise for the intrusion," I exclaimed with heavy mockery, "but being wealthy, famous and handsome is a terrible burden for one man to carry." Marlene, while stroking my hand acted out a parody of sympathy and pity to an invisible orchestra of violins before replying, "My heart goes out to you, Gunty. The gods seem to have given you everything a man could desire and yet, your wealth is only dependent on how little I spend. You certainly are good-looking but there are signs of fraying around the edges. I noticed touches of grey in your hair and you are beginning to carry some small bags under the eyes. As for your fame, it is only as good as your last part. You know what they say in your business don't you Gunty, fame is short, you're only as good as your last picture and as the saying goes, *'Who is this Gunther Conrad? Get me Gunther Conrad. Get me the new Gunther Conrad'.*"

Leaning towards Marlene and looking her straight in the eyes, I replied, "Thank you, Mrs Conrad, for keeping my feet firmly planted on the ground. There certainly is no danger in my getting a big head while you are around. Seriously though, you are quite right in what you say. An actor's life is very mercurial and shallow, but as long as I have you by my side, whatever lies ahead of us doesn't amount to much more than a hill of beans. Changing the subject, Mrs Conrad, I believe that you owe me a promise."

Suddenly, I felt her hand gently caressing the inside of my leg and after giving me a lingering kiss she said as she arose from the table.

"I accept your challenge lover-boy. How about following me upstairs? But as you are getting older, I wouldn't leave too long in case you run out of steam before you get there." With that, she slowly sauntered out of the restaurant leaving the few remaining diners electrified by her exit and me hastening after her, doing an imaginary impression of Groucho Marx.

I will draw a veil on what happened when we reached our suite, except to say that it is not up to me to disclose our most intimate moments. However, if one could imagine Clarence Brown's most passionate film as a prelude, and Cecil B. DeMille's most extravagant *Opus* as the second act and finally, George

Cukor's brilliant finale of *The Battle of the Sexes*, you will know that the climatic finish was accompanied by the waves crashing on the shore, a chorus of thunder and lightning and finally, a gentle breeze brushing through the bedroom curtains. In other words, we both were exhausted by our passion and fell asleep in each other's arms.

The following morning, we enjoyed a leisurely breakfast in our suite whilst enjoying the sea air, having discussed the choice of either taking a drive starting at Hove and then turning back onto the coast road through Rottingdean, Newhaven, Seaford and Eastbourne, or spending the day in Brighton visiting the Lanes and the Regency Pavilion, Marlene chose the latter. I was pleased with her decision because I think that this was the first time that we were truly relaxed after leaving Germany. Looking outside, it appeared that we were in for a perfect summer's day as the skies were blue and the sea was calm. In other words, a perfect opportunity to leave the car at the hotel and see Brighton on foot. It didn't take me long to shower, shave and dress. Unfortunately, the same couldn't be said for Marlene who like most women, tended to take three times as long. After a suitable wait, I called out to her that I was going downstairs and would wait for her in the lounge, after Marlene finally shouted out from the bathroom that she wouldn't be long,

I proceeded to take the lift down to the lobby where I collected some *What's On* brochures and the previous day's copy of the *Evening Argus* newspaper to pass the time while I waited. Eventually, after what seemed a long wait, the lift doors opened and out stepped Marlene, looking radiant dressed in a blue silk blouse and white skirt with a pair of elegant beige sandals and finally, as an accessory, a light-coloured tan, shoulder-length bag. Even before she had reached me with her now familiar long-legged stride, my senses had already detected the aroma of her Coco Channel perfume. Having spent a few minutes confirming our original intention to explore Brighton on foot, we set off, stopping only briefly, to ask the hotel commissioner for directions to the Lanes, which turned out to be no more than a five-minute walk from the hotel.

Olivia had been right, the Lanes were as enchanting as we had hoped they would be with one central lane winding through a myriad of small Regency shops offering antiques, jewellery, books and paintings. Now and again, a tea shop or a fine dining establishment would pop up. Very quickly, Marlene's eagle eye spied a Victorian bracelet in the window of a jewellery shop, made of gold with Ruby inserts. It did look stunning on her wrist and I didn't need much persuasion to buy it, especially when it gave her so much joy. It was early afternoon by the time we had finished exploring and we finally gave our feet a rest by dining in one of those quaint English cafés that abounded in the Lanes, where you spent a leisurely hour devouring a selection of assorted sandwiches and pastries accompanied by a large pot of tea.

The next stop on our agenda was the Brighton Pavilion, which on enquiry was only a short walk away, near the Old Stein. It certainly was worth seeing. The first stages of the building work had commenced in 1787 by the English Prince Regent, later to become King George IV and were finally completed by him in 1811. Its style was quite unusual for the period, very much in the character of an Indian palace with a flavour of China. One of the architects involved had been the famous John Nash, noted for his terraced houses which could be seen, I was told, in Brighton, London and Bath.

As a bonus for what had been a very pleasant day, Marlene and I decided to walk through the pavilion gardens which led us out to a theatre situated amongst a row of shops. This turned out to be the Theatre Royal. With our curiosity truly aroused, we hurried across the road to read the theatre's playbills from which I discovered to my pleasant surprise, that both Noel Coward and Gertrude Lawrence were appearing in his latest play, *Tonight at 8.30.* I had met both of them socially in America during the late twenties and had found Noel Coward not only to be a clever and scintillating playwright but also, a marvellous bon vivant with a rapier-style wit, which could very easily put you in your place. As for Gertrude Lawrence, her light comedic touch put her amongst the great musical comedy stars of our age. Much to my surprise, the theatre box office was open for business with a considerable amount of activity taking place. It was only on further investigation that I realised that it was a matinee day and although I expected to be told that the house was sold out, I had the good fortune to be told that there were two seats available in row C of the stalls for the following night due to a last-minute cancellation. I quickly acquired the tickets, as well as leaving a message for

Noel, telling him that I was staying at the Metropole and that both my wife and I hoped to see him after the show tomorrow.

We took a slow walk across the Old Stein to the seafront and though we were tired from the physical exercise of the day, we decided on the spur of the moment to take a look at the attractions on Palace Pier. It was our first experience of the British love for the seaside and in particular, its fondness for piers. Palace Pier was a hurly-burly of people, with arcades overflowing with machines that enticed you for the price of one penny, to have a go on a variety of amusements such as, 'Read your palm', 'Pinball', 'What the Butler saw' and many others. As we walked further out, we encountered rifle ranges, a castle from which you slid down a chute on a mat and finally, a hall of mirrors and a ghost train. At the end of the pier was a theatre, advertising a variety show which was on every night for the summer season. The headliner on the playbill was an English comedian that I was not familiar with by the name of Arthur Askey. As we turned around and began to retrace our steps, we were gradually drawn into the magic of the moment. Stopping by a stall, I bought Marlene a large candy floss on a stick and we both happily posed for a photograph taken by a stout gentleman wearing a pink bowler hat and a striped suit of many colours. We collected our photograph from his booth for the price of six pennies and as we laughed at ourselves in the photo, we strolled arm-in-arm from the pier.

The following day, we drove to Eastbourne along the coastal route through Rottingdean and the port of Newhaven which was a ferry terminal for the channel crossing to France and then on to the quaint little town of Seaford and from there, eventually, we arrived at Eastbourne, where we had lunch in a bistro-style café situated near the beach. Eastbourne turned out to be a charming seaside resort and from our observations, appeared to have quite a high percentage of retirees. However, Marlene and I were tired from a healthy abundance of sea air and physical activity and because we had experienced a wonderful time in Brighton, particularly as we had been able to do as we pleased, virtually incognito, we decided there and then to drive back to Brighton and spend a few extra hours in the hotel before our anticipated visit to the theatre that evening.

After a leisurely drive back, which included a stopover on the Sussex Downs to take in the scenery, we finally reached the hotel around four o'clock in the afternoon. There were two messages waiting for me as we collected the keys to our suite. The first message was from Noel Coward who was looking forward to seeing us and that we should go backstage as soon as the final curtain had dropped. Unfortunately, the second message was from Olivia asking me to phone her as soon as possible. Giving the receptionist our home number, I asked her to place a call for me which I would take in my suite. Marlene and I made a quick dash upstairs just in time to hear the phone ringing. Picking the receiver up, I heard Olivia's unmistakable voice.

"Is that you, Gunther? I'm so sorry to have to interrupt your holiday but I received two urgent phone calls earlier this afternoon, one from a producer at Gaumont British film studios by the name of Ted Black and, one from Robin Cox. Apparently, Ted Black is asking you to do him a big favour by reporting to the studio this Friday for a script run-through in preparation for the start of principal photography on Monday. He apologises to you for having to bring you in a week earlier than scheduled. Apparently, it has something to do with studio politics concerning Hitchcock and the studio chiefs, Maurice and Isidore Ostrer. If possible, Mr Black would like an answer from you by late afternoon. The other call was from Robin, essentially saying the same thing but that you were not contractually obliged to start earlier than intended. However, as you are about to re-energise your career in the English-speaking film world, a gesture of goodwill might not come amiss."

"Okay, Olivia, it seems an instant decision is required, so get in touch with Robin Cox confirming that I will start Friday and would you ask him to pass that information on to Ted Black immediately. Obviously, Marlene and I will be home tomorrow, which is a great disappointment for both of us, as much as we wanted to see London, I guess we'll have to put that trip off for another day. Although come to think of it, I shall be working there for the next few months, during which time, I shall be travelling backwards and forwards between home and London and I would think by that time, I would be no stranger to the city. By the way Olivia, when you ring Robin, could you find out whether they're filming at Islington or Shepherd's Bush? I would hate to turn up at the wrong studio. You can always ring me here if you need me and if not, then as I mentioned earlier, Marlene and I will be home tomorrow."

As I put the receiver back on the hook, Marlene called out from the bathroom, "I heard the bit about see you tomorrow, so I take it that we won't be going to London after all. Perhaps it was for the best? It was a little selfish of me to drag you off for a short break when we had only just arrived. Whilst you are filming in London, I shall have more than enough to occupy me with the house and gardens. I think we should let our hair down tonight and have a great evening at the theatre. I've brought along that cocktail dress and matching bolero jacket that you like so much, so now you will have to make the effort and put on a black tie and dinner jacket."

"I'll tell you what we will do, sweetheart. Whilst we get dressed, I'll order a light dinner with a bottle of Dom Perignon and have it bought up to the suite, whilst at the same time, I will order a cab for ten minutes past seven to take us to the theatre. I don't know when we will get the opportunity to visit Brighton again, but I do know that these last two days that we spent here will be treasured memories of our first days of freedom."

When we drew up outside the Theatre Royal, we still had ten minutes left before 'curtain up' and as the traffic of theatregoers in the theatre lobby had thinned out leaving just a few parties of late arrivals such as ourselves, we found an usher who then proceeded to lead us down the central aisle of the stalls towards our seats. It had become part of our lives that whenever Marlene and I attended public events, we inevitably attracted attention and scrutiny and tonight was no different. Wearing that stunning cocktail dress and her general deportment exuding glamour as she moved, she looked magnificent and I must admit that even I, who by this time, was a veteran at public appearances, was both proud and slightly overwhelmed by the buzz of excitement that swept through the stalls and didn't subside until we had taken our seats and the house lights had dimmed.

Glancing quickly over the programme notes, I noticed that the original production had been written as ten one-act plays, the performances to be announced in advance in various combinations of three. The opening play-let for this evening was to be *Red Peppers*, followed by, *We were Dancing* and the last, *Shadow Play*. Obviously, because of Noel and Gertrude's star power, they could do no wrong with the audience's critical appreciation. However, I much preferred *Red Peppers* which was about a husband-and-wife music hall act on tour and their relationship with each other, with most of the action taking place in a dressing room. It was droll, witty and acerbic as only Noel could write and both stars were firing on full cylinders. Both we and the audience thoroughly enjoyed it and when the curtain fell at the end of the evening's performance both Noel and Gertrude received tumultuous applause from the audience as they took their repeated curtain calls.

The auditorium gradually emptied as the audience's filed through the exit doors leaving the two of us to approach an usher, who, on hearing that we were expected backstage, immediately took us through a door situated by the proscenium. This led straight onto the backstage which was a hive of activity with stagehands moving flats and furniture and shutting the lights down on the gantries. The usher finally deposited us at the stage doorkeeper's cubbyhole whilst informing him that Mr Coward was expecting us. The stage doorkeeper, who apparently went by the name of Fred and spoke with the broadest of Cockney accents, asked our names and then proceeded to reach for the phone and press a button before speaking. Within seconds, he put the receiver down and informed us that somebody would be along immediately to take us through to Mr Coward. True to his word, a man who I took to be in his early fifties and was wearing a white porter's jacket and black trousers came down the corridor and greeted us.

"Good evening, Mr and Mrs Conrad, my name is Murray and I am Mr Coward's personal dresser. Please follow me. He is expecting you."

Very quickly, we reached the dressing room and upon Murray opening the door, we were ushered in. The master himself was seated at the dressing table removing the remaining remnants of his stage makeup and immediately swung around and stood up when he heard the door open, walking towards us with one hand extended in greeting and the other holding his signatory cigarette holder and cigarette and speaking in his familiar clipped accent, greeted us enthusiastically.

"Hello, Gunther, dear boy. How nice to see you again and this gorgeous creature can only be your lovely wife, Marlene."

Taking her hand, he bent and kissed the back of it before continuing, "My dear, you'll never know how heartbroken I was when I read of your marriage to Gunther. I first set eyes on him in 1926 when I had gone to Hawaii to recover from a disastrous relationship. We met one night at a fashionable party. He was with a typical American flapper girl, something to do with the cinema, I believe. I was smitten, the moment I set eyes upon him and knew in an instant that the two most beautiful things in life were Gunther's profile and my mind. However, I realised then, that my passion would never be consummated and so did the next best thing, I composed a little ditty called *Mad about the Boy*. He burst out laughing at the momentary look of bewilderment on Marlene's face, but she soon realised that this was Coward being Coward and joined in the laughter.

It didn't take long for Marlene to fall under Noel's spell either, hanging on every word as he explained that the company would be soon off to Broadway for the American première of *Tonight at 8.30* and thanked God that he had no longer any contractual obligations to remain in a production for more than three months. Apart from the fact that he loathed appearing in long runs, three months was about all he could take of the fast way American life. At that precise moment, a tall, striking looking lady burst into the dressing room filling it with a huge burst of energy from which she simply proceeded to take over with her commanding presence. It was, of course, none other than Gertrude Lawrence who, after giving Marlene and myself theatrical embraces accompanied by 'darling this' and 'darling that', proceeded to have us in stitches as she went about describing her and Noel's antics in tonight's performance. Talk about life imitating art, it only proved that Noel richly deserved the accolade of being one of Britain's foremost playwrights of his generation. We didn't stay much longer after that because after all, it had been still very much a working day for both Noel and Gertrude and out of consideration to them both, we didn't wish to overstay our welcome. Also, we faced a tiring journey home to Medmenham in the morning. Just before we left, Noel took me to one side and in his best master and pupil mode, told me that it was most important that I re-establish my position as a major international film star with the English-speaking public.

"Take all the parts that you are offered, whether they be big or small, Gunther. Remember, dear boy, there are no such things as small parts, only small actors! You are young enough to take on the challenge of *Hamlet, The Merchant of Venice* and *The Taming of the Shrew*. Accept the challenges and push the boundaries of your talent."

It was gone midnight when we finally left the theatre and as luck would have it, there was still one or two taxis for hire waiting outside. We very quickly pulled up in front of the hotel and after paying the taxi driver off, Marlene and I then decided on the spur of the moment to walk across the road to the seafront and enjoy a few moments listening to the waves gently washing over the stones of the beach while inhaling the sea air.

"Two days aren't much in terms of a lifetime, but I shall always remember this short time out that we spent together. Britain may be a small island, but I feel very secure and unafraid by being here. Have you noticed, Gunty, the absence of marching boots and martial music, the slow and insidious indoctrination being fed into the average German that they are members of a master race and the total absence of free speech? We are a very fortunate couple and enjoy a very privileged life and I hope that we shall continue to do so but I feel that I should give something back by giving some of my time and money in opposing Hitler in any way that I can."

"I totally agree with you, Marlene and will fully support you in any decisions that you make. It may be wise to concentrate for the moment on bringing your parents and any other members of your family out of Germany. I think these decisions will come naturally to us over the next few months. Meanwhile, let us be grateful for a new start in life and enjoy every moment of it. Let's just see how many of our dreams are fulfilled in the coming years. Apart from the ones that I have already stated, I have one more and that is for you to restart your career over here and then to retire at the top of your game."

"I too, have one more dream, Gunty and that is that we have a family of our own one day and bring them up in a world that has no prejudices. Meanwhile, it's you and me against the world, baby. As a matter of interest, I think it's best that we go back into the hotel. There are a lot of passers-by who are beginning to give us second glances. God forbid that I should have to stand by and watch you signing more autographs for your adoring female fans at this time of night when I have only got to take you up to our suite to have my wicked way with you." Bursting out laughing, I grabbed her in an embrace and gave her a lingering kiss, then I pulled away and looked her straight in the eyes.

"I can always rely on you, Marlene, to bring me firmly back down to earth but can I just say that actions speak louder than words, so give me your hand and let's make a run for it back to the hotel."

Chapter 9

Establishing New Roots

A lot of water had passed under the bridge since those peaceful days in Brighton. Marlene and I had made an offer to purchase the house which had been accepted. We were now the proud owners of Falcon House. By the time Marlene had finished renovating the rooms, refurbished the guesthouse and employed a gardener, I had spent a small fortune. This expenditure was offset by Marlene having a keen eye for interior decorating and negotiating great deals with contractors. The previous years of 1936 and 1937 had also helped financially: my first film with Alfred Hitchcock had not only proved a success with the British public but also had achieved distribution with major American cinema chains throughout the north American continent. Thankfully, this exposure had brought me fresh recognition on both sides of the Atlantic and two years of busy engagements which included amongst other things, three months at the Old Vic in London, a film for Gainsborough and one for Gaumont British. Finally, just when I thought I had enough work on my plate, I went and signed a three-picture deal with producer, Alexander Korda of London Films.

Unfortunately, the first film to be scheduled of the trio was to have been a film adaptation of Robert Graves' book, *I Claudius* which started filming in the autumn of 1937. What might have been a classic British film, turned out to be an unfinished masterpiece. The iconic director, Joseph von Sternberg, was at the helm with the charismatic actor, Charles Laughton, playing Claudius supported by Merle Oberon, yours truly, Flora Robson and Emlyn Williams. But it wasn't to be. With artistic differences on interpretation between Sternberg and Laughton and a car accident involving Miss Oberon serious enough for her to be hospitalised, the film went well over budget and was shut down. I suspect that Korda never really had sufficient funds to finish it, although I was paid for doing very little. Had it been completed, there was every possibility that it would have been a better film than Korda's previous box office hit, *Henry VIII*.

The European continent was beginning to make the headlines, but not in a good way. In March, Hitler's Germany had gained unification with Austria, bringing it under Nazi domination. Then, during September, with the acquiescence of both Britain and France, Hitler had occupied the Sudetenland, exposing Czechoslovakia to the further danger of German territorial demands and confirming the world's misguided view of the German leader. The American magazine *Time* had chosen him as their 'Man of the Year'. This inexplicable appeasement of the German dictator had started in 1936 with the Olympic Games being held in Berlin despite the Nazi government's persecution of the Jews. It didn't help that Germany came first in the table of nations with a total of eighty-nine medals, confirming Hitler's belief in the Teutonic master race. In the same year, Edward VIII abdicated the throne for the love of his mistress, making way for his brother George to become King George V. Meanwhile, Edward took the title of the Duke of Windsor, married his mistress, Wallis Simpson and then proceeded to visit Germany and by doing so, bestowed a further seal of approval on the Nazis.

It was the beginning of autumn that October 1938 and the lawns at Falcon House were beginning to develop a carpet of fallen leaves. Marlene, with the help of Bill and the gardener, had spent most of Friday morning preparing the outside grounds for winter, whilst I was going through the script of my second film for Alex Korda, due to commence shooting at the start of the following week. Olivia, bless her, had completed our nationalisation papers and that morning, had them ready for posting to our immigration lawyer. Some time back, Marlene and I had made a joint decision to become British citizens feeling that we had a lot in common with the British way of life, especially considering how we were so easily accepted in a non-judgemental way by everybody. As far as my career was concerned, the great British public was treating me as one of their own. In whatever medium I had appeared in, be it radio, film or theatre, I had managed to build a loyal following.

For all that, Marlene's determination to resume a position in the British fashion industry had filled me with immense pride. She had, on her own initiative and after many attempts, been granted an interview with Norman Hartnell, the couturier and dress designer, who impressed by her enthusiasm, had hired her as a model for his 1937-38 collection of evening wear aimed specifically at the wallets of the high society parents whose daughters would be attending the annual Debutante's Ball in which they would be presented to the King and Queen. Her début as a Norman Hartnell model had attracted considerable attention from the press which had raised her profile within the fashion industry and in turn, had placed her in a position, where she was being offered more assignments that she could cope with.

As I stood at the window, watching her moving backwards and forwards amongst her beloved plants, closely followed behind by Bill trundling a wheelbarrow with gardening tools, I must admit that she looked rather fetching, dressed in Wellington boots, a heavy tweed skirt, a high-necked pink jumper and finally, a fleecy lined short coat. I also noted with some amusement that Marlene still attracted the protective instincts of the opposite sex without arousing any animosity of her own gender. In other words, the menfolk of the house accepted from her, far more than they would from me, when it came to getting things done. My train of thought was interrupted by the phone ringing. It was Robin Cox.

''Hello, Robin. Nice to hear from you. No problem on Monday's start date, I hope?''

''No, Gunther. That only happens now and again just to keep you on your toes. Seriously though, I have just received a phone call from a Doctor Xavier Jurgens who apparently, is the Cultural Secretary at the German Embassy. He requested your number which I refused to give. However, he was rather insistent saying that the matter was urgent, so I told him to give me his number and I would get you to ring him as soon as possible. I hope I didn't exceed my authority old chap, but he really did get my backup, not that I wish to tar all Germans with the same brush, but those Nazis are really something else. That last German ambassador, what was his name? Oh, I remember now, von Ribbentrop. What an absolute shower he turned out to be. Anyway, the number he gave me is St James' Park 1504. Best of luck, old boy. Hope it's nothing serious.''

''I hope so too, Robin. Thank you for going to so much trouble which I appreciate and by the way, I am completely in agreement with your opinion of the Nazis. What we need now is a strong leader to stand up to Hitler. Before you go, Robin, I read the script that London Films sent me and I am certainly excited by its concept. It's something completely different for me. It's a fantasy, and it's aimed at a family market and it gives me the opportunity to play a nasty guy, so just let Korda know that I accept the part. Take care of yourself and I'll see you at the studio."

As soon as I had finished the call, I re-dialled the St James' Park number and on being connected, was informed that it was the German Embassy. Unfortunately, as it was late Friday afternoon and most of the offices were closed for the weekend, Dr Jurgens would not be available until Monday morning. So much for urgent! Well, this Jurgens fellow could jolly well wait now until I was ready to speak to him.

Socially, because we had obtained such a high public profile, it had become very difficult to have an evening out either together or with friends. Marlene and I intended to spend more of our leisure time at home in our own company or occasionally, invite friends over for a dinner party and tonight was to be no exception. With me starting a major film on Monday and Marlene having two modelling assignments mid-week, we had decided on a quiet weekend at home. In the morning, Olivia was going to visit relatives for the weekend, so I thought it would be nice for her to join Marlene and I that evening for one of Lucy's culinary feasts and to relax by the open fire with a few drinks.

The grandfather clock in the hallway was just striking eight thirty in the evening when we finally finished dinner which had been a superb start to the evening. Bill had laid out an excellent table with some of our best China silverware and crystal glasses and finished off with lighted candles in the centre of the table which set the room off in a warm glow. Lucy had prepared a starter of King prawns in garlic butter followed by a saddle of lamb for the main course, finished off with a dessert of good old-fashioned rhubarb and apple crumble, all served by Bill with his usual aplomb. Once the remainder of the dinner plates had been cleared from the table, with her usual spirit of thoughtfulness, Marlene had Bill bring Lucy from the kitchen and had proceeded to thank them both for a lovely night and inform them that not only should they close the kitchen down as soon as possible but that Bill should choose a bottle of wine and then both of them should go upstairs and relax for the remainder of the evening.

Alcohol and good company can introduce a sense of well-being and sentimentality and this was especially the case when

Marlene and Olivia mentioned Irving Thalberg, who had died suddenly three weeks earlier and wondered whether I had known him that well. I reminisced over the silent days of Hollywood and Marlene and Olivia sat spellbound as I talked about the privilege of being a young actor working at the great MGM film studios at the time that Thalberg had been its head of production. He had been the same age as me but apart from Louis B. Mayer, was the most powerful man in Hollywood. Unfortunately, he had been born with a degenerative heart disease which had always made him very frail and sadly, it was to claim his life at the early age of thirty-seven. However, the legacy he left behind would go down forever in Hollywood history. He had helped to create several of the best-known silent stars including Greta Garbo, John Gilbert, Lon Chaney, Joan Crawford and just below that pantheon of stars, me. I had been very fortunate to have been in my early twenties when I was summonsed to MGM and had earned my reputation playing alongside great actresses such as Garbo, Lillian Gish and Norma Shearer. More importantly, I had learnt my craft as a film actor under the tutelage of the great directors of my generation; Alan Dwan, Clarence Brown, F.W. Murneau and King Vidor.

Both Marlene and Olivia asked if I thought that the sound cinema had reached the same quality that the silent film had accomplished? Taking a sip of Jack Daniels and after giving the question some thought, I proceeded to reply to their question.

"No, not yet. But we are slowly getting there. In the last few years, the camera has been released from its static booth and thanks to the simple invention of the microphone boom, dialogue is beginning to sound far more natural, as well as allowing the actors greater freedom of movement. The best examples I can give you are the Western films which have become trailblazers for outdoor filming rather than being confined to interior sets. I think that by the end of the decade, all these innovations will come together to create some film classics. I refer, in particular, to the emigre composers from Germany such as Franz Waxman, Max Steiner, Alfred Korngold and Dmitri Tiomkin. And don't forget, a new breed of theatre-trained actors from Broadway, such as Clark Gable and Spencer Tracy plus, of course, Katharine Hepburn, have all brought a new sense of naturalism to the movies. I also believe that all these improvements will eventually be enhanced by the switch from black-and-white photography to colour."

"I have a feeling, Gunty," Marlene interjected, "that in the future, you will end up on the other side of the camera either as producer or director."

"What was it that Sam Goldwyn said when he heard that Charlie Chaplin and Mary Pickford had formed their own production company called United Artists? The lunatics have taken over the asylum. Well, Marlene, I have a feeling that you could be right and that somewhere in the future, that's where my destiny could take me."

"Well, you two lovely young people," Olivia announced, I'm going to go upstairs now. I would like to keep up with you as it has been such a lovely night, but I have an early start in the morning and I'm not as young as I used to be. If you're not up when I leave in the morning, have a peaceful weekend and I will see you next week."

Rising from the table, Olivia stooped and kissed Marlene on the cheek wishing her good night before walking around the table to me. Placing her hand on my shoulder she said, "Good night, Gunther. Good luck on the first day of shooting on Monday. I am sure you will give it your best and neither you nor Marlene are to worry about anything concerning the house or office. I assume, of course, that you will drive home from the studio every night. It will help if you let us know your estimated time of arrival back so that Lucy will have dinner waiting for you."

With Olivia gone to bed, Marlene and I pulled our chairs around to face the glowing embers of the fire which with the lighted candles, gave the room a warm glow as well as giving off a kaleidoscope of flickering patterns on the walls. We sat in silence for a little while holding hands, just staring into the golden embers of the logs.

Presently, Marlene turned towards me and lighting two cigarettes proceeded to pass one to me whilst at the same time breaking the silence by speaking quietly, "I have to tell you, Gunty, that I received a letter from mother today, in which she writes that both she and papa have had enough and have reached the end of the road as far as remaining in Germany despite Grandma and Granddad's insistence on remaining. Now that Hansi and Lothar are both safely in America and Greta and Philip have settled in Holland, they are beginning to feel very vulnerable. Papa has applied for visas to Great Britain but has been told that the applications could take at least a year just to be processed. She has also written that although she doesn't want to worry me unnecessarily, papa is now required to report once a week to the internal security offices where his papers and movements are checked vigorously and he has also been told that he is now considered a Jew of personal interest. Mama asks if perhaps, with your connections, you could expedite the process for them to leave Germany? She finishes by sending us her love and thanking us for the supply of money they have received by our underground couriers."

"I hope that the same persons unknown delivered the letter discreetly before it was sent on to you," I quickly interjected. "I don't want to alarm you, darling, but you must realise that the Nazis are censoring all activities in and out of Germany and that the less they know, the better so that we can protect the safety of your mother and father."

"Don't be silly! Any communications that we have with mama and papa are sent through a pipeline of volunteers who travel in and out of Germany. You would be surprised how many people in the fashion industry loath the Nazis and will do anything they can to help those who are being persecuted."

"Forgive me, darling. I didn't mean to offend you, it's just that you can't be too careful. Now that your mother and father have made a commitment to emigrate, I do have a plan that I was unable to use before because of their indecisiveness. I happen to know of several Swedish intermediaries who could deliver messages from me to those closest to Hermann Goering. I expect that you may have forgotten my mentioning Emmy Goering nee, Sonnemann and Hermann's brother, Albert, whom I had frequently met socially in the past. Apart from Emmy and I knowing each other in our drama student days, I had often been in the position to help her get acting jobs and to advance small loans to tide her over difficult patches between jobs. Albert was as different to his brother Hermann as chalk is to cheese. Hermann has risen to the top, becoming both commander-in-chief of the Luftwaffe and after Hitler, the second most powerful man in the Third Reich. Also, although Hermann is regarded publicly as a rabid anti-Semite, privately, he is not as ideologically driven as other senior party comrades. His anti-Semitism is purely materialistic, based on financial gain and power. Albert, by comparison, is a completely normal human being and made it quite clear that he was a fervent anti-Nazi and would, whenever he could, assist Jews and other so-called enemies of the state, to escape Germany. During the early twenties, Albert had been involved in film production which is how I first met him. We took an immediate liking to each other, but unfortunately, we lost contact when I went off to Hollywood and we only met a few times after I returned to Germany. By then, Albert had left the film industry and become a businessman."

"You know, sweetheart, I'm not being melodramatic when I tell you that the Democratic countries of this world need to sit up and take notice. Hitler has seized the moment both by seducing Italy and encouraging Japan into forming an axis of evil. He is only waiting now for the last piece of the jigsaw to complete his grand design, whatever that may be. I must be totally honest with you, darling and tell you that I received a phone call from Robin Cox this morning informing me that the German Embassy wishes me to get in touch with them. I don't know why because there is nobody available until Monday to tell me. I know I have drunk a lot of alcohol tonight, but let me tell you, sweetheart, there is one thing I do share with the British and that is that I may be slow to anger, but when I am, watch out. I've had enough and I am as mad as hell now. Even though I am filming next week, I will find time to put into motion plans to extradite mama and papa. All I ask of you, Marlene, is not to worry and to believe me totally when I tell you to have complete faith and confidence in the promise that I have made to you."

"Oh, there is no question in my heart that you won't succeed in bringing mama and papa out of Germany safely, Gunty. One of the things that I love about you is the passion that you have for the things that you believe in. I think, for the moment, we must concentrate on getting as many members of our family as possible to Britain and out of harm's way before it is too late. From what you have just told me about the phone call, time is of the essence and obviously, there are signs of something more sinister beginning to emerge. I do think, darling, that once we have got the family to safety, we should give some thought to what we can give back to society. After all, we have both been very fortunate over the years and have obtained the fulfilment of most of our dreams. I think we need to be more socially conscious and become part of a moral crusade, such as joining an anti-fascist organisation to fight the evils of Nazism, I have had many conversations as I'm sure that you have with friends and colleagues on the subject of what is happening in Germany and the general consensus is that all of us could start up a foundation to combat racial prejudice by making people aware how damaging intolerance can be, especially amongst the very young."

"I think that is a marvellous idea, sweetheart. I can think of so many people who would be more than willing to lend their support, but as you said earlier, we will keep that idea in reserve until the time is right. In the meantime, let us enjoy the peace and quiet of the moment. Talking of which, I've noticed the bottle of Chevrey Chambertin on the table waiting to be finished off and whilst we do that, accompanied by a cigarette, it will give me the opportunity to tell you that of all the wonderful things that have happened to me. You, are the best."

"Sweetheart, that's a lovely thing to say. It's the best Christmas gift that I could wish for, apart perhaps from two others."

As I emptied the remainder of the bottle into our two glasses, I hadn't been listening to Marlene as I was fully occupied thinking of the tasks that lay ahead of me during the next few weeks.

The sound of Marlene's voice intruding on my thoughts soon brought me back to earth, "When I said two additional gifts for Christmas, I actually meant three. Obviously, my second gift would be having my parents here."

I interrupted her at that point, "I think, sweetheart, that your second wish may be achievable in the very near future, God willing. However, I am intrigued as to what your third wish would be, knowing now would certainly save me a lot of heartache on wandering what to get you. Mind you, we are still only in October and have several weeks to go before we start putting the Christmas decorations up, so I think that we are racing a little bit ahead of ourselves."

Marlene promptly burst out laughing at my comments before answering me, "Oh, sweetheart, do you really think that I am that shallow that I only desire the materialistic possessions in life. I consider myself a very lucky girl to enjoy a lifestyle that most people would give their back teeth for, but having said that, none of it would be worth a hill of beans without each other. As to the third gift, it is something special to me and you. Quite simply, I want a baby, a child that will grow into adulthood with our unconditional love and support. Time goes so fast and my body clock is ticking away and before we would know it, the opportunity would be gone for good and we both would end up as a self-centred couple with an abundance of unrequited love.''

I was completely taken aback not only by the earnestness of her remarks but by the depth in which she spoke, so much so, that I butted in with a mixture of both German and English.

''*Gott in Himmel*, Marlene, don't go getting profound on me. I couldn't wish for anything better than for you to tell me that you're pregnant. By the sounds of it, I may have to go out and buy a copy of the karma sutra and perform some new moves on you, sweetheart.''

''Hark at the big screen lover!'' she replied with a mischievous smile. ''By the time that you have read the karma sutra, I will be an old lady and you will have been reduced to a spear carrier, third from the left, in a DeMille biblical epic! Seriously, Gunty, life isn't as simple as that. When our doctor expressed surprise that despite me being in good physical condition, I hadn't conceived yet, without wishing to burden you, Gunty, darling, I went up to Harley Street to see a specialist who gave me a thorough physical, including x-rays. His prognosis confirmed our doctor's opinion that I was in good health and that I was to relax and let mother nature take its course and if that failed, it may be necessary for you to be checked out as well.''

Our conversation flowed backwards and forwards into the early hours of the morning filled with humour and serious matters including the topic of Neville Chamberlain, the British Prime Minister who, on returning last month from a meeting in Germany with Hitler, had made declaration 'Peace in our time', one that neither Marlene nor I had any faith in, because we both sensed that Hitler had a hidden agenda which certainly didn't include peace! We finished the evening off by attempting to dance to a swing version of Tommy Dorsey's, *I'm Getting Sentimental Over You*. We started off by giggling like schoolkids as we attempted to master the beat but very quickly, the mood, the music and the alcohol had us dancing in a more sensuous and romantic way which finally led us upstairs hand-in-hand.

I suppose when we kissed each other goodbye, early on Monday morning, neither of us had any inkling what the future had in store for us, but as I drove away from Marlene as she stood at the front door, I was already going through all the things that I had to deal with during the next few weeks. I had spent Saturday and Sunday closeted in the office memorising my lines for the first part of the film, *Council's Opinion* which was being shot at Denham studios, meaning that I only had a short distance to travel from home. My co-star was the gorgeous Merle Oberon who I hadn't seen since her car accident and I certainly looked forward to working with her again, this time on a completed picture rather than an unfinished one. A bonus for me was that the film music was being composed by a friend of mine from the past, Miklos Rozsa, a Hungarian, like Alex Korda, the producer of the film. Finally, the film was being directed by an American, called Tim Whelan, whom Korda had brought over to London to direct several British films, the last one being *The Mill on the Floss*. As the car carried me to the studio, I remembered that I had to phone the German Embassy and speak to Xavier Jurgens, after which I would have to try and contact a Swedish friend of mine, Lars Holquist, who had business connections with many Nazi bigwigs, including Hermann Goering. I might get lucky in persuading Lars to act as a go-between in negotiations with Goering which hopefully, would result in the extrication of Marlene's parents from Germany. Obviously, there would be a price to be paid and the sooner I knew what that was, the better.

Once the car had arrived in the studio car park, I was installed in the makeup department and whilst there, being prepared for the cameras, Jenny Bush, the script supervisor, came in and took the opportunity to go through the scheduled shoot. After a strong cup of coffee, I proceeded through to the set, where Tim Whelan and I introduced ourselves. Shortly after, Merle came through with her makeup artist and gave me a hug and within minutes, the set began to come alive, humming with activity. We were soon joined by Cecil Parker and Miles Malleson, two prominent British character actors due to appear in the scene with us. Unfortunately, as most of the morning was used up by technical details such as setting up blocking moves by the cinematographer, Harry Stradling and Merle and I modelling for costume shots, it became obvious that we would not start filming until mid-afternoon. To prevent any further embarrassment to his cast, Tim Whelan told us to take a long lunch break and apologised to Cecil and Miles for keeping them sitting around all morning. However, it did give me the opportunity to catch up on some private business. Whilst the cast and crew trooped over to the studio commissary, I slipped over to the outside telephone line situated off set in the studio hangar.

The first call I made was to the German Embassy in St James' Park and on being connected was put through immediately to the mysterious Xavier Jurgens, at which point I, introduced myself.

"Good afternoon, Herr Jurgens. My name is Gunther Conrad and I understand that there is a matter of some urgency which you wish to discuss with me?"

"My dear Herr Conrad. How good of you to respond so quickly. I am wondering if perhaps, we could arrange a meeting at your convenience. This is not only a subject of urgency but a delicate one as well and …"

At that point, I interrupted him in a tone of measured coolness, "The first thing I have to say to you, Herr Jurgens, is that I have just commenced a new film this week and there is no gap in my schedule that would allow me to interrupt filming to meet with you. The second thing is what is this urgent matter that can't be discussed over the phone?"

"I quite understand, Herr Conrad and believe me, I do sympathise with your growing irritation, but I have been instructed to deliver to you covertly, an important message from a very senior German minister that can only be delivered person-to-person. Perhaps if I tell you it concerns members of your wife's family, that may facilitate an opportunity for us to meet? Hence, the urgency. If I may add, the sensitivity of the message requires the utmost delicacy in protecting its source."

"That, Herr Jurgens, sounds like a threat of some sort, so for the moment, I will be diplomatic and pretend that it doesn't exist. Because I am intrigued at the contents of the message and your reference to my wife's parents and immediate family, I am prepared to meet with you here at Denham studios this coming Wednesday at one o'clock in the afternoon, where you will find a pass waiting for you at the front desk. I'm certainly looking forward to meeting you and I am somewhat intrigued by what you may have to say. I hope that this appointment will meet with your approval and bid you goodbye until eventually, we meet, Herr Jurgens."

"I look forward to seeing you this Wednesday, Herr Conrad and bid you goodbye, until then."

As soon as I had disconnected the call, I redialled the number of a Swedish business in London by the name of the Norvasc Petroleum Company and asked to be put through to a Lars Holquist. Eventually, a voice came on the line with an unmistakable Swedish accent which I recognised immediately as belonging to Lars.

"Hello, Lars, you mangey old sea dog. How are you doing? I bet that you have added yet another million to your considerable fortune since we last met. And how about your lovely wife, Viveca? Don't forget to send her my love and remind her what a lucky guy you are."

"Same to you, Gunther, you old reprobate. Still think you are God's gift to all women? The last time that I saw you up there on the big screen was in one of those 'Tits and Sand' movies with all those 'Come with me to the Casbah' lines. Seriously though, it's nice to hear from you, old chum. We will have to meet up with the womenfolk and have a meal out somewhere. Meanwhile, what can I do for you? Are you after a donation to the actors old folks home or something?"

"No, Lars, it's a personal favour I'm asking from you this time. Marlene and I are very concerned for the safety of her parents who are German Jews, as you know. The situation in Germany is becoming increasingly fraught with danger for them as it is for all Jews and despite our entreaties, they have, until now, refused to leave the Fatherland. But due to Hitler's ever increasing economic and the physical pogrom against the Jewish population, they have now changed their minds and decided to leave. It appears that there is added threat to their well-being, insofar as the German security police are now treating them as 'persons of interest'. I know Lars, that you and several other Swedish businessmen travel to Berlin a lot and have access to the highest circles in the Nazi government. So, is there any way that you could obtain exit visas on their behalf?"

"I won't lie to you, Gunther. This is going to be difficult and will be needed to be handled very delicately. I can't guarantee success, but as it happens, I have been invited to Carinhall, the country estate of Field Marshal Goering, to join his shooting party. He has a weakness for collecting titles and medals and apart from being Commander-in-Chief of the Luftwaffe, he also holds the office of Reich Minister for the Economic Four-Year Plan and as if that is not enough, he also holds the title of Reich Head Huntsman for all of Germany! Strange to say, that although he is both ruthless and corrupt, the German public have a great fondness for him, far above all the other Nazi leaders and they refer to him as 'our fat Hermann'."

It was at this point in the conversation that I interrupted him, "I think, Lars, that the invitation to Carinhall has come at a most opportune moment. You see, the Field Marshal's wife and I were young drama students in the old days and later on, as I became successful, I often helped her to obtain acting roles wherever I could and kept her away from the poverty line when she divorced her first husband. Whilst over there, you may get the chance to speak to her privately on my behalf and gain her support. After all, she may be able to persuade her husband to be more sympathetic to our petition."

"Gunther, that piece of information will be of great help to us for you see, not only is the Field Marshal anxious to do business with us as a consortium because of his desire to obtain a stockpile of gas and petroleum, but his brother Albert, also does business with us in a small way. As you know, he has been responsible for helping many Jews to obtain exit permits from Germany. What I would like you to do, Gunther, is to supply me within the next few days, all the pertinent information of your in-laws. Just one last thing, Gunther. The consortium normally clubs together to grease Goering's palm with an expensive work of art and obviously, the more value it is, the greater our chance of success. Would you object to contributing if we are successful?"

I needed no persuasion in agreeing to Lars' proposal and promised that I would send him all the details of Marlene's mother and father immediately. We spoke together for a few minutes longer, covering the usual subjects: family, gossip and world affairs and I finally signed off, wishing Lars the best of luck and thanking him for all the efforts that he would be making on our behalf.

I made one last phone call home speaking first to Olivia, instructing her to forward all the details of Marlene's mother and father to Lars whose address would be in our files and then to Marlene, mentioning that I had now spoken with Lars, who would do everything that he could to bring her parents safely out of Germany. We agreed that we should keep our fingers crossed in the meanwhile. I also mentioned that I had made arrangements to meet this sinister character from the German Embassy at the studio on Wednesday mid-day and finally, ended the conversation by telling her I would see her that evening despite the fact that we hadn't commenced filming yet.

By the time Wednesday morning arrived, the whole cast on the film including the director, Tim Whelan and cameraman, Harry Stradling, were in a state of mounting anxiety with tensions running high on the set. This was due to the arrival, on Monday afternoon, of a certain lady by the name of Natalie Kalmus, a colour supervisor for the Technicolour Corporation. The film was being shot in Technicolor and it transpired that all films using the Technicolor process required to have the technical support of Miss Kalmus on set. She was the ex-wife of Herbert T. Kalmus, the founder of the organisation and it was mandatory for her to be on set as colour supervisor.

To say that she could be awkward was an understatement, as from the moment that she arrived, she had taken Tim and Harry to task over the vivid colours of the set. In her eyes, too much colour was unnatural. Consequently, the set was being altered to mute it to her satisfaction. Whilst all this was going on, Merle and I were going nowhere fast with constant interruptions on our opening dialogue and by Wednesday morning, the film had fallen way behind schedule with Binnie Barnes and Ralph Richardson being sent home as their scenes were no way near ready to be shot. Marlene, who had decided to come with me for the day, had been taken off by Merle to the commissary where I joined them still wearing evening tails and makeup.

Though the commissary was busy, I soon located them ensconced in a booth having an animated conversation with a young fair-haired fellow with the languid good looks of a junior leading man. When I reached the table, Merle introduced him to me as Paul von Henried, a young actor friend of hers who had just recently arrived from Austria seeking work. Listening to all three chatting away, I was struck by Paul's easy-going charm and slight Austrian accent. It certainly wouldn't have surprised me if some time soon, with the help of lady luck, he didn't become prominent in our profession and that was before I had seen him act. I was beginning to become anxious as to whether Xavier Jurgens would turn up in time before I had to return to the set. I needn't have worried, for at that moment, a studio runner arrived at our table to tell me that I had a visitor at the front desk. I instructed for him to be brought over to the film set immediately. As soon as the runner had left, I apologised to Merle for leaving and turning to Paul and speaking in German, wished him good fortune and said that I hoped to see him soon. Then, taking Marlene by the hand, she and I walked out of the commissary towards the sound stage where the film was being shot.

When we arrived back to the studio set, it was bursting with sound and activity; carpenters hammering away, grips shouting and pushing huge klieg lights into position and painters working feverishly to change the colours of the set, whilst Harry Stradling and Natalie Kalmus stood to one side, communicating aggressively with each other, accompanied by a lot of arm waving and finger pointing.

Catching sight of Tim, I walked over and asked him how much time I had left before I was due back on the set. He looked at his wristwatch and then over at Harry and Natalie and then back to me and with an expression of resignation, replied in that mid-Western drawl of his, "Gunther, judging by the ruck-us going on between Harry and that damn broad, Kalmus, I would say you have got about forty-five minutes, so tell me exactly where you will be and I'll send the assistant director to fetch you when I'm ready for you"

I continued, "Just now, I have a visitor from the German Embassy. Marlene and I will take him to my dressing room which is where I will be when you want me. Just as a matter of interest, Tim, might it not have been easier to have filmed in black and white?" Shooting me a glance of mock anger, Tim told me to get the hell out of there.

Just at that moment, as we arrived at my dressing room, a ray of daylight flooded the set as the sound stage doors opened and through the light, stepping gingerly over the cables, appeared Jill, the assistant director, followed by a gentleman of at least six foot in height, slimly built with a saturnine but handsome face. I sensed immediately that women would be attracted to him by the way Jill looked at him as he bent his head and kissed the back of her hand and thanked her for escorting him over to the set. Whilst enquiring whether this was his first visit to a film studio, I proceeded to introduce Marlene and myself and out of courtesy, I extended my hand in greeting which he accepted. At the same time, he announced himself as Dr Xavier Jurgens, attaché at the German Embassy. There was an awkward silence between the three of us until Jill had left the dressing room and even after that, there was only desultory conversation concerning the weather. It didn't escape my attention that he had made no overtures to greet my wife, so that seething with inner embarrassment and anger for Marlene, I forced the issue by introducing her yet again to him. His only acknowledgement was a slight nod in her direction and a perfunctory, "Frau Conrad." After that open display of bad manners, there was no way that I was going to give an inch to this specimen of the alleged master race, addressing him in an icy manner.

"How can we be of any assistance to you, Herr Jurgens? I'm afraid I don't have a lot of time to spare as I am expecting to be called to the set at any moment so I would be grateful if you could be as brief as possible. Please be seated and tell us what this is all about."

Pulling two chairs together, Marlene and I sat down facing him whilst making a point by holding each other's hand. The first thing that struck me about Jurgens was that he seemed uncomfortable without a desk in front of him and the very fact that there was just empty space between us appeared to make him feel vulnerable. However, having reached down and unlocked his briefcase, he sat up straight, crossed his legs and as he cleared his throat, started to speak.

"First, I must apologise to you once again, Herr Conrad for insisting on this urgent meeting, but I am here to act as an emissary on the instructions of both the Ministries of Foreign Affairs and Propaganda. As you are no doubt aware, during the past five years, the Fuhrer, in his divine wisdom, and greatness has succeeded in restoring Germany's honour and placing her in the forefront of European nations. Earlier this year, not only did he complete the incorporation of Austria into the Third Reich but in September, reoccupied the German Sudetenland which was taken from Germany by the so-called Treaty of Versailles. There is no doubt that the Fuhrer sees great triumphs for the German Volk in the future and fully intends for the Third Reich to last a thousand years."

It was at that point that I butted in, continuing to refer to him in a way that I knew was disrespectful to his title and would irritate him, "Forgive me for interrupting you, Herr Jurgens, but surely you haven't travelled all this way just to deliver this piece of political propaganda, because if you have, I'll have to remind you that I have heard this rhetoric before."

Jurgens completely ignored the interruption and continued, "Now is the time for all German nationals living overseas to rally to the Fatherland and join the party and by doing so, become true National Socialists."

I quickly interrupted him again at this point, "I'm sorry, Herr Jurgens but what has this exactly got to do with my wife and myself? You seem to have overlooked a simple fact and that is because we don't agree with the politics of Adolf Hitler that we choose to live in exile."

At this, Jurgens' demeanour underwent a subtle change. Whereas, up to that point, he had appeared conciliatory towards us, now, he adopted a sterner approach, almost in the manner of a teacher giving a stern lecture to recalcitrant pupils.

"Pardon me, Herr Conrad, but I think it is you that has overlooked the simple fact that it is the Fuhrer's visionary policies that are making Germany both strong and great. It is the Fuhrer who has given the working-man back his self-respect by creating new jobs for projects such as a network of autobahns stretching across Germany; the creation of new buildings in Berlin reflecting the emerging glory of a Third Reich that will last one thousand years; the revitalisation of German industry, particularly in the area of rearmament; and finally, the burden of which the Fuhrer has placed upon his own shoulders, the removal of the malignant tumour of the Jewish and Bolshevik influence from all walks of German life. It is now incumbent on all German nationals living abroad to either return home to the Fatherland or to show support for National Socialism in any way that is demanded of them. For prominent German citizens such as yourself, it is vital that your name is placed in a register of loyal Germans who are willing to serve the Fatherland in whatever capacity is necessary. In your case, Herr Conrad, you have been given a choice: either to return home to the Fatherland and take your rightful place in the German film industry with all the privileges that entails or to remain abroad promoting the interests of the Third Reich and acting in a position of unofficial ambassador."

I had no doubt in framing my reply, "Whilst Herr Hitler pursues the policy of anti-Semitism and the loss of free speech, Herr Jurgens, my answer will be an emphatic no to both choices. Frau Conrad and myself will remain in the free world, where my wife will enjoy the privileges of not being humiliated or persecuted. You will forgive me, I'm sure, if I end this conversation now, as I can see no point in continuing it. Herr Jurgens, I am in the middle of a tight schedule and I do not wish to see my wife endure any further unpleasantness."

"I quite understand, Herr Conrad, but before I go, may I leave you with a piece of advice, particularly as it is of interest to your wife. Anticipating your reaction, I have been instructed to tell you that the door has been left open for you to reconsider your decision. My personal view is that you haven't thought this through properly, bearing in mind that your wife's father, Professor Bachman, has now been placed on the 'persons of interest' list by the security police and though technically, he is already under house arrest, he can be detained at any time if he appears to be in breach of public order. Unfortunately, because he appears to be an outspoken and militant member of the Jewish Council in Berlin, it is giving the security services some cause for concern, particularly when his daughter is illegally cohabiting with a prominent German of questionable loyalty to National Socialism. I think, having a few weeks to think things over, you will make the right decision and Professor Bachman's present and future difficulties will be resolved. I will give you my card so that you can reach me at any given time should you need to do so. Just before I take leave of you, Herr Conrad, there is one other matter of interest to you. His Excellency, Foreign Minister von Ribbentrop has appointed me to oversee your well-being and should there be any difficulties in the future, I am authorised by him to bring such matters to the attention of the Reich Fuhrer of the SS, Heinrich Himmler. Of course, I don't visualise any difficulties happening as I'm sure, in the end, you will prove to be a loyal patriot. I will, therefore, take my leave of you, as I think we now understand each other very well. I will find my own way out as I am sure that if I get lost, someone will kindly show me the way to my car. Once again, I bid you farewell, and I look forward to hearing from you soon."

It was at that moment that Marlene interrupted the conversation, "As my husband has already said and I will reiterate to you now, you represent everything that is a danger to this world and though I do not know how long your remit will last or how much pain that you will inflict upon myself and my family, I will oppose you with every breath in my body by helping to put an end to your master's evil policies!"

Jurgens rose slowly from the chair and extricated a card case from his waistcoat pocket and slowly placed it on the makeup table. Then, turning to us, he raised himself to his full height and as he simultaneously clicked his heels together and raised his right hand, called out "Heil Hitler." Then, gathering up his briefcase and Homburg, he quietly left the dressing room. Marlene reached into her handbag and taking out her cigarette case took out two cigarettes placing both in her mouth and lit them. Inhaling on one, she gave the other to me. Neither one of us spoke as we allowed the nicotine to calm our nerves. Then, Marlene said to me calmly, "That, my darling, if I may say so, was one hell of a bastard! What kind of hell hole did they find him in? If mama and papa had been here listening to him, they would have told him where to go, regardless of their own safety. However, the reality of the situation is entirely different. How we go about saving the family from the clutches of Nazi Germany is now dependent on how we respond to the threats of this political gangster."

It was obvious now that Lars Holquist had to be our only chance of succeeding and feeling less than confident and trying not to show it, once again, I told Marlene that Lars was leaving for Germany at the end of the week and that I would phone him that evening to let him know how urgent the situation had become and that however much money would be needed, whether it would be in cash or gifts, I would pay it.

At that moment, there was a knock on the dressing room door and Betty, the continuity girl poked her head around to let me know that Mr Whelan was now waiting for me on the set and that Madge the makeup artist was standing by as well. By the time Marlene and I reached the set, she was totally in control of her emotions and as she sat down in the chair with my name on it, to observe the filming. She was looking very cool and sophisticated. Having given Marlene a kiss, I gave Betty my undivided attention whilst she applied some Max Factor makeup to my face to comply with the Technicolor cameras. By the time that she had finished, Merle had already taken her place upon her camera marks and was busy conferring with Tim, as I approached them, they both greeted me warmly.

The scene that we were about to shoot was where Merle and I first met each other. The set had been dressed as a hotel suite and we were wearing evening clothes with Merle looking particularly stunning in a figure-hugging evening gown. This was supposed to be our first introduction to each other and I was supposed to be annoyed because Merle was trying to usurp my suite for herself as the hotel was full due to the London fog having paralysed all traffic and brought it to a standstill. Once Tim had issued further instructions to us both and ensured that we were standing directly under the microphone boom, he walked off the set to the director's chair. As he did so, the large Bell and Howell camera slowly inched forward towards us and that the same time, the massive klieg lights were switched on, bathing the set in a hot glow of light, leaving Merle and I looking out beyond the perimeter of the set into what we assumed was total darkness. Then, we froze momentarily as the clapper boy held his clapper board up, upon which was noted details of the forthcoming scene. Once he had left the set, we heard a voice shout out the mandatory instruction, "Quiet everybody please … Roll them."

Time was passing very quickly. It was already mid-November, and I was keeping extremely busy. The filming at Denham was back on schedule thanks to a lot of late nights, which I was grateful for in a way as it helped me take my mind off worrying about Marlene's family. The same could not be said for Marlene who didn't have the divergence of work to distract her. Despite keeping up appearances in public and appearing not to have a care in the world, all of us at Falcon House knew how much she was suffering. It must have been all of three weeks since Lars Holquist had returned from Germany and initially, all the signs had been favourable. He had managed to be in contact with both Emmy Goering and her brother-in-law, Albert. I was surprised to hear that Emmy had bothered to remember me as it might have brought back memories of when she was just a poor jobbing actress in search of work. However, not only did she choose to remember me, but she also sent her regards and hoped that I would return to Germany. According to Lars, she showed some sympathy for the plight of Marlene's family and would mention it to her husband but only at a time of her own choosing and when her husband was at his most receptive. As for the Goering brothers, it was Albert, who had been involved in the German film industry during the twenties and had known me socially, who sent me a message through Lars, telling me he would do everything he could to obtain exit visas for Marlene's family. Finally, Lars filled me in on his official visit to the Air Ministry on the Leipziger Strasse in Berlin, in which he headed a small consortium of businessmen who were about to enter into negotiations with Field Marshal Goering regarding the supply of petroleum for the Luftwaffe.

Having concluded a successful deal to the satisfaction of both parties, the jovial Field Marshal then spirited the businessmen out of Berlin to Carinhall, his country estate near the Schorfheide Forest, where he entertained them to two days of hunting wild boar. Apparently, Lars impressed Hermann by shooting down an impressively large and ferocious male who was charging them head on!

When I asked Lars what sort of man Hermann was, he had great difficulty in analysing Goering's personality. Lars described how one moment Hermann was like an excited schoolboy even to the point of showing off to them his model train sets laid out in a huge room, the next, like a modern-day Nero surrounded by fawning courtiers, liveried footman and unimaginable luxury and ostentation. However, on many occasions, whilst they were there, Goering revealed a razor-sharp mind and was quite capable of winning most arguments. As an example, he elaborated on the Fuhrer's policy regarding the Jews, totally agreeing that the Jews had had their own way for far too long, manipulating German politics and financially, almost destroying the German economy. The two best examples of this were the defeat of Germany in 1918 and the Wall Street crash of 1929. As Head of the Reich Four-Year Economic Plan, he intended to soak the Jews for every pfennig until they squealed. Of course, he had gone on to say, some minor party officials had advocated physical punishment to all Jews, something which he did not agree with, preferring to see them removed from German society and resettled on an island, Madagascar perhaps?

It was, at that moment apparently, that Lars delicately raised the subject of Marlene's family and after listening to Lars' petition, feeling in an expansive mood, Hermann told him to give the particulars of the case to his adjutant after which he would consider what action to take. Lars told me that he felt some hope, as Goering didn't strike him as being a fanatical anti-Semite. Indeed, apparently, there was some history of him helping Jewish acquaintances from the past and in his summing up of his character, Lars felt he was more like what one would have imagined a pirate buccaneer to have been like several centuries ago.

Knowing it would be some time before we got any good news, if any, I tried to get Marlene to actively participate in charity work to take her mind off the present situation. There was one particular organisation which I knew would be very close to her heart and that was called *Suffer Little Children*, who were busy raising money to bring Jewish children out of Germany under the umbrella of the programme *Kinder Express*. We had been aware for some time of the general feeling of repulsion against Hitler's government, but we hadn't realised how much money had been raised, not only to bring children out of Germany by train - hence the name *Kinder Express* - but also, to settle them in Britain. So far, from what Marlene and I had learnt, over eight thousand Jewish children had been resettled in this country. This example alone was responsible for making us more than anxious to volunteer our time and money.

Another opportunity for taking Marlene's mind off her present worries, was that the shooting of my present film was due to be completed by the end of November and it was my intention for her to help me in promoting the film by attending the film premiere at the Odeon, Leicester Square in central London. The only piece of good news now was that in the first week of December, Marlene and I would swear allegiance to the King and thereby, become British citizens. We would definitely be holding a party at Falcon House to celebrate the occasion and I hoped that in doing so, it would brighten up Marlene's spirits, especially as she would be surrounded by her friends in her own home.

I did not have a good night's sleep on the ninth of November so consequently, overslept. I barely gave myself time to grab a coffee and a slice of toast and say goodbye to Marlene before I was heading off to the studio. It was only when I arrived there that I learnt in the daily papers and BBC news, that a German diplomat by the name of Ernest von Rath had been shot by a young Jew at the German Embassy in Paris.

Unconfirmed reports filtering through suggested that von Rath had since died of his wounds and for the remainder of the day, during breaks in the filming, I learnt from the radio that the German press was working itself up into a frenzy, demanding retribution. As soon as filming had finished for the day, I started off for home and arrived back just in time for the world news on the BBC Home Service. Marlene and Olivia were already seated by the radio consul when I joined them.

As I was asking about their day, the announcer broke in with the day's news. The bulletin confirmed that von Rath had died of his wounds received at the German Embassy in Paris and that tensions had been rising all afternoon in Germany. A statement had been issued by the French police that the assailant was of the Jewish faith by the name of Herschel Grynszpan who was so angry at the harsh treatment of his parents by the German government, that he bought a gun in Paris with the express purpose of shooting a German diplomat. It turned out that his parents were amongst the thousands of German Jews expelled from Germany because they were of Polish origin. Hitler had decreed that their visas should be withdrawn and that they should be deported within twenty-four hours of notice back to Poland by October the twenty-eighth. Unfortunately, the Polish government only took in four thousand, decreeing that they would not take any more after the end of October, leaving approximately eight thousand stranded between the two borders, many of whom were without food and water and even shelter for the nights to come. Meanwhile, all of this was taking place in the worst weather of the autumn with continuous heavy rains and extreme cold. The BBC closed the bulletin by saying, that reports were coming in from foreign correspondents that a synagogue and some shops were already on fire and that there were signs of shop windows being smashed in Berlin!

At that point, Olivia stood up and smoothing her skirt down, marched over to the radio and turned it off. She faced us and said, ''People can do terrible things to each other but that doesn't mean that we have to sit and hear about it all night long. I dare say we shall wake up to it in the morning and in the morning after that, to the sounds of politicians who will either make excuses for it or that Germany should be punished. But in the end, nothing will be done about it. The only suffering that will still occur will be by the ordinary people. I am going to go and help Lucy and Bill put the dinner on the table whilst you two have yourselves a pick me up and join me presently.''

When Olivia had closed the door behind her, I turned to Marlene and said, ''She's right you know. There's very little that we can do at this moment in time. I'd go as far as to say that as long as the family stay inside their homes and do not venture out, they will be safe. From experience, I would imagine that the Nazi thugs will be encouraged to take to the streets, smashing and looting what few Jewish businesses are left. Tomorrow morning, we will try to get a message to your parents through some of our mutual Aryan friends who I am sure will do their best to find out whether that they are safe or not.''

As I sat wondering how Marlene would cope if the situation in Germany became worse, the question was immediately answered, for she stood up and went to the drinks cabinet where she poured two glasses of Jack Daniels. Returning to me, she handed me one and then leaning over, kissed me on the cheek.

''Gunty, I have a confident feeling that mama and papa will survive this storm, but I am worried about grandma and granddad. I think their refusal to leave Germany will place them in jeopardy. For the first time, I feel frightened for the future of civilised society. Hitler has so often been appeased by weak politicians that he no longer cares about world opinion and is now revealing his true intentions. I don't, for one moment, believe that what is happening in Germany now is just any old anti-Jewish pogrom but an accelerating policy of the complete removal of all Jews from Germany. I don't know what Hitler's final solution to that matter will be but after today's events, I fear that there is a hidden agenda to Nazism, one that advocates conquest and extermination. From tomorrow, I am determined to support officially any movement that will politically oppose the Nazis, although it does appear that Britain and France do not have the backbone for it. It reminds me of a rerun of 1914. They have just exposed Czechoslovakia to the mercy of Hitler which country will be next I wonder ..."

At that point, both with admiration and humour, I interrupted her, "Well, darling, my little political firebrand, you certainly have my full support and not only that, if by chance they do a new production of Bernard Shaw's *St Joan*, I shall be nominating you for the part. Seriously though, we are both in this together and listening to your enthusiasm about opposing Hitler has jogged my memory. Not so long back, when I was appearing in a revival of *The Master Builder* at the Old Vic, a conservative politician came backstage to complement me on my performance. His name, if I remember correctly, was Winston Churchill. He was a member of the government a long time ago but is now a Conservative backbencher. Anyway, I digress. From what I gathered at the time, he is fervently anti-Nazi and anti-appeasement and is one of the few Conservative MPs who will stand up and say so. He left me his card if I ever want to get in touch with him. I must say that when I met him, I felt that I was in the presence of a fellow actor, such was his charisma. The thing that struck me about him most was his voice. When he spoke, you listened. This was an Englishman who spoke the King's English as it should be spoken and as a vocal tool, it gave him the advantage of being a powerful orator and as if that wasn't enough, he could easily be the caricature of a British bulldog. Without a doubt, I shall take him up on his offer and be in touch with him very shortly, for I have a feeling that he is one of a small group of politicians who will emerge from the gathering storm with any credibility. Now, my darling, I think we should go into dinner before it becomes ruined and Olivia becomes irritable with hunger pains."

It is quite true what they say about adversity: when it happens, you usually find your true friends and it couldn't be more accurate than this evening. It was almost as if the black cloud hovering over the house no longer existed. Although Lucy had prepared another excellent meal, our appetite was more for alcohol than food. Whilst Olivia surpassed herself in her satirical assessment of the political establishment and show business folk, Marlene further lifted the mood of the evening by giving some exaggerated impersonations of the reigning film stars such as,

Claudette Colbert, Carole Lombard, Bette Davis and Joan Crawford. As I sat there in the dining room listening and laughing, temporarily isolated from the outside world and all its worries, I studied Marlene from across the dining table and realised, yet again, how fortunate I was to have married her. Not that she was aware of herself in any way, as everything that she did came naturally and everybody who came in touch with her ended up adoring her. To say that she was a paragon of virtue was nonsense. She was simply just a free spirit upon which fate had dealt the best cards; looks, intellect, humour and a strong belief in right and wrong. Oh! And I almost forgot, when she was minded, she could curse so well that she could make a stevedore blush. When in the mood for a drink, she drank well but was a happy drinker and tonight, I think she was in the mood. As for Olivia, the old trout, I swear that she was deliberately leading Marlene on so that she could escape the worry of her parents. As far as I was concerned, Olivia was a kindred spirit to Marlene in every way except that she was older and boy, she could certainly put away the wine. I swear to God that she had to have hollow legs. Poor Bill made the mistake of popping his head around the dining room door to ask if we needed anything else.

Before he and Lucy retired for the night, there was a momentary silence as Marlene studied the question. Then, standing up from the table and speaking in that husky voice of hers, she replied.

"Bill, you will immediately go back into the kitchen, fill a bowl with snacks and then, taking Lucy by the hand, you will lead her into the lounge where I will be putting some records on. Oh, and by the way, you had better bring some glasses with you because we are having a small get-together tonight."

I don't think Bill and Lucy had needed much persuasion, for by the time we reached the lounge, they weren't that far behind us. Marlene started the party going by placing a stack of records on the console turntable. The first record that she put on was one of the hits of the season, *The Harry James Band* playing, *Don't be that Way*. The lounge was soon reverberating to the sounds of Gene Krupa performing a solo spot on the drums followed by the next record from a young black artist called Ella Fitzgerald who was fast becoming an acclaimed jazz singer. This record had become very popular with the public this year, called *A-Tisket, A-Tasket*, which soon put us in the party mood. Acting as a barman, I kept up a steady flow of booze and it wasn't long before Bill and Lucy gave the rest of us an exhibition of jiving to the music of Cab Calloway's *Jitterbug*. As I have matured in life, I have developed many beliefs, one of which was 'when drink's in, truth's out' and that expression was never truer than tonight, where it appeared that Marlene had observed some grazing on the knuckles of one of Bill's hands and being the inquisitive soul, she enquired as to how he his hand became damaged. But the more Bill hummed and hawed, the more mysterious it all became, particularly when Bill and Lucy were exchanging furtive looks between each other.

I suppose we could have gone on all night trying to get to the bottom of it, but Olivia soon brought matters to a head by exclaiming, "Come along William, I heard from reliable sources that you had been involved in a fight at The Swan with Two Necks public house a few nights back and that the landlord had to break it up."

Whilst Marlene laughed and wagged her finger at him as if he was a naughty boy and Lucy stood looking pensive, I asked Bill what it was all about, adding in a jocular manner, "Was it because the beer was cloudy?" After a while, we dragged the reason out of him, though I suspect Olivia had known all along. Apparently, there had been some out-of-towners drinking in the public bar that night, one of whom Bill described as a bar-room lawyer. Anyway, this particular character was praising Hitler, saying what a great man he was and that he was right in going after the Jews, especially as they were responsible for the First World War and had also caused the stock market crash which created massive unemployment. The atmosphere in the bar became tense when somebody whispered to this character that Bill worked for us and that really put the cat amongst the pigeons. He wanted to know what it was like to work for a Jewess. Was she tight with the wages, making him work long hours? Anyway, the man continued, she must be a whore to have ended up marrying such a world-famous film star.

That was when it all kicked off. Bill squared up to this idiot telling him that as it happened, he worked for the best people imaginable and as for Marlene being a whore, this bloke wasn't even good enough to kiss the ground that she walked on. Then, Bill landed two punches, sending the bloke halfway across the bar.

The final outcome of the punch-up saw the landlord and some of the customers chasing the bloke and his mates out of the pub. Bill then downed a pint of bitter and proceeded to order a fresh pint after which he sat down to an evening game of cribbage.

When Bill had finished recounting his tale, Lucy grabbed hold of his arm and gazed up at him, her face glowing with pride while the rest of us applauded. As she said later, she was proud of her Bill standing up for the underdog. In fact, had she been there, she would have given the bloke a right good hand bagging. Marlene, having given Bill a kiss on the cheek, then called him her knight in shining armour which made him blush. The party then continued its merry way, until unfortunately, we had to end it. I had to be at Denham for an early morning start for filming and it was already two o'clock in the morning. Somehow, Marlene and I turned the last dance into a slow romantic waltz to the sounds of Billie Holiday singing, *I'm Going to Lock up My Heart and Throw Away the Key*. By the time the record had finished, everybody else had discreetly withdrawn, leaving Marlene and I to check all the doors and put the lights out one by one until finally, we stood at the bottom of stairs in a lingering embrace. Breaking away from me, Marlene took my hand and with that mischievous look in her eye, started upstairs with us both warbling off key to Tommy Dorsey's *Pecking with the Penguins.*

I had hardly got into bed before I was getting up again at five o'clock in the morning which barely gave me enough time to shower, shave, dress and drive to the studio by seven o'clock. As I stumbled down the stairs, I could smell the tempting aroma of freshly brewed coffee and as I pushed open the kitchen door, low and behold but who should be standing there with a coffee pot in one hand and a mug in the other but none other than the goddess herself, with no makeup on, wearing one of my dressing gowns over her negligee and a pair of my slippers.

"Good morning, darling," my goddess said, as she poured me a steaming mug of coffee. "How is my Lord and master's head this morning? Not throbbing, I hope, from last night's over-abundance of jungle juice. I am having a terrible vision of the screen's great lover in close-up on the set this morning, gazing with smouldering desire into the beautiful face of Merle Oberon, desperately trying to uncross his bleary and red-rimmed eyes."

I grabbed the coffee mug from her with one hand and with the other, gave her a playful tap on the backside, remarking to her at the same time, "Never mind about the state of my eyes sweetheart, I can still see the bags under yours and what is more important that fresh piece of buttered toast is looking very inviting on that plate."

Laughing, she put her arms round my neck and kissed me. Then, lighting a cigarette, she watched me eat the toast before making sure that I had my script and cigarettes to take with me. Winter had arrived very quickly this year and it was a very cold November morning, so I didn't want Marlene coming with me to the front door to see me off. I told her to phone me at the studio if there were any further developments concerning her mother and father. We embraced each other, and putting on my overcoat and scarf, I left her standing in the kitchen doorway as I left the house.

By mid-morning, news began filtering through on the newswires from Germany. Each fresh bulletin brought worsening news and with it a sense of outrage within the studio itself. Between takes, Merle, Ralph Richardson and I, plus members of the crew, gathered around a portable radio listening to the incoming news. According to the reports, during the night, there had been at least two dozen synagogues vandalised and set on fire. Apparently, local fire services had been instructed not to put the fires out but to stand by and ensure that surrounding buildings were safe. All known Jewish shops and businesses were looted and had their windows smashed in. A recurring newspaper story was emerging from the reports, time and time again, the burning and looting was being identified as 'the night of broken glass' or as spoken in German, *Kristallnacht.*

Reports were now beginning to include many Jewish fatalities. The numbers had already passed a thousand and there had been a massive round up and detention of many more. The Minister of Propaganda, Joseph Goebbels had issued an official statement saying that despite the attempt of the Third Reich law enforcement agencies to safeguard property, the will of the people had proved stronger and could not be denied. For far too long, world Jewry had ridden roughshod over the rights of ordinary people and the final straw of the murder of a decent German diplomat had roused the German nation in all its fury to retaliate against them. Then, he finished by saying that law and order was now being gradually restored throughout Germany. I attempted to carry on working but was constantly fluffing my lines and missing my chalk marks causing retake after retake, which gradually exasperated my co-stars. Eventually, Tim took me to one side explaining to me that it was obvious that I was under enormous stress and that it might be better if I went home and looked after Marlene. He could easily shoot around me for the rest of the day, then by tomorrow morning, we could all try again. He added that if he could be of any help to me, I should call him. As he walked me back to my dressing room, he added that Alex Korda had already been in touch, expressing his shock and anger at the news coming out of Germany and that Tim was to do all he could to support me, if necessary, shutting the film down until I was ready to return, as he fully sympathised and understood what these terrible events would do to Marlene. Thanking Tim, I assured him that I would be back in front of the cameras tomorrow morning and would he please get in touch with Alex and tell him how much I appreciated his support.

I had recently purchased an expensive Ferns Fulltone car radio, and despite the car radio industry still being in its infancy, I was able to listen to the news as I drove home. Law and order appeared to have been fully restored in Germany with the Nazi gangs having been called off the streets. However, the amount of damage to Jewish property had considerably increased since this morning and in the face of international condemnation, both Hitler and Goebbels were trying to play down the wanton savagery, as acts of over exuberance on the part of many Germans whose patience had finally snapped at the latest Jewish-Bolshevik transgression.

After a while, I grew tired of listening to the depressing intrusion of the flow of bad news and switched the radio off and to escape the stark reality of the situation, my mind wandered off on a tangent. I started thinking about the fact that I was a prisoner in a mechanical bubble. For example, although I could receive information, I couldn't impart any, especially at a time like this, when instead of having to wait until I arrived at my destination before I could have a conversation in person, I could instead, have a phone with me in the car and then could speak to them person-to-person immediately. Ah well, perhaps someday in the future, some bright spark would invent a car-phone.

Time slips by very quickly when you are immersed in your own private thoughts and before I knew it, I had arrived outside the house. As I entered through the front, I bumped into Mary who was busily hoovering the hall carpet. I popped my head around the office door to let Olivia know that I was home and that I would join her in a little while. I then headed towards the kitchen, where the loudest amount of activity was emanating from and as I passed the back door of the house, I could see through the window, Bill and John engaged in a conversation and gesturing towards the rhododendron bushes. On opening the kitchen door, I saw Marlene sitting at the kitchen table, drinking coffee and talking to Lucy who was busy rolling pastry.

As soon as Marlene saw me, her face lit up but without missing a beat in that laconic style of hers she said, ''Hello, big boy. You're home early. Have you had a bad news day at the office? I should imagine it's about the same as we have had here even though Lucy and I have been trying to overcome it. Lucy has been showing me how to make an apple crumble which hopefully, will be ready for tonight's supper. I don't suppose that you have had anything to eat since you left this morning, so why don't you go through to the office whilst I make you up a tray of sandwiches and coffee and follow on behind you. Before you go, take that worried look of your face and come over here and give me a kiss. Lucy loves it when we get romantic; she says it's like sitting in the pictures.''

Walking around the table, I kissed Marlene and whilst looking over at Lucy standing there blushing with a rolling pin in her hands, I remarked casually to her as I strolled through the door, ''Don't you worry, Lucy. Whilst you continue to entrap me with your delicious sticky toffee pudding, I shall remain your slave for life.'' As I walked down the hallway, I could hear them laughing and because of that, suddenly a small ray of sunshine entered the house.

When I entered the office, Olivia was standing at her desk with a sheath of papers in her hand and looked up at me with a smile remarking, ''Gunther, you look better now than when you came in, which makes me believe that both you and Marlene are now in command of today's events. There have been some phone calls this morning. One of them was from that gentleman, Mr Jurgens from the German Embassy. He wanted to know how he could get in touch with you at the studio. I told him that you would get back to him as soon as it was most convenient for you to do so. There was one other phone call from a Mr Holquist, who asked for you to ring him, as he had some news for you, and also, in the post this morning, was a contract accompanied with a note from Robin Cox, asking you to sign it and return it as soon as possible. Oh, and while I remember it, there was also a letter from an organisation called The League of Democratic Europe who were holding a meeting in April next year at Wigmore Hall in London. The guest speaker was, I hope I can pronounce his name right, Prince Werther Freudenberg. You might need to find out a bit more about them before replying to their letter, Gunther."

"Thanks, Olivia," I replied. "I think the priority is to return the call of Lars Holquist but before you do that, have you had lunch yet? If not, it might be better to have some now as I need to have a brief chat with Marlene."

At that precise moment, both Marlene and Lucy entered the room carrying trays which they placed side-by-side on the small coffee table between the desks.

"There you go, Olivia," Marlene said, "Everything stops for tea. Lucy's made you some assorted sandwiches, some apple strudel and of course, a pot of tea. Now, stop doing whatever it is you're doing and relax for a little while. Gunther, would you please carry your tray through to the lounge. I need to have a private conversation with you regarding mama and papa." I followed Marlene through to the lounge and placing the tray on a table, proceeded to sit down beside her on the sofa.

"Well, darling, you obviously have had some news this morning and I can only hope that it is nothing too serious. From what I can gather from the news reports, order has now been restored, thanks to the flood of international outrage descending upon the Nazi government. I can only hope that international opinion may halt temporarily any further harassment to the Jews."

"I spoke to mama earlier on today, Gunther. Somehow or other, she had been able to get through to me on the phone and despite her being distressed and speaking in both German and English, I was able to understand the following facts. Two days ago, papa reported to the local police station as usual but this time, he did not return home. By this time, feeling very worried, mama went around to the police station to enquire about him and was told that he had been detained and transferred to the Moabit prison in Berlin and that she was to go home as no further information was available. Then, she spent the next forty-eight hours worried sick about papa and having to endure the terrible things going on outside the house. She witnessed men and women being beaten up on the streets and a Jewish lawyer, who lived across the road, being dragged out of his house, all the while, being beaten by thugs, who then threw him on to the back of a lorry. She was weeping uncontrollably when she told me that our local synagogue, which I had attended growing up as a child, had been looted and then set on fire. The fire brigade had just stood back and let it burn to the ground. Many of the houses had paint daubed across the front doors proclaiming, 'Jews Out' and several had their front windows smashed in. She says that things have now quietened down, so she was able to slip out and buy a few essentials, not that there was much, as every shop that she visited, had been smashed up, making it very difficult to buy milk and bread. Mama says that, by tomorrow, hopefully, order will be restored and that she will be able to go to the local Gestapo offices for further news on papa. As soon as she gets any, she will let me know. Meanwhile, I was not to worry as God will protect us all. With that, she said goodbye to me and put the phone down. Olivia has been a tower of strength, calming me down and bringing me endless cups of tea. Indeed, sometimes I wonder what the British would do without tea. Anyway, without Olivia's calming presence and sensible approach, I would have probably gone to pieces and as she says, what can be done about it now? Worrying won't solve the situation. Meanwhile, I have been busy compiling our Christmas card list and the guest list for our nationalisation party and I have been through our social engagements for December.''

I stopped her there and taking her in my arms, whispered to her that everything would be all right. We must have remained like that for several minutes because eventually, there was a knock at the door and Olivia poked her head in.

''Lars Holquist is on the phone, Gunther and I suggest that you bring some of those sandwiches with you, otherwise you'll be collapsing with lack of nourishment.'' As I reached the desk, Olivia handed me the receiver and there were the guttural tones of Lars.

''Hello, Gunther. This is hardly the best of times for you and Marlene, especially considering the dreadful pogrom that has been unfolding in Germany. Hitler's treatment of the Jews simply beggars belief and I cannot understand why the democratic nations of the world, including the Vatican, are not pursuing a more aggressive rebuke to the Nazi government instead of all these wishy-washy platitudes. I think there may be a light at the end of the tunnel for both you and Marlene. The reason why I haven't been in touch with you since we last spoke is that I have been back to Berlin at Field Marshall Goering's invitation. Did you know that his first wife was a Swedish aristocrat? Her father was Baron Carl Fock and that her remains are interned at Carinhall, which he had built in memory of her. It appears that he has strong ties with Sweden and in the process of doing business together, he appears to have taken a shine to me. He considers me a fellow hunter-in-arms and such is his growing confidence in me, that he is now beginning to treat me as an unofficial emissary, carrying messages back and forth between the British government and himself. Strictly between you and me, I think Hitler is using him to sound out public opinion abroad, particularly in London. Anyway, as I said earlier, I was summoned to a meeting with him last week, during which, he brought up the case of Marlene's mother and father. It seems that Emmy Goering had finally petitioned her husband on your behalf and what with my petition and a word from his brother, Albert, he finally agreed to do what he could to help. Of course, the fact that my company was prepared to offer him a generous discount on his purchase of petroleum clinched the matter and as he said to me whilst giving me a hearty slap on the back, one good turn deserves another. That evening, my partners and I had arranged a private dinner for him and two of his closest associates from the Air Ministry, Generals Erhard Milch and Ernst Udet and it was during the course of the evening that he told me he had discreetly instructed the Berlin Chief of Police, Count Graf von Helldorf, to issue exit visas and the appropriate documentation for Marlene's parents to leave Germany. To be frank with you, Gunther, all this took place before the terrible events of the last two days, so I don't know how quickly this will work its way through the system before Marlene's parents are granted permission to leave."

"Unfortunately, Lars, Marlene's father has been detained in Moabit prison during the last forty-eight hours and I am sorry to ask another favour of you but is there any way that you can pull some strings and get him released?"

"Jesus, that does make things difficult, but I'll see what I can do. Just give me twenty-four hours and I'll get back to you. There is some friction between Goering and Goebbels going on at the moment. Goebbels is an ideological anti-Semite and therefore, a dangerous fanatic, whilst Goering is a financial anti-Semite who is only interested in monetary gain. He thinks that Goebbels is going much too far in pushing his extreme hatred of the Jews and inciting public unrest against them, believing that it is both damaging to the economy and counter-productive when it comes to world opinion."

"Lars, I can't thank you enough for the help that you have given us and I will await your return call, hopefully, with good news."

"Don't worry, Gunther. It's been a privilege to have helped you. However, you owe me big-time pal. The least you can do for me is a couple of invites to some showbiz parties and if you really want to thank me, I'm just dying to meet Ingrid Bergman. Boy, is she the cream in my coffee! Please don't tell the wife, but I have been a fan of hers since she became a star and it's only just recently that I saw her in the German film, *The Four Companions*. Now she is off to America where I think she will be a huge hit. Well, I have to go, but do give my love to Marlene and I hope we all meet soon in better circumstances."

After I had repeated Lars' conversation to Marlene and Olivia, I could see Marlene's face beginning to lighten up and thought that it might be wiser to add a cautionary note into the conversation. So, I told her to be patient and not to count her chickens before they were hatched and that it might be more helpful if she could contact her mother and gently tell her what could be happening very soon without giving too much away. It was more than likely that international calls were being tapped by the Germans so the least said, the better. Once again, Olivia proved her weight in gold. Moving across to Marlene, she enveloped her in a hug and told her not to worry and that nothing bad was going to happen as she had a good husband, a loyal staff who cared about her and some strong friends. Only good could come from such a strong combination of love.

She then went on to say, "Of the three of us, Marlene, you are the driving force and organiser behind the social calendar for the remainder of the year: there is a party to be organised for celebrating your citizenship; the house has to be decorated for Christmas; there are two major Christmas parties that you said you wanted to throw for your friends plus invites to be replied to; and whilst you are busy doing all that, master Gunther here, has a film to finish so that he can justify the huge amount of money that he is paid and that, in turn, keeps us all in the lifestyle to which we are accustomed. Furthermore, it's about time that we ate something. Those poor sandwiches have been hanging around for so long that they are beginning to curl up at the edges, so while I take my share of them to the kitchen and asked Lucy to make some fresh coffee and tea, you two Lumpkin's can decide what you are going to do."

That little speech seemed to have done the trick, for both Marlene and I burst out laughing simultaneously. "Right, you two heartless creatures," Marlene replied theatrically, "Get yourselves off to the kitchen and take your sandwiches with you whilst I try and get through to mama, after which, I will join you for a fresh cup of tea."

It did seem that Olivia's morale building speech and Marlene's return call to her mother had taken the heat out of the situation, for when she joined us in the kitchen, she had become her usual buoyant self. Inwardly though, I prayed to God that we would be successful in getting her parents out of Germany for I knew that to fail, would have a disastrous effect upon her emotional state.

Chapter 10

It's a Wrap

For all of us, the next two days proved a tortuous time. When a phone rang near one of us, we jumped and yet after about forty-eight hours, we had become so obsessed that thankfully, nature kicked in, and we became less fixated and the everyday rhythm of life gradually resumed its course as we settled down to meet the challenges of each day.

I had just finished a scene with my co-stars Merle Oberon, Ralphie Richardson and Binnie Barnes, when I was summoned off the set to take an outside call. I wasn't really anticipating anything when I picked the receiver up, but when I heard Marlene's voice, I tensed up.

''Oh, darling, you've done it.''

''Done what? Marlene''

''Mama has just finished speaking with me. Papa is being released and mama has been told that they will have forty-eight hours in which to put their affairs in order and to make the necessary travel arrangements for leaving Germany. They are only allowed to take one small suitcase each and a small amount of money. All their other assets and possessions will be confiscated by the state as compensation. I told her that as soon as Papa had been released and they were reunited that she was to ring me straight away regardless of the time so that we could have some information on their travel arrangements. She sounded heartbroken at the thought of losing all her personal possessions and having to leave the remainder of our family behind. I tried to explain to her that her safety was far more important than possessions and that they could be replaced and that her memories would last forever. I am afraid that I ended up crying with her. However, in the end, she had become resolute in her determination to save Papa and herself. She confirmed that as soon as she had any new information, she would phone me.''

''That is marvellous news, Marlene, '' I replied. ''However, I won't breathe a sigh of relief until they have actually left Germany and are on their way to us. I am afraid I can't talk any more as I will be holding up the shooting schedule. So, I would like you to do something for us. Ask Olivia to phone our immigration lawyers and ask them what legalities are involved in getting your parents through British customs and give them the authority to act on our behalf. I am afraid, sweetheart, I have to go now, as the bell is ringing, so I will see you this evening. Love you."

It was not until I got into the car late that afternoon that I finally had a moment with my thoughts. Since I had spoken with Marlene, it had been a madhouse on the set. We had fallen behind schedule yet again and Tim Whelan was facing pressure from the front office to finish on time. So, it was a pleasure finally to drive home and think things through without any outside interruptions. Renovating the outside cottage had proved its weight in gold. Now, Miriam would have a place to call her own and be safe in. With the tranquillity of the Buckinghamshire countryside surrounding her, I didn't think it would be too long before Hiram and she had put the horrors that they had endured behind them. God willing, I could visualise Marlene and her mother having the time of their lives choosing furniture for the cottage and preparing for Christmas. On a practical level, I would have to transfer some extra funds not only to meet the cost of refurbishment but also for the purchase of new clothes as when they arrived, their only clothes would be the ones they would be standing up in. Boy, Marlene would be in seventh heaven at the realisation of all that spending. As I reached the outskirts of Marlow, my brain was spinning with the number of thoughts running through it. So, mentally, I shut down, turned the radio up and put my foot down on the accelerator.

By the time I reached the drive, there were a few flurries of snowflakes, but I reckoned according to the forecast, that they would be gone by the morning. However, it did look like we might have a white Christmas as it certainly was cold enough. I put the car in the garage and made a beeline for the kitchen door and on entering, I was overwhelmed by a mouth-watering aroma. I spied Lucy in front of a row of saucepans placed on the Agar seemingly trying to catch up with herself putting a spoonful of this and a spoonful of that into various receptacles. She reminded me of a witch from Macbeth.

"There are some delicious smells coming from this kitchen Lucy. What have you got planned for us tonight?" I asked her.

"Mrs Conrad asked me to try my hand at making a curry. She said it was time that we tried something new and exciting, so for tonight, you will be having a madras beef curry, with side dishes of basmati rice, Bombay potatoes and vegetable aloo and if you don't mind me saying so sir, if that lot doesn't give you a good clear out, nothing will! Laughing uproariously, I strode through to the office and was surprised to see Olivia still working.

"You're working late, Olivia. You should be upstairs putting your feet up before dinner, which by the way is to be a curry evening, although I'm sure that you already know that by the rich aromas drifting through from the kitchen. Incidentally, we would be more than happy to have you join us for a taste of the mysterious East by way of Lucy's cooking. By the way, have you seen Marlene? I am wondering whether there may have been any further developments since I last spoke with her."

"Marlene went upstairs a few hours ago for a shower and a lie down. She just needed to freshen up after the events of the last two days. There have been many phone calls for you today but only two worth mentioning. One was from that Mr Jurgens, yet again requesting that you get in touch with him. I have told him that when you get the opportunity, you will phone him. The second one was from Mr Holquist requesting that you phone him back as soon as you can. The rest of the day has been taken up by a dozen return correspondences, all needing your signature and I have laid those out for your attention in the morning. Now, I'll just dial this number for you and then I'll slip away upstairs via the kitchen and tell Lucy that there will be three for dinner. I am getting too old not to live dangerously and I suggest that when you have made that phone call, you call it a day and relax."

True to her word, as soon as Olivia had dialled the number for Lars, she handed the receiver to me and left. Lars could not have been far from the phone because he answered immediately.

"Gunther, I am glad that you have phoned. I have a dinner date with a gorgeous English rose and I think I may be in with a chance even though she is my wife. Talking of which, I think you may have to deliver on our side bet with reference to the gorgeous Ingrid Bergman being my date. You will be pleased to know that I received a phone call from Albert Goering, who has informed me that true to his brother's word, fresh passports and travel documents enabling Marlene's parents to travel out of Germany and through France will be handed to Marlene's father when he is discharged from Moabit prison within the next twenty-four hours. From what I gather, he will have to make his own way back to his house and will only have a further twenty-four hours to leave Berlin with his wife. Take my word for it, there is some urgency to this timeline. It appears that the Reich Minister of Propaganda, Joseph Goebbels and the German Foreign Minister, von Ribbentrop are attempting to use Marlene's parents as pawns against you. However, luckily for you, next to Hitler, Field Marshal Goering is the most powerful man in Germany and he is not to be messed with, so it is vital that the matter is over and done with as quickly as possible before dark forces prevail.''

''Bless you, Lars. On behalf of Marlene, I can't thank you enough. I would expect Marlene's mother or father to be telephoning by tomorrow night so that we can make any arrangements that are necessary to expedite their exit. Meanwhile, if you are going to spend Christmas in Britain, there will be several invites on their way to you and your lovely and tolerant wife!''

''Glad to have been of assistance, Gunther. Just because I have to do business with the Nazis, it doesn't mean I have to like them. I think their political ideology is loathsome and I have a horrible feeling that Hitler intends to impose those views on other European countries by force of arms. Anyway, I am running late, so must put the phone down. By the way, I expect to see those invites arriving through the mail shortly. Best regards to you both and see you soon.''

Deciding that I would give Marlene another hour to rest before I called her, I poured myself a large Jack Daniels and soda, and just at that moment, as I turned, through the office windows, I saw John pulling up and unloading a big Christmas tree which he placed inside the garage. Opening the front door, I called him into the house and though it had stopped snowing, there was an icy chill to the air. John looked particularly cold and his breath was vaporising as he breathed out.

''John, come into the office for a moment. The way the weather is looking at the moment, we could be in for a frost tonight, so you might as well join me with a whiskey to warm the cockles of your heart before you go home. I noticed that you had been shopping for a Christmas tree. I imagine that will keep the womenfolk busy decorating it and putting up the other Christmas decorations over the next few weeks. I wanted to have a word with you because during the next two or three days, I am going to need you to drive us to London where we hope to collect madam's parents, probably at Victoria Station. Obviously, we need to take the Humber, as there will be a maximum of five of us. However, there will be a minimum amount of luggage, but I do have to tell you that not only are madam's parents elderly, but they have also been through a very traumatic experience and are likely to be quite frail. I suggest that you put two more travelling rugs in the car just in case they are overwhelmed with the cold. While I think about it, could you make sure that the cocktail cabinet is stocked up with whiskey and brandy. One other thing, John, I don't think that you're going to be needed tomorrow, so take the day off and I will notify you as soon as I have definite news of their pending arrival. I would imagine that it will be an early start in the morning for us, as they will either come in on the mail train from Newhaven or boat train from Dover."

"Thank you for the extra day off, sir. But if you don't mind, I will pop over tomorrow for a couple of hours just to make sure that the Humber has a good going over plus a valeting. You can count on me, sir. We will bring them home safely. I'll be off now and thank you for the whiskey. It went down a treat, sir."

I poured myself another drink and lit a cigarette after John had left and sat for a few minutes alone with my thoughts. Whilst drawing on the cigarette, I suppose I must have become deep in thought, for suddenly, I heard Marlene's voice calling my name and the door to the office opened. There she was, standing in the doorway with a welcoming smile her face.

"Hello, darling. Have you been home long? I am sorry to have missed you, but I thought I would pop upstairs and freshen up for dinner. Unfortunately, it seems I fell asleep on the bed. If you don't mind me saying so, you look pretty washed out yourself. Why don't you come into the lounge and put your feet up for a few minutes and relax?"

"I'll do that after I have told you the good news. I have just finished speaking with Lars and he tells me that he has it on good authority that your father will be released within the next twenty-four hours. He will also be supplied with all the necessary travel documents for leaving Germany, both he and your mother will have exactly a further twenty-four hours to comply. I would imagine that sometime during tomorrow, you will be receiving a phone call from them giving you some information on the time scale of their arrival in London. When that happens, I want you to leave a message for me at the studio so that I can call you back immediately. I think it is marvellous, but I shan't relax until I know that they are both safely on the way to us. Meanwhile, why don't we go upstairs and whilst I get changed, you can fill me in on what sort of a day that you have had. By the way, I have invited Olivia for dinner tonight. I think that she was intrigued when I mentioned that Lucy was making a genuine Indian curry. I got the feeling that Olivia had never tasted curry before, well you know what they say: there's always a first time and besides, she's always good company and at a time like this she would take our minds off other matters.

Lucy had certainly done herself proud. The meal that she produced was absolutely first class and with the help of copious amounts of chilled champagne to cool our throats, we emptied the serving dishes completely. Marlene and Olivia had developed a rosy glow to their faces and Marlene had become totally relaxed and happy and while we waited for the dessert, Marlene and I began reminiscing over our early years in Berlin with Olivia, an avid listener, particularly when we talked about our personal encounters with many of the Nazi big wigs.

Lucy's final culinary masterpiece for the evening was a baked Alaska which was a perfect complement to the curry and rounded off a wonderful evening. Once again, I called Lucy back into the dining room and thanked her for a magnificent meal. I insisted that she and Bill have a large Martell brandy to retire to bed on. Olivia finished the night off with her usual dry humour observing that if she were to drink like this every week, she would end up a raving alcoholic and that her wages would have to include danger money. The evening drew to a close with the grandfather clock in the hall striking midnight and leaving just Marlene and myself once more having a final dance to Cole Porter's *The Way You Look Tonight* before we put the lights out and drifted upstairs holding hands.

The following morning was taken up at the studio with the filming of the final sequence in the hotel suite. For this, Merle and I were required to wear evening clothes and then had to do a change into daytime clothes for a day scene. All of this required a lot of hanging around whilst Tim and the production staff changed the scenery and rearranged the lighting. It also required our stand-ins to double for us whilst camera angles were worked out and whilst all that was taking place, we had to find time for a photo shoot of Merle, myself and Ralph Richardson for *Screen Legend* magazine. Finally, just after one o'clock in the afternoon, we were given a long enough break to have something to eat from the mobile canteen. Most of the time whilst eating was taken up with a debate on Hitler's intentions in the Balkans and his treatment of the Jews. The views expressed were sharply divided between the pacifists and those who thought we should be standing up to Hitler. Being the only German amongst them, it was assumed that I would know all the answers, but the only opinion that I did express brought an uneasy silence to the debate. I said that the only way to stop Hitler and his stooge, Mussolini, was by a strong and united front of European leaders backed up by a force of arms.

Just at that moment, I was summoned away by a phone call which I sensed was from Marlene. As soon as I picked up the receiver, I could hear her excited voice down the line. "Gunther, they have released Papa. Apparently, he found his own way home early this morning. Mama says that he is not in a good place mentally and is looking very drawn. At the moment, he is resting in bed to try and regain his strength. The Nazis have discharged him with all the necessary travel documents that will enable them to leave Germany and they have been given twenty-four hours to comply or they will be re-interned. Mama says they are going to take the early morning mail train from the Lerter Bahnhof Station and hopefully, arrive at Victoria, via Dieppe and Newhaven, sometime on Saturday morning. She told us not to worry and that they were just about to walk out of the door leaving everything behind. Also, a friend of theirs was kindly going to take them to the station in his car. She told me not to worry once again and that they would see us soon. She also sent us her love."

"That is wonderful news, Marlene. Although I won't rest until I see them step off the train. The first thing you must do is to ask Olivia to check the timetables for the arrival time of the mail train on Saturday morning and get hold of John to tell him to have the car ready. I dare say you will have your hands full getting the house ready for their arrival. More than likely, I will be late home tonight as Tim Whelan is under a lot of pressure from the front office to wrap this film up. So, just have a cold plate waiting for me when I get back. Love you."

When I returned to the set, it was still in a state of pandemonium with a dozen or so jobs all being done the same time. Spying Tim huddled in a corner with the script girl, I strolled over to them and waited until they had finished. Taking out a packet of cigarettes, I took one and lit it whilst offering the packet to Tim.

"Thanks, Gunther, I needed that," he grunted, inhaling deeply on a cigarette. "I reckon that we have about thirty minutes before we start shooting which will give you enough time for some fresh makeup. Don't forget that there will be a break in filming later, as you will have to change into pyjamas. By the way, I hope I have your approval in case you're not aware, but Alex Korda has assigned me to direct your next picture, *Ali Baba*. I am sure that you have already been informed that this is going to be a big production and that Alex is determined to make this as good as any Hollywood extravaganza. I thought I would tell you this now because I have enjoyed working with you, Gunther. I hope that you have felt the same about me?"

"To be honest with you, Tim, I have had family problems and haven't had much chance to study the script, but I do know that it is going to be something special, a fantasy film and that I will be playing a villain for a change. It's a risk for me, as I don't know how the public will accept this new persona. Plus, judging from what little I have seen of the script, I have some very good lines. You can be rest assured that I won't be exercising the director's clause in my contract. I look forward to working with you again on a film that will require one hundred percent effort from both of us. I wanted to ask you if you're going to be needing me on Saturday. Unfortunately, I cannot work that day as Marlene's parents will be arriving in London. You probably are not aware of it, Tim, but they are victims of Nazi persecution and have lost everything they possess."

"Gosh, Gunther. I wasn't aware of your personal situation, but don't worry, as there was nothing scheduled for Saturday. I thought everybody needed a weekend break. In fact, in view of what you have just told me, I wouldn't have dreamt of asking you to work. Just tell Marlene that my thoughts are with her and her parents. Meanwhile, Gunther, you and I have a film to complete, and whatever else, the show must go on. I will be waiting for you on the set in thirty minutes."

It was becoming a ritual for me to use the time spent driving to and from the studio to analyse everything. I now saw the car as my thinking bubble. On reflection, I believed that Marlene's parents would not have suffered quite as much if I had not been their son-in-law. There was a fallacy that actors and modesty did not go hand-in-hand, so I could only speak for myself when I say that I was rather like an oxymoron: I was actually quite a shy man in company but had no fear facing hundreds of people on stage. Of course, I craved recognition for my work, but celebrity and adulation could be an enormous burden. In my case, having achieved international film stardom, I was considered an icon in my country which was why the Nazis wanted me back, to be part of the respectable face of the party. That, in turn, was the reason Marlene's parents were used as pawns to blackmail me into returning. I hoped and prayed that Field Marshal Goering had more political influence than Goebbels or von Ribbentrop.

As soon as the headlights of the car swept across the front of the house, the front door opened, revealing Marlene silhouetted in the doorway. After giving me a hug and a kiss, we went into the house. As I removed my coat, Marlene told me that she had instructed Lucy and Bill to finish early and that they were just leaving to listen to a variety show on the radio in their apartment. Olivia had begged a lift off John to go into Marlow to see a picture. She then told me the piece of news that she had been holding back to last. Her mother had telephoned her again that evening to tell her that they were leaving Berlin tomorrow evening and they would be changing trains at the Franco-German border and on crossing into France, would eventually take the channel steamer from Dieppe to Newhaven. After crossing the Channel, they hoped to arrive at Victoria Station at around about ten o'clock on Saturday morning. It had been a long time since I had seen Marlene so happy and she couldn't stop chattering as she took me by the hand and dragged me into the kitchen. Laid out upon the table was a selection of cold cuts, salad and freshly baked bread. The only thing missing was a chilled glass of Liebfraumilch which I promptly took from an open bottle in the fridge as Marlene started slicing the loaf. I hadn't realised how famished I had been or that Marlene had waited for me before having anything to eat herself, so both of us soon made short work of the food.

Eventually, we just sat back, full to bursting, discussing the things that needed to be done before Marlene's parents arrived. Marlene had decided that they would stay in the main house until such times as the cottage was ready for them to move into. It was obvious that she was very much looking forward to taking her mother shopping for clothes and household goods. I shared that enthusiasm, for I enjoyed the pleasure of watching other people's enjoyment at receiving. Without being pompous, the joy of giving was the greatest gift of all. I think, because of the pressures of the last few months and that now everything was moving towards a happy conclusion, things suddenly became anticlimactic. Suddenly, both of us felt very tired and just wanted an early night. So, grabbing a hot water bottle, we made our way upstairs to bed, leaving the hall lights on for Olivia when she returned.

It was early Saturday morning. Friday had gone in the blink of an eye and had been a busy day for both of us and I suspect more so for Marlene. When I returned home to Falcon House that evening, it was obvious that it had undergone a makeover. Marlene proudly took me around the house and when she finally showed me the bedroom that her parents would be sleeping in, I was struck by the effort that she had made in planning everything down to the smallest detail. Personal items, such as nightwear that had been laid out on the bed, his and her bathrobes hanging in the wardrobe and hairbrushes and perfumes laid out on the dressing table. One item that caught my eye was a shawl with fringes hanging from its corners that had been carefully placed on one of the armchairs. I was sufficiently intrigued to ask Marlene what the significance of the garment was.

"The shawl, darling," Marlene replied, "is called a tallit, known as a Jewish prayer shawl, to be worn over the outer clothes. The hanging fringes are called tzitzit. I have placed it on the chair as a welcome home gift for papa and to make him even further at home, I asked John to place a small container at an angle to the right-hand side of the door of the cottage. That object is called a mezuzah in which you place a small parchment scroll, thereby placing the home under God's protection. Every time you pass through the door, you are supposed to touch it and then kiss your fingers."

It just goes to show that after all these years of living with Marlene, how ignorant I was of her religious customs. I think Marlene would have stayed up all night if she could, as she was that keyed up with the anticipated arrival of her parents. However, by the time that we arose the following morning, dressed and had a light breakfast, she was more settled and it wasn't long after that before John had pulled the Humber up outside. The car was sparkling in the winter sunshine and as arranged, he had not only placed two rugs on the back seat of the car, but he also looked immaculate in his suit and chauffeur's cap whilst Marlene looked stunning in a mink fur coat and matching hat. Bill and Lucy had got up a little earlier than usual to see us off and had packed us a flask of hot tea and as we settled in the back seat of the car, they waved us off as John took the car down the drive and turned right towards London.

Apart from a few lorries, there was very little traffic on the roads and it didn't take John very long to reach central London. A clean, crisp and dry winter's morning, London was beginning to throb with the sound and activity of buses disgorging their human cargoes and as we sped past Buckingham Palace, we had a brief glimpse of the Palace sentries in their red tunics and bearskin hats before we were away up Buckingham Palace Road and on to Victoria Station. We had overestimated the length of time that it had taken to drive from the house to Victoria, so that by the time John had parked the car, we had left ourselves just over an hour before the mail train arrived. I felt that it was prudent that I send John for a quick break and to check the arrivals board whilst Marlene and I remained in the car. I was being cautious by habit, as normally the press would routinely cover the arrival of the boat train or the Golden Arrow for the possible arrival of celebrities or persons of news interest. The last thing I wanted at this moment was a private family matter turned into a media circus.

As it turned out, John had parked us alongside what I assumed to be the arrival platform for the mail train. There were four or five trolleys being lined up along the platform edge and at the same time, post office vans were beginning to park up around us, so if my assumption was right, we would be able to collect Marlene's parents and be away very quickly. Then, we both remembered that Lucy had packed us a thermos flask of tea, so whilst we sat back enjoying a hot cuppa, we had the opportunity of observing the flow of people going about their daily lives, some arriving and some leaving and some like ourselves, waiting to pick up relatives or friends. I also noticed a greater number of military personnel with their kit bags either arriving on leave or returning to camp. Eventually, John arrived back at the car. He had found a small café round the corner and had himself a cup of tea and a bacon sandwich. He had also checked the arrivals board and our train was running twenty minutes later than scheduled which meant that we still had at least an hour to wait. He suggested that Marlene and I spend that time in the station news theatre which would be as good a place as any to hide from the press, while he would remain in the car. Marlene and I thought that was an excellent idea and very quickly, were out of the car and walking briskly through the main concourse, where I located the news theatre above us on the second floor. We climbed the main stairs and purchased two tickets and went through the double doors into a darkened auditorium where we found two seats at the back and quickly made ourselves comfortable.

News theatres served a useful purpose with the public. They were an ideal place to spend an hour if you had time to spend, most of the main railway stations in the capital had them and I have even seen one in Trafalgar Square on the corner of Whitehall and one near the clock tower in Brighton. Their programme consisted of all the same standard fare, including cartoons, newsreels, travelogues and Pete Smith specials and ours was no different, so whilst watching the clock at the side of the screen, Marlene and I settled down to watch a Barney Bear cartoon a Pete Smith special, called *Hot on Ice,* a James Fitzpatrick Travelogue, showing us places of interest to visit and a *Crime Does Not Pay.* Both of us enjoyed the experience and before we knew it, forty minutes had elapsed and it was time for us to walk down to the arrival platform. It was a strange sensation coming out of a darkened cinema into the morning daylight with all the accompanying sounds of a railway terminal and by the time we had walked down the stairs to the main concourse, the station Tannoy was announcing that the ten-thirty mail train from Newhaven would be arriving in fifteen minutes time at platform number eight.

We could plainly see a newshound and a photographer hovering between platforms seven and eight, so whilst Marlene walked over to the booking office to purchase two penny platform tickets, I pulled my homburg further down over my eyes and pretended to study the newspapers and books on display at the WH Smith stall. Marlene returned and together arm in arm, we attempted to blend in amongst the scurrying crowd, ducking and diving behind pillars and trolleys carrying all manner of cargoes but soon enough, the mail train appeared with its engine belching smoke. As soon as it had stopped in front of the buffers, it proceeded to shoot out great clouds of steam temporarily obscuring the disembarking passengers. As Marlene and I walked closer to the barrier, we observed the ticket inspector opening the gates as a large group of children disembarked carrying small cases with labels pinned to their coat lapels. They all congregated together on the centre of the platform looking very confused and disorientated until four adults travelling with them formed them up into twos and proceeded to shepherd them in crocodile formation towards the barrier where they were met by what I assumed to be a delegation of mostly women of which the two most prominent were holding clipboards. As soon as the photographer started to take pictures of them, I began to realise that this was part of the *Kinder Express* programme designed to save Jewish children from the Nazi terror machine and with the news reporter walking alongside the women and the photographer snapping pictures, the children marched off towards the station exits.

It was now easier for Marlene and me to go through onto the platform and as we walked, we observed the passengers scurrying past us. There were many trolleys banked up alongside the first two coaches. One, presumably, was the mail van judging by the number of sacks that were being thrown onto the trolleys and the other coach appeared to contain trunks and large packages. As we moved along the platform peering through the open doors of the carriages, the volume of passengers disembarking began to thin out, making it far easier for us to see down the length of the train. Just as we began to get a little anxious, we saw them alighting from the last carriage. Momentarily, I watched the tabloid of an elderly couple carrying two small attaché cases between them whilst holding hands and looking very vulnerable and fragile. The moment was broken when with a cry "Papa! Mama!" Marlene began running towards them and when she reached them, she threw her arms around them both. By the time I reached them, all three were caught up in the emotion of the moment crying with tears of happiness and speaking rapidly in German.

As I embraced them both, I was struck by the physical deterioration of Hiram. Although it had been a few years since I had last seen him, he appeared at least ten years older and had lost a lot of weight. He also needed a walking stick in assisting his mobility. As for Miriam, she still retained her patrician looks although her hair had turned grey with white flecks and she too, was considerably thinner, especially in the face, which also had a haunted look. I didn't think it wise to be hanging around on the platform, so picking up their small cases, I walked ahead, leaving Marlene and her mother to assist her father. I looked back at them from time to time to make sure that they were alright, but they seemed happy enough, talking amongst themselves. As I reached the parking area, John had already seen me and had got out of the car and taking the two cases from me, placed them in the boot. By the time Marlene and her parents had arrived at the car, I had taken the opportunity of lighting a much-needed cigarette whilst John opened the rear passenger door. Marlene paused for a moment and then spoke to John.

"John, may I introduce you to my parents, Hiram and Miriam." Then, turning to her parents, she spoke slowly in English "Papa, Mama, this is John who works for us and he is a very good man". Hiram extended his hand to John exclaiming in pidgin English.

"Good Morgen, John, mien wife and mien self, have been pleased to have seen you." I shared a gentle chuckle with Marlene as she said to John.

"As you can see, John, they do not speak very good English."

"That's all right, madam," he replied and at the same time, touching his hat, "We will soon have them speaking the King's English which probably will be a darn sight sooner than before we speak German. Oh, I am sorry, madam, I didn't mean it to sound like that. I meant to say that none of us at the house would have enough patience to learn another language." Whilst Marlene and I carried on chuckling and with her parents looking perplexed, we placed them in the back of the car with Marlene getting in with them. As John started the car, I slid in beside him as he took the handbrake off. He then turned the car around and headed out of Victoria Station.

Once we had left London behind us, it did not take us long to arrive at Marlow. As it was a weekend and midwinter, the roads were quiet and John was able to put his foot down. In the back of the car, Marlene and her parents, speaking in German, kept up a steady flow of conversation, mostly concerning family matters, whilst John and I took the opportunity to discuss the merits and general performance of the Humber. Finally, we reached Falcon House and as we turned into the drive, I heard Hiram and Miriam gasping in amazement at its size and its grounds with Miriam exclaiming in German.

"We have always been proud of your achievements as an actor, Gunther, but you must be earning a lot of money to afford such a beautiful house and one set in such magnificent grounds. I think our daughter is a very lucky girl."

Chuckling, Marlene leaned forward, patting me on the shoulder.

"I am a lucky girl, Mama. Gunther and I have an incredibly good life together and so shall you and Papa from now on."

Even as she finished speaking, John had swung the car around to the front door, revealing Olivia standing on the porch acting as the welcoming committee. Olivia being Olivia, she had soon shepherded everybody into the house and after taking Hiram and Miriam's coats, she vanished into the kitchen to organise some lunch whilst Marlene made her parents comfortable in the dining room. Very soon, Olivia reappeared with Lucy and Bill carrying lunch which consisted of a quiche, a salad bowl, a bowl of new potatoes and the basket of freshly baked rolls and after introducing Lucy and Bill to Marlene's parents, the four of us were left to enjoy some catch up time over lunch. By the time Bill had brought the dessert in, consisting of hot apple pie and custard, Marlene and I sensed that having just endured a nightmare forty-eight hours plus the excitement of finally arriving, her parents were beginning to wilt under the strain.

When lunch was over, Marlene suggested to her parents that they might want to take an afternoon rest before dinner and if they were ready, would take them upstairs and show them their room. Obviously, they were tired for they didn't need much persuasion. Marlene told me afterwards that on entering their bedroom, her parents, especially Hiram, became very emotional on seeing the tallit and she admitted that she was overcome with sadness when she opened her mother's suitcase to discover such a small number of possessions. A blouse and skirt, some underwear and many photographs represented the sum total of her life's journey. Her possessions, her religion, her country and her family had all been stolen from her. She told her mother and father there and then that as of that moment, they would have back all that they had lost except their country and for that, they would have to wait some time. Then, turning the bedcovers down and closing the window curtains, she left them to take an afternoon nap.

Later that evening, the grandfather clock was just striking nine o'clock, as we all settled down in the lounge. Hiram and Miriam had been greatly refreshed by their afternoon sleep and despite the early evening darkness, had wrapped up well and had a short walk around outside of the house. Of course, Marlene couldn't resist showing them the cottage, whilst gently telling them that it was to be their new home and when Hiram noticed the mezuzah attached to the right-hand side of the door frame, he was once again overcome by the moment and before entering the cottage, he touched it with his fingertips and kissed them. Even I was impressed upon entering the cottage. It appeared to me that whilst I had been away filming during the day, that Marlene had been very busy supervising and buying decorating materials and carpeting for the floors. Miriam fell in love with it immediately whilst poor Hiram could not believe his good fortune. It took some persuading on Marlene's part to convince her father that we could easily afford for them to live in the cottage.

Eventually, the combination of the cold night air and the fact that the heating in the cottage was off, forced us all back into the main house, where we were met by Bill, looking very professional, dressed in his white jacket and black trousers. Whilst taking our coats, he whispered something into Marlene's ear, resulting in her disappearing towards the kitchen, leaving Bill to announce that dinner was about to be served and leaving me to marshal Hiram and Miriam into the dining room. It seemed to me that somebody had worked very hard to create an atmosphere of tranquillity. The wall lights and the candles on the table bathed the room in a copper glow which, in turn, were bouncing tiny crystals of light off the wineglasses. The log fire had been lit and as it burned, you could hear the occasional spit of wood and on the sideboard, Marlene had placed a seven-branched candelabra which I had been told by Marlene a long time ago was called a menorah which was used as a symbol of celebration.

Once Marlene had returned from the kitchen and we were all seated, Bill and Lucy proceeded to serve a magnificent kosher dinner consisting of chicken soup with asparagus and roasted fennel, followed by a main course of Mediterranean baked chicken on the bone with prunes, accompanied by fresh potatoes and assorted herb vegetables and for dessert, we had red velvet cake. After we had eaten, I was compelled to call Bill and Lucy from the kitchen and thank them for their first attempt at cooking and serving a kosher meal and in particular, Lucy, who had excelled herself. Lucy replied that madam deserved the credit for helping her with the preparations and guidance and that if madam's parents had enjoyed the meal then that was a reward in itself. When Marlene had translated Lucy's comments back to Hiram, he immediately arose from the table and walking around to Lucy, took her hand and kissed it which left her in a fine old state not knowing whether to curtsy, jump for joy or to pass out. The remainder of the evening gently wound itself down, with Lucy and Bill eventually closing the kitchen down and going up to Olivia's apartment for a game of cards, leaving the rest of us to move into the lounge. Whilst Marlene and her parents exchanged reminiscences, I took the opportunity of studying Hiram and Miriam. Of the two, Miriam was the one who appeared to have altered least apart from losing a lot of weight and looking gaunt, she still appeared to physically be the same person. It was Hiram who seem to have physically altered the most, his hair was almost completely grey and his face was sallow and drawn, I also noticed that he had developed a slight tremor in his right arm which on occasion, at the dinner table, had prompted Miriam to gently steady it.

All in all, as I had observed earlier, his appearance was that of a man looking ten years older than his sixty-five years. I reminded myself to have a chat with Marlene later regarding any health issues they may have as well as getting our family doctor, who I am quite sure, given time, would restore them to good health, to accept them as patients. Also, the thought occurred to me that Marlene was going to have her hands full, settling her parents in, getting the house ready for Christmas and the organising of our festive social calendar. My daytime commitments at this time of year were leaving me very little time for anything else and inevitably, meant that I would be spending less time at home. It would appear to me that I needed to have a talk with Olivia for she too, would have an increased workload. Apart from her normal office routine, Olivia would have to deal with extra issues relating to Hiram and Miriam, such as setting paperwork in motion regarding their permanent residency status in Britain, assuming of course that they would want to stay here. They might have wanted to go to America and be with their sons or live in Holland with their daughter. Either way, Marlene would have to discuss it with them very soon.

The remainder of the weekend was spent continuing to show Hiram and Miriam the house and grounds plus the cottage, their home-to-be. We walked with them through the orchard down to the river's edge where they stood watching the occasional pair of swans regally sailing down the meandering Thames. It was also an opportunity for them to get to know the staff and despite their limited English, had soon won them over and gained their trust, particularly Olivia who was an opera fan and was already aware of Miriam's career and fame.

By late afternoon, the womenfolk were gathered in the kitchen planning out the evening's menu helped I may add, by quite a few glasses of wine. Marlene and Miriam were helping Lucy in making dumplings, whilst Olivia in her best Edna May Oliver mode, assigned herself the position of chief taster and wine pourer. I wasn't entirely sure with the way things were developing, what the odds would be on whether there would be any dinner at all. On the spur of the moment, I turned to Hiram and asked him if he fancied a short walk to my local pub, the Dog and Badger to try a half pint of Wethered best bitter. Working on the assumption you should try anything once, Hiram agreed and after telling Marlene what we proposed to do, whilst dinner was being prepared, I went and fetched our coats and when I got back to the kitchen, Marlene insisted on fetching gloves and a scarf for her father, as well. After ensuring that he was well wrapped up against the cold night air, she told me that we were to be back for dinner no later than seven-thirty. Then, giving us both a hug, she pushed us out through the kitchen door.

Once we had reached the end of the country lane, we turned right onto the Marlow Road and within ten minutes, had reached the pub. Across the road, the lights were on in the village hall with a fair amount of activity going on inside. It seemed as if the locals were decorating the hall with Christmas decorations. Other than that, it was pretty quiet. We certainly appreciated the warm environment as we entered the public bar for the temperature was dropping rapidly outside. As it was still early evening, there weren't many customers about. There were two elderly men hunched over a game of dominoes, smoking pipes and drinking mild and at the other end of the bar, there were three younger men engaged in the game of darts and while Hiram stood watching the game, I ordered two halves of bitter. I was acquainted with Mike, the landlord and though he certainly recognised me, he never let on, which was one of the reasons why I occasionally called in after a long walk. The other reason was that the pub also offered me a safe haven and whenever I called by, I always used the public bar where my privacy was respected and I was able to mix with people and listen to their opinions. I had encountered quite a few bar-room lawyers in my time and in the end, it was all grist to the mill. I ended up learning a lot on how the so-called ordinary folk thought and lived.

Hiram took a liking to English beer that night and we had hardly sat down at a table before his glass was empty. I offered to get another round and although Hiram made a show of saying no, it was obvious to me that he meant yes, so I returned to the table with two pints this time and we both settled down to watch the world go by. I shall always remember that evening for it was when Hiram began to relax and come alive again. He told me of his plans to practice medicine again in Britain and to continue as a surgeon and that he would also learn to speak fluent English so that he could be granted a long-term visa and work permit. He was quite adamant that more than likely, he would end his days in Britain because at the moment, none of the leading nations in Europe were prepared to stand up to Hitler who had got away with the occupation of Austria and the German Sudetenland and Hiram was quite convinced that either Poland or Czechoslovakia would be next. Eventually, he foresaw a Second World War erupting as the only way to stop Hitler from leading the German nation into destruction. Already, the moral fibre of the nation was being eroded, by the tacit approval of the people who were turning a blind eye to a programme of euthanasia that was being carried out on the mentally ill and the brutal treatment of Jews, gypsies and other minorities such as homosexuals.

I reckon that my idea of taking Hiram for a walk so that we could get to know each other better had worked, with the help of the ye old English pub. We were becoming more at ease in each other's company and Hiram was beginning to reveal more of himself to me. Suddenly standing up, he collected our empty glasses and took them to the bar for a refill. Just as I was wondering how he was going to pay for them, he put his hand in his coat pocket and pulled out a five-pound note. Obviously, Marlene, bless her, had slipped some money into her father's topcoat to maintain his dignity. Unfortunately, not being familiar with the English currency, Hiram had tended a note of a large denomination for the price of two pints of bitter which had come to the grand total of one and eight pence. It did not matter how many times Mike asked Hiram if he had anything smaller, Hiram simply did not understand, leaving poor Mike to go upstairs to get change for a five-pound note. Fortunately, Hiram redeemed himself upon Mike's return, by buying the other five customers a round plus a whiskey for the landlord. Whilst all this had been going on, I had moved up to the bar with the intention of offering a ten-shilling note to pay for the drinks but then I really did not want to run the risk of embarrassing Hiram, so I let him get on with it because the only way that he would learn would be by experience.

It is quite true what they say that time passes very quickly when you are enjoying yourself and when I next looked at my watch, I discovered that we had roughly thirty minutes to get home in time for dinner, otherwise we would be facing the wrath of both Marlene and Miriam. It took me a little while to persuade Hiram to drink up and it hadn't taken him long to learn some English phrases, one in particular, much to my amusement, was 'one for the road' which he kept repeating. After telling Mike that he would be returning for some more beer because he had a most enjoyable evening, I got him outside. But I still had to go back in again to collect his walking stick and after making sure that he was well buttoned up against the cold night air, we set off for home.

There had been a complete change in Hiram that evening and it wasn't because of the alcohol because there was no way that you could say he was drunk. I sensed that his real personality was finally reasserting itself. He appeared stronger and fully in command. It was almost as if somewhere in the past, his self-esteem had gone into hiding to escape the terrible deeds that had been going on around him. I think he had been about to tell me earlier on in the pub about those experiences but had thought better of it. I am quite convinced that one day, he would tell me if only to cauterise some terrible memories that he had experienced.

The walk back to the house gave us both an opportunity to cement our relationship. I took comfort in this, for apart from Hans and my first agent, I had never really had a father figure to look up to, so perhaps this could be the beginning of a wonderful friendship. My thoughts were interrupted at this point by Hiram taking my arm and starting to speak in German.

"You know, Gunther, that I am very beholden to you and owe you a huge debt of gratitude and it may very well be some time before I can repay you. However, I don't want you to think that you and Marlene will be responsible for our keep in the twilight of our years. Apart from having a respected name in my profession, there is no reason why I cannot continue to practice for the next ten years. I shall apply as soon as possible to the British Medical Association for a licence to practice in Britain. Miriam shares the same view on this matter as I do. In fact, it is her intention to resume her operatic career and I do know she will be asking you soon for the name of a theatrical agent who specialises in handling opera singers to help her in restarting her career. I cannot express myself sufficiently enough to tell you what it means for us to be here and to become financially independent. Last week, we were in hell and now, we are in the heaven of the English countryside and Miriam and I would like to end our days here particularly in the cottage which is where we want our home to be."

"Hiram, the only thing that Marlene and I ask of you both is to stop worrying and relax. It is quite true when you say that both of you still have a lot to give society before you retire but it is important that you spend the next few months building up your physical and mental strength. Meanwhile, there will be more than enough to keep you both occupied if Marlene has anything to do with it. She will be advising her mother on the choice of new furniture for the cottage whilst you will be relegated to the role of doting husband and father. Don't look to me for support as I shall be working, so you are on your own. By the way, Hiram, how are you at decorating Christmas trees and putting decorations up in the house? If you haven't had much practice, you are certainly going to have plenty now. I can see the lights of the house appearing down the lane, so before we go in there are two things that I want to tell you. The first is that from now on, you only speak English because that is the only way you're going to learn quickly and the second is that I have thoroughly enjoyed your company tonight and I sincerely hope that it leads to a lifetime of close friendship. For as much as I love Marlene and are very fond of my staff, it would be nice now and then to invite you over to the house for a game of chess or to unwind over a glass or two."

With that said, we both proceeded to walk up the driveway and around the house to the kitchen. As soon as we entered, we were met by the rich aromas percolating from the kitchen Agar and the whole place was seething with activity. Apart from Lucy, who was wearing her chef whites, the remainder of the womenfolk were wearing aprons whilst Bill was busy laying the kitchen table with crockery and wineglasses.

"Hello, darling," Marlene said, as she walked over to me and gave me a hug. "Supper is almost ready. You know I really didn't think that you would be back quite so early. I do hope that you haven't been leading Papa astray." She laughed as she planted a kiss on her father's cheek.

"I must say that the pair of you smell like a brewery. God help you if you don't eat your supper after all the effort that has been put into cooking it. In case you are interested, we are having spaghetti Bolognese accompanied by small balls of garlic bread and a dipping dish consisting of virgin olive oil and Parmesan cheese finished off by a dessert of upside-down rhubarb and apple crumble. I also have to tell you that Bill and Olivia went foraging in your wine cellar and brought back three bottles of your precious Barolo and in case you're wondering why we are eating in the kitchen tonight, I thought it would be nice to finish the week end off with a proper homecoming for Mama and Papa. I expect it will be the Christmas holiday before we all get together again as a family unit, as Gunther, you will be working flat-out during the day to finish your picture and coming home tired, we have our nationalisation coming up very soon and finally, we have to decorate the house for the Christmas festivities and begin to organise the forthcoming parties that we will be holding here. So, Bill, while you do the honours and start pouring the wine, Gunther, you can go and hang the coats up whilst Mama and Papa can sit down at the table as Olivia and I help Lucy serve the food."

When I returned from the hall, everybody had seated themselves around the table upon which had been placed in a large bowl of steaming spaghetti Bolognese and the sundry other dishes. I had only just sat down when Marlene stood up with a glass in her hand calling for everybody's attention.

"I just want to take a quick moment before the food goes cold to say how happy I am to have my Mama and Papa safely home. I would also like to thank Gunther for working so hard to achieve that and for Olivia, Lucy and Bill for being so loyal to us over the past two years. I want to say that I consider them very much part of our family. For the moment, John and Mary have been unable to be here tonight due to a prior family commitment but I am including them in my toast. Everybody, please raise your glasses and drink to a long and happy union of us all and without further ado, let the meal begin."

Watching Miriam have an emotional moment and the rest of us raising our glasses and calling out, "Cheers," tipped me momentarily into a parallel universe where all of us were dressed in Dickensian clothes seated around the table upon which candles were illuminating a large roasted turkey, while outside the window would be a large camera mounted on four wheels attached to a movable arm operated by Jimmy Howe, the great Hollywood cameraman who was gradually tracking back from the window revealing snowflakes falling upon a group of Yuletide singers holding lanterns and all fitted out in Victorian clothes with stove-pipe hats and bonnets et al, straight from the wardrobe department at MGM. Finally, there would be a cry of "CUT" from George Cukor the director. This would signify the ending of yet another great MGM picture and later, the composer Alfred Korngold would record the necessary mood music that helped make the MGM studio the Rolls-Royce of the American film industry. I was quickly back in the present by the sound of Marlene's voice calling to me to tuck in.

As I helped myself to the spaghetti amidst the family laughter and chatter, I realised at that moment, what many older actors had told me as I rose through the ranks of my profession;

the more work that you received in the theatre, the harder it became to differentiate between life and art. That is why tonight I finally learnt that important lesson. There was a thin line between being genuine and becoming shallow. I was very fortunate to have married a woman who was my soul mate and most certainly kept my feet firmly planted on the ground. I must admit that I spent a lot of my time observing the daily routines of people's lives, collecting their accents and mannerisms and storing them away in my mind to be used again on some other part that I would play. I had taught myself that once I had closed the front door on the outside world, I would be able to leave it all behind and with Marlene I had found the perfect actor's wife: no theatrical nonsense, no emoting, just say it as it is and be your natural self. The weekend had started with uncertainty but finished on a high note with everybody having enjoyed the communal supper, especially with the assistance of my precious supply of Barolo, one of the great wines of northern Italy, but what the heck. Wine is for drinking, especially amongst friends and family and not for collecting as a possession to be hidden away in a cellar and occasionally brought up to be admired. Once supper was finished, we all mucked in washing-up the dirty crockery and putting the kitchen to rights ready for the morning, after which we spent the remainder of the evening in the lounge playing charades. Olivia emerged as the winner of the evening. The final charade in which she beat us all with was the film called *Captains Courageous,* after which everybody started drifting away.

The first to go were Bill and Lucy who, of course, had to be up reasonably early in the morning. The next to go were Hiram and Miriam who I was surprised, I must admit, to be still active, after such a tumultuous weekend, but as Marlene said to them as she kissed them good night, there was no need for them to get up in the morning until they were ready. Olivia being the last to leave, gave me the opportunity to have a quick word with her regarding the most important items to be dealt with in the coming week. The most urgent of these was contacting Xavier Jurgens at the German Embassy asking him to phone me at the film studio if he had anything further to discuss with me since our last meeting. Finally, Olivia said good night and departed upstairs leaving Marlene and I alone with just the sound of the ticking grandfather clock to keep us company.

Later, we tidied up the lounge and finally turned the lights off after gathering up the empty wine glasses and carrying them through to the kitchen where we washed them up and put them away. After making sure that the kitchen was clean and tidy for Lucy to come down to the following morning, we then stepped outside and braved the cold night air for one last smoke and a chat. Despite the lateness of the evening and the drop in temperature, we covered a multitude of topics ranging from inviting her sister Greta and her husband to come over from Holland for a visit, drawing up a list with Olivia of people she would be inviting to any one of the three parties that she would be holding over the Christmas period and most importantly of all, she would be commandeering John for the next few days to drive her and her parents shopping for furniture and fabrics, a shopping expedition that I am sure would have my accountant tearing his hair out when he started receiving the bills.

The cold air made us both realise that we would be better off indoors continuing the conversation that we were having tucked up snug in a warm bed with two mugs of hot chocolate. Marlene was still chatting away whilst she made the chocolate and I had locked and bolted the kitchen door leaving me to just stand there, nodding wisely accompanied by the occasional, "Yes dear," but in the end, she flung her arms around my neck and kissed me, while telling me that she had just had the best weekend of her entire life and that she was extremely lucky to have such a gorgeous man for a husband. Well! What could I say to that other than to tell her to go upstairs while I followed behind with the chocolate and once in the bedroom, perhaps she could elaborate on the statement that she had just made? She gave me one of her enigmatic smiles and teasingly replied that she had nothing more to add though she may possibly be able to better illustrate with movement what she had been trying to say with words. I certainly did not need any further explanation for despite being handicapped carrying two hot mugs of chocolate I was right behind her all the way up the stairs.

Because I had an early call at the studio that morning, I was the first person to be up, but boy was the house cold. It certainly didn't take me long to get showered and dressed and to find Marlene buried beneath the bedclothes fast asleep. I snatched a quick kiss on her forehead before rushing downstairs to turn the central heating on. I reminded myself to update the heating system of the house as soon as possible. What we needed was a timer of some sort so that it would turn itself on and off automatically. I brewed a cup of coffee accompanied by a slice of toast which would keep me going until I reached the studio, after which, I let myself out of the house. There had been a heavy frost during the night which forced me to spend five minutes scraping ice off the rear window and windscreen and having to sit in the car freezing whilst I gently eased the choke out without flooding the engine. I then spent another couple of minutes running the engine so that the heat it generated completely defrosted the windscreen and restored life once more to my nether regions. Once I had achieved a clear vision of the view in front of me, I set off.

It did not take me long to reach the studio as the traffic on the roads was only just starting to build up. I was pleased to see as I parked the car in my reserved space, that I wasn't alone, for as I got out of the car, I recognised Ralphie Richardson's motorbike and Binny Barnes' car already parked up. Sure enough, when I walked into the makeup department, Ralphie was already ensconced in a chair taking a quick nap whilst June, one of the makeup artists, was gently applying a powderpuff to his nose. As I plonked myself down in the makeup chair next to Richardson, I glanced in the mirror facing me and groaned, thinking it would take a miracle to make this face of mine photogenic in time for this morning's shoot. Fortunately, April, one of my regular makeup girls, well used to my early morning grumpiness, was already beside me with a mug of hot coffee as we greeted each other.

"Morning, Mr Conrad. Try this coffee. It will soon get rid of your grumpy head. Goodness, I do have a bit of work to carry out on your face, this morning. Have we been having a good time enjoying ourselves this weekend?"

"Morning, April. You'll have to use all your skills to make me look presentable for the cameras this morning. I look and feel bloody awful. But I must admit it's been well worth the suffering we have been celebrating the arrival of my wife's parents from Germany who are going to be living with us."

"Don't you worry, Mr Conrad. I'll soon have you looking as handsome as ever and I am ever so pleased that your wife's parents are going to be living with you. I think that Mr Hitler is a terrible man and it's about time that we started giving him a piece of our mind."

Just at that moment, Ralph Richardson woke up from his catnap and noticed me sitting beside.

"Morning, Gunty. How are you, dear boy? Are you ready for this morning's histrionics? Probably not, judging by the look of you. What you need is for me to take you out for a spin on my Harley Davidson. That will soon blow away the cobwebs. Anyway, if I were you, I would just relax. It will be some time yet before we are needed on set. Binny is having her hair done and Merle, according to the studio grapevine, has not turned up yet. I couldn't help but overhear that your in-laws have successfully arrived from Germany. It must have been a great relief for you all, especially Marlene. I do think that the politicians should stop chasing votes and listen to the people and tell this Mr Hitler that enough is enough."

"I don't think that will happen, Ralphie. I am afraid that in my opinion, Mr Chamberlain will continue to appease Hitler until it is too late to stop him. I can't tell you how glad I am to have finally managed to get Marlene's parents safely out of Germany but unfortunately, many members of her family will not leave thinking that the persecution will blow over but that I fear that will not happen. Changing the subject, I hope that this film of ours will be finished by the end of next week as per schedule, as I am committed to start a new film in January and as I seem to recollect, you are as well."

"Have no fears on that score, dear boy. Korda is juggling several film projects in the air at the moment, one of which, as you know, is that darling Merle is due in Hollywood in the New Year to start work on a film version of *Wuthering Heights* for Sam Goldwyn whilst in January, Larry Olivier and I are due to start filming one of those spy dramas titled *Q Planes* to be directed by the dependable Tim Whelan. Who do you think Goldwyn has cast in the male lead opposite Merle in *Wuthering Heights*? Why none other than Larry, of course. You see, Gunty, it is in Korda's interest to wrap this film up by next week. In fact, I'll wager you a fiver on it."

Eventually, Merle arrived with her hair in curlers and with her hairdresser and makeup artist in tow. She promptly vanished into her dressing room, leaving the three of us, Ralph, Binnie and myself, to go over our lines and have a gossip. I have said this before about the acting profession insofar that you never know where it will lead you. Most actors intend to end up on a treadmill playing variations of the same old character. Binnie Barnes was a case in point. She had been born in London, in a place called Islington and had been learning her trade in the theatre and in the early thirties, she had made the transition to films, finally establishing a name for herself with British cinema audiences. Her screen persona came over as a feisty, no-nonsense, straight-talking female. Hollywood soon came a wooing and consequently, she ended up a star on both sides of the Atlantic. So, while the three of us marked time waiting for Merle, she told Ralph and myself that she was off again to Hollywood in the New Year to play a dance hall girl in a western, opposite the actor Randolph Scott, The film was to be called *Frontier Marshal*. I remembered that she had already partnered Scott some time back in the film, *The Last of the Mohicans* which had been successful and now she was off again to the United States and I rather suspected that she would eventually settle there permanently. Like all of us who tread the boards, she had worked hard and taken life's knocks, but unlike most, she had the benefit of a lucky break. I hoped that she grabbed her good fortune with both hands.

Once Merle had appeared on the set, Tim Whelan soon had the principles and supporting cast whizzing through take after take and by Wednesday, Merle and I had our final scene together on board a channel steamer which in reality was part of a mock-up of a steamer's deck, placed on rollers to give the impression of being at sea. I had a feeling that Ralph would be collecting on his bet and I would gladly pay it. It was also on Wednesday that I finally received a phone call from Xavier Jurgens. I had previously requested that an outside line be put in my dressing room to afford me some privacy and fortunately, the call came through during a break in filming. Speaking in German, Jurgens' attitude came over as being polite but cold.

"Good afternoon, Herr Conrad. I apologise for the delay in replying to your last phone call, but things have been rather busy here at the Embassy, especially with the change of ambassador. With reference to our previous conversation concerning your return to the Third Reich, recent events concerning your family lead me to the conclusion that your answer is no. It seems that your connections go right to the very top of the party and supersede my superiors. It has also been noted that your in-laws have left

Germany and are residing here in Britain, a fact that has not gone down well with either the Minister for Foreign Affairs or the Minister of Propaganda and I must admit, it does seem unbelievable that you have chosen to turn your back on your Fatherland for the sake of a Jewess. You do realise, of course, that your name will now be included amongst those who are enemies of the state and will be subject to retribution if you should fall within the boundaries of the Third Reich. I personally, will be following your career with great interest, Herr Conrad because I know that sometime in the future, due to the Fuhrer's genius, that if our paths cross again it will be to your detriment. Finally, Herr Conrad, I am sure that you now realise that any protection that your wife's family had received will now be removed and that they like all other German Jews will be subject to the Fuhrer's whim."

"I have taken note of your comments, Herr Jurgens and would expect nothing less from one of Hitler's acolytes but let me tell you, Herr Jurgens that I truly believe that one day your beloved Fuhrer will overreach himself and it will be you and other Germans like you, supping currently at Hitler's table, who are going to need a very long spoon to avoid the consequences of their actions."

"Oh dear! It is very easy, Herr Conrad, to criticise from a safe distance whilst others nearer home will have to bear the brunt of your stupidity. I refer, of course, to the remainder of your wife's family who have now been designated as high-risk to the Third Reich and will not be able to travel outside the borders of the Fatherland under any circumstances. As to your sneering reference to patriotic Germans, all of us would be proud to sit at the Fuhrer's table. His genius and strength of character has finally restored Germany to its rightful position as a world power and only the Fuhrer has the determination to destroy world Jewry and its insatiable appetites for corruption and money. Still, I mustn't keep you as I know you are busy prostituting your talent for a handful of silver from your Jewish masters. As I said earlier, I will leave you now with the words, until we meet again."

I sat there for a few minutes after I had put the phone back on its cradle. Jurgens had left me with a feeling of both guilt and fear. It seemed that I had abandoned Marlene's family to a permanent climate of intolerance which now I would be unable to do anything about. I thought it would be better if I kept this conversation to myself rather than share it with Marlene and her parents for there would be absolutely no point in placing any more stress on their shoulders. At that moment, the studio runner poked his head around the door to tell me that I was needed on the set.

The final scene of the film was set in a divorce court and would probably take until the end of the week to complete and as my character in the film was a barrister, my costume was quite simple, just a wig and gown over an everyday suit and when I emerged from the dressing room suitably attired, I was surprised to find the studio runner waiting for me. He was going to guide me to another part of the studio where a new set had been put up showing the interior of a court room. It was fortunate because I probably would have got lost finding my way having spent many weeks going to the self-same adjoining sets. When we finally reached the new set, I was astounded at the layout of the courtroom. Apart from a wide area between the judges dais and the benches of the King's Counsel to allow for Harry Stradling and the camera crew and of course, the director, Tim Whelan, there had even been built a small gallery which was already occupied by film extras waiting for Merle to take her place on the front seat for reaction shots, whilst I conferred with Tim over the script pages for that day.

Most of it would be concentrated on me as I had a long summation speech to make, which in turn, involved some time being spent setting up reaction shots of me addressing the jury. The supporting cast on the front benches waited patiently for their final instructions whilst behind them, stood roughly a dozen extras dressed in the assorted costumes of solicitors, policeman, court ushers and spectators. Tim Whelan calculated that we would complete the final scene by Friday morning, but he would still need me next week on standby as they were re-shooting the ballroom sequence due to Technicolor problems and though I wasn't in that scene, I might be needed for retakes on my arrival at the hotel during the London fog. Just as Tim told me to take my mark so that Harry Stradling could look through the viewfinder to determine the composition and positioning of myself and the extras in the well of the court, Merle walked onto the set wearing a fetching beige suit and a brown leopard skin pillbox hat. She was closely followed by the character actor, Morton Selten, who was playing the part of the crusty but lovable old judge, Lord Steel, who was also the father of Merle in the film.

We finished filming by the following day as it only took five takes of my speech before Tim approved my performance. The remainder of the time was taken up with the reaction shots of Merle to my closing arguments and likewise to Morton Selten and then finally, it was a wrap and I was free to go home. As I said cheerio to everybody until next week, Tim reminded me that the official wrap party would be the following Wednesday afternoon for the cast and crew and it was also going to be extended by inviting prominent members of the profession, so it looked like it was going to be one hell of a do. He also told me that late last night, he had looked at the rushes with the film editor of the first shots of me arriving in the fog at the hotel and had declared them perfect, so I could take myself off for a long weekend and he would see me on Wednesday.

That weekend was idyllic for me. Marlene was looking in the best of health as were Hiram and Miriam who were physically recovering in leaps and bounds. Marlene and her mother were out hunting for suitable furniture for the cottage whilst Hiram had very wisely opted out by staying behind and brushing up his English with Olivia as well as learning some Cockney phrases from Lucy. He had even done odd jobs for Bill and Mary around the house. I spent part of Friday afternoon with Olivia helping Hiram to make a start on the paperwork required for a long-term visa application to remain in Britain. Also, we had started to list his qualifications as a surgeon for his curriculum vitae for the British Medical Association, so that they could grant him a licence to practice in Britain. I couldn't foresee any problems in the granting of his licence as he already had an international reputation as a noted surgeon. The only problem that I could envisage was his limited command of the English language and that could be rectified with tuition and constant practice. It was only as the grandfather clock in the hallway chimed four o'clock that I realised we had lost all sense of time and called a halt to the afternoon's work. It was just as well, as Hiram, feeling tired, went upstairs for a lie down, leaving Olivia and myself to finish off for the weekend.

We had only just finished tidying up when the heavens opened with a torrential downpour of rain virtually wiping out any daylight left in the day. As Olivia and I began to worry about Marlene and Miriam making it home soon, the headlights of the car swept the study as it pulled into the driveway and simultaneously the phone rang giving us both a start leaving Olivia to answer it. I made a dash for the front door and grabbing an umbrella, went out to the car and shepherded Marlene and the Miriam indoors, leaving John to bring in any parcels. I had barely time to give Marlene a kiss before Olivia was calling me back into the study and handing me the receiver while letting me know that it was an urgent call from Robin Cox.

"Hello, Robin. Don't you ever stop working? I would have thought that you would have been sliding off for the weekend to spend time with your family by now," I said, greeting him.

"Sorry to have disturbed you at the end of the week, Gunther, but Gainsborough studios have got themselves in rather a tight situation and need a replacement star urgently for a film they are due to start shooting in early February. Knowing that you have just about finished your commitment with Korda within the next few weeks and are not due to start your next film with him until midsummer, they are hoping that I will be able to persuade you to help them out. It will be no more than an eight week shoot and they are prepared to offer a contract for twenty-five thousand pounds and a guarantee for you to meet your deadline with Korda for commencing your next film. Obviously, it is going to be an 'A' picture and they have already cast Margaret Lockwood to be the female lead plus a rising young emigre actress by the name of Lilli Palmer. It is also going to be helmed by one of Britain's best directors, Carol Reed and the part itself is a bit of fluff; Ibsen, it is not. The script has been written by Frank Lauder and Michael Pertwee who, as you know, are both excellent at writing comedy dialogue. The character is a wealthy European aristocrat, being pursued by two gold-diggers, who is finally won over by love. To be honest with you, Gunther, I can't see it doing you any harm at the box office for it is sure to bring in the female audiences in droves."

"You know me very well, Robin. I won't turn down any part if the money is right. My philosophy is that if you keep working long enough eventually, from all the dross, a few great performances will emerge that the public will remember you by. Go ahead and tell Gainsborough that the answer is yes and I will leave you to do the usual crossing the t's and dotting the i's on the final contract and while I remember it, I hope to see you at the wrap party at Denham next Wednesday although I am quite sure that you will be there if only to count the number of your clients that will be in attendance. Seriously though, thanks for thinking of me and I do appreciate the efforts you make on my behalf. Take care of yourself and my love to the family."

"I am glad that you said yes, Gunther. The salaries from this film and *Ali Baba* will put you well ahead of the game for next year leaving you in an enviable position of being able to pick and choose projects in the latter part of 1939. Perhaps, I shouldn't mention it, but the scuttlebutt from across the pond is suggesting that both Warners and MGM are showing some enthusiasm in adding to their roster another European star who will appeal to the American public especially for women's pictures. In particular, they are showing interest in placing you under contract so you might want to think about it if the prospect of negotiations should arise in the future. I will notify Gainsborough immediately and will meet up with you next Wednesday. Give Marlene my love and tell her I hope to see her then."

The remainder of the weekend and the beginning of the week was spent with Marlene, Miriam and Mary putting the finishing touches to the cottage. In between furniture being delivered and essential services being checked, the womenfolk were hanging curtains, cleaning and stocking up with China and cutlery and whilst all this was going on, poor Hiram was using Bill to practice his English on but to be honest with you, I wasn't sure who was teaching who. It was quite possible that Bill would end up speaking better German than Hiram spoke English. My time was fully taken up in catching up with correspondence that had needed my attention and signing cheques for Olivia to send to various suppliers. There was also a stack of scripts for projects from film producers, half of which, would never see the light of day and as for the rest, there might be a part buried in there somewhere worth giving your high teeth for. There was a thought growing somewhere in the back of my mind that I needed to re-establish the direction in which my career seemed to be travelling. I had this feeling of wanting to do more theatrical work and be more selective in my film projects but thinking and doing are two separate things. I had fairly substantial overheads which required a lot of liquid income and more importantly, Marlene and I were still trying for a baby. There was no reason, according to the doctors, why nature wouldn't take its course and Marlene would finally become pregnant. Bearing all that in mind, I guess that I was still stuck on the treadmill of playing wealthy playboys or swashbuckling heroes in 'Tits and Sand' movies. Probably that is why I was looking forward to the challenge of taking the part of the wicked Vizier in *Ali Baba.* It could create a new persona for me with movie audiences, thereby creating an opportunity for better parts.

Knowing that we had the studio wrap-party to attend the following day, plus the fact that Alex Korda had also invited us to a cocktail party in the evening of the same day at his Park Lane townhouse, Marlene and I had taken the opportunity of retiring early on the Tuesday night. It was not often that we had the luxury of snuggling up together in bed reading with a warm mug of Ovaltine, particularly as we were night owls by habit. Marlene was reading a novel titled *Gone with the Wind*, which had been a worldwide literary sensation back in 1936. It had been written by an American by the name of Margaret Mitchell, a southerner by birth and the book depicted both the decline and defeat of the South during the American Civil War. David O. Selznick the American film producer and brother of my American representative, Myron, had acquired the film rights and since 1937, had mounted a search for an actress to play Scarlett O'Hara, the heroine of the novel. Virtually every Hollywood actress had been tested for the part, although a young actress by the name of Paulette Goddard was emerging as the front-runner. However, there was some insider gossip surfacing, suggesting that Vivien Leigh, one of Britain's own film actresses, fresh from a British film starring Robert Taylor titled *A Yank at Oxford,* could be a serious contender. Anyway, the book had certainly captured Marlene's attention, for not only could she not put it down, but she was also unable to stop talking about it. I was trying to work my way through William Shakespeare's *Julius Caesar* as I had an idea that sometime in the future, I would like to both star and produce a film version playing Marc Anthony, a brave concept if I may say so, as filmed versions of Shakespearean plays were not exactly popular with the movie public. However, Marlene had other ideas for she kept breaking my concentration by butting in with comments.

"Oh, Gunther, that Scarlett really is a wilful girl. She is now trying to steal Ashley Wilkes away from Melanie. That Rhett Butler is really a dish. You know there are only two actors that could play Rhett Butler. One is Clark Gable and the other is you. I am surprised that you have not been considered for the part I can just imagine you drinking mint juleps and sweeping Scarlett off her feet."

"Oh, for goodness sake, Marlene," I laughed as I interrupted her, "The part calls for a genuine American actor from the northern states, not a European one with a slight accent. You are quite right that there is only one actor who can play Rhett Butler and that is Clark Gable. Unfortunately, he is under contract at MGM and knowing Louis B. Mayer as I do, he'll want a small fortune to loan him out to Selznick."

"Maybe you're right, Gunther. Perhaps I am being a little bit greedy? Perhaps, I should let Scarlett have Clark? After all, one out of two isn't bad and you are all mine aren't you, sweetheart?"

I am afraid that as I felt her hand sliding under the bed clothes, William Shakespeare surrendered and beat a hasty retreat.

We both rose early the following morning, with Miriam helping her daughter pack an overnight case and in particular, helping her choose a cocktail dress to wear that night, whilst having already brought down a change of clothes and put them in the hallway ready to be loaded into the car, I went into the kitchen where I joined Hiram and the rest of the staff in a light breakfast. I had decided that John would drive us first to Denham studios where he would drop us off and then, after picking us up again later, would proceed on into London to the Dorchester Hotel. Meantime, whilst he was waiting for us, he was more than welcome to join Marlene and myself at the after-wrap party and mingle with some showbiz personalities. If not, he could carry on driving to the Dorchester in London and deliver our overnight cases to the hotel concierge before driving back to Falcon House and collecting us the following morning from the Dorchester, leaving us to organise a car from Denham to the Dorchester. As for Lucy, Bill and Mary, they were more than happy to serve Hiram and Miriam and take instruction from them whilst we were away. Miriam was well used to running a household and had a natural flair for getting on with staff. As for Olivia, I asked her to do me a favour, which was, that if necessary, would she arrange transport and accompany Hiram and Miriam if they wanted to go on a shopping trip perhaps to Marlow or High Wycombe. She would be a great help to them with any language or money problems and perhaps even stop for high tea. Eventually, Marlene joined us all in the kitchen looking as if she had just stepped off the front cover of *Vogue* magazine wearing a blouse and a two-piece suit over which she had a winter coat plus an ankle length pair of winter boots topped with fur. She exuded high octane glamour and such was her personality, that it was easy to see how she made all those within her orbit enthralled to the point of becoming some of her most devoted admirers. Whilst she was chatting with them all, I helped John carry the luggage out and load it into the boot of the car and to start the engine up so that the windows could be defrosted whilst I went back inside the house to fetch Marlene. It took several minutes for her to say goodbye to everybody. You wouldn't have thought that we were only going for one night, what with Miriam fussing whether Marlene had put clean handkerchiefs in her bag, Hiram being the doctor that he was, advising us not to drink too much (as if that's likely not to happen!) and Lucy and Mary hoping that there would be some news about it in tomorrow's papers. I finally got her into the back of the car with everybody crowded in the front door waving and shouting out have a good time as John finally pulled the car around to drive off down the drive and turned left into the main road and head for Denham in Berkshire.

Chapter 11

Citizenship

Despite the late November weather, it was still a pleasure to drive along the roads through Berkshire and Buckinghamshire. To me, these counties formed part of the fabric of the English countryside. At times, you could be driving along country roads with their hedgerows on either side and then just as suddenly, you would be driving on main arterial roads. When we passed through Windsor, I was able to point out to Marlene not only the castle, but Eton College as well and as luck would have it, she was able to see some of the boys from the school dressed in their black top hat and tails on the way to college. Then we drove on to Slough, finally arriving at Denham studios.

It was just after midday when we entered the main gates at Denham and as John swung the car up towards the main offices, I couldn't help but marvel at the sheer size of the studio complex. I'd read somewhere that only three years before, with the financial backing of a major British insurance company, Korda had purchased one-hundred and sixty acres of land right here in Denham. With the help of designer, Jack Oakey whom incidentally, I had met socially in Hollywood many years ago and who had just finished his completion of Paramount film studios, Korda had built a massive studio complex consisting of at least seven sound stages, dressing rooms, workshops and several restaurants, one of which was to be the venue for the after-wrap party. I had enjoyed the benefit of a short-term contract with Korda and had appeared in several films for him. Indeed, the next one was to be *Ali Baba* and having also worked for Louis B. Mayer, I was able to compare the two and Korda was certainly the equal in pursuing the same determined and ruthless quest for quality moviemaking.

Having waved John off, Marlene and I sauntered over to sound-stage number four where Tim had been re-shooting the ball sequence and where we joined a few technical staff waiting to go in. We had hardly had time to exchange pleasantries when the green light came on and we all trooped through onto the soundstage. I just had time to catch a glimpse of Merle hurrying from the set in the direction of her dressing room still dressed in her evening gown whilst the extras were slowly moving off, chatting amongst themselves in the opposite direction, towards the changing rooms. Seeing Tim Whelan, Harry Stradling and Jill, the continuity girl, in conversation, we walked over and joined them, stepping over the odd cable and dodging the occasional grip pushing a heavy klieg light.

"Well, hello, you two," Tim said, whilst giving Marlene a peck on the cheek, leaving me to introduce Marlene and Harry to each other. "You will be pleased to know, Gunther, that the film is finally finished. Harry is very pleased with the photographic composition of the ball scene, so all I have to do now is to supervise the editing and hope that Miklos Rozsa's music score will blend in perfectly with the storyline. Then, come next year, you and I will be working on *Ali Baba*, a project that I am really looking forward to. Alex Korda is due to arrive any time soon with his brother Vincent as well as Vivien Leigh and Larry Olivier, I know that you are aware that Larry is off to the United States to play Heathcliff in *Wuthering Heights* for Sam Goldwyn, but I bet you didn't know that Vivien will be joining him. Apparently, David Selznick wants to meet her with regard to playing Scarlet O'Hara. I have a feeling that she is going to beat Paulette Goddard to the winning post and get the part. I am sorry but I will have to temporarily leave you both as I have to tidy up a few loose ends. By the way, I forgot to mention to you both that there's been a change of venue for the party. It is now being held here on the ballroom set. The front office decided, in their wisdom, that as there was already a set standing for the ballroom sequence, we might just as well use it. As well as the band that they had already hired for the scene. Speak of the devil, I think that the caterers have just arrived which means our grips will start racing to get the studio equipment put away so that they can start laying out food. I am afraid that's my cue to leave you both as I've said, I have a few things to deal with before I join you at the party."

"Go right ahead, Tim. Marlene and I will walk over to Merle's dressing room for a gossip. I am quite envious of her, for she is going to be one of the main stars in one of Hollywood's biggest productions for next year. It will be interesting, as she will have Larry as her leading man who will be playing Heathcliff to her Cathy and if what you say is true, that Selznick is considering

Vivien favourite for the part of Scarlet O'Hara in *Gone with the Wind*, then I would imagine that once the Hollywood press get wind of Larry and Vivien's romance, then all hell will break loose and the pair of them will really be under the spotlight. Anyway, we won't hold you up any longer, Tim because we know you're busy. We'll catch you later."

We made our way slowly across the studio floor occasionally stopping to say hello to various people, in particular, one gentleman getting on in years by the name of Billy Brewster who it so happens, was my dresser and gopher and had been with me on all my English films in the past years. After introducing him to Marlene and having a general chat, we were just about to move on when I remembered that I had some good news to give him.

"By the way, Billy. I am glad we bumped into each other because I have something good to tell you. I know you'll be looking after me when I start *Ali Baba* next year, well it so happens that Gainsborough have had a problem with casting on their new film due to start in January and I have agreed to step in at the last moment. I'm wondering whether you will be available to look after me?" Billy's face lit up. He was what I would call one of the old-school theatre people. In the past, he had been part of a successful music hall comedy duo, but his partner had become a chronic alcoholic and the partnership had been dissolved and unfortunately as a consequence, Billy had fallen on hard times never having been given the opportunity to re-establish himself by finding himself a new partner or as a single act.

"You don't have to ask me twice, sir," he replied. "That's the best Christmas present I could have received. That extra job means that I will be able to give the missus a few extra luxuries this year. If I may ask, sir, will it be a period or modern film? I know that those period films can take a lot out of you, sir. What with all that fighting and leaping about that you must do, you must make sure that you look after your health." Marlene and I burst out laughing at his comments for as it happened, there was some truth in his observation, not so much from the health issue but that I was getting to that stage in life where I possibly should be looking for parts in the very near future more befitting to my age. In other words, it might be time to hang up my tights and as I patted him on the shoulder before moving on, I re-assured him.

''Don't worry, Billy, I'm not that old yet. I'm more in danger from those bottles of beer you keep bringing in. God knows where you get them from but they're strong enough to knock an elephant off his feet! Anyway Billy, it's a modern dress part and I'll be in touch with you before Christmas to confirm the start date and that Gainsborough will be including your name as part of the crew. Meanwhile, I'll see you later this afternoon for a drink and whatever you do, behave yourself and remember to keep your jokes clean. We don't want you offending any ladies.''

As it turned out, by the time we reached Merle's dressing room, she was unable to receive us as she was only halfway through changing into her everyday clothes, so rather than hang around getting in everybody's way, I decided to walk over with Marlene to the wardrobe department which I knew would be of great interest to her. She had, of course, been a visitor to quite a few film sets in the past but her visits had mainly been confined to the actual film set itself, so that the opportunity of visiting other parts of the studio intrigued her. When we did arrive at the wardrobe department, I was amused at the look of amazement on Marlene's face when she first saw rack upon rack of costumes representing the styles down through the ages. I don't think that she was expecting to see a warehouse filled to bursting.

Gemma Tyler, the wardrobe mistress was only too happy to show Marlene around. I was surprised, as we moved along the rows of racks, just how many films had been made by Alex Korda. Marlene was captivated by the costumes that had been made for them, in particular, *Things to Come*, *Fire over England*, *Knight without Armour*, *The Drum* and *The Private Life of Don Juan*, the latter starring the late Douglas Fairbanks senior. I had to drag her away from Marlene Dietrich's wardrobe for *Knight without Armour*, in particular, the fur hats which she insisted on trying on. She was fascinated by the costumes for the film, Henry VIII, noticing how heavy Charles Laughton's costumes were and she was enthralled by the colours of the dresses worn by his wives. In the end, we ran out of time such was Marlene's enjoyment, we had spent nearly an hour before we realised that we should start back for the party.

By the time Marlene and I had walked over to the set where the after-wrap party, which had begun officially at two o'clock, was being held, it was already beginning to get into full swing and apart from the cast and crew, guests and uninvited guests were already swelling the numbers. Trestle tables had been laid out with a variety of buffet foods and a drinks bar had also been installed which was already becoming busy, there was also the original four-piece band previously hired for the film, playing popular songs. Once I had collected drinks for Marlene and myself, we began to circulate amongst the visitors until suddenly, we came across Vivien Leigh and Larry Olivier, chatting with some fellow guests. Marlene, having recognised one of the group, immediately grabbed my hand and started pulling me over towards them exclaiming as we went.

"It's Ursula, darling, you know? One of my best friends, she had a part in that film last year, what was it called? Oh yes, I know, *Storm in a Teacup* with Viv and Rex Harrison, I have invited her and Roger to our New Year's Eve party.

It didn't take long to become part of the group swapping gossip and stories. They were all part of our circle of friends. Just to mention one, Tony Bushel, who had been in America at the same time as me. Tony had made a name for himself over there both on Broadway and in Hollywood, playing romantic second leads. Now that he was back in Britain, he appeared to be moving away from acting to getting behind the camera and concentrating on production. The other male in the group was not only a friend of ours but was also one of Britain's rising character actors for this generation. His name was Cecil Parker and he had just finished a film for Alfred Hitchcock titled, *The Lady Vanishes*. It just so happened that he had also appeared in the same film as Vivien and Ursula which had been filmed last year, namely, *Storm in a Teacup*. Cecil played either droll or pompous parts but off screen, he enjoyed a reputation within the industry for being a gifted raconteur.

Most of the conversation centred around the possibility of Vivien's chances of winning the part of Scarlet even though not only had she not had a screen test, but she hadn't even met David O. Selznick yet. Somehow, I sensed that she was made of sterner stuff and that she had set her heart on playing the role and that is exactly what would happen. As for Larry, it was obvious that he was deeply in love with Viv. Most of the time, they only had eyes for each other and there was no doubt that they made a very glamorous couple. Some time back, Larry had suggested that it would be a marvellous idea for me to play Iago to his Othello at the Old Vic and even to exchange roles. It was an exciting idea and I was all for it but so far, the opportunity to put it into practice had eluded us. Eventually, Marlene and I, both feeling hungry and in need of another drink, broke away from the group and made our way towards the buffet tables. While we were helping ourselves to a variety of canapes, I felt a hand on my back accompanied by a booming voice.

"Hey hoe, Gunther, you old Kraut! How have you been doing? How about you and your lovely wife joining Donald and myself for a drink?"

I turned and recognised Bobby Newton and to his side, another well-known character actor by the name of Donald Calthorpe, both of whom possessed larger-than-life personalities and prodigious appetites for booze. Bobby Newton, I suspect, was on the verge of becoming an alcoholic. He appeared to be able to keep it under control, as it never seemed to interfere with his work and there was no doubt that he was an impressive actor both on stage and in film. Poor Donald Calthorpe was an entirely different story. Only a few years back, he had been destined for a long career as a major film actor having already appeared in several Hitchcock films, when tragedy struck. I think it was at Shepperton film studios where he was filming and he had invited a young chorus girl by the name of Nita Foy up to his dressing room for a drink. Unfortunately, her flimsy dance costume caught fire when she brushed up against an electric heater, the result being that she died from massive burns and Donald having witnessed the horrific scene, never recovered from the experience. Not only did it cost him his marriage, but his career had never fully recovered its momentum. I was anxious not to become too involved with the pair of them as it was getting late and I really wanted to be back in London so that we would both have time to get ready for our dinner engagement, but Marlene had become deep in conversation with them both. That was something that I had noticed about her in the last few years, her rapport and understanding of other people's problems. She seemed to sense their inner turmoil. Maybe, this was due to the centuries-old persecution of her race.

"Come on, Gunther," Bobby Newton had bellowed at me, his features contorting with various expressions and his eyes rolling feverishly. The thought crossed my mind that one day, he would make a fine Captain Hook in *Peter Pan* or even Long John

Silver from *Treasure Island*, nevertheless that fine instrument of a voice that he possessed continued to boom out., I'm sure most of the studio must've heard it.

"Don and I would like the pleasure of taking our favourite couple up to the West End for dinner and a few drinks ..." Marlene, cutting him short whilst gently putting her finger to his lips, responded by telling him that if it been any other time, we would have loved to have joined them but unfortunately, we were committed to a dinner party with Alexander Korda that evening. Not only that, she went on to say with an impish smile, but she would have her hands full trying to keep three gorgeous men, one of whom was her husband, on the straight and narrow. I had to admire her for the way in which she handled them both without causing offence and although we stayed with them a little while longer, we parted company knowing full well that the pair of them would be painting the town red well into the early hours of tomorrow. As luck would have it, we came across Alexander Korda and his brother Zoltan appearing to be having a serious discussion with Tim Whalen whilst Merle stood nearby with Binny Barnes and the character actor, Morton Selten, obviously sharing and enjoying an amusing anecdote between the three of them. When Alex caught sight of us, he beckoned us over and after embracing Marlene on both cheeks, put his arm around my shoulders declaring in his thick Hungarian accent.

"Gunther, I must congratulate you. You have succeeded in delivering a great performance. Both you and Tim have performed miracles with a bit of fluff that undoubtedly will show a profit at the box office. I can tell you now that your next film, *Ali Baba,* is going to be really big. No expense will be spared. Not only will it be in colour, but I have also allocated a huge budget, particularly in the special effects department. Not only do I want this film to be better than *The Private Lives of Henry VIII,* but I also want it to be the equal of any Hollywood extravaganza. I will discuss this further with you later this evening. You will be interested to know that one of my guests tonight is a backbench Tory MP who is very keen to meet you. He has held high office in previous governments and has a reputation for being a firebrand. His name is Winston Churchill and currently, he is in the political wilderness because of his views on Hitler and the Nazis. In other words, he has been labelled a warmonger. I personally don't go along with that opinion. I think there's a limit to how far you can go with appeasement and right this moment, Britain needs a politician with some backbone. You will have to forgive me, Gunther, but Merle and I are about to leave so that we can make sure that the house is ready for you both and our other guests. By the way, how are you two getting back to London? Is your car waiting for you outside, Gunther, or are you going to hire a car?"

''No, Alex. I left it open with my chauffeur with an invite to the party here at the studio or to drive straight back to the house. Obviously, he has chosen the latter so I'm about to phone for a car to take us back to the Dorchester where we are staying overnight.''

''No need, Gunther. Merle and I will be more than happy to give you a lift back into town. My Rolls is parked up in the back lot ready to leave, so I won't have it any other way. You will get a lift back with us to the Dorchester during which time, we can have a chat about a few ideas that I have for some future projects. As an example, I am thinking of producing a remake of *Anna Karenina*, but this time, in colour and I think you will be ideal for the part of Count Alexei.''

We jumped at the opportunity of a lift and graciously accepted. After all, it's not every day that the boss not only offers you dinner but gives you a lift as well. I was not so sure about the part of Count Alexei. Although it certainly was a good part to be offered, there was a big difference in age between the character and myself with Alexei being considerably older. The one thing that has made me uncomfortable was watching younger actors being made to look old on-screen and it simply doesn't work. The camera was too analytical and never lied and therefore, destroyed the actor's credibility with his audience. Eventually, after having an official studio photograph of cast and crew taken, we made our way out of the studio and climbed into Korda's Rolls Royce and proceeded to set off for London.

It was an uneventful journey that was made considerably more relaxing by the well-stocked liquor bar that enabled the conversation to flow. I was particularly fascinated by Alex Korda's lament regarding his rival, J. Arthur Rank, who controlled most of film distribution in Britain with his chain of Gaumont and Odeon cinemas, leaving Korda's London Films just the ABC and Essoldo cinemas to exhibit his films. Also, to add further insult to injury, as far as Korda was concerned, Rank had built a studio at Iver Heath and named it Pinewood, thereby ensuring a supply of films for his chain of cinemas. He was particularly incensed by the logo that Rank had adopted for the introduction to his films, featuring prize fighter, bombardier Billy Wells striking a large gong with the announcement, 'J. Arthur Rank presents'. Korda felt that it was far too Americanised, unlike his own trademark of 'London Films presents' with the shot of Big Ben striking, which he felt, reflected the true values of Britain. I admired both these men and there was no doubt that they were the giants of the British film industry. Both shared the same dream which was to make London the equal of Hollywood. However, as I counted Alex Korda one of my friends as well as my employer, my sympathies lay entirely with him.

I had been in the film business far too long not to know its weaknesses and strengths and it was all quite simple really, money equalling art, equalling profit. The film moguls needed to produce the films that the public would pay to see. Far too often, the road to hell was paved with good intentions. Many a film project that looked a sure-fire money maker at the box office with a good script, a top-notch cast and a fine director, would prove a dud with the public, a cycle that repeated itself time and time again. Still, nobody knew the answer. That is why I sympathised with Korda. He was an individual producer with a studio that each year cost a fortune to maintain but was unable to produce the necessary number of films to break even. Not only that but the American film studios each owned their own chains of the cinemas as well, thus operating a closed shop to European film makers.

A light fog had descended over the capital as we reached Hyde Park Corner and thank goodness, it was nothing like the peasoupers that normally would reduce visibility in London to zero at this time of year. Once we had entered Park Lane, we were soon drawing up outside the Dorchester and as the hotel doorman, resplendent in his liveried overcoat and top hat, opened the passenger door for us to exit the car. Alex lent forward from the back seat and reminded us that dinner would be at eight-thirty before closing the car door and speeding off. As soon as we had been ushered through to the reception desk and identified ourselves, an assistant manager escorted us up to our suite. Our luggage had preceded us and had been unpacked and Marlene's dress and my dinner suit had been hung up. After enquiring whether there was anything else that we might need, the assistant manager excused himself and left and the door had no sooner closed behind him when Marlene commandeered the bathroom which was all right by me, as it would give me at least thirty minutes, if not more, to relax and have a cat nap. I must have been a little more tired than I thought, for the next thing I knew, Marlene was shaking my shoulder and telling me to get ready as time was getting on. It didn't take me long to have a shower and a quick shave and by the time I had finished looking for my cufflinks, Marlene had already applied her makeup and was ready to slip on her dress. I must admit that as she put the finishing touches to her ensemble with a white sable coat with a high collar which she proceeded to wear over her black sheath of an evening gown, she looked the epitome of glamour and sophistication. By the time we finally got down to the lobby and asked for a cab, all eyes were upon her and boy did she make the most of it.

It didn't take long to reach Alex Korda's house as it was only just around the corner. Located in a mews, it was one of several town houses which all had a similar outward façade and about three stories high and naturally, being Park Lane, looked very elegant. The front door was opened by a butler who bore a strong resemblance to the actor, Arthur Treacher, who I had last seen at the movies performing a dance with little Shirley Temple, the immensely popular child star of the thirties. After taking our coats, he proceeded to guide us through to the salon which, by now, was quite full. Upon seeing us enter, Alex and Merle broke away from their company and welcomed us. Merle was another extremely beautiful woman who possessed both a touch of exotic mystery about her coupled with a commanding presence. We had now worked together on two films, one of which had only just been completed this very day and the other was the aborted *I Claudius* and she had my total respect, for despite her love affair with Alex, she was a major film star in her own right. Unlike so many other talented and beautiful girls, she had seized whatever opportunities that had come her way and obviously Korda, not only admired her beauty but adored her. There was certainly no doubting that, for he had been totally involved in launching her Hollywood career.

As we were introduced to our fellow guests, I recognised many of them. Eric Maria Remarque was the internationally acclaimed author of the magnificent anti-war novels *All Quiet on the Western Front, The Way Back* and *Three Comrades*. He was, at present, living in exile with his wife, Zambona and because of his anti-war stance, his books had been publicly burnt and forbidden in Nazi Germany, hence his taking up residence in Switzerland. Next, I was introduced to Louise Rainer and her husband, Clifford Odets. Louis was a screen actress and winner of the Oscar for Best Actress in two consecutive years for her roles in *The Great Ziegfeld* and *The Good Earth*. I was not over-familiar with Clifford's work, but I was aware that he had a growing reputation in America as a left-wing playwright, espousing the cause of the working man. He was also a supporter of communism. Two of his plays had caught my attention. The first was *Waiting for Lefty*, written in praise of the working man's right to union representation, in this instance, taxi drivers. Secondly, his play, *Golden Boy* was an expose on corruption in the boxing world. Another guest that I was unfamiliar with, was Prince Hubertus Wertheim Freudenberg, an historian and politician and his wife, the Princess Helga Maria. They too were living in exile, refugees of Hitler's policies. The other two guests were politicians, the first was of medium height and bald with a cherubic face and his striking-looking wife by the name of Clementine. This, of course, was Winston Churchill whom I had heard so much about, a maverick backbencher in the House of Commons who had no liking for Adolf Hitler.

The first thing he mentioned to me after the introductions was that our paths had nearly crossed way back in the twenties when he had gone out to Hollywood and stayed at Pickfair as a guest of Douglas Fairbanks and Mary Pickford. In fact, he distinctly remembered the making of *Robin Hood* with Fairbanks and Charlie Chaplin clowning around on the set for the benefit of the press. Now that he had mentioned it, I did remember at that time, the Los Angeles daily papers were full of his visit for he was, after all, a British celebrity, having been made famous during the Boar War for his daring escape as a prisoner of war and having also served in the British government during the Great War. I also remember having received an invitation to attend a party in his honour at Charlie Chaplin's house but unfortunately, had fallen ill and had been unable to attend.

The other guest who, as it turns out, was also Minister of State for War in the present government was introduced to me as the Right Honourable Leslie Hore-Belisha and his lovely companion who it so happened I knew, Jacqueline Delubac, a

French actress. Earlier in the evening, whilst driving to the Dorchester, Korda had given Marlene and myself a short history on Belisha. Prior to his appointment into the government, Leslie Hore-Belisha had been Minister of Transport and had introduced the now famous Belisha Beacons which allowed pedestrians to be able to cross major roads without fear of injury from traffic. However, the main thrust of Alex's conversation was that the poor chap was being given a hard time by the top brass of the army and certain MPs in the House of Commons for being a Jew and that he was using his position as Minister of War to invoke a crisis with Germany because of Hitler's anti-Semitic policies. Naturally, Hitler had wasted no time in accusing the British government of being in the hands of international Jewry. The last guest was the newspaper tycoon, Lord Slade and his wife, Alice. The newspaper magnate's publishing empire consisted of several major daily newspapers, all right wing in their political views and many weekly and monthly magazines. He was a very influential man and was certainly powerful enough to make or break a prime minister.

As the evening progressed, there was no doubt that Alex Korda and Merle Oberon complemented each other very well as host and hostess and everything about the dinner was superb; the wines, the food and the service were all above reproach and Merle certainly stage-managed it brilliantly. It was no secret that they had been a couple for some time. Alex had been grooming Merle for stardom since 1936 and having achieved that objective, it was obvious they would marry. However, there had been no official announcement of any intending nuptials but there were plenty of rumours flying around that suggested that Alex and Merle would marry very soon.

After the dessert had been concluded and the plates cleared away, the ladies retired to the salon leaving us menfolk to our brandies and cigars. It was inevitable that politics would enter the conversation and sure enough, Clifford Odets posed the question as to how long it would take Europe to wake up to Hitler's lust for territorial gains. After all, he had successfully helped General Franco to destroy democracy in Spain, as well as having seized Austria after a phony plebiscite, marched into the Sudetenland and now, had designs on Czechoslovakia with presumably Poland following on soon after. He finished the question with another, as to when was the supine League of Nations was going to fulfil its mandate for the protection of native inhabitants? He went on to refer to the conquest of Ethiopia by Mussolini and Hitler's cleansing of the Jewish communities within Germany's borders.

Churchill answered by saying that he had been one of the few voices advocating a stronger position against Nazi Germany but unfortunately, the seam of appeasement ran deep through the political establishments of both France and Britain and if neither country was prepared to honour their treaty obligations, then Hitler would continue to gain bloodless victory after bloodless victory. The sad truth was that after the Great War of 1914, neither country had any enthusiasm for any further military adventures that would require spilling of the blood of their countrymen. However, he went on, like all gangsters, Hitler would eventually overreach himself, forcing France and Britain to stand up to him. The tragedy was that if we did it now, the sacrifice would be small but if we left too late, we would pay a very heavy price indeed.

Hore-Belisha interjected into the conversation, remarking that the general staff of both Britain and France had no enthusiasm for a potential military action and that now, even he had come around to the view that we must strengthen our armed forces. Despite his ministerial position, his efforts were being thwarted by strong resistance from the general staff. Unfortunately, as Winston rightly pointed out, there was a deep seam of appeasement running through not only the government but the upper classes as well. Hore-Belisha confirmed that he never thought for one moment when he accepted the post that it would be easy. However, he had not banked on the vicious anti-Semitism that was personally directed at him, particularly from the general staff of the army and the ruling classes of the nation. Once again, it was the ordinary people of the country who showed the most common sense and certainly a spirit of fair play. One only had to look at how just recently, a large percentage of the public had seen off Sir Oswald Mosley and his black shirts from the East End of London and interrupted his rally at Earls Court. Hore-Belisha continued his train of thought by remarking that it had been wrongly assumed that Anthony Eden had resigned his position as Foreign Secretary because he was firmly against appeasement. Unfortunately, that wasn't the case at all but instead involved simple protocol issues between Mussolini and Britain over Spain and the Mediterranean.

At the end of a long debate over European politics, the general consensus around the table was that eventually, military intervention would be the only option available to prevent Hitler from further conquests and despite Winston Churchill's misgivings about Stalin and his communist regime, that it might be wise for both Britain and France to seek a rapprochement with Russia rather than to keep them at arm's-length and in a state of isolation. The final discussion of the evening concerned the persecution of the Jews and Britain's reluctance to increase the quota of Jewish immigrants allowed into the country. It was at that point that Lord Slade broke into the conversation by stating that it would be madness for Britain to allow unlimited immigration into the country. Since 1933, there has been a huge increase in Jewish refugees and the danger was that unless we maintained a strict quota, our social structures would start to collapse under the volume of immigrants arriving in our country, regardless of whether they were political or economic. There was also something else to consider, that with the injection of so many foreign cultures the British way of life could also be threatened. It was just incomprehensible that Britain would risk peace by offending Hitler simply because he was a strong leader.

It was during this discussion that Merle poked her head around the dining room door to see if we needed anything else which was an obvious signal for us to join the ladies. Even when we had joined our partners, Lord Slade persisted in his argument against the so-called warmongers in Britain and their attempt to interfere with Hitler's internal policies. Marlene picked up on the thread of his conversation and after listening to him for a little while longer, interrupted his monologue. She began by saying that Lord Slade was entitled to his opinion, but he did not know the facts. He had obviously been misinformed, for Hitler was not a strong democratic leader but a ruthless dictator who had successfully destroyed all opposition by placing his opponents in concentration camps where they were either beaten into submission or murdered. Then, with his obsession for a master race, Hitler had quietly targeted the mentally ill with a programme of euthanasia and at the same time, began herding German Jews into ghettos and denying them the rights of German citizens as well as forbidding them to work in their chosen professions and as if all that wasn't enough, he had successfully, apart from a handful of courageous pastors, brought the Catholic and Lutheran churches to heel. Having put the German house in order, so to speak, it was logical that he now required more living space for the master race that he had created. It was only natural that he would destroy a democratic Austria and incorporate it into the greater German Reich and do likewise to the German Sudetenland. It didn't take much imagination to see that the remainder of Czechoslovakia would soon be gobbled up by Hitler and to be followed by Poland perhaps? Meanwhile, those refugees who had been fortunate enough to reach Britain had not only brought doctors, scientists and leading figures in all the arts but also the teachers, the builders and the shopkeepers, all of whom wanted to work and contribute to society. How did she know all this you may ask? Well quite simply, she was a Jewish refugee herself and but for her husband who had stood by her as a Gentile and sacrificed his country of birth, she and her parents would be in Berlin living in a ghetto and by law, would have to wear the Star of David on their clothes identifying them as members of what Hitler and his party defined as a subhuman race. Perhaps Lord Slade wasn't aware that there were Jewish veterans from the 1914 war who had fought with distinction for their country, such as her father, who was the proud bearer of the Iron Cross First Class and who had now been reduced to living in ghettos, stripped of their civil rights. It seemed such a pity that Lord Slade, whom from her first impressions of that evening had appeared to be an erudite and pleasant gentleman, could not instigate through his papers an enlightened immigration policy that offered a safe haven to these victims of persecution.

When she finally stopped for breath, not only was there a round of applause from her fellow guests, but even Winston Churchill stood up and rumbled, "Hear, hear." Lord Slade and his wife sat looking rather uncomfortable, as no doubt, they were not often spoken to in such a forthright manner. I realised then that I would never ever get a good review published again from the Slade publishing empire and certainly, somewhere down the road, I would expect one of his columnists to write an unsubstantiated expose piece about Marlene and myself. But what the hell. I was proud of my girl for standing up against ignorance and prejudice.

The remainder of the evening was spent in discussing the more important feminine issues of the day such as, gossip, fashion and the theatre. Most of the women wanted to hear from Merle what Gary Cooper was like off-camera and who did she consider was her favourite leading man from all her films? She replied that she didn't really have a favourite but the three that she enjoyed working with, were myself (she would say that wouldn't she!) Gary Cooper and Joel McCrea. There were times in the latter part of the evening when I was slightly embarrassed. Unfortunately, there were some subjects that when discussed, became very animated, so it was understandable when Louise Rainer, Eric Remarque, Marlene and me, would lapse into our native tongue becoming oblivious to our English-speaking friends. Fortunately, Alex, who also spoke fluent German, reminded us of our bad manners by gently pointing out that not everybody spoke German.

As the evening wound down, with most of the guests having already left, Winston Churchill, who had been in a conversation with Alex, beckoned Marlene and myself over to them and once again, congratulated Marlene on her forthright views whilst Clementine Churchill patted Marlene's hand, exclaiming how impressed she had been with Marlene's independent opinion. Winston Churchill's last words to me before his cab's arrival had been announced, were that if I was agreeable, he would like to meet us both again soon, perhaps at the House of Commons, where he would be delighted to show us around that ancient symbol of democracy. Perhaps, after Christmas, we could both spend the weekend as the guests of Clemmie and himself at his beloved Chartwell House. If the idea appealed to me and Marlene, maybe I could get in touch with him at the House of Commons so that he could arrange some specific dates. Marlene and I were delighted to accept his invitation and told him we looked forward with eager anticipation.

After the Churchill's had departed, it just left Marlene and me. As we waited for our cab, we sat and chatted with Alex and Merle where most of the conversation was taken up with my up-and-coming fantasy film that Alex was producing and Merle's impending departure across the Atlantic to Hollywood to commence filming Goldwyn's *Wuthering Heights*. I was somewhat intrigued by Alex's conspiratorial body language as Merle and Marlene walked ahead to our cab waiting outside, stopping for a moment and speaking in a low voice, Alex told me that there was a possibility that events in Europe would come to a head and that Neville Chamberlain, the present Conservative Prime Minister would stake his reputation and office on preserving peace at all costs and if he should fail in that endeavour, the man to watch would be Winston Churchill. I was somewhat taken aback, for I hadn't realised how far Alex had come in being accepted within the establishment, to be privy to such confidences. Neither had I been aware of his involvement in politics. As we stood on the doorstep, we thanked Merle and Alex for a wonderful evening and wished Merle good luck on her new film and looked forward to seeing them both in the future. Alex Korda's final words to us were to keep our chins up for we were not alone in our fight to help persecuted minorities.

The following morning, after having phoned the house to ask John to come and pick us up, Marlene and I vacated our suite and whilst waiting for John to arrive, decided to have coffee downstairs in the main lobby. I had been feeling guilty since my last conversation with Xavier Jurgens and the fact that I had deliberately kept it from Marlene with the best of intentions, especially the threats that he had made concerning the remainder of her family in Germany. Keeping secrets from Marlene did not sit well with me. I felt as if I was betraying her and I realised now that bad news shared together was far easier to deal with than hiding it away. I also had to consider Marlene's parents who were equally entitled to any knowledge regarding the well-being of their own parents. I made the decision to tell her there and then holding both her hands in mine I went on to explain.

"I never told you, Marlene, the content of the last conversation that I had with Xavier Jurgens. It seems that we were only one step ahead of his masters in Berlin in extricating your parents from Germany and that they were far from happy at the outcome. Jurgens made it quite plain that they would not make the same mistake twice and that your grandparents were now on a special list of people who would not be granted exit visas and neither would any other members of your family still living in Germany. I kept it from you because I didn't want to spoil your happiness at your parents' safe arrival in Britain. I am afraid that being who I am looks like it has worked against your grandparents and I feel guilty for that reason. All we can do now is to wait until things either settle down or Hitler gives way to international censure."

"Oh, Gunther, you can be so silly sometimes. Mama and papa have been aware of this situation for quite a few days. Papa had a contact number and had used it to let them know that Mama and he had arrived safely. It was then that they had told him that they were under house arrest and could only go out to obtain supplies. However, they told him not to be unduly alarmed as they were physically all right. Through my contacts within the fashion industry, I have arranged for small sums of money to be delivered to them from time to time ensuring that they won't want for anything. So, you see, Gunther, you have been worrying unnecessarily. We have learnt to live with the situation and pray for things to improve. We never told you because we didn't want to worry you either and as Papa said, you've already done more than enough for the family, so let's put everything to one side and look forward to our forthcoming British citizenship and Christmas."

Our first engagement before Christmas was the most important one for both of us and that was the ceremony of citizenship. Marlene and I opted for Kensington Town Hall to take our oath of nationalisation which was conducted by the mayor and some councillors of the Kensington Borough. The proceedings consisted of the ceremony of citizenship and the oath of allegiance. Apart from the dignitaries present, we could bring two guests. We chose Olivia and Robin Cox and as we filed into the chamber, we were offered light refreshments which we thought was a nice gesture not knowing exactly how long the swearing-in would be. In fact, it lasted just over thirty minutes at the end of which, we collected our certificates, presented in the form of scrolls. It was fortunate that unless otherwise tipped off, the press did not normally bother to cover that type of event, as the last thing that Marlene and I wanted were newshounds and flashing photographers intruding upon a private moment in our lives. As it was, it was a great feeling to be mingling with other newly granted British citizens, all excitingly chattering with family or friends in either fractured or fluent English. Even the mayor was circulating wearing his chain of office adding a touch of history to the occasion and from time to time, someone would approach me asking me for an autograph which I was more than happy to give.

Considering how special the occasion was, I added a few extra words to the autograph so that perhaps later, down the years, it would bring back happy memories to the recipients. For all said and done, we were embarking on a new journey and even Olivia dabbed her eyes before giving us both a hug whilst Robin embraced Marlene and shook my hand telling me with a twinkle in his eye, as I was now a pukka Englishman, he would have to find me extra work to pay for my additional tax liabilities.

Having bid our farewells to all concerned, the four of us left the town hall and proceeded up Kensington High Street to where John had parked our car down a side street alongside Derry and Toms, the famous Kensington departmental store, which Robin informed us, had just opened their rooftop gardens. That piece of news gave me the opening to suggest that as it had just gone midday, now would be a good opportunity to visit the rooftop garden and have a light lunch at the same time. Having made that decision, Marlene gave me a knowing look. Since the day we first met, we had been capable of anticipating each other's thoughts, so it was no surprise to me that after giving me a kiss on the cheek, she told us to wait a few minutes while she walked to the car. I knew what she was about, for sure enough, she soon returned with John beside her as I sensed that she would. John shook my hand rigorously whilst congratulating the both of us on becoming British citizens. He suggested that he would wait in the car until we were ready to leave but I wasn't about to have any nonsense and I told him so. This was mine and Marlene's moment and we both wanted to share it with those closest to us, so whether he liked it or not, he was coming to lunch with us.

So, that is how we spent our first hours as Britishers, walking around Derry and Toms' rooftop gardens in a cold October climate, admiring the arches and pathways surrounding the trees, the flower beds and the pond, after which, we descended to the restaurant and had a light lunch finished off with two bottles of champagne to celebrate the occasion. The downside to being famous, not that I had any regrets on that score, was that I could never linger too long in a public place without eventually attracting attention. So, quite soon, we had to call time on a memorable occasion and leave. Robin parted company with us on leaving the departmental store as he had an afternoon of business meetings to fulfil and turning down our offer of a lift, said it would be far easier and quicker to take the tube rather than to take a taxi or accept a lift from us with the way London traffic was these days. As we watched him walk up to Kensington High Street tube station, he turned towards us as he was about to enter and gave us a wave. We would, however, see him later in the evening, for not only would he be a guest at our party, but he and his wife would be stopping over for the night.

We needed to start back to lend support to Lucy and Bill who would be supervising the outside caterers in laying out the cold buffet. The company responsible would have been there most of the morning, erecting the marquee and furnishing it with tables and chairs as well as ensuring that it would be suitably heated. The caterers realising that it was the month of October and cold, had sensibly erected a tunnel connecting the house to the marquee, ensuring that the guests remained warm as they passed backwards and forwards. Marlene had planned it all, including the hiring of a few girls from the village for temporary waitressing and the preparation of four bedrooms for some of our guests. The remainder would either be staying at the Complete Angler or driving home afterwards. I dare-say that there would be one or two who would end up sleeping on the downstairs couches.

Once we had arrived back at Falcon House, the remainder of the afternoon sped by in the blink of an eye. Everybody concerned had worked wonders whilst we had been in London, particularly Bill and Lucy who had worked in tandem with the caterers to produce a stunning looking marquee, lit by Chinese lanterns reflecting a warm glow against the colour scheme of old rose and copper. As I have mentioned before, I had the good fortune to have a very astute business manager by the name of Geoffrey Halifax to represent my interests in the commercial world, who on receiving an invitation to our citizenship party, had promptly joined forces with Robin to approach the champagne company, Moet and Chandon, to broker a successful deal. In return for advertising their product, I would not only receive a substantial fee, but they would also supply a champagne bar with a heavily discounted supply of champagne for the evening's event. For some music, Robin had engaged a young Trinidadian by the name of Edmundo Ross who was just beginning to make a name for himself in the music world with a recently formed band that specialised in calypso and Latin American music.

Marlene and I had barely enough time to get changed before the guests started arriving. The first were Robin and his wife Rebecca, quickly followed by close business associates such as Joe Bloomstock and friends and other colleagues from the theatrical profession. As an example, girlfriends such as Ursula Jeans and her husband, Roger Liversey, Margaret Lockwood and Lilli Palmer. As a bonus, I had been keeping a surprise secret from Marlene. Whilst we had been in London, I had arranged for Greta and her husband Philip to travel from Holland and they had arrived at the house early that afternoon, where at present, they were secreted away in the cottage with Hiram and Miriam, awaiting my signal to spring the surprise on Marlene. Gradually, the downstairs part of the house began to fill up with arriving guests giving us the opportunity to take the first arrivals through to the marquee where Marlene and I positioned ourselves at the entrance to greet everyone whilst leaving Bill with backup from John and Mary to usher them through the connecting tunnel.

When I spied the film composer, Miklos Rozsa and his companion, Margaret Finlayson, walking towards us, I gave Olivia the nod to fetch Marlene's family from the cottage. Meanwhile, we spent a few minutes chatting with Miklos who, incidentally, had worked on several of my previous films and was about to write the film score for my next one, *Ali Baba*. Though Miklos was Hungarian by birth, he was still a refugee from Hitler's Germany which was where I had originally met him. You could say that along with Peter Lorre and Billy Wilder, we were part of the Berlin crowd during those early years. The trouble with Miklos was that one got the feeling that he felt composing for the cinema was slightly beneath him and that his true love was classical music. Unfortunately, as we all had learnt, if you wanted to put bread on the table and enjoy some of the good things in life, you had to learn to take the studio shilling.

I would probably have paid a king's ransom just for the look on Marlene's face as she saw her sister walking towards her. Within seconds, they had fallen into each other's arms crying and laughing at the same time whilst I grabbed hold of Phillip's hand and pulled him towards me for a hug. Obviously, with so much to catch up on, I told Marlene to grab a table for her family and I would join them as soon as I had welcomed the remainder of the late arrivals with the help of Olivia. Meanwhile, Edmundo Ros was creating a party atmosphere with a Carmen Miranda number called *Camista Listada*. Very soon, the marquee began to generate a cacophony of sound and movement, both the buffet tables, champagne bar and the drinks bar were hives of activity and from where I was standing with Olivia, I could see that the poor waitresses had their work cut out, delivering trays of champagne to the various tables. As I was about to call it a day and join our table, who should suddenly make a grand entrance but none other than Marlene Dietrich, swathed in furs and looking uber glamorous. Whenever Marlene and I held a social evening, it was inevitable that we issued La Dietrich with an open invitation, purely on the basis that she never knew where she would be half the time. However, as she was another old friend from the Berlin set of the twenties and early thirties, it was always a joy to meet up with her.

"Darling Gunty," she said in that famous husky voice, as I kissed her on both cheeks. "May I introduce you to my travelling companion, Mercedes de Acosta. My secretary told me of your invitation and as we were already on our way to Rome, I decided to stop off in London and come and visit you. You know, Mercedes, I never understood why this gorgeous hunk and I never had an affair. I think our friendship got in the way and now it is too late for I would never be able to compete with that beautiful wife of his. By the way Gunty, where is Marlene?"

"She is sitting over there at the table with her family. I have just surprised her by re-uniting her with her sister. We have so much to talk about you and I. Why don't you and Mercedes grab a glass of champagne and wander over to Marlene's table and say hello and I will join you very shortly."

I watched her making progress towards our table being greeted left and right by such luminaries as Cole Porter, Jack Buchanan, Cedric Hardwicke and Sir C. Aubrey Smith. I was very fond of La Dietrich but not necessarily of some of her lifestyle choices, which I found, perhaps selfishly, I was uncomfortable with. She was, in many ways, very similar to Greta Garbo with whom I had co-starred with in several silent films. She too, represented a new age of independent woman projecting a mysterious aura of sexuality not only in her persona but also the way she dressed, crossing over from female to male attire from time to time and was not above having affairs with both male and female partners, hence Mercedes presence there at the party.

Once Marlene and I had dispensed with our duties as hosts, we were able to relax and it turned out to be a great night. We had, officially, invited sixty guests but I'm pretty sure we ended up with at least seventy. Edmundo Ros was worth every penny of his fee creating a very relaxed atmosphere and the dance floor was constantly in use. The caterers had fed everybody very well, Moet and Chandon had kept the champagne flowing and I didn't run out of liquor, thank God. However, the piece de resistance was persuading La Dietrich to sing *Falling in Love Again* accompanied by Cole Porter on the piano which brought a standing ovation from all of us in the marquee and finally, that part of the evening was rounded off by the companion of Cole Porter, who went by the name of Monty Woolley.

I knew very little about this man, other than that he was the son of a very wealthy New York family and had a part-time career as a character actor. Also, he was a close friend and confidant of Cole, which explains why he was here tonight. He had a commanding presence, was well built with grey hair and moustache and beard. His intellect was equally as impressive supported by a lightning, rapier wit. Therefore, it came as a complete surprise to Marlene and me when he got up on the stage and on behalf of the guests, thanked us both and the staff for a wonderful night. He then went on to deliver a very witty speech on our achieving British citizenship and at one stage, brought the house down by suggesting that should we ever return to Hollywood, we could eventually outrank Sir C. Aubrey Smith as Lord and Lady Conrad, governor of the Hollywood Raj.

Olivia had had the foresight to book rooms at the Complete Angler in Marlow for forty guests and had arranged the coach to ferry them from the house to the hotel, otherwise, I am sure we would have been going all night and into the following day. It was only after the band had played its last number and departed that we were able, with some difficulty, to get the twenty couples onto the coach. Marlene's parents had thrown the towel in earlier on and retired to bed so that eventually, it left just a mere dozen of us sitting at one table whilst around us the catering crew were packing up the tables and clearing away the debris of the night. I had no idea what time they'd get back to their prospective homes, but I know Marlene had made sure that they spared time in which to help themselves to food and as well, thanks to Moet and Chandon, a few bottles of champagne.

It seems to be a fact, that if you put a group of actors together, they will inevitably either talk about themselves or talk shop such was the case tonight. La Dietrich started the conversation by informing us all that she had recently been voted box office poison by the American Film Distributors and on her return to the United States, she was going to start on her first film in two years.

"Believe it or not, darlings," she said, "All I have been offered is the part of a saloon bar madam in a western to be shot at Universal studios, of all places. One of the main reasons for accepting the part is the fact that gorgeous Jimmy Stewart will be my co-star." Listening to this, Sir Cedric Hardwick gave a chuckle, replying that he too, was leaving very shortly, to start work with the actor, Spencer Tracy, in a film that told the story of the explorer and missionary, Dr Livingstone and the newspaper reporter Henry Morton Stanley, sent out to Africa to locate him. Cedric told Marlene Dietrich not to be too concerned, as in his opinion, God felt sorry for actors, so he created Hollywood to give them a place in the sun and a swimming pool and the only price they had to pay was the surrender of their talent. "Mark my words, Marlene," he finished by saying, "Hollywood being Hollywood, in all probability, this little Western you're going to make will turn out to be the smash hit of the year and you will become the sensational new Marlene Dietrich."

Cole Porter and Marlene Dietrich had already decided that they would be driving back to the Savoy Hotel in London with their companions. I had nothing but admiration for the pair of them, for between them, they personified the very words sophistication and glamour. Marlene and I walked them out to their Rolls-Royce where the chauffeur was waiting patiently for them and after a flurry of farewells, stood and waved them goodbye as they sped down the drive and vanished into the night. The remaining few of us left congregated in the lounge for one last nightcap or two. Cedric and his wife Helena were the first to say goodnight and retire upstairs followed soon after by Maggie Lockwood and her husband Rupert Leon. Miklos remained for a little while longer, mainly because we all reverted to speaking in German.

The conversation revolved around the uncertainty of being Jewish and living in Europe. Miklos somewhat surprised me by informing us that as soon as his contractual agreement with Korda had expired towards the end of next year after the completion of his music score for *Ali Baba*, he would take up the offer from Hollywood to work at MGM. Eventually, he and Margaret also retired for the night after thanking us for the wonderful party. There was a sense of unease lurking at the back of my mind. Occasionally, I felt like a wild animal sensing danger in the wind and not sure of the form that it would take. Many of my friends from the old country were responding to the call of America and leaving. With the responsibilities that I had, I too, began to feel vulnerable. There was only four of us left now. Marlene and her sister Greta, Philip her husband and I just talked mainly about their life in Amsterdam which seemed pretty good for them.

Despite Phillip's family having lost their German business to the Nazis, they still had considerable assets in Holland and they were able to live in a peaceful and liberal environment. Unfortunately, Peter said Holland did have a home-grown Nazi Party under the leadership of a Dutchman by the name of Anton Mussert, yet another far right extremist, who was attempting to stir up political unrest with the usual Nazi propaganda about how the Jews must be controlled and that Holland should ally itself with Germany rather than France and Britain. Marlene was particularly forthright with her sister, telling Greta and her husband that they should seriously consider leaving Holland with whatever assets they had and either emigrate to Britain or America before Europe succumbed to Hitler's domination over the next few years. Greta and Philip felt that we were both unduly alarmed, as the combined military might of Britain, France, Poland, Holland and Belgium would keep Hitler firmly in his place. But as Marlene pointed out, it wasn't the military strength that would be the deciding factor but whether the Allied leaders would have the political courage to outwit Hitler and eventually defeat him. She was adamant enough in her beliefs to ask Greta and Philip to promise her that they would consider giving serious thought to emigrating. On that serious note, we ended what had been a momentous day for us, one filled with magical memories that would live with us for the rest of our lives.

The remaining weeks of 1938 were filled from one day to the next with either social or professional activities. The first major event was putting the Christmas tree up in the lounge and decorating it from top to bottom with Christmas baubles and fairy lights, a mission the ladies of the house eagerly took part in. When they had finished with the tree, they proceeded to work on the adjoining ground floor rooms, eventually turning them into a winter wonderland, before moving on to the cottage, to add a touch of Christmas cheer there. Greta and Philip gave in to Marlene's entreaties and decided to stay on through Christmas and New Year, a decision that brought great happiness to Hiram and Miriam who were now more confident within themselves after their initial arrival in Britain and now that their youngest daughter and her husband had decided to spend the Christmas season with them, Falcon House came alive.

Everybody was constantly entering and exiting with Marlene taking her family on sightseeing tours of London and in between, Hiram was learning to drive on the left-hand side of the road in preparation for gaining his British driving licence and Miriam, having been welcomed with open arms by the concert world, was already booked to perform a selection of operatic arias for one night in January at the Wigmore Hall in London. As far as work was concerned, the only two commitments that I had this side of Christmas were for the BBC Home Service drama department for two plays to be broadcast in the New Year. Both were adaptations of novels. The first one was *Little Women* in which I was to play the character of Professor Bauer and the second was to be *Murder on the Orient Express* in which I had been cast as Hercules Poirot. The remaining weeks of the year were mine to do as I pleased, so Marlene and I took the opportunity to spend as much time with the family as the opportunity presented itself with Greta and Philip now guests over the Christmas period.

I had scaled back on my social engagements apart from those that extended their invites to cover Marlene's family as well, preferring all of us to spend quality time as a family in the privacy of our home. We spent Christmas Eve and Christmas Day mucking in together giving the staff an opportunity to spend Christmas with their own families apart from Olivia who, having no dependants of her own, was always included as part of our family at holiday times. Christmas this year was the happiest that I had spent so far and I am sure the same applied to Marlene. The girls had taken over the kitchen completely, making it their headquarters for all operations regarding food. Olivia was put in charge of front of house, responsible for the dining room whilst we three men were responsible for the drinks, lighting the fires and moving the furniture around as required.

Marlene had booked a transatlantic phone call to her brothers in Tampa, Florida so that she and the whole family could wish the festive season's greetings to Hansi and Lothar. However, because of Florida being five hours behind us, she had booked it for two o'clock Christmas Eve and dutifully, at the given time, we all crowded around the telephone as the call was connected. The brothers were doing well at university, consistently achieving high grades in their chosen subjects of aerodynamics and were, at present, working on a thesis regarding interplanetary rocketry. It sounded like something out of an H. G. Wells novel and they also had part-time jobs at a restaurant called Harvey's to supplement their income. It was an emotional phone call but one of a happy nature, for when we ended the call, it was generally agreed that the brothers had landed on their feet and were doing well.

Come Christmas morning, after the women had spent important time doing the preparation for our Christmas lunch, we all sat in the lounge eating toast and marmalade and drinking champagne cocktails whilst opening our Christmas presents. My gift to Marlene was a pair of diamond earrings while in return, she presented me with a leather-bound edition of Omar Khayyam's *Tales of Arabian Nights*. By the time we had finished unwrapping the gifts and gathered up all the wrapping paper, midday was almost upon us. So, whilst the girls retreated to the kitchen, we mere males put on our winter coats and trudged along to the Dog and Badger for a quick pint. It was a crisp morning with a thin layer of snow on the ground and when we arrived at the pub, there was a fire merrily blazing away in the saloon bar and the landlord had placed some bowls of diced cheese and peanuts on the bar top for his customers. The bar was reasonably full, mostly with refugee males having escaped from sundry kitchens up and down the village. We didn't have long to down a couple of pints as the landlord only had a special Christmas Day licence for two hours after which he was closed for the rest of the day. Two pints of Courage best bitter had the desired effect of giving the three of us a great sense of well-being. There was even some talk of having a third pint, but discretion became the best part of valour when we considered the dual force of female power and food confronting us, so we opted for a small whiskey and were soon merrily on our way home.

The first thing to hit us as I opened the front door was the delicious aroma of roast turkey coming from the dining room followed by a procession of the womenfolk carrying bowls of vegetables, roast and creamed potatoes. There was a general stampede for the dining room and as we entered, we could see that Olivia had done her work well. The table was aglow from the colours of the China and the charges upon which the plates sat. The crystal wine glasses were shimmering in the light of the log fire and the turkey was sitting upon a silver salver patiently waiting for me to commence slicing and to finish the setting off, were Rosewood candelabra, aglow with candles with bases covered in holly and berries. Scattered around the table were gaily covered Christmas crackers.

Taking my place at the head of the table, I said a short prayer of thankfulness for what we were about to receive and as I was about to pick up the carving knife and fork, Hiram began chanting in Yiddish, something that I presumed to be a prayer with the rest of the family joining in, leaving Olivia and myself sitting in respectful silence until it was time for me to start carving the turkey. The walk to the pub and back in the fresh air had given us menfolk a sizeable appetite so it didn't take long with the help of the ladies for the turkey to be demolished and as soon as we had all got second wind, we formed a human chain ferrying dirty dishes and leftovers to the kitchen. Once the task had been completed, Marlene ordered us, apart from Philip, to return to the dining room and once we were all seated, she reappeared with Philip carrying a dish upon which sat a flaming Christmas pudding accompanied by a sauce boat filled with brandy sauce. As she placed the pudding on the table, she received a spontaneous round of applause whereupon she proceeded in serving helpings out to everybody and as there were no refusals, the dish was soon emptied.

It had been a magnificent Christmas lunch and when the grandfather clock in the hall struck two-thirty, it gave us all the opportunity to help clear the table and stretch our legs before the

King's speech at three o'clock. As soon as the King had delivered his speech to the nation, we all cleaned the kitchen up, after which those of us who were brave enough, wrapped ourselves up in coats and scarves and took a brisk walk down to the river's edge inhaling the crisp winter's air into our lungs. We had brought some stale buns with us which Marlene proceeded to break into small pieces to throw into the water. Very soon, we had quite a few Mallards congregating along the riverbank and the trouble was that every time we threw the bread to the furthest bird away from us, the majority would turn and make a dive for it. The situation changed dramatically when two majestic Swans regally glided up, demanding their royal prerogative and proceeded to swallow Marlene's last two buns.

Eventually, we started to walk slowly back towards the house with my arm around Marlene. Greta and Philip had already gone on ahead and we stopped briefly to admire the orchard covered in a blanket of frost.

"You know," Marlene said softly, looking up at me, "I may not have been bought up with Christmas, but these holiday celebrations and especially today, have been perfect and I feel very privileged to have so much. I often wonder when life will rear its ugly head and teach me a lesson in humility by taking it all away. I hope God will answer my prayer and grant us a child of our own. Then, I think my life will be truly complete."

"Marlene, I swear to God that the Jewish race is collectively born with a streak of fatalism. Enjoy what you have today and stop worrying about tomorrow and what might be. Yes, you are right that we are very fortunate, compared to most people, but that's the luck of the draw and not something to feel guilty about and do you know, my darling, I have a feeling in my bones that one day soon, we will have a child of our own. Just be patient. Nature will take its course when it is ready and now, I think we best get you back to the house as you are beginning to look cold."

As I kissed her on the lips, I grabbed her hand and ran towards the house. It seems that whilst we had been out, Hiram had taken a cat nap on the sofa, leaving Miriam and Olivia pottering around in the kitchen making hot drinks for us for when we arrived back which we were grateful for as there was now a definite chill in the air. Hiram must have caught the aroma of coffee because he woke up and joined us in the kitchen. Planning how we would all spend the rest of the day was an event in itself, but we did decide on a family game of monopoly, followed by a cold buffet. The evening's entertainment would be a choice between showing a film, which in this instance, was Alfred Hitchcock's thriller *Young and Innocent,* featuring Nova Pillbeam and Derek De Marney or to watch a transmission of Noel Coward's *Hay Fever* at nine o'clock, which was being presented by the BBC on a new medium, called television. To be honest, although I had bought a set some months ago, our reaction to it in its present state was one of disappointment. The screen was too small, and the camera was static reminding me of the early days of sound cinema and finally, the viewing hours were restricted and the choice of programme limited. However, once the novelty had worn off, a combination of technical improvements, a larger choice of entertainment and the added factor of cheaper prices for a set, the new medium could soon amount to a serious threat to the cinema.

By general consensus, we opted to watch the film. While the family were laying the Monopoly game out on the dining table, Philip gave me a hand in lowering the screen in the lounge and preparing the projector which involved threading the film onto the sprocket's which, in turn, carried the film through the apertures. Once we had accomplished that task, we commenced the game of Monopoly, which after a few pleasant hours, had Marlene emerge as the winner. With foresight, she had acquired Park Lane and Mayfair right from the start, thereby gradually eliminating us one by one. The rest of the evening was spent watching the film which after *The 39 Steps,* had firmly established Hitchcock as Britain's premier director, although I hadn't been able to obtain a copy of his latest film *The Lady Vanishes,* which was supposed to be even superior. There is no doubt that the family thoroughly enjoyed the plot of a man wrongly accused of murder and his efforts to prove his innocence. For my part, I was fascinated by Hitchcock's emerging trademark of using a long tracking shot, as in this instance, the camera gliding through the front entrance of the hotel and through the hotel restaurant towards the band playing in the background, finally focusing on the drummer, who was the true villain of the piece, with a tight close up of his twitching face.

The evening was rounded off with a few bottles of Prosecco and happy reminiscences of times past and it gave me great satisfaction to watch Marlene and her family interacting with each other remembering incidents from the past and enjoying each other's company. I did, however, have a sense of sadness at watching a family who under normal circumstances would be a credit to any community, being made a victim of persecution. Just briefly, Olivia and my eyes met and I knew in that instant that she was thinking the same as I was.

The remaining days of the old year was spent recovering from the excesses of the Christmas festivities and preparing for New Year's Eve celebrations. Marlene had settled for a party at home just for the family, staff and a few neighbours that we had got to know over the years. The plan was for the party to start at around ten o'clock in the evening, giving me the opportunity to take the menfolk out to the Dog and Badger for a pre-party drink or two. Meanwhile, prior to that, for the last few days, I had been busy familiarising myself with the script, *A Girl Must Live*, a film that I was about to start in the first week of January. Most of New Year's Eve had turned Falcon House into a hive of activity, despite the small number of guests that would be attending that night, Marlene had organised a gang of volunteers from the family to blow up balloons to fill the nets that she had attached to the ceiling of the lounge where they would be released by pulling a string dead on midnight.

It was just before eight o'clock in the evening when we entered the public bar of the Dog and Badger as it had been agreed by the men of the house to have a game of darts, but we hadn't foreseen that the pub would be full of villagers and that the dartboard was fully occupied and booked by a long list of customers waiting for a game. As the bar was already two-deep with thirsty customers, we cut our losses and walked around to the saloon bar where we grabbed one of a few empty tables left. Within half an hour, the place was heaving with customers and the atmosphere gradually thickening with tobacco smoke and the rising crescendo of chatter. In the end, because of the time it took to order a round, we only managed to get three rounds of drinks in because of the crush around the bar, so by general consensus, we decided to call it a day and start back to the house. By the time we reached home, the combination of the night air and the alcohol had put us all in a very happy festive mood. The house itself, was a welcoming sight ablaze with lights and when we entered the hallway, we were greeted with the sounds of Cab Calloway singing *Mini the Moocher* reverberating on the record player over the sounds of people chattering. No sooner had Marlene rushed up to me, I knew by the mischievous look in her eyes that she had a surprise in store for me and sure enough, after giving me a kiss, she opened the lounge doors to reveal a group of guests that I hadn't expected to see standing there and who, on my entrance, raised their glasses and in unison, shouted out, "Happy New Year, Gunther."

I was soon amongst them all, shaking hands with Lars Holquist, who the family owed so much to, Peter Lorre with cigarette holder and drink in hand, Oscar Levant with whom I'd become firm friends in the late twenties whilst in America and finally, Billy Wilder and Conrad Veitd from our Berlin days. It didn't take long for the party to really take off and Marlene dazzled everybody with her charm and energy, going from one group to the next, alternating between German and English. She even persuaded Oscar to play a medley of George Gershwin songs accompanied by her mother singing *Somebody Loves You* in German, which was received with rapturous applause, so much so, that the pair performed an encore of another Gershwin standard titled *Embraceable You*. The performance was so impressive that I suggested to Miriam that she and Oscar should cut an LP titled *Opera goes Pop* which could be a new concept in bringing music to the masses.

At three minutes to midnight, I sneaked over to the radio console and turned the volume up full blast which had the immediate effect of stunning everybody into silence. Then, Big Ben boomed out across the lounge and everybody began counting down in unison, whilst Marlene and Olivia stood by, ready to pull the strings of the balloon nets. Five! four! three! two! one! finally calling out, "HAPPY NEW YEAR, EVERYBODY!" The partygoers responded back as the coloured balloons descended and the party poppers were pulled, sending out paper streamers. We all started putting on party hats and joining hands, all sang *Auld Lang Syne,* after which, we all joined in with Oscar and Miriam singing *We'll Meet Again*. It all got rather emotional with people hugging and kissing particularly amongst the immigrants, many who were going back to the United States. Marlene's family were particularly vulnerable and were emotional which was understandable under the circumstances. I took hold of Marlene and embraced her wishing her a very Happy New Year. By the time we had all kissed and hugged each other, Olivia had put a party record on and in no time at all, we had formed a chain and were dancing to the Conga, out through the lounge doors and into the gardens back into the house and through the downstairs rooms, after which the majority of us descended upon the food and drink like a plague of locusts. In between, many of us, led by Marlene and me, danced to the popular melodies of the moment.

Finally, in the early hours of the morning, Oscar and Miriam, well fuelled by champagne, performed a duet singing *There's No Business, Like Show Business* and we all joined in enthusiastically, practically taking the roof off the house. They finished the evening off with *Now Is The Time To Say Goodbye*. Apart from Oscar Levant, Billy Wilder and Lars Holquist, who stayed overnight with their partners, everybody else made their own way home, leaving us standing in the middle of what can only be described as a building site. Bizarrely, whilst we were all standing there surveying the wreckage and finding something to drink, Oscar supplied us with a memory of a lifetime, which was a picture of him sitting at the piano with a cigarette out of the corner of his mouth, playing Gershwin's *Rhapsody in Blue*. What a memorable experience! So began the year 1939.

The third of January was the day that Greta and Philip had decided to leave us and return to Holland. It was a particularly grey and dismal day weather-wise. I suppose you could say that it was in keeping with the mood. We were setting off early in the morning. John had already pulled the car around to the front door and as Marlene and I waited by the car, Greta and Philip said their farewells to Hiram and Miriam, something not to be lingered upon, as all parties were visibly upset. But with one final hug, Greta and Philip climbed into the car with us and John quickly pulled away. The journey down to Liverpool Street Station was very subdued and although Philip and I tried to brighten the atmosphere, the girls were very conscious of the fact that the time for parting would very soon be upon them. I made every effort, with the help of Philip, to dwell upon the positives, that we should not leave it so long before we all met up again and certainly Marlene and I would love to visit them both in Holland probably around May this year. As for themselves, they only had to phone us to let us know that they were on their way and we would have the bedroom made up. Marlene, meanwhile, made one last pitch to Greta and Philip to seriously reconsider their position in Holland and indeed the whole of Europe. She felt that they should restart their lives either in Britain or the United States and certainly, at the very least, they should have an emergency plan in place should the worst scenario occur and if that felt like scaremongering, just remember Germany. I sensed in the confines of the car that Philip was becoming rather like a donkey, insofar as the more you pulled him, the more he resisted. He gave a final retort on the matter.

"Please, Marlene. Do not upset yourself any more on this matter. There is no way that I would place Greta in any position of danger. Despite a slight upsurge in fascism, not only does Holland remain an overwhelmingly democratic country, but also a liberal one. I also believe that the strong military buttress of Britain, France, Belgium and Poland will be more than enough to keep Hitler in his place."

John, meanwhile, had become very adept at finding spaces to park the car without bringing attention to us, as he proved again this time, sneaking in amongst the Royal Mail vans as unobtrusively as possible. While we waited for him to check the platform and departure time, I said my farewells to Greta and Philip by the car. I would not see them off from the departure gate. I did not want my presence to attract unnecessary attention at a time like this, so it was best if Marlene saw them off on her own. John was soon back with a luggage porter and after their cases had been loaded onto the barrow, I embraced both of them and wished them Godspeed and watched as Marlene and Greta followed the porter and Philip to platform six to catch the train to Harwich where they would board the ferry for the Hook of Holland. As I watched them cross the concourse, I observed to John that at least they were going to a country where they would be safe from the evil clutches of Hitler. Winding the window down, I lit a cigarette and sank into the back seat while I watched and waited for Marlene to reappear, wondering to myself what 1939 would have in store for us.

Chapter 12

Descent to War

The months had flown by. It was already the closing days of April as Marlene and I returned home after spending three weeks on holiday in Portofino, Italy. Despite enjoying the experience of working with the young British director, Carol Reed and the cast, including Margaret Lockwood and Lilli Palmer, it had been a much-needed break after three months of filming at Gainsborough film studios. The film itself which had only just recently been released, had proved a disappointment as indeed had the previous one which I had finished in November. Neither film had much substance to them and all we seemed to do in them was to rush in and out of scenes asking, "Anyone for tennis?" whilst appearing to have no visible means of support and the only social class depicted seemed to be that of the upper class. Without a doubt, I needed to find better scripts if I wanted to remain at the top of my game. Hopefully, my next film for Korda would be the beginning of that process and would signal a complete change of screen persona for me. For one thing, my character was completely villainous, which I fully intended to give more depth too, thus avoiding the stereotyped baddie. The plot was set in ancient Arabia, the film was to be shot in Technicolor, thereby enhancing the various costumes and it was to have many special effects such as a flying carpet and a genie appearing from out of a lamp and a clockwork flying horse.

So far this year, if there had been any good news at all, it had surely been Vivien Leigh acquiring the role of Scarlett O'Hara in *Gone with the Wind*. However, in some quarters the fact that a Britisher had been awarded the most sought-after part had not gone down well. Personally, I thought it was an inspired piece of casting, especially as Clark Gable had been cast as Rhet Butler, making them Hollywood's dream team. I understood from the news coming out of Hollywood that there had been problems with the production and that George Cukor, the director, had been replaced by Victor Fleming. According to studio scuttlebutt, Gable had not been comfortable with Cukor, feeling that he was too much of a ladies' director and that consequently, his part was being diminished. It seemed that David O. Selznick had agreed with Gable and had replaced Cukor with Victor Fleming, a director with a flair for bringing class to action films, to helm the picture and to give Gable's part more depth.

The political climate in Europe had deteriorated drastically despite the British Prime Minister's triumphant return from Munich in September of last year with a piece of paper, proclaiming 'Peace in our time'. Hitler had proceeded to ride roughshod over the English and French policy of appeasement by reneging on the Munich agreement, with the result that by March of this year, Czechoslovakia had been occupied by the Germans with a puppet government installed and the Czech territory, previously known as the Sudetenland, had become Bohemia and Moravia, totally under the heel of a Berlin appointed Reich protector. There was now a growing awareness amongst European nations that the policy of appeasement towards Hitler had failed and that he now had ambitions for further territorial gains in the East, with Poland being the number one target.

Despite pro-German support from some of the British upper classes, there was a general feeling amongst ordinary British folk that there would be an inevitable showdown with Hitler in the near future, all of which created an atmosphere of unease, coupled with a determination to enjoy life while you could. Despite the political uncertainties in Europe, the good news was that despite their advancing years, both Hiram and Miriam were re-establishing themselves in their chosen professions. Hiram, after a successful application to the BMA, had gained his certificate to practice medicine in Britain and had already established a practice in Woking, as well as obtaining a position at Charing Cross Hospital as a consultant surgeon. As for Miriam, because of Hiram's successful resumption of his career, she was now able to pursue hers on a part-time basis. Not only was she a member of the D'Oyly Carte Company but also, she did occasional radio work for the BBC.

As for myself, I would be reporting for work on Thursday at Denham for the first day's shooting of *Ali Baba*. I must admit I was looking forward to working on this production. Apart from my change in film persona, I would also be working with some old friends from previous productions such as Tim Whalen and Harry Stradling and my dear friend, Miklos Rozsa, who would be composing the musical arrangements for the film. From the technical side, I was intrigued that I would be anticipating in a new process called blue screen where apparently, we actors could be separated from the background sets that we were filmed in and placed in new environments such as flying carpet's and mechanical horses.

Despite our success as a family, the cloud of uncertainty hanging over Falcon House dominated our lives. Communications between Marlene and her relatives in Germany were being severely restricted, causing great concern to both her and her parents. Marlene had developed a sense of foreboding and was urging her sister to persuade husband Philip to move from Holland to Britain and make a more stable future for themselves. Once again, Philip took the view that it was impossible for Hitler to conquer France, Belgium and Holland especially with the invincible Maginot Line of individual concrete fortresses blocking his way, so as far as he was concerned, it was pointless to sacrifice so much for so little.

Despite fears over her family, with the help of our staff, Marlene had transformed Falcon House into a magnificent country estate, especially with the development of the gardens. With the help of Bill and our gardener, she had planted a new vegetable garden and rejuvenated the flower beds plus extended the lawn straight through to the water's edge. As if that wasn't enough, she had also supervised a partial redecoration on the interior of the house. Marlene had been gradually withdrawing from professional modelling and devoting more time to becoming a much sought-after hostess and fund-raiser, particularly for anti-fascist organisations.

She also gave support whenever she could to emigre artists who had fled Germany, Austria and now, Czechoslovakia. Only last weekend, she had put on another well-organised and memorable soiree for a mixture of guests from both sides of the camera in the hope that many of them could find employment in the British entertainment industry. She had put up yet another marquee on the lawn and had dragged me around from one group to another in the role of a fixer. Some of these groups I met were already becoming established in the public eye. Those who had just arrived in this country, I hoped would become acquainted with producers, directors and agents. Marlene and I constantly found ourselves reverting to German to overcome some of our guests' pidgin English. I had an interesting conversation with a young actor by the name of Paul von Henried who had recently had a small but eye-catching part in a recently released film starring Robert Donat, titled *Goodbye Mr Chips*. I had met him briefly before and I believed that he possessed sufficient drive and charisma to make a name for himself. The only advice I could give him was that even though he was a genuine Austrian aristocrat, it might be wise, in view of the current political situation, to drop the middle part of his name and just call himself Paul Henried.

Another young actor I came across had only just recently arrived as a refugee from Czechoslovakia. He had anglicised his name as Herbert Lom. All I could do for him was to put his name about and tell him to stick at it. I had a feeling that he was a survivor and would also make a name for himself. It was also at that weekend that I was able to catch up with an old friend of mine by the name of Ben Lyon. Our friendship went right back to the late twenties when we were both stars of the silent screen and our social life revolved around golf and tennis. Anyway, in 1927, Ben had been signed up to star in an epic aviation film to be called *Hell's Angels* which was being produced and financed by a young man by the name of Howard Hughes who, as it turned out, was totally independent of the Hollywood film industry.

Not only was Hughes immensely wealthy, but he had also inherited ownership of a company producing drilling bits for the oil industry. Unfortunately, within weeks of the start of filming, Hollywood had started to change over to sound and Hughes made the decision to close the picture down whilst he changed over from the silent medium to sound. One of the first casualties of that decision was his leading lady, Greta Nissen, whose voice proved to be totally unsuitable. Her Norwegian accent was too guttural for the microphones. Hughes, being the maverick that he was, cast a virtually unknown girl by the name of Jean Harlow as his leading lady and as they say, the rest is history. Jean went on to become an international screen icon whose life was tragically cut short in 1937.

Meanwhile, whilst the film lumbered on, with Hughes finally taking over as director, poor Ben was contractually tied down to the one role and although his salary fully compensated him there, was a lot of time wasted between filming. I well remember one Saturday morning having a game of golf with Ben as my partner. Whilst playing against Howard Hughes and James Hall, Ben's co-star on the film, when halfway through the round, Hughes decided to fly us all down to Tijuana in Mexico to spend a long weekend relaxing. A weekend turned into a long week. I could not calculate how much that decision must have cost him financially to shut *Hell's Angels* down whilst he and his two co-stars were somewhere in Mexico living it up. I do believe that Ben and I became very familiar with all the bars in Tijuana and then some. As for Howard Hughes, all I can say is that he was one hell of a character. Incidentally, the film *Hell's Angels* was finally released in 1930 as a talkie with some amazing aerial combat footage. It became a smash hit. As Marlene and I stood talking to Ben and his wife, Bebe Daniels, Ben suddenly reached out and grabbed the arm of a man walking past us accompanied by a striking-looking girl with the red hair. He pulled them both into our circle exclaiming.

''Gunther, I would like to introduce you to an extremely talented musician and comedian and his lovely wife. I am sure that you have heard of them. They are Vic Oliver and Sarah Churchill. I know Sarah won't object if I tell you that her father is Winston Churchill, the politician.'' From what I gathered, Vic Oliver was the son of an Austrian baron and had served in the last war and after being discharged, had become a musician of some repute, eventually going to America where he became a noted orchestral conductor. It was during that time that his talent as a comedian emerged after combining the two talents together. He had arrived in Britain making a name for himself in musical comedies in the West End, which was where he met his wife Sarah, who he then married.

I had known for some time that Ben and his wife Bebe, had decided to make London their home, having become Anglophiles and so it appeared, had Vic Oliver. Apparently, from what Marlene and I gathered, the three of them were working on an idea for a new radio show in which they would play themselves in daily situations. They were thinking of calling the show, *Hi Gang* and both of us thought it could have a lot of merit. Strangely enough, I always felt that Bebe and Ben always interacted with each other in their private lives in a similar way that the American radio stars George Burns and Gracie Allen performed in their double act.

Their routine was built on the fact that with Gracie, being such a scatterbrain, it took George most of the time to understand what she was thinking. So, it was more than possible that their idea for a new radio show could be a success.

Whilst Marlene was conversing with the other three, I took the opportunity of telling Sarah that I had recently met her father and was full of admiration for his political beliefs. From our conversation, I felt her desire to be independent in her own right and escape the shadow of her father's name. From an early age, she had wanted to be an actress and had spent her early childhood years being taught ballet, a firm foundation for her all-round and exceptional dancing ability. I don't know whether she had given up all pretensions to becoming a full-time professional actress now that she was married or whether she was just biding her time waiting for the right opportunity to occur, but either way, she and Vic made an odd couple. I couldn't put my finger on it, but they did both come from different worlds. Even though he was a talented violinist, Vic had gone to America in the mid-twenties, having made a name for himself as a musical conductor. At the same time, excuse the pun, he added a second string to his bow by becoming a comedian. He was the son of an Austrian Jew, Baron Victor von Samak, a member of the Austrian aristocracy. Vic was considered by all those who met him, to be a thoroughly decent and cultured man who vocally, somehow had adopted up a strong New York accent whilst in America. That appeared to be at odds with his native tongue which came out fractured making him sound something like Harpo Marx. All in all, it had turned out to be a successful night and I like to think that we may have created the opportunity of some future work for some of our guests.

I duly reported at Denham studios to commence filming for London Films' *Ali Baba,* in which I was to play the evil Grand Vizier Jaffar. As with most Korda productions, it was chaotic. I was pleasantly surprised to find that an old friend by the name of Ludwig Berger was directing the film. He and I were friends and colleagues from way back in the twenties when he directed many German silent films in Berlin. He had then gone to Hollywood but had not been successful. Consequently, he had returned to Europe and recently had a box office success with George Bernard Shaw's *Pygmalion* starring the fine Shavian actress, Wendy Hillier and the international star, Leslie Howard. I was, nevertheless, still disappointed by the fact that I had assumed Tim Whelan would be directing but unfortunately, his previous film, *Q Planes* had overlapped with the start of *Ali Baba*. On some days, there were endless delays whilst the script was rewritten, driving poor Miles Malleson, up the wall. He was not only a member of the cast but the script writer of the film as well. One minute, he would be told by Vincent Korda to remove some lines from the day's shooting script, then the next day, Zoltan Korda, would ask him to add another two pages. It came as no surprise that Ludwig became exasperated with the Korda brothers and was replaced by young up-and-coming director who I was not familiar with by the name of Michael Powell. Despite the delays, the whole cast and crew got on very well together and unlike some film sets I had been on, there were no prima donnas to disrupt production apart from Natalie Kalmus perhaps, who was, yet again, the mandatory Technicolor consultant. I had experience of her dictatorial methods on my last film and this time, things were no different. Filming was constantly stopped as she locked horns with Harry Stradling, the film's cinema photographer and it was not unusual for Alex Korda to be called on to the set to mediate between his brother Vincent, the art director and Kalmus.

The atmosphere between cast and crew between takes was a relaxed one, particularly amongst the younger members of the cast. On this occasion, seeing as it was the last working day of the week, Marlene had accompanied me to the studio to watch a day's shoot. As we had been invited to stay at Jack Buchanan's Knightsbridge house for a weekend party, having found herself a canvas chair alongside that of the continuity girl, she settled down to watch the day's proceedings with good-natured amusement, particularly when I arrived on set dressed in the costume of the Grand Vizier. She stopped her conversation with Miles Malleson, as soon as she saw me and immediately burst out laughing, exclaiming that I looked perfect for performing the Egyptian sand dance and that Miles should accompany me. It would be perfect for the Royal command variety performance.

The bell sounded for the final preparation of filming for the afternoon's scenes. I took my place on the set along with a young actress by the name of Mary Morris who was playing my assistant, Halima. In the guise of a six-armed mechanical dancing doll, she was about to kill the Caliph, played by Miles. Mary was having a slight case of nerves and as this was her first major appearance in the film, she was tense, especially as she had to have two female dancers strategically placed behind her so only their arms could be seen, as she performed her dance of seduction for the Caliph. After fluffing her lines on the first take, sensing her anxiety, Miles waddled up to her and whispered some words into her ear. Immediately, Mary burst into a fit of laughter followed by uncontrollable giggles after which she very quickly settled down, so that after the three of us had taken our marks again for the camera, the scene was completed without any further problems. As the set was being prepared for the next take, we waited off-camera and I was intrigued enough to ask the pair of them what had been said that have given Mary a fit of giggles, Mary began laughing again.

''There I was, standing on my mark, dressed in an exotic Eastern costume, preparing to speak my lines on cue, but also, to move my arms in coordination with the other two girls hiding behind me. I was beginning to suffer from a panic attack when dear Miles sidled up to me holding onto his turban to stop it falling off and whispered in my ear: 'Come, come, my dear, don't be downcast. Just think what a wonderful night of love you could have with those six arms, a veritable night of passion that any man would willingly die for'.'' When I repeated these remarks to Marlene, she began to laugh, telling me that it might be difficult to find a man robust enough to keep up with her and that as Miles was the scriptwriter for the film, perhaps he could get my character to build a mechanical male model to keep up with her demands. Mary played the joke out for all that it was worth, making it very difficult for the sequence to be completed without her fellow actors and production crew involved breaking up with a fit of the giggles at her antics, especially with her fellow actor Miles, whom she persistently goosed.

There is more than enough truth in the expression 'time flies' for before any of us knew it, we were in August. Britain was doing what it did best to 'Keep Calm and Carry On' as the slogan suggested. It was a saying that was beginning to become a popular phrase with the public. Because Britain was enjoying a hot and dry summer, more people took advantage of the August Bank Holiday by spending the weekend at the seaside, particularly at Blackpool in the north and Brighton in the south. Meanwhile, Alex Korda had made the decision to complete *Ali Baba* in Hollywood because the special effects and blue screen were technically more advanced over there. As I had previously mentioned, my old friend, Helmuth Berger, had departed and a new director by the name of Michael Powell had been assigned to share the screen credit temporarily. Michael was one of the small handful of British directors who were becoming internationally known. Despite still being a young man, he had built up an impressive catalogue of films since 1930 and had only just recently finished *The Spy in Black* when Korda asked him to help. It was the first week of August and the British sequences of *Ali Baba* had nearly been completed. Consequently, there was very little to do other than being forced to wait around most of the day to do blocking shots. Alex Korda was already preparing his departure to Hollywood, taking my friend, the film's musical composer, Miklos Rozsa and some senior members of the special effects department with him. As for the leading cast members, Jean Duprez, John Justin and Sabu, they would get the additional bonus of an all-expenses paid trip to Hollywood to complete the film, whilst having completed the majority of my part, I had agreed to go over to the United States at a later date, if needed.

It was on the Thursday morning that Robin decided to visit me on the set with some possible life-changing news and as soon as he had arrived, we sauntered over to the studio commissary for a coffee. After the usual pleasantries had been exchanged, I asked him. "Well Robin, as I'm sure that you haven't come all this way just to enquire about my health, so, in the vernacular of Jimmy Cagney 'What do you hear, what do you say?'"

"How would you react, Gunther, if I told you that you could be offered a contract paying you over one-million dollars!"

"Well, Robin, as you have mentioned dollars, that to me suggests Hollywood, which in turn, means moving and I'm not so sure that I want to do that anymore."

"Let me fill you in first, Gunther, as to what is on offer. Realising what is involved, I wanted a complete picture of the terms of the contract before getting in touch with you. I also insisted that they give you a month's grace to consider the offer and I have also brought with me a rough copy of what is being offered so that you can study it at your leisure. I'll start from the beginning and tell you now that we have received a tentative offer from Warners offering you a five-year contract at a salary of two-hundred and twenty-two thousand dollars per annum. Your name will always be above the title. You will also have director and script approval and you will be legally classified as a star character actor which if I am honest, is quite an honour. The only actor that I can think of in that class is Lionel Barrymore and perhaps, Claude Rains and Walter Brennan. As your agent, I must tell you that the advantages are enormous. You will receive a salary that will set you up for the rest of your life. You will continue to have access to a huge cinema audience worldwide for five years and will have the full support of a major film studio behind you. The only downside that I can see, is that you will have to move lock, stock and barrel to the United States. I'll tell you now, Gunther, this offer could not have come at a better time in your career. To be honest with you, the British and continental film industry are no longer able to offer the roles suitable for a star of your stature. Since you last left Hollywood, you have gained considerable experience on stage and screen by working both in Berlin and London continuously. Not only have you maintained your reputation but have enhanced it and that is why I believe Warners have come after you. They are looking for some gravitas to add to their stable of stars, unlike MGM and 20th Century Fox who seem to have cornered the market, particularly with British actors. Rumours have been flying around for some time that Warners have been looking for a star with the glamour of Charles Boyer and the dramatic appeal of Spencer Tracy and they think that you fit the bill. Now, do me a favour and take these papers away, study them and talk it through with Marlene. Then get back to me and remember, Warners have left us some room to negotiate. My final word to you on the subject is to think it through very carefully for this could be your opportunity of a lifetime.''

''Strangely enough, Robin, this offer has indeed arrived at a time when I seem to be at an impasse in my career. I feel as if I have become stuck in a rut and have a need for a worthwhile challenge to revitalise myself. Don't worry, I shall talk this through with Marlene and the family and get back to you very quickly. I do have one reservation though: Warners do have a reputation for being particularly tough on their actors. If you remember, Betty Davis had a run-in with them over her contract, particularly when she refused to accept any more trashy parts and was placed on suspension unable to work elsewhere and the time lost was added to her existing contract. Although she took them to court, let's not forget that she lost the case."

"I hear what you're saying, Gunther, but all the Hollywood studios operate on the same principle and they jealously guard their assets. It is the only industrial system in the world where the product walks out of the factory at the end of the working day and somehow, despite this conveyor belt system, there are quite a few works of cinema art produced. I am afraid that it comes with the shingle and that is a price that you must pay for a highly rewarding and privileged job." We parted company after spending the remainder of the morning discussing what few projects were on the horizon for the remainder of the year, the most tempting being a short winter season at the Old Vic, which would hardly pay the rent. By the early afternoon, after completing some reaction shots, I was finally released from *Ali Baba* and was on my way back to Falcon House.

The slow drive home on a warm August afternoon gave me the opportunity to be alone with my thoughts as I navigated the Buckinghamshire roads which were reasonably quiet, owing to the peak August holiday season, I suppose. The offer from Hollywood had certainly shaken me out of my complacency and if I was honest with myself, I had certainly got into a rut as far as my career was concerned. Even though I had managed to appear in a few quality pictures, the majority had been dross and it looked like I would continue in that cycle with ever diminishing returns. The other bone of discontent in our lives was the threat to European peace by that megalomaniac, Hitler. Britain was far too close to the continent not to be yet again involved in a war with Germany. Finally, there was the issue of Marlene and I wanting children. According to our doctors, there was no physical reason to prevent that and given time, nature would take its course. When that day finally arrived, would we want to bring a child into a world of such conflict? Obviously, I needed to find out Marlene's views on these matters and then we could discuss them with her parents. There is no doubt that the Warners offer had opened a whole new can of worms. When I had left for the studio that morning, I lived in a world of complacency, but now, it was full of turmoil, what the heck! I had promised Marlene that we would take her mama and papa to the pictures in Marlow. The old county cinema there had been recently taken over by the Odeon chain and this week, it was showing Betty Davis in the film *Dark Victory*. Both Marlene and Miriam were avid fans of La Davis and ironically enough, it was a Warners production which to my superstitious mind, was an omen itself. Perhaps a higher force was trying to tell me something?

Come the evening, we drove down the main shopping street of Marlow and turning left, parked outside the Odeon cinema. Whilst I waited in the car, Marlene and her parents went ahead and purchased tickets, giving me the opportunity to put some sunglasses on so that when I joined them in the foyer, we could go straight in without bringing attention to ourselves. The picture was well received by the girls though I'm not so sure about Hiram. I had the feeling it was too much of a woman's picture for his liking. As for myself, looking at it from a professional point of view, it was a typical Warners 'A' film, professionally produced and straight off the assembly line. However, two ingredients made the picture iconic; one was Betty Davis and her magnificent portrayal of the doomed heiress and the other was Max Steiner's musical score, which acted as a perfect partner to Davis' emotional range, none more so than at the end, when he matched the musical composition perfectly to her death bed scene. Fortunately, the gap between the cinema lights going at the end of the picture and the national anthem being played, gave the female members of the audience time to put their handkerchiefs away. We lingered a little longer as the auditorium emptied so that we could file out without bringing any unnecessary attention to ourselves, not that we had any problem with the citizens of Marlow as they tended to respect our privacy as well as the other celebrities living amongst them. It was only the visitors to the town that tended to be intrusive.

Once home, we settled down in the lounge with assorted sandwiches that Mary had prepared for us accompanied by cold bottles of Chablis to wash them down. It was a perfect ending to a pleasant evening out, finally finishing up with the four of us discussing the merits of the film that we had seen earlier on in the evening.

It was after Miriam and Hiram had decided to retire for the night that I took the opportunity to discuss with Marlene the offer that I had received earlier on that day. After listening intently to what I had to say, she sat quietly for a moment then began speaking.

"Well, Gunty. I am not sure what to make of that offer. If you feel that it is in the best interests of your career but also will give us a better quality of life than we already have, then you must go with your instincts and I will support you wholeheartedly in that decision. I have never been to America and therefore, have no experience of it, so I must rely upon your judgement as to what is best for us both. Obviously, I can think of two reservations. One is what will happen to my parents if we leave them behind? I would not be happy leaving them in a vulnerable position. The second reservation is that it would be quite an emotional sacrifice to leave Falcon House with all its happy memories. However, having said that, I also believe Hitler will not rest until he has plunged the continent into war, which means Britain will also be dragged into the conflict. Do we both need to endure so much uncertainty again, particularly if I should become pregnant. Also, do we really want to bring a child into this world under those circumstances?"

I responded, "Marlene, I have no intention whatsoever of jumping into this situation feet-first. As it is, the contract is still subject to negotiation and until terms are mutually agreed by both parties, we won't be able to say yay or nay. I'm putting you in the picture now so that you will have time to think things out. I will always keep you informed with each new piece of information. As for your parents, once you and I have decided one way or the other, we will sit down and talk it over with them. There are a few questions that will need to be answered. For example, what will Miriam and Hiram response be? Do we sell the house or keep it? What about our staff? All I'm doing tonight, darling, is letting you know that new horizons could be beckoning."

"Don't worry, Gunty. Whatever decision is made, it will be made together, regardless. As a matter of interest, if we did somehow end up going over there, would we get to California in a covered wagon? I sure hope all the Indians are tame now." With that she threw her arms around me laughing.

It was now officially in the trade papers, that Korda had closed production down on *Ali Baba* and would be moving a small group of actors and technicians to Hollywood where the director, Tim Whelan had been signed on to finish the film. So, my commitment was now finished unless something untoward occurred and my services were required. Seeing that I was now officially resting between engagements, I began toying with the idea of Hiram and myself driving up to Scotland for a week of golf at St Andrews, taking our wives with us, of course. None of us had been to Scotland before but many of our friends told us how wonderful the scenery was and that the bagpipes, the whiskey and the locals, wearing tartan skirts would be an experience to remember.

Unfortunately, on the twenty-third of August, Hitler pulled off a surprising diplomatic coup, by signing a non-aggression pact with Russia. This act sent a seismic shock through all the continental foreign offices including Britain's. No country had foreseen that two dictators ideologically the opposite of each other, would sign a pact of mutual assistance. Now, the cat was well and truly out of the bag. The democracies had finally woken up to a nightmare. Hitler had his sights set upon the East so that he could create more space for his Nazi empire and now he no longer needed to pretend otherwise, so began a repeat performance of the previous year which had resulted in the conquest of Czechoslovakia. This time, it was to be Poland's turn. Informing the world, Hitler now declared, that his patience had been exhausted. He issued an ultimatum to Poland that unless the Polish government ceased in its persecution of the German minority, he would have no choice but to place the German military forces in readiness to cross the Polish borders.

Now began a mad scramble between France and Britain to confirm their staunch support of Poland and in the event of her being attacked by Germany, they would come to her aid. However, the German leader appeared to have accurately assessed the moral weaknesses of the democracies and it appeared to the ordinary man in the street, that Hitler was about to call their bluff. The general feeling of the public and national newspapers was to get on with it, give Hitler a good hiding and send him packing.

Meanwhile, life still went on in that glorious month of August. People in Britain still went about their everyday lives either going on holidays or commuting to work by bus or train whilst I am ashamed to say, that I had recently bought a two-berth cabin cruiser which I had christened the *Marlene* for sailing on the Thames and further afield. I had been playing the role of captain with the help of family, friends and staff, frequently cruising through Sonning and Henley feeling very much like a character from *Three Men in a Boat*. That last week in August unfolded like a film in slow motion. It seemed that we were all on two different planets, with one populated by the politicians and newspapers pumping out useless information whilst the rest of us, on the other hand, pretended that they didn't exist.

On Thursday night, I took the boat out with Marlene and cruised downriver to Cookham, where I birthed along a quiet stretch of the river. Mary had prepared a picnic basket for us which Marlene, as the one and only crew member, laid out in the stern of the boat and we sat watching the sun go down, observing the occasional cruiser go by and sometimes the odd punt, crewed by a young man and his girlfriend. As the water lapped against the sides of the boat, we could feel the gentle motion lulling us.

"You know, Marlene, this is a night that will go into our chest of special memories, whatever road we take, whatever fate has in store for us. Being alone together without any pressures, just each other, will be justification for my love for you."

I was about to say more when the sound of a banjo and singing grew louder. Sure enough, around the bend, came a riverboat festooned with fairy lights carrying day trippers enjoying an evening trip on the river and as they came alongside us, they greeted and waved at us and as they passed by. The riverboat created a gentle swell which rocked our boat, but it didn't stop us from waving back and raising our glasses in a toast which after emptying, we then threw into the river.

"Gunty Conrad, I love you too much, for despite all your faults, you are a rare breed, a good and loyal husband and where you go, I shall go. However, having said that, why not take me into the back of the boat and have your wicked way with my body. After all said and done, we can then say that the boat has been well and truly christened the 'fair' *Marlene*.

The sun had set by the time we arrived back at Falcon House and after birthing the boat and securing her to the embankment, Marlene and I commenced a slow stroll back to the house, all the while chatting about the uncertainty of making any plans in the current European crises. As we passed the cottage, Miriam opened the front door and beckoned us in. Marlene and I exchanged glances having noted that Miriam seemed a little agitated, leaving us to wonder whether she had received some unpleasant news. We both knew that Hiram was working late at Wycombe General Hospital. Having followed her into the front room, Miriam started by saying that she was sorry to be a nuisance to us, but could we spare her a moment. After some gentle persuasion from Marlene, Miriam told us how she had just finished speaking on the phone with Greta who was concerned about the rise of Dutch National Socialism. Its leader, Anton Mussert, was campaigning in Holland for the Dutch people to ally themselves with Hitler and was proclaiming that once again, international Jewry was responsible for the present political unrest. It seemed that Philip, was attempting to reassure her, telling her that there was no way that the Dutch people would vote for a demagogue such as Mussert and that if Hitler tried anything on against the Allies, he would come a cropper at the Maginot Line and sent packing back to Germany with his tail between his legs. Nevertheless, Greta's anxiety had communicated itself to Miriam who felt that Greta and her husband should leave Holland as soon as possible before it became too late. No amount of reassurance from either myself or Marlene could persuade her otherwise.

Eventually, however, Marlene managed to calm her by promising to ring Greta within the next few days and at the same time, instead of staying at the cottage on her own waiting for Hiram to return, why didn't she walk over to the main house with us and keep us company. Although by now, fully composed, she declined our invitation saying that having discussed it with us she was in a far better frame of mind and that once Hiram had arrived safely home, they might walk over for a nightcap with us.

I am afraid that within days, our complacency was shattered. Under the pretence of a so-called incident at the Gleiwitz radio station on the German-Polish border, carried out by supposed Polish militiamen, who having attacked the station by force, had then proceeded to broadcast anti-German propaganda, Hitler had mounted a full-scale invasion of Poland on the first of September. Promptly, both Britain and France served notice on Germany that if she had not withdrawn her troops back across the German border by the third of September, there would be a state of war between the three countries. As Hitler refused to comply with the ultimatum, the British nation was informed by the Prime Minister, Neville Chamberlain, in a speech broadcast to the British Empire at approximately eleven-fifteen on Sunday the third of September that Britain was now at war with Germany.

All of us at Falcon House, family and staff, had gathered around the radio to listen to Chamberlain's announcement and when he had finished, we all sat in stunned silence. Miriam sobbed quietly into her handkerchief whilst being comforted by Marlene, Olivia and Mary slipped into the kitchen arm in arm, presumably to cheer everybody up by making some tea and we three men went out into the garden for a smoke.

"*Gott in Himmel,*" Hiram said. "The bastard has finally brought about the apocalypse. Hitler won't stop now, until he has subjugated the Eastern nations and eliminated the Jewish race."

"I don't think it will be as easy as that, Mr Bachman," Bill said, "Herr Hitler will be facing the combined might of Britain, France, Holland and Belgium and don't forget the impenetrable Maginot Line. Oh no, I think Herr Hitler has bitten off more than he can chew. You mark my words, gentlemen, it will be all over with by Christmas and that is an ex-soldier from the First World War speaking."

I said little as I stood there listening, whilst drawing on my cigar. I would like to have believed Bill, but my instinct told me that Hiram was right. Hitler was a gambler and was on a winning streak. Since 1938, he had sensed that his opponents were morally weak and like all gamblers who were winning, he would go for broke. I sensed that he would launch a different type of warfare that the Allies were used to. I had only read the other day that twenty-five per cent of the Polish army were cavalry and I well remember way back in 1935, a fellow dinner guest by the name of Colonel Guderian enthusiastically singing the praises of a new type of warfare which he named the blitzkrieg comprising of tank battalions racing ahead of the infantry, destroying everything in their path. Now, I wondered all these years later, how Polish horses would defeat German tanks.

Marlene called us in to the house at this point. Apparently, there was a long list of announcements being made on the radio concerning the introduction of certain wartime regulations to take effect almost immediately. Most of them were common sense, such as petrol rationing, the distribution of gas masks to the population and a new terminology including words like the 'blackout' which would require all buildings to have windows and doors covered with curtains or black paper. This regulation would be strictly enforced by either a heavy fine or imprisonment. The one regulation that I thought was rather heavy-handed and not because it affected my profession, but purely on the basis that it was bad for the public morale, was the immediate closure of all cinemas and theatres. There was also going to be further announcements regarding food rationing.

Most of the day was taken up with short bulletins advising us what to do. These instructions included tips on wearing a bright stripe on our clothing when walking out in the dark and gas masks were to be carried at all times after distribution to dwellings or through local schools. The government would also begin distributing free Anderson air raid shelters to all householders earning less than two-hundred and fifty pounds per annum, whilst the rest of us would have to make our own arrangements. Petrol rationing was the one regulation that would have an impact on our lives. Although it did not become mandatory before the sixteenth of this month, the quantity issued would be based on the rating of the vehicles registration book. The basic ration would be one gallon per coupon and if more was required under special circumstances, then an application would have to be made to the local divisional petroleum officer. Also, all vehicle bumpers would be required to be painted white and headlights to be blacked out. It seemed that the government had already commenced evacuating children from the age of five upwards to the countryside from London and all the major cities. Volunteers were being sought to take them into their homes and in return, they would be compensated with seven shillings and sixpence per child per week.

We all realised how serious that it had all become when news began seeping through the day's special announcements that a British Expeditionary Force was already sailing for France to join with the French Army. Although the news had been expected, we were all still stunned by the fact that after twenty years of peace, we were now in conflict again with the same nation that we had beaten in a war to end all wars just two decades before.

That afternoon, Marlene and I decided to go for a walk along the Thames. It would give us a chance to discuss the day's events and to put them into some form of perspective. As we strolled arm in arm along the embankment, there was a slight breeze rippling the surface of the water and the trees seemed to be whispering as the breeze danced through the branches. Finding a spot, we sat down and lit a cigarette, all the while taking in the stillness of it all. Not unsurprising, the normal weekend activities were missing except for the occasional couple who, like us, were dealing with the enormity of it all.

"Facing up to Hitler and making all the sacrifices necessary doesn't worry me at all. In fact, I welcome the opportunity to be able to contribute to his defeat, Gunther," Marlene said, drawing deeply on her cigarette, "But I am worried about his intentions towards the German Jews within his borders which obviously includes the rest of my family. I am just as worried about Greta and Philip. I ask myself if they going to be safe remaining in Holland? Again, I ask myself about mama and papa. Will they be treated as enemy aliens and if so, what will become of them?"

"My darling, there are no reassurances that I can give you with any certainty that would give you peace of mind," I said to her. "However, we should try and make some of our worries a little easier to deal with. First, regarding Hiram and Miriam, I have a feeling that as you and I are now British citizens, it will put them in a better position regarding their proposed classification. It might well be that they will fall into the category of friendly aliens. First thing tomorrow morning, I will get some legal clarification from our solicitors. As for Greta and Philip, how certain are we that Hitler will be defeated and that the war will be over with by Christmas? If that turns out to be the case, we should have no worries about their safety. However, if the unthinkable was to occur, it might be wise to put an alternative plan to them now. Perhaps, they should be considering emigrating now whilst there is still time, on the grounds that they could become a persecuted minority in the future?"

I thought it best not to mention to her that I had already tried to contact them by phone, but the telephone lines to Holland had been shut down. As for the remainder of her family still living within the borders of Germany, I am afraid this would be down to the decisions of history. If Hitler were defeated by the Allies and overthrown by the German nation in a coup, then there would no longer be a problem. However, if things were to go the other way then we could only hope and pray. I left the rest unsaid as I knew that Marlene was way ahead of me in my concerns. By the time we had returned to the house, we had talked ourselves out on the impending hostilities and its ramifications and indeed, when we entered the house, we could sense the same feeling from everybody else. So, after the evening meal and a generous helping of alcohol, I showed the latest George Formby film, *Trouble Brewing,* which not only took the tension out of the air but had everybody laughing at George's antics.

Over the next few months, despite being in a state of war, the country appeared to be in limbo. With the introduction of compulsory blackouts, the evacuation of children from the major cities, the distribution of gas masks and the introduction of ration books to cover meat, bacon, eggs, butter, sugar and tea, the feeling amongst us all in the country was that we had entered into what became known as the 'Phoney War'. It seemed that both sides had drawn breath during the winter months whilst they engaged in strengthening their forces. I had been aware that my friend, Lars Holquist, who had been responsible for getting Marlene's parents out of Germany, had been acting as an intermediary between London and Berlin. It appeared that Hitler did not accept the fact that Britain was prepared to go to war over such a silly trifle as Poland and that had she been offered the right terms in the first place, she would willingly have signed an armistice. The good news for the nation was that after some second thoughts, in their wisdom, the government decided to reopen the cinemas and theatres with the proviso that they were closed by ten o'clock in the evening, thus giving a massive boost of morale to the country.

As for our own small world at Falcon House, for the last time, Marlene had put together a great family Christmas with a few shortages. Hiram and Miriam, as I thought, were classified as friendly aliens and had to report once a week to Marlow police station. Unfortunately, to add to her worries, she was no longer able to communicate with her sister or her family in Germany, a burden that she shared with Hiram and Miriam.

The call up of young men between the ages of eighteen and thirty-six had spared our household as both John and Bill were over the age. However, John's son had already received his call-up papers and had been posted to Aldershot. My working life was in turmoil. Because of the war, the film industry had been hit by a shortage of nitrate, building materials and manpower. Quite a few technicians had already been called up, leaving a shortage of experienced filmmakers. Consequently, there were a few films in production. I was being kept busy making short films for the Ministry of Information and appearing on current affairs programmes and guest appearances on light entertainment shows for BBC Radio. Because of petrol rationing limiting my mileage, I had mothballed one car and was sharing the other with Hiram who was now a consultant surgeon in High Wycombe. I had also taken a lease on a small flat in Hampstead, just north of central London, thereby conserving our petrol coupons for emergencies. Whenever possible, we had been using public transport into London but usually, I either walked or took taxis to my destination and by doing so, avoided bringing attention to myself. Everywhere I went in central London, people seemed determined to give off an air of normalcy, even though all government buildings had sandbags stacked shoulder high outside the main doors with armed sentries in attendance, all the departmental stores and shops had the mandatory black tape running horizontally across the glass windows and the streets were filled with office workers and military personnel hurrying backwards and forwards from their various tasks carrying their gas masks over their shoulders. Even on the underground, preparations had been made for the citizens of London to bed down during the night on the platforms if the need should arise.

One good piece of news was that Winston Churchill had become a member of the war cabinet as first Lord of the Admiralty, at long last, an indication that the government was finally acquiring some backbone. On our own home front, Marlene joined the St John's Ambulance Brigade whilst Hiram became a senior consultant surgeon at RAF Uxbridge, specialising in prosthetic limbs. As for Miriam, she had become a part of the BBC propaganda unit beaming anti-Nazi material to Germany. I had yet to find a worthwhile role that I could fill to contribute to Hitler's downfall. I had tried to enlist in the air force but, although I was physically in good shape, I was classified as being above the enlistment age. In other words, I was too old. I kept myself occupied by appearing in Ministry of Information films such as *Careless Talk Costs Lives* and *Think of Others Before Yourself.*

Marlene and I had spent one long evening discussing how we could best contribute to defeating Hitler and had arrived at a decision that the best thing that we could do right there and then was to put our money where our mouth was. I had been very fortunate in comparison to most of my fellow actors insomuch as I had been gainfully employed as a star for the past fifteen years and with a small permanent team of professionals, had built up a substantial balance of wealth consisting of real estate and stock holdings on both sides of the Atlantic. Consequently, once we had arrived at that decision, I had approached the government through intermediaries to loan them sixty per cent of our savings in the shape of war bonds and also, ensuring that in doing so, we received no publicity whatsoever. The upshot of that was, that we received a very gracious reply from the Prime Minister's office thanking us for our contribution to the war effort. Our other contribution was to hold a party for some of the officers from RAF Medmenham. From what we understood, it had now become a specialist unit dealing in aerial photography and other important intelligence work. Regardless of whether it was a fully operational airfield or desk-bound was immaterial, we felt that it was our moral duty as civilians to support the armed services who were fighting for us.

Marlene had performed Herculean efforts to persuade as much glamour from the fashion, the theatre and film world to attend. When the night of the party had arrived, on the last weekend of May, not only did we have a full house, but the phone was constantly ringing during the day from the girls who had only just heard about the party, pleading for an invite, even though most of them had a fair distance to travel to get to us. Naturally, because Marlene found it difficult to refuse, I had to ask Hiram and Miriam if they would let us use the downstairs of the cottage as an extension for the possibility of potential guest sleepovers. They had no hesitation in agreeing despite their advancing years and were soon throwing all their energy into helping Marlene organise the party. Together with Mary, Lucy and Olivia, they all performed miracles in providing the food for the buffet despite the restrictions imposed by rationing. Whilst John and Bill helped me stock the bar with enough beer, wines and spirits to start a brewery. I guess that either one, or both, had connections with a lot of pub landlords in the area. I had also hired three girls from the village for waitressing and bar work.

Come that night, the house was heaving with a mixture of civilians and air force personnel. We had pilot officers and Flight

Lieutenants plus members of the women's Royal Air Force. Leslie Hutchinson was at the piano, ably assisted with vocals by Jack Buchanan, Ivor Novello and Pat Kirkwood. Olivia did a great job at spotting unattached people and introducing them to each other and whilst Marlene and I were in continuous orbit around the house, I happened to notice many of the young officers had wings on their tunics signifying that they were all pilots. I presumed that they would be due for posting out of Medmenham when the need arose. I felt a twinge of apprehension watching them, for their average age was about nineteen and yet they seemed to be living as if there was no tomorrow.

We finished the evening off with a massed singsong of *We're Going to Hang out our Washing on the Siegfried Line* and the *Lambeth Walk*. But afterwards, guests formed into groups and reflected on when the real war would start. Amongst our own friends and colleagues who were immigrants, only Paul Henried had been offered the opportunity to leave for America. Bebe Daniels and Ben Lyon were determined to stay in London and entertain the nation as were Lilli Palmer, Herbert Lom and Anton Walbrook. That seemed to be the general view shared by most of the showbiz fraternity, who all said that they would join ENSA and tour military hospitals and camps entertaining the troops if called upon to do so.

It certainly had been a party to end all parties and none of us really had any desire for it to end but at its conclusion, the majority had slipped away with most of the officers setting off on foot, back to camp. Poor Marlene, who had to endure many sloppy kisses and hugs from everyone thanking her for the party. I had the foresight a few years back to build four extra guest rooms above the stables which came into their own that night as we had been left with quite a few inebriated guests. Hiram and Miriam rose to the occasion by taking three young ladies to the cottage, taking being the operative word, as they were what you would call 'legless'. Whilst Olivia, Mary and Lucy were cleaning up the kitchen, Marlene, with the help of the young waitresses, was collecting all the dirty glasses and plates. With the help of John and Bill, I had managed to get some of the more inebriated guests bedded down in the stables and the last three standing, were made makeshift beds on the settees in the main lounge and gradually passed out onto them one by one. Within minutes, a heavenly silence fell over the house. Soon after, we waved goodnight to John and Mary as they drove off, taking the young waitresses with them, leaving the seven of us to congregate in the kitchen with a pot of coffee reflecting on how we had a hard day's work in front of us in cleaning up the house. In the end, we called it a day and went to bed, accompanied by the sound of snores reverberating from all over the house.

The so-called 'Phoney War' ended abruptly in the first week of May 1940 with the Germans launching a massive Panzer attack through the supposedly impassable Ardennes region, thereby bypassing the invincible Maginot Line and isolating it, placing the French and British forces in danger of being trapped in a pincer movement. Disaster came upon disaster. The French Army was now beginning to disintegrate and the British Expeditionary Force, otherwise known as the BEF, was being forced back to the coastal town of Dunkirk, whilst meanwhile, the Maginot fortresses fell to the German army with virtually no effort at all, the unthinkable was occurring, the way to Paris was now open to the Germans. Here at home, the Chamberlain government fell on the eighth of May when the MP Leon Amery addressed Neville Chamberlain in the house with these comments.

"You have sat here too long for any good that you are doing, depart I say and let us be done with you, in the name of God, go!"

Winston Churchill was asked to form a government and became Prime Minister on the tenth of May at the age of sixty-five. He very quickly flew over to Paris in a vain attempt to rally French morale, but it proved a hopeless cause. By now, both Holland and Belgium had fallen to the Germans and the BEF was now fighting what appeared to be an organised retreat. The pipe dream of an easy victory over the Germans was shattered. Our family was now facing the cold reality. We had no way of being in contact with Philip and Greta. We didn't know if they were safe or were making plans to escape. All I could do was to remain in touch with the Home Office and keep tabs on refugees entering Britain.

I had been invited to the House of Commons to listen to Churchill's maiden speech as Prime Minister. The invitation to attend had come out of the blue and was sent from the office of the Right Honourable Hore-Belisha, the prominent Conservative cabinet member whom Marlene and I had the pleasure of meeting previously at Alex Korda's house. Also enclosed was a pass to the

Strangers' Gallery with a request that I meet him in the central lobby after Churchill's speech. It was a day that I was never likely to forget for many reasons. Apart from all else, it was the thirteenth of May and the previous day, my agent had phoned me and told me that Warners had agreed to our terms and were ready to exchange contracts at Burbank in California, so that all that was needed now was my was my signature. Because of the wartime conditions now prevailing in Britain, I asked for a week's grace to make my mind up. Obviously, there was going to be a long debate with Marlene and her parents, whether to accept or remain in Britain.

I took the underground and got off at Westminster embankment and arriving at street level, crossed over the main road and walked around to the Houses of Parliament and presented my invitation at the visitors booth just inside the front door. Upon passing through, I was escorted by an usher dressed in white tie and morning coat and he led me through an archway and up a stone flight of stairs which led into a small gallery with bench seating. I was lucky enough to find a seat in the second row which enabled me to look down upon the chamber below which was divided by a long and heavy looking table. On the left side, seated on leather benches, were the government ministers and their fellow MPs and on the right facing them across the desk, was the opposition party and at the top of the chamber, situated on a platform, stood a large chair similar to a throne in appearance and seated upon it, was I presumed, the speaker of the house and just below him, two clerks attired with wigs and black robes. Unfortunately, visitors were not allowed to make any notes of the proceedings but to my dying day, I shall never forget the historical proceedings which enfolded before me.

The chamber was packed with MPs, many of which were standing at the back and when Churchill rose and stood at the desk ready to address the house, I knew instinctively, as an actor, that I was going to listen to a great performance. I felt that I had gone back in time to the fields of Agincourt and was listening to Henry V, not only was it surreal, it was magic, it was history. I remember his speech well, part of which I will quote here.

"You ask what is our aim? I can answer in one word: it is victory, victory at all costs, victory in spite of the terror, victory! However long and hard the road may be. For without victory, there is no survival, let that be realised. No survival for the British Empire, no survival for all that the British Empire has stood for, no survival for the urges and impulses of the ages that mankind will move forward towards its goal. I feel sure that our cause will not be suffered to far amongst man. At this time, I feel entitled to claim the aid of all, and say, come then, let us go forward together with our united strength."

When he sat down, the house stood and erupted into a foot-stomping and arm-waving round of cheers. As I descended the stairs from the gallery, I knew then that though the road ahead would be of hardship and sorrow for the nation, we would eventually win this war. Standing in the central lobby later whilst waiting for Hore-Belisha gave me the opportunity to study my surroundings. The House of Lords and the House of Commons faced each other on either side of the module, the windows were set in stone walls with the central lobby adorned with several marble busts of prominent parliamentarians of the past. The lobby had quickly filled up with MPs spilling out from the chamber. Most were standing in groups talking and laughing excitedly. There was no doubt that Churchill had jump-started the atmosphere and awoken the house up from its malaise. Apart from his rousing speech, he had also informed the house that he was forming a national coalition government for the duration of the war and that probably explained why the MPs appeared to be so animated. There were many representatives of the armed services coming and going carrying their mandatory gas masks over their shoulders. I also noticed a small group of people who I took to be American because of the style of clothes they were wearing, being ushered through by a guide who was pointing out various objects of interest.

I saw Hore-Belisha striding towards me, accompanied by a distinguished gentleman of about fifty years of age. Once they had reached me, Hore-Belisha introduced me to his companion. Apparently, he was Commander John Burton, who asked if he could tag along as both he and his wife were great fans. After the usual round of opening chitchat, I was asked if I would like to go downstairs to the Strangers Bar for a quick pint. I agreed to that suggestion and duly followed them down some stairs and along a carpeted corridor until we arrived at our destination. It wasn't a particularly large bar, but it was certainly busy. There was a tradition that only MPs could buy drinks for their guests and I learnt quite quickly that it was a sensible custom to discreetly slide a pound or two in advance to one's host, so that the MP would not be out of pocket. Once the drinks had been purchased, we were lucky enough to grab a table with three stools. I was asked what I thought of Churchill's speech and replied that at last, the right man had come along to supply Britain with the will to fight. Both men nodded in agreement and the conversation continued in the same vein until looking at his watch, Hore-Belisha suddenly said to me.

"First, I must apologise to you, Gunther, for bringing you here in a roundabout way and under false pretences. I am sure that you will understand the reasons why when everything has been explained to you. I would first like to convey to you on behalf of the Prime Minister's office, his heartfelt thanks for your very generous loan towards the war effort I would also ask you once again to forgive my duplicity in bringing you here. It wasn't I who was responsible for your invitation this afternoon but the Prime Minister, who specifically asked for this meeting to be arranged between Commander Burton and yourself. Very shortly, if you agree, we would like to take you to a private committee room where two other gentlemen are at present awaiting our arrival. I would like to stress to you that you are under no obligation to come with us and if you should say no, the matter will be dropped without any further inconvenience to you. If, however, you agree to come with us then as of that moment, you will be part of the Official Secrets Act and there will be no record of this meeting."

I must admit that I was momentarily stunned by these revelations but then I became intrigued. I sat there feeling like a character from a John Buchan spy novel which immediately appealed to my sense of dramatics. Feeling that I was up for an audition, I agreed to go along immediately!

I was soon following the two B's as I now thought of them, along a labyrinth of corridors and up two flights of stairs until finally stopping before a door marked 'Room Six' which we then entered. The room itself was furnished with a conference table and ten matching chairs upholstered in green leather, all showing the portcullis motif, as did the carpet. There were several oil paintings on the walls, one of which, depicted Charles I, addressing Parliament and finally, to finish it all off, was a leaded window looking out over the Thames. As we entered, two men rose from the conference table and were introduced to me as Mr Ian Lang from the Foreign Office and Mr David Hislop, the designated British Consul of the State of California. Having made all the introductions, Hore-Belisha turned to me with his hand extended.

"I shall be leaving you now, Gunther, but before I go, I would like to thank you once again on behalf of his Majesty's government for your unstinting patriotic support and I would like to conclude by saying that if we can produce more men like you to support our fighting services, we shall certainly give the Nazis a run for their money."

With that, he shook me by the hand and bid good afternoon to the other three gentlemen and left the room. Commander Burton then took his place at the head of the table with the two Foreign Office officials facing me across it and then began to address me.

"I must thank you for being so patient, Mr Conrad and I certainly don't wish to keep you any longer than is necessary. I do have one question to ask of you and your reply will determine whether we proceed with this conversation. The question is, would you be prepared to take a more active part in fighting the Nazis?"

"Of course," I replied, "My wife and I spent three years living under Nazi tyranny and I can assure you that the evil that they have done in the past is nothing compared to what they will do in the future if they are not opposed. The answer has got to be yes, although I am intrigued to where all this is leading. I have already been rejected for the armed services on the grounds that I am too old and to be honest, the idea of confronting my fellow countrymen on the battlefield does not appeal to me, even though Britain is my adopted country. It's Hitler and his gang of National Socialist thugs that I would want to take on." Commander Burton held his hand up and smiled.

"Good gracious, Mr Conrad, your strengths are of far greater value elsewhere than on the battlefield. The Prime Minister, like you, believes that this is a war between good and evil and that our darkest days are yet to come. The Prime Minister has, with some foresight, been looking to woo the most powerful industrial nation in the world, one that he believes will eventually be dragged into the war. I am, of course, referring to the United States. However, though we have many things in common, like the same language, the founding fathers and we maintain a special relationship with them, since the end of the Great War, America has developed a very powerful isolationist lobby both in Congress and the Senate supported by the American Bund, an organisation which is made up of German Americans and Nazi sympathisers. They have been holding rallies recently in New York very similar in style to the Nuremberg rallies held by the Nazis. They have even taken to wearing the brown stormtrooper uniform. All this has been a big problem for President Roosevelt who happens to be a fervent believer in the Anglo-American relationship. As much as he would like to support Britain in her hour of need, the president is very much a prisoner of American public opinion of which a large percentage is either isolationist or anti-British. For example, the Irish community have very little love for the British and raise funds for Sinn Fein to support their activities in Northern Ireland. There are also, several cliques in Hollywood who are on the extreme right of the Republican Party, some of which contain some well-known celebrities such as, Adolphe Menjou, Ginger Rogers and Robert Taylor and although they are staunch Americans, they also happen to be keen isolationists.

Against this backdrop, lies the main thrust of the Prime Minister's thoughts. He feels that it is vitally important to seek the American public's support in Britain's fight against Hitler. If he can accomplish this with the support of high-profile celebrities such as yourself, then it might be possible for Roosevelt to introduce a fourth Neutrality Act, permitting the United States to trade in arms, with perhaps an inclination to favour Britain rather than Germany. Now I think that it is only right and proper I should come to the crux of the matter and the reason for this meeting. Putting it bluntly, as we already know that you have been offered a contract in Hollywood, would you be prepared to accept that offer and whilst there, act as an unofficial counterpoint to the American Bund and isolationist lobbies in the interests of Britain."

"Good God, Commander. To say that you have caught me left-footed is an understatement. I was only made aware of that offer just the other day and if you don't mind me saying so, I rather resent the fact that you might be spying on me."

"I can assure you, Mr Conrad, that there is no question whatsoever that we were spying into your private life. The fact is that even to get as far as this meeting, we had to vet your history and we wouldn't be here now if we had not been satisfied by your commitment to this country. As to the matter of your proposed contract from Warners, without being derogatory to your profession but it is always rife with rumours and gossip. You are already aware of Mr Lang and Mr Hislop who are here representing the Foreign Office, but what you may not know is that I represent British intelligence and that our two departments are already placing high profile people to represent British interests abroad. As you are now covered by the Official Secrets Act, I can now tell you that if you do volunteer, you will be in the company of Alexander Korda, who has already gone ahead of you and is in Hollywood. Also, Leslie Howard will be covering Spain and Portugal in the same capacity. With that in mind, British intelligence would like you, shall we say, to become a covert agent in plain sight, one that while in a neutral country, will be with some subtlety unlike our Nazi counterparts I may add, persuade the leaders of the cinema industry in Hollywood and the politicos in Washington to swing their support behind Britain. As a matter of interest, you will not be required to form clandestine organisation with the object of disrupting the American way of life. If, after discussing the proposed move with your immediate family, you make the decision to accept, your controller would be David Hislop. Hence, his presence here. He will be taking up the appointment of British Consulate in Los Angeles, shortly. Whilst we are on the subject, Mr Hislop, who is an Under-Secretary at the Foreign Office will oversee and share the running of the mission with my department. I am sure that you will have some questions for me but before you put them to me, let me assure you that this mission could be of the utmost importance to the country. Our view is that the next few weeks will be the testing time for Britain. The French high command is badly demoralised and the French government appears to be infected by a sense of defeatism and in those circumstances, the BEF could be in danger. On that question lies our survival. I think that under Churchill's leadership, we will continue to fight on. That is why it will be vitally important that somewhere in the future, we must have access to America's vast military arsenal. Perhaps now, you may be able to understand how important your contribution to the war effort could be?"

"Commander, I certainly understand a little more now the significance of what you are asking from me. Even before this meeting, the proposed contract with Warners required a lot of serious thought. It is one thing to move over four thousand miles to a semi-tropical environment, but this would be for five years. I have yet to hear my immediate family's opinion or their reaction, and I have also to consider the future of my staff. There is also the reaction of the British press. Do I really want to be labelled as a rat leaving a sinking ship when it is the complete opposite to what my family and I feel? Though I must admit, I do feel selfish when somebody such as Leslie Howard places themselves in harm's way by travelling in and out of Spain and Portugal whilst I am being offered a safe birth in America! I can tell you now, if it was only my decision that was needed, I would probably say yes, but because I have family commitments, I would ask you to give me a week's grace in which to give you an answer."

"I perfectly understand, Mr Conrad and willingly agree because even if your answer is in the affirmative, it will be several months before we could send you on your way. Travel documents have to be arranged, your briefing will take some time, there will have to be a blackout with the press on your activities which would minimise the public's reaction to your leaving the country and of course, some time will be required for you to obtain visas to enter the United States. Once again, I will reiterate that upon your acceptance, his Majesty's government will take care of every detail. Unfortunately, as I am already late for another meeting I must attend, I shall have to take my leave of you. Shall we finalise this meeting by you agreeing to notifying us of your decision in a week's time?"

"I certainly agree to that, gentleman," I answered, "and may I say that I am flattered at the opportunity that you have given me to serve my adopted country."

Commander Burton rose from the table and shaking each one of us by hand, bade us goodbye. But before leaving, paused briefly in front of me with a twinkle in his eye.

"I caught your performance as Marc Anthony in *Julius Caesar* at the Old Vic last year and was spellbound. I think the time is ripe for you to do a revival of Shakespeare's *Henry V*, either here or in America. Just think how well Henry's speech on the eve of the Battle of Agincourt would be received by today's audiences. If I remember, it starts something like this, *"Once more into the breach, dear friends."* It really shouldn't be difficult to find an angel to back such a production. Oh, and how silly of me, the thought has just struck me that I haven't left you any instructions on how to communicate with me. Ian will give you some contact numbers at the Foreign Office which will connect you speedily to him. Well, once more, Mr Conrad, goodbye and let us hope our paths cross again."

After the Commander had left, the three of us stood at the window looking over the river Thames at the landscape of London with only the anti-aircraft balloons above the city to remind us that we were now at war. After some desultory conversation, Ian Lang handed me a card with several telephone numbers and then with his colleague, David Hislop, gathered up their files and proceeded to accompany me back downstairs to the central lobby where we parted company. As I stood on the pavement outside, viewing the sandbags piled outside the entrances, with an occasional ARP warden passing by and the increasing traffic in military personnel going about their business, I felt that it was all very surreal, for despite the fact that Marlene and myself had experienced first-hand, the evil of Nazism, we were now actually going to do battle with them.

Chapter 13

Decisions Made

The train back to Marlow was packed with commuters returning home from work and though I had managed to get a first-class seat at Paddington, the train was delayed by endless stopping and starting, no doubt due to the increased wartime traffic. Fortunately, things improved when I changed trains at high Wycombe for the Marlow branch line which I was able to do without waiting. I was denied total privacy as the only first-class carriage in the service was occupied by a mother and her son who were already seated in the carriage. Having recognised me, the lady let her boy, who was aged about ten years of age, know who I was. We soon struck up a conversation and I ended up telling the lad about the forthcoming fantasy film, *Ali Baba*, with its Arabian nights theme which greatly excited him, especially when I told him that I was playing the wicked Vizier. I signed an autograph for them both and watched them get off at Cookham and as the train pulled away from the platform, I waved goodbye.

As luck would have it, when I arrived at Marlow, I was able to commandeer the one and only taxi, despite the recently imposed rationing of petrol. I must admit that war was a great leveller of the social classes, for normally I would be using my own transport. So, it became a pleasant surprise to me to be brought firmly down to earth by the cab driver who proved to be very sociable over the short journey to Falcon House, telling me that he had lived in Marlow both as man and boy for the last fifty years and although little had changed in the town these past years, having an air force station in the immediate area had boosted the local economy. I discovered that his name was Bert and that the one question everybody was asking soon came up, "Do you think the war will be over with by Christmas?" Realising that I now had some doubts on the matter, I remained non-committal, preferring to make vague comments.

Finally, as we neared the house, he mentioned that his wife was badgering him to take her to see *Gone with the Wind*, the film adaptation of the Margaret Mitchell novel. Unfortunately, it was only being shown at ABC cinemas, the nearest being High

Wycombe. He asked me if I thought that the film would be worth the extra effort? And being that I was a famous film star, perhaps I would be able to advise him? It was with some humour that I told him that the film was worth seeing and that his wife would never forgive him for not taking her to see it. As we pulled up outside the front door, I asked him whether he was in the telephone book so that we could call upon his services when needed. Without further ado, he pulled a business card out of his pocket telling me that I would always be able to count on him.

Once inside the house, I was greeted by Marlene who threw herself into my arms and kissed me and appeared to be in an extraordinary good mood. I also sensed the same from Olivia as she greeted me from the doorway of the office. I had hardly taken my raincoat off before I was being told that her mama and papa and Olivia were having dinner with us that evening. She had then grabbed me by the hand and was pulling me down the hallway into the lounge. After pushing me down onto the sofa, she proceeded to pour a Jack Daniels which she handed to me as she sat down beside me. I had sensed by now, just looking at her, with her eyes shining with excitement and her face covered in a rosy glow that good news was about to be delivered and I had a rather good idea what it would be.

"I paid the doctor a visit this morning for a check-up, Gunty and you will be pleased to know that some time, around Christmas this year, the stork will be arriving bringing us both a bundle of joy." For a few seconds, I was speechless, then the emotion of the moment overcame me and bursting with happiness, I grabbed her and gave her a big kiss. Once the initial reaction had passed, she told me all the details, on how she had missed a period and waited before going to her doctor earlier that day. Once he had confirmed it, she was so overcome with excitement that she had to tell someone. Because her mother was working at the BBC and her father was performing several operations, there was nobody to turn too to share the good news with other than Olivia, who soon put everything in its proper perspective spending the remainder of the afternoon in girl talk. As she was talking, I suddenly realised that I had my own news to tell her. I was not so sure that I wanted to tell her right at this moment, but I had really no choice. To delay might make matters even more complicated. I needed Marlene's decision and support on whether we should go to America, before telling the rest of the family. There was also the uncertainty and lack of knowledge concerning the fate of her sister and the rest of the family, all the while hovering over us like a dark cloud. Since Holland had been occupied by the Germans, there had been no communication with her sister or nor were we any clearer on the whereabouts of the remainder of her family in Germany. I really didn't have much choice, so I quietly gave her a blow-by-blow account of the day's proceedings, studying her face all the while for any indication of how she was taking the news. But she gave none. She just sat there holding my hand and listening intently to what I had to say.

When I had finished speaking, she sat for a moment contemplating the impact of my remarks, then started speaking.

"You know, Gunty, when we discussed this a little while ago, I had already made up my mind to fully support you if you made the decision to go to America. My decision at that time was because it was good for your career and that opportunities don't come along that often in one's lifetime. Now, I would think poorly of you if you didn't go. You are being given an opportunity to strike back at that monster, Hitler and his band of thugs and by doing so, will more than likely contribute to the destruction of his vicious regime. My goodness me, I think that we all best eat first tonight before giving mama and papa such an avalanche of information. As far as they are both concerned, I know that they will consider it all good news.

As far as I can see, we have more than enough time to consider the welfare of those who work for us and to see their immediate future safeguarded if we must let them go. I am also quite sure that it won't take too long for our accountants to put our business affairs in order before we leave. As for the rest of it, I am convinced that the British government will smooth the way for you, whenever necessary. As for mama and papa and Olivia, once they have been told tonight, we will go along with any decisions that they arrive at and I'm sure that you agree with me that it doesn't have to be today."

We spent most of the dinner time that evening discussing Churchill's speech to the House of Commons and how long the French government would hold out before they capitulated, but as soon as the dessert plates had been cleared away and the coffee served, I gave them the good news and the not so good news, with

Marlene adding her own comments. Our announcement of a forthcoming baby had Miriam jumping up from the table and smothering Marlene with kisses whilst Hiram shook my hand vigorously, congratulating both of us. The second part of our announcement provoked a more muted response. Hiram was the first to speak but not before he had helped himself to a small brandy.

"You know, the pair of you should not be feeling guilty simply because you have been given the opportunity to make progress with your career in the United States or that it could be helping the war effort in some way. I know that I speak not only for myself but for Miriam as well when I say that we both have reached an age when we are too old to go through all the upheaval of starting a new life. We went through the trauma of all that when we left Germany and were allowed into Britain as your dependants. Britain is our country and our home and we both still have plenty to contribute to it in its hour of need and as I have taken up specialising in trauma surgery, my skills will be required even more. As for Miriam, she couldn't be happier than working for the BBC and I suspect that she will be kept busy soon, broadcasting anti-Nazi propaganda to all of Europe. The only thing that we will regret, will be missing the birth of our grandchild but that will be a small price to pay in comparison to the sacrifices that will be made by our armed services so that future generations will be born into a better world. Let this be a night of joy and celebration and brace ourselves for what lies ahead." Olivia was the next to speak but not before raising her glass in a toast to the Conrad family. Then she addressed both of us.

"Gunther, I started work for you when you both first arrived in Britain in 1936 and gradually, over the years, you have made me a member of your family. We have shared happiness and sorrow together and despite your fame and wealth I have always found you both honest and straightforward in your dealings with everybody that you have encountered. I have experienced with you all the terrible religious persecution that both Marlene and her family been subjected too. Now is the time for all of us to stand together and to do whatever is necessary to defeat this monster at our gates before he destroys all that is good and true in the world. Meanwhile, I agree with Hiram that all our personal problems will be worked out over the coming weeks, but tonight is a night for celebration. Let's adjourn to the lounge and plays some records and drink some wine and bring Bill and Lucy in to celebrate the future arrival of a new member of the Conrad clan and to reaffirm our unity and determination for whatever lies ahead.''

None of us had expected such an emotive speech from Olivia and much to her discomfort, we all gathered around to embrace her. Hiram then asked all of us to hold hands and bow our heads in a short prayer. Then he, Marlene and Miriam recited a prayer in Yiddish, after which, as Olivia went to the kitchen to fetch Bill and Lucy, the four of us drifted into the lounge and as we waited for the others to arrive, I thought I would start the mini celebration by placing a stack of Glenn Miller singles in the turntable and turning the volume up, so just for an hour or two, we could forget the outside world.

The following morning, my first call was to Ian Lang at the Foreign Office informing him of my decision to operate in an undercover capacity for the British government whilst working in the United States. I also thought it best to add that because it involved a long stay, I would also be taking my wife with me. Ian Lang thanked me for the decision that I had made and he wanted me to know that it was greatly appreciated. He then asked me for the address of my solicitors so that he could send them the appropriate visa application forms for the United States which needed to be filled in promptly and returned to him. He also said that he would be informing Commander Burton of our telephone conversation, who no doubt, would get in touch with me very soon and finally, before ringing off, thanked me once again for my decision to do my bit for the war effort.

My second call was to Robin Cox telling him to go ahead and inform Warners that I was ready to sign the contract but to please make sure that a clause allowing me time off to do the occasional play was included. After listening to me, Robin replied that he would notify the legal department at Warners right away and was quite sure that from a professional point of view, I was making the right decision. However, he felt that the offer had come at the wrong time and it might be wise to give it as little publicity as possible, as it could turn the British cinema going public against me. I told Robin that I fully appreciated his concern and had already taken that on board. Unfortunately, that was a risk that I had to take. I asked him to only think the best of me as there were other ways of serving your adopted country without wearing a uniform. It might be best, therefore, to think only of it as a confidence to be shared strictly between us. Robin remained silent for a few seconds before replying.

''Reading between the lines, Gunther, if what you are telling me is for some reason a matter of national security, then I shall be supporting you unreservedly with no questions asked.''

The third important call was to my accountants. Because of the little time that I had left before leaving for America and having loaned the government a considerable portion of my liquid assets, I needed to safeguard the remainder of my property in our absence and of course, I would also need monies to draw on when we arrived in the United States.

Both Olivia and I had kept busy that morning gathering important documents from our files and generally bringing the office up to date. Marlene had popped her head around the office door insisting that as it was now two o'clock in the afternoon, it wouldn't be a bad idea to stop for something to eat, a thought we instantly agreed with. In fact, after we had arrived in the kitchen, I decided to call it a day. The weather was perfect for the end of May and the gardens were alive with colour. Obviously taking advantage of the fact, both Bill and John had brought out the garden furniture whilst the womenfolk had carried out the lunch. After a hearty communal al fresco buffet, I immersed myself in the daily papers and even reading between the lines of the censored dispatches, I realised things were getting pretty dangerous for our troops and that they were being forced back to the coast and in particular, to the town of Dunkirk. It did not take me long to get fed up reading the depressing news, so grabbing Marlene by the hand, we proceeded to walk down to the riverbank.

When I had bought the cabin cruiser, at the same time, I had erected a boathouse to accommodate it and as we both stood there gazing at the boat gently bobbing up and down with the rhythm of the river, I remarked to Marlene that we were hardly likely to find a buyer now for the boat, so the only solution would be to mothball it for the duration of the time that we would be spending in America.

''Whilst we are on that subject, Gunty, have you come up with any ideas regarding the house. Personally, I would not like to see it put on the market as it holds too many happy memories. This is where we first gained our freedom to live without fear of persecution and where mama and papa gained refuge from the tyranny of Nazism and where our child was conceived. One day, we will return to Britain and it is my desire that Falcon House will be waiting to welcome us home."

"I too, have been giving that a lot of thought, my darling. I can see no reason why Hiram and Miriam cannot continue to live in the cottage and neither can I see any reason why Lucy and Bill can't continue to live in their apartment above the garage. Also, John and Mary could continue in the present positions. As for the house itself, it wouldn't be a bad idea for us to lend it to the government, providing that they were willing to commission it for the duration of the war, perhaps as officers' quarters for the camp at Medmenham."

"I think that's a brilliant idea, Gunty. The very thought that our house could somehow contribute something towards Hitler's defeat would give me a great deal of satisfaction. I also have been thinking a lot about Olivia's position and I think it is only fair to her that the three of us get together to discuss any plans that she may have for her future. I don't know whether you have thought about it, but I would like us to offer her the choice of going to America with us. There would be no better choice than Olivia to continue as your private secretary and being somewhat selfish, I would feel far more secure having her there with me when my delivery date arrives. It might well be that she has other plans which is why we should discuss it with her as soon as possible."

"I think you are quite right in your thinking, Marlene and it certainly seems like a very good idea, one that we should discuss with Olivia, if only for the fact that should she agree, we will need some time in which to get her passport and visa approved. It seems that I'm going to be kept busy in the next few weeks, what with dealing with accountants, my agent, my business manager and the Foreign Office. I think for the moment, you and I should take a leaf out of the book of that family of Swans and their cygnets regally gliding down the river and just lean back and let the world go drifting by."

This was a feeling that was never going to last long, either for us or for the other millions of British couples. It was during the following morning that the reality of war came home to us and I mean that literally. Olivia and I were in the office when we saw the car draw up to the front door out of which stepped two men, one of whom was a naval officer. They stopped briefly to talk to Bill then waited patiently while he came into the house to inform me that they wished to speak to me. Accompanied by Bill, I walked out of the house to greet them. The naval officer introduced himself as Captain Johnson and his companion as a Mr Dickinson from the Ministry of Shipping. It seems that I had missed a radio appeal for seagoing boats owned by the public. They were now carrying out a physical search for all suitable craft up and down the Thames. Apparently, the initial broadcast for civilian boats had been so successful that they had exhausted the pool of naval personnel to crew them. Unfortunately, the Navy still needed more. The upshot of their visit was that as I was a registered owner of a seagoing motor cruiser named *Marlene*, could I, therefore, spare the time for them to examine the craft for suitability. I agreed and asked them to follow me down to the boathouse.

As we passed the kitchen, Marlene caught sight of us and being naturally inquisitive started to follow us. Once Captain Johnson set eyes upon the boat, there was no holding him. He jumped on board and disappeared below deck re-emerging several minutes later and started the engine. After listening for a minute or two, he cut the engine and jumped back onto land where he re-joined us. Looking straight at Mr Dickinson, he nodded his head, whereupon he pulled a black notebook out of his jacket pocket and made some entries. During all this time, both Marlene and Bill had joined us just in time to hear him address me.

"I'm sorry to put this on you, Mr Conrad, but I shall have to requisition your boat. It is well within the guidelines laid down by the Ministry. She is more than thirty foot in length and of the required shallow draught. I am afraid that to add insult to injury, we are also suffering from a shortage of naval manpower. We are looking for civilian volunteers to crew their own craft. The British Expeditionary Force is in serious trouble, enough to say that it is trapped in a pocket surrounded by German forces, in a place called Dunkirk with its back to the sea and although the Royal Navy is there, the water is too shallow for our home fleet. What we need urgently, to solve the problem of evacuating our soldiers from the beaches to the naval ships, are small seagoing craft that can lift them from the beaches and ferry them to our larger vessels. That is why I have been ordered to commandeer as many civilian boats as I can find. Your vessel is exactly what we want I'm afraid and I shall need to requisition it immediately. Now comes the hard part. As I said earlier, because of the large amount of commercial shipping and civilian pleasure boats that we have already sent over, we have drained the pool of naval and merchant marine personnel to man these boats. I am afraid because of that situation and time being of the utmost importance, I must ask you if you would volunteer to sail your craft downriver to Sheerness where it will join an armada of small boats ready to sail for France. Although this is not mandatory and I must emphasise that this is only a request to volunteer, would you be prepared to continue to skipper your own boat from Sheerness on towards France? I must make it clear to you, Mr Conrad, that it would be no picnic. The Germans are quite determined that they will wipe out the British forces. They are at present attempting to smash through the Anglo-French defensive lines safeguarding Dunkirk whilst the Luftwaffe is busy both bombing and strafing the beaches. I cannot emphasise enough that your life would be at serious risk, but to put it bluntly, the country is in mortal danger and needs every pair of hands that it can get so that Britain has the breathing space in which it will need to recover from this debacle. Hopefully, that will give Britain time in which to rebuild its shattered forces and fight the Germans on another day."

Just for a second or perhaps a heartbeat or two, I stood and looked at both Marlene and Miriam and there was just simply no contest. The woman that I loved and her whole family had suffered appalling humiliation and cruelty based purely on their religion and many of them were still in the clutches of that evil government. Turning to Captain Johnson, I delivered my answer.

"I am prepared to volunteer to take my boat over to Dunkirk, captain. Just tell me when and where I will receive my orders and whatever else I will need."

"Mr Conrad, just for now, I would like to thank you on behalf of his Majesty's government. I am afraid that you must set off for Sheerness within the hour and must be prepared to be away for at least forty-eight hours. When you arrive at Sheerness, you will be briefed and given charts by which you will navigate the route to Dunkirk. Depending on the lateness of the hour, you will probably rest over until dawn. You will also require one extra crew member though looking at the size of your boat and what you may have to go through I would say two would be wiser. I'm sorry that I can't stay longer but I have other boats on the river I must look at before sunset. I think Mr Dickinson has now recorded all the relevant details and a rough estimate of your departure. So, we will leave you now but don't forget when you reach Sheerness, report to the harbourmaster's office for further instructions. Goodbye then, Mr Conrad and good luck.''

As Captain Johnson and Mr Dickinson departed towards the house, Marlene momentarily stood looking at me then turned and arm in arm with her mother and Olivia, slowly started back, leaving just Bill and I standing by the boathouse. Bill had always been a somewhat laconic type of character and inevitably, kept his thoughts to himself. Fetching a packet of cigarettes out of his pocket, he offered me one which I took. Having placed one in his mouth, he took out his lighter, offering me first light, after which, he lit his own. After drawing deeply, he exhaled smoke and looking me straight in the eye, asked me a question in such a matter of fact voice he could almost have been asking me the time of day.

''So, what time do you reckon we will be starting off then, Mr Conrad?''

''We! What do you mean we, Bill? There is no way that I am taking you with me. You have Lucy to consider as your dependent, plus your family and besides, you are getting a little long in the tooth for gallivanting around on the high seas. Seriously though, I shall be happy enough knowing that you will be here holding the fort and ensuring that everything is running smoothly.''

''Sorry, Mr Conrad, but it's not only just your war. It's mine as well and like many Brits of my generation, we still have a score to settle with the Huns. No, Mr Conrad. I am afraid that you are stuck with me and the only way that you can stop me from going is to sack me. Besides, your film fans would lynch me if they knew that I had let you wander off on your own.'' I couldn't help but smile to myself at the thought of Bill being chased by angry fans.

''Putting it like that, Bill, you give me no choice but to take you with me and may I add that I am proud of you for volunteering. You do realise that you have got to tell Lucy and that might be a more frightening experience than facing the Germans. I suggest that as time is running short, we go up to the house now and face the music.''

"Okay, Mr Conrad and don't you worry your head about Lucy. She may put up a bit of a show, but she'll come around before we leave. Just before we set off for the house, I'd better top up the tank. It's a good job John had the foresight to store up a few cans of petrol because we have got a fair distance of river to travel before, we reached the Medway River and Sheerness."

When Bill and I finally reached the house, I must admit that I opened the kitchen door with some trepidation not knowing what sort of a reception I would receive and especially not knowing how Lucy would react to Bill's decision to come with me. It was all rather anticlimactic for the scene before me was of Olivia, Miriam and Lucy preparing a large cardboard box with provisions. Before I had a chance to enquire where Marlene was, Lucy had stopped what she was doing and folding her arms across her chest, gave her husband such a look of reproach that it's a wonder the pair of us weren't jammed in the doorway as we tried to make a fast exit.

"I know what you're up to William Jackson," Lucy said to her husband. "I haven't been married to you for all these years without knowing what you are capable of. You think that you're going to go off with Mr Conrad on some sort of an adventure to France. Well, let me tell you, William Jackson, it won't be no adventure. You could more as like get yourself blooming killed and if that was to happen, don't expect me to speak to you again." As soon as she had spoken, her features softened. She lifted her hand and gently touched the side of his face. Looking him straight in the eyes.

"Oh Bill, you are a big lump! I know it's what you want to do and I'm proud of you. Just make sure that the pair of you bring yourselves back in one piece. Mr Conrad, madam is upstairs packing a few overnight things for you to take with you, so I'm going to whip over to the flat and pack a few things for Bill as well." Leaving them all in the kitchen, I went looking for Marlene upstairs and found her in the bedroom placing clean underwear and socks, plus a shirt, into a small, brown attaché case. As soon as she saw me enter the bedroom, she stopped what she was doing and walking up to me embraced me.

"For a few moments out there on the riverbank, Gunty, I felt moments of anger. I couldn't understand why you would want to put yourself in harm's way knowing that I was pregnant. Then, as

I walked back to the house, I began to realise that I was being selfish and that, as hard as it was to realise, there were thousands of men fighting for their lives, who in all probability, had families of their own or wives who were also expecting a baby and some of those men would not live to experience that joy again. I also thought about the humiliation and persecution that my parents had endured under Nazi rule as indeed I had endured and the continuing hatred still imposed upon the remainder of my race still trapped in Europe. It was then that I realised not only why you had volunteered but how proud I was for your courage in doing so. I just hope and pray that the Lord will protect you and send you safely home to me. As you can see, we are busy making a box of food up for you. Where I am being selfish is that Lucy seems to feel that Bill will go with you and if that is true, I will be a lot happier knowing that you won't be alone.''

''Oh, my darling, you don't know how guilty I feel in leaving you at a time when we should be celebrating the forthcoming birth of our baby. But we won't be parted for long. I am determined to return as quickly as possible. Promise me that you are not going to sit around fretting. I am afraid that Bill and I must leave as soon as possible, not only do we have a fair distance to travel to Sheerness, but we also have to be briefed when we arrive on how to navigate the distance to Dunkirk and also, on how to respond with what lies ahead of us when we reach France, I don't think it will do either one of us any good to prolong our goodbyes. Just remember, before we go downstairs, you're the girl for me, always have been and always will be.''

When we went back downstairs to the kitchen, Olivia and Miriam were just putting the finishing touches to our ration box. As Lucy and Bill were absent, I assumed that they had gone over to their flat to pick up some clean clothing for whilst he was away and to say their farewells to each other. Knowing Bill as I did, he probably made light of it as if he was only going down to the local pub. Both Miriam and Olivia responded to the occasion in their own way. Miriam rushed over to me and taking my face between her hands, kissed me on both cheeks assuring me that I was under the Lord's special protection and that she would say a prayer for me tonight, one to watch over me and a second one for having made sure that Hiram had been working this day and therefore, had kept him out of harm's way. As for Olivia, she was so British, so stiff upper lip and so nonchalant. But so much loved. She reminded me of that marvellous actress, Dame May Whitty, in the film of *The Lady Vanishes,* just standing there noting down the contents of the amount of food that that we would be taking with us. Then, having completed that task, she moved around the kitchen table and putting her hand in her jacket pocket, spoke to me as she placed an object in my hand.

"Right, Gunther, I have placed a list of all the provisions in the box, so that you won't need to rummage through it to find out what you have to eat. Furthermore, while we are on the subject of your intended absence, are there further instructions regarding any urgent matters that are likely to come up that you would like me to deal with? More importantly, how long do you think you'll be away for? The reason I am asking is it might be prudent for you to sign one or two cheques to cover any emergency that may come up. As for the more mundane matters, I am sure Marlene will deal with the everyday running costs out of petty cash as they arise. Finally, it would give me peace of mind for you to accept this St Christopher medallion, the patron saint of travellers. It was carried by my father throughout the Boar War campaign and brought him safely home and I expect nothing less than that for you. Take good care of yourself and do not do anything foolhardy. Do not worry about Marlene. We will all make sure that she will be well looked after." With that said, Olivia stepped back, and taking out a handkerchief, blew her nose very loudly whilst mumbling about having caught a summer cold.

Whilst waiting for Bill and Lucy to return, I took the opportunity of darting into the office. I suddenly remembered where I had put several navigational charts referencing the port of Sheerness and the northern coast of France. Once I had retrieved them, I was able to do a quick calculation in my head and reckoned that with an average speed of twenty-five knots per hour, we should be able to reach Sheerness in just under two hours. Either way, we would arrive well before sunset. So, gathering up the charts, I walked back into the kitchen to find that Bill and Lucy had arrived. Bill was carrying a half-filled kit bag presumably filled with clean clothes, I imagined that the kit bag was a left over from the First World War. Who would have imagined that in just over twenty years, the same kit bag would be in service again to fight the same enemy? I attempted to reassure our womenfolk that all would be fine and that Bill and I would be looking out for each other. I knew that it was time for us to leave before we caused any more unnecessary heartache to our loved ones. Once we had checked off all the items that were necessary for our journey, the five of us gathered them all up and set off towards the boat. I had taken the opportunity earlier to change into what I called my boating clothes; dungarees, a plaid sports shirt and a windcheater, whilst Bill was sporting a pair of old khaki army trousers and a heavy Shetland isle polo necked jumper. I suppose to an outsider looking in, the pair of us probably looked like two guys out for a day's fishing and would never have guessed that in fact, we were sailing off to a war zone.

As soon as we had loaded our rations on board, I reversed the boat out and brought her around to the embankment where Bill tied her up so that I would have her facing down river when we were ready to leave. As I stepped ashore, Marlene emerged from the boathouse carrying my Wellingtons. As she handed them to me, she gave me a look of reproach.

"You are going to need these and the four pairs of socks I've packed to ensure that your feet will be both clean and dry. Remember, don't try to be heroic, just do what you can and come home. Don't forget that you have two of us to come home too. Now get going, big lug! This is no film set and I'm not going to stand here weeping buckets of tears so give me a kiss and go."

I pulled her close to me and kissed her gently on the lips and finally, whilst running my fingers through her hair gently, I told her.

"I love you and I shall be back within the next few days, so you don't get rid of me that easily."

Having embraced Miriam, Olivia and Lucy, I jumped back on board and started the engine up giving Bill enough time to say goodbye to Lucy. Once he was on board and had cast off, I pulled away and the last view I had, as we turned the bend, was of the four women standing on the embankment waving us goodbye.

We were able to keep up a consistent speed which enabled us to reach the port of Sheerness well within two hours. It took us some time to find a birth as the harbour was filled with ships of all sizes. I spotted a naval corvette and a minesweeper plus motor torpedo boats and the little ships like ours. Bill and I also spied five or six anti-aircraft balloons hovering in the sky above us.

Eventually, having found a birth, we wandered along the harbour wall until we found the harbourmaster's office. On stating the purpose of our visit, we were directed to a building on the other side of the road which had a board fixed on the front of the building with the words, 'North East Naval Command'. Like all government buildings these days, it had its mandatory columns of sandbags on either side of the front doors, between which flowed a steady stream of people coming and going. Judging by the fact that most of the men was similarly dressed like us, I assumed that there had been a huge response for volunteers. One thing I did notice was that most people were wearing their gas masks over their shoulder, something Bill and I had forgotten to bring with us as we had left them on the boat.

Once inside the building, we were directed by a naval rating to a room on the ground floor marked new arrivals. It was a large room with rows of empty chairs facing a small stage upon which stood a table and a blackboard. The only other physical activity was that of a naval officer whose rank I was unfamiliar with (probably a lieutenant) judging by the single ring upon his sleeve and a petty officer, who were both in the process of gathering up various charts and papers. Looking up, as we made our way towards them, the petty officer enquired our business there and once I had told him, he looked at his superior, who immediately extended his hand towards me.

"Good afternoon, gentlemen or perhaps I should say evening. My name is Lieutenant Mason and this gentleman here is Petty Officer Billings. I am afraid that you have just missed the briefing of our latest group of volunteers. However, in view of the urgency of the situation, we will take you through the briefing now. Have you, by any chance, got the form on you that designates the type of boat that you own?" It took me a few seconds to locate the paper from the recesses of my windcheater and hand it over to him.

"I see here that you own a forty-foot Teal-Rampart 30, built by Thornycroft which is about as good as it gets when it comes to civilian small craft. Is that correct? I also assume as well, that you are, Mr Conrad, the owner of the boat and may I ask who this gentleman is?"

"The answer to the first two questions is yes, Lieutenant Mason and as to the third, this is my fellow crewman, Mr William Jackson."

"Thank you, gentlemen. Perhaps, if you would like to step around, I will show you the best route to take. There were originally two but unfortunately, the Germans have now intensified their attacks on the beaches, making it, I am afraid to say, extremely hazardous. The safest route remaining now is route X which, if you follow my finger on this navigation chart - Petty Officer Billings will give you a copy before you leave - which means that you will sail from Dover around the Goodwin sand and north of the Goodwin light ship and through the Ruytingen pass and on to Dunkirk, a distance of thirty-eight nautical miles. With a boat such as yours, it shouldn't take you much longer than two hours. Because there are sections of the channel nearest France that are heavily mined, it would be wiser to proceed to Dover this evening and set off for Dunkirk at sunrise tomorrow morning. Once you arrive at Dunkirk, you will realise the importance of why the Navy has sent out an SOS for small boats. Although we have many naval ships ready to evacuate the troops, they are simply too far out for the soldiers to reach. However, if we can raise enough small boats, the Tommies could wade out to them and then be ferried to the larger vessels. The beaches are very wide but would give the soldiers a chance to be rescued by only having to wade through a hundred yards of sea to the waiting small craft."

"Do you mind if I ask you a few questions, Lieutenant Mason?" I asked.

"Not at all, Mr Conrad. Fire away and I'll do my best to answer them."

"How many troops do we need to evacuate from the beaches? How many boats will make up the armada to accomplish that mission? And finally, how long are we to remain in harms' way?"

"Good questions, Mr Conrad. There are approximately two-hundred and seventy small craft already there or on their way and about thirty following on behind including your good selves. Most of that group are made up of speedboats, motor lifeboats, cabin cruisers, car ferries and paddle steamers. Then there are the big boys, who are there to carry out the main evacuation and to defend the perimeter from the sea. They are made up of one anti-aircraft cruiser, thirty-nine destroyers, thirty-six minesweepers, thirty-four tugboats. As to the number of men to be evacuated, I can only guess at a figure of about four-hundred thousand. As to your final question, only you will be the best judge in that situation. My advice would be to return home as soon as your fuel begins to run low or, if your boat runs into difficulties, to abandon it and return home on one of the naval vessels. Finally, I can only tell you that it's going to be rough out there and a lot is being asked of you civilian volunteers but Godspeed and may he protect you. Now, as I said earlier, if I were you, I would start out for Dover and get a few hours rest overnight there. One more thing, Mr Conrad. Just to satisfy my curiosity before you leave. You aren't, by any chance, Gunther Conrad the film star? Because if you are, I would like to shake your hand as a representative of all the civilian mariners taking part in this massive evacuation of our embattled soldiers. I also think that for somebody in your position it is very courageous thing that you are doing."

"Thank you for your comment, Lieutenant Mason, but for my part, I would be grateful if you left it as a case of mistaken identity. As you said earlier, it's best that we get off now and reach Dover before nightfall and just before we leave, I would like to thank you for your patience in dealing with two civilian novices."

We sailed to Dover through calm waters. The weather was as perfect as it possibly could be. There was a mild and balmy breeze in our faces and as it was the first day of June tomorrow, we could be facing a warm month. We reached Dover harbour by six-thirty that evening and having found a birth for the boat, Bill and I repeated the same routine as we had at Sheerness, in trying to find a naval command centre. Once we had located the building and our identities and information were duly logged, we were then issued a chitty for cans of petrol with the advice that on reaching Dunkirk, we should locate Bray Dunes where the largest amount of beach evacuation was centred. The meeting was terminated with the shaking of hands and with good luck ringing in our ears, we left the building for the nearest telephone kiosk so that we could phone home and let the girls know that we had arrived safely at Dover. Unfortunately, when we did find some telephone kiosks, there was a queue of six fellows presumably with the same thing in mind. It was obvious that it was going to be some time before it was our turn, so giving Bill a pound note, I suggested that he get as many pennies as he could for the coin box whilst I stayed in the queue. It was almost an hour before I was able to make the call home and Marlene was the first to pick the phone up.

"Hello, darling," I said. "We have finally ended up here at Dover and will be leaving for Dunkirk at sunrise tomorrow. Although there are quite a few boats assembled in the harbour, I get the feeling that we are the tail end of the rescue armada and that the majority of vessels are already at Dunkirk. I know it's silly to tell you not to worry about us because I know that you will. I anticipate that it will be about forty-eight hours before I can contact you again, but the time will soon fly by. I am afraid, darling, that I can't speak for long as I am in a call box and apart from Bill, there are another seven blokes waiting to make the same phone call. I just want you to know that I love you that you are to take care of yourself and the baby whilst I am away and give my love to everybody there and if Lucy is there with you, I am going to hand over to Bill. Before I go, sweetheart, I will say cheerio and knowing how much you enjoy listening to Tommy Handley in the radio show *ITMA* I will just say T.T.F.N. Love you and see you soon."

With that, I stepped out of the kiosk and handed the receiver to Bill. As Shakespeare would say, parting is such sweet sorrow and boy, did I feel depressed. Reaching into my windcheater, I pulled out a packet of twenty Players' cigarettes. Pulling one out of the packet, I lit it and inhaled deeply whilst I offered the pack to those in the queue. Whilst I waited for Bill, I thought about Marlene's words to me and I had to admire her stoicism and courage. It also brought a smile to my face when she said, "Cut out all that bullshit nonsense and don't overdo the courage; there's only one hero in pictures and that's Errol Flynn and don't you forget it, lover boy."

As soon as Bill came out of the telephone box, we started walking back towards the Quay looking for a pub and it didn't take us long to find one, with the sign above the door announcing the Railway Tavern. The tap room was busy and filled with tobacco smoke. Somehow, they had been able to squeeze in an upright piano which was being played ferociously by a very plump gentleman upon whose head sat a bowler hat. The tune that he was playing was *Doing the Lambeth Walk* lustily sung by half of the patrons many of which I suspect had consumed a few pints already. Finally, when we caught the landlord's eye, I asked him for some of what most of his patrons seemed to be drinking as they appeared to be having a great time. "Two pints of Fremlin's best bitter, will it be, sir?" I also asked him if he had anything to eat? He replied, "I can get the missus to knock you up a couple of cheese and ham sandwiches, seeing as I know a local farmer. It pays to know people in times like these, 'cos then we can all help each other. I mean, for instance, take half my customers in here tonight. They'll be off to France in the morning and if you don't mind me saying so, sir, I suspect that you will be too. So, as I see it, sir, a little bit of ham and cheese under the counter don't hurt nobody, especially if they're one of them picture actors trying to do their bit for King and country. Know what I mean, sir?"

With a smile and a wink, he called out to his wife, "Marge, do two rounds of ham and cheese sandwiches." Then pulling two pints, he pushed them towards us asking me at the same time for three shillings. Whether it was the sea air or the several more pints of bitter, but the sandwiches went down a treat. We left the pub early before because we both thought it wise to have an early night. Hopefully, we hadn't left it too late to buy petrol. As it happened, luck was with us. As we walked back along the harbour to the boat, we spied a ramshackle hut with a battered sign, proclaiming 'Petrol Station' and just in front of the hut was a solitary petrol pump, manned by an old sea dog whom I took to be his sixties. Once again, lady luck was smiling upon us for he was just about to shut down for the night. We presented him with our Royal Naval chitty and were able to buy four cans of petrol which according to my rough calculations and added to what we already had on board, would be enough to cover our needs. By the time we had struggled back to the boat, we were ready for our bunks and a few hours' sleep.

I was awoken after what seemed only a few minutes, by my shoulder being shaken. Bill was standing over me, holding a mug of tea.

"Time to get up, Mr Conrad. It's six o'clock and it looks like it's going to be a good sailing day. Although the sea seems a little choppy, we should make good time across the Channel. Now get this tea down you and when you are ready, there are some sausage sandwiches on the table that my Lucy made yesterday and whilst you are doing that, I will go up on deck and prepare the boat for sailing." By the time I had a quick wash and shave and had dressed, Bill had already navigated the boat past the harbour wall and was out to sea. As soon as I came up on deck, I could feel the sea air on my face and smell the brine. Bill was standing at the wheel with a mug of tea in one hand and as soon as he noticed me, called out.

"Good morning, Mr Conrad. Ready for what lies ahead of us? Several boats have already gone on and I think that there is one more behind us. Our speed is averaging thirty knots, so we should reach Dunkirk within two hours."

"Good morning, Bill. As you said, it's a great morning to be out at sea but very soon, we shall have to keep our wits about us. Whilst you man the steering wheel, I will just check the chart, for once we are past the Goodwin Sands and become closer to the French coast, we will need to keep our eyes peeled for mines and enemy aircraft."

"You know, Mr Conrad, whilst I have been standing here, the thought struck me how strange life can be in its twists and turns. Twenty odd years ago, we were mortal enemies sworn to kill each other and now, we are comrades-in-arms facing a shared enemy. Godspeed to us both and pray that we both emerge unscathed from what lies ahead."

Chapter 14

Whatever the Cost May Be

We didn't have to see our destination to know that we had arrived. The sounds of warfare and the flashes of heavy artillery identified by black clouds of smoke heralded our arrival to the shoreline of Dunkirk. It was a weird feeling, almost as if we were being drawn into an oil painting depicting two opposing forces attacking each other. There was no mistaking the British naval forces protecting the trapped British soldiers. I lost count of the number of destroyers arriving and leaving and certainly couldn't fail to miss the lone battle cruiser extending a protective shield to all the other ships, in particular, the tugboats who were ferrying the exhausted British soldiers from the beaches to the safety of the destroyers, it was at that moment that Bill and I had our first baptism of combat.

No sooner had we arrived than the Luftwaffe launched an aerial attack consisting of Heinkel bombers, Stukas and Messerschmitt fighter planes. The bombers were concentrating on the big ships whilst the fighter planes were targeting the small craft and the beaches. The Stuka fighter known for its intimidating whine when it dived on its helpless victims, proceeded to rake the water and the beach with machine-gun fire, as it pulled out of its dive. Bill and I watched hopelessly in horror, as we saw our soldiers running backwards and forwards desperately trying to escape the deadly fire. Suddenly out of the sun came a small group of Spitfires, who without any effort, overtook the Dornier bombers despatching two very quickly into a watery grave. They then peeled off into individual sorties, one climbing almost horizontally before diving to take up a position behind the tail of a Messerschmitt, which it quickly dispatched with a burst of cannon fire. We watched spellbound as the pilot of the doomed Messerschmitt bailed out of the smoking cockpit and slowly parachuted down into the sea whilst his plane disintegrated on impact with the water below him in a cloud of smoke. The whole scene was like a real-life version of Pablo Picasso's painting of the bombing of Guernica.

Bill and I had made a choice of heading for a spot on the beaches called Bray Dunes and it certainly was not difficult to find, as it was quickly identified by a long line of army lorries tied together and stretching out head to tail from the beach and acting as a makeshift causeway where from the beach side, soldiers were queueing up in orderly lines ready to proceed along it to the small boats such as ours. The boats were waiting to embark them and then shuttle them out to the waiting destroyers, minesweepers and tugboats. As well as the artificial causeway of lorries, there were five or six lines of soldiers stretching far back on the beach whilst snaking far into the sea. I reckoned that the first twenty men at the head of each line, had the sea water up to their armpits. I waited patiently until the boat in front of me, having successfully pulled on board survivors, pulled away and headed for the big ships. As I throttled back, Bill took up position halfway down the boat ready to haul on board the soaked soldiers. Between us, we had calculated that we would be able to take some fifteen soldiers, but we were sure that our estimate would be more precise after the first trip.

The first man to grab the side of our boat was a sergeant who, calling out to Bill, asked him how many men we could take. Leaning over the side of the boat, Bill grabbed the sergeant's arm replying.

"I reckon we can take fifteen lads, sarge. I'll pull you on board first and then the two of us can haul the rest in."

"Not for me this time, mate. I'm here to make sure that this lot get away in an orderly fashion without any panic. Right, you horrible lot, the first fifteen men wade up to me ready for embarking. Pacey, pacey we haven't got all day."

As soon as the first man had reached alongside, Bill and the sergeant hauled him aboard by his webbing. It didn't take long to fill the boat up and with careful placing of the soldiers, I found that we could accommodate another three, even though I was somewhat anxious about being awash in the water and adrift. Anyway, it was time to pull away, especially as there was another small boat waiting in turn behind me. Having got the last three men aboard, I steered away from the queueing men and headed out to sea towards the flotilla of naval ships. As there was no system to follow regarding the embarkation on to larger vessels, I came alongside a minesweeper which had rope netting hanging down the side. Having got into a position of touching alongside, I dropped a large bag into the water to stabilise our boat whilst the

Tommies made their way by climbing up the netting where there were seaman waiting to haul them over the railings. As soon as the last Tommy had left the boat, Bill pulled up the sea anchor and we commenced our journey back to the beach. We had hardly travelled a quarter of the way back before there was an almighty explosion followed by a second one. As I turned to look in the direction of the sounds, I heard Bill shouting out.

''My God, Mr Conrad. One of our destroyers has been hit.''

Looking at the direction in which he was pointing, I could clearly see a destroyer erupting in flames and smoke amidships. At the same time, a delayed shock sent a tidal wave of water of such force that I had great difficulty from preventing our boat from going on her beam ends. Simultaneously, the stricken destroyer started breaking up in front of our eyes, subjecting us both to the full horrors of war as the crew abandoned ship. Our little boat was one of many who made their way quickly to the danger zone though it proved a hazardous journey and required all my skills in navigation to avoid the floating debris and the ever-increasing amount of floating dead bodies.

As we neared the area which I called the rescue zone, all of the boats which had made the dash with us, made a circle on the outer perimeter of the stricken destroyer and waited until there was a lull in the enemy aircraft strafing us. We then raced in to pick up survivors as quickly as possible before another attack. Once we were approaching the main bulk of the survivors, I cut the engine and dropped my sea anchor and proceeded amidships to help Bill. We were soon hauling aboard sailors who were suffering from burns and bullet wounds, plus many were covered in oil. One of the men that I rescued was a boatswain's mate who told me that their ship was *HMS Havant* and that he was sure that they had been hit by torpedoes. Even as he spoke, *HMS Havant* turned on her beam ends and began to slide beneath the waves. With as many on-board that we could safely carry, I wasted no time in speeding away and quickly located a group of tugboats busy relieving the small craft of their survivors that they had picked up. As Bill and I helped unload the sailors onto the first available tugboat, the captain leaned from the bridge and shouted to me.

''Ahoy master. Proceed back to the beach and continue to evacuate the soldiers! There are enough boats here to deal with the abandoned sailors. You certainly don't want to be hanging around here, otherwise you may be a sitting target for those bloody Germans."

I didn't take much persuading as courage wasn't exactly the top of my agenda. I quickly opened up the throttle to its maximum knots and ducking and diving between my fellow mariners and the diving Stukas and Heinkels, arrived back in the same place of departure where we proceeded to continue the same process of evacuation. I am proud to say that between Bill and myself, by late afternoon, we had evacuated one-hundred and eighty troops and had ferried them to the mother ships. During a long day, we had seen two destroyers sunk and endless small craft destroycd by enemy machine-gun fire at a cost of many civilian lives. There was one moment in the day when I knew that we had been truly blessed by the Lord. We were doing another pick-up when a Dornier swooped in, dropping its load of bombs right on the beach where we were embarking troops. The detonations caused a considerable number of casualties amongst the scattering soldiers. Not only did the blast rock the boat but sent Bill flying overboard into the shallow water and blew me off my feet straight into the cockpit temporarily concussing me. I came to with the sensation of my face being slapped but had difficulty on focusing for the moment as my vision was obstructed with blood. However, I was able to identify the unmistakable voice coming from the blurred shape beside me as Bill's.

"You all right, governor? I had to give you a slap or to bring you around. Just lie still whilst I wash the blood off your face. Fortunately, there are two army medics tending to the wounded alongside, so don't worry, I've called out to them and they'll be with us as quick as they can. The good news is that some of our boys in blue came out of nowhere in their Hurricanes and chased those Kraut bombers off but not before shooting one down! So at least they won't be back for a little while. The bad news is that we have taken some damage on board and that we are awash, but we are still afloat, I'll soon get the pump working. There now, I've cleaned your face up the best that I can. You do have a nasty gash on your forehead, so hold this clean cloth to the wound until the medic arrives."

"Give us a lift up, Bill. I want to go aft and sit in the open air. Where possible, I can also give you a hand until I get my full strength back. At the same time, I will also be able to act as a sentry watching the sky for any marauding fighter planes."

As soon as I stood up, I became unsteady on my feet, but putting his arm around my waist, Bill eased me out of the cockpit and semi-dragged me to the stern where he sat me down. Sitting there gazing at the beach, I couldn't help but admire the fortitude and discipline of the British Army in retreat. Nevertheless, I am sure that in the last few days, there would have been quite a few acts of panic and mutiny as there are in any army. That, I'm afraid, is human nature.

Having satisfied myself that our zone was free from enemy fighters, I went back to scanning the beach. After the last aerial attack, several field ambulances had drawn up on the sand and were waiting with their engines running whilst stretcher bearers were ferrying the wounded back to them. The medics, by this time, were almost alongside the boat, working their way along the casualties and I noticed that they efficiently separated the living from the dead. Many of the dead soldiers had been caught out while standing in the sea. Consequently, they were being pulled ashore and laid out in rows on the sand where an army padre and a sergeant major were going from body to body saying the last rites and collecting the identity tags from each corpse. I also noticed two army lorries standing by like two chariots of death waiting to receive the bodies. My head hurt like hell but the rest of me seemed okay, certainly well enough to stand up and slowly make my way towards Bill. Pulling out a very crumpled packet of players cigarettes, I pulled one out and lit it.

"How's it going, Bill? Apart from my bloody head, I feel a lot better, so is there anything I can do to help?"

"No, governor. The motor is in good shape and the pump is working and apart from a few bullet holes aft and a whack to your head, I would say that we are in good shape and ready for sea. Now go and sit yourself down and rest for a little longer and I'll join you in a few minutes for a smoke."

I barely had time to make my way back to the stern and to sit down when an army medic carrying a large khaki shoulder bag with the Red Cross emblazoned on it waded up alongside.

"Excuse me, sir, but I can see that you are the gentleman that has been wounded. Mind if I look at it and fix you up?" On hearing his voice, Bill walked over to the side of the boat and leaning over, helped him clamber onto the deck. Straightening up and taking a good look around, the medic came towards me, putting his bag down beside me he started talking as he bent over to look at my forehead.

"I am Lance Corporal Jackson, sir and that if I may say so, is quite a gash that you have on your head. I am afraid you are definitely going to need stitches for that wound. The best that I can do for you right now is to clean it and cover it with a bandage, as well to give you some pain relief. As to closing the wound, the only choices that you have is to either get over to one of the destroyers or to tough it out and sail back to Blighty."

As he started to treat me, he chatted away, presumably to divert my attention away from what he was doing. Informing Bill and I that he had enlisted in the army as a regular just before war had been declared and that he had been born and bred in Hackney, East London.

"Cor! talk about Bob's your uncle and Fanny's your aunt, I had no sooner done my basic training than I was over here in the blink of an eye and then those bleeding Jerrys took us all by surprise with the speed of them Panzers! Talk about a cock-up. The only thing that prevented all of us from being taken prisoners was a couple of British and French divisions keeping the Jerrys at bay and that situation won't last for long. If you ask me, it's a race against time, though I will say this, between our navy and you civilian volunteers, most of us might get away yet. But four days ago, it was a different story. There were literally hundreds of thousands of troops pouring into Dunkirk and everywhere you looked was chaos with abandoned trucks, field guns, rifles and tanks everywhere. Gradually, order has been restored and what is more important, over half of those troops have now been evacuated. I reckon that the rest of us could soon still slip away. All we need is a bit more luck! And it's all down to you lads basically, to carry on what you are already doing and rescue us all from becoming prisoners of war. If you ask me, every one of you deserves a medal. There, I've fixed you up now but remember, it's only temporary. Sometime in the very near future, that wound has got to be properly attended to, otherwise you will suffer from some pretty serious repercussions."

With that, he jumped back into the water and as he was about to wade back to the beach, Bill called him back to the side of the boat and handed him a flask of hot tea and a couple of apples, "Take these, mate and enjoy them if you get a quiet moment," whereupon the Lance Corporal tucked them inside his tunic and gave Bill and myself two thumbs up as he turned and started back the shore. It was quite true what the Lance Corporal had said. Looking along the shoreline, there was an obvious reduction in personnel waiting for boats. The number of queues were not only diminishing but shortening as well, there was also a continuous non-stop shuttling of troops between the beach and the destroyers and I lost count of the number of channel ferries and pleasure steamers heavily laden with evacuated soldiers trundling away from the Dunkirk docks back towards dear old Blighty.

As for my sore head, there was too much going on around me for me to worry about it. The Germans were getting nearer for they had managed to bring up heavy artillery and were busy shelling Dunkirk docks with high explosive shells. From time to time, an occasional salvo would land on the beaches, sending up great fountains of sand and debris. Once we had put the boat in order, we beckoned to the nearest queue of soldiers and took another eighteen on board. We couldn't help but notice that the men were getting to the end of their tether. They were all showing signs of exhaustion. Their uniforms were soaked through to the skin where they had been standing in the water for at least one to two hours and I don't suppose for one moment they had been able to have anything hot to eat or drink.

Bill and I were getting to the point where we needed some physical respite. The boat was proving hard to control with our diminishing strength combined with the overload of the soldier's extra weight. There was something else for us to worry about too. The weather was beginning to turn. The sea was becoming choppy and even though deteriorating weather conditions would keep the Luftwaffe out of the sky, we small mariners could be in for a bumpy ride. On the way back to the beach, Bill and I discussed the pros and cons of what to do for the best. As he said, my physical condition was only going to get worse unless we found proper medical treatment. There was also the changing weather to consider and it might perhaps be wiser to either seek a safe haven for the night and find a hospital to have my wound seen to or to break off and run for home.

As it turned out, our questions were soon to be answered, as we approached the shallows. Two naval officers who had been walking along the shoreline must have seen us coming in for they stopped in their tracks and stood waiting for us. We came into the shore as near as possible without scraping the bottom of the boat and after throwing the sea anchor over the side, we both waded onto the beach where we were greeted by the two officers. Just as we came abreast of them, the four of us instinctively ducked as a German shell landed further up the beach sending soldiers diving everywhere for cover. As the four of us stood there brushing the wet sand off our clothes, I had the opportunity to do a quick study of the officers in front of me. The oldest of the pair and the most senior in rank, judging by the egg on his cap, was wearing a grey polo necked jumper over which was a duffel coat plus naval trousers tucked into green wellingtons turned down at the tops. His colleague was dressed exactly the same but was carrying yet another clipboard upon which were resting a stack of papers.

"Good evening, gentlemen. I am Captain Markson of the Royal Navy and I am the Beach Master in charge of all the beaches and have the responsibility for all the boats in this area. This officer is Lieutenant Joseph, my second-in-command. I take it one of you gentlemen is the captain of this motor cabin cruiser?"

"I am, captain", I said. "My name is Gunther Conrad and I am the owner of this boat which is registered in the name of the *Marlene.* This gentleman here is my fellow crewmen, Bill Jackson."

"It's nice to meet you, gentlemen but I wish it was under better circumstances as I'm sure you do. Lieutenant Joseph will register the boat and your names so that we have a record of those civilians who took part in the evacuation. If I may, we would like to fill you in as quickly as possible as to the general situation here. Just over ten miles away, the perimeter to this area is being defended by one French division and one Scots Guards division, the 51st Highlanders. The consensus is that we have just under two days to complete the evacuation of Dunkirk before the Germans breakthrough. Although the Dunkirk docks have been damaged beyond use, we have been using the east and west moles of the harbour to continue the evacuation. I'm pleased to say that thanks to the courage and fortitude of small boats such as yours, we have been able to evacuate the main bulk of the British Expeditionary Force and any men left on these beaches now will be moved to the harbour moles. I'm sure you won't mind if I give you some advice, Mr Conrad. At some stage soon, the wound that you have is going to need proper medical attention! You have two choices that you should consider. First, you can leave your boat and accompany me back to the field station for treatment and afterwards transfer to an available destroyer sickbay. However, because of the huge influx of wounded men waiting to be attended to, it could take a long time to be seen to. On the other hand, it might be just as quick to head back for Blighty in your own boat assuming of course that the *Marlene* is seaworthy. The weather is likely to remain relatively calm for the next twelve hours and if you follow the safe route back to Dover via the Goodwin Sands behind a flotilla of ships that will be leaving here very soon, you should be relatively protected from enemy fire."

"I appreciate your advice and concern, Captain Markson," I replied as we all ducked again as a fresh salvo of shells landed from overhead, but as we straightened up, I continued speaking. "I must be honest, my inclination now, Captain, is to head for home. There aren't many small boats left now so I think our job is done here unless, of course, you tell me otherwise. If I leave now, I would like to transport ten extra soldiers back to Dover, but as a lot of the physical workload will fall on Bill's shoulders, I would like to ask him what his opinion on the matter is. Well Bill, what do you think?"

"If you're asking me my opinion, Mr Conrad," Bill replied, pausing whilst he took a deep draw on his cigarette, "I have to say that I agree with you. If we remain here now, the chances increase of us being blown right out of the water and as most of the civilian craft have departed, it would be a pointless sacrifice. It's obvious that we small boats have made a big difference to the evacuation and the remainder of the troops left will be lifted off the beaches and harbour by the larger vessels. If we take ten lads back with us, one or two would be able to give me a hand if needed just in case, you should pass out. That is, of course, looking at it from the worst possible angle. Well, that's my opinion, gentlemen, for what it's worth. Seeing as my governor's been wounded, I want to get him home to his wife and I want to get home to mine. As for the seaworthiness of the boat, I have just finished checking her out and making any repairs that were necessary. Apart from some damage caused in the cockpit by enemy fire, she's sound and will have no trouble in getting us home. I've said what I've got to say, so it's up to the rest of you."

"Right, gentlemen," Captain Markham replied, when Bill had finished speaking. "I think you have come to a sensible decision. The Germans are certainly putting on the pressure now and I shall be advising all remaining small craft to leave. I shall also be clearing the beaches and moving the remaining BEF back to the moles for evacuation. Even as I speak, I can see a convoy of ships steaming away from the fleet towards Britain. As the lieutenant and I walk back to the harbour, we will send the first ten stragglers that we see back to you. I am afraid I shall have to leave you now, but I wish you both a safe journey home and for what it's worth, on behalf of all the troops that have been trapped here, a massive thank you for your contribution. Now, I shall have these men here within minutes and that is as long as it should take you to up anchor and be gone. Cheerio."

True to the captain's word, a group of ten soldiers appeared running along the beach and as soon as they saw Bill waving, turned as a group and started wading towards us through the surf. As we waited for them to reach us, I went rummaging for a bottle of aspirin that was in our first-aid box. Apart from feeling queasy, I had a rotten headache and the vision in my left eye was becoming slightly impaired by the swelling on my forehead. By the time I had returned to the deck, the soldiers were alongside us and after some pulling and pushing, we soon had them all on board. In all, there were two corporals and eight privates all looking very wet and bedraggled. They had no rifles or kit, but Bill made them as comfortable as possible. He had also managed to brew some hot tea up on our primus ring and though we only had six mugs, we managed to share them amongst all of us. We also cleared the food cupboard out, distributing the remaining fruit and chocolate bars and even two sandwiches, amongst the soldiers. After we had settled all of them down, I started up the engine whilst Bill pulled up the sea anchor. Swinging the boat around, I opened the throttle up and made a run to catch up with the convoy gradually fading over the horizon.

The further we travelled out, so the waves became increasingly choppy and I could see on the horizon, paddle steamers and tugboats and much smaller boats bringing up in the rear of the convoy. There were also three minesweepers on the perimeter guarding them like a mother hen and finally, leading the convoy, were two destroyers. I must admit the motion of the waves wasn't doing my poor head any good whatsoever and it wasn't much consolation to me either, to notice that a few of the lads had their heads over the side. On a rare occasion, a squadron of Spitfires flew overhead on the way to Dunkirk. It was at least reassuring that their presence in the area would keep the German Luftwaffe off our backs. Glancing aft, I noticed a few boats in the distance trailing us and asked Bill to identify them with his binoculars. They were about five tugboats followed by some large cabin cruisers and even two yachts. After a while, Bill came ahead and stood beside me checking the compass and the gauge.

"You feeling all right, governor? I can take over for a while and give you a chance to rest up or to go and sit and have a chat with the lads. Fingers crossed but so far, everything is okay. Strictly between you and me and the gatepost, I shall be happier still with a few more miles nearer to Blighty under our belt, because we represent a tempting target at this moment. Anyway, enough of all that nonsense go and sit yourself down and have a chinwag with the squaddies. It'll take your mind off the pain." Nodding in agreement with Bill, I moved over so that he could take over the wheel and giving him an affectionate slap on the back, gingerly, I made my way aft to the lads, four of which were asleep in the births below deck. The other six, two of which had been, or were suffering from seasickness, were laid out in what little space there was, whilst the other four were quietly having a smoke. As I inched towards them, they pushed up a little more so that I could have somewhere to sit. There had been a few films in which I had been either shot or stabbed but this was real. Boy, did I ache!

Pulling a fresh packet of cigarettes out of my pocket, I offered them around telling them to put one behind the ear for later. One of the lads introduced himself to me as Len and went around each one of his mates introducing them by name, which I am sorry to say soon went out of my head. Apparently, they were part of a Lancashire regiment that had been encircled by the Jerries, and having fought their way out, had joined the retreat to Dunkirk, where they had seen a lot of their mates either killed or wounded on the way to the beaches. The first few days after their arrival had been bloody awful. The dock had been bombed out of action and the beaches were filling up with fleeing troops. They were being constantly bombed by the Luftwaffe and the first twenty-four hours were filled with panic and it wasn't until the arrival of the military police that order began to be restored.

Once the evacuation began and the small ships started to arrive, things started to move along, even though he and his mates had to stand in the sea with the water up to their armpits. Len asked me how long it would take to get back to Dover and I told him, just before nightfall. His face lit up as he nudged me in the ribs with his elbow. The first thing he told me that he was going to do when we reached dear old Blighty was to have a plate of cod and chips washed down with a bottle of Newcastle Brown ale. Bill had been right. Listening to their private lives and sharing their personal photographs had taken my mind off my own personal discomfort. It had certainly done them a lot of good as well especially as Bill had craftily placed a hip flask of whiskey in my jacket pocket. Having taken a large nip myself, I passed it around. The next time I glanced at my watch, a good forty minutes had passed which meant that that we must be near the Goodwin Sands. It was also about time that I relieved Bill at the wheel.

As I excused myself and rose, Len asked me if I would help settle a bet with the lads, I replied that I would do my best.

"Well, it's like this, sir," he told me. "The lads seem to think that you look very much like a certain famous film star. I've told them they're wrong. You wouldn't be stuck out here looking like shit! After going through hell, the same as what we have."

"How much did you bet, Len?" I asked him.

"Half a crown," he replied.

"Then, I am afraid that you lose," I told him.

"Blimey!" he exclaimed looking at me and then back at his mates. "He bleedin' well really is that Gunther Conrad. Who would have thought it in a million years? You wait until I get home and tell the missus. She will never believe it. Come to think of it, I'll get a free pint every night at my local, on the strength of this story. Well, I'll tell you something, Mr Conrad. I would like to shake your hand because for somebody like you to do what you have done has gained my respect in a big way."

I felt a proud man when he spoke those words and for me personally, it justified everything that Bill and I had done that day. Len, of course, being Len, had to gild the lily.

"Just one other little thing, my missus will never believe me unless I show her some evidence. It so happens that I have got the last letter that I received from her before I was shipped out to France. Could you do me a favour, Mr Conrad and just sign it to Madge. It will make her day."

Anticipating what would follow once I had signed my autograph, I told the other lads to jot down their names and addresses and I would make sure that they received a photograph. Turning the side of the envelope over, I wrote, 'For Len and his lovely wife, Madge. Just a reminder of Len and my lucky escape from Dunkirk. Affectionately yours, Gunther Conrad'.

Once I had made my way forward, I relieved Bill and took over the wheel, telling him to take the weight of his feet and join the lads in the stern. Looking at the compass, I could see that we were on course heading south towards Dover and by my estimation, the white cliffs would be appearing any time soon on the horizon. Bill was still standing beside me, nudging my elbow with an offer of a cigarette which I gratefully took. He also offered me a large piece of clean gauze at the same time.

"You need to wipe your eyebrow, Mr Conrad. There is a lot of blood coming through your bandage. Seriously, you should listen to me. I can take the boat from here on in and dock her and the couple of the lads will help me to do what else is necessary. Not only that but dusk is nearly upon us and we are going to need perfect vision to sail into Dover harbour, so do the right thing, Mr Conrad, sit yourself down again and let me do the donkey work."

"You're right, Bill," I mumbled, "I'll let you take the *Marlene* in, whilst I sit down and recover my sea legs. Once we land, I don't think that we will be able to go anywhere else tonight, so just in case I get banged up in hospital to be patched up, promise me that you will phone home and let the womenfolk know that we are alright."

Just at that moment, a squadron of Spitfires flew over us heading for Britain dipping their wings as they passed overhead though there certainly weren't as many coming back as went out. Obviously, some poor bugger had been shot down. In fact, maybe one or even two had been forced to ditch in the sea for an air-sea rescue launch came whipping past us out of nowhere, heading towards France. You could feel a change in the weather as nightfall closed in. The sea was becoming increasingly turbulent and I could feel the vibration of the boat's motor under my feet as it attempted to power through the strong waves. Len and his mates started to sing a melody of pub standards such as, *It's a Long Way to Tipperary, Doing the Lambeth Walk* and appropriately for the occasion, *White Cliffs of Dover*. It was infectious and in no time at all, both Bill and I were joining in, or at least Bill was, for I must admit that I was now beginning to feel distinctively under the weather and could barely mumble the words.

You could almost feel the collective sigh of relief as land came into sight and the mood amongst the squaddies brightened up. A mouth organ had been produced which greatly enhanced the squaddies' vocal talents and their repertoire. By the time we were ready to enter Dover harbour, they were already into the eighth verse of that well-known rugby song, *She Stood on the Bridge at Midnight Throwing Snowballs at the Moon*. As Bill cut the engine, the squaddies had grown excited with the air of expectancy of finally standing on firm ground.

The destroyers had unloaded the evacuees and steaming back out of the port, thereby easing the pressure on the other boats waiting to unload. Whilst the main port was used by the larger vessels to unload the cargo of their rescued soldiers, smaller vessels such as ours, were endeavouring to land their passengers on the quays, so we were forced to be patient, with our engine ticking over as we waited for a space to become vacant at one of the wooden jetties. Within a few minutes, hawk-eye Bill spied an empty gap in the moorings and sailed in. He docked the *Marlene* perfectly alongside the jetty, where there were assembled a small band of army and naval personnel directing the disembarking soldiers to the end of the jetty where there were army lorries parked ready to pick them up. It certainly was a chaotic scene but somehow, it seemed organised. Every time one lorry was filled up with men, it would take off to be replaced within minutes by the arrival of an empty one.

As soon as Bill had thrown the mooring ropes to a couple of naval ratings so that the boat could be secured, we were instructed to disembark our group. As the lads stepped off the boat one by one, they shook both of us by the hand with the promise from both of us that we would keep in touch with them. Len was the last one off and I supposed, the most senior of the two NCOs. The lads had lined up in twos and once Len had said his farewell to us, both he stepped onto the jetty and immediately barked out, "Attention, left turn, quick march" and with that, the group marched off in step towards the waiting lorries. I watched them marching away and though they were a sorry and bedraggled looking bunch, I felt extremely proud of them for if they represented an army in defeat then Hitler had a lot to be afraid of, for this was Britain at its best and a nation that would never give way to bullies; a nation that had beaten the French at Agincourt, had seen off the Spanish armada and defeated Bonaparte at Waterloo. I suppose I realised then, with my natural sense of theatre, that all the British people needed was a leader who would harness their fighting spirit and at that moment, I instinctively thought of Winston Churchill.

Meanwhile, Bill had come back on board, accompanied by a naval officer. Apparently, Bill had mentioned to the officer that I had been wounded at Dunkirk and that he needed to moor the boat overnight whilst he got me to a hospital. Having introduced himself as Lieutenant Markham and having been told of my condition and the circumstances, he thought it might be wiser to have the boat taken to the naval yard and moored up for the night. He also said that he would arrange an ambulance to be waiting for us to take me immediately to naval command headquarters situated in the subterranean tunnels blasted into the Dover cliffs where, apart from all the other amenities that were needed to protect both military and civilian population, it also boasted a fully operational hospital which by the looks of me, I needed to be admitted to, as soon as possible.

In next to no time, with a naval rating on board to guide us, we had arrived at a boatyard where with the help of Bill, I was put into a waiting ambulance and driven a short distance to a cavernous entrance leading into the bowels of a cliff face. I was quickly transferred to a wheelchair and accompanied by Bill, was pushed by a male attendant along a passage until we came to a triage centre. This medical centre was primarily for the officer commanding and his staff and any civilian population that was sheltering in the tunnels from bombing raids. All the other wounded being landed from the disembarking vessels from Dunkirk were being dispersed elsewhere to other military and civilian hospitals. So, I was rather fortunate to have a doctor on hand to give me a primary medical examination and thank God, his prognosis was that though the wound was deep and had some wooden splinters embedded in it, all that would be necessary would be a whiff of gas to put me out whilst they removed the splinters, a clean for the wound and a few stitches to bind it together. By the morning, I should have made a good recovery and be ready for discharge. Whilst the operating theatre was being prepared, it gave me the opportunity to tell Bill to phone the house and to tell our loved ones that we had landed back in Dover safely and that apart from a small wound that I had received, we were otherwise both fine and with a bit of luck, we should be sailing up the Thames and reach the house by early tomorrow afternoon.

Finally, realising how exhausted Bill must be feeling, I told him not to hang about any longer and to go and get himself something to eat and find a bed for the night, with what little money I had on my person, I gave to him, urging him to leave right away. As luck would have it, the doctor attending me overhearing our conversation told Bill that the tunnels had been designed for the civilian population as a shelter in the event of Dover being bombed as well as for the military personnel. There were facilities not only for sleeping but also a recreational area including an around-the-clock NAAFI. The doctor would be happy to sign a document authorising Bill a bed for the night and Bill was happy to take him up on his offer. Shaking my hand, Bill told me to keep my chin up and that he would see me in the morning and with that, he lumbered off back towards the triage station.

From that moment on, everything seemed to move with precision and quickly, I was in a surgical gown being prepared for the operating theatre. It was while I was waiting for surgery that the one thing occurred that I didn't want. Two young nurses had arrived at my bedside to remove the dirty bandage and wash and clean my face and I knew immediately they had recognised me. After that, the game was truly up when a staff nurse arrived to take down my personal details and other relevant information such as my occupation and how I had received the injury. As soon as she had completed the forms and wandered off, I was left to my own devices until eventually, she returned with the doctor dressed in a white gown and a surgical mask hanging from under his chin, who introduced himself as Dr McFarland R.N. He told me that he would be performing the minor surgery on my head. He explained the procedures involved and that it would be all over in no time at all and unless there were any complications, I should be ready for discharge tomorrow morning.

We were soon talking about Hitler's easy victories and what the outcome would be and whilst we were having that conversation, he enquired how I had received my head wound and further went on to say.

"It appears, Mr Conrad, that you have the nurses' station in a complete state of excitement. I gather from a rumour that is apparently flying around the medical centre that we have a famous film star in our midst being treated for wounds received in a war zone and even my theatre staff are waiting in anticipation for you to be wheeled through, believing no doubt, that it is you. Once the rumour has been confirmed, I think it might be fair to say you won't lack for care and attention from the nursing staff during your stay with us. Somehow, if you do not mind me saying so, life appears to be imitating art, because all the nurses here not only think you are the bee's knees, but that you are a hero as well."

"I'm no hero, Dr McFarland. I was called upon by my adopted country to do my bit for her in her darkest hour as indeed, were literally hundreds of small boat owners, like myself. Quite a few sacrificed their lives as well in the process. I was just fortunate that I made it back alive?"

"Well, Mr Conrad, I admire your humility, but you are still a hero, one of dozens. I suspect we will see a few more of them being admitted here in the next few days suffering from injuries, some of which are likely to prove fatal. Just let the nurses enjoy the experience of looking after you, Mr Conrad. For a brief time tonight, whilst you are in here, you will be perceived by the British public as representing all that is best in the British character. I think that you have earned their respect and their adulation, wouldn't you agree, Mr Conrad?"

I soon found myself being wheeled through swing doors into the operating theatre and it was with some trepidation that I found myself surrounded by masked nurses. However, I had no time to dwell upon that for an ether mask was placed over my nose and mouth with the instructions to breathe in. I don't think I took more than four intakes of breath before I was drifting off.

I came to with a light slap on the face and the voice intruding on my subconscious, "Wake up, Gunther, wake up." I opened my eyes to behold a young nurse leaning over me smiling as she spoke.

''There you go, Gunther. Just making sure that you have come out of the anaesthetic and that there have been no complications. I am sure you will be pleased to know that your wound has been successfully cleaned and stitched up. As it's only just gone midnight and you're going to feel very groggy, just close your eyes and take advantage of a good night's sleep. Dr McFarland will pop around to see you in the morning before he goes off duty to discuss the results of the surgery and whether any post-operative treatment may be required. My name, by the way, is Sister Jimpsome. I am the ward night sister and I shall be checking in on you from time to time during the night.''

What must have been many hours later, I awoke to the sounds of activity followed by the unmistakable noise of squeaking rubber-soled footsteps around my bed. It took a second or two for my vision to clear before I noticed Sister Jimpsome from the night before, with another nurse, examining the chart at the foot of my bed. When she saw that I was awake, her face lit up with a big smile.

''Good morning, Gunther. Just in time for us to take your blood pressure and temperature and as soon as we have done that, you can get up and have a wash, by which time, nurse Saunders here will have brought you a cup of tea and some toast. Dr McFarland will also be doing his rounds shortly to tell you whether you are fit to be discharged.''

Apart from feeling a little unsteady on my feet at first, I had little trouble in performing my morning ablutions and I had barely got back into bed before Dr McFarland arrived accompanied by the staff nurse and Sister Jimpsome. The doctor examined my charts and finally, my head wound. When he had satisfied himself of my general condition, he started to speak to me.

''Well, Mr Conrad, you will be pleased to know that you have made a very good recovery and I have no hesitation in sending you home this morning. You have been a very lucky man, a harder blow to the scalp could have resulted in severe trauma to the brain. I am going to give you some strong painkillers. Please take them as prescribed and please contact your GP as soon you arrive home. I recommend complete rest for at least a week. Now is there anything that you would like to ask me?''

"Just one question, Dr McFarland," I replied, "Will I be left with a permanent scar and if so, how prominent will it be?"

"The answer to the first question, Mr Conrad, is yes and as to the second it won't be noticeable at all unless you search for it. Obviously, I realise that you are a professional actor, but I think any light makeup will cover it over or in the worst-case scenario, a reputable plastic surgeon will improve any damage to your features. Before I leave you, Mr Conrad, I would just like to say that it has been a pleasure to have treated you even though it hasn't been under the best of circumstances. I do have one favour to ask of you. Would it be possible to have a photograph taken of yourself and the nurses who were on the night shift last night?"

"I would be honoured to, Dr McFarland. Whilst I get myself dressed, perhaps you could organise a group photograph outside, one I hope you will be also be taking part in?"

After trying to make myself look as presentable as possible under the circumstances, I popped out into the main passageway stopping the first orderly I came across and asked him to point me in the direction of the nurses' station so that I could collect my discharge papers. He did better than that by escorting me directly to it. As I walked towards the station, I saw Dr McFarland, the ward sister, plus Sister Jimpsome and at least eight other members of the nursing staff all obviously waiting for me. I was soon besieged by a forest of outstretched arms all holding out notepads requiring my autograph and although I soon felt physically tired, I realised that this was no ordinary group of fans but a group of wartime nurses sharing with me a brief moment of glamour and excitement. We were all in this war together now so who the hell was I to feel tired, compared to what these girls were going through every day, tending to the sick and wounded.

Quickly pulling myself together, I poured on the charm and started chatting to each and everybody. Eventually, Dr McFarland brought some order to the proceedings and soon had us all in a group. Out of nowhere, a photographer appeared and after arranging us in some form of order, began to take a series of flash photographs and as soon as he had finished, a few of the nurses produced box cameras which immediately triggered a series of individual photos being taken. Fortunately for me, the ward sister put an end to it by briskly clapping her hands, reminding them that they had ward duties to perform and for those who had just finished their shift, it was time to go and get some rest. It was Dr McFarland who suggested that it might be a good idea as I was already at the nurses' station to use their outside line to notify my next of kin that I would be on my way home very soon, an offer which I took up immediately.

My call was answered very quickly by Marlene. As soon as she heard my voice, she started bombarding me with a series of questions. Was I all right? Was I fit enough to leave hospital? If so when did I think that I would be home? When I finally managed to get a word in, I told her that Bill and I would be setting off from Dover as soon as possible and we should be home by mid-afternoon. I told her not to worry and that I loved her and would see her very soon. Dr McFarland's final act of kindness was to walk me to the NAAFI where Bill had been waiting for me. Pausing briefly at the entrance, he shook me by the hand and wishing me all the best, turned on his heel and briskly walked away.

Having seen me arrive, Bill had gone to the counter and brought back a cup of tea to the table where I had joined him.

"You look a darn site better this morning than you did last night, governor. Are you sure that you're fit enough to make the journey back home? Or do you want to spend another night in Dover resting up. There are quite a few hotels still open, so I don't think there be much of a problem getting rooms. There is another alternative. I was only thinking last night that in the event of you still not having fully recovered to face the journey home by water, we could take the train and I could return another day and collect the boat."

"I'm fine, Bill and I've made up my mind that we are going home this morning. I've already phoned the house to tell them that we will be on our way and should be home by the afternoon, so as soon as we have drunk our tea, we will go and collect the boat and depart."

"Okay, governor, I'm ready when you are. Earlier this morning, I took the liberty of collecting our remaining quota of petrol which should see us safely back. Also, the weather forecast for late afternoon is stormy with heavy rain forecast and at the moment, the sea is a little choppy out there. However, if we set off now and hug the coast all the way to Canvey Island and then slip into the Thames estuary, we should be sheltered from any bad weather that might be coming in."

As we headed out of the relative calm waters of the inner harbour, we left behind a maelstrom of organised chaos; naval ships of various class, civilian tugboats, holiday boats and even a few pleasure craft still advertising their destinations. The quays and the surrounding side streets of the docks and harbour were awash with military vehicles of all types, including buses upon which were being loaded with disembarking troops from the vessels. The soldiers represented a sorry looking sight bless them. Most of them only had the uniforms they stood up in whilst the rest descended the gangplanks with just a blanket wrapped around their bodies. The walking wounded were being helped by their comrades and their less fortunate colleagues were being stretchered away to the waiting ambulances. Now and again, to ease the shortage of transport, the more fortunate amongst them would be lined up in columns of three and quick-marched away to a distant depot. None of them were carrying any side arms and throughout the whole panoramic view of activity, there was a complete absence of any military equipment. However, for me personally, I detected a strong feeling of fortitude and dignity mixed with that famous British sense of humour which gave me a strong sense of confidence that somehow or the other, this small island nation would give Hitler more than he bargained for!

It took us a little time to receive authorisation for leaving the harbour to return home in our boat, but once we had registered our intended route and destination, we were soon granted clearance. We wasted no time in embarking on the *Marlene* and by a process of a quick-thinking and slow manoeuvrability, we darted in and out of the wash of the outgoing naval vessels and avoiding being hit head-on by the bows of the incoming ones, we were soon able to leave the security of the harbour walls and head out to the open sea.

The weather forecast was proving Bill right. The sea was beginning to work itself up and the waves with their white caps were pounding against us broadside on and outside the cockpit, we quickly became damp with the spray of the sea water. Once we had the left Dover, we had stuck strictly to hugging the coastline past Ramsgate and the North Forelands, but as Margate passed us by, the weather was becoming angrier with the clouds above us scudding rapidly by and the waves forcing the boat to rise and dip in the increasingly angry troughs. Bill had taken the wheel at this junction and I must admit if only privately to myself that I was glad, for not only was I in awe of the sea's might but physically, I was beginning to feel a little queasy and for the first time, a little scared, even with the experience of Dunkirk. Thank God, once we had passed Whitstable, we entered the swale which offered us immediate protection from the open sea and continued to do so until we reached Sheerness and entered the River Thames. From then on, we were home and dry from the rough weather of the open seas and proceeded to sail on past Gravesend and Tilbury and on to Erith. Once we had chugged our weary way past Woolwich, both of us relaxed completely. Out came the cigarettes and Bill even managed to find a half empty bottle of Jack Daniels. Even the good ship *Marlene* perked up after her battle with the angry seas and was responding well to the flowing River Thames. Even the engine had now settled down to a quieter and regular rhythm.

Very soon, we came into sight of Westminster Bridge and the Houses of Parliament above which, high in the sky, were the floating anti-aircraft balloons and both of us noted that there was still a high volume of traffic crossing the bridges, including lorries, buses, taxis and pedestrians. You could be under the misapprehension that it was a typical early start to the month of June, but of course, it wasn't. The nation had been at war nearly nine months, most of which had been called by most of us a 'Phoney War' but now, within the next few days, I am sure the nation would wake up to the fact that the honeymoon was well and truly over and that we must now turn the defeat in France into victory.

Suddenly, out of nowhere, a Thames police boat had come up alongside us requesting that we cut our engine. A police sergeant lent over with a grappling hook and pulled both boats together.

''Good afternoon, gentlemen,'' he said in a strong cockney accent. ''Where have you come from and where are you bound?''

Bill produced the document authorising us to travel and handed it to the sergeant and at the same time, both of us passed him our I. D. cards. After examining the documents carefully, he then proceeded to run his eye over the boat and then finally ourselves. Speaking softly to us both he explained.

"It seems to me, gentleman that you have been having a rough time of it in France. Both of you look as if you have been to hell and back and the boat doesn't look much better either! In the last couple of days, there have been a few boats limping home upriver towards Oxford, all returning from the evacuation of Dunkirk and all in the similar state to yourselves. We lads of the river police would like to salute the courage all you blokes in risking your lives in the evacuation of our Tommies. We had all sorts returning, civilians, doctors, bank managers, accountants and even a judge, plus some who were old enough to be tucked up in bed with their Horlicks. I must confess though you're the first film star that we've come across so there's been no problem in identifying your good self. My wife is forever dragging me around to the pictures whenever one of your films is showing. If you're sure that you need no assistance from us, we'll let you get on your way for you still have some distance to travel before you reach Marlow. Have a safe journey home, gentleman and God bless you."

We waved to them as they sped away from us. We both felt that now we could really start to relax as we headed for home. We proceeded to continue on our way passing from historical Westminster, past Chelsea and Battersea, on through Putney and Barnes until eventually, we reached Staines, at which point I took over the wheel, giving Bill a chance to have a break and also to rummage around for something to eat. Finding a half-eaten bar of Cadbury's chocolate which we shared, accompanied by a mug of hot tea, we proceeded to relax and enjoy the ever-changing scenery. After a while, we could see ahead of us the town of Windsor and its famous castle. It seemed almost surreal that only yesterday, we were surrounded by death and destruction and now, we were part of a quiet and tranquil pastoral landscape. I turned to Bill and told him it was good to be nearly home and he agreed with me. We spent some time after that recollecting our experiences and then I decided I would discuss my future plans with Bill and his possible place in them; it is strange how we humans pick our moment to communicate life changing events to each other, I started by saying.

"You know, Bill, I have to tell you that I have recently received an offer of a contract from an American film studio which could involve me living in the United States for some years. There are other reasons for accepting the offer which I cannot discuss with you. However, if I do decide to accept, in view of Mrs Conrad's pregnancy, I will, of course, be taking her with me. I am telling you this as I would like both you and Lucy to remain in your present positions and look after Mr and Mrs Bachman, while we are away. There is no immediate hurry for you to give me an answer because if I do decide to leave, I won't be leaving much before August. I must tell you Bill, that I have grown very fond of both you and Lucy over the years, as has Mrs Conrad. It goes without saying that as well as enduring the experiences of the last few days, we also have become brothers-in-arms which as far as I am concerned, has only strengthened that feeling, so if you do say yes, it will make me a very happy man."

Bill replied without hesitation, "You can be rest assured, governor, that without even asking the wife, we will only be too glad to stay on looking after the house and Mr and Mrs Bachman. I know with confidence that when you have made your decision that you will discuss your plans with us for the future."

Once we were past Windsor, we were on the home stretch and whilst we cruised towards the bridge at Marlow, I sat smoking a cigarette, taking in the view on both sides of the river, observing as we passed through several locks, the canal boats moored to the riverbanks, soldiers hand in hand with their sweethearts strolling along the river foot paths until finally, we rounded the bend in the river and spied Falcon House set back behind the apple orchard. After we had manoeuvred the *Marlene* into the boat house, we spent at least half an hour putting her under wraps for the duration and though she had taken some damage to her bow, it was nothing the local boatyard wouldn't put right. We stored most of the non-essential gear at the back of the boat house, to be collected later at our own convenience and after putting the padlock on the double doors, we picked up our attaché cases and side-by-side, started strolling back towards the house.

Chapter 15

Convalescence

We had barely reached the lawn when the kitchen door flew open and Marlene, Lucy and Miriam ran outside and very quickly were hugging us both simultaneously, half laughing, half crying. After ensuring that Bill was physically alright, Lucy started dragging him into the kitchen whilst affectionately calling him all the names under the sun, leaving the three of us embracing each other. Marlene made a great fuss of the injury to my forehead and insisted that the doctor came out on a home visit despite my protestations that I had been well looked after by the doctors in Dover. Listening to the two women, it was difficult to believe that I'd only been away for forty-eight hours such was the number of questions that I was expected to answer and I reached a point where I really couldn't keep up with the torrent of information that I was receiving either. Fortunately, as we entered the kitchen, Olivia and Mary were waiting for me and both of them gave me a hug and a kiss. I also noticed John in the corner of my eye giving me a wave and telling me that it was good to have me back home. I felt a change of mood within myself. I felt tired, I felt stressed. Everybody seemed to be talking at once with most of the conversation going over my head. I don't know whether my body was naturally closing down after what it had endured but emotionally, it all felt something of an anti-climax and everybody I was looking at, appeared as if through a distorted mirror. I also began to experience a slight case of vertigo making it necessary for me to grip Marlene's hand tight for support. Suddenly, I could hear her voice, it seemed to be coming from far away, perhaps she was speaking to me from an echo chamber?

"Gunty, I think that you have done too much. Let's get you upstairs and get you rested. John! Bill! Help get Mr Conrad upstairs and Olivia, could you ring the doctor's surgery and ask if Dr Vincent could manage a house call today for Gunther. Come on sweetheart, let's get you upstairs to bed."

"Don't worry about me folks. I don't need anybody to get me upstairs except myself and Marlene. All I need is a few hours rest and I shall be as right as nine pins. Bill is the one that needs looking after. He did all the donkey work bringing us both back from Dunkirk and I am sure I speak for him when I say it's good to be home and to see all your faces again.''

With Marlene supporting me with arm around my waist, it didn't take us long to climb the stairs and despite my protestations, Bill and John insisted on standing at the foot of the stairs in case I fell. Once I had entered my own bedroom, my spirits lifted as my nostrils caught the familiar smells of fresh linen and Marlene's toiletries and perfumeries, especially her Van Cleef and Arpels. Sitting myself down on the edge of the bed, I pulled her towards me and whispered to her.

''You know, sweetheart, I should never have left you the way I did, but I just did it instinctively, feeling at the time, that it was the right thing to do for both of us. They may not realise but it was the start of payback time for Mr bloody Hitler and his gang of thugs. The things that I have seen and experienced in the last few days have changed my perspective on life completely. Before Dunkirk, I had felt a sense of guilt for even thinking of leaving Britain in her hour of need for the security of the United States. Quite honestly, it made me feel like a rat leaving a sinking ship but since Dunkirk, I have been able to view it from different perspective. It doesn't matter how small a part we may be asked to play or how insensitive we may appear to be towards public opinion, if I can use my celebrity for whatever it is worth as a civilian soldier in bringing the United States out of her state of neutrality and with all of her industrial might at her disposal, get behind Britain in her defence of the free world, then you and I, sweetheart, will have done our bit for the war effort.''

''Shush, Gunty,'' Marlene whispered, placing her finger on my lips. ''Stop talking and give your head a rest. You don't have to justify your actions to me. I understand the reasoning behind them. If anything, I think you are a hero. For the moment, I think we best get you showered and into some clean clothes. By the look of things, that bandage will need changing and until Dr Vincent arrives, we best keep it as dry as possible.''

''As soon as I have showered and put on some clean clothes, I will go back downstairs as I have no desire to go to bed yet. When Dr Vincent arrives, he can see me in the lounge. Come to think of it, we needn't have bothered him as your dad could have seen to me as soon as he arrived home. By the time I have showered and had something to eat, I should be as right as rain. Then you and I can curl up on the settee with a bottle of Prosecco and enjoy the sun setting."

As soon as I had convinced Marlene that I wasn't going to go to bed, reluctantly, she helped me into the shower and then laid fresh clothes out on the bed for me. I must admit that by the time I had showered and put on some clean clothes, I felt a new man and with Marlene's help, I made my way carefully down the stairs and into the lounge. I had no sooner sat down when the chimes of the front door were reverberating throughout the hallway. Having heard us coming down the stairs, Olivia poked her head around the door and in her usual matter-of-fact way, said, "Doctor's here to see you" and showed him in. After checking my vital signs, the doctor then took the soiled and wet bandage from around my head and after examining the wound, declared himself satisfied with the stitches. He then proceeded to dress the wound with a fresh bandage, all the while, giving me a running commentary on the evacuation of Dunkirk and how the daily papers and the radio were full of updates on it. His verdict on my general condition was favourable, the wound was clean and well stitched and provided I rest for the next few days, I would be as good as new. Meantime, he would leave me a prescription for some painkillers and then I should make an appointment to come and see him at the surgery where the practice nurse would remove the stitches. As he snapped his black bag shut ready for departure, he looked up at me, "All you civilians that took part in that evacuation did a very brave thing and you have my full admiration." Then, glancing at Marlene, he continued, "Don't you forget, Mrs Conrad, I shall be expecting you to see me very soon so that we can start monitoring baby's progress towards his full term."

By the time that Hiram arrived home from the hospital after going through the day's list of his patients, Miriam and Marlene had made Lucy finish early so that she could take care of Bill. John and Mary, having completed their jobs for the day, had also departed for home. Meantime, I had taken a catnap from which I had eventually awoken feeling considerably better. As I lay there on the settee pulling myself together, I could hear the familiar sound of the grandfather clock in the hallway accompanied by the familiar clacking of the typewriter keys as Olivia worked her way through answering the day's mail. Pulling myself onto my feet, I folded the blanket that Marlene had lovingly spread over me and walked down the hallway towards the kitchen where I could hear voices. When I entered, both Marlene and Miriam were busy washing and preparing a salad, including items such as, tomatoes, lettuce, beetroot and radishes which obviously, they had picked from the vegetable garden. Hiram, who had been drinking a cup of tea, was the first one to notice me and came straight over and enveloped me in a hug, saying how pleased he was to see me home again. He looked tired to me, but I put that down to the end of a hard day in the surgery.

Apparently, I had awoken at the right time as the girls were just finishing preparing supper. Looking at the spread, I had to admire Marlene's foresight from way back in planting vegetable gardens, for with the introduction of food rationing, the small amount that we were allowed per person from the available food stock on offer was making life very difficult. Fortunately, Miriam had baked an apple strudel from the apples that she had picked from the orchard, but even that, she told me was becoming a luxury as flour and other baking ingredients were becoming difficult to get hold of. Once we had all helped lay the table, I went and fetched Olivia to make sure that this would be a true family meal. By this time, I was that hungry, I could have eaten a horse. I was ready to dive in, but Hiram insisted that we all join hands whilst he recited a prayer of thanks to the Lord in Yiddish for delivering myself and Bill home safely.

Boy did that meal taste good, especially as Hiram had obtained a large jar of pickled cucumbers, known in the East End of London as 'pickled wallies'. These were one of the side dishes that I was addicted too, along with pickled role mops both of which were some of my favourite Jewish foods. Obviously, the topic of conversation around the table was the evacuation of Dunkirk and what Hitler's next move was going to be. Maybe, he thought that we, as a nation, might capitulate and sue for peace or he may have to do it the hard way and the prepared to make plans for the invasion of the British Isles. Anyway, as far as I was concerned, this was not a night of fear and speculation. I remembered that as it was Thursday, the night when we all gathered in the lounge religiously at eight-thirty and listened to one of the nation's popular comedy shows called *Hi Gang* with our favourite comedian Vic Oliver and apart from lifting all our spirits up, every week, it also featured a guest appearance of two of my old pals from the Hollywood days of the twenties, Ben Lyon and his lovely wife, Bebe Daniels. The British public had taken them both to their hearts and considered them one of their own. After all said and done, there weren't very many American film stars who would choose to live in London when it was facing its darkest hour and especially at this moment, with the Allied defeat in France, it would be standing alone against the Nazi war machine.

At least once the broadcast of *Hi Gang* had finished, we could all say that the day had ended with a laugh and after some small talk, Olivia said good night and as she left the lounge, she told me to rest up as she would take care of everything to do with the office in the morning. During the evening, I had felt an atmosphere of tension between Marlene and her parents and I wasn't prepared to go to bed until I found out the cause. I have always been a great believer in facing troubles head-on rather than having them smouldering away beneath the surface and I wasn't going to be any different this time around. It took a few minutes of denials until finally, after my persistent probing, Marlene and Hiram told me what was on their minds. It appears that the sudden capitulation of both Belgium and Holland and the occupation of the low countries by German forces had left the family without any contact with Greta and her husband or, for that matter, any of the remaining Bachman family in Germany. I knew in my heart of hearts that both Marlene and her father realised the peril that their family were now in and had resigned themselves to the situation. It was only Miriam who was refusing to accept the reality of the situation, that they felt the need to protect her.

There was, however, some good news. Marlene's brothers, Hansi and Lothar, had called from America and told us that they were doing fine and that we were to keep our spirits up. Not only were they doing well in their chosen subject of aerodynamics, but they had also attracted the attention of a man called Philip Oppenheimer who was a physicist and felt that they had a potential for a future in rocket science. With Hiram supporting me, we were able to put a positive spin on the situation and feel grateful that the two boys were safe and beginning to develop a future for themselves in America. On that note, we decided to call it a night. I gave Miriam a bear hug and told her not to worry so much over matters that she had no way of resolving and that the only way any of us could deal with it was to contribute in our own small way to the fight for their freedom. Marlene and I then walked both of them to the front door and as we watched them make their way over the gravel from the main house back to the cottage, we called out after them that we would see them in the morning.

By the time we had finished locking and bolting the front door and making sure all the curtains in the downstairs rooms were all securely drawn, thus preventing any light acting as a beacon for the enemy bombers, the pair of us then went back into the kitchen. After washing up the remaining cups and glasses left over from the earlier part of the evening, I switched the kitchen lights off and taking Marlene by the hand, led her upstairs to the bedroom. By the time that we both had got ready for bed and finished talking about anything and everything, we barely had time for a kiss and cuddle before I was fast asleep. According to Marlene the next day, one minute I was amorous and the next I was snoring my head off. I have to say what with my extreme exhaustion and the recharging of my libido, we never got up until mid-afternoon the following day!

Marlene and I spent the next week in seventh heaven protected from the outside world by our loyal staff. Within the borders of Falcon House, we enjoyed an idyllic existence of each other's company doing exactly what we wanted without being under any duress or pressure to keep to a commitment of either business or social engagements. In other words, we were just plain lazy, doing nothing and thoroughly enjoying the experience. The days were spent in getting up late, going for walks along the Thames and picnicking on the front lawn. We also spent time with the gardener tending to the flowers and in the orchard picking apples. Our evenings were spent with the family and staff usually playing cards or the odd board game.

On one evening, Lucy had managed to get enough ingredients together to bake a chocolate cake which we all had as a treat whilst watching a copy of *Fire Over England,* a film that Alex Korda had kindly lent me, starring my old chums, Larry Olivier and Vivien Leigh. It had come as no surprise to me that both had now acquired international stardom, Vivien for *Gone with the Wind* and Larry for both *Wuthering Heights* and *Rebecca.* The story of the film that we were watching was very relevant to the moment, as it was about England's defeat of the Spanish armada, after Queen Elizabeth's defiance of King Philip of Spain. The story was running parallel to Britain's present-day conflict with Hitler's Nazi Germany with comparisons being made by all of us to Winston Churchill and Adolph Hitler. The film had acted as a great tonic for our morale.

My convalescence and our time together would not have been possible without Olivia acting as the gatekeeper. Diplomatically, she fended off an irate Robin Cox who had heard a rumour that I had been over to Dunkirk and likewise, several daily broadsheets had been pestering her all wanting some confirmation of a rumour that had been circulating, that I had taken part in the Dunkirk evacuation and had been seriously wounded and God knows how many other calls that she diverted by using her wits and diplomacy. Eventually, time ran out on us and our brief honeymoon was over. It was time to return to reality. I wasn't looking for any work for the obvious reasons. I had put myself on hold pending a green light from Hollywood and therefore, was not able to accept any work that required a long-term commitment in Britain. This meant that I was able to stay at home with Marlene and the only sacrifice that I had to make was to give her a kiss whilst in transit either from the bedroom or the kitchen to the office.

On the first morning back, I straightened my shoulders and marched into the office fully expecting to face the music for being absent from the outside world due to my enforced time off. However, Olivia had turned the radio on for the first bulletin of the day on the BBC World Service, so I was just in time to hear the newscaster saying that they were going to run a repeat of Winston Churchill's address to the nation. Marlene and I had missed the original broadcast as we had been out for a late afternoon stroll. However, as everybody else had heard it, I now had the opportunity to catch up with it, shouting out to Marlene in the kitchen to come and join us. The three of us gathered around a small radio and listened. There was absolutely no doubt at all in my mind listening to this great Englishman, delivering such a stirring patriotic speech, filled with such amazing highs and lows and spine-tingling phrases, that he would have made a fine actor. What he would have done with Henry V's speech at Agincourt or Marc Antony's speech in Rome beggars belief. He began by saying that the nation could not turn the defeat of France into a victory at Dunkirk. However, he continued, his voice full of resolve.

"We shall defend our island at whatever the cost may be. We shall fight on the beaches. We shall fight on the landing ground. We shall fight in the fields and the streets. We shall fight in the hills, but we shall never surrender."

There was more to the speech and by the time he had finished speaking, I instinctively knew that Churchill had grabbed the nation by its shoulders and shaking it out of its stupor, it was no longer a nation wallowing in pacifism but one full of obstinacy and a determination to win. My gut reaction had never been stronger that somehow, Hitler would finally meet his match and that even though it would take time and a lot of sacrifice by the British public, it would in the end bring Hitler's evil Empire crashing down around him.

Olivia had placed in front of me a list of call backs. The first one that I moved to the top of the list was Robin Cox. As soon as I was put through to him, I had to hold the receiver away from my ear.

"Gunther! Where the hell have you been? What is going on? Olivia keeps telling me that you are convalescing. Convalescing from what? There are rumours flying around town like nobody's business. One is that you sailed over to Dunkirk and were rescuing British soldiers. Secondly, that you had been seriously wounded in the process and thirdly, that you had a nervous breakdown due to shellshock. Let me tell you that I am suffering from number three already."

"Calm down, Robin. Yes, I did go to Dunkirk. I went on the spur of the moment because I felt it was the right thing to do. It was just an instantaneous decision and I'm glad that I did it. Yes, I did suffer some minor injury and I was advised to take some time out so that I would recover. More importantly, I wanted to spend some quiet time with Marlene who is now pregnant with our child and thanks to Olivia, who was acting on my instructions, I achieved that. Let me apologise to you right now for not putting you fully in the picture but it wasn't intentional."

"Jesus, Gunther. Don't ever do that to me again. Despite what you have put me through that certainly was a brave thing that you and all those other men did but you are not out of the woods yet. Fleet Street knows that there's a story there somewhere and they won't rest until they get it. I think it might be wise if I arrange a couple of press interviews at your house as soon as possible, otherwise if you don't, they will invent and run their own stories. By the way, one of the two important reasons why I wanted to speak to you was to congratulate you and Marlene on your forthcoming happy event. The other reason for me trying to get in touch with you is that Warners definitely want you on board by the autumn and want you to sign a contract of intent ensuring that you will be in Hollywood by September. I must tell you, Gunther, that looking through the draft copy of the contract, it ticks all the boxes. It will guarantee you gainful employment with your name above the title for at least five years. It will certainly make you a very wealthy man and above all, will give you peace of mind with regards to the future of Marlene and the baby. Profits are the driving force behind the studios over there and they are worried that the lucrative European markets are gradually being closed to their product. As you are aware, Hollywood has no love for Hitler and his politics especially as ninety per cent of the American film industry is run by Jews. Consequently, because of the German embargo, the gloves are coming off. Despite America's neutrality, Hollywood is beginning to take a stand against Nazi Germany. The opinion of the liberal Hollywood elite is that sooner or later, America will be dragged into the European war supporting Britain."

"I agree with you, Robin, but I think that we have a lot of persuading to do before that happens. President Roosevelt can do little to help us whilst Congress and the American public wish to remain neutral and prefer a policy of isolationism. I am afraid that for the moment, all that stands between the total defeat of democracy in Western Europe is Britain. I am pleased that Warners want my services and I would be grateful to you Robin, if you can finalise the deal as quickly as possible. I think that it will take some time to put my affairs order, so it won't be much sooner than late August before I am able to leave."

"Don't worry, Gunther, I'll get onto the legal department at Warners right away. I think where we might have a problem is when we submit your visa applications to the American Embassy, as the Foreign Office may have something to say on the matter as well, considering that wartime regulations and restrictions now apply to any overseas travel. I don't think that you would have stood a chance on obtaining an exit permit if you had been legible for conscription. As it is, you are now too old for call up. If you don't mind me being frank with you, Gunther, but you do know I wouldn't be doing my job properly if I didn't advise you to consider whether leaving Britain now in her darkest hour might not be a bad career decision. It may not sit well with the British public or the British film industry if they think that you are going for reasons of self-preservation. It could possibly have the effect of destroying your career later on."

"I need you to help me as much as you can this matter, Robin. You see, as I have previously told you, I really am not in position to justify my actions. Perhaps it will help you understand if I tell you that my travel arrangements will be handled by the Foreign Office and that once again, as I have said before, there are other ways to serve your adopted country besides wearing a uniform. I think that when we eventually win this war as I know we surely will, the British public will understand and will continue to give me their loyal support. Meanwhile, whilst I am waiting to leave for America, see if you can get me any work on a short-term basis, such as any public information films or radio work. One last favour that you could do for me is to play down all this media interest on the Dunkirk business. I am not seeking public recognition as an individual or because I am famous actor for what is all said and done, a patriotic act of duty, carried out by hundreds of other private citizens in addition to myself.

"Well, Gunther. Thanks for putting me in the picture for as much as you feel you can. I certainly won't pry any further. You can also rely on me to handle the press to the best of my ability. Meanwhile, give my love to Marlene and make sure you take care of her and don't forget, you going to be a father soon. Speak to you later and before I go, one more question. You mentioned previously that you had been wounded. I hope that you are recovering successfully from it and hasn't damaged your profile in any way."

Very quickly, I told him a white lie in that it had only been a minor wound and that I was a hundred per cent intact. As soon as I had put the receiver down, I asked Olivia to ring the Whitehall number for Commander Burton. I had barely lit up a cigarette before she was holding the receiver towards me whilst mouthing that I was connected.

"Hello, am I speaking to Commander Burton?'

"You are indeed and am I right in thinking that I am speaking to Gunther Conrad?

"That's correct, Commander. I am ringing you to let you know that I am accepting the offer of the five-year contract from Warners which we had discussed previously."

"That is good news, Mr Conrad. The Prime Minister is determined that this project gets off the ground as soon as possible and has marked it top priority. Looking at my calendar, can you make this Friday for a briefing at the Foreign Office? Shall we say, eleven o'clock in the morning? I am afraid that I must again remind you that you are now covered by the Official Secrets Act, so that it is imperative that you guard what you say very carefully. This is now classified as 'For your eyes only', so there will be no further conversation on this matter on the phone."

"I do understand perfectly, Commander and look forward to meeting you on Friday at eleven o'clock."

"Thank you, Mr Conrad and before you go, let me just say that was a foolhardy but brave act that you indulged in last week. Just remember to liaise with me before you do anything else equally as brave and stupid. Otherwise, you may be putting the Prime Minister's plans in jeopardy and neither of us wants his wrath descending upon our heads. Look forward to speaking to you on Friday."

Putting the receiver back on the cradle, I was thinking that this Commander Burton was a bit of a laidback character and I certainly was looked forward to working with him. When all said and done, it wasn't every day you were involved in a cloak and dagger operation that was straight out of a John Buchan or Dennis Wheatley novel. I spent the next hour sifting through film scripts, projects that I would never be able to accept because of my imminent departure for America. Fortunately, Marlene broke the morning up with a tea break, which was gratefully received by Olivia and me. It came at just the right time for both of us as we had been kept busy answering calls from friends and colleagues, all enquiring on the state of my health and that wasn't even including the ones from the trade press. As far as I was concerned, it was all a complete waste of a good morning when better things could have been accomplished. It was only as we were drinking our tea and I was quietly mulling things over in my head that I suddenly realised that we were keeping Olivia somewhat in the dark. She was very aware by now that I was planning to go to America so that it was right and proper that I put her in the picture as to our intentions and this couldn't be a better moment with the three of us together.

"Olivia," I began by saying, "It is time for Marlene and myself to share with you any plans that we might have for the future. I know by now that you must be aware that I have been offered work in America which means that we will be temporarily moving over there. We certainly wouldn't like you to think that we were deliberately keeping you in the dark, but we did think it was important that we arrived at the right decision before bringing you into the picture about all the details. What we would like to say to you is that before you consider any alternative plans, based on what you have heard, what do you think about coming with us? If these were normal times, the offer that I had received from the Hollywood studios would without a doubt be the next logical step to take in my career. However, when you throw in the fact that we are at war as a nation, my first reaction was to turn the offer down and by remaining, contribute to the war effort. However, life is never as simple as that, for low and behold, the government have muddied the waters by making proposals to me that I cannot explain to you at this time as I am now bound by the Official Secrets Act, hence the reason why we have been less than upfront with you. From the professional point of view Olivia, you are irreplaceable to me. You understand the world of theatre and cinema as much as I do, you certainly can handle the press better than I can and you certainly have a keen eye when it comes to scripts. Equally as important is the fact that you have become one of the family, always there for both of us but never intrusive. As for Marlene and I have no doubt she will tell you this herself, next to her mother, there is no other person she would rather confide in knowing that her confidences would be respected than yourself. Having already discussed this with Miriam and Hiram who have both decided they are too old to make the journey across the Atlantic and would prefer to end their days at Falcon House, Marlene would be over the moon, if you would go with her and be a support to her in her final months of labour."

I thought it would be a good moment for me to leave the room and have a quick cigarette in the garden whilst Marlene and

Olivia talked it through. It would give me the opportunity to figure out where Bill and Lucy and John and Mary would stand in any plans. Providing that they were agreeable, it seemed logical to me that Bill and Lucy should stay on in their present positions and look after Miriam and Hiram, especially as they could continue to occupy the outside apartment. As for John and Mary, their situation might require a little more thought as in my absence as there would be no requirement for a chauffeur whereas Mary would still be required for domestic duties. As I stubbed out the remainder of the cigarette, I thought to myself, that was a problem for another day and promptly walked back into the office. I was just in time to see Marlene and Olivia embrace and on hearing me enter, Marlene turned to me, gripped my hand and with a smile told me that Olivia had something to say. Clasping her hands over her chest and giving me her beady-eyed look, she commenced speaking carefully pronouncing every word.

"It is quite obvious to me, Gunther, that somebody has to go with you both to protect you from yourselves and although I am not inclined to travel to a country that offers Red Indians, chewing gum and something called 'Boogie Woogie', I would be failing in my duty if I had allowed Marlene to be exposed to such frivolities, particularly in her present condition. I have decided, therefore, to accompany you both. I have no family ties to bind me here apart from a married niece living in Bath and I am certainly of no value to my country's defence other than to clack away on some typewriter in a government ministry in London. Besides, Gunther, my intuition tells me it is not self-interest that takes you to America but a desire to contribute something towards the war effort and if that is to be the unspoken aim then I shall willingly share it with you.

"Olivia, You don't know how relieved I am to hear that," I replied enthusiastically. "Although I must warn you that is going to be a long and exhausting journey to get there and even when we arrive on American soil, we shall have to cross a continent by rail to get to California and when we do finally arrive, you must expect a semi-tropical climate. I have a feeling that the three of us are going on an adventure and with God's blessing, will end up as four. There should be a spare E2 application form for the United States somewhere in the office. If you can find it, just take the trouble to fill it in with your personal details and I will take it with me on Friday when I go to the Foreign Office."

The next few days passed with lightning speed. Marlene and I spent an evening with Hiram and Miriam at their cottage making sure that they were happy with the arrangements that we were making. Hiram was adamant that with his salary as a surgeon and Miriam's salary from the BBC as well, that there would be no problem in them footing the bill for the running costs of Falcon House. Further to that, it might not be a bad idea with the number of spare rooms that we had available to approach the Air Ministry with view to housing some of their staff from RAF Medmenham. By the time the evening had finished, Marlene and I had no concerns about her parents. They were not only rising to the challenges that the war had brought but were also looking forward to the inevitable results that would have to be overcome and were determined to contribute to the defeat of Hitler and his gang.

Despite the meeting with Commander Burton having been arranged for Friday morning, I had decided to accept Noel Coward's invitation to spend Thursday night at his townhouse in London. It had been originally our intention for both of us to spend two days in London, but unfortunately, morning sickness had been taking its toll on Marlene leaving us no choice but for her to stay behind in the security of her own home and rest. This wasn't the best of times for a woman to be pregnant. Rationing was beginning to bite deeply into our everyday lives and even with ration books, it was becoming difficult to acquire essential items, particularly new shoes. It was even difficult to get old ones repaired. Our local shoe repairer in Medmenham could only offer us rubber, if our shoes required resoling and one of the biggest sacrifices that we were required to make was with heating the house. This wasn't so bad during the summer months. However, with hot water, it was a different matter. Bathing was difficult as we were only allowed a few inches of bath water which was hardly enough to cover one's essentials! It wouldn't be long before Marlene would be needing maternity outfits and like most women, she would want to look her best. The problem was that even though clothing had not been rationed yet, there was still a shortage of materials and what few maternity items were on offer were pretty drab affairs. Despite all this, we had no real reason to complain and if I'm honest, I think the pair of us felt guilty in the knowledge that very soon, we be leaving it all behind us.

On Thursday morning, Marlene and I took advantage of a bright sunny morning by having an egg and bacon breakfast outside at the patio table. Lucy had obviously found an under-the-counter source for obtaining sausages, bacon and eggs, a practice most people given the opportunity were indulging in. I admit it was easier to do if you lived in a rural area, for the simple reason that you had your local farmers and freeholds to call upon if you were in the know. Of course, the proviso was, don't get caught. Marlene, who was still going through the cycle of early morning sickness, remained her usual laid-back self, especially to the things that she must do to stay healthy. She had readily accepted that smoking could be bad for the baby's health but refused to give it up completely confining herself to three cigarettes a day. As to alcohol, goodness gracious, that was another area of contention. She would contain herself to two glasses of wine a night and she saw no reason why, if Winston Churchill could smoke cigars and drink whiskey galore to relieve the stress whilst saving the country, then there was no reason why she should not do the same whilst expecting.

As we walked around the house to the front door, I told her to make sure that she rested whenever necessary and not to do too much whilst I was away in London. John was waiting for me with the car and had already painted the bumpers and running boards white in accordance with wartime regulations. It was becoming increasingly difficult to gain any benefit from having a car on the road. A car of our horsepower had an allowance of fifteen gallons of petrol per month, the equivalent to roughly three-hundred miles. This was just about enough to take us to the station at Marlow every day and a trip, once a week to High Wycombe, for shopping. Neither was John very happy with the petrol that was on offer to the motorist as the government had replaced premium fuel with a diluted version called 'pool' and at one shilling and six pence a gallon, gave him cause to grumble. As he said in his own words, it mucked the engine up. It seemed obvious to me that once we had left for America, the larger car would have to be taken off the road for the duration of the war, just leaving the run-around for Hiram to use for work.

As I kissed Marlene goodbye, she asked me to do her a favour which was to bring her back as many pickled gherkins as I could carry, as she had a terrific fancy for them. I was still laughing at her through the rear window as John and I pulled down the driveway. The train journey to London took twice as long due to constant stopping. As it was packed to the limit, it was virtually impossible to leave the compartment. The corridors were filled with passengers either standing or sitting on kit bags as a very high percentage of them were military personnel, particularly from the RAF. Whilst I had been fortunate enough to get a seat in first-class, these were now different times and a few vacant seats that there had been in the carriage were soon taken on a first come first-serve basis. It was not that I was being snobbish. God forbid, it was the fact that being who I was and trapped in a carriage with nowhere to escape meant I had to sacrifice my privacy by being involved in a question-and-answer session with cinema fans. It was an experience that had not happened to me for a long, long, time considering the privileged world that I lived in. In the end, I was humbled by the experience, realising that we were all just human beings and that I was very fortunate for being who I was. One thing that was really annoying was that all the station names had been taken down making it extremely difficult, I would imagine, to know where to get off, especially at night, something I would have to watch on my return journey, otherwise I could end up in Oxford or God forbid, even further on up the line in Birmingham! I dreaded to think what it must be like travelling at night-time by train with no lights and only your memory of the landscape to guide you as to which station to get off at.

When the train arrived at Paddington, I sat where I was whilst all the passengers around me made a dash for the platform. When the carriage had emptied, I stepped onto the platform and made my way to the underground. The station was swarming with people, mostly in uniform, squaddies in full webbing and kit bags, sailors with just their kit bags and the boys in blue, now beginning to be known as the Brylcreem boys. All this was before the late afternoon rush hour when the civilian workers would make a run for their trains to take them home. It was no different on the underground, where I was caught up in a melee of people rushing in all directions and even on the down escalator, where you would think you'd be happy to stand still and let the stairs do the work for you, people were still charging past you as if they were somehow competing in beating the escalator to the bottom. When I finally located the southbound platform for the Bakerloo Line, that too was three-deep all the way along the platform.

Soon enough, the indicator board lit up and I began to hear the rumble of the approaching tube train. People moved forward in unison towards the platform edge ready to swarm into the carriages and then suddenly, like a huge beast emerging out of a black hole, the train appeared, gradually coming to a stop and filling the whole length of the platform. When the sliding doors opened, there was a mad scramble of people trying to get off, meeting a mad scramble of people trying to get on and over all of this on the Tannoy, came the stentorian voice of the platform announcer calling out, 'Mind the gap'. I was propelled forward with my inner voice telling me to go for it! Pulling my grey fedora hat further down over my ears I charged forward, just managing to get myself into the carriage and just to add insult to injury, the ticket inspector was marching along the platform attempting to push passengers further into the carriages so that the doors would slide shut.

Finally, the doors did slide shut and the train started off. I soon reached Piccadilly Circus, which was my destination and looking back, I am still debating whether I fought my way out onto the platform or was thrown out! Anyway, I finally made my way to the surface and close by, I found the Piccadilly Hotel with its covered colonnades and proceeded to walk across the road, avoiding the traffic to reach my destination, the food emporium at Fortnum and Masons. Walking into their grocery department, I enquired of the young female assistant whether they had any pickled gherkins in stock and on checking, she informed me that they had large jars of them in stock and at the moment they did not require coupons. So, I bought four jars plus some various cheeses which I knew Marlene liked and asked the young assistant if she could have them boxed up so that I could take them with me. Whilst I was waiting, I noticed that although customers were leaving, no new ones were arriving. Intrigued, I stopped a passing floor manager and asked him what time they closed? He replied that under the new wartime regulations, the larger West End stores such as theirs were required to open at ten in the morning and close at four o'clock in the afternoon and he couldn't apologise enough for any inconvenience this may have caused me. Eventually, my purchases were brought to me suitably packaged in a Fortnum's box which fortunately, had handles, making it easier for me to hold as it turned out to be a cumbersome package to carry.

Once outside, I was able to hail a London taxi but not before time for as I stood at the curb's edge trying to waive down a cab, I became aware that passers-by were beginning to give me a backwards look as they passed me, by making me feel in the process, rather vulnerable. The last thing I wanted was to create a public disorder merely by being recognised. Fortunately, a cab pulled up, so I jumped in and gave the driver Noel Coward's address in Kensington. It wasn't a great distance to travel and the cab driver made it shorter by keeping up a continuous stream of chatter over his shoulder as he drove. However, one of his comments deflated my ego when he enquired whether I was starting a new film yet? He'd seen my last one and thought that it was a bit of a stinker. Too much talk and too much swanning around was his opinion. When he dropped me off outside Noel's flat, I made sure that he had a handsome tip. After all, if you wanted an honest appraisal who better to hear one from than a London cabbie.

The concierge in the lobby, having given me Noel's flat number and floor, directed me to the lift and in no time, I was ringing the doorbell. I had a silent chuckle to myself as I handed Marlene's box of pickles to his manservant, the unexpected weight nearly knocking him off balance. Just at that moment, Noel appeared from nowhere immaculately turned out in a double-breasted suit and his trademark cigarette holder jutting out the corner of his mouth.

"Hello, dear boy," he said in his clipped vowels. "You are looking as ravishing as ever, even if you are approaching middle age. I'm sorry to hear that Marlene can't be with you tonight. I had been looking forward to seeing her again but as you have put her in the club, you must invite me down to Falcon House so that I can give her my commiserations."

With that, he took me by the elbow and guided me through double doors into his large sitting room. I would guess that there were roughly a dozen people gathered there, including some faces that I recognised instantly. First, I spotted Joyce Carey, the stage actress and friend of Noel, Gladys Allthorpe, the stage designer, also closely associated with his stage productions and in a corner of the sitting room, I spied Leslie Howard, a fellow film actor fresh from his triumph in *Gone with the Wind* in conversation with a young man who was introduced to me as David Lean, a young film cutter apparently making a name for himself as an up-and-coming name in the film industry. The rest of the company was made up of people that I was not familiar with. However, there were two handsome young men who needed no introduction and were inevitably replaceable in Noel's private life.

Poor Noel lived life on the edge having to be very careful of societies perception of him, for you see, his sexual persuasion was that of a homosexual and in the times that we lived, if that were to become public knowledge, it would ruin any man. However, we theatre folk were far more tolerant than the general public when it came to a person's sexual persuasion and Noel was very discreet when it came to his romantic affairs. After having a glass of wine shoved into my hand, I was propelled around the room by Noel who introduced me to people I hadn't met before while I reminisced with those that I had. It was a great privilege to be able to socialise with talented artists at the top of their game. Normally, showbiz parties became rather boring and self-indulgent with people talking incessantly about themselves or sharing scandalous gossip about some unfortunate actor. A gathering such as this was entirely different, usually young innovators or a varied group of professional artists talking about their new projects or future ones.

Noel's domestic staff had somehow managed to put on a buffet, even if it was somewhat spartan in choice thanks to wartime rationing. I think we all were becoming more accepting of the shortages and were becoming resigned to second-best. I think in compensation for the buffet, Noel decided on a little cabaret at his piano singing in his inimitable style some of his famous compositions such as *Mad Dogs of an Englishman, Don't Let's Be Beastly To The Germans* and *London Pride*. During the medley, a young army officer arrived and joined the gathering. His face was familiar to me, but it was when he was introduced to me as Second Lieutenant John Mills that I recognised him as another young actor beginning to make a name for himself. In fact, I remember seeing him with Bob Donat in the film *Goodbye Mr Chips*.

As the evening wore on, guests started to leave early because of the blackout restrictions. That left a small group of us in conversation. It appeared that Noel had recently been searching for young film technicians to work with him on a film project that that he was hoping to direct in the near future, whilst David Lean meanwhile, was working on a film that they had lined up, a story about a naval corvette on active duty and the lives of its crew. Noel was not only writing the script but apparently would also be playing the main role of the Corvette's captain, with David Lean collaborating and directing the film. They already had a rousing title for the project, which would be known as, *In Which We Serve*.

After conversing with us about the difficulties he was experiencing in writing another play, Noel excused himself and wandered over to the two young men, leaving me talking to Leslie Howard and David Lean. During the conversation, I asked Leslie Howard whether he had any plans for either a play or a film lined up, as it was well over a year since the release of *Gone with the Wind*. He replied that he had been travelling extensively to quite a few neutral countries such as America, Portugal and Spain. He had, however, been playing with the idea of writing a modern adaptation of Baroness Orczy's *The Scarlet Pimpernel* and instead of rescuing the French aristocrats from the guillotine, he would be rescuing the Jews from the clutches of the Nazis. He felt that it would take him some time to write a film script and after that, a few more months in which to set the production up. He remarked to me it was usually the same for everybody in the theatrical profession, in that one minute you were idle with nothing to do and the next, you were being overwhelmed with work. He had only just recently heard from the director, Michael Powell and co-producer and writer, Emerick Pressburger that they were thinking of doing a film next year. It was to be about a crew of a German U-boat that had been sunk in Canadian waters, being forced to flee across Canada to gain sanctuary across the American border so as to avoid being interned for the duration of the war by the Canadians.

It was only natural, if only out of politeness, that I would be asked if I had any projects lined up and when Leslie Howard asked me that question, I had no alternative but to speak the truth. As a matter of fact, I replied, I have just accepted a contract from Warners in Hollywood and as I would be required to live there, I would be taking my Marlene with me. My announcement was followed by what one would call a pregnant pause until Leslie replied.

"Congratulations, Gunther. As it happens, I was under contract to Warners during the thirties and had some good times whilst I was there. I have to warn you that Jack Warner runs the studio like a factory without union rules. In fact, he has been attributed to the saying that Hollywood is the only manufacturing town where the product walks out of the factory doors at the end of the working day. If you don't mind me saying so old chap, you could have picked a better time to go to America. A lot of people are going to criticise you for leaving Britain in her darkest hour and many will be observing that although you may be too old for call up, you could still contribute to her defence in other ways."

"I appreciate your concerns, Leslie. However, the key word here is 'contribute', as I am sure that you will understand exactly what I mean by that comment."

Just at that moment, Noel had joined our group. "What is going on, dear boys," he drawled, "Don't tell me that I have just missed some juicy gossip?"

"Far from it, Noel. Gunther here was just telling us that he's off to America soon," Leslie responded and went on to say, "In fact, I rather suspect that he has become a member of our happy band of brothers, wouldn't you agree, Noel?"

Noel Coward linked arms with Leslie and myself as he steered both of us away from the remaining group to a quiet corner of the room where I had to repeat my intention of going to America to him. Noel gave a sly chuckle and slapped me on the back.

"Leslie is quite right, Gunther. I can't quite picture you in the role of a rat leaving a sinking ship but rather as someone joining Churchill's theatrical troupe. It is infinitely more exciting, to do something for one's country rather than spend the time taking endless theatrical tours around wartime Britain playing the same old *King Lear* with a rapidly diminishing geriatric cast. Naturally, the downside, dear boy, is that you are going to take a hell of a lot of criticism from certain members of the press, some of it I am sure will be verging on the unprintable! But I am sure you will be able take it on the chin as you lie in your swimming pool in tropical weather enjoying unlimited supplies of luxury food. No, I am afraid Leslie wasn't entirely correct. It is true when he says that we are a band of brothers but of the three of us, I guarantee he'll come out smelling of roses whereas you and I will be vilified for some time."

I went to bed that night in Noel's guest room reflecting that he had said everything that was to be said without saying anything at all, but at least, if I was going to be ostracised and cast out as a leper, I wouldn't be alone.

The next morning, Noel waited with me for the arrival of my taxi and as we stood at the front entrance of the flats. We both observed that there was no indication other than the anti-aircraft balloons floating above us and the Londoners themselves, carrying the mandatory gas mask slung over their shoulder, that we were a country at war. We both knew that eventually, once Hitler could not enforce his will on Britain by diplomatic means, he would attempt to break our spirit by terror bombing and then conquer us by invading. Noel had made it quite clear to me the night before that both he and Leslie Howard had their bit to play but I had the most important role. If Britain could hold out for as long as possible, until America was persuaded to actively support us with arms and ships, Churchill knew that the tide would turn against Hitler. That is why it was important that I went to America, regardless of what public opinion would be towards me in Britain. My job in America would be to turn American public opinion in favour of Britain's cause. His last words to me as he handed me Marlene's box of pickles, as I got into the taxi, were "Just do as your heart tells you, dear boy and bugger everybody else! I think it will be some time before we meet again so give my love to Marlene and tell her that I would be most affronted if I am not chosen as a Godfather by proxy."

It was exactly a quarter to eleven when my taxi dropped me off at the front of the Foreign Office overlooking St James' Park. I stood for a moment watching the trickle of civil servants going in and out, all dressed in the same black jacket and striped trousers with just a variation of a black homburg or bowler hat on their heads to differentiate them. I also took in the armed sentries standing at ease and the sandbags both situated on both sides of the doors, all the windows and there were a lot of them, were taped against the possibility of bomb blasts. Picking up Marlene's cucumbers and cheeses, I walked into the main vestibule only to be temporarily stunned by the sheer magnificence of the swooping grand staircase and magnificent ceiling. I was soon brought back down to earth by being stopped in my tracks before I had even reached the reception desk, by two policeman who politely enquired what my package contained. Equally politely, I replied that they were jars of pickled cucumbers and some cheeses for my wife. I somehow got the feeling that they didn't believe me as their expressions told me to pull the other one.

Once I had convinced them of my identity, they reluctantly allowed me to get one of the receptionists to phone upstairs to Ian Lang's office asking him to verify my appointment with him. Having obviously confirmed it as genuine, the receptionist asked me to wait while someone from Mr Lang's office came to collect me. Sure enough, after a few minutes, a lady appeared by my side. She was quite an attractive looking girl and I surmised her to be in her mid-thirties. She introduced herself to me as Miss Philips and turning to the two constables, she informed them with great charm that she would now take responsibility for me, whereupon they both gave me a salute and apologised for any inconvenience they may have caused me. Miss Philips then proceeded to walk me over to the lift and whilst we waited for it to descend, she enquired whether I shopped at Fortnum and Masons a lot and yet again, I had to explain for the umpteenth time that the package contained jars of pickled cucumbers which I was bringing home for my pregnant wife. As we stepped into the lift, she commented on how sweet it was for me to be so considerate. Also, she asked how many months did Marlene have to go? By the time we reached the door marked 'International Affairs', the knuckles of my left hand were practically scraping on the ground such was the length of the corridor from the lift to the office and the weight of those damn pickles.

After Miss Philips had knocked on the door, I followed her through into an office which happened to have a large window overlooking the park. Mr Lang was seated at a desk with the window behind him and Commander Burton was seated at the other side of the desk. As both gentlemen rose to greet me, Miss Phillips left the office carrying my precious pickles! This was followed by an interlude of small talk between the three of us until finally, we got down to the real business of the day. Once Ian Lang had requested and received from me the three visa applications to the United States plus our passports, I was assured no further work would be required by myself on this matter and that any further action regarding these permits or travel arrangements would be handled by intermediaries of the Foreign Office. Once we had lit up cigarettes and settled down with the traditional British cup of tea, Commander Burton then proceeded to brief me.

"As I explained to you when we last met, Mr Conrad, the Prime Minister feels that we must leave no stone unturned in the fight to win the propaganda war in America. There is no doubt whatsoever that President Roosevelt dislikes both Hitler and Mussolini and the cause of fascism that they espouse. He also has grave concerns over Hitler's territorial gains and further aspirations in Europe and believes that he is a megalomaniac that needs to be stopped. However, much though he would like to help Britain, his hands are tied by public opinion and in turn, by Congress, who favour isolationism and have no desire to be dragged into yet another World War over Europe. Unfortunately, there are two further obstacles that we must overcome and they are the substantial Irish American community who in general, are anti-British and the other being the American Bund, an organisation made up of German Americans, financed by Nazi Germany and certain sections of American big business acting in concert with their German counterparts. I refer to Henry Ford, the founder of the American car manufacturing giant and I. G. Farben, the German international pharmaceutical company. All of these are joined by yet another organisation called the America First which has, as its national spokesperson, America's great hero, the aviator, Charles Lindbergh and an anti-Semite priest by the name of Father Charles Coughlin whose loathing of the Hollywood Jews is well recorded. The Prime Minister feels that it is only a matter of time before American public opinion will shift in favour of Britain but until that moment occurs, it is essential that celebrities such as yourself discreetly campaign to hasten that moment."

Commander Burton went on to say that my being offered a contract to work in Los Angeles could not come at a better time. Having worked there in the past and the fact that I had made many friendships and contacts in the film capital of the world, made me an ideal candidate for helping to tip the balance in favour of America's intervention on Britain's side. There was also another area of vital importance and that was the South American countries, where I could be useful in counteracting against the axis propaganda machine operating south of the border. He concluded.

"You are not to be anything else but yourself and that you certainly aren't going to be involved in any espionage activities but was simply to discreetly win over Hollywood's mighty film industry into persuading the American public to support Britain in her lone fight against the Axis powers. David Hislop will be discreetly supporting you behind the scenes and he has already taken up his post as British Consul in Los Angeles. He will be in touch with you after you have arrived from Britain. I know that what you are being asked to do does appear on the surface to amount to much, Mr Conrad but very soon, Hitler will become frustrated by Britain's refusal to accept his peace overtures and will unleash his armies in a full-scale attack on Britain but first, he will have to destroy our naval supremacy and home defences and for that, he will need to deploy his Luftwaffe. It is on the outcome of that potential battle of the skies that will determine our survival. If our forces, plus a little bit of luck, can buy us enough time, it is people like yourself and America's admiration for the underdog that will eventually bring her to our aid. Finally, I anticipate it will be something like five to six weeks for your permits and travel documents to arrive on your doorstep plus another few weeks for you to start on your travels. I am afraid from the public relations point of view, you may come in for some flak from certain quarters, which will last for a little while, but don't worry, we won't leave you out to dry. We will put things right for you down the road. Now if you have any questions to ask me, now is the time to ask. If not, it just leaves me to say good luck to you both and that your wife has an easy confinement when her time arrives and that she delivers a bonny baby. Though I probably won't be seeing you again for some time, our man in Los Angeles will keep his eye on you and don't forget to let him know where your new home will be when you finally arrive."

Shaking hands with me, Commander Burton was the first to leave allowing me to linger over the details of my departure with Ian Lang. He thought it best that to avoid any unnecessary suspicion, they use their own specialised travel agency, so if I could kindly give Miss Phillips the address of Robin Cox, my agent on my way out, they would liaison directly with him. He reminded me that if anything urgent came up, I was to contact him immediately. Once we had said goodbye to each other, I walked next door to Miss Phillips' office. She had obviously been expecting me as Marlene's package of pickled cucumbers and cheeses was waiting for me on her desk.

"I think," she said, whilst giving me a gorgeous smile, "That you have an address to give me Mr Conrad and whilst I am doing that, I might as well take your current home address and phone number so that I can update your file and of course, don't forget as you leave to take your package." I lingered a little while longer talking with her about the war and the effect that it was having on all of us, during which she mentioned that her husband whom she had only just recently married was a fighter pilot, stationed somewhere in Britain. Both of us left unsaid what we knew lay ahead and instead, concentrated on the inconveniences of rationing and the blackout until finally, just before I took my leave, she actually asked me for an autograph, for her older sister, she explained, giving me a sly wink.

As soon as I had left the Foreign Office, I took a cab straight to Paddington as my only wish now was to get home. Whilst I was waiting for the next train, I took the opportunity of phoning Marlene from one of the six phone boxes situated in the main concourse to tell her that I would be home soon and that I would be taking a taxi from the station when I arrived. I just gave myself enough time to tell her that I loved her and that I would tell her all about my adventures in London when I got home. There were still twenty minutes left before my train arrived, so I took the opportunity of finding a discrete seat away from public eyes and settling down, took out a cigarette and lit up. It was going to be a busy two months for the two of us, plus one and I wondered how quickly things would change from the present calm, before Hitler unleashed Armageddon upon the British people. During the last few weeks, I had rapidly become very streetwise when it came to travelling on public transport. I am afraid it was very much a case of dog eat dog as far as getting a seat even in a first-class carriage. I found myself standing not so far back from the front of the queue waiting to be allowed onto the platform.

As soon as the passengers had disgorged themselves from the newly arrived train, the departure gate was opened by an unfortunate ticket collector who was swept aside as we all poured through onto the platform. In a strange way, I quite enjoyed the experience for the first time in many a long year, nobody was interested in me. They only had their eyes set on one goal and one goal only and that was to get a seat on the train. By a combination of shuffling and running and with one hand holding Marlene's package of well stirred up pickles and cheeses, the other hand holding down the hat on my head, I was able to reach a first-class carriage and fall in. Even so, it was three quarters full and apologising profusely as I trod on one or two toes, I was able to secure a seat. Placing Marlene's package on the rack above me, I flopped down onto the seat exhausted. Once I had settled myself down, I took the opportunity of glancing around the compartment. It was filled with the usual mixture of city gents most of whom were wearing the mandatory black jacket and striped trousers and a sprinkling of military personnel of officer rank. When the whistle finally blew, the train started moving off during which time the corridor was already full of standing passengers.

I was only just thinking that I better keep my wits about me to ensure that I got off at Marlow when a naval captain sitting opposite me offered me a cigarette. It turned out that he lived in Medmenham and was going home on seven days leave. We hadn't been talking for long before he made the observation to me that I might be an actor. He was quite sure that he had seen me somewhere before, but he wasn't sure where, as he didn't go to the theatre or cinema that often. That came as a relief to me as I was able to mumble quietly that, yes, I was actor but mostly in Shakespearean plays. He apologised by saying the last time he had done any Shakespeare was when he was a schoolboy. He wished me luck and hoped that I would eventually land a part in a film as he understood that was where the money was!

It turned out that I had no trouble getting off at the right station as it was easily identifiable in daylight and the naval captain was also getting off. I noticed that the train was disgorging most of its passengers, mainly air force personnel and a smattering of civilian workers and several ladies returning from a shopping expedition in London. Despite the large amount of people, I was lucky in obtaining a taxi and low and behold, in no time at all, I arrived back at Falcon House. Marlene was the first person I saw standing outside and as I bowed before her, I handed her the package exclaiming, "Your pickles, madam."

Chapter 16

Departure Imminent

Events began to pick up momentum during the remaining days of June and I can remember quite clearly the two that stood out the most. It took a great worry off my mind when Robin notified me by phone that Warners had sent a cablegram, acting as a letter of intent, confirming their offer of a contract and that they would expect to see me in Hollywood by the twentieth of August 1940 ready to start work. I arranged with him to spend a long weekend with us and besides bringing any paperwork that required my signature, he was also to bring his family as well. It would be pleasant to hear the laughter of two young boys in the grounds of Falcon House and Marlene was happy to go along with the idea, throwing herself wholeheartedly into preparing the house for their impending arrival. The second event was Winston Churchill's speech to the House of Commons on the eighteenth of June in which he said, in part, "The Battle of France is over the Battle of Britain is about to begin. Let us, therefore, brace ourselves to our destinies and so bear ourselves that, if the British Empire and its Commonwealth last a thousand years, men will say, this was their finest hour." The speech not only overwhelmed me by its oratory and content but also made me feel, as I'm sure it did for most British people, a participant in British history in the making.

By mid-July, we were all into the full swing of leaving for America. Our travel documents and passports had duly arrived and upon reading through them even as a seasoned traveller, I had to admit that our journey to America appeared quite a daunting prospect. We would start by travelling up to Liverpool by rail and then take one of the few remaining civilian flights from Speke airport across the Irish Channel to Dublin in Southern Ireland. Then we would travel on to County Limerick by road and proceed to a small seaside town by the name of Foynes, situated on the banks of the River Shannon. There we would board a Pan Am Boeing 314 flying boat which would take us via Botwood situated in Newfoundland and on to Shediac, New Brunswick, finally arriving in Port Washington, just outside New York City. I estimated by the arrival and departure schedules that it would probably take us between two to three days to accomplish the first part of our journey. Then after a two-night stopover in New York, we would then take the train to Chicago arriving at La Salle Street station at nine o'clock the following morning. We would then proceed to Dearborn Station where we would be connected to the Super Chief, the flagship of the Atchison, Topeka and Santa Fe Railroad which would then proceed to take us to Los Angeles passing through Albuquerque and Gallup, New Mexico, the whole trip taking another two days. It would be one hell of a long journey.

To start with, I had some concerns for Marlene and our child that she was carrying and then there was the worry of the crossing to Ireland, though a neutral country there were still plenty of German aircraft operating in the Irish Sea, so it wouldn't take much for the Neutrality Laws to be broken by one fanatical Nazi Luftwaffe pilot to shoot down a neutral passenger plane. I made a point early that evening of sitting Marlene and Olivia down in the office and going through the itinerary of the travel documents, stressing very carefully the length of the journey and the danger involved. To my surprise, rather than finding it a daunting task, the girls took the opposite view. Olivia immediately assumed her prim and no-nonsense look and speaking first.

"You certainly don't have to worry about me, Gunther. The journey would to be an experience of a lifetime. The furthest I have travelled outside of Britain is to France and that was by boat and train. Now I am going to travel four-thousand miles to America by plane and face the dangers of Indians and gangsters! As for any other dangers, well I say a farthing for your dangers. What's good for our fighting lads is good enough for me." When Olivia finished speaking, Marlene gave her familiar gurgle of laughter and standing up, came around to the back of my chair and putting arms around my neck, she kissed the top of my head.

"Don't be so silly, Gunty. I'm not made of china that I would fall apart so easily. I am not even at three months, so even when I arrive in America, I would still have four months to go to my confinement. Doctor has assured me that I am in good physical shape and carrying well. As Olivia has just said, it's an adventure and remember, I have not been to America before, so the both of us will enjoy the experience together. What you will have to worry about is that Olivia and I will be let loose spending your money on some new outfits so that I will look my best as your glamorous wife when we arrive in the States."

I finished up the month of July by appearing in a BBC Radio production for Saturday night theatre of R.C. Sheriff's *Journeys End*. It was to be my last engagement in Britain. Its theme was very much in tune with the times as it depicted life in the trenches during the First World War. Talking of war, Hitler finally decided to launch daylight attacks on our southern airfields, particularly those nearest the coast. It seemed that growing weary of having his peace overtures continuously rejected, he had decided to soften Britain up by destroying our air defences, so as Winston Churchill had forecast, the Battle of Britain had indeed begun. So far, thank God, our lads were giving the Luftwaffe as good as they got. We were also fortunate that RAF Medmenham was a non-operational station, thereby sparing the residents of both Marlow and Medmenham from aerial bombardment.

Marlene and I had made a joint decision to offer Falcon House to the Air Ministry for the duration of the war. It would make an ideal additional officers mess to the main camp as it could accommodate at least eight officers. The ministry had accepted our offer with enthusiasm and had already arranged with us a site inspection of the property with a view to turning it into a billet for the AOC (Air Officer Commanding) of the area.

As we went into August, I became involved in a whirlwind of activity signing a mountain of paperwork, giving my solicitors joint power of attorney with Hiram to manage my English estate in my absence, as well as formalising the requisition of Falcon House with the Air Ministry. During a hot August evening, sitting in the garden, Marlene and I had discussed with her parents about whether they had any doubts or anxieties about the direction our lives were taking us. For instance, we not only felt guilty for leaving Britain but also for denying them both the opportunity of welcoming the arrival of their grandchild. Also, I couldn't help feeling that their only reason for staying behind was that they didn't want to be a nuisance by coming with us. Hiram put it very succinctly when he answered my questions.

"Stop trying to convince yourself, Gunty! You have no reason to be ashamed of yourself for making the decision to go to America. I am aware of the dominant factor as to why you are going and believe me when I say that I am proud of you. As for your concerns about us wishing to stay behind, let me assure you that both Miriam and I are done with running from the Nazis. We are simply getting too old for that nonsense. Should the unspeakable occur, that Britain would fall and there is no doubt in my mind that she will not, then Miriam and I will fall with her alongside many of our friends. I don't think we need to dwell any longer on that morbid subject. In a lighter vein, since I have been licensed to both practice medicine and perform operations as a consultant surgeon, I am fully independent and able to share the running costs of Falcon House with you. As to the Royal Air Force moving into the main house, you can be rest assured that Miriam will be in her element. She will be like a mother hen to those officers and I'm sure that the air force catering corps will have a job keeping her out of the kitchen. All you have to do, Gunty, is to make sure that you take care of Marlene and our grandchild and bring them back to us safe and sound."

The four of us spent the remainder of the evening conversing in German about the old days before Hitler came to power, how he had utterly destroyed the moral compass of the nation and that he had to be stopped before he continued to poison the minds of future generations of Germans. After Marlene and I had gone upstairs and were getting ready for bed, we were discussing how the future would turn out. It struck me at this moment in time, that all over the free world, there would be people like us, from all walks of life, from all nationalities and from all religious denominations asking the same question. We both snuggled down underneath the bed clothes and wondered what sort of future our child would be living in when it reached our age. After Hitler and Mussolini had been defeated, how many more tyrants would be coming along? How many more ethnic minorities would be persecuted? It was the Jews today, but who would it be tomorrow? Take your pick as there were plenty to choose from and as an afterthought, what about the 'Isms'? At present, we had communism and fascism but what would come next? Ah well, as Hiram would say, 'Enough already'.

It was only a matter of days now before we would be leaving Britain and it had been my intention to take Marlene down to London but there had already been several isolated bombing attacks on the capital which made it unwise to risk her health in her present condition. Olivia had been gradually closing down the office and apart from bringing me endless thank you notes to sign for all those friends and acquaintances who had sent us bon voyage cards, she also brought me a short correspondence from Commander Burton wishing us a safe journey and in view of Marlene's forthcoming event, had thought it wiser if we spared her a long and arduous journey up north and so was enclosing additional petrol coupons which would cover the consumption needed for our journey by car to Liverpool where we would be picking up the flight to Dublin. Some other good news that also arrived, was that Myron Selznick, my American agent, had received an offer from William Haines, an acting chum from the old days of silent Hollywood. He was kindly offering to place his house in Bel-Air at our disposal whilst he was away at Palm Springs for the season. It was a thoughtful gesture on his part as it would enable us to have a little more time to purchase a property suited to our needs.

I held a last briefing with Bill and Lucy confirming that they would be happy to stay on looking after Marlene's parents and the same applied to John and Mary, with Mary continuing to carry out housekeeping duties for the cottage and John taking responsibility for the gardens and the maintenance of the garages and cottage. I then went on to explain to them that the Air Ministry would be taking over responsibility for the maintenance of the main house and would be supplying their own personnel to staff it and last but not least, Miriam would be responsible for paying their wages at the end of each week.

The battle of the skies over Britain was now being identified in the psych of both the German and British public as the *Luftshlact um England* or the Battle of Britain. Though there had been a few bombs dropped on London, the main concentration of the battle was still on airfields and coastal installations. The good news, if it could be called that, was despite the overwhelming superiority of the German Luftwaffe, we were inflicting heavier losses on the Germans than they were on us. I hoped and prayed that despite the courage and skill of our young pilots, we weren't going to lose the battle through attrition and the sheer weight of numbers.

Marlene came up with a wonderful idea of holding an American themed dinner for our last weekend in the country as a token of our appreciation to those American friends of ours who had decided to stay in London cementing the Anglo-American relationship. At first, I was a little wary of the idea until she had contacted Ben Lyon and Bebe Daniels who had asked her, would it be okay to bring along a young American broadcaster by the name of Edward R. Morrow who was working as a news correspondent for the American Broadcasting Company. Apparently, he had only just recently arrived from Europe, where he had been covering the German takeover of Austria and the Sudetenland in Czechoslovakia and had now begun broadcasting direct to America from London with the opening line, "This is London calling." It seems that the American public were becoming spellbound with his reports from London and that they were slowly being persuaded to turn away from isolationism by his on-the-spot recordings of Hitler's conquest of Europe. Now that he was in London, they were listening first-hand to the Luftwaffe's bombardment of Britain and how the average man in the street was standing up to it.

Somehow, Marlene had put together a party for that weekend consisting of Joseph Kennedy, American ambassador to the United Kingdom, Vic Oliver and his wife, Sarah Churchill, Ben Lyon and his wife Bebe Daniels, Edward Morrow and a late addition to the list, an American actor by the name of Douglas Montgomery. I was just beginning to worry again that perhaps Marlene had taken on more than she could cope with especially as she was about to embark on a long and hazardous journey that could be stressful for her. I needn't have worried, for Marlene casually informed me that she had taken on two extra kitchen staff and two additional waitresses to assist Bill in waiting on table.

On the day of the dinner party, I spent the morning with Olivia and John carefully packing our more precious ornaments into several tea chests and then, after moving them into the garage had proceeded upstairs to the bedroom and done the same thing with our bric-a-brac and surplus clothes, many of which Marlene had already given to the girls. Because the wartime restrictions on food and clothing were beginning to affect the ordinary man in the street, both Lucy and Mary were delighted with the range of couturier clothes that she had given them. In the early afternoon, we went for one of our favourite walks along the Thames. We took in the scenery, the sounds and smells of the countryside, knowing it would be some time before we experienced them again. As we strolled along, we talked about our fears over the lack of communication from her sister in Holland and the remainder of her family in Germany. We didn't dwell on the subject for too long as it was far too depressing knowing that there was nothing that we could do but hope and pray that they would be safe and sound.

Later in the afternoon, as we discussed our guests whilst we were dressing, I could not help but express my reservation to Marlene over the wisdom of inviting Joseph Kennedy. The only connection I had with him was our business association in Hollywood where he had dabbled in financing films such as *Love of Sunya,* a film in which I co-starred with Gloria Swanson who at that time, was having a discreet affair with Kennedy. The affair had lasted for some time but was to end after a great deal of acrimony over the production of her film, *Queen Kelly* when the director, Eric von Stroheim was fired by her and Kennedy after he had lost control over the final cut of the film due to his overrunning the film's budget. However, what was more disturbing to me was that he had a reputation for being anti-Semitic and supporting Hitler. He also had very little regard for Britain as he felt that she would very soon be conquered by the Germans and therefore, there was very little point in assisting her. Obviously, that sort of attitude did not go down well with the British government or for that matter, President Roosevelt. It was also noted that Kennedy preferred to stay outside of London because of the threat of bombing. As a matter of fact, there was a quip circulating amongst the political fraternity that a senior civil servant at the Foreign Office had remarked, 'I thought my daffodils were yellow until I met Joe Kennedy'.

Marlene agreed with me and felt the best course of action was to tough it out and try and avoid any politics whatsoever. I had been so busy talking and dressing that it was only as I slipped on my dinner jacket that I noticed Marlene standing by the bedroom door waiting for me. She looked stunning! Despite a slight thickening of the waist, she had poured herself into a black sheath dinner dress and now that she had overcome morning sickness, she stood before me the very picture of Hollywood glamour. "You look gorgeous tonight, Marlene," I said, as I took her arm ready to escort her down the stairs. "One thing's for sure: a year in the Californian sun will have the studio moguls chasing after you with long-term contracts."

"There's one thing that you can be sure of, Gunty. There is no way that I would want to be part of that world. One film star in the family is more than enough. My only ambition now is to be one hell of a hausfrau and mother and to keep you safe from all those Hollywood she-cats."

As we descended the stairs laughing, I could hear the telephone ringing its heart out and by the time we reached the bottom of the stairs, it had stopped. Olivia very quickly appeared from the office to tell me that the American ambassador was on the line and wished to speak to me. Quickly walking into the office, I picked up the phone and announced myself.

"Hello, Mr Ambassador. Gunther Conrad speaking."

"Hello, Gunther. I am afraid you'll have to excuse my bad manners in letting you know so late, but Rose and I will not be able to make it for dinner tonight. To put it bluntly, the crap has hit the fan in so far as Washington is becoming concerned over a news reporter by the name of Ed Morrow who is at present broadcasting live from London direct to the American public. Despite my strong protestations to him not to be so anti-German, he has, so far, refused to do so. Unfortunately, I am at present tied up at the Embassy dealing with the matter. Once again, please accept my apology and give my regards to your lovely wife. I hope that we will meet up again in the future."

After I had given my commiserations to the ambassador, I put the phone down and joined Marlene in the lounge just as the sound of the car bringing the first guests swept through the inside of the house. Whilst Marlene and I welcomed our guests, Olivia had been able to let Bill and Lucy know that we would be two guests short.

Fortunately, the ambassador's absence did not spoil the party. In fact, it was a relief as I am sure that had he been able to attend, the atmosphere would have been unbearable though I can't say in all honesty that it was an occasion for too much merriment, considering the nation was under attack and facing its darkest hour and we the hosts were about to leave for a safer climate. Unbeknown to us, having not read the morning's papers, Sefton Delmer of *The Daily Express* had written an article on the list of entertainers who were contributing to the war effort and my name was amongst those that he listed.

From our point of view, it turned out to be a successful evening. Most of the guests were people that I looked upon as my close friends. Ben Lyon and Bebe Daniels, I had known since the late twenties when Ben was working for Howard Hughes, the director-producer and Bebe was singing her heart out in early sound films such as *Rio Rita*. As to the young man that they brought with them and introduced to us as Edward Morrow, he turned out to be a tall Texan with dark good looks and an unmistakable Texas drawl. Both Marlene and I took to him immediately because of his easy-going charm and the fact that he had similar mannerisms that reminded us of Gary Cooper. Vic Oliver, of course, was another matter altogether. As soon as he entered the house, he was entertaining us all with his wisecracks and one-liners. He had even brought his violin along. The thing about Vic was that he had a private and public personality and despite having what I thought was a rather exaggerated American Bronx accent and the persona of a funny man, was a rather thoughtful, erudite and an accomplished musician. The other tantalising aspect of Vic was that he had fallen in love and married Sarah Churchill the red-haired and beautiful daughter of Winston Churchill, our Prime Minister. Sarah had chosen to make a career in show business which is where she first met Vic Oliver after his return from the States after a successful career as a concert violinist and raconteur. At first sight, it seemed an odd marriage: a Jewish entertainer and the daughter of one of Britain's premier aristocratic families, the Marlboroughs. It seemed to work, as they made a vivacious couple and appeared to complement each other. One of the other guests was a young actor by the name of Douglas Montgomery who I wasn't familiar with, but I did know had become a major star in the early thirties playing good-looking and dependable co-starring roles to many of Hollywood's leading actresses such as Katharine Hepburn, appearing with her in the film *Little Women*. During a visit to Britain, he had fallen in love with the country and was at present living over here.

Lucy had once again performed miracles tonight in the kitchen, with ration books now beginning to dominate our lives and shortages beginning to appear. Somehow, she had acquired a string of rabbits which she had served baked with a tasty sauce and accompanied by vegetables and potatoes and for a dessert, she turned the simple bread-and-butter pudding into an art form. As for the wines, over the years, I had laid down many excellent reds and whites, most of which I had now transferred over to the cottage for Hiram and Miriam to dispose of as they wished but for tonight's last dinner party, I had brought up the last remaining six bottles of an excellent red from the region of Veneto in northern Italy and some first-class Prosecco from the same region. The result was that by the end of the meal, the atmosphere around the table was completely relaxed and as an example, Ed Morrow who was seated next to me, gave me a slightly different version of the tale told to me by Ambassador Kennedy a few hours earlier. It appeared that the broadcasting of his reports from London by ABC to the American people, was beginning to cause a shift in public opinion in favour of Britain and cause a shift from isolationism to intervention in helping Britain and that Kennedy's assumptions that Britain was already a defeated nation was contrary to the views of the Roosevelt administration. The upshot of that was that the American State Department was instructing the ambassador to adopt a more conciliatory tone in his dealings with the British government or else face the possibility of being recalled, hence the panic at the Embassy. I made the point of thanking Ed for his reporting and asked him how much longer that he would remain in London. His answer was, "As long as it takes and if the Brits can take it, I sure as hell can too."

The main consensus around the table was that if the Luftwaffe failed to knock out the RAF, they would switch to bombing civilian targets such as London, full-time. Despite my own lack of enthusiasm for leaving Britain so soon, everybody assured me that I would do more for the war effort by being in America fighting our corner than being over here lost in the shuffle and in any case, as Ben said, the reverse could be said for all the Americans who were over here helping to keep up British morale. In the end, Vic Oliver had us all trooping into the lounge where he proceeded to entertain us on his violin with a rendition of *Nessum Dorma* from Puccini's opera *Turandot*, accompanied by Miriam singing the lyrics. They eventually rounded off their voluntary recital by giving us *A Nightingale Sang in Berkeley Square*. As soon as Vic and Miriam had finished their star act to great applause, Marlene placed a stack of records on the turntable and then went and made herself comfortable on the settee with her legs curled up underneath her, holding court with our guests. Meanwhile, whilst

Bill and I acted as barmen, I managed to spend some time talking to Sarah Churchill not only about her show business inspirations but whether her father's national prominence as war leader would have any effect on her ambitions to succeed in the theatre. Her reply to that was yes, it was indeed very difficult to have a famous father and that one had to work twice as hard to achieve one's own identity and to be a success in one's chosen profession. I certainly wished her all the best and encouraged her not to give up her dreams. I must admit that even though she was vivacious and had her mother Clementine's good looks, I couldn't help feeling a twinge of sympathy for her, for not only did she have a famous father, but she had also acquired a famous husband. Would she have enough talent to overcome those twin millstones around her neck?

I spent the remaining hours of the evening reminiscing with Ben and Bebe over the golden silent years of Hollywood and how they and Vic had created such a great morale booster for the British public with their radio show *Hi Gang*. We eventually brought the evening to a close by putting everybody up for the night for the simple reason that most of our guests had partaken one glass too many and the remaining few had no way of getting home. Unfortunately, their prospects of a breakfast when they awoke were nil. The most that we could offer them would be tea and porridge.

It was to be nearly midday before the last guest finally left Falcon House with most being ferried to the station at Marlow and as we said goodbye to both Ben and Bebe, I promised them faithfully that I would be sending them food parcels from America. By the time we had stripped the beds and cleaned the house, we were all completely exhausted by a combination of late-night partying and hard work. We spent the remainder of the afternoon sprawled out in the lounge but even then, there was to be no respite, for as the hours started ticking down to our departure, our personal belongings would have to be selected and packed. Also, there were constant interruptions of phone calls, as friends and acquaintances called to bid us bon voyage and safe journey. As we had a very early start in the morning for the long drive to Liverpool, our luggage consisting of a trunk and several large suitcases had already been brought downstairs ready for loading into the car. I had also taken it upon myself to keep both Marlene and Olivia from thinking too much of tomorrow's journey. The radio proved a godsend with shows such as Tommy Handley's comedy, *ITMA* and *Mystery Theatre* with Valentine Dyal. As to the war itself, the Germans were really throwing everything they had at Britain's defences and were also carrying out sporadic bombing of London which was now becoming known as the blitz. If Hitler thought that by bombing London, he would break the spirit of the civilian population he was mistaken, for the Londoners were determined to prove him wrong. The King and Queen and the two Princesses had made the decision to remain in Buckingham Palace whilst ordinary folk carried on with their everyday lives. Nobody was in any doubt that if Hitler and Goering failed in crushing the R.A.F., they would turn their full attention on bombing the civilian people into submission, as they did with Poland and Holland.

Already, the government had taken steps to protect the civilian population by ensuring that London tube stations would remain open all night serving as underground shelters where people could bring bedding so that they could sleep on the platforms. Most children living in London were being sent into the countryside as evacuees to live in villages and farms so that they would be out of harm's way from the impending bombing of the capital. However, despite the good intentions behind the government's proposals, it was heart rending to see so many mothers being forced to part with their sons and daughters. As for myself, I had never achieved peace of mind in the decision that I had made to go to America and as each week that had gone by had weighed more heavily on my shoulders. I could only rationalise that by leaving, I could play some small part in bringing the United States into supporting Britain with their massive industrial muscle, thereby making whatever sacrifices the ordinary British citizen in the street made, it would not be in vain.

It was seven o'clock in the morning and we were ready to leave. John had brought the car around early and between us, we had just about managed to fit our luggage into the large boot. Whilst we had been doing that, Lucy had rustled up two thermos flasks of tea and some sandwiches for our long journey up north. Once again, despite my best of intentions to avoid an uncomfortable farewell, it was an emotional parting. Hiram and Miriam, Lucy and Mary were moved to tears as they had embraced Marlene in farewell. I too, had difficulty in controlling my emotions as I shook hands with Bill and gave Hiram a hug. However, Olivia maintained her British stiff upper lip and composure throughout the farewells only to give herself away with a light dab at the corner of her eyes with her lace handkerchief and then finishing with a vigorous nose blow. When we finally set off down the drive, it was with a heavy heart that we looked back through the rear window at the five people that mattered most to us standing on the porch of Falcon House waving us goodbye. It was to be only a fleeting moment for as we turned out of the drive, the tableau disappeared out of sight.

It wasn't until we had been driving for a while that normal conversation was renewed within the car as three of us had been lost in our own private thoughts and it didn't take long before we were commenting on the passing countryside. Apart from John, none of us had been this far north before. After a few hours, we passed Birmingham and after another long stretch John informed us that if we had kept straight on, we'd be in Scotland but instead, we would be turning off now and heading for St Helens in Lancashire. We had long since eaten the food and drink that the girls had brought with us on the trip so after many hours, there would be an opportunity for John to pull over at a transport café that he knew, so that we could stretch our legs. When we pulled into the parking area, there were already several heavy goods vehicles of all descriptions plus an army lorry and four armoured tanks. Once inside, we ordered four bacon sandwiches with teas and grabbed a table. The atmosphere was heavily laden with tobacco smoke with the squaddies occupying one corner of the café and the remaining civilian lorry drivers and us occupying the remainder. Within minutes of seating ourselves a middle-aged waitress appeared with our order, "Here you are folks," she said. "Four bacon sandwiches and four mugs of tea. Enjoy" and off she sashayed leaving the three of us to watch John lift up his slices of doorstop bread and pour some brown sauce over several slices of bacon and after having banged the bread back down, he then proceeded to take a large bite. "Lovely," he said upon which the three of us followed suit. I did have a quiet chuckle to myself as I watched Marlene and Livy, as we now called her, attempt to manoeuvre a mug of tea to their lips without losing their femininity and then to try and proceed to eat a large bacon sandwich with a paper napkin wrapped around it. I think from the moment that we entered the café, the whole concept of the journey that we were undertaking changed the girls. They became more relaxed and I think they looked upon it now more as an adventure than something to be endured. It so happens that the waitress who I now knew as Maggie, had recognised me and had the good grace to wait until we had finished eating before she approached me asking for an autograph which I willingly gave. Unfortunately, it didn't end there as the café owner came over with a box Brownie camera, asking if I would mind having a photograph taken with him so that he could hang it behind the counter. With that mischievous look in her eyes that I knew so well, Marlene volunteered to take the photo of myself, the proprietor and Maggie and then having accomplished that, the minx then sauntered over to the squaddies who, by now, were well aware of who I was. She spoke to the young lieutenant and as I found out afterwards, she had informed him that I was full of admiration for the British Armed Forces and would be more than happy to pay their breakfast bill! The young officer came over to thank me personally and wondered if we could have a group photograph taken as a souvenir. Low and behold, Marlene once more volunteered to be the chief photographer. It must have taken up all of fifteen minutes to arrange chairs and set up a shot for eighteen soldiers plus myself and once that had been accomplished, I had to go through the same process again with the civilian lorry drivers! By the time we left the café, I could have done with a large whiskey. However, I knew deep down that I had brought some excitement into the lives of a few people and it certainly had lifted the spirits of both Marlene and Livy. As for John, he seemed to achieve some pleasure out of it purely by association.

Once we had left St Helens, it was just a short drive to Liverpool. Unfortunately, we saw very little of the city as Speke airport was on the edge of the city's suburbs and then, we only arrived there with an hour to spare before our plane's departure. There was hardly enough time to say another emotional goodbye to John, who finally stood and watched us checking ourselves through all the stages of the formalities. I looked back just to see if John was still there. Indeed, he was, if only for a brief second longer, then with a wave, he was gone. We were soon walking over the tarmac towards an Aer Lingus Lockheed twin engine passenger plane and being welcomed by a male steward who very quickly had us comfortably seated. As we were the last to embark, there was a murmur of recognition as we entered the cabin from the other passengers and by the time we had stowed away our hand luggage in the overhead lockers, the cabin door had been closed and we were slowly taxiing down the runway.

Only stopping for a minute or two, there was a surge of power and with escalating speed, the plane finally lifted off the ground and was soon climbing above Liverpool and out over the Irish sea, after which we settled down to a steady cruising speed. We were now flying above a low cloud formation although there were occasional breaks allowing us brief glimpse of the water below. Marlene, who had been holding my hand tightly during the take-off, had now relaxed and accepted tea and sandwiches from the air hostesses. By the time we had finished our light refreshments and talked amongst ourselves, because of our early start, we were soon drifting off into a light sleep, only to be awakened by the captain announcing over the cabin sound system, that we were now approaching Dublin airport and would be descending very soon. He hoped that we had experienced a comfortable flight. We spent a very pleasant fifteen minutes or so watching through our porthole windows as we broke cloud and had a panoramic view of Dublin. We had circled the airport several times, lining up for our runway but eventually, we descended, watching the ground rising up towards us at great speed and then landed with a bump and a jar of the airplane frame as our wheels hit the tarmac. Our plane then braked and slowly taxied towards the main airport building.

Whilst we were waiting for the steps to be wheeled up to the cabin door, we had the opportunity to take in our surroundings. As far as I could make out, work on the airport terminal was still only half finished, although even then, it was still very impressive, designed so I was informed, in the shape of a liner with a white exterior. As I understood from one of the stewardesses, the airport had only been opened in January, but that work would be completed on the terminal by the end of the year. Clutching our hand luggage, we proceeded to walk the short distance from the aeroplane to a temporary building where we passed through Irish immigration and customs. I had telegraphed ahead from Speke for a large limousine to be waiting for us, so once our luggage had arrived from the plane, it was loaded it into the car while Marlene and Livy got themselves seated comfortably. The chauffeur, as it turned out, was solidly built, with a ruddy complexion and a mass of curly blonde hair upon which a chauffeur's cap sat precariously. He went by the name of Patrick O'Rafferty. Of course, he recognised me at once exclaiming in a thick Irish brogue, "To be sure, sir, are you not the famous 'filum' star, Gunther Conrad?" When I replied in the affirmative, he seized my hand and whilst pumping it vigorously, said, "Welcome to Dublin." I had already wired ahead that we were to be driven to the Perry Square Hotel in Limerick, as it was only a short distance from Foynes and our connecting flight was not due to leave until twelve-thirty the following day. I felt it wiser for us to recharge our batteries by staying overnight in Limerick before we faced a long journey across the Atlantic, particularly as I didn't want Marlene physically overdoing it.

We covered the ninety odd miles to Limerick with Patrick keeping up a constant flow of repartee as only an Irishman could. It seemed that none of us had stopped laughing from the moment that we had left Dublin until we arrived in Limerick. Once we had arrived at the Perry Square Hotel which was only a stone's throw away from St Mary's Cathedral, I had the baggage unloaded and not only paid Patrick his fare but also added a handsome tip for his good company. Judging by his reaction you would have thought that I had tipped him a king's ransom. Robin had phoned ahead some weeks back for a suite and a large bedroom to be reserved for me and accordingly, as soon as we had checked in at the reception desk, the manager appeared from his office and immediately proceeded to escort us to the lift and take us to the top floor where our suite was located. Livy's room was situated on the same floor and was well furnished with en suite facilities and after inspecting it, she declared herself more than happy with it. The manager then escorted Marlene and I to our suite which was situated on the same floor and with a flourish, opened the double doors which led into a sitting room with bay windows which gave a marvellous view of the Cathedral. There was another set of double doors which lead into a bedroom with a large, canopied four-poster bed and beyond that was a door leading into an en suite bathroom. We also noticed that the management had placed some fresh flowers and a bowl of fruit in the sitting room as a welcoming gesture to Marlene. I also happened to note that there was a small dining table and chairs situated near the window which prompted me to ask Marlene whether she would like to dine in the privacy of the suite or downstairs in the public area. Her preference was for downstairs, providing we could have a secluded table. The manager assured her that as it was a quiet night, he could guarantee us total privacy which satisfied Marlene.

Our luggage, minus the trunk which we left in the porter's lodge, arrived followed by a maid who proceeded to unpack and put away Marlene's things whilst at the same time, enquiring whether madam would require any of her dresses to be ironed? All in all, it turned out to be a very pleasant stay. True to the managers word, the dining experience was unobtrusive, the food was excellent and the staff very attentive. It was a good idea to have broken the journey up with an overnight stopover as it had given the three of us an opportunity to unwind and recharge our batteries for what would be the longest and most demanding stage of our journey.

Finally, to round up what had been a very pleasant night, we took in the tranquil night air of Limerick with a slow walk to St Mary's Cathedral and whilst on our return journey to the hotel, I spied a pub and dragged Marlene and Livy in. I bought them two half pints of Guinness, their first taste of the famous Irish brew and also, we enjoyed the experience of listening to a folk singer accompanied by two fiddlers giving us a rendition of foot-stomping Irish ballads. Once again, Marlene proved a natural with her beauty and charm, even to the point of singing along with the other customers and of course, it went with the shingle, so to speak, that the mandatory camera was produced from somewhere so that the landlord and his wife could have their photo taken with us. It had been a very relaxing interval with both Marlene and Livy being reluctant to leave. However, Marlene was insistent that I leave a substantial tip behind the bar so that everybody could have a drink on us. That, of course, brought forward a large cheer of all those present as we left and continued our walk back to the hotel.

The next morning, we were soon on our way to Foynes, with Patrick our driver from the day before chauffeuring us. We were expecting to arrive at somewhere around ten-thirty in the morning and Patrick quickly assured us that he would have us there in no time at all. The morning was already turning into a bright and sunny day and it was certainly bringing out the best in the Irish countryside. Every so often, we would pass a pony and trap driven by a man in a peaked cap and a pipe firmly clenched in the corner of his mouth or an elderly woman on foot with a traditional Irish shawl around her shoulders. Such was the atmosphere that I fully expected to see John Ford to pop out from behind a bush chewing a corner of a handkerchief whilst directing Barry Fitzgerald or Ward Bond! Both Marlene and Livy were quite happy in the back of the car chatting about the hotel and how quaint Limerick had been, which was a good thing, as whilst they were chatting about Limerick, it would take their minds off the journey ahead.

We arrived at Foynes before we realised it. I would have described it as a small town perched on the banks of the River Shannon and as we drove down to the Quay, I could see that some building work had been carried out. Apart from a maintenance hangar having been built, there was also a prefabricated building which I assumed acted in the capacity of an arrival and departure terminal. I could also see quite clearly a large flying boat stationary in the water some yards away from a jetty. There also appeared to be a considerable amount of activity, both inside and outside the aircraft, with a launch at the tail end, unloading luggage into the baggage hold whilst at the front end, just under the cockpit a cabin door was wide open revealing a uniformed crew member passing backwards and forwards within the interior, I also noticed the Pan Am logo on the fuselage.

Once we had entered the reception area, I took in the various desks and on seeing the first one marked 'Checking In', I ushered the girls over, whereupon once our reservations had been confirmed, our luggage was weighed in. Unfortunately, though we had a free baggage allowance, we ended up by having an excess which placed me in the position of having to pay a surcharge of an additional thirty pounds. Once I had sorted out that little financial matter, we were handed individual boarding cards and passed through to the customs desk where once again, our identities were confirmed by checking a photo match on our passports. Our hand luggage underwent a cursory examination and after that, we passed through to an area which was obviously the departure lounge.

I don't think that there were more than thirty other passengers seated around, some engaged in conversation others just reading and we had no difficulty in finding a leather settee and table to park ourselves and whilst Livy wandered over to a magazine stall, it gave me the opportunity to ensure that Marlene was comfortable. "Of course," she had replied, "It is at least four months too early to be fussing over me and with that, she bent over and kissed me on the lips. We had barely started talking about the layout of the lounge when Livy returned with an armful of magazines and papers and she had no sooner settled down beside us when a public announcement was made that the Pan Am Boeing 314 would soon be ready for departure and would all passengers proceed to embarkation.

We joined the tail end of a small queue of passengers filtering through the embarkation door and once we had passed through, it was a short stroll onto a jetty where, a tender was moored and with the assistance of a crew member, we came aboard and once we were seated, proceeded to ferry us over to the flying boat which was about a hundred yards away. The nearer we came to it, the more impressive the aircraft was. Our boat was brought alongside what I first believed to be a platform but according to the crew man standing next to me, it was actually known as a sponson, which apparently had the dual purpose of being both part of the flying boat's design for landing on water and a platform for entering and exiting through the cabin door. For passenger safety, there were two ground staff members to assist passengers from the boat to the plane. Marlene being Marlene, was a hoot! She displayed her impish charm by removing her high heel shoes and making the transition from boat to plane in her stockinged feet, ably assisted I may add, by the ground staff. As for Livy, she made the short journey as any colonial Englishwoman would, totally independent of any assistance, her head held high with her nose in the air.

Once we were on board, a charming stewardess dressed in a light blue Pan Am uniform showed us to our seats which we were informed could be converted into bunks during the night and whilst we were making ourselves comfortable, she also told us, that at the back of the cabin there was a door that would lead us through to a lounge. If we carried on from there, we would find a dining room with seating for sixteen and beyond that, there were separate dressing rooms for male and female passengers. Once past those, there was a recreational room for the comfort of the passengers. Marlene and Livy headed straight for the ladies powder room giving me the opportunity to study my fellow passengers. I don't think that there was more than thirty of us on the flight and of that number, I could only see three couples. The remainder were either businessmen or senior civil servants travelling between Ireland and America. As I looked out of my window, I could see the tender heading back to the jetty which suggested to me that we wouldn't be long before we took off and sure enough, the mighty engines burst into a roar as the propellers of the twin motors started to turn. The girls soon came back and took their seats just as the captain's voice came over the speaker.

"Good afternoon, ladies and gentlemen. This is Captain Romano speaking. Very shortly, we will be taking off and I would ask you to remain seated until we are fully airborne, after which you will be informed that you are free to leave your seats. You will be pleased to know that the weather forecast for our journey across the Atlantic is temperate and we will be making two stops. The first one will be Botwood, Newfoundland and the second, at Shediac, New Brunswick. Our cruising speed should be at about one-hundred and seventy-eight miles per hour and based on our present weather forecast, our estimated time of arrival at Port Washington, New York should be in thirty-two hours."

Within minutes of the captain concluding his announcement, we began moving and gathering speed. As we sped along the surface of the water, the twin motors on both wings were now at full throttle and eventually, as we watched out of the windows, the massive flying boat lifted itself slowly out of the water and began gradually climbing, leaving the estuary and Foynes below us until they disappeared from view as we entered the cloud formation. Finally, we climbed above the clouds and we felt the aircraft bank to the right and head out over the Atlantic. Once it had levelled out, the captain's voice once again came over the speaker to inform us that we were now free to move about the aircraft and enjoy the amenities on offer.

We certainly didn't need any second bidding as most of the passengers were soon on their feet, some rummaging through their hand luggage for personal items, whilst others proceeded to explore the length of the flying boat. The dining area was certainly something to behold, furnished in the style of a first-class restaurant and whilst we were passing through, two waiters dressed in white monkey jackets and black trousers were already laying out silverware on the white tablecloths. In the background, we could hear the subdued sound of the cascading strings of Mantovani and his Orchestra playing through the discreetly hidden speakers. The next apartment was the lounge area with comfortable chairs to relax in and finally, the last apartment was a recreation room fitted out for the relaxation of the passengers with card tables and the selection of board games. I was informed by one of the air stewardesses that on all the other long-haul routes that the Boeing 314 flew, such as to Honolulu, Asia and Africa, a luxury bridal suite had been installed but that had been removed from the route we were taking since the outbreak of war. In its place, Pan Am had extended both the lounge and recreation rooms. It was without doubt, a most impressive testimony to the rapidly advancing aviation technology and design. It made one wonder where it all would end once the war was over. It did seem likely that somewhere in the future, we would see passenger planes that would carry as many as four-hundred people and with that advancement would come a huge drop in airfares, allowing the so-called masses to travel the world. I reflected that the price of the air tickets that I had paid for the three of us, would undoubtedly pay the full market price for a three bedroomed detached house plus a car in Britain!

It was obvious to the three of us, as we took our places for the second sitting in the dining room, that the whole experience of the trip was specifically designed for the luxury end of the market. To be able to dine flying above the clouds with a choice of gourmet cuisine and fine wines served to you by immaculate waiters was an experience in itself and certainly the equal of any fine hotel in any city in the world. Marlene had never been impressed by the trappings of power and privilege adopted by our so-called 'betters' but she did firmly believe that everybody had the right to travel first class through life, especially if it was through their own endeavours. That was one of the reasons why I loved her so dearly. It was a pleasure to be with her that evening. There was no side with her, no pretence and no acting the grand dame. She just sat at the table spreading good cheer with her natural sense of good humour which gradually created its own atmosphere. Fellow passengers were soon talking to us across tables and the waiters soon became her devoted subjects. As for Livy, she had become totally relaxed, temporarily seduced by the sheer luxury of it all and enjoying every moment of it, she had even let her guard down by exclaiming that even if I discharged her next week, the experience for working for us would be the highlight of her life and it was a pleasure to serve us both as an employee and a friend and furthermore, if this was what the Americas was all about, then she was glad that she had made the decision to come with us, if only to protect us from the Yanks' fast talking ways. That little speech set Marlene off into fit of throaty laughter and only subsided when she bent over and gave Livy a hug.

By the end of the dinner, we were on first name terms with our fellow passengers many of whom occupied prominent positions in their respected professions. These included two American senators returning home after a fact-finding mission, three directors from the Pan Am board and two scientists. It was great for me just to be able to totally relax and be myself in the company of people who respected my privacy. By mutual agreement, we all decided to have a nightcap in the lounge, thereby vacating the tables for the last sitting and it was during our after-dinner drinks that we were introduced to Irish coffee. With Marlene sticking to soft drinks, Livy and I took up the challenge and ordered one each. Apparently, it was a concoction dreamed up by a local chef in Foynes for a group of American passengers on a cold and wet night and they had liked it so much that it was incorporated into Pan Am's transatlantic standard fayre. After waiting in some anticipation, it was finally served up to us in wineglasses and consisted of whiskey and brown sugar and coffee finished off with a head of double cream. It carried quite a kick, so much so, that I ordered a second one, even though Livy, being more sensible, stuck to one. Marlene, on the other hand, had a sip of mine and her verdict was that it was a drink to die for.

The rest of the evening was spent debating world affairs with the other passengers, the main talking point being how long it would be before America entered the war, if at all. It was quite a divisive topic amongst our American fellow passengers with about half saying that they should and half saying they shouldn't. In the end, it all came down to which political party they supported. I guess we must have had an equal number of Republicans and Democrats on board!

The girls decided to call it a night and retire. Even with a night's stop-over in Limerick, it had still been a long and tiring journey all the way from Falcon House for them and I reckoned it wouldn't be long before they were fast asleep in their bunks. As for me, I carried on with a couple of glasses of Jack Daniels whilst I finished my cigar and then called it a night.

We were all woken up and served a hearty breakfast in preparation for our arrival at Botwood in the territory of Newfoundland, Canada. After touching down, we refuelled and took off again. With the rigours of the trip now taking their toll on me, while Marlene and Livy chatted away about our life ahead in Los Angeles, I fell asleep again in my comfortable seat.

Our next scheduled stopover was at Shediac, New Brunswick, in Canada. It was a blessing that the second phase of our journey took only just over five hours to complete. Thanks to the weather remaining calm, when we touched down on Point Du Chene Bay, we had the opportunity to stretch our legs on dry land as the stopover was scheduled for a couple of hours, whilst mail was loaded on board and the aircraft was refuelled for the last stage of the journey.

Once ashore, the three of us took a short stroll along the shoreline towards the small town of Shediac. However, our stroll was cut short when we came across a picturesque Victorian hotel by the name of Maison Tate House and decided instead of proceeding any further, we would take an afternoon tea on the Veranda before setting off back to the bay. We couldn't have picked a better afternoon to view the Canadian scenery. Livy kept herself busy with her camera, taking pictures of everything around her and finished up by getting our waitress to take a picture of the three of us. Marlene was looking well. Instead of showing signs of travel fatigue, she was looking the opposite. The Canadian sunshine proving a tonic to her complexion. Whilst we posed for a picture with the owner of the hotel, we learnt that Shediac was known by the locals as the lobster capital of the world which pretty much told me that during the remaining stage of our journey to New York, there would be lobster on the menu! Indeed, when we arrived back at the jetty, there were several crates of fresh lobsters being loaded on to the flying boat. The three of us couldn't help looking at them with some anticipation for as Livy remarked, she couldn't remember the last time that she had tasted a lobster and it was way beyond her imagination and wildest dreams that she would be having it for her dinner aboard a flying boat. Once again, we were the last three passengers to board and as I stepped off the sponson and into the cabin, Captain Romano was standing there talking to a stewardess. However, when he saw me, he came towards me with his hand outstretched.

"Good afternoon, Mr Conrad. As you might have gathered, I am Captain Romano. I noted from the manifesto that you were on board and have been meaning to introduce myself to you sooner. So far, since our inaugural flight last year, I haven't had the opportunity of flying a world-famous film star across the Atlantic, so I do hope that we have been looking after you well? I also wonder perhaps if you'd like to be shown around the cockpit and experience the Atlantic Clipper taking off?"

"You don't have to ask me twice, Captain Romano. I would be absolutely thrilled and if you would just give me a moment, I will go and tell my wife where I will be."

"No need, Mr Conrad. Melanie, our chief stewardess, will be only too happy to notify your wife and companion of your whereabouts. As we are due to take off very shortly, perhaps you would like to follow me upstairs."

I certainly was surprised as I entered the cockpit and saw how large it was. There was a crew of five already installed in their own designated spacious areas and I was introduced to the co-pilot, the navigator, the wireless operator and two engineers. There were so many instruments and gears that it would frighten the life out of me if I had to use them. Anyway, the captain found me a seat out of everybody's way and then sat himself down at the control panels. Finally, after going through some form of checklist with the cabin crew, the captain then made an announcement for all passengers to take their seats and for the cabin crew to ensure that all exit doors were closed. This was then followed by the twin engines on both wings bursting into life which was then accompanied by a constant flow of communication between land and the cockpit until finally, Captain Romano shouted out, "It's a go" and commenced to ease forward the throttle until the flying boat, having swung out into the bay, gradually began picking up speed until once again, she began riding the waves until eventually, they began dropping away beneath her. This time, I had the pleasure of observing the territory of New Brunswick beneath me as it was a cloudless day and gave me the opportunity of viewing both land and sea in one panoramic view.

I could have stayed with the flight crew for the rest of the journey, but I wanted to make sure that Marlene would not forget to order me a lobster for dinner. So, saying cheerio to Captain Romano and thanking him for his hospitality, I left the cockpit and made my way down to our seats where I joined Marlene and Livy for an early evening cocktail. I also took the opportunity of booking a table for first sitting in the restaurant as it would now appear that we were scheduled for a late arrival in Port Washington. After finishing their cocktails, the girls went off to freshen up for dinner and whilst they were gone, I took the opportunity of reading the day's edition of the *Shediac Times*. Even though we had only been gone just over thirty hours, the news from Britain was not good. The situation had worsened as the Luftwaffe increased their blitzkrieg of the capital, but the RAF bloodied, but not bowed, was giving as good as it got. The bombing of London was increasing daily and there was a picture in the paper of the King and Queen visiting a bombsite. It certainly didn't do my feelings of self-worth any good to be flying in the lap of luxury to America when my adopted country was in mortal peril.

Well, we finally got our lobster dinner even though we had a moment of merriment at Livy's expense. As our waiter attempted to place a bib around her neck, her first reaction was one of outrage as she attempted to thwart the waiter's efforts. It wasn't until we explained that the bib was there to protect her clothes from the messy effects of eating the lobster that she accepted the situation. After we had eaten, we retired to the lounge but not before I had sent a note to the galley chefs accompanied with a substantial tip as a mark of our appreciation. After all, it was not every day, that you were served lobster straight from the sea and so well prepared and presented. Whilst Marlene stayed on soft drinks, I ordered a bottle of Prosecco for Livy and myself. As Captain Romano had announced that we had entered American airspace, we spent the next couple of hours both relaxing and preparing ourselves for landing.

Sure enough, Captain Romano once again announced that we were preparing for touchdown and that if we looked out of our windows, we would see a panoramic view of Long Island which was bathed in a myriad of lights and as we followed the coastline and began to descend upon Port Washington, I was able to see the water glistening in the half-light on the bay. Once we had touched down, the Clipper taxied over to the landing jetty and was quickly moored ready for our disembarkation. After we had said our farewells to our fellow passengers and collected our hand luggage, we proceeded to leave the flying boat in a leisurely and orderly fashion and once on shore, followed the air stewardess to the main terminal building where we proceeded to the immigration arrivals desk.

There were three immigration officers but unfortunately, the one we chose to present our documents to, was a rather surly looking individual who reflected his own self-importance by taking an unnecessary amount of time to examine our passports and asking the most obvious questions. In the end, having ascertained my artist's visa was in order and that Marlene was my spouse, he then proceeded to stamp our passports and then turned his attention towards Livy, performing the same ritual as he had with us, except this time, he added an extra question; how would she financially support herself during her stay in America? Livy gave him one of her sweet, sarcastic smiles that she normally reserved for naughty children whilst patiently informing him that, as it clearly stated on her visa, she had been brought over as Director of Corporate Affairs for Falcon House Arts Incorporated, a limited company that my astute financial advisers had set up for me whilst I was staying and working in America. This had been how I had been able to bring Livy over as an employee with specialist skills. I don't think that the immigration officer had seen many British subjects like Livy before, but after giving her a long hard stare, he stamped her passport and waved the three of us through.

I had barely enough time to say welcome to America before a Pan Am official had come up to me and asked me if I would mind meeting the press, as they had patiently been awaiting my arrival, after which he would escort my party to a waiting car which had been placed at my disposal by Warner Bros. He ushered us into a side room which consisted of a table and four chairs facing a William Randolph Hearst news camera, a radio announcer from NBC and about a dozen news hounds, all with pad and pencil and accompanied by their press photographers. There had been a young man standing front of them issuing some form of instructions, but as soon as he saw us enter, he came right over and spoke to me.

"Good evening, Mr and Mrs Conrad. My name is Clinton Kelly and I have been assigned by Warner Bros., New York office to accompany you all the way to California. I have booked a suite at the St Regis Hotel in New York so that you can rest up for two nights before continuing the last leg of your journey. As you can see, the press is here to interview you and I have told them that they will have fifteen minutes in which to get their story."

It was at this moment that Livy decided that she would be out of place in the forthcoming proceedings and that she would step outside for a cigarette while she waited for us, explaining that she would only be superfluous to requirements as she had nothing to contribute towards all this American razzmatazz! Wishing us good luck, she left the room. I had no sooner made Marlene comfortable and sat down beside her when the room was lit up by a barrage of flashing cameras. When that ritual was over, Clinton stepped forward and introduced us, informing the press that I was over here to complete some technical sequences for my latest film, *Ali Baba,* pointing out that the film had already been completed in Britain but because of the wartime restrictions, London Films would be completing the film in Hollywood and whilst in America, I would be appearing in several Warner productions.

As I sat there, I realised that Commander Burton had done his work well. I had a legitimate reason now for being in America without having the label of opportunist and coward placed upon my shoulders. Consequently, all that followed on would be coincidental. There then followed the usual onslaught of questions, some private, some topical and many asked just for the sake of it. However, there were some that did have honesty and depth, such as, how was London taking the blitz? Was I glad to be back in America? Was it true that my wife was expecting? Did I believe that Britain would win the war against Germany? Would Marlene resume her modelling career in America?

There were a few more questions besides those, plus a short question-and-answer radio interview and then we were done. Once Clinton had led us out of the room, he guided us out of the terminal to a large Packard saloon car which had already been loaded with our luggage. The car was large enough to accommodate the three of us on the back seat whilst Clinton sat in the front with the driver and without waiting any longer than was necessary, the car moved off. Knowing that Clinton would now be part of our company for the next four or five days, as Eddie Strickland had helped me on my first trip to the United States, I made a point of trying to get to know him. Apparently, he worked in Warners' New York office as Junior Vice President of Public Relations and as his family lived in Los Angeles, he was assigned the job of delivering me to the studio. During our conversations, he came over as a likeable and dependable guy, although I did have one word of caution to say to him and that was, "No more press interviews until we arrive in Hollywood."

Even though the hour was now late in the day, New York was throbbing with the sights and sounds of a huge Metropolitan city which came as a cultural shock to the three of us, having by now, endured nearly a year of blackout and wartime restrictions back home in Britain. The cornucopia of multicoloured lights on every building, the sounds of bells and horns emanating from all types of vehicles and even the occasional traffic policeman standing at an intersection with a whistle firmly clenched in his lips whilst he waved his arms about, all this was a sight to behold when it came to watching Marlene and Livy's faces, as they took it all in. Marlene was spellbound. She was no slouch when it came to travel, having lived in Paris, Rome, Berlin and London, but New York seemed to have hypnotised her by its frenetic pace and vibrant atmosphere. As for Livy, I'm afraid she wasn't giving an inch. However, although there was a flicker of a twinkle in her eyes, she still had time to comment.

"This is like being in a jungle and instead of trees, there are tall buildings reaching for the sky and instead of canyons, there are roads all appearing to go nowhere. It is just as I thought it would be, simply everything has got to be bigger and better."

"Livy, you should have been writer," I said, "Just remember though, it was your forefathers that colonised this land and made it the great nation what it is today."

Soon after that, our car pulled up outside an imposing building, whose façade was lit up by golden lights and had a green canopy stretching from the hotel entrance to the curb-side and upon its front was written, St Regis Hotel. A commissioner, attired in a top hat and a green overcoat with gold buttons, finished off with a gold lanyard from his right shoulder, came over to the car and opened the rear door. He escorted us up through the revolving doors of the front entrance into a magnificently decorated foyer which immediately to our right was the hotel reception. Clinton, who had been giving instructions to the bellboys regarding our luggage, had swiftly caught up with us and was already talking to a receptionist who picked up a phone and in the twinkle of an eye, there suddenly appeared in front of us, a gentleman dressed in a black frock coat and striped trousers who proceeded to introduce himself to us as Mr Halliday, the night manager. On behalf of the St Regis Hotel, he welcomed us to New York and if we cared to follow him, he would take us straight up to our suite.

He had us whisked up to the fourth floor where he proceeded to lead us along a thickly carpeted hallway to a set of double doors marked La Guardia suite where, with a flourish, he opened both doors exposing a luxuriously appointed sitting room which he promptly lit up by pressing a wall switch. Meanwhile, one bellboy had darted past him and proceeded to draw the heavy balcony drapes. At the same time, three more bellboys marched in carrying our baggage and finally, a waiter followed behind, pushing a trolley carrying chilled champagne in an ice bucket. There was also, of course, the mandatory bowl of fresh flowers on the coffee table. Marlene kicked off her high heels and made herself comfortable on a red velvet couch, leaving Livy to instruct the bellboys to put our luggage in the appropriate bedrooms. Whilst the waiter opened the champagne, I accompanied Mr Halliday on a tour of the suite. In the double bedroom, there was a king size bed as a centrepiece. There was also an en suite bathroom which also included a walk-in shower. Livy's bedroom was equally well apportioned and also included an en suite bathroom. Finally, after expressing my satisfaction to him, Mr Halliday enquired if there was anything further that we needed. I thought it best to order an assorted tray of sandwiches with tea and coffee. The suite rapidly emptied out as Clinton handed out a fistful of dollars bills to the bellboys and finally, having satisfied himself that all was well, Mr Halliday proceeded to bow himself out of the suite. It finally came to me who he reminded me of. He bore a remarkable resemblance to the actor, Fritz Feld, who Marlene and I had seen a few years back in a film called *Bringing up Baby* in which he had played a very funny caricature of a maître d'. The last to leave was Clinton who very casually gave us tomorrow's itinerary. At the top of the agenda was to be a meeting with Harry Warner the President of Warner Bros. film studios. Although Jack Warner ran the West Coast operation producing the company's films, it was his brother Harry who was the powerful President of the company overall, so I guess there was no way of refusing a summons from the Almighty.

Chapter 17

All Aboard

The following morning, we were up with the birds. I guess our journey across the Atlantic had played havoc with our body clocks for although we had slept well, we had no desire to sleep in. Having ordered our breakfast to be sent up, we spent a leisurely hour on the terrace enjoying the view and watching New York below us as the city gradually woke up and gathered momentum. Exactly on time, Clinton was waiting for us in the hotel foyer and he seemed surprised when only Marlene and I turned up. Earlier on, Livy had already decided in her wisdom that it wasn't her place to be meeting the boss and if we didn't mind, she'd much prefer to do a little sightseeing on foot and to take stock of the local natives and by the time that we returned, she would be comfortably ensconced in the lobby with a pot of tea. Without any further delay, we were back in the Packard limousine making our way to Warners' headquarters. Whilst on our way, on my request, we performed a minor detour so that we could we pass by the famous Radio City Music Hall situated on Sixth Avenue in the Rockefeller Centre where the dancing troupe known as *The Rockettes,* formerly known as *The Roxyettes*, performed live on stage and I'd remembered correctly, the last time I visited, way back in the early thirties, when the movies were king, it had been built by a consortium of film producers under the logo of the RKO Film Corporation. Architecturally speaking, it was a temple to the silver screen, ankle-deep carpets, a sweeping staircase to the mezzanine floor which led into a huge auditorium decorated in an art deco style and had a seating capacity of more than five thousand. It also included a mighty Wurlitzer organ plus an orchestra pit to accommodate at least fifty musicians.

Once we had arrived at Warners, Clinton escorted us up to the executive offices where, having announced our arrival to the receptionist, we had barely sat down before a middle-aged woman was in front of us, introducing herself as Alysia Simpson, Mr Warner's private secretary. She led us into a large office where an imposing gentleman rose from his seat and came around his desk to greet us. Introducing himself as Harry Warner, he proceeded to welcome us to America and the Warner family. He said he hoped that the journey from Britain hadn't been too strenuous and he also asked many questions about how Britain was holding up against Nazi Germany. He was quick to point out that his studio was one of the first to release an anti-Nazi movie despite strong opposition from both home and abroad. He went on to remind us that it was called *Confessions of a Nazi Spy*, starring one of the best movie actors around, Edward G. Robinson. Once he became aware that Marlene was a mother-to-be, he became extremely considerate of her well-being and using his intercom, instructed Alysia Simpson to wire the West Coast to ensure that the best paediatrician available would become Marlene's personal physician once we arrived in Los Angeles. He finished the meeting by concluding that his brother Jack had big plans for me and was convinced that it would not be long before America entered the war.

The studio was currently short of a romantic star to meet the present-day moviegoing public's desires and although the company had Errol Flynn, he was firmly associated in the public's mind as a handsome swashbuckler in period movies, or Westerns, particularly when he was paired with the beautiful Olivia de Havilland. What Jack was looking for was a male star with a cynical and world-weary exterior who had experienced it all before and had the chemistry to excite the female fans at the box office. As it happened, the studio had already received positive feedback from Goldwyn studios about my performance in Korda's epic Arabian adventure, *Ali Baba*, which apart from some final editing, would be ready for its film premiere very soon. That development would help the studio to build up my public image.

I took a shine to Harry Warner but sensed that he was in the wrong profession. He was too much of a straight-as-an- arrow type of guy and therefore, could easily be taken advantage of. We carried on talking for a little while longer until once again, Alysia Simpson came back into the office and whispered something in his ear, whereupon he rose from his chair, exclaiming that regretfully, he would have to cut short our meeting as he had a luncheon engagement with the governor of New York. Having wished us a safe journey to California, he left it to Miss Simpson and Clinton to accompany us out of his office and we continued on the itinerary that Clinton had organised for us on our short stay in New York, the entire expense of which, including our hotel bill, would be met by the company.

True to his word, Clinton led us on a whirlwind tour of the city, taking in lunch at Sardi's followed by a visit to the Empire State building and then, a sightseeing tour of the Guggenheim Museum, Carnegie Hall and Manhattan. There was little time to relax. By the time we had got back to the hotel, the girls had just about enough time to change before we had a light supper and were on our way to the Shubert Theatre where we would see Katherine Hepburn in the smash hit, *The Philadelphia Story*. In some ways, I was a forgotten face to the Broadway audiences. However, it was Marlene's entrance into the auditorium and the walk down the aisle that drew the audience's attention and she looked stunning in a black dress which had a slight ballooning effect from the waist and coupled with her long hair, it certainly caused a ripple of sound through the stalls as we took our seats.

It was an enjoyable evening of madcap shenanigans amongst the long island high society set, with Katherine Hepburn giving a scintillating performance, ably supported by the actors, Joseph Cotton and Van Heflin. After the curtain had fallen on the last act, Clinton took us backstage to meet up with Katherine Hepburn. I had not had the pleasure of meeting her before but as we entered her dressing room, I was struck by the physical similarities between her and Marlene and even though I was biased, I think that Hepburn lacked the sensual aura that Marlene possessed. Nevertheless, we spent several minutes congratulating her on her performance which was not far removed from her natural persona. She conveyed all the tributes of an upper Manhattan socialite being very articulate and opinionated and indeed I suspect, that without the disciplines of a script the sound of her voice, could be slightly irritating.

Presently, we were joined by her two co-stars, Joseph Cotton and Van Heflin. Cotton exuded good old-fashioned Southern charm which he used to great effect upon Marlene, while Heflin was the opposite, having a more reserved and serious disposition. It transpired that the play was ending its run and that the three stars were off to Hollywood very shortly. Hepburn was to reprise her role for MGM in their forthcoming movie adaptation of *The Philadelphia Story*, a topic by the way that rankled Heflin, as his part in the play and been given to MGM star, Jimmy Stewart. Heflin was under contract to the same studio but all he had been given was a supporting role in an Errol Flynn Western whilst on loan out to Warners. Personally, I thought he was far too good an actor not to eventually become star. As for Cotton, he was off to Hollywood with his pal, Orson Welles, to make several movies for RKO after having set both radio and Broadway alight with their Mercury Theatre productions and scaring the wits out of the American public with their radio adaptation of H.G. Wells' *War of the Worlds.*

It was certainly a great finish to a perfect day. We were soon deposited back at the St Regis Hotel. The three of us were ready for bed. Before we called it a night, we did, however, decide to unwind with a nightcap and hors d'oeuvres. The first thing Marlene did was to throw her shoes off and plunk down on the settee whilst I gave her a foot massage. Livy too, kicked her shoes off and collapsed into an armchair whilst removing her hat. Between small bites of her appetiser, she informed us that it had been a day that she would never forget. In fact, she went on to say that if somebody had told her that one day she would fly to America with a famous actor and his wife, she would have told them that they were talking absolute nonsense. She also said that the play was wonderful and of course, Miss Hepburn was enthralling. Raising our glasses, the three of us toasted a successful finish to our long journey with Livy having the final say by rounding the toast off with an Amen and hopefully the Indians would not be on the war path on our journey west.

After Livy had said goodnight, Marlene and I lingered for a little while longer talking. She told me how she had been completely blown away by her first experiences in America. She had never actually seen a skyscraper and to see so many dominating the skyline was truly awe-inspiring. She could feel the rhythm and vibrancy of the city and from this moment on, she would be for ever reminded of New York whenever she heard Gershwin's *Rhapsody in Blue.* I knew exactly what she meant, for she reminded me of my own personal experiences when I first arrived in New York. As soon as we had finished our drinks, I took her by the hand and walked her to the bedroom and whilst we shared the bathroom, we carried on talking about our plans once we had arrived in Hollywood. We were still talking in between Marlene removing her makeup and me taking a shower, but she eventually gave up the conversation by tapping on the glass door and exclaiming.

"Gunty, I am going to bed now. The condensation in here will play havoc with my hair if I stay any longer. Besides, I am beginning to feel very tired. I'll see you in bed."

By the time I had dried myself down and put on a bath robe, I was beginning to feel tired myself, so I wasn't particularly surprised to find Marlene fast asleep on the bed. Gently pulling the bedclothes over her, I turned the bedside lights off and climbed into bed beside her and drawing her close to me, I put my arms around her and was soon fast asleep.

It was getting on for eleven o'clock in the morning by the time we had risen and had breakfast and as we had time on our hands, it was on Clinton's suggestion that we decided to take the car and visit Macy's departmental store. Apparently, our train, the Broadway Limited, was not due to depart from Penn Station until six o'clock that night. So, while we got ready to go down to the lobby and await the car, it gave Marlene the opportunity to place a call through to her brothers, Hansi and Lothar. I could hear her voice picking up with happiness as she was speaking to them and I thought to myself that at least that was another two close members of her family safe and sound from the clutches of Hitler's tyranny.

The girls certainly enjoyed Macy's. The sheer volume of merchandise on every floor was in stark contrast to what we had left behind. My cheque book did not escape unscathed for Marlene and Livy soon located the maternity department and before I knew where I was, several outfits had been purchased including accessories. The trouble was that when she had finished there, she had then made a beeline for the toy department and I had to gently remind her that it was a little too soon to be thinking of buying teddy bears and other such toys and in any case, once we were settled in Hollywood and in our own house, she would have no problem in buying just as many nice things in Los Angeles as they were in New York.

By the time that we had returned to the St Regis Hotel, collected our luggage and checked out, we were beginning to run out of time for boarding our train. However, we needn't have worried for under Clinton's expert guidance, we arrived at Penn Station with thirty-five minutes to spare before the Broadway

Limited departed. Clinton summoned three red caps to carry our luggage to the train. It was quite an impressive walk to the track where our train was waiting, as there was a crimson carpet laid down on the platform showing the logo of the Broadway Limited's owning company, the 20th Century Limited. All along the length of the train, there were white jacketed Negro attendants stationed outside each sleeping car. Clinton eventually stopped outside one marked 'C' and showed our reservations to the attendant who promptly had the red caps take our overnight luggage on board whilst I and the two girls followed. Livy's was the first sleeping compartment we stopped at and whilst one of the red caps stored away her two suitcases, it gave us the opportunity to give the compartment a once over. It consisted of two overhead bunk beds, a small reading table situated under the window and a sliding door which led into a bathroom just big enough to accommodate one person. Our next stop was a drawing room which was nice, as it gave the three of us the opportunity of some privacy. It also had an adjoining door into our sleeping berth which was laid out the same as Livy's. Our sleeping car attendant introduced himself to us as Roscoe and informed us that he would be our attendant for the journey and then proceeded to give us a run through of the Broadway Limited's amenities.

The dining cars were two carriages further down, as well as a private dining room called the Turquoise restaurant, the clubroom and observation parlour, plus the pleasure dome bar which were back towards the rear end. The start of breakfast would be announced every morning with a gong and during the course of the early evening, he would prepare the beds and turn the sheets down and finally, if we required any coffee or tea, there was a buzzer in the state room to summons him. As to the journey, we were scheduled to arrive at La Salle Station, Chicago at about nine o'clock the following morning where we would remain in our carriage to be shuttled over to Dearborn Station. There, we would be connected to the Super Chief and at the same time, we would be offered the services of the Ambassador East Hotel to freshen up or take a quick bath after which we could take lunch in the hotel's famous pump room. Whilst I slipped him a couple of dollars, I enquired who else was travelling on the train.

"Well, Mr Conrad, I do know that we are pleased to have the company of Mr Henderson and Mr Brown, the famous songwriters, who are already aboard in this carriage and I have seen Miss Bette Davis boarding further down. I have heard on the grapevine that Mr Gable and Miss Lombard are also on board too." Punctually, at six o'clock, the Broadway Limited moved slowly out of Penn Station and by the time it had reached the outer suburbs of New York, it had picked up momentum and was belting along at a fair speed. Whilst Marlene was putting the finishing touches to her makeup, I went through to the stateroom and ordered a bottle of champagne from Roscoe. As I sat there, gazing out of the window watching the houses and fields slipping by, I had a feeling of déjà vu, only this time, I had a wife to enjoy the experience with all over again. By the time Marlene joined me, Roscoe had already brought the chilled champagne with flutes in an ice bucket and as soon as Livy joined us, I filled the glasses with champagne and proposed a toast, "California here we come."

Hunger pangs eventually forced us out of the comfort of the drawing room and with me leading the way, we began to transverse in crocodile fashion along the corridor towards the restaurant cars. We couldn't have picked a worse time to get a table. The first restaurant was full, with no table available for at least an hour and the Turquoise restaurant was also fully booked. When we finally arrived at the third restaurant car, we were greeted by the restaurant steward and this time, we were lucky in our timing, for although the dining car was almost full, he immediately escorted us to the one remaining empty table. Once again, Marlene caused a ripple of interest as she walked along the aisle following the maître d', it was only as I was nearly upon our table that I felt a hand on my sleeve and a loud voice exclaiming in a strong Brooklyn accent.

"Hocha! Hocha! If it isn't my amigo from the old days. Dare I intrude and venture to ask what brings you to this moment?"

I turned at the sound of the voice and found myself staring at a jolly pixie of a face, eyes that were full of merriment, a head that was topped off with a bald pate and the nose that had to be the largest in show business but so happened, was also his trademark. It was none other than Jimmy Durante, one of America's most lovable and loved comics, whom I had become firm friends with, back in the twenties, when he was part of the Clayton, Jackson and Durante trio. He had moved on as a single act and just before I left for Germany in the early thirties, he had been starring in movies with Buster Keaton. After giving me a hug, he insisted on being introduced to Marlene and bending low, he kissed her hand murmuring to her what a lucky guy I was to be married to such a beautiful broad. He made the same introduction to Livy by kissing her hand, but when he heard her accent, he made a great thing out of doing a double take and placing his hand upon his heart declaimed to the heavens.

''Goodness me, this is one hell of a highfalutin, limey dame. I got to hand it to you, Gunther, you are certainly travelling first-class with this band of feminine pulchritude. Please tell me that you are travelling through to Los Angeles with these delightful creatures so that I may have the pleasure of your company. Don't forget to look for me in the Pleasure Dome bar so that we can talk over old times.''

Seeing that he was making life difficult for the waiters by blocking the gangway, Jimmy repeated his invitation before moving back to his table. There was no doubt about it that Jimmy had completely overwhelmed the girls and even a hard professional as Clinton was won over with his explosive personality. However, with the help of the Broadway Limited's champagne dinner, which consisted of fresh Romanov caviar, followed by sirloin steak, I was able to bring them gently back down to earth and by the end of the meal, Marlene was ready for retiring after a long day. Livy agreed with her decision, telling us that she too was ready for bed and although she had the latest Agatha Christie mystery novel, she was sure that it wouldn't take long for her to fall fast asleep, especially with the rhythm of the train. Sure enough, the girls were the first to leave the table and make their way back to their births leaving Clinton and myself to finish the champagne. I was gratified when Clinton told me that Warners would be picking up the tab for the meal, as it gave me a sense of security knowing that the studio felt highly of my talents. After some small talk about studio politics, Clinton decided that he would wander into the bar for a late-night drink and wondered if I would like to join him. I regretfully turned him down, telling him that the journey across the Atlantic had finally caught up with me but we would make a night of it the following evening. Telling him not to drink too much, I said goodnight and made my way along the carriages to our birth. When I entered the stateroom and walked through to our sleeping berth, Marlene was already sitting up in the upper bunk with her hair in curlers reading *The New Yorker*. When I queried with her whether she would be comfortable, she came right back at me with a gurgle of laughter saying that if she was going to spend the night with me, she preferred being on top.

It took me some time to finish both washing and undressing for bed in such a close confinement and by the time that I had accomplished those two tasks and returned to the sleeping compartment, my beautiful and pregnant wife was fast asleep, leaving me no choice but to spend the night in the lower bunk on my own. I really didn't have much time to dwell on my thoughts, as the rhythm of the train riding the tracks coupled with the gentle swaying of the carriages, soon had me falling into a deep sleep.

I was awakened the next morning with a kiss and the aroma of Channel No. 5. When I was finally able to focus my eyes, I saw Marlene fully dressed and as fresh as a daisy.

"Come on sleepyhead," she said, as she ruffled my hair. "It's time to get up. We shall be arriving in Chicago within the next thirty minutes and we should try and get some breakfast. Livy is already up. We have decided to use the services of the Ambassador East Hotel and I have asked Roscoe to make the necessary arrangements. I wasn't sure whether you would want to come with us or would prefer to stay on the train and avoid any unnecessary attention from the press and just relax."

As far as I was concerned, there was no decision to make. I was more than happy to remain on the train and use its facilities whilst Marlene and Livy went off and pampered themselves. So, it transpired that after a hearty breakfast, the girls left the train at Chicago's Dearborn Station after the train had made the short transfer from La Salle Station. Carrying their vanity cases, they set off for the Ambassador East Hotel for their makeovers with the strict instructions from both Clinton and I that they should be back on the train no later than five o'clock in the afternoon as the Super Chief was scheduled to leave the station by mid-evening. I took the opportunity of seeing them off by making myself comfortable in the observation car and watching them exit the platform accompanied by a representative of the train company. Unfortunately, even then, they were denied their privacy, for as they left the platform gates, several press photographers managed to take some shots of them. Fortunately, they weren't held up for more than a few minutes. As for the stars, such as Jimmy Durante, they would have gone back to bed after changing trains. As for the other passengers disembarking the Broadway Limited, it appeared that Chicago was to be their destination.

With the help of Roscoe, I spent the rest of the morning transferring our luggage across the platform to the Super Chief, during which, I was gratified to learn that Roscoe would be transferring over to our train as well as deputising for a sick colleague and that he would be the attendant of our sleeper car, named Kiethia. You certainly couldn't get much luckier than that. I spent a few more hours in our drawing-room catching up on showbiz news and gossip from *Variety* newspaper, the bible of the entertainment world. For the world news, I read *The New York Times* and I also whiled away the time watching the teams of cleaners systematically going through the carriages and the kitchen staff, supervising and inspecting the fresh fish and meats waiting to be loaded on board. Strangely enough, I didn't meet up with any of the other passengers remaining on board, I knew that it would be unlikely that there would be any sightings of Bette Davis for she valued her privacy and no doubt, would be secluded in her state room. As for the stars such as Jimmy Durante, they would still be sleeping, no doubt recovering from the previous night's roistering in the cocktail lounge.

Towards midday, I decided to stretch my legs and get some fresh air in my lungs, as I arrived at the door of the carriage, I passed Roscoe busily loading fresh linen and towels into a small linen cupboard, so I took the opportunity of telling him that if my wife and my personal assistant were to return whilst I was out, would he just let them know that I'd gone for a walk and would be back soon. Roscoe was more than happy to oblige and very considerately pointed out that the restaurant car would be closed until the train departed that evening and if I began feeling hungry before then, he could recommend a 'ma and pa' diner just outside the station and it so happened that they did the best New York deli club sandwich and fries that you have ever tasted. Thanking him for his helpful information, I slipped him a buck and ventured out onto the platform.

The first thing that attracted my attention amongst all the hustle and bustle going on around me was the diesel locomotive that was just attaching itself to our carriages. It was a sight to behold, as it had been painted in red with the logo of an American Indian's war bonnet. It certainly was a magnificent piece of machinery, so much so, that I spent several minutes inspecting its length. Roscoe was quite right to remind me about eating for I had no sooner walked through the main concourse of Dearborn Station than I began to feel hungry. I had no trouble in following Roscoe's directions and soon found the family diner and ordered his recommended club sandwich and fries plus coffee. It was every bit as good as he said it would be.

Whilst I sat there eating, I began wondering about my plans in Hollywood. It had been ten years since I had last made a movie in the country and in the film industry, an actor is only as good as his last film. I obviously had become a forgotten star as far as the American public was concerned and I gave full credit to Warners for offering me a contract under those circumstances. Therefore, my first hope was that I would be offered a once in a lifetime part, rather than emphasising star billing over the title. I was keeping my fingers crossed, as my first test of public opinion would be the soon to be released, *Ali Baba*. If the movie proved to be a smash hit, my stock would rise considerably at Warners and would hopefully, give me a greater choice of parts. As I left the diner and walked back to the station, I was still mulling over my options. I knew from experience working at MGM that you were a well looked after and pampered star but that wasn't the case at Warners, who had a reputation for working their stars until they dropped. However, they were very much tuned in to what the public wanted and intended to make great stars out of their contract artists despite their ethos of turning their films out like an assembly-line product.

Back on board the Super Chief, I once again came across Roscoe sitting in his little cubicle having a smoke. He seemed more than happy to shoot the breeze with me and as we chatted, it transpired during our conversation that he was putting both his children through Washington State University and that despite the heavy financial sacrifice, he was quite determined that they would have the opportunity of a better education and in turn, a far brighter future than either he or his wife had experienced. He hoped that he may live long enough to see coloured folks take an equal place in society. I must say that I wholeheartedly agreed with his sentiments having experienced first-hand, the results of racial intolerance. I must admit I could have gone on talking with Roscoe for a lot longer, but our tête-a-tête came to an abrupt finish when Marlene and Livy came aboard the sleeping car followed by a red cap carrying a brand-new leather Valise which he promptly deposited in the drawing room. The girls had had a leisurely morning at the Ambassador East Hotel where a bedroom with en suite facilities had been placed at their disposal. They had eaten a light lunch and then gone shopping in down-town Chicago, where Marlene had bought, in her own words, some accessories and cosmetics which were to die for. I was left pondering how only a woman could finish a journey with more luggage than when she started! However, it was nice to see the pair of them relaxed and happy, especially after I received a kiss from Marlene. I spent some time listening to their first impressions of Chicago, or the Windy City, as it was called and in particular, from Livy, who was not at all surprised when she learnt that the notorious gangster, Al Capone, who had recently gone to prison on tax evasion charges, had treated Chicago as his personal kingdom. Giving her usual snort of disapproval she finished by saying, "Only in America."

The three of us had decided that we were going to make a night of it and paint the train red, so to speak. By the time that we had dolled ourselves up and made our way to the restaurant car, it had already gone eight o'clock and the Super Chief was already eating up the miles, having pulled out of Chicago an hour before. The restaurant steward immediately showed us to our table and after receiving our menus and ordering a bottle of champagne, he left us, whilst we decided what we would eat. Whilst the girls were making up their minds, I looked around the car to see if there was anybody that I knew. Sadly, there wasn't, regrettably. I had been away from Hollywood for too long and although I was considered a big European star outside the American continent, I was considered a Mr Nobody as far as Tinseltown was concerned. When we had decided early on to paint the train red, I hadn't realised how seriously the girls were intending to go! During the meal, in which both the kitchen and restaurant staff excelled themselves, the three of us managed to drink our way through a bottle of Châteauneuf-du-Pape, a bottle of Semillon Chardonnay and two bottles of Prosecco. Once we had got our second wind, we went seeking further excitement in the cocktail bar. In all honesty, despite the copious amounts of alcohol that we had consumed,

Marlene was a pretty cool looking hot potato, whilst Livy was the epitome of cool Britannia and looking every inch a member of the British Raj.

Having successfully manoeuvred the corridors of the swaying railway cars, we finally pushed open the door to the cocktail bar. What a different ballgame that was to the one that we had just left behind in the restaurant car. The air was heavy with tobacco smoke, vibrant with the sound of chatter and occupied by all the night owls on the train. There was Jimmy Durante, Ray Henderson and Lew Brown occupying the upright piano and as we entered, they were playing *You're the Cream in My Coffee*. Contrary to my earlier belief that I had become unknown in Hollywood, I was greeted by quite a few faces from the past. Wallace Beery was one. We went back as far as the last days of the silent cinema at MGM and Wallace, since then, had reinvented himself as one of the moviegoing public's favourite stars at the same studio, portraying gruff and irascible rogues with a heart of gold, especially in partnership with the late Marie Dressler, in a series of *Tugboat Annie* films. There was also Billy Wilder who I had lost contact with since our early days in Berlin and Miklos Rozsa, who had recently written the musical score for *Ali Baba* and finally, a guy who was physically short in stature but huge in talent and sporting an outsize cigarette holder which very nearly poked my eye out, none other than the prankster, raconteur and friend, Peter Lorre.

That night would certainly go down in my book of memorable evenings. Apart from the fact that Marlene was the centre of attention, there was also the added ingredients of some of the most talented people in show business who, in the privacy of being away from the public eye, became totally relaxed and gave free rein to their personalities. It was a privilege to hear Henderson and Brown duetting, *I'm Sitting on Top of the World* and Jimmy giving us countless choruses of *Dinky Dinky Doo* and of course, with the endless supply of alcohol, the more the jokes flowed and the reminiscences became more and more exaggerated. As the evening wore on, Marlene and Livy became much sought-after partners amongst my friends for a dance shuffle around the bar. Because of her straight talking and no-nonsense attitude, Livy had rapidly been nicknamed 'Limey Liv' and been adopted as the mascot for the journey and as for Marlene, she just had a natural talent for creating admirers, especially as she already possessed both a glamorous and alluring mystique, coupled with the capacity for holding an intellectual conversation.

I was busy catching up on all the Broadway and Hollywood gossip as well as gauging the reaction to the war in Europe. It was gratifying to know that most of the people that I talked to that night believed it was a foregone conclusion that America would enter the war on Britain's side. The general belief was that the American public had had enough of Germany's aggression in the First World War and certainly weren't prepared to watch Britain stand-alone against the Nazi hordes goose-stepping over the European democracies.

It was around two o'clock in the morning when both Marlene and Livy retired gracefully to their beds, leaving me with a diehard group of friends to continue to try and put the world to rights through an alcoholic haze. I must admit I was one of those fortunate people that had what I would term hollow legs. In other words, I could consume a lot of alcohol without becoming drunk. I was being given a lot of advice from both Jimmy Durante and Wallace Beery, especially on the subject of how hard a taskmaster Warners were towards their actors and the two of them were all too eager to remind me that Bette Davis had taken the studio to court in order to challenge the studio's right to automatically extend the contracts of its talent. They had done this after suspending some people because of their refusal to accept parts in films that were derogatory to their industrial status. They would then add the suspension onto the end of stars' contracts. I didn't need reminding that Bette Davis had lost her legal challenge for I liked to consider myself as being fairly streetwise when it came to dealing with the Hollywood studios, having worked there in the twenties. I was already aware that Warner stars James Cagney and Olivia Haviland were unhappy at the way they were being treated by the studio.

With that in mind, I had signed my contract with them with the clause 'script approval' written in, to protect myself in any future negotiations. The sun was already rising in the sky when we finally called it a night and after going through the ritual of a hearty farewell, I was left with the task of half carrying the inebriated Clinton back to his sleeping berth. Fortunately for me, Roscoe was up early and gave me a helping hand in putting

Clinton onto his bunk after which I shared a pot of coffee and a smoke with Roscoe and finally, wishing him good morning, made my way to bed. I went out like a light.

When I finally awoke, it was midday by my watch and I certainly had no desire to get up. However, the effort had to be made. For the first few minutes of standing up, my head felt as if it had been invaded by a tribe of Caribbean drummers and by the time I had washed, shaved and freshened myself up, I was dying for a cup of coffee. Fortunately, Roscoe proved my angel in disguise, seeing me attempting to leave the drawing room and sensing my need for a giant pick me up, he brought me coffee and a glass of tomato juice and Worcestershire sauce with an extra ingredient of a raw egg, telling me to drink the concoction down in one go and in no time, I would be fine and dandy.

I must admit that by the time I was on my second cup of coffee, I had regained my equilibrium and was ready to face the world. As I could see no sign of Marlene in the restaurant cars, I carried on through the swaying carriages to the observation car where I was pretty sure that she would have deposited herself. Sure enough, I spied her and Livy in conversation with a couple at the top end of the car. As I approached them, Marlene caught sight of me and gave me a wave and as she did so, the woman that she had been talking to, turned her head in my direction and despite the wide brimmed hat and sunglasses that she was wearing, I had no trouble in recognising her from the movies that I had seen of her back in Britain. Marlene confirmed her identity by introducing her to me as Bette Davies and her male companion as Arthur Farnsworth, whom apparently, she had only just married.

Once I had a hair of the dog that bit me, I quickly joined in the conversation. It turned out that Bette was in between movies having just completed *All This and Heaven Too* and after completing a publicity tour for that movie in New York, was returning to Hollywood with her husband to commence filming on her new movie, *The Letter* at Warners. Studying Bette, I was left in no doubt that she was master of her own destiny and when push came to a shove, she was quite capable of manipulating studio politics to her advantage. She was already fully aware that I had signed on with Warners and was quite certain that we would soon co-star together in a film as soon as the right movie script came along. She also told me in no uncertain terms to be wary of Jack Warner, who was nothing but a shark dressed in a Vicuna suit. I listened to her reminiscing about her legal battles with him and how she had fled to Britain to obtain work and also, how much she had admired seeing my Hamlet at the Old Vic. Once again, she emphasised the point that now we were both under contract to the same studio, we would make a great screen team just as Warners had achieved with Errol Flynn and Olivia De Havilland. Somehow, I didn't think that piece of casting would happen, as Bette intended for her leading men to be played off against, rather than to be a challenge to her by dominating a scene.

During our conversation, I had the opportunity of observing her and though she was more than charming towards me and Marlene, she did come across as being very forthright in her opinions. Nevertheless, if the opportunity arose for us to work together, I would certainly take it, for to be honest, I would readily accept the challenge of working alongside an actress of her calibre. I was also made aware of how she valued her privacy, for as the observation car filled up with passengers, she started to become both fidgety and irascible until she bent forward and said, "I am sorry, Gunther, but when I am off duty, so to speak, I cannot stand being gaped at by the public because before you know it, we will be surrounded by autograph hunters. So, you will forgive me if I leave you now and retreat to my sitting room and I look forward to seeing you in the near future, for Hollywood being Hollywood, it would be difficult for us to miss each other."

With that, she arose and with her husband, Arthur Farnsworth, trailing behind her, regally swept out of the observation car. The Super Chief had already made its first stop at Kansas City and was scheduled for a stop at Albuquerque, later that evening, before proceeding on to Gallup, New Mexico and then finally, to our destination in Pasadena, California. This all gave us ample opportunity to just simply relax. Clinton finally appeared in mid-afternoon, looking decidedly hungover and moaning that the last time he had felt as bad as this was when the front office assigned him to chaperone John Barrymore around New York, to keep him sober for an NBC radio broadcast. He only half succeeded. Having finally got Barrymore to the radio station, apparently three sheets to the wind and then having spent an hour sobering him up sufficiently to perform, Clinton then lost the battle completely after the show went off the air by ending up in an off-Broadway bar until the sun came up over Times Square!

The remainder of the journey was spent at a very sedate pace and although after we had dinner, we had gone back to the bar, this time, it just for a nightcap. In any case, it was just as well as a few of our friends from the previous night were missing and from what we could gather, there was a card game going on in one of the sitting rooms organised by the Broadway die-hards, Jimmy Durante and Phil Silvers. Clinton was the first to call it a night and head for bed, followed soon after by Livy doing likewise. Marlene and I spent an enjoyable hour each other's company until she finally pulled me out of my chair saying.

"Time to call it a night, Gunty. If we have any more to drink, we won't need to pack our bags because you will be carrying them under your eyes in the morning."

Fortunately, I slept like a log that night and woke up naturally. Marlene had beaten me to the bathroom which gave me the time to have a look through the blinds at the outside world. I was met with a view of mountains and the landscape of desert and cacti. The sun was already high in the sky and judging by the shimmering haze hovering over the desert in the far distance, I imagine that it could already be pretty hot out there for a greenhorn to be lost in. From all this, I assumed that we were travelling through the state of New Mexico and therefore, we should be arriving very soon at Gallup which was a whistle stop before reaching our destination of Pasadena. Indeed, by the time Marlene and I had taken a seat in the dining car for breakfast, the train was beginning to brake and slow down. Livy had already arrived before us and was being served coffee and orange juice, so in the short interval between our catching up with her with our own orders, I enquired whether she had a good night's rest? She replied that she had slept well. It was at this point that the Super Chief came to a halt at Gallup. It was just a two-track station, one going east and one going west and as far as we could make out, beyond the stop was a small city centre. From information that I had learnt from Roscoe, it had a population of some nine-thousand inhabitants and had been named after a railway engineer by the name of Gallup who had built that particular section of the railroad through the reservation of the Navajo Indian tribe. Indeed, we caught glimpses of several native American Indians dressed in traditional costume selling souvenirs from the track. All this of course came as a surprise to Livy as she had been expecting her Indians to be whooping, chanting and rain dancing savages rather than small-town American citizens trying to make a living in the twentieth century. All of this kept Marlene and I busy for the next thirty minutes, pulling her leg.

Clinton was the last member of our party to join us and he looked far better than he had done the day before. He was able to join in the conversation, adding certain bits of information in reference to Gallup, which due to its nearness to Hollywood, was used frequently by the studios for filming Western movies, particularly by the director, John Ford. Gazing out at the landscape, it wasn't difficult for me to envisage John Wayne, saddle in one hand and rifle in the other, bringing the stagecoach to a halt on one of those dusty tracks that inhabited the desert beyond their whistle stop.

With a cry of, "All aboard," from the train conductor, with a jerk, the Super Chief began to move forward into the heat of the desert and before long, was forging ahead towards Pasadena. As soon as we had finished breakfast, we spent the remaining part of the journey packing up our personal belongings and making ourselves presentable for our arrival. Having accomplished those tasks, we sat quietly in the sitting room drinking coffee and watching out of the window the ever-changing landscape. Of course, I had travelled this route before, some fourteen years previously and although I had the luxury of being blasé, both Marlene and Livy were full of anticipation at their intended arrival. Any fears that I may have had upon the effects that the journey across the Atlantic may have had on Marlene's well-being were quickly dispersed, for as I glanced at her across the table, she was the picture of glowing good health and although she was showing a slight thickening of the waste, she was unmistakably still a very glamorous woman.

My reveries were eventually interrupted by a knock on our sitting room door and with Roscoe standing there.

"Next stop, Pasadena, folks," he drawled. "If your baggage is ready, I'll take them up to the carriage exit. In the meantime, it has been a pleasure for me to have looked after you all and I hope that you have had very comfortable trip."

Eventually, the Super Chief pulled in at Pasadena and having given themselves a last-minute check in their mirrors, the girls gathered up their vanity cases and slowly made their way to the carriage door where Roscoe was waiting, having placed a small set of steps for the passengers to be able to step down onto the tracks. I was the last one of our party to leave the train and as I did so, I shook hands with Roscoe and slipped him a fifty-dollar bill. It was gratifying to my ego that I had not been entirely forgotten for there was a small group of news photographers waiting for me and under Clinton's supervision, took a series of photographs to the sound of popping bulbs of Marlene and I posing in the bright sun. No sooner had they moved on looking for more celebrities than I noticed two men walking towards us, one of which was carrying a bouquet of flowers and who I immediately recognised as my American agent, Myron Selznick. When he doffed his hat and presented Marlene with the bouquet exclaiming, ''Welcome to Hollywood, Mrs Conrad','' I knew that our journey was finally over.

Chapter 18

Tinseltown

A lot of things had changed since the last time I had lived in the city of Angels. Los Angeles had now become a spreading metropolis buzzing with vitality. The parochial hamlet, where silent movies had been made was now a company town dominated by the big five film studios: MGM, Warner Bros., 20th Century Fox, Paramount and Universal with RKO struggling in sixth place, followed by what were known as the two 'poverty row' studios, Columbia and Republic. Finally, came the three independents, Selznick International, Sam Goldwyn and United Artists. I had settled the three of us into the Wiltshire Palms Hotel situated on Sunset Boulevard and a short hop from the two B's, Bel-Air and Benedict Canyon. True to his word, Billy Haines offered me his property in the near-by Holmby Hills on a short-term lease, so that I would have some time to purchase a suitable home for Marlene and myself, so we moved in there once we had recovered from our long journey. Billy was one of the nice guys in Hollywood. He had been a major silent star at MGM, but unfortunately, not only was he homosexual, he made no secret of the fact and when it finally became public knowledge, MGM gave him an ultimatum: dump his partner Jimmy Shields or walk. Billy walked. Not only had he remained in a stable relationship with Jimmy, but he had also built up a successful interior design business to the stars. The other important matter that needed to be taken care of was registering Marlene with a reputable paediatrician which, by way of Harry Warner's timely recommendation, I was finally able to manage by acquiring the services of a doctor, Manual Escobar, who was practising out of the Cedars of Lebanon Hospital.

As for my settling in at Warners, Myron accompanied me to a meeting with Jack Warner, the head of the studio who, after our introduction, spent some time in assuring me that only the best would be good enough for me and that the number one producer on the lot, Hal B. Wallace would be overseeing my career. The impressions that I had been given by my friends on Jack Warner appear to have been fairly accurate. He seemed to be the exact opposite in personality to his brother, Harry. Where Harry was quiet and introverted, Jack was very much the showman and whilst giving off an aura of bonhomie and geniality, one could not help but sense that underneath the surface, he was perpetually scheming at what was best, for Jack particularly, when it came to self-aggrandisement. Fortunately for me, the moment was in my favour. Korda had finally put the finishing touches to *Ali Baba* and released it to the American market. It had become an instant box office hit and had received rave reviews by the critics. I was gratified to note that my performance had been singled out as outstanding, a point not lost on Myron, who proceeded to use it as a bargaining tool in his dealings with the studio. What he did achieve in his meetings with Hal B. Wallace was to get me two months in which to settle in Hollywood and two novels by a writer called Henry Bellamann, one titled *Grey Man Walks* and the other, *Kings Row*, both of which were being prepared for script adaptation with an eye on one of them being the perfect vehicle for my first American movie.

It certainly didn't take long for us to settle into the social scene of Hollywood with the likes of Basil and Ouida Rathbone, Alfred and Alma Hitchcock and Ronald and Anita Coleman hosting welcoming parties on our behalf. It was on one such event that we were given a tip off that a house had just come on the market which possibly might appeal to us. Its present owner had got into some financial difficulties and was prepared to sell it below its market value. Marlene quite rightly wishing to have a home of her own for our baby's arrival, badgered me incessantly until I finally gave way. I located the realtor who was handling the sale. Her name was Rona Ingleby and she took us out to view the property. The house was situated at 138 South Carolwood a subdivision in Holmby Hills and the minute that we drove through the wrought iron gates and saw the house, built in the style of a Spanish hacienda, we were both hooked.

The house itself stood resplendent in two acres of land and as we drove up the driveway, was flanked by palm trees on either side. I could see the heavy wooden front door leading out onto the Veranda with a balcony directly above it on the second floor. Once through the front door, we were not disappointed in our expectations as we momentarily stood in a large hall viewing a circular stair leading up to the second floor. The ground floor consisted of a well-equipped kitchen, a large dining room and two lounges one of which led directly out into the backyard, which comprised of a tiled courtyard with steps leading down to a swimming pool with a waterfall as a feature at one end. The pool was surrounded by lush vegetation with all manner of semitropical flowers including sycamore ferns and vines and beyond the pool, was a well-kept lawn with sprinklers maintaining its pristine condition. Once back inside the house, we were taken upstairs and briefly stood looking over the balustrades at the reception area beneath, before viewing all five bedrooms which were all en suite. Despite Miss Ingleby leaving us in private to discuss and make any decisions regarding a possible purchase of the property, I don't think that she would have arrived at the bottom of the stairs before Marlene had already made up her mind that she wanted to live there.

That is how 138 Carolwood Drive became our permanent American home. Within a month, the seller had accepted my price for the property plus all the furnishings, the warranty deed had been signed at the local offices of the title company and we were ensconced, lock, stock and barrel in our new home. Once I had placed staffing needs in Livy's capable hands, we soon had on board a housekeeper who ensured that the house was kept to a high standard and also, a Filipino houseboy, Jose who dealt with the multitude of jobs that needed doing around the house and his wife, Consuela, a talented cook, who looked after all our meals. As soon as I had opened my cheque book, it remained open, for with the help of Billy Haines, Marlene then embarked on a slight makeover of the house which included new drapes for most of the windows and more importantly, the creation of a nursery.

Meanwhile, as for the rest of our world beyond the shores of the United States, Britain was standing alone against the Nazi empire and although she was still holding her own, her back was very much to the wall. London, Manchester, Liverpool and Coventry were being bombed incessantly by the Luftwaffe who were inflicting heavy casualties on the civilian populations. The nation itself was preparing to repel a German invasion whilst in North Africa, the British Eighth Army was busy repulsing the Italians and despite mounting an attack on the west African port of Dakar, had been pushed back by the Vichy French.

The pretext of sorting out some minor visa problems was the cover that was arranged for me to visit David Hislop at the British Consulate. He had certainly benefited physically from his new posting. When I shook hands with him in his office, he was already beginning to develop a Californian suntan and was putting on weight. When I mentioned this in passing, he smiled replying.

"Yes, I know. Unfortunately, I have been put on a strict diet as I suffer from a congenital heart problem, something that prevented me from being able to enlist in 1939. Hence, the downside in being posted to America. The food portions over here are bloody enormous. We don't know how lucky we are in comparison to our fellow countrymen back in Blighty."

"You don't have to remind me, David. I already have this sense of guilt that hangs around me like a cloak. Having said that, the reason why I am here is, in part, so that I can contribute to the war effort."

"I can sympathise with you, Gunther, because I understand how you must feel. However, you must put all feelings of guilt out of your head as your worth and contribution is noted where it counts the most! I am going to give you this envelope which contains a brief history of all the leading contenders of all the anti-British movements in this country. You will be able to identify the following; Gerald P. Nye, Republican Senator of North Dakota; William Dudley Pelley, founder of the Silver Legion; Burton Wheeler, Democratic Senator for Montana; Gerald L. K. Smith, Minister of the Disciples of Christ; Charles Edward Coughlin, Roman Catholic priest; Charles Lindbergh, international aviator; Henry Ford, auto-mobile industrialist, pro-Nazi with links to German industrialists such as I.G. Farben; and Alfred Krupp, the German steel industrialist. All of these men are known and self-proclaimed anti-Semites. Apart from their racial prejudices, these men are either isolationists, members of America First or the German American Bund. Your task will be to convince Hollywood society either through your social connections or through your workplace at the studio that America must help Britain in her hour of need. Just remember that we have an ace which is that ninety per cent of the film studios are controlled by Jewish businessmen and once they can be persuaded to produce anti-German propaganda films, it will go a long way in persuading the American public into supporting Britain."

We carried on talking for a little while longer and finally parted with the understanding that if I needed assistance or advice, I was to get in touch with David at the Consulate.

That old and trusted expression, time waits for no man, certainly applied to both Marlene and me. It was now the beginning of November and Marlene was well into the fifth month of her pregnancy and although, by now, she had a substantial bump, she still looked very glamorous in maternity wear. Also, she still had a passion for pickles but by now, she couldn't get enough of cheeseburgers. On the home front, we were now exchanging letters on a regular basis with Hiram and Miriam. Whilst Hiram's workload as a surgeon had doubled due to civilian war casualties, Miriam had become den mother at Falcon House to the air force personnel billeted there. Indeed, she had enclosed a photograph of herself dressed in a Red Cross uniform looking very proud, surrounded by air force officers. Marlene was also overcome with joy at a surprise visit by her two brothers, Hansi and Lothar, both of whom had become strapping young men in their late twenties and who were now working together, having been seconded to Yale University, working on various projects one of which was mysteriously titled, the Manhattan Project. Other than that, they didn't expand any further on what they did. It did seem that they didn't appear to have a worry in the world. Both were seriously courting beautiful young ladies by their own account. Of course, Marlene insisted that they bring them out on another visit very soon as it had been a very happy week for the three of them.

Unfortunately, I was unable to spend as much time with them as I would have wished. In the strange world of filmdom, the two projects that I had been offered were cancelled and put on-hold. In a matter of days, I had been offered a script which I had accepted and in a matter of weeks, I suddenly found myself on the back lot at Warners, filming a movie entitled *Marrakesh*, playing a character called Steve Blake, one of life's drifters who was the owner of a nightclub in Marrakesh called Steve's Place. The plot concerned the reuniting of Steve and an old flame from the past by the name of Sam Lane, an ex-chorus girl that he had met in Paris and fallen in love with. Complications arose when she re-entered Steve's life with a man by the name of Henri who was on the run from the Germans for being a member of the French underground. The script was no better than a dime store novel, but it was topical and I felt that I could do something with the part, besides which, it had one of Warners' best directors, Michael Curtiz at the helm and a strong cast plus the cinematographer, James Wong Howe and an acquaintance of mine from the past, the composer, Wolfgang Korngold.

It was during photographic tests for wardrobe fittings, that I received a nasty surprise. Apparently, the German legation in Los Angeles had caught wind of the script's content and had requested that its cultural secretary be allowed to visit the set to ensure that the studio maintained its neutrality. You can imagine my horror when on the second day of wardrobe fittings, who should come onto the set but none other than Xavier Jurgens, our old adversary from back in Britain, accompanied by a party of assorted personages, all there, I presumed, to ensure that the studio remained neutral. Because the American State Department had included a representative in the party, Jack Warner, never one to miss an opportunity, was personally conducting the tour and had gone the whole mile by putting on a buffet for his visitors. But despite Jack's big show for his guests, including getting his stars to sign autographs for them, Herr Jurgens remained aloof and at times, made no effort to disguise his arrogance. Of course, he made no effort to disguise his contempt for me either.

However, as far as I was concerned, due to the seriousness of the situation in Germany, I had no qualms in humiliating myself by asking for his help in locating Marlene's family and seizing a fleeting opportunity, I was able to have a quiet word with him. I could have anticipated the tone of Jurgen's reply but had to ensure that I had done everything possible to establish the whereabouts of Marlene's relatives even if that meant providing Jurgens with an opportunity to humiliate me further by unleashing more of his foul and abhorrent Nazi rhetoric. His first words to me set the tone for the rest of the conversation.

"Well, Herr Conrad, I see that you and your Jewish wife have deserted yet another sinking ship! You appear to be doing very well in your new country. By the way, how many is it now, three?"

I replied, "Herr Jurgens, I do not wish to trade insults with you or to take offence at your remarks but merely to seek your help in obtaining any information on the whereabouts or well-being of my wife's family, an act of kindness that I would be eternally grateful for."

"You know, Herr Conrad, that you are a perfect example of the dangers of mixed marriages with inferior races. The Fuhrer has been warning the German people for years of the disease of Judaism and the many forms in which it strikes. In your case, you appear to have been contaminated with manipulative treachery. Having thrown Reich Minister Joseph Goebbels' generous offer to you right back in his face and rejected his hand of friendship, you then, by an act of sheer deviousness, take advantage of Reich Marshall Goering's good nature. Now you have the audacity to appeal to my good nature. Unfortunately for you, your wife's family is under the personal attention of Reich Fuhrer Himmler and I can tell you now that they have been re-allocated to Warsaw in Poland, where they will remain under the jurisdiction of Hans Frank, the Reich Governor of Central Poland, leaving just your sister-in-law at large in Holland. But rest assured, we will eventually hunt her down. As for the parents of the Jewess, Marlene Bachman, I shall no doubt look forward to meeting them when we conquer Britain. I hope that I have now made my thoughts plain to you and sincerely hope that you make the best of your stay in America while it lasts."

My first overwhelming desire was to beat the living daylights out of him, but I knew that he wanted me to attack him as we both knew that it would have led to the revoking of my visa by the United States government. Instead, keeping my emotions strictly under control, I looked him steadily in the eye and quietly replied.

"Enjoy your Fuhrer's triumphs whilst they last with the emphasis on whilst, for some time in the future, the German nation will face a day of reckoning and you will be made accountable by the free world. I will bid you goodbye, Herr Jurgens, until we meet again and when we do it will be on our terms." Briefly, Jurgens stood glaring at me as if something unpleasant had crawled under his nose. Then, he turned on his heel and walked away from me.

I kept my feelings well under control until Jack Warner had escorted the party off the set and then I beat a quick retreat to my dressing room where I poured myself a large Jack Daniels. I was just starting in on my second shot when there was a knock at the door and Mike Curtiz poked his head around. It was an indisputable fact that Mike only spoke fractured English, being that he was a Hungarian refugee who had fled Europe from Hitler's tyranny. Consequently, his conversation with me went something like this.

"Vot did that arseholes of a Kraut haf to say to you that wasn't already full of shit! You should have told him if I vant idiots, I go myself."

I burst out laughing, which obviously didn't please him too much. However, despite his reputation for being rude and abrasive with colleagues, he had still found time to see if I was okay after noticing Jurgens and I in conversation. I quickly passed it off as a petty exchange of words, I didn't think for one moment that he accepted my explanation, but he very quickly reverted back to his normal self and barked at me that he expected to see me punctually on time the following morning and here I quote, "Vid your lines firmly in your head."

Dressed in a white tuxedo, I made my way through the throng of patrons strolling from one gaming table to the next. Occasionally, I would stop to sign a slip for extended credit for a regular gambler, until eventually, I reached the bar. Then, I turned to survey the casino and as I placed a cigarette in my mouth and raised my hand to light it, the customers in front of me parted, leaving a corridor, in which there was a large camera mounted on a mobile dolly and carrying a small platform attached to the side upon which sat Michael Curtiz and standing beside him, looking through a viewfinder, was James Wong Howe. The camera stopped inches from my face, allowing me to give reaction shots with my eyes and then I heard, "Cut," followed by the bell to signify the end of sequence and allowing the soundstage to spring back to life. There was organised pandemonium everywhere with grips, carpenters and electricians busy fulfilling their allotted tasks. Whilst I was finishing my cigarette, the script girl went over the lines of my next scene with me and after that, I spent a few minutes talking with Mike Curtiz and Jimmy Howe and then slipped outside to grab the opportunity of some fresh air.

As I lit yet another cigarette, I took the opportunity of observing the comings and goings of the studio workers. Just by standing in the alleyway connecting these six large sound stages, I could watch dozens of extras dressed in all manner of costume ranging from, Roman centurions, Arabian dancing girls, cowboys and foreign legionnaires all heading for either sound stages, wardrobe department or to take a break in the studio cafeteria. On the odd occasion, a golf buggy drove by, carrying a studio executive or a star, such as Eddie Robinson. It was while standing outside that I received a pleasant surprise, for suddenly, standing beside me, was an attractive woman whom I instantly recognised as Lotte Palfi, a German actress that I had last seen in Berlin during the early thirties. As we fell into conversation, I learnt that she had had fled from the Nazis in 1934 and had ended up in America. She had found it difficult to adjust, but somehow, had managed to survive by playing small parts in Hollywood movies, hence our meeting each other on the set of *Marrakesh*. It was a common enough story that I heard all too often and it made me realise how lucky I was. Lotte was an all too familiar tragedy, a former distinguished German actress reduced to fleeing from her native country because of persecution and living out an existence on bit parts that came her way from the Hollywood studios. In my effort to help, I foolishly offered her money which she refused, with great dignity. However, I did regain her respect and gratitude when I gave her Marlene's number and told her to call her as Marlene would love to hear from her. At the same time, I asked her to leave her address and phone number with me so that I could ensure that she would at least get some work on any movie that I would be working on.

That encounter brought home to me sharply the extent of how many European Jews were in exile from Nazi tyranny. It so happened that since then I had developed a practice of examining the cast sheets of my movies, if only to remember the names and faces of the minor actors just to indicate that I have worked with them previously and it was no different with *Marrakesh*. On that film alone, besides Lotte Palfi, there was my old mate, Peter Lorre, S. Z. Zakall, Marcel Dalio, Curt Boise and Leonid Kinsky besides several others who did not even have speaking parts. My reflections came to an end as the assistant director came to tell me that Mr Curtiz was waiting for me, so without further ado, I escorted Lotte back inside the sound stage.

Livy had proved herself a pillar of strength. She had organised the employment of household staff and with the help of Billy Haines, had carried out Marlene's wishes transforming the house on South Carolwood into our home. Marlene had very quickly been accepted by Hollywood society. Women such as Irene Selznick, Benita Coleman and Carole Lombard had rallied around and organised a baby shower. My own time had very quickly been taken from morning until night with either working at the studio or becoming a board member for various organisation such as the Relief for European Actors, Finding American Homes for British Orphans, as well as giving lectures to the members of these groups with the title, 'Why Britain Stands Alone'.

The weeks just flew past and before we knew it, we were into November. *Marrakesh* had been completed and was on general release to the public. I had not thought much of it, seeing it as a double bill filler in the theatres. Well, it shows just how much I know, as it turned out to be what we call in the trade, a sleeper, becoming a box office hit by word of mouth. Really, when I think about it, I had missed all the signs for it had a great director in Curtiz, brilliant photography by Jimmy Howe and a stunning musical score by Miklos Rosza, who above all else, had turned an old standard composed by Gus Kahn titled, *I'll See You In My Dreams*, into the year's number one hit in the music charts and a movie sensation out of a composer-piano player by the name of Hoagy Carmichael who had played my sidekick in the movie. What was all the more gratifying was that Jack Warner was pushing the movie for Oscar contention in the New Year with a massive publicity boost.

However, it didn't stop him from starting me immediately in a new film, playing the part of the Spanish explorer, Hernan Cortez and his conquest of Mexico titled *Conquest of the Sun*. Hal Wallace, who was producing the movie, had allocated it a massive budget so that it could be filmed in Technicolor and shot on location. Meanwhile, Marlene and Livy were about to experience their first American Thanksgiving, which always fell on the fourth Thursday in November. Americans intended to give it precedence over Christmas Day, as family members travelled from all over America to reunite with their loved ones.

Marlene had already anticipated the looming Christmas holidays by dispatching a large food hamper containing tinned hams and fruits, assorted chocolates, cigarettes and all other unobtainable luxuries to her parents in Britain whilst we spent the American Thanksgiving as guests of the Hitchcock's at their home in Bellagio Road. As the month of November fell away from the calendar and moved into December, Marlene now was only a few weeks away now from her due date and her physician, Dr Escobar was more than happy with her condition and could see no problems arising when her time came. Once again, Livy held a firm hand on the situation and kept me firmly in control of myself whilst Marlene continued to remain cool, calm and very much in charge.

I had already done a fair amount of location work in Mazatan, New Mexico, when Hal Wallace decided to bring the unit back to Hollywood because of the impending Christmas holidays, to film most of interior scenes at the studio. As far as Britain was concerned that December, despite Hitler's aerial blitzkrieg on Britain, she was still standing proud and resolute and that any invasion plans that Hitler may have had in invading her appeared to have been postponed. The other good news was that President Roosevelt had been able to push through Congress a bill that would enable America to provide Britain with materials under what was called a Lend-Lease deal. There was no doubt now that American public opinion was no longer in favour of neutrality and was putting pressure on congressmen and senators to act accordingly.

We spent Christmas Day of 1940 lounging around the pool and enjoying the company of our friends and even in the semi-tropical weather of California, Marlene still managed to remain cool and laid back, even though she intended to waddle like a stricken battleship. We had planned to see the New Year in at Nigel Bruce's and I had promised her prior to that to take her shopping on Rodeo Drive for artwork. She had begun to develop a taste for collecting rare paintings by the Masters, such as Manet, Toulouse-Lautrec and Mark Chagall. All the way down from our house to the art showrooms, I had been kidding Marlene that her sudden passion for paintings could possibly bankrupt the pair of us. Rightly, she pointed out that it might be a passion, but just remember it was an investment as well. A good example, she went on to say, of mixing pleasure with business, was Edward G. Robinson, who had started early in the thirties collecting and now had one of the finest art collections in Hollywood.

By the time I had pulled the car into a parking space outside the art gallery, I had to agree with her logic. As I walked around to the passenger door, I was laughing at some remark that she had made and opening the door extended my hand to help her out of the car. Instead, she sat there looking at me and then gripping my hand tightly quietly said.

"Gunty, my waters have broken."

Feeling somewhat like a headless chicken, I ran around to the driver's side and proceeded to drive like a bat out of hell towards the Cedars of Lebanon Hospital, all the while rambling inane comments such as, "Are you all right? Hang on we will soon be there, don't have it now." Marlene just sat there stroking my arm, telling me to stay calm which only made me more hyper. I must have broken a land speed record in trying to reach the hospital. Indeed, by the time I screeched to a halt outside the hospital's main doors, there was a motorcycle cop right on my tail. Completely ignoring the world around me, I sprinted into the hospital vestibule shouting out for an orderly and a wheelchair. By the time I had sprinted back to the car, the policeman was standing there with his notebook out. Right behind me, came an orderly with a wheelchair accompanied by a nurse. Fortunately, the policeman, sizing up the situation, put away his notebook and before turning on his heel to leave said, "Congratulations to you both." As for the nurse, she took charge of the situation immediately, advising me to calm down, as Marlene was now in safe hands and it would be wise to park the car up and follow them through to the maternity wing. Meanwhile, Marlene quietly reassured me that she was fine and that I was to phone Livy and ask her to bring an overnight bag that she had packed, ready and placed in her wardrobe closet. Turning to the nurse, she asked her to notify Dr Escobar as he was her paediatrician and with that, she was gone, leaving me standing there as if I had just been hit with a wet kipper.

By the time I had finished dropping dimes and quarters over the telephone kiosk floor and got through to Livy, I was in a right state of panic, but Livy calmly talked me down and told me to pull myself together, assuring me that she would be with me shortly. I soon found the maternity wing and as soon as I arrived at the nurses' station, they told me that they had been expecting me. Once Marlene had received her initial examination, I could go in to see her. Meanwhile, I could wait in the private waiting room until Dr Escobar, who had already been paged, had spoken to me. I was gratified to see a jug of coffee percolating on a hot plate when

I entered the waiting room and that plus a packet of cigarettes kept me going. It seemed that I had been waiting hours, but it was no more than thirty minutes before Dr Escobar arrived dressed in scrubs. In appearance, he was a well-built man of Latin American heritage with a jovial and calm exterior and was extremely well thought of as a baby doctor within the Hollywood community. Grabbing himself a cup of coffee, he sat down beside me.

"Well, Mr Conrad, I will just bring you up to speed on your wife's condition. You will be pleased to know that after carrying out an initial examination, she is on course for a natural and healthy delivery which will occur when mother and baby are ready. Further to that, I have more good news for both of you. While I am about it Mr Conrad, I have to tell you that you will be the father of twins. By one hiding behind the other, they successfully fooled us by disguising their dual heartbeats as one."

It was at that moment, as he was speaking, that Livy arrived carrying a small case and when I told her the good news, her face lit up and without thinking, she gave me a hug, before realising that she had momentarily lost her British reserve. Dr Escobar continued.

"You may go in now to see her and remain with her until she begins to go into labour. My team and I will now be in attendance until her delivery, so please do not worry. She is in good hands."

Livy and I proceeded to follow Dr Escobar to the private suite that Marlene had been placed in. Marlene was certainly in fine form, ad-libbing with the nursing staff around her bed and as soon as she saw me, she held out her arms and as we hugged whispering in my ear, "Look what you have done to me, you big lug! Not content with just giving me one baby you have given me two." We spent the next ten minutes talking with Marlene who gave strict instructions to Livy to ensure that within the next twenty-four hours, another cot was placed in the nursery. It was whilst we were discussing whether we were going to have boys or girls that she started her contractions. Dr Escobar took over whilst asking us to leave.

Once again, I found myself back in the waiting room, pacing up and down and chain-smoking, whilst Livy kept me in constant supply of coffee. It was exactly five minutes past six in the evening when Dr Escobar came to fetch me.

"Congratulations, Mr Conrad. You will be glad to hear that you are the father of healthy twin girls weighing in at 5.6lbs and 5.4lbs respectively and that mother is doing fine. Now, if you would like to go in to see them, please remember not to stay too long as mother will need some rest. The first sight that greeted me was of Marlene propped up in bed holding our daughters, one in each arm. Despite just giving birth, she looked radiant and as I bent over and kissed her, I murmured, "Thank you, sweetheart." It was a very private and emotional moment between us and the next thirty minutes or so passed all too quickly as Livy and I took turns holding the girls. I must admit I was very much the proud father looking down on their angelic faces with their tufts of blonde hair.

Marlene and I had already decided on their names; one was to be called Inger Melanie and the other, Kim Alexis. However, being identical twin girls, I could see that it would take a little time in recognising who was who. That certainly wasn't a problem, as we were too busy taking photographs of their first moments upon this planet. It wasn't until Dr Escobar gently reminded us that it might be time to give Marlene the opportunity to get some sleep and that I could take the opportunity of viewing our daughters through the observation glass of the baby unit. As I kissed Marlene good night, Livy had unpacked all her personal things, leaving out her nightgown and negligee for her to change into, plus some cosmetic creams and perfumes. I also ensured that a phone would be plugged into her bedside so that in the event of her needing anything, she could phone home and I would it bring in tomorrow morning. There was no doubt I was feeling a proud father standing at the observation window looking down at my two daughters lying fast asleep in their cribs just like two little angels. In between 'ooing' and 'ahing', Livy made a point of reminding me to have flowers sent over in the morning and to buy a second cot for the nursery. She suggested it also might be wise to contact a staff agency as soon as possible to hire a nanny to assist Marlene in looking after the babies. It had certainly turned out to be an eventful day, one which had left its main participants happy but exhausted, whilst the main cause of it all slept blissfully unaware tucked up in their cribs.

Both national and local press had picked the story up, so that not only had our friends and colleagues been dropping by delivering cards of congratulations accompanied by assorted cuddly toys, but my fans had been sending cards as well. Poor Livy had to borrow a clerical assistant from the firm that handled my public relations to help her in dealing with the barrage of telegrams and the large increase in mail. I had also booked a transatlantic call to Marlene's parents and was finally able to give them the good news at four o'clock the morning American time, that they were now grandparents to twin girls. They were, of course, overjoyed, as were Marlene's brothers, when I was finally able to get in touch with them.

Forty-eight hours after the birth, Marlene was discharged from Cedars of Lebanon by Dr Escobar. The moment arrived when Livy and I came to bring Marlene and the twins home from the hospital. It was a case of the two women sitting in the back of the car in a cramped space, one holding Kim and the other holding Inger which brought home to me the fact that I needed to trade in my present run-around and buy an estate wagon so that we could accommodate two carry cots. What a homecoming it was for Marlene and the girls. Within a week, from a list of girls from the employment agency, Marlene had selected a young Scottish lass by the name of Mary McConachie, who by some miracle, had obtained a green card to work in the US. Marlene had also hired a dietician to bring her weight down and to get rid of her spare tummy fat. She even had the foresight to remind me to have a gate installed leading into the swimming pool area with an alarm built in so that we could ensure the safety of the twins when they became old enough to get into mischief.

I am afraid at this point, I was forced to take leave of Marlene and my daughters and report back on location to Mazatan, Mexico to complete exterior footage on my present movie about the Spanish explorer, Hernan Cortez and his conquest of the Aztec Empire. It had already been given a provisional title by the studio of *Conquest of the Sun*. The film's director, Victor Fleming, had already arrived at Mazatan with his camera crew and I was due to fly down there the following Monday. It was not an absence that I desired but I had always prided myself on being a professional and was a strong believer in the motto, the show must go on.

In all honesty, as a male I was rather superfluous to requirements in the household. Marlene was off and running when it came to the re-organisation of her household routines ably assisted by Livy and now that Mary McConachie had settled in so well, it enabled Marlene to make a speedy return to her old self. I spent the weekend before departure to Mexico in quality time with Marlene and our daughters, mostly in the evenings, as daytime was interrupted by endless visits of the Hollywood wives, all coming to pay their respects and to coo and sigh over Kim and Inger. Of the two girls, Kim proved to be the most vociferous when it came to her feeds during the night and Marlene made it quite clear that she alone would take care of their needs during the night-time, as quite rightly, she felt that it would quickly establish the bond between them.

Incidentally, I had grown a beard for my role in *Conquest of the Sun* which Marlene did not like at all, referring to it like kissing a broom, a remark which only encouraged me to try and kiss her all the more and that usually reduced her to fits of giggles. I rose early on Monday morning and after giving both Kim and Inger a kiss, went down to the kitchen with Marlene where we shared a coffee and some toast and then walked through to the front door and took the opportunity of breathing in the fresh morning air. All too soon, the studio car appeared, coming up the drive and as I gave Marlene a lingering embrace, I reminded her that I would phone every evening and would be back on Friday night. With that, I picked my bag up and slung it in the trunk of the car and climbed in the back. As the car travelled down the drive, Marlene and I waved to each other until she vanished out of sight.

Chapter 19

The Mexican Brigade

It didn't take long for the car to reach La Jolla airfield where there was a private plane waiting for me. As I climbed aboard, I was pleased to note that I would not be travelling alone as there were several of the cast members on board already. I recognised Gilbert Roland and Donald Crisp, two Hollywood veterans who, in turn, introduced to me a young Mexican actor just beginning to make his way in Hollywood by the name of Anthony Quinn. By the time that we landed at Mazatan, with the help of a few bottles of tequila, the ice had been broken and we were all getting on famously. After settling in at the hotel, we arranged to meet at the bar that evening but before I went down, I put a call through to Marlene and we chatted for some time with her final words to me that we were not to drink too much as she didn't want to read in the papers that I'd been flung in the Caboose.

Unfortunately, there was no mistaking that I was in for a boisterous night for apart from my fellow travellers, the company had grown with the presence of Victor Fleming and another Mexican actor who I was introduced to as Arturo Cordoba who had been cast to play Geronimo de Aguilar, the father confessor to the expedition. Arturo was not widely known outside of Mexico, but his reputation preceded him as being a fine actor. He certainly had an impressive personality, very much the bon vivant and raconteur and I took a great liking to him. With a happy mix of flamboyant personalities and booze, there was no way that the evening wasn't going to be anything but a great night.

Victor Fleming, our director, was known in the business as a man's man and was noted for being opinionated and forthright in his views. In fact, as the evening progressed, he had bet me a hundred dollars that Britain would capitulate to the Germans by the end of 1941. Despite his image as a macho man of action, he was in my opinion, in the top ten film directors, having pulled off a double in 1939 with *The Wizard of Oz* and *Gone with the Wind*, where he had been a re-placement director for George Cukor. It was past midnight when we all voluntarily called it a night being very much a case of needs must, when the devil drives. Victor warned us that he had scheduled an early call in the morning and that he expected all of us to turn up on time or else! The 'Mexican Brigade', as I had now nicknamed my fellow actors, insisted on one final drink for the road just to show their independence and that is how I left them.

When I arrived at the location for the exterior filming which was further along the coast from Mazatan, the Warners unit was already a thriving hub of activity. I counted at least six trailers, one of which was to be mine for the purpose of makeup and costume changes and relaxation between set-ups, as well as quite a few trucks for transporting the heavy Klieg lights and cameras, not to mention the sound equipment and of course, the obligatory catering wagon. Looking out at the mouth of the inlet where I was standing, I was surprised to see two sixteenth century galleons anchored and was intrigued enough to ask Tony Gaudio, the film's cinematographer, where they had been acquired. He told me that they had originally been built for the Errol Flynn swashbucklers *Captain Blood* and *The Seahawk* and were to be used extensively in the opening sequences of the Spanish landings.

I spent the first two hours in makeup, something that I was never comfortable with. I had no problem in its application for the theatre. Due to the stage lighting and the distance of the proscenium to the audience, it had to be heavily applied whereas for the screen, it had to appear more natural. Consequently, I always felt somewhat uncomfortable between takes, probably because it made me feel somewhat effeminate. As I had already been fitted for my costumes, it didn't take long to get dressed in doublet, hose, breastplate, knee-length boots and helmet and giving myself the once over in the mirror, I looked every inch the Spanish conquistador, especially with my beard. Having been called to the set, I quickly made my way down to the beach by car where Victor Fleming awaited me, accompanied by the script girl. Giving me the once over, he growled, "You look fine, Gunther," before launching into a detailed summary of what he wanted.

"We are going to try and film several sequences today, Gunther, providing our luck holds and we have no problems with any unforeseen circumstances arising. The first sequence will be of you, Gilbert, Tony and Pedro, landing on the beach. The second sequence will be of you and your lieutenants gathering your troops together with all the necessary dialogue involved and after lunch, the third sequence will be the most difficult, involving some very complicated camera work as we will be tracking you on rail whilst filming you on horseback with your officers, leading your column of foot soldiers up from the beach to the high ground and with your baggage mules following behind. Tony Gaudio will have his work cut out. Not only have we had to lay a track down to film you from a side view, but he will also require full frontal shots of both you and the column wending its way up the mountain with a view of the ships in the bay below in the rear. Finally, we may have problems recording the interchange of dialogue between yourself and the other principal actors. I'm telling you all this, Gunther, because the front office has given me exactly two weeks to film the landing of the Spanish expedition, their journey through the Mexican jungle and finally, the first meeting between Cortez and Montezuma."

Having filmed us disembarking the galleons before Christmas, the cast climbed into the first longboat but not before the continuity girl had checked our costumes. It was just as well, as I'd forgotten my sword, although, fortunately, my dresser hadn't and helped me buckle it on. Once we were all on board, the boat was towed out a little way from the shore, the Mexican extras took up the oars and waited until the clapper boy had registered the scene. On the word "Action," we started rowing to the shore. Once we hit the beach, I jumped ashore followed by Tony Quinn carrying the Spanish flag. It was at that moment the first of our technical problems arose. It had suddenly become windy with intermittent gusts which caused problems with our dialogue which, in the end, meant that we all faced re-recording once we were back in Hollywood. The second problem arose after lunch when the setting up of the two large cameras halfway up the mountain trail, had taken far longer than anticipated. The dense vegetation on either side of the trail was restricting the mobility of the cameras and sound boom, so despite the valiant efforts of the technical crew and grips, Victor was forced to abandon filming late that afternoon. This decision was greeted with some relief amongst us actors, as we had been forced to sit around all afternoon in the sultry heat in heavy costumes twiddling our thumbs.

The next day, we all re-assembled back at the starting point and once the remainder of the technical issues had been resolved, we were instructed to mount our horses and be ready for action.

There followed a few minutes, while we sat astride our horses as the camera angles were worked out by Tony. Fortunately, our mounts proved to be quite placid being kept calm by their Mexican handlers but then unfortunately, after "Action," had been called, the weather became overcast with the light becoming temperamental which, in turn, caused problems with the continuity of the photography. So, once again, it would be mid-afternoon before we were able to commence filming and finally, to finish. Then, it was a further wait whilst the camera cinematography was worked out to film the whole column from front to rear and also, to encompass the bay below us. Victor had no sooner called "Action," when we were engulfed by a heavy shower which, thank God, only lasted a few minutes. It was fortunate that the camera was protected from the rain and the tropical sun by a tarpaulin which was the only excuse needed for Victor to continue filming. His determination paid off, for when the rain stopped, the sun came out in spades, bringing with it, not only a rainbow but a cacophony of bird calls emanating from macaws and parrots. I just hoped that the sound engineer had been able to record those natural sounds which I am sure would provide a bonus to the scene by providing additional atmosphere.

Although my fellow cast members and I took some pride in having completed the scene, it didn't alter the fact that we were all soaked to the skin and when we finally dismounted from our horses, the air was full of Spanish curses from my co-stars and it certainly didn't help to see Victor standing by the camera, dry as a bone and grinning like a Cheshire cat. That to me, was akin to rubbing our noses in it, so exercising my rights as the star of the film, I squelched over to him and yelled.

"The hell with this, Victor. I am going back to camp to change out of this wet costume and I sure hope that wardrobe has a duplicate outfit because I am not putting this one back on until it has been cleaned."

On hearing this, Victor burst out laughing. Jumping down from the lorry, he strode over to me, putting his arms around my shoulders.

"Calm down, Gunther. It's only a bit of water. Besides, I want to congratulate you and the rest of the actors for producing such a great scene. I can guarantee you that by the time it reaches the screen, it will be a memorable sequence. While I'm about it, I might as well tell you that I've got some more goodies in store for you all. I have decided that next week, we will film the battle sequence which promises to be fun and for the remainder of this week, we will shoot your first meeting with Montezuma. I know it's no fun working in this unpredictable climate, especially having to wear those heavy costumes. However, you will be pleased to know that I will be shutting the production down on Friday midday for a long weekend, so as the cars are waiting to take you back to camp, I suggest you all get going. Oh, and by the way, I don't know whether you have any plans for tonight, but apparently, there's supposed to be an excellent Chinese restaurant in Mazatan and I was thinking of booking a private room there for some of the cast and crew. It would be a pleasant way to unwind and shoot the breeze whilst having a good meal and some drinks."

"You can count me in on that, Victor. It will certainly beat being on my own with just a bar to prop me up."

Later that day, Pedro Armendariz, the last major actor of the cast who was playing King Montezuma, flew in and arrived at the hotel in the early hours of the evening in readiness for the following morning's filming. I had only just finished freshening myself up with a shower after spending an extremely hot day climbing on and off a horse and trying to avoid the midges or mosquitoes, as they were formally known, when there was a knock at the door of my suite. When I opened it, Victor Fleming was standing there with a Mexican gentleman whom Victor introduced as Pedro Armendariz. He certainly was a handsome and well-built guy with a presence that commanded attention. I guessed that he was about six-foot tall, dark-haired and with a moustache which gave him a rather saturnine look. I put his age at roughly ten years younger than myself and it turned out that after the introductions were over, we both had something else in common. We were both new fathers, his son having been born in April of last year by his wife Carmelita. During the getting to know each other session between Pedro and myself and the sharing of a few glasses of tequila between the three of us, I was about to suggest that we book a private room in the hotel for a meal as we had done the night before and invite the same people, particularly the Mexican brigade who I knew would make Pedro feel right at home. Then, I remembered that we were going to have dinner at the Chinese restaurant that Victor had mentioned earlier in the afternoon.

Having made the arrangements for the evening's relaxation, I sent Victor and Pedro ahead whilst I made my regular evening call to Marlene. She sounded contented and was certainly pleased when I told her that I would be home Friday evening. Kim and Inger were both very contented babies and Mary, their new nanny was already proving indispensable. Marlene also added that her brothers Hansi and Lothar were flying in for a quick visit on the following Tuesday, and her final words to me were before we disconnected our call was the usual caution about not staying up taking part in late night drinking with my cast members.

After a wonderful meal at the Chinese restaurant, we returned to the hotel bar but there wasn't much chance of having just a few drinks as it was filled with members of the crew, a crowd that was not only a hundred percent macho but was not about to give up the opportunity for having a big night. Aside from the Mexican brigade and Victor Fleming, there was Donald Crisp who apart from being a member of the inner circle of John Ford's company, was also a leading character actor in the Warners' pantheon of players. Jokes and reminiscences were swapped backwards and forwards between us as the quantity of booze we all consumed increased. Apart from showbiz gossip, sport and women, there was very little room for more serious conversation. However, that didn't stop the topic of the European war being brought up and Victor was still adamant that Britain would capitulate any time now. It made me feel a sense of pride that most of my drinking companions didn't see it that way. Being the only member of the group present who could speak for Britain from a first-hand experience, it gave me the opportunity of contributing my two-penny worth to the debate and I like to think that the views I put forward that evening would ripple out from the bar to a wider audience beyond. As for Victor, in his enthusiasm, he was taking bets of ten-to-one that Britain would go under. I didn't stay to the end, as it was a case of getting to bed before too much damage was done. I was not alone, as Victor and Donald called it a night as well. When it came to the big hitters in the league of drinkers, I had to doff my hat to the Spanish lads.

The following morning, I rode up with Victor to our new location which was situated on a plateau just a few miles above where we had been filming previously and by the time we had arrived, the assistant director and Tony Gaudio, the cinematographer, were already busy setting up the forthcoming scenes. There were two large coaches deputising as wardrobe departments parked up alongside a large marquee which I assumed was being used as a changing room for the local population who had signed on as extras. Victor told me that there were at least five-hundred extras involved. Two hundred would be kitted out as Aztec courtiers and warriors with the remaining three hundred as Spanish foot soldiers. The set was just a hive of activity with the noise to match with grips and electricians darting everywhere accompanied by the sounds of hammering, generators humming and orders being barked. I made my way to my trailer where the makeup and costume departments were waiting for me and where I could go over my lines. As it turned out, I had more than enough time to revise the script as it was something close to two hours before I was finally called to the set and when I arrived, I was surprised at the transformation.

The Spanish foot-soldiers and pack mules were already in position with our horses at their head just quietly grazing with their Mexican handlers standing by. On the edge of the forest facing them, were our Aztec warriors and noblemen who had been impressively fitted out in gold costumes and multicoloured feather head dresses. Between the two sides, a portable track had been laid down, upon which stood a large platform on wheels carrying the camera for close-ups. I could already see that the supporting cast fully costumed, were standing around smoking. From where I was standing, which was on a mound, I could see right across the plateau which to me, was a perfect spot for filming. Both Victor and Tony obviously felt so too, for they had a couple of flat-top lorries parked close to me carrying the main cameras and sound equipment. It appeared that the assistant cinematographer, Frank Weston, would be handling the long shots and that Tony would be shooting the close-ups of the two protagonists meeting for the first time.

I stood by, as Victor gave his instructions to the assistant director, Johnny Dobbs and Frank Weston. Then, having satisfied himself that all was well, he departed with me in the station wagon. It didn't take more than a couple of minutes to reach the main camp and during that time, the remainder of the principal actors were onset waiting for us. Pedro Armendariz, having arrived straight from wardrobe and makeup, was standing by a golden litter which was to be carried by four muscular Mexican extras. Pedro looked very imposing, dressed in a white robe with a gold breastplate and gold accessories, plus a magnificent and colourful headdress. I had to smile at how incongruous he looked reading the sports pages and smoking a cheroot and as for Arturo, for a moment, I thought he had wandered off the set of Robin Hood dressed as he was, in monks robes.

Finally, at just about mid-morning, shooting got under way for the first historic meeting between Cortez and Montezuma. As soon as "Action," had been called, I led the Spanish extras from the forest trail onto the plateau towards the already encamped Montezuma and his Aztec chiefs, who on sighting us, advanced towards us, being carried in his litter, accompanied by his nobleman and a group of musicians omitting strange sounds from the horns that they were carrying. Unfortunately, the first take was ruined as Pedro Armendariz was supposed to step out of the litter with great dignity to greet me, but instead, accidentally, he fell out to the great mirth of all of us on the set. Being the trouper that he was, he then proceeded to bow to one and all, receiving applause in return from the crew. That wasn't the only re-take of the day. Later in the afternoon, as I was delivering my dialogue, I became a recipient of bird droppings on my helmet. I'm not entirely sure whether the bird was expressing his opinion of my acting, but once again, the crew certainly saw the funny side of it.

It was early Friday afternoon when Victor closed the set down for the weekend. Considering the logistics involved in the filming of the sequence that we had just completed and the retakes involved due to technical and human error, Victor was reasonably satisfied with the amount of film in the can and more importantly, so was the front office who under any normal circumstances would be far from happy on any film that was being shot on location and beyond the studio's fiscal control. But when you add in a location in a foreign country and a cast of hundreds, they start panicking about potential runaway costs. However, Victor was only two days over budget, which was something that he would no doubt make up as the shoot progressed. To guarantee a return to California for the weekend, I had hired a private aircraft to be on standby at Mazatan airfield that Friday afternoon and so, as it turned out, was able to give a lift to a few other cast members who were as anxious to get home as I was, such as Donald Crisp, Gilbert

Roland and Anthony Quinn whose wife was director Cecil B. DeMille's daughter, Katherine.

It was only after we had taken off that the three of us relaxed and began talking amongst ourselves. I was surprised at the professional history and the volume of work that the veteran character actor and director, Donald Crisp had and was still involved in, all of it in class 'A' features. He had only just recently completed three roles virtually moving from one part to the next and all three films had been box office successes, *Dr Ehrlich's Magic Bullet* and *Brother Orchid*, both starring Edward G. Robinson and the Errol Flynn swashbuckler, *The Seahawk*. It seems that he had commenced his career in the movies at the beginning of the century. Then, he had interrupted his career and returned to Britain to serve in the First World War as an intelligence officer. Returning to America, he had resumed where he had left off and continued both as director and character actor, in the silent and sound period of the cinema, right up to the present day. As well as the excellent company, it also turned out to be a perfect day for flying, the weather was clear with not a cloud in the sky which enabled us to have a clear view of the Sonora Peninsula and the Baja Sur before landing at Holmby Hills flying club, Los Angeles.

It didn't take long to reach the house from the flying club and Marlene was waiting for me with open arms. I went straight up to the nursery to see my daughters and I was quite surprised at how quickly they seemed to have developed in only five days. However, it soon became obvious to me that I had no role to play other than to 'coo' over them. What with Marlene, Mary the nanny and even Livy to take care of their every need, I was certainly superfluous to requirements. I showered and changed whilst Marlene filled me in with all the local news. We went downstairs and sat on the patio with Livy, enjoying an early evening drink before dinner. Amongst the things that we talked about were that Hitler appeared to have abandoned his invasion plans for Britain for the moment, that the civilian population were taking it on the chin and that morale was still high, despite the Luftwaffe's intensified bombing of Britain's cities.

Meanwhile, Livy filled me in with the week's business amongst which had been an invitation from Louis B. Mayer to attend a party that he was throwing the following night at his home. Marlene had quite rightly accepted in my absence once she had learnt that there would be several important people attending, knowing that it would be a great opportunity for me to espouse Britain's cause, especially as she understood there would be at least one senator attending. Later that evening, when we were both cuddled up in bed, I whispered to her that as she had missed out on her last visit to Simpson's art gallery and that I was going to take her down there in the morning because it so happened that they had a Mark Chagall for sale. Marlene, of course, was over the moon and remarked how coincidental it was that during the week, she had driven down to Walgreens for some baby products and had bumped into Vincent Price who not only, was accomplished actor from Broadway, but was just beginning to make his mark in Hollywood. He also happened to be an art expert of some distinction and whilst talking about their favourite subject, he had mentioned to her that if she ever had the opportunity, she should attempt to acquire a Mark Chagall, for its value would rise considerably during the next few years. She must have been mightily impressed by him, for she babbled on long enough on how suave, handsome and tall he was and how she was quite convinced that he would have a long career in movies playing sophisticated villains, because even talking to him in a drugstore, he gave off an aura of mysterious devilry. That is how we finally went off to sleep, with my wife snuggled up in the arms of her husband who also happened to be one of this year's Oscar nominees and voted in the magazine *Screen World* as America's fifth most romantic star, listening to her giving a domestic science lecture on babies and talking about the sex appeal of fellow actors. Hey ho, an actor's life for me!

I spent the first part of Saturday morning with Livy going over my professional affairs and reminding her that we needed to arrange a meeting with my business manager with the reference to purchasing some real estate in an ever-growing Hollywood and also, some time in the future, the possibility of setting up my own production company. It was as well that I had plenty to occupy myself with, being that rightly so, Marlene's priorities lay with the best interests of our daughters and that I would have to take a temporary back seat whilst she looked after their welfare and the running of the house. Nevertheless, when her duties were done, we managed to get away together and drive down to Simpson's art gallery where, after a very pleasant late morning, examining paintings, she was happy for me to buy her a Mark Chagall as a present. After that, we drove over to the Brown Derby for an order of hamburger and fries with a Coke. It was a magic moment, for we felt briefly, that we were in a time vacuum, enjoying the freedom of having no responsibilities, a feeling that we had not experienced since we were both youngsters a long time ago.

As I sat across the table from Marlene, I couldn't help thinking how she had blossomed physically in motherhood. It seemed that all the stress and anxiety of the previous years had been wiped away and that motherhood had made her appear younger. She was wearing a cream silk blouse with a fashionable long skirt in which the hem reached halfway down her legs and the ensemble was finished off with white bobby socks and suede loafers. All in all, she made a very modern mother and as we left the Brown Derby and walked over to my recently purchased Chevrolet convertible with its bright red bodywork and white tyres, the thought crossed my mind that in the eight months since I had left Britain, I was living the American dream. It was especially confirmed when we took off up the freeway for home, the car radio blasting out the voice of a young crooner by the name of Frank Sinatra singing his latest hit single, *Our Love Affair*, whilst Marlene lounged back in her seat. With her hair blowing in the breeze and sunglasses on, she certainly looked every inch the goddess on the front cover of any national magazine.

That night's social affair requested black-tie and having dressed in a dinner jacket, I popped into the nursery to kiss my daughters goodnight, only to find Livy helping Mary to tuck them up in their cots.

"Well, I do declare," Livy said, seeing me enter, "That beard and suntan certainly do wonders for you, Gunther. You look very distinguished tonight. I am certain that you will make a very good impression on the ladies at tonight's soirée." She was laughing as she said it and as an afterthought, reached up and straightened my bow tie. After spending some time in the nursery, Livy and I went downstairs where I poured two whiskeys for us. We had hardly said "Cheers," when Marlene appeared at the top of the stairs and began descending them. The sight of her took my breath away. She had arranged her hair in the peekaboo style and was wearing a simple, black cocktail dress with a white mink stole covering her shoulders, black, high-heeled court shoes, all accessorised with a diamond necklace while holding in one hand a silver clutch purse. As I walked to the foot of the stairs, I greeted her.

"We have some time to spare, Marlene. Would you like me to pour you a drink? Oh, and by the way, if you don't mind me saying so darling, you look absolutely fabulous tonight and I wouldn't be surprised if Mr Mayer doesn't take one look at you and put you under contract."

"I don't think that will happen, Gunther," she laughingly replied, "From what I have seen of Hollywood, I know which side my bread is buttered on. I'd much rather be a stay-at-home wife and sooth your bruised ego when you come home from a bad day in Tinseltown. What do you think, Livy, am I right or am I wrong?"

"I think you are quite right, Marlene," Livy replied, "I can't help but sympathise with all those beautiful people out there never knowing where their next movie is coming from and taking life far too seriously."

"Hold on, girls. I was only trying to pass a compliment not the Bill of Rights."

Marlene raised a glass to her lips and tossed the whiskey down in one gulp and taking my face in both hands, kissed me full on the mouth before whispering.

"Come on, you handsome lug. Let's go partying with the good and the powerful and we will see you in the morning, Livy."

It took about twenty minutes to drive to East Gate, Bel-Air and a further ten minutes to find St. Cloud Road. However, there was no problem in locating Lewis B. Mayer's palatial mansion. Once through the electrified main gates, it stood out like a monument with all its lights full on. I had no sooner pulled up outside the imposing entrance than we soon had a taste of how grand the evening was going to be. A young man dressed in a green monkey jacket and black trousers and who obviously was a parking valet, opened the passenger door for Marlene to step out and then proceeded to walk around the car and do the same for myself, after which, having given me a numbered cloak ticket, he then proceeded to drive the car away into the darkness leaving Marlene and myself to climb the steps to the double doors and ring the bell which was promptly opened by a butler who was obviously British and had a look of Alan Mowbray about him.

It never ceased to amaze me on how many butlers were employed in Hollywood on the basis on either being British or having a strong physical resemblance to expat British character actors. Having handed Marlene's wrap to a maid, he then proceeded to escort us to yet another set of double doors which he opened, revealing an extremely large reception room filled wall-to-wall with the cream of Hollywood's A-Listers, a lot of which were employed by MGM. I immediately recognised Lewis B. Mayer and his wife Margaret, threading their way through the guests towards us. Physically, Mayer was a short but powerfully built man, wearing glasses. He came from a Russian Jewish background and had immigrated to Canada in the latter part of the 19th century. After a short stay, the family had crossed over to the United States and settled in Long Island. After spending his early adult life in the scrap merchant business, he had made the decision to change the direction of his life by purchasing a six-hundred-seater Nickelodeon called The Gem. He soon proved that he had a natural flair for show business and very quickly, by sheer hard work, had built MGM film studios into the largest entertainment factory in the world. He was also the most powerful man in Hollywood and the highest-paid executive in America. After I had introduced Marlene to them both, Mayer stood looking at me quizzically whilst he grabbed hold of my arm.

"You know, Gunther," he said, "We were slow picking up an option on your when you were available. If you remember, you started your international career at MGM in the twenties, when I signed you to a contract in Berlin all those years ago. You were very young then and under our guidance, became a great star, but you chucked it all up and went back to Europe to make movies and all because of the threat of sound. Now you are back in America as good as you ever were, if not better, which unfortunately is MGM's loss and Jack Warner's gain. If I have any advice to give you, it would be to fight your corner for the best scripts and parts, otherwise Jack will work you like a mule for the last dollar. Now, I want to introduce you to some of the new stars on the MGM lot and also, more importantly, to some United States senators. Having just arrived back on a factfinding mission from Britain, I think that they will be very interested to hear from you on the way the British public are coping with the way things are over there. With Ed Morrow broadcasting to the American people direct from London and the British bulldog still standing up to Hitler, I don't think it'll be too long before Roosevelt finds a way to supply Britain with material to carry on fighting. So, if there is anything that you can do tonight to persuade these politicians to go back to Washington to vote for aid for Britain, then you will have accomplished something.''

With Marlene beside me, Mayer introduced us to the actor Walter Pidgeon and his wife, Ruth Walker and to Robert Taylor and his wife, Barbara Stanwyck. Then, she moved us on to introductions with Greer Garson who had just gained acclaim with her role in the movie *Blossoms in the Dust* and her husband, Edward Snelson. Two people that I was overjoyed to meet again were Lionel Barrymore and his sister Ethel. They and their brother John had been the toast of Broadway over twenty years. I had the pleasure of meeting them and becoming friends with them when they moved to Hollywood. Despite being confined to a wheelchair now, Lionel was still a major movie actor, whilst brother John was just a caricature of his great talent having succumbed to extreme alcoholism. Ethel, on the other hand, was rapidly becoming the grand dame of the cinema and it didn't take long for her, Marlene and Margaret Mayer to be chatting away to the democratic senators for California. I spent some time with them as they were very eager to hear what I had to say about the situation in Britain, particularly when it came to the only object standing in in the way of Hitler's domination of the world was my vulnerable adopted country. Eventually, the catering staff broke up our conversation when they started circulating amongst the guests with trays of hors d'oeuvres as a prelude to the buffet tables becoming available.

Margaret Mayer had commandeered Marlene and was busy introducing her to all and sundry, leaving me to my own devices. Fortunately, I was either acquainted with or knew many, of the people who were attending the party on personal terms. It was whilst I was helping myself to smoked salmon and potato salad that I felt a tap on my shoulder. Turning around, I found myself looking at another face from the past. This time, it was the burly physique of Eddie Mannix, accompanied by his wife, Toni Lanier. I had known Eddie socially way back in the twenties, when he was then Louis B. Mayer's right-hand man, the keeper of MGM's secrets and the go-to guy for fixing the stars indiscretions, a role he still performed.

''Hiya, Gunther. I knew that you were back in town, but this has been the first opportunity we've had to meet up again. I was surprised when the old man neglected to sign you up when you became available. How are you doing over at the Warners factory? I see that your first film for them has been nominated at the Oscars for Best Picture as well as yourself as Best Actor so that makes you in contention with our own *Philadelphia Story* and Jimmy Stewart for Best Actor. All I can say to that is to wish you luck, pal. By the way, your old flame, Trixie Montana, is supposed to be here tonight. I expect that you know by now, she is one of the biggest stars in Hollywood and has only just recently signed with us. As you probably already know, whilst you have been away, she made a series of hit musicals in partnership with Gene Fredericks and has built up a huge public following. If memory serves me right, you and she were very much an item. In fact, the general consensus at the time was that the pair of you would marry, but instead, you've married a beautiful German model by whom you have twin daughters, so congratulations.''

I am afraid that the position of enforcer and Mr Fix-it, fitted Eddie Mannix like a glove. He was a great guy to know if you wanted your indiscretions to be hushed up but a deadly enemy if you crossed him. Fortunately, whilst I had been under contract at MGM, my youthful misdemeanours had been small, so I had avoided being one of many of his skeletons in his closet.

''Well, it's nice to see you again, Eddie. I can quite clearly see that you have still got your fingers in all the pies and yes, I do look forward to seeing Trixie after all these years. I am sure that after I have introduced her to Marlene, they will get on like a house on fire, talking of which, I am going to go and see if I can find her, so you'll have to excuse me. But no doubt I will see you at the Biltmore Hotel for the Oscars at the end of February.''

I finally caught up with Marlene still being accompanied by Margaret Mayer as they moved amongst the other guests, but this time, they appeared to have been joined by her daughter, Irene and her husband, the producer, David O. Selznick, who, of course, was the brother of my agent, Myron Selznick. As I have so often thought before, Marlene had a natural capability of enchanting the company that she was with at that current moment in time and so it proved, even though I had joined her, she remained the centre of attention, leaving me the opportunity to survey the room. It certainly contained the cream of Tinseltown and beyond, for I noticed the opera singer, Laurence Melchior in deep conversation with the concert pianist Jose Iturbi. Even the younger generation were represented for I suddenly spotted Judy Garland and Mickey Rooney talking animatedly to a young man whom I didn't recognise. Both Judy and Mickey had been voted America's favourite teenagers. Both had been child stars and had risen to the top of their profession with two recently released movies, *Strike Up The Band* and *Babes on Broadway*. It certainly was my intention to introduce Marlene to them, for in my opinion, as far as modern music goes, they were the most talented youngsters on the planet. But then, who should suddenly be standing at the door but Hollywood's reigning star of musicals, my ex-girlfriend, Trixie Montana.

She had certainly matured into a strikingly glamorous woman and the way that she drew all eyes in the room towards her suggested to me that she had already perfected the art of being a diva. As Marlene was deep in conversation, I stood and observed Trixie. She had already seen me and slowly began working her way towards me accompanied by her escort, the choreographer, Busby Berkeley, stopping now and then to acknowledge somebody, a kiss here or a hug there, until she arrived in front of me. Employing all her histrionic skills, she threw her arms wide open declaring, as she gave me a rather too personal hug.

"Hello, darling Gunther. I knew that you were back in town, but I simply haven't had the opportunity to get in touch with you. Belated congratulations on your marriage and on you becoming the proud father of twin daughters. You certainly hit the ground hard since your return from Europe, Gunther; already an Oscar contender as well as making a movie on location in Mexico. Now that's what I call a great comeback."

"I haven't really been away Trixie, or don't you read the foreign press! Anyway, it's nice to see you again. You look fabulous and from what I gather, you seem to have achieved all that you have wished for. Now I would like to introduce you to someone very important to me. Trixie, this is my wife, Marlene; Marlene this is Trixie Montano."

Both women gave each other the mandatory peck on the cheek and then stood exchanging pleasantries whilst eyeing each other up. Marlene was well aware of my past history with Trixie but nevertheless, gave her the full charm offensive, even going as far as to invite her to dinner one night which rather caught Trixie off-guard and it was at that moment that Louis B. Mayer called the room to order by announcing that Judy Garland and Mickey Rooney, accompanied by Roger Eden, the MGM musical arranger, would sing us a couple of songs. The trio made their way to a grand piano to the sound of polite applause from the room and after some clowning around by Mickey, both he and Judy broke into song, their first number being *How About You*, a song from their latest smash hit film, *Babes on Broadway*, followed by a second song from the same movie, *Yankee Doodle Boy*, both which brought a standing ovation from all of us. After that, the evening could easily have descended into an anticlimactic mood but after witnessing a display of such considerable talent, the opposite effect was achieved.

Marlene and I once again quietly worked the room, talking to senators and power brokers, espousing Britain's solitary stand against the might of Hitler's Germany and his egomania. He would never stop in his thirst for conquest, which was why it was so important that Britain needed the help of other freedom loving countries to prevent that from happening. That was our message that night: Hitler's ambition was Europe today, tomorrow the world. Eventually, we ended up in the company of Louis B. Mayer and his wife Margaret. When I asked him where he stood regarding the European conflict, he told me that he was well aware of the importance of opposing Hitler through the media of film. However, he disliked message movies as MGM's success was built on providing family entertainment for the average American so that just for a few hours, he could escape from the realities of life and be part of the world of glamour and good family values such as the *Andy Hardy* and *Dr Kildare* series.

He had, he went on to tell me, produced *The Mortal Storm*, which was a veiled portrait of Nazi Germany. Also, he had only recently purchased the rights of a new book by the authoress, Jan Strother, entitled *Mrs Miniver*, which was about an English family standing up the trials and tribulations of wartime Britain. He was determined to have the production completed within the next two months and had already assigned Greer Garson and Walter Pidgeon to play the Minivers but I suspect, when all is said and done, he would have preferred to have kept the European markets available for MGM products rather than to antagonise Adolf Hitler. Before I left his company, he did take the opportunity of informing me that he would endeavour to have a quiet word with the Hollywood arts council regarding a possible tour of South America with myself as part of the delegation. I couldn't think of a better opportunity to espouse the cause of Britain whilst visiting the capitals of South America.

It was whilst I was discussing with Irene Selznick her ambition to one day, produce a play on Broadway, that Marlene slipped away to the powder room to freshen up and she had barely left my side when I felt a tug at my elbow. When I turned at the slight distraction, Trixie was standing there with a mischievous smile.

"I shall be leaving now, Gunther, for an early night. I have an unbelievable heavy work schedule and I need my beauty sleep to stay ahead of the game. However, we can't possibly pass each other by like this without meeting some place to talk over our memories."

"It would be great to have a get-together, Trixie," I replied.

"But I too, am tied up on out-of-town location work for a couple of weeks, after which I will then be finishing up on interior filming at Warners. I tell you what, give me a contact number so that Marlene can phone you for a chat and arrange a dinner party at home for a get-together with a few of our friends. I imagine, however, that because we both have busy film schedules, that we are more likely to meet up at the Oscars in February before we can arrange a dinner date."

"I look forward to that moment, Gunther, but don't let's leave it too long because you still occupy a special place in my heart and I still consider you one of my dearest friends. Oh, by the way, Gunther, good luck at the Oscars."

With that, she kissed me on the cheek and slinging her silver box over her shoulder, proceeded to sweep out of the room but not before stopping to have a few words with Louis B. Mayer and his wife Irene. We spent the rest of the evening in conversation with various friends and acquaintances, especially the actress, Greer Garson, who was up for Best Actress at this year's Oscars in another MGM picture, *Blossoms in the Dust* and a young actor by the name of Van Heflin who we had already met when we first arrived in New York. Meeting him a second time only confirmed my previous opinion of him that whilst he appeared reserved in the company of others, it was when he was performing that he projected enormous charisma compelling you to watch him.

Having exchanged good luck wishes with her, Marlene decided that she was ready for home. It took a little while to say good night and to thank our hosts for a great evening before we eventually collected our car and drove off. Considering that it was early February, it was a warm evening and after winding my window down, I turned the radio on to the sounds of Glenn Miller whilst Marlene snuggled up to me as I drove.

"I rather think that Trixie Montano would like to rekindle her lost love for you and being the type of woman that she is, what she wants she gets."

"You need not have any worries on that score, darling," I replied. "All that happened a long, long, time ago and since then, I fell in love with the most beautiful girl in the world and from that moment, I now have two lovely daughters. Trixie made her decisions many years ago by choosing a career over love and now she is the queen of Hollywood. Unfortunately, there always seems to be consequences for any woman who strives to be the best, especially in our profession. Inevitably, there comes the moment of realisation when age starts catching up with your looks and a younger Trixie Montano comes up behind you to usurp your position and when that happens, there is nothing to fall back on other than money and loneliness. I would be a hypocrite to deny that I still have feelings for her but only regarding her future well-being. I can only hope that she finds a soulmate who will look after her for the rest of her life so that she can retire gracefully from the pinnacle of her success rather than to fall into a lonely oblivion."

"You know, Gunther, if you ever get fed up with being an actor, you could become a politician, as you always have an answer for everything." I couldn't stop laughing at that gentle put down. There was, however, some truth in it, for I could think of several actors who could easily make that transition. Who knows, one of them could even one day end up in the White House as President of the United States.

The remainder of the weekend was spent enjoying each other's company and relaxing by the pool, catching up with paperwork with Livy and being an observer to my baby daughters. At this stage of their lives, there wasn't much interaction that I could indulge in with them as both Marlene and Mary

McConachie were quite rightly the centre of their universe. However, I am sure that soon enough, I would have my hands full with them, a day I looked forward to. Monday morning, I would be flying down to Mazatan to resume exterior filming. Thank goodness, this would be the last week and then it would be back to Burbank for completion of the movie.

I arrived back at Mazatan early on Monday afternoon but not before a delay in take-off. I was forced to wait in the aircraft with its engines ticking over. Sure enough, within minutes, a man carrying a small holdall came running over the tarmac towards us. Climbing aboard, he proceeded to sit down across the aisle from me. After apologising to us all for the delay, he introduced himself to me as Yakama Canutt. I certainly knew of him, for he was widely recognised in Tinseltown as one of Hollywood's leading stuntmen and second unit directors. Physically, he was the image of his profession, ruggedly built and over six-foot tall with granite features and a dimpled chin. During the flight, he told me that Victor Fleming had requested him to supervise the battle sequence that was being filmed this week. He also mentioned that he had lost count of the number of injuries that he had received over the last twenty years and indeed, it was only as recently as last year that he had suffered severe internal injuries which had necessitated him convalescing for the last six months. He went on to remark that he was getting too old for the physical side of the job and was now making a career as both a stunt co-ordinator and second unit director for action sequences. By the time we touched down at Mazatan, we had got on so well that we were on first name terms with me addressing him as Yak.

Because of the logistics and sheer scale of the battle sequence, this week was going to be entirely different from the previous one. I knew that because of the large financial overheads involved in this week's filming, that a lot of pressure and stress would be on Victor Fleming's shoulders and sure enough, I had only just arrived at the hotel before I and the supporting cast involved in the sequences to be filmed, were summonsed to a script conference where amongst other things, the cast members were asked not to indulge in any heavy drinking, as we would be expected to be on set fully costumed ready for action by eight o'clock every morning.

It was early evening when we finally finished the conference but not before Victor had asked me if I would be prepared to lead the cavalry charge in the opening sequence without having to use a double. Seeing that my compardres, in the Mexican brigade, would be involved in that sequence and that I considered myself a good horseman, I agreed. I am quite sure that Victor would be keeping his fingers crossed just as much as I would be during the filming of that sequence, for if anything should go wrong, God forbid, then the picture would be right up the Swanee River. That evening, as I am sure that you have already guessed, instead of carousing around the town, the crew stayed in the hotel bar and soon made short work of Victor's edict on no heavy drinking. Where would we be without alcohol and good companionship? Nevertheless, after a bellyful of beer and tequila shots, I called it a night and was ready for bed but not before calling home and wishing Marlene a good night.

The following morning, I was up with the birds having put in an early call for six o'clock and was soon downstairs in the hotel restaurant, sharing a breakfast table with Victor Fleming and Yak Canute before the three of us piled into a studio car which promptly took us up to the location. When we arrived, I was surprised at how much the crew had achieved in preparing the scene so early in the morning and despite the bedlam and activity, there were strings of horses tethered and already saddled up, their grooms brushing their coats, whilst all around them, squatting or standing drinking coffee and eating or smoking, was literally an army of Mexican extras, either dressed in Spanish or Aztec uniforms. There were at least three large generators humming away with cables spewing forth from them like tentacles from an octopus. I also noticed two big vans housing the sound equipment with sound engineers setting up mic booms on trolleys. More importantly, I noticed that the day looked set for some fine weather and not wanting to be accused of wasting any of it, I hurried off to my trailer to change into my wardrobe and receive makeup.

By the time I left my trailer, I had been made up and was dressed in the full attire of a sixteenth century Spanish grandee. God knows how they had endured the heat in such cumbersome clothing, what with a heavy woollen jerkin, breastplate, pantaloons and a short cloak, plus heavy, thigh boots and a helmet. Life must have been just about unbearable in the tropical heat. I envied the grips going about their tasks stripped to the waist and already, I was thankful for the cool breeze that was sweeping over the plateau. As I approached the set Vic, Tony and Yak were deep in conversation which I inadvertently interrupted when I finally reached them. As it turned out, I had arrived at an opportune time. The three of them were working out camera positions for the charge that I would be leading in the character of Cortez.

Today would be devoted to filming close-ups of myself and the other leading actors and tomorrow, Victor intended to repeat his masterly shot from *Gone with the Wind*, only this time, instead of using a crane shot to open up a panoramic view of endless rows of wounded, he intended to film with the second unit under the supervision of Yak, the cavalry charge of the Spanish conquistadores against the forces of Montezuma. It was at this point that a fourth man joined us who was introduced to me by Yak as a veteran stunt rider by the name of Billy Clements who somewhat took me aback by his close physical resemblance to myself which it now emerged was the reason for him being here. He would apparently be my stunt double for tomorrow's long shots. Today's sequence consisted of me leading the Spanish expedition force in retreat after the death of Montezuma (interior sequences to be filmed on sound stages later in Hollywood), breaking out of the jungle, hotly pursued by the Aztec warriors, only to find ourselves in danger of being encircled, hence our charge to break that circle which would be filmed tomorrow.

It turned out to be an arduous day with many retakes either caused by fluffed lines or miscues. But in any event, we finally wound up by four o'clock in the afternoon having taken all day to film five minutes of screen time. Thank God Victor finally called quitting time. I think for all of us, it had been a long and laborious day. I don't know who was more fed up; the horse, or me, for the number of times I climbed on and off the poor creature. As well as the endless sitting around between takes, there was also the debilitating and humid heat to contend with which in turn, resulted in the constant retouching of makeup to our faces.

I was never more grateful when I finally got back to the hotel and was able to luxuriate in a long, cool shower after which, whilst I was waiting for a telephone connection to Hollywood, I had lain down on the bed and with the telephone receiver cradled to my ear watched the ceiling fan rotating, bringing some relief to the humidity. Finally, the call was put through and I heard Livy's, business like voice.

"Hello Livy, it's Gunther," I shouted down the receiver. Why we shout on long distance calls I don't really know. Perhaps it's something to do with the distance! Anyway, I carried on speaking.

"How are things? Not that I need ask, you are so efficient that by this time of day, you have nothing else left to do."

"As it happens, Gunther, there has been a large amount of incoming mail today, most of which are from your fans requesting signed photographs. It's a good job that I had the idea of having a stamp made with a facsimile of your signature because it enabled Marlene to get through a huge stack of photographs whilst I put them in envelopes. Needless to say, looking at you all day long can be pretty wearisome. The only other thing of note was that your passes for the Oscars have also arrived as well. Marlene is here now, so I will pass you over to her and will, no doubt, see you at the end of the week. Cheerio for now."

"Hello, handsome, you just can't do without me for five minutes, can you?" Marlene's voice came down the line through the receiver with that unmistakable gurgle of laughter. "You have only been away two days and already those two daughters of ours are breaking all records when it comes to changing nappies. I tell you something, Gunty, Mary is a treasure. She has both girls changed, fed and asleep in no time at all. Make sure that you look after yourself, do you hear? Make sure that you change your socks regularly and eat plenty, stay away from the booze and those Mexican señoritas and I expect to see you home at the weekend." We spent several minutes laughing together over the phone until we blew each other kisses and disconnected.

Later, I joined Victor Fleming, Joe Gaudio and Yak Canute for dinner in the hotel restaurant, where I learnt that Vic was reasonably content at the progress being made in filming. He felt that we should be able to wrap up the location work by Friday and be back to filming on the back lot at Burbank by the following Monday which was very good news for me. At least, I would be permanently back at home base by Friday for the conceivable future. After the meal, the four of us split, with Vic and Tony going off to do some planning for tomorrow's big scene, whilst Yak and myself sauntered over to the hotel bar for a nightcap.

As to be expected, a lot of the crew were already there, some either playing pool or cards with the remainder scattered around the bar sitting at tables with the customary Budweiser and Jack Daniel chaser. Standing at the bar itself or sitting on bar stools, were a few of the supporting actors, among whom one I recognised as my stunt double, Billy Clements. Having spotted us first, he beckoned us over and offered to buy us a drink. Under normal circumstances, people working in Hollywood could be just as bad as the British when it came to class distinction. Directors and stars did not mix socially with supporting players but when you are hundreds of miles away from home on location, there was a relaxation of the system, particularly if the star preferred to be one of the boys. It just so happened that I did consider myself one of them and as far as I was concerned, we were all in it together, each with a job to do and I saw no reason not to socialise under those circumstances with the crew. One of the benefits from being on location was that just by listening to the reminiscences of the old timers, you could learn an awful lot about the history of Hollywood and so it transpired that night, particularly as I listened to the stories of Yakama Canutt and Billy Clements on their early days as stuntmen working in westerns at Universal.

Such was my enthralment at listening to their tales that the next time I looked at my watch, two hours had passed in the blink of the eye as well as many large glasses of Jack Daniels. Because of the importance of the filming tomorrow, I reluctantly decided to call it a night, with Yakama, deciding to do so as well. As we left the bar together, we decided to step outside the hotel for a breath of cool night air. As we stood outside the hotel, Yakama told me the story of Billy Clements. In the twenties, Billy had been the top stuntman of his day. He had not only taken young Yakama under his wing but also taught him most of the tricks of the trade. Billy had also been a long-time associate of the western star, William S. Hart, performing as a double and a stunt arranger on most of on his films. He also worked in 1925 on Hart's last film before he retired called *Tumbleweed*. Unfortunately for Billy, soon after the completion of that movie, he was involved in a serious automobile accident which left him badly crippled with serious leg injuries and his wife paralysed from the waist down and from that moment on, the quality of his life went downhill rapidly. What with the medical bills and the inability to work, life became very hard and so, by the time Billy was able to work again, time and age had passed him by. Yakama had never forgotten Billy and was able to give him small jobs which gave him a small income per year and despite the fact that Billy was nearly fifty-five years of age, Yakama had been able to secure him a week's work in Mexico as my stunt double on this movie. In a roundabout way, I was listening to the story of Hollywood. It wasn't all about its success stories but about the thousands who struggled to find work and those who overcame adversity just to keep their place in the sun. On that philosophical note, I bade Yakama a good night and went up to my room.

Once again, on the following morning, an early start was scheduled as this was to be one of the spectacular highlights of the movie. I spent the morning doing close-ups followed by a break for lunch, after which, in the early afternoon, the battle sequence was ready to be filmed in long shot. I would not be needed until later when my horse was supposed to fall and an insert would be filmed of me being rescued by Gilbert Roland. As Yakama was directing this action sequence, I had climbed onto a platform with Vic to watch the sequence being filmed below me. A camera had been set up on a flat-top truck which would be filming parallel to the charge as it raced alongside. From my vantage point, the set up looked very impressive with the plateau filled with at least two-hundred Mexican extras dressed in costumes of all colours of the rainbow, Billy Clements was already mounted and from a distance, it was difficult to tell that it wasn't me. Gradually, everything began to gather momentum until the moment arrived when I heard the word "Action" boom out across the plateau and the charge began. From where I was standing, it all looked a very spectacular sequence until, to my horror, tragedy struck.

Somehow, in the melee of the staged battle, Billy Clements horse took flight and despite Billy's efforts to control him, bolted. In attempting to jump over some fallen trees, the horse fell, rolling over Billy in the process. To our consternation, the horse got up revealing that poor Billy's foot had been trapped in the stirrup and even worse, he appeared to be unconscious as he made no attempt to extricate himself. Fortunately, some extras grabbed hold of the horse's bridle before he attempted to canter off. By the time we arrived, the studio doctor was already kneeling beside Billy performing chest compressions and was soon joined by the company's nurse. Suddenly, everything around us became very still and quiet. Everybody had moved away as if to give the doctor and nurse more room with Yakama standing alone over them watching. Meanwhile, the company ambulance had backed up to the scene whilst two fellow stuntmen stood by ready with the stretcher. It seemed like an eternity as we all stood there in silence watching until just as suddenly all activity around Billy stopped. I could see the doctor bent over Billy, listening to his chest with his stethoscope. Seconds later, he had removed them from his ears and appeared to be looking at the nurse as he made a gesture with his hand. He appeared to say something to the two men with the stretcher because they immediately came forward and lifted Billy's body onto it whilst the nurse covered the whole body with a blanket. It was then loaded into the back of the ambulance. The doctor, having closed his black medical bag, said a few words to Yakama and after patting him on the shoulder, climbed into the ambulance beside the driver who promptly drove off with siren wailing, leaving behind a stunned crew and cast. It seemed hard to comprehend that in just over thirty minutes, we had all gone from an act of creativity to witnessing the termination of a life. I stood beside Victor Fleming as the studio nurse informed him of the outcome.

''I am sorry, Mr Fleming but the patient's heart had already stopped by the time Dr McRae and myself had arrived and despite Dr McRae's efforts to revive the patient by restarting his heart, it was of all to no avail. I can only surmise that he suffered massive internal injuries and that will only be determined by a post-mortem. I am sure that I speak for Dr McRae as well as myself when I say that this was a tragedy beyond our capabilities. All the more so, when our expertise was to prevent the crew and actors from suffering from the more mundane accidents of life, such as broken limbs, cuts, bruises and sunstroke. If you haven't anything else to ask me Mr Fleming, I'll get along now to write a secondary report of the incident with the doctor for the coroner's office and the studio. I'd just like to say that I'm very sad that our best simply was not good enough to save this man's life.''

It was obvious to both Victor Fleming and I that Yakama Canutt was not only in a state of shock but was also suffering from remorse as well and we did our best to console him. Victor made the decision to call a halt to the filming for the day out of respect but made a point of saying that he expected everybody onset on the following day to resume completion of the battle sequence. Leaving the assistant director to close the set for the day, Victor and I helped Yakama into the company estate wagon and drove back to the hotel. Once we had arrived back there, Victor and the script girl left us to attend to the business of notifying Warners of the fatality and that Billy Clements wife was to be notified immediately before the press got hold of the story. This was a sad task that Yakama undertook personally to perform, having known the family for many years. As for me, I took it upon myself to keep Yakama's mind occupied with reminiscences of the old days, so by the time that we had reached the hotel, he had pulled himself together. Because of the increased heavy traffic on the telephone exchange between the two countries, it was to be almost an hour before I was finally connected to Marlene in Los Angeles. I updated her on the tragic happening and to explain to her what Billy's role had been in the industry.

That evening, most of the company held a wake for Billy with Victor and Yakama organising a collection for Billy's widow. Apart from the booze, there were also three foot-stomping fiddlers supplying a continuous background of country and western music. It hadn't taken long for the local señoritas, to get wind of the wake and pretty soon, the hotel bar was not only full but was also reverberating to the sound of music which coupled with alcohol, produced as the evening wore on, line dancing, hoe downs, Mexican flamencos and I swear to God, even Indian rain dances! My compardres, Gilbert, Tony and Pedro from the Mexican brigade had joined forces with the stuntmen to create a school of hard drinkers who gave no quarter. Everything was up for grabs that night; politics, old-time Hollywood, sex and who could drink who under the table!

Eventually, I began to lose a sense of time because I was beginning to hold onto the bar for support, but I assume it was probably around midnight when the three of us, Victor Fleming, Tony Gaudio and myself arrived at a mutual decision to call it a night and retire as gracefully as possible. But before we left, we deposited the remains of any cash that we had left on us into a large Mexican cooking pot which somehow or the other had been acquired. It was already filled with dimes and quarters, bills of various denominations plus quite a few cheques from the senior members of the cast and crew, myself included. Boy, did I feel sorry for the guys behind the bar having to deal with filmland's stuntmen and hardened drinkers. The three of us didn't get off scot-free either, for as we attempted to leave, we were being offered yet one more drink for the road so that by the time we reached the hotel lobby, the three of us more or less fell into the elevator. Anyway, the last words that Victor said to me that night were that he was going to put back shooting until two o'clock that afternoon so that it would give the company more time in which to pull themselves together. Have you ever tried to put a key in a lock after having consumed a lot of booze? It's not easy, you know. Somehow, I managed to accomplish that simple manoeuvre and I thanked God that there were no news photographers hiding in corners, snapping away, for I could just imagine the Hollywood tabloids making it front page news.

Fortunately, as I became older, I did not tend to suffer to much from hangovers on the morning after, so that when I finally arose from a good night's sleep, I was soon able to pull myself together with a brisk shower and shave. Then it was off downstairs for a hearty breakfast. Although it was past ten in the morning, there still weren't many cast members in attendance and what few there were, looked decidedly hungover. As soon as I had finished breakfast, I strolled over to reception to see if any messages had been left for me. There were none, but I did learn that Victor Fleming and Tony Gaudio had already left for the location. However, before he left, Victor had ensured that there would be a studio car waiting for me outside the hotel. Putting on my sunglasses and carrying a small holdall, containing my dog-eared script plus other small essentials, I ventured outside the cool confines of the hotel into the blazing sun and quickly located my car. Although there was a couple of hours still to go before the commencement of the day's shooting schedule, when I finally arrived on location, considering the size of the wake from the night before, there was surprisingly, quite a big percentage of crew already hard at work. I quickly located Victor, deep in conversation with a mug of coffee in one hand and the sheath of memos in the other, involved in an animated conversation with his secretary and script girl. However, before I joined their company, I was enticed by the aroma of coffee from the catering wagon situated nearby and once I had availed myself of a mug, I wandered back towards Victor, who was certainly glad to see me.

"Morning, Gunther. I am pleased to see that you have got here earlier than anticipated. I was about to send for you as most of the crew and the on-call actors have already turned in and as the weather today is so good for photography, I have decided to bring the shooting schedule forward by an hour."

"That is good news, Victor," I replied. "In which case, I will immediately rush away for makeup and a quick change into costume. Just send a runner to me when you are ready."

"Before you go, Gunther," Victor said, "You will be pleased to know that amongst the memos that I have received this morning from Warners says that they will be picking up the tab for Billy's funeral and that the amount raised last night for his widow came to one thousand five-hundred dollars which will be sent to her immediately along with a letter of condolences from the cast and crew."

As I made my way to my trailer, I was filled with both with sadness and pride; sadness for the occasion and pride in the knowledge that Billy's widow would not feel alone and unsupported and that Billy's friends back home would gather around her and protect her. Incidentally, according to the coroner's report, Billy died from a broken neck which was attributed to a freak accident when his horse was spooked. By Friday morning, Victor Fleming brought the location shoot back on schedule. Everything had run smoothly and the weather remained perfect for the rest of the week. There was also a feeling of determination amongst the crew to make the action sequences in this movie the best. It was as if we all wanted Billy to look down on us and be proud of his last movie.

I was certainly glad to be back home in Los Angeles. I had never experienced location filming before having been previously confined to studio sets for all my past movie productions. I can't say that I would be too eager to do it again. It is true that from my recent experience, you had the companionship of your fellow cast members. However, as outdoor location work was confined mainly to action movies, the cast was usually all-male which, in turn, meant most evenings of heavy drinking. It also could be a lonely life filled with soul destroying days spent sitting around whilst waiting for camera set-ups. There was also the temperamental weather to contend with and a constant diet of greasy food. I suppose the truth of it was that I didn't like being away from Marlene and our daughters.

Chapter 20

Oscars and Bonds

The next few weeks were spent working flat-out and I thanked the Lord that my agent had the foresight to have inserted into my contract the stipulation that I would finish work at four o'clock in the afternoon. I was already aware of Warners' reputation for treating their actors like cattle and working them around the clock, so as far as I was concerned, working ten hours a day was enough. The big social event for Marlene and I was the Oscars ceremony, held at the end of February in the Biltmore bowl room in the Biltmore Hotel. I had been nominated in the Best Actor category for my part in *Marrakesh*. In all honesty, I really didn't think I was worthy of the accolade. My part wasn't as well written as it should have been and although I had given it my best shot, it simply wasn't good enough. It was, however, a great honour to be nominated and the Oscars ceremony which had grown considerably in importance since its inception, was the number one Hollywood social event of the year, full of glitz and glamour and it would give Marlene the opportunity so soon after her pregnancy to feel glamorous once more.

When the evening had finally arrived, I was already downstairs waiting for the studio car to take us to the Biltmore and Marlene, like all women, was still putting the finishing touches to her makeup and wardrobe. Of course, meanwhile, I was waiting downstairs, well in to my second large whiskey which was necessary to steady my nerves. All I have to say is that it was well worth the wait for as she descended the stairs, she looked a million dollars. She was dressed in a sea blue taffeta evening gown set off by emerald necklace and finished off by a white mink stole. I quietly stepped up to her at the foot of the stairs and gazing into her eyes remarked.

''Wow! Are you going to give those girls at the Oscars a lot of competition tonight sweetheart? I may be the one that is up for a Best Actor award, but all the attention is going to be focused on you.''

''Now don't you go fretting, Gunty. I'm just going along for the good time to be had. I don't need a little gold statuette to prove that my husband is the greatest. I already know that.''

We were soon joined by Livy, Mary and Jose, our Filipino houseboy and his wife Consuela, who were all waiting to wish me luck. Mary McConachie was so overcome by Marlene that she couldn't help blurting out in her Irish brogue that she had never seen such a beautiful creature in all her life and then promptly did a small curtsy which had us all laughing and as Livy gave me a peck on the cheek, she told me that as soon as we had left, they would be tuning in to the NBC radio broadcast live from the Biltmore. Once we had pulled away from the house, we soon reached downtown Los Angeles, but it was a different story when we reached Grand Avenue where the Biltmore was situated, as there was a long line of cars backed up waiting to unload their passengers which left us no choice but to relax in the back of the limousine while we waited our turn. Marlene held my hand as we inched slowly forward to our destination. Eventually, as we reached the head of the queue, we could see a crowd of people consisting of stars, photographers and radio presenters all milling around on a huge red carpet which on both sides, was roped off and contained bleachers for the fans. It was only when we finally arrived and our passenger door was opened by a greeter that the hubbub hit us.

As I guided Marlene onto the red carpet, we were enveloped by a cacophony of cheering fans, the shouted greetings from attendees to each other and the pleas from photographers for just one more picture. There were camera bulbs going off from every direction and as soon as we had stepped onto the red carpet, we were quickly surrounded by press photographers busy snapping away at us as we stood there. I would say, on reflection, because of Marlene. I was merely an appendage as we were hit by a barrage of flash photography. We had no sooner navigated that gauntlet, than I was shaking the outstretched hands of the fans and signing the many programmes being thrust under my nose, which also provided me an opportunity to speak to a few of them. Then, we stepped into the foyer of the Biltmore Hotel to be met by an NBC radio commentator who remarked on how lovely Marlene looked and asked me what my chances were for winning the Oscar. Once we were past that obstacle, we slowly made our way into the

Biltmore, mingling with fellow guests and nominees, stopping briefly to exchange greetings with Walter Brennan and his wife Margaret and wishing him the best of luck for his nomination as Best Supporting Actor for his role as Judge Roy Bean in *The Westerner*.

Once inside the room, we made our way to our table which was near the front of the podium from which the Oscars were to be handed out. Our table was occupied by Warners personnel with their partners, which meant, of course, Harry Warner himself, Michael Curtis, Victor Fleming, James Stevenson, yours truly, Peter Lorrie, Bette Davis, William Wyler and Barbara O'Neill, all of whom, with me included of course, were in contention with other studio artists for Oscars. Jack Warner, as head of the studio dominated the table as a king would, with his courtiers. I had never been prouder of Marlene than that evening, for she kept everybody's spirits high, including Jack Warner's who was eagerly anticipating a clutch of Oscars for his studio. My feeling was that only Bette Davies and William Wyler would bring home the bacon for their film, *The Letter*.

As soon as the food was out of the way and the booze was being served discreetly, the proceedings then began. The first person to open the proceedings was the president of the Academy of Motion Pictures and Science, Walter Wanger. After a brief synopsis of the aims of the Academy, he then introduced the President of the United States, Franklin Delano Roosevelt, via a recorded film message, extolling the virtues of the American film industry. Next, Walter Wanger introduced the toastmaster for the evening, Bob Hope, who strode on to the musical arrangement of his signature tune, *Thanks for the Memory* and he certainly bought the evening alive with his repartee, after which it was down to the serious business.

Unfortunately for Jack Warner, the only award for the studio that night was for Lawrence Butler for Special Effects: the surprise upset was that Bette Davis lost out to Ginger Rogers and that the other Warners hopeful, Barbara O'Neill, up for Best Supporting Actress, lost too Jane Darwell, for *The Grapes of Wrath*. As for myself, it certainly didn't come as any surprise when Jimmy Stewart won for *The Philadelphia Story*. It was a much-deserved honour and in truth, it hadn't been my best shot. As far as Jack Warner was concerned, he took the results in his stride, taking the attitude that the studio being honoured for so many Oscar nominations was reward in itself. In any case, there was always next year, a view that Marlene agreed with, whispering to me, to just turn up for work give it my best shot, collect my paycheck and I would get the brass ring in the end.

The rest of the evening was spent pleasantly with Marlene and I exchanging greetings with our far more relaxed contemporaries. This was the first major social event where Marlene was seen by the cream of Hollywood society. I suppose you would call it her baptism of fire before being accepted into the exclusive Hollywood wives club. I exchanged gossip with Barbara Stanwyck and her husband Robert Taylor. There was a rumour circulating around the studio that she and I were about to be paired in a comedy about a stripper who seeks refuge with a group of professors to escape her gangster boyfriend. We both thought that it was a great idea and hoped that it would be green-lit by the studio. One girl who instantly bonded with Marlene was Carole Lombard, the golden girl of screw-ball comedy, who got on like a house on fire with her. I think because they both shared the same zany humour and vaguely resembled each other, it rather left her husband Clark Gable and myself somewhat on the side lines, as they laughed and chatted. Nevertheless, it gave Gable and I an opportunity to talk and I was taken aback somewhat by some of his remarks. For example, despite being voted the King of Hollywood and forever being associated with his role as Rhett Butler in *Gone with the Wind*, he was not happy at the way MGM persisted in casting him in all his movies as a sex symbol. Anyway, we parted that evening with an invite to a Gable-Lombard cook-out the following weekend, where I hoped he and I would continue the conversation about our careers. After accepting many commiserations for not winning the Oscar, Marlene and I decided to call it a night. After spending five hours in that atmosphere of showbiz, glamour and the glorification of self-importance, combined with alcohol, all that we wanted to do was to get home to the babies, kick off our shoes and relax with a nightcap.

The following weeks seemed to fly by. My weekdays were very busy finishing *Conquest of the Sun*, as our new movie was being titled, on the sound stages at Warners and leading a fairly hectic social life, as Marlene was considered a much sought-after guest. It didn't do my ego much good but secretly, I was very proud of her. She certainly helped me considerably by accompanying me to many pro-British gatherings where I would do the talking and she would supply the glamour.

On the home front, I was overjoyed in March when President Roosevelt announced the Lend-Lease programme by which America would supply Britain with ships, supplies and aircraft. Within hours of the announcement on the radio, I received a phone call from David Hislop at the British Consulate thanking me for contributing to that decision. The Nazi blitzkrieg of Britain appeared to have abated, although British civilians were still suffering casualties and the cities were suffering considerable bomb damage. It was not nearly as intense as it had been the year before. It also seemed that Hitler had postponed his plans for a long-awaited invasion of the British Isles. According to David Hislop, that decision had given Britain the breathing space it needed to start rebuilding its armed forces and replace the material lost at Dunkirk.

Due to the Lend-Lease Act, Hitler was now facing a stronger and more deadly adversary. At present, the only active theatre of war was North Africa, where we had soon put an end to Mussolini's grandiose plans for the conquest of Libya and Egypt by forcing the Italian forces into retreat. Unfortunately, that victory had its downside insofar as it forced Hitler to come to the aid of his humiliated ally. He had dispatched an army to North Africa under the command of a German general by the name of Erwin Rommel whose army was already being known by the general public as the Africa Korps and it appeared that Germany had the advantage at the moment and was regaining lost Italian territory. David Hislop felt, however, that Churchill and the British government were far more optimistic now than they had been since 1940. It was Churchill's opinion that although the British Empire faced many defeats to come, the tide was slowly turning in our favour. As Hitler had been forced to intervene in North Africa, he now faced a war on two fronts and now that Britain had the availability of America's vast industrial muscle, there were signs that Hitler was being placed at a disadvantage for the first time.

As far as the domestic front was concerned, Marlene's mother and father were being kept busy in Britain contributing to the war effort and her brothers, Hansi and Lothar, still visited us from time to time and appeared to be working permanently at a place called Los Alamos. We were none the wiser as to what they did as they always clammed up when asked, but life appeared to be good for them as they appeared to be both well and prosperous and having inherited their parents' good looks. The New Mexico climate had turned them into bronze gods. When it came to the rest of Marlene's European family the news was not so good. Despite some very discreet enquiries by the American Embassy both in Berlin and the Hague, all we could find out was that a high percentage of Berlin Jews were being shipped out of the capital many of whom were being resettled in Warsaw. As for her sister, Greta, there was no trace of her whereabouts in Holland and as much as Marlene maintained a brave face, I knew that she was worried sick. I told her that there was no need for her to punish herself for she was in no position to be able to do anything about it. At least, she had the knowledge that both her parents and her brothers were safe. Despite her obvious concerns for Greta and Philip, she had to devote her energies to the upbringing of her babies. As I knew she would, with her usual level-headed approach to life, Marlene just tucked her worries into a mental chest of drawers situated in the recess of her mind to be retrieved when necessary.

I finally completed my part in *Conquest of the Sun* by the end of March with the film completed by the first week of April. Not so long after, I had the opportunity of attending a private screening of the finished product at Warners. My reaction to it was as expected for although it was a full-blown action epic and would fall into the category of a road picture and would no doubt earn the studio a considerable profit, it had nothing special about it that the moviegoing public would remember and certainly, my performance appeared dull with my character badly underwritten. As an actor, if you worked at Warners, you weren't given much opportunity to sit around all day long watching your navel. I was quickly given a new assignment which I approved of. It had a strong script by Billy Wilder and Charles Bracket and was based on a short story by Edgar Allen Poe. Once again, the film would be directed by my old friend, Mike Curtiz and the final clincher was that it had a great supporting cast including Peter Lorre, Sidney Greenstreet, Zachary Scott and last, but not least, the beautiful Irish actress, Geraldine Fitzgerald.

Marlene and I, along with most of the European actors in Hollywood, received earth shattering news this June. Hitler had unleashed a full-scale invasion of Russia, taking the Russian dictator Stalin, completely by surprise for despite the two countries having signed a non-aggression pact, Hitler had, for some time, been preparing a covert sneak attack on his ally under the codename of Operation Barbarossa. According to David Hislop, the impending invasion had been no secret to Britain and that Stalin had received many warnings but had chosen to ignore them. David was delighted with the news for this meant that Hitler had now opened up a second front by attacking Russia in the East, a war according to David that he could not possibly win and also, in the meantime, one that would give Britain a greater breathing space to gather her strength together with which to eventually defeat Hitler. The other good news that occurred at the end of May had been the sinking of the German battleship *Bismarck* in the North Sea and coupled with the previous loss of the German pocket battleship, *Graf Spey* outside of Montevideo, had put paid to any further serious threat from Hitler's Navy. The only downside to the encouraging news was the defeat of our soldiers in Greece, giving Hitler yet again another piece of territory.

Our two daughters, Inger and Kim, were growing rapidly and were already displaying individual personalities. Inger was physically the plumper of the two and already had great strength in her chubby little legs. As for Kim, she would laugh and chuckle at anything, whether it was pulling faces at her or making funny noises. One of the things that they did like was being taken into the swimming pool at the shallow end and being held in our arms whilst they exercised their arms and legs splashing with the water. As for the rest of our domestic life, things could not be better. I had hired a Filipino gardener, Max, with the task to revitalise the grounds with a programme of re-planting and to give the pond a new lease of life by restocking it with various fish. During the few months that he had been employed, he had transformed the slightly run-down estate into a thing of beauty with the emphasis on green vegetation and palm trees.

Marlene was never happier than when she was working alongside Max or cutting flowers for the house. She had also accumulated a small circle of girlfriends, so was forever organising poolside brunches, a hobby which gave her an immense pleasure.

She also enjoyed tennis and always ensured that the court was well looked after. I suppose we Europeans, on arriving in California, were very quickly seduced by its climate, our first priorities being owning your very own swimming pool and being the proud possessor of a tennis court. It was during this time that Livy decided that she would take the plunge and become a property owner. I think that she probably realised it would be nice to go home at the end of the day to your own little house and close the front door to the world. She had located a bungalow at Santa Monica beach very close to the Santa Monica stair which also happened to be a local landmark and was considered a keep fit challenge by the local community and beyond, in either walking or running its entire length. It also had one other notable feature in so far as that I recognised the stair from a Laurel and Hardy short called *The Music Box*, the plot which had the pair of them attempting to deliver an upright piano to a house situated halfway up the stair. Livy had fallen in love with it, so I was happy to underwrite the mortgage, thereby making her the proud owner. Of course, it goes without saying that Marlene and Livy spent a lot of time together busily scouring local antique and furniture stores and by the time they had finished in their quest, they had turned the bungalow into a small piece of home in Britain and so, it now became an everyday ritual of Livy arriving and departing in her roadster always to the sound of her honking horn.

It was in September that one of my dreams was fulfilled. True to form, as I had completed my previous assignment, Warners immediately pencilled me in for a psychological drama about a mental hospital with a provisional title, *White Corridors*. I think they visualised this intended masterpiece to be an answer to MGM's *Grand Hotel*, but this time, set in a hospital. It was Warners' intention for this to be one of their big movies of the year and had bestowed a large budget upon it, as well as the cream of Hollywood's supporting actors. One of my dreams was to come true, as they included Claude Rains, an actor so good at his craft that he was considered amongst Hollywood film studios as being classified as a star character actor. An Englishman by birth, he had been born in London where eventually, he became both an actor and a drama teacher. It wasn't until he was in his early forties that he finally made his début in Hollywood in 1933, playing the invisible man. Essentially, it was his voice that propelled him into stardom as he wasn't seen for most of that film. For me, it was an honour to be sharing a movie with him after idolising him from the stalls of many a West End theatre production and I knew that any ability that I had as an actor would be fully tested as Claude was noted for not taking any prisoners when it came to scene stealing. Apart from Olivia de Havilland, who would be my female co-star, there would also be two other great scene stealers, Charles Coburn and Raymond Massey, plus another young actor that Warners was grooming for stardom by the name of Ronald Reagan. Altogether, with such a great cast, the movie had every possibility of being a challenge, although the script needed a lot of work. I had a distinct feeling that the cast alone would turn dross into gold.

From the start of the movie in September, to its finish in November, it turned out to be an exhilarating period in my life. For a start, it gave me the opportunity to enjoy a stable family life. Finishing shooting late afternoon every day allowed me the opportunity to spend quality time with my family. It was amazing how quickly the twins were growing. They weren't far off being a year old and had quickly discovered the joys of mobility and now that they were crawling, it was becoming a full-time job for we adults to keep an eye on them. Thank God for the playpen is what I say, at least it contained them in one place, even though Inger was forever trying to break out and scamper off to greener fields. As for Marlene and myself, we were both happy and life was good, not that we wanted to dwell upon that fact, for life has a habit of throwing you a curved ball and everything could change in the blink of an eye.

Working on the set during the day was also a joy. I was quite right in my summation of Claude Rains, for in my scenes with him, I had to pull out every trick in the book to prevent him from dominating my performance. Between takes, it was entirely different. He had recently purchased a farm in Pennsylvania and was forever reading and discussing agriculture and husbandry. I suppose, like all townies, there was an urge to get away from the hurly-burly of city life and enjoy the pastoral countryside. It really was a privilege to be able to spend quality time in conversation not only with him but also with my other two fellow actors. For instance, I hadn't realised that Raymond Massey, not only being Canadian by birth, was also related to the Massey family that had produced the world-famous Massey farm tractor and that he had an older brother who was heavily involved in Canadian politics. Ray had decided he wanted to be an actor rather than to stay in the family business. Subsequently, he had come to America via Britain, where he had struggled for many years learning his craft before finally earning recognition and fame on Broadway and earning the respect of the American theatre world by playing, of all people, the American president, Abraham Lincoln, who he had gone on to portray in film. As for Charles Coburn, he had made his name playing irascible millionaires, judges and grandfathers, all with a softer side and to be honest with you, he wasn't much different off-camera. As for my co-star, Olivia de Havilland, she intended to be treated as a favourite amongst the rest of us and she too wasn't much different from her screen persona, although she could be quite direct with you when she wanted to be. We all teased her about carrying a torch for Errol Flynn, the swashbuckling actor whom she had been paired with eight times. She always became indignant and vehemently denied the accusation but explained that there was no doubt that both she and Errol had a lot of chemistry between them which is what made them such a popular romantic team with the public. All in all, it was a pleasure being part of the crew and if all my other future film work were to be like this one, I would be a happy man.

By the time that we had celebrated Thanksgiving on the last Thursday of November, I had completed *White Corridors*. I was in the happy position to enjoy all of December with my family as the studio had no immediate projects lined up for me until January. Marlene and Livy immediately began planning for the Christmas festivities and organising all the Christmas invitations both the ones we were sending out and those we were receiving. On the morning of the seventh of December, I spent the first few hours with Livy going through a stack of business papers that I had received from my management team that required my signatures. I was pleased to note that my earnings for 1941 had reached one-hundred and eighty-five thousand dollars, before tax, of course. Nevertheless, I asked Livy to make a note to arrange an appointment with my accountants in January to explore ways of investing any surplus income. We were in the midst of a conversation on that topic when Marlene suddenly came through the office door looking very white-faced and agitated. Speaking with a slight tremor, she said to the pair of us.

"News is just coming through on the radio that apparently, the Japanese have attacked the American fleet at Pearl Harbour. So far, official reports state that there has been considerable damage to the fleet coupled with heavy losses to naval personnel. On the evidence supplied so far, the radio commentator had gone on to say that it had all the hallmarks of a surprise attack carried out by the Japanese Air Force."

All of us including, the staff, went into the lounge to listen to the NBC broadcast, but it wasn't until late afternoon that a true picture began to emerge. The Japanese government, it seems, before formally declaring a state of war between the two nations, had mounted a sneak attack on the American naval base at Pearl Harbour. The operation had been carried out by a squadron of Japanese aircraft carriers who had launched a series of air-strikes against the unsuspecting American Navy and its port facilities, resulting in the sinking of the battleship *Arizona* as well as three cruisers and three destroyers plus the destruction of one hundred and eighty-four aircraft on the ground. The loss of life had been horrendous with over two-thousand military personnel having been killed. It was a stunned household that went to bed that night as I'm sure was the case across the length and breadth of America. The following day, President Roosevelt announced to Congress that America was now at war with Japan and that the seventh of December, the day on which Pearl Harbour was attacked, would go down in history as a day of infamy. Within days, the mighty American continent began flexing its industrial muscle and even before compulsory call up was introduced, American men were rushing to the colours. On the eleventh of December, Hitler and Mussolini honoured their pact with Japan and formally declared war on America. Now, we were all in it together and that night, Marlene, Livy and I stayed up into the early hours of the morning discussing the situation and what we could possibly do to contribute to the war effort. When we finally went to bed, the general feeling was of euphoria because we felt that this was the beginning of the end, for even though there would be inevitably be a few setbacks the Axis powers would eventually be beaten.

Because the world was apparently being relentlessly driven on over the edge of the abyss, despite our efforts, Christmas proved to be a rather subdued affair. Even though we celebrated the birth of the twins in January earlier in 1941, it was difficult to believe that the year had already gone past. I would imagine that most families across the United States were coming to terms with the knowledge that their menfolk were likely to be put into harm's way in the foreseeable future. From what I sensed at the time, the nation was enraged by the sneak attack carried out by the Japanese on the United States Navy, the general feeling being that whatever the cost or sacrifice, that Japan must be punished and brought to its knees. Like most British people, Marlene and I were already feeling the effects of war and even though the average American would be now sharing that burden with us, it would be hypocritical for us to say that we weren't glad that we no longer stood alone and that our American cousins had now joined us in the fight against the Axis powers. I believe that the citizens of America from coast-to-coast, from city to town, from farmland to mountains were preparing themselves for defeats and for the sacrifices that would entail but, in the end, they were determined that the joint Allied crusade would eventually defeat the Axis of evil.

Meanwhile, the Hollywood dream factory started to mobilise itself for the coming battles. That manifested itself in the 1942 Oscar ceremonies, when it went from glitz and glamour to a more sombre mood, in keeping with the times, with the girls dressing in two-piece suits or dresses and us fellows in double-breasted suits. Jimmy Stewart set the tone of the evening, by presenting Joan Fontaine the Oscar for Best Actress, dressed in the uniform of the United States Air Force and even Donald Crisp received his Oscar for Best Supporting Actor wearing his reserve army officers uniform and finally, Gary Cooper received tumultuous applause when he received the Oscar for Best Actor for his betrayal of Sergeant York the hero from the First World War, with the film of the same name picking up the Oscar for Best Picture. The film proved immensely popular throughout America and Britain, in reflecting the people's defiance and the urge to strike back. Elsewhere in Hollywood during the coming months, many of its stars and technicians were joining the colours. These included Robert Taylor, Tyrone Power, Mickey Rooney, Robert Montgomery, John Payne and on the wings of tragedy, Clark

Gable, who lost his beloved wife Carole Lombard in a plane crash whilst she was raising war bonds.

I had applied to return to Britain to serve her in a more active role, but the British Foreign Office had advised David Hislop, the Los Angeles Consulate that I was to remain in in the United States. Their advice was because of my age and my married status. I was to remain in America flying the flag for Britain through radio, theatre and films. Marlene and I started contributing to the war effort. Marlene threw herself head-first into organising with co-founders Bette Davis and John Garfield, a rest and relaxation centre for all members of the armed services passing through Los Angeles on their way to or from theatres of war. It was to be free and would supply food, dancing and entertainment and would be manned entirely by volunteers from the film industry. This would include stars giving their services either as waitresses, bus boys and girls, kitchen hands, hostesses and greeters with the musical entertainment supplied by the big bands of the day and guest vocal artists such as Ginny Sims, Dinah Shore, Doris Day and the Andrew Sisters. It was to prove a project that she firmly believed in and as the war progressed, took up a considerable amount of her time. Even I would accompany her on occasions and do my bit, serving food in the canteen not just to American servicemen but to all the Allied forces from around the world who were just in transit.

Warners had released me for three weeks to contribute my services to an episodic movie in support of Britain. It was to be called *For Ever and a Day*, a story about an English house situated in London owned by two families over the last several centuries. It featured a large cast of British expatiates such as Ronald Coleman, Claude Rains and Cedric Hardwick and a young American star, Robert Cummings, who acted as an anchor bringing the story lines together by coming to London to sell the family home. The film then told the story of the various family occupants through the centuries in flashbacks. I then volunteered my services to sell war bonds on a special train that Warners had put together called the Hollywood Caravan. The train would carry Warners stars through many states between Los Angeles and Washington, DC, stopping at large cities along the way for the express purpose of selling war bonds. Inevitably at each stop, we would progress through the city in question in a caravan of vehicles for the benefit of its citizens.

Several of us, like Charles Boyer, James Cagney and Jimmy Durante, took the ride from start to finish, whilst many others joined the train along the way whenever their commitments made it possible. As usual, when there was a group of actors, there was alcohol and this was no exception. The most overcrowded coach every evening was the one containing the bar, where all of us took the opportunity of unwinding in privacy away from the public eye. It was there, four days into the journey, that I came across Trixie Montano who had joined the train that day with Greer Garson. The years had treated her well since we parted. She had gone from a guileless young starlet to a sophisticated woman of the world as well as becoming one of Hollywood's big box office stars. In the years that I had been away in Europe, she had built up a solid fan base partnering Gene Frederic, Hollywood's top dancer, in a series of musicals which had become very popular with cinema audiences. However, it seems that she had sensed a wind of change in her career for she gradually started easing herself into straight dramatic parts, so successfully that she had all but abandoned Hollywood musicals. From what I had heard on the Hollywood grapevine, it seemed that she could be up for an Oscar nomination for Best Actress in the next Oscar ceremony.

I was having a conversation with fellow actor, Walter Abel, when both she and Greer Garson swept into the refreshment coach and immediately, she came right over and after embracing me, apologised for not having been able to accept Marlene's previous invitation for dinner due to a heavy work schedule. As Trixie showed no inclination to leave our company, Greer Garson decided to move on. I admit that it was very pleasant reminiscing about old times with her and as the evening wore on, I began to find it disturbing that Trixie was awakening in me emotions for her that had long since faded. It didn't help to be trapped in the close confines of a train with your ex-lover, who you had nearly married so many years ago, but as luck would have it, I managed to extricate myself from what could have become an embarrassing situation, by Greer Garson returning with a group of friends. I was able to make my way back to my state room while Trixie's attention was distracted elsewhere in the club car. Mind you, I felt that somehow, I wasn't emotionally out of the woods yet by any means for I knew that sooner or later, the moment of truth would arrive between Trixie and myself as there were still four days to go, before we arrived in Washington to be formally welcomed to the White House by President Roosevelt. I knew that tomorrow morning, our next stop was to be Kansas City, where we were all due to take part in a motorised caravan to drive down Main Street, after which booths had been set up outside the town hall for us to sign war bonds to the public. We would then finish up posing for propaganda photos and with all that to come. I put out the bedside light and settled down for a much-needed night's rest.

I was awakened by our coach attendant knocking on the door telling me that we would be arriving at Kansas City within the hour. I washed and shaved and having selected a matching tie and suit, made a dash for the restaurant car so that I could at least have some coffee and toast. The restaurant car was only half full, so I had no problem in finding a table and neither did I have to wait long for my order. I was halfway through eating my toast when I was joined by another pair of late arrivals, Mr Yankee Doodle Dandy himself, James Cagney and his screen nemesis, Pat O'Brien, both of whom, along with their fellow Irishmen, Frank McHugh, had been socialising the previous night in the club coach. I suspect that quite a few of the male contingent, including myself, were suffering from sore heads this morning and if I am honest about it, several female stars would also be reaching for the Alka-Seltzer bottle. By the time, the three of us had finished off several pots of coffee, the train was beginning to brake as it approached Kansas City. As we glided to a halt, we could plainly see out of the restaurant car window, literally a horde of newspaper photographers, reporters, studio news cameras and personnel from Warners publicity department.

It took a hell of a long time for us to disembark from the train. First, we were formed into groups of six celebrities with three girls in front standing on the steps of the coach and three male stars standing behind them in the doorway, all of us with fixed smiles on our faces. My small group consisted of Gary Cooper, Jimmy Cagney and myself with the female contingent comprising Barbara Stanwyck, Olivia De Havilland and Ida Lupino. I suppose if you are doing the same thing day after day, it does become a little cheesy. However, it was all for the war effort and our lads overseas would be suffering a darn sight more than we were. Once we had been filmed or photographed, we were herded out of the station where there were a line of open topped cars awaiting us. I finished up sharing a coupé with Trixie Montano cuddling up to me on the back seat with Dennis Morgan, Warners' popular male star sitting up front. Once everybody had climbed into their allocated cars, we were off down the main street of Kansas City. Heading the cavalcade was a flat-top lorry carrying a combo of musicians, who at that precise moment, were playing the popular tune, *Hooray for Hollywood*. Both sides of Main Street were packed with fans and as the parade proceeded on its merry way, we were greeted with a cacophony of applause and cheers, the biggest roar of approval being reserved for the leading car, carrying Jimmy Cagney and Merle Oberon.

Eventually, we came to a stop outside the town hall and were marshalled into the main lobby which had been decorated with flags, pennants and stalls with 'Buy Bonds' logos plastered all over them. Once we had sat down at our designated stall, the general public were allowed in and immediately began forming a queue in front of their favourite movie star. I don't think it mattered whether we were popular or not. What was important was just the fact we'd stepped out of the silver screen and were there before them in real life. When it came to giving, the American public proved itself no slouch. United States war bonds came in several price categories, the lowest and most popular being the twenty-five-dollar bond which you could purchase for eighteen dollars and seventy-five cents and in ten years, if you wished to cash it in, you would have made six dollars and twenty-five cents in interest. The Treasury Department, it appears, had set itself a target for 1942 of eight billion dollars-worth of sales in war bonds and so far, in only the first six months of the year, six billion had already been raised. Judging by the public turnout today, I would imagine that the target would have been exceeded nationwide by the end of September.

It so happens that both Trixie and Dennis would be accompanying Glenn Miller and his orchestra that afternoon in a special matinee at the local Warners movie theatre. Laurel and Hardy would be appearing on the same bill, providing the comedy routines and finally, the vocalists were to be Ginny Simms and Dinah Shore. Being at a loose end, a few other stars and I went along to give support by watching the show from the wings. The movie palace was packed floor-to-ceiling with a full house of exuberant movie fans and as soon as Glenn Miller appeared with his band to open the show playing his signature tune, *In the Mood*. The audience went wild and their welcome was so noisy that I'm sure that you could hear it in the next state! After playing a medley of top hits, Ginny Simms and Dinah Shore accompanied by Tex Beneke, Glenn Miller's saxophonist and male vocalist and the popular backing group, *The Modenairs*, launched into a medley of Glenn Miller's hits including *String of Pearls, Moonlight Serenade* and *The Chattanooga Choo Choo*. If I were ever in a position in the future to look back on this moment in time, I am sure that it would rank as one my special memories of the Second World War.

Whilst I stood in the wings of Kansas City's premier movie house, watching the cream of America's popular music and dance industry performing to middle America, whose husbands and sons were either being drafted or were already, in transit to overseas theatres of war, I don't think any of us in that movie theatre that afternoon were not unaware that many of their loved ones would not be coming home and that sacrifices would be made. However, just for a few hours, the outside world was forgotten as the movie audience responded to the magic of the music. The audience had risen to its feet clapping to the beat of the music with even some jiving in the aisles and when the show was finally bought to a close with a rendition of the *Star-Spangled Banner*, sung by the coir of the University of Missouri, Kansas City, listening to the whole audience accompanying the choir left me in no doubt that Mr Hitler, the Emperor Hirohito and Benito Mussolini better start looking for somewhere to hide.

As soon as the show was over, we were all transported back to the railway depot where our victory train was waiting to transport us to our next venue. It came as a shock to see so many fans waiting to give us a send-off. The police and railway officials had been forced to create a neutral zone on the track so that we had access to the train. It took a little while to reach it as our progress was considerably slowed down with the constant demand for autographs. Once on board, most of us trooped through to the observation car and as the train finally started to pull out, as many of us as possible stood on the observation platform waving goodbye. As soon as Kansas City faded from view, many of us took the opportunity of winding down with an early evening cocktail. The occasion also provided me with the opportunity of meeting with some of my European ex-pats, three of which I noticed sitting at a table in the observation car as I stepped through from the platform. I had instantly recognised Paul Henried from the last time we had met at one of our weekend parties back in Britain. I also knew that he had just completed a movie with Bette Davis titled *Now Voyager* and judging from the scuttlebutt feeding back from the early previews, he could be the next continental heartthrob. The older man needed no introduction for it was none other than Jean Gabin, the great French actor who had just escaped from Paris by the skin of his teeth and was known as the French Spencer Tracy. The third and youngest man present had escaped from Austria and had recently just completed a small but important part in a Greer Garson movie over at MGM and introduced himself as Helmut Dantine.

It didn't take long for the conversation to come around to the occupation of Europe. Jean Gabin was rather forthright in his views, particularly on the Hollywood style of film making. He made no bones about the fact that as soon as the Allies landed on the European continent, he would be going back to join the free French under General de Gaul. Eventually, the desire for a good meal gave me the opportunity to excuse myself from the present company, just in time I might add, as the Warners' starlets were beginning to hover around the tables and it was becoming obvious to me that quite a few of my fellow thespians would be forgoing the restaurant car and instead would be heading for the bar and a sandwich. After a sluice and a change of shirt, I made my way back along the train to the restaurant car and as luck would have it, as it was getting late, the restaurant manager found me a vacant table. It was the first time since this morning that I had a little time to myself so whilst I waited for the dining car steward to take my order, I had the luxury of sitting back in my seat with a pre-dinner Jack Daniels in front of me, looking out of the window as the landscape bathed in a sunset glow flew by me.

Thoughts flew through my head like gadflies as I contemplated the events of the past eight months since the attack on Pearl Harbour. We British had lost Singapore after being defeated by a numerically smaller Japanese force. Whilst in North Africa, the German general, Irwin Rommel and his Africa Korps, had driven us back almost to the gates of Cairo and our American cousins had fared no better in the Pacific having been driven out by the Japanese from the Philippines and the Solomon islands, with the Japanese even posing a threat to the Australian continent. I would say that 1942 was proving a bad year for the Allies with only the invasion of Russia by the Germans providing a ray of light. Hitler's boast that Russia would be defeated within six months was beginning to sound hollow. Russia's greatest weapon, the harsh winter, had already brought the spectacular German advances to a halt, catching them totally unprepared for the severe sub-zero temperatures and vicious snowstorms and to add further insult, had caught Germany left-footed by throwing in fresh armies against them in the spring.

As far as our private life was concerned, it was proving to be both one of joy and melancholy to Marlene and myself. The joy was in watching the girls grow, as they were now in their toddling stage and were into everything, having to be constantly watched as their curiosity drove them into new adventures. Marlene's mum and dad were managing very well back at Falcon House and her brothers kept in touch on a regular basis despite living and working in this mysterious place called Los Alamos. However, a cloud of despondency was always in the background. We both knew that a lack of contact from any of Marlene's European family was ominous especially as the rumours were beginning to circulate that Jews were being driven from their homes and resettled in ghettos or camps. We could only console each other with the thought that we must remain strong together in the face of the things that we could change.

I was brought back from my thoughts by the voice of the restaurant car manager enquiring whether I would mind sharing the table with three other people which, of course, I had no objections to whatsoever. Turning around to see who it might be, I spied Trixie Montano in the company of Ann Sheridan and George Brent, two fellow Warners stars, all obviously heading my way. George was a tall and good-looking Irish American, who specialised at Warners in supporting the studios reigning female stars such as Bette Davies and his name on the cast list for any Warners movie usually guaranteed a certain amount of ticket sales at the box office. As for Ann, she was a striking redhead known for studio publicity purposes as the 'oomph girl' and her screen persona was that of a no-nonsense, all-American girl, who wasn't afraid to speak her mind, an image that was wholeheartedly endorsed by the American movie public and helped her to become a major star. Incidentally, Ann and George had only just recently become husband and wife.

The four of us spent a pleasant hour swapping studio gossip and reminiscences of the present tour so far. I have to admit that I was in admiration of Ann's and George's stamina, for it transpired that so far this year, they both had appeared in three movies each and were pencilled in for two more before the end of the year and besides which, they had got married to each other and found time to raise money for the war effort. However, the main topic of our conversation was our impending arrival in Washington and being welcomed at the White House by President Franklin D. Roosevelt, to be followed later that evening by a gala fund-raising dinner. At some stage, Trixie and I suddenly found ourselves with only each other's company as the Brents decided to slip away for what they euphemistically called one last nightcap! This left Trixie and I to bring each other up to date with our lives. I don't know who suggested it, I think it was Trixie, but we decided to adjourn to the observation coach for coffee. Considering it wasn't late in the evening, the coach was practically empty. I can only assume that my fellow actors were either crammed into the bar or had retired to their state rooms for an early night.

As we waited for the steward to bring our coffee and brandies, the thought crossed my mind that I was in danger of either being indiscreet and thoughtless or incredibly stupid. Just being in the company of Trixie in this type of situation would create gossip but when you are having a relaxing evening and are in good company, caution tends to fly out of the window. Trixie was exactly the way I remembered her from all those many years ago, full of fun, leaving me in stitches of laughter as she recounted to me her journey up the Hollywood ladder. I guess that if she ever wrote her biography, it would be a best seller. Mind you, she would have to wait until most of the people had passed away, such was her assessment of most of them. I was completely lost in the moment enjoying Trixie's company until the tone of the conversation changed. Suddenly, Trixie placed her hand upon mine and leaning forward looked deeply into my eyes.

"You know, Gunty, don't you, that I still love you and that the biggest mistake of my life was not marrying you when you asked me all those years ago. Putting career before love has gained me nothing but heartache. There is no denying that I have achieved a successful career along with fame and fortune, but I am nobody's fool. Neither career nor fame will last because eventually, the public will grow tired of me and a younger and vibrant copy of a Trixie Montano will replace me. I have been an absolute failure when it comes to relationships. I have been married twice and I have not found a single saving grace amongst the men that I married. I can tell you, Gunty, that I certainly have had plenty of experience in dealing with greed, unfaithfulness, physical abuse and finally, to rub salt in the wound, it has cost me a small fortune to get rid of the bastards."

"I am sorry to hear you say that Trixie." I replied. " It grieves me that so far, you haven't been able to find true happiness in your private life and I get no sense of satisfaction from hearing you say so. If it is any consolation to you, there will always be a special place for you in my heart. However, decisions have been made and cannot be undone. After years of wandering aimlessly from relationship to relationship, I suddenly found the love of my life, a union which in turn, has blessed me with two lovely daughters, so, Trixie, at the risk of sounding a boring and one-dimensional character, I simply cannot visualise a life without Marlene and the children. By the same token, I want you to know, I shall always be there for you should you ever have any problems. Remember just call me."

A few hours and a few more drinks later, we decided to call it a night and made our way slowly along the swaying corridors of the train. We arrived at Trixie's compartment first and momentarily stood watching the scenery flying by. Suddenly she flung her arms around me kissing me passionately on the lips forcing me to fall back against the corridor windows with the force of her passion. When she sensed that I wasn't responding, she stopped and whilst still pressed up against me, she gently caressed my face all the while looking deep into my eyes.

"Oh Gunty, Gunty," she whispered, "Why spend the night alone? When you can spend it with me. I can feel that you want me you know. So why fight nature? It is not as if you are being a bad boy on a one-night stand. You have already admitted that you have a place in your heart for me. I want you, Gunty. I want you tonight. Nobody needs to know if we remain discreet."

"Whoa, back, Trixie," I said, as I gently pushed her back by her shoulders. There is no way of saying this without hurting your feelings but as I want us to remain close friends for the remainder of our life, I will say it only once and pull no punches in doing so. A standing prick has no conscience and I am not about to allow mine to destroy my marriage. You know, Trixie, I think that you are far better than you think you are, so be a good girl and retire gracefully and I will see you during the next few days.''

Trixie stepped back from me, her eyes blazing with anger and in the matter of a second, had delivered an almighty slap across my face which sent me rocking back on my heels. But just as quickly as it had arrived, the storm passed from across her eyes and was gone, just leaving me with one hell of a stinging cheek.

''I am sorry, Gunty,'' Trixie whispered ''I tried to take advantage of the situation and I was wrong to do so. Please forgive me. I certainly don't want to lose your friendship. It is, if truth be known, the only constant thing which I have in my life that prevents me from being destroyed by Tinseltown. Now that you are back in Hollywood, it has given me a sense of security, as I know that I will always be able to count on you. I'll be seeing you over the next few days, so that we will be able to reminiscence over old times and have a laugh together. By the way, you do know, we sure as hell would have had one hell of a great night in the sack together don't you!''

Flashing that famous smile at me, she turned and entered her compartment leaving me standing in the corridor, massaging a stinging cheek and smiling ruefully. I certainly took no satisfaction from being in the situation that I had been placed. I am no 'Holy Joe' and I have never believed in the saying, 'Why go out for hamburgers when you can have steak at home'. In truth, I had been only a few seconds away from accepting Trixie's invitation but then I realised that I would never be able to betray Marlene. I suppose that puts me in the category of being boring! I suddenly thought that it might not be such a bad idea to retrace my steps to the bar and have one well-deserved last drink for the road and to remember in the morning to phone home at the next stop we make.

Once we arrived in Washington, we all participated in a bond drive on Pennsylvania Avenue before proceeding to the White House where we had a photo shoot for the press corps, but prior to that, we had the honour of being introduced individually to the President of the United States, Franklin D. Roosevelt, after which, we then formed ourselves into a semicircle with the

President placed in the middle of us in his wheelchair, whilst the news photographers bombarded us with popping flashbulbs.

Later that evening, we were all bused back to the White House to attend a fund-raising dance, which both the President and his wife Eleanor would be attending. Once we had arrived and been met by a welcoming party, we went on a guided tour and I have to say that I was in awe, as we soaked in the historical atmosphere of the White House. We were then ushered into the state ballroom which, on this occasion, was furnished with large round tables accommodating seating for ten. I was intrigued to notice that many of the tables having been laid for ten persons had only nine chairs, the reason became all too clear to me and others later, as the evening progressed. There was also a United States Marine band playing as we entered. Not only would they be supplying the music, but they would also be accompanied by the opera singer, Rise Stevens and the United States Air Force choir. On our designated table, I had the pleasure of the company of George Brent and his wife Ann Sheridan, James Cagney and Pat O'Brien, Bette Davis, Jane Wyman and Jack Carson. Once we had eaten and the plates had been cleared away, Bob Hope and Al Jolson held an auction for a Norman Rockwell painting.

It was only after, as we were being served dessert, that the president started table hopping by means of a wheelchair both guided and pushed by a marine sergeant. It's only when you enter the private world of the president that you realise how badly he had been stricken by polio and how his presidential advisers had kept the severity of the infliction from the American public. Most of the time, the public image of him was either sitting behind a desk or in a chair. I guess now that it didn't matter, as we were now involved in a global war and that he was already into his second term of office, which if it hadn't of been for that conflict, would have been his final term as president. I suppose it wasn't important any more for his public image. Anyway, there he was, the President of the United States, approaching our table and like his soulmate, Winston Churchill, he too, had an iconic trademark. Whereas Churchill was always photographed with a cigar, Roosevelt favoured a long cigarette holder and so it came to pass that he arrived at the empty place setting on our table. As we instinctively rose from our seats out of respect, he quickly beckoned us all sit down again.

He began by enquiring whether we'd had a good meal and were enjoying the entertainment. He then went on to say how he and the American public were grateful to the Hollywood industry for its magnificent input to the war effort. He continued by saying how grateful he was for our efforts in raising money on the 'Bonds for Victory' tour. He then singled out Jimmy Cagney, informing him that he had already had a sneak viewing of his movie *Yankee Doodle Dandy* and how moved he had been by his portrayal of George M. Cohan. The performance itself, he further went on to say, would give the American public the moral boosting shot in the arm to win the war. He stayed for a few minutes more before being wheeled on to the next table and after he had departed, we all observed how fragile he was looking. It was bad enough to be struck down by polio but then, to add on the heavy burdens of state, plus the responsibility of a wartime presidency was asking a lot of a person. I certainly wasn't alone that night in thinking that he was looking ill.

Later in the evening, Eleanor Roosevelt and her son Major James Roosevelt, who apparently, was home on a forty-eight-hour pass before shipping out, made the rounds of all the guests' tables and stopped by ours for a brief chat. She had the patrician looks associated with being a member of the one-hundred Boston families. Nevertheless, she was very down to earth and not above trotting out one or two jokes. She also had the gift of being able to hold a conversation with you on a one-to-one basis. As the evening wound down and just to prove that there were no hard feelings, I did a turn around the dance floor with Trixie who was bursting with pride.

"I never thought, Gunty, that this girl from a Minnesota working class family would end up dancing in the White House with one of the world's most famous film stars. This sure is the stuff that dreams are made of."

"Well, Trixie, the same could be said of me. I too, would never have dreamt in a million years that I, a lad from humble beginnings in Hamburg, Germany would become very famous, married to a beautiful wife and have two lovely daughters and that at some stage, would be dancing in the American White House with a very famous actress as my partner. It only goes to show how lucky we have both been. It has nothing to do with talent or determination but just the fickle finger of fate. So, Trixie, this will be the last time that I will preach to you. Don't rely on other people to give you happiness and contentment. You must find it yourself. Share that luck with somebody that you both love and trust. Forget about the Hollywood hunks of beefcake with features of a Greek God. You will only end up paying for misery and a lonely and empty life. I think the party is beginning to wind down here as the president and his good lady have already retired for the night. How about we both grab a cab and go back to the Union Station on Massachusetts Avenue where our train is awaiting and where I can guarantee the bar will soon be filled with half of Warners' roster of stars which will give us the opportunity for one last hurrah before we return to Hollywood?"

Chapter 21

The Holocaust

Two days later, we arrived back in California. Leaving the train at Pasadena, I managed to avoid the press and grab a cab to take me home. No goodbyes were necessary to the majority of my fellow bond sellers as we would be bumping into each other at various times on the sound stages at Warners. Also, there was the weekend social circuit where we all intended to let our hair down after the long weekday schedules, which more often than not, required us to be at the studio by seven o'clock in the morning and where the less fortunate of us would be required to be on call to at least seven o'clock in the evening, unless you had some clout as a star such as yours truly, by having a cut-off clause of no work after four o'clock in the afternoon built into your studio contract. Before I left the railway station, I took the opportunity of phoning ahead to let Marlene know that I was on my way to the house. Livy answered the phone, saying that she was pleased that I had finally arrived back and would let Marlene know as she was at present poolside with Kim and Inger. She would also ensure that a freshly brewed pot of tea would be waiting for me.

The drive back to the house was soon over and after giving Livy a hug, I headed for the pool area where I found Marlene and Mary in the shallow end, playing with the girls who appeared to be having the time of their lives splashing with the water. As soon as Marlene saw me, she stepped out of the pool holding Kim and gave me a welcoming embrace. Kim held out her arms to me and immediately, I took her in one arm as Mary placed Inger in the other. It had been less than a week since I had last seen them but in that short time, they seemed to have acquired even more energy and were proving to be very much a handful. Marlene had the good sense to place a large playpen on the lawn over which she had placed an awning to prevent them from becoming sunburnt and into which I very quickly deposited the pair of them.

That weekend turned out to be a combination of relaxing, playing with the kids, catching up with some scripts the studio had sent over for my attention and spending quality time with Marlene. On the Saturday night, I decided to take her out to a newly opened nightclub on Sunset Boulevard called the Mocambo, a place in town that everybody was talking about. We weren't to be disappointed. The owners had spent a heck of a lot of money on its furnishings which included an aviary, consisting of glass cases set into the walls, each containing an exotic group of birds. There were cockatoos, parrots, macaws, a few other species and as a further attraction on that night, there was a guest appearance of Xavier Cougat and his Latin American orchestra, who was temporarily in town, filming over at Columbia.

It was one of those evenings that unexpectedly turned into a great night out, particularly with the music which constantly lured Marlene and I back onto the dance floor, where in my own clumsy way, I attempted the rumba, samba and a few other Latin American numbers. Not only did Marlene look gorgeous but she looked every inch the Spanish señorita when dancing. Consequently, she had many requests to dance from our inner circle of friends such as Victor Mature, Gilbert Roland and Caesar Romero. I was more than happy to watch them wear themselves out while I sipped a Jack Daniels on the rocks and chatted with my fellow studio worker, Humphrey Bogart and his wife, Mayo Methot. Though our paths crossed frequently, both professionally and socially and I was fond of them both but I sensed that they were in a dark place. They had acquired the title of the battling Bogarts. When they weren't drinking, things were peaceful. But when drink was in, so to speak, it was an entirely different story. Things descended into major rows and on occasion, Mayo was alleged to have seriously assaulted Humphrey to the extent that Bogey needed hospitalisation.

It seemed ironic that after all those years appearing as a supporting actor, fate had stepped in and made him a major star and all because Hollywood's reigning screen tough guy, George Raft, had turned down two films as not being suitable for his image. The first one was *The Maltese Falcon* in which his replacement, Bogie, was very well received by the public and the second, *The High Sierra*, which once again, with Bogie as his replacement, proceeded to turn Humphrey into a major star. Just as suddenly, Warners, never slow to recognise a cash cow, started showing some respect to Bogie both in salary and status. Sadly, what should have been a sense of satisfaction and accomplishment in his life turned out otherwise. Instead, he appeared to be battling the demons within his marriage, in public. Most of us who counted ourselves as his friends hoped that he would eventually find peace and contentment.

The trouble with America was that because of the Second World War, it was only just beginning to wake up to the fact that there was another world out there beyond its shores and unfortunately, it took even longer for the inhabitants of Hollywood to realise that life was real and not just an extension of a studio script! I suppose that I was as guilty as anyone else in this respect. It certainly was all too easy not to be too worried about the dangers to the democracies when one lived such a pampered existence. Every day was a sunshine day and the only worries you had revolved around if you would be able to get away to Catalina Island for some sailing or to Aspen to enjoy the sun and skiing. Nevertheless, Marlene, Livy and I had our own routine of assimilating daily news from the papers and the radio so that we could put together a general picture of the situation in both Europe and the Pacific.

The first signs of recovery for the Allies occurred, in the Coral Sea with a naval battle between Japan and America and though Japan came out slightly on top, sufficient damage had been inflicted on her naval forces to lead to her Pacific fleet being defeated in the Battle of the Midway a month later. This was a significant turning point, as it marked a halt to Japanese expansion and because of serious losses imposed upon the Japanese Navy, prevented her from securing Port Moresby which would have been used as a springboard for the invasion of Australia. For the European theatre of war, it was a mixed bag of good and bad news. The good news was that a British general by the name of Montgomery was gradually turning the tide of war in North Africa by slowly driving the Germans back and likewise, on the Eastern front, despite his spectacular advances into Russian territory, Hitler was now being met with fierce resistance from a never-ending supply of fresh Russian forces. The bad news came in the form of a Jewish refugee by the name of Laszlo Horta who had miraculously escaped from Warsaw via London and New York and the story he had to share. I had just recently met him at a gathering of members who collected funds for an organisation called the Friends of Europe. Anyway, it transpired that he had been a pre-war scriptwriter in the Polish film industry and what he told us seemed unbelievable.

To start with, the information that he was about to give us had already been given by him to both the British Foreign Office and the Department of State. On both occasions, his report had been met with some scepticism and in his opinion, had been quietly shelved for the duration of the war. What he told us was shocking and deeply upsetting. On the occupation of Poland by the Nazis, an area in Warsaw, the capital city, had been sealed off and was being used as a dumping ground for Jews taken from all European-occupied territories and by mid-1941, not only had it become so overcrowded that its inhabitants were dying in the streets through lack of food and medicines, but it had also become the norm to find children and the aged lying dead in alleyways and on the pavements. Because of their fear of an epidemic of typhus breaking out, the Nazis began shipping out Jews in freight trains to ease the overcrowding in the ghetto. It was at this point in Laszlo's narration that the atmosphere in the room became heavy with foreboding. People around me were becoming uncomfortable, as if they were hearing too much information and as Laszlo continued speaking, he withdrew from a document case a sheaf of what I took to be transcripts to which he referred to as a notarial account by one Moshe Vartec. Clearing his throat, he then proceeded to read from the documents.

"To the best of my beliefs, this is a true and accurate account of what befell me Moshe Vartec, on the morning of the twenty-second of July 1942. The previous day, the inhabitants of the buildings, one of which I and my family lived and was located on Masaryk Street, situated in what was now known as the Warsaw ghetto, an area specifically designated for Jews only and sealed off by a wall and its entry and exits guarded by a mixture of German troops and Polish police. The Nazi authorities allowed the ghetto to self-govern itself but insisted that its counsel provided all essential services for its inhabitants such as, food, power, law and order, health and education. As I had mentioned before, we were issued with notification from the Jewish Council that the buildings were to be vacated the following day and that the inhabitants would be transported to the nearest rail terminal and that they were only to pack overnight clothes. It was on that following morning that German troops descended upon our area of the ghetto and commenced to seal it off. Shortly afterwards, they were followed by two detachments of Waffen SS who then proceeded to enter every building. Whilst this was going on, a convoy of trucks started to arrive outside the buildings where they proceeded to park up with their engines running. Within thirty minutes to the sounds of shouting and banging, the SS emerged escorting the Jewish families, all of which, were either carrying attaché cases or bundles. The children and the elderly were being helped along by their relatives and whilst many of the groups were calm, there were others who were agitated, with the women in those groups crying and yelling which, in turn, frightened the younger children.

"As I lived in one of the top floor apartments, I was one of the last groups to leave and once we reached street level, we were pushed along to one of the last lorries where with great difficulty, my parents and I, with the help of some who were already in the lorry, finally got my grandparents on board. Once my parents and I had followed them, the lorry moved off. After a short journey, we arrived at a railway goods siding where we were ordered off the lorries and after being told to leave our belongings behind were forced to climb into freight wagons. No provisions had been made for seating or supplying food or water and there were no toilet facilities. Each wagon was filled to overcapacity leaving men, women and children packed like sardines. The journey itself was long and arduous with frequent stoppings and all too often, many of the elderly died from dehydration and the cold. Eventually, we arrived at our destination and were ordered to disembark, whereupon we were forced to line up and undergo an inspection by several SS officers, some of whom were wearing white coats. From what I could tell, it was only the able-bodied males, myself included, who were formed into a separate group. Once the selection process had been completed, the women, children and elderly were marched off. Eventually, the remainder of us, after having a number tattooed onto our right arm, were also marched off and distributed throughout a series of wooden huts each consisting of basic wooden bunk beds. It didn't take very long before I was fully in the picture as to where I was and how long my life expectancy was to be. I had arrived at a concentration camp called Treblinka, located somewhere in Poland and according to my fellow inmates, I had become a slave labourer with a very short life expectancy. Even worse, all our women and children and aged parents had been marched off on arrival to a killing factory where they had all been gassed!

"In the nine days before I succeeded in escaping, I experienced the full horror of being in hell. The tall chimney in the centre of the camp was belching out smoke continuously, day and night. The inmates, too physically exhausted to work, were beaten to death where they lay and the bestiality of the prison guards towards their fellow human beings was beyond description. There is no doubt in my mind that the German forces of occupation are carrying out a policy of extermination across Europe and it is only because of my own tenacity and the courage of my fellow inmates that not only did I escape, but that I was also able to make my way into Switzerland, where I was brought to London. It became obvious to me that even if the Allies were prepared to believe me, they did not have the strategy or, at this moment in time, the resources to deal with it.

"I could understand this decision but what I could not accept was the deliberate suppression by the newspapers of what was going on, thereby denying to those organisations that cared, the opportunity to lobby either the British House of Commons or the American Senate which, in turn, could have possibly saved many Jewish lives. I just want to finish by saying, ladies and gentlemen, that what I have said is once again the truth and that before Nazi Germany is finally defeated, there is a state sponsored policy of extermination now in operation throughout Europe that will amount to millions of European Jews being put to death."

Under ordinary circumstances, it is normal for a speaker to receive a round of applause after he has finished speaking but tonight was an exception. After Laszlo had sat down, he was met by a stunned silence from an audience who seemed to be unable to cope with what they had just been told. Turning to my fellow actor, Johnny Garfield, who also happened to be Jewish, to sound out his opinion, I was met instead by a man just shaking his head in bewilderment, speaking in that staccato voice so familiar to the moviegoing public he asked.

"Is this guy for real, Gunther? Is this guy really trying to tell us that the Nazis are murdering the entire Jewish community and not only that, but he'd have us believe that they are doing it on an industrial scale and that they already have several camp-factories in existence which are already exterminating Jews by the thousands?"

"I don't think, Johnny, that any right-minded person would believe that fellow human beings would be capable of such barbarism but having lived in Germany in the early thirties and experienced first- hand, Hitler's anti-Jewish laws, I have an uneasy feeling at the back of my mind that it could be true. As far as my feelings are concerned on this matter, I shall be asking around and calling in favours from certain quarters to see if there is any truth in any of it."

I went home that evening with a heavy heart, knowing that it would be unnecessarily cruel to burden Marlene with the knowledge of the evening's events, knowing the stress and anxiety that would cause her. It would be better to check it out first and then decide on what course to take later.

The following morning, I telephoned David Hislop at the British Consulate in downtown Los Angeles and fortunately, not only did I find him in, but he also had some spare time to talk to me. I repeated to him what I had heard the night before and what the reaction of both the British and American government had been. Having listened to me, he went on to say that he had no knowledge of any government department meeting with individuals to discuss the extermination of the Jews by Nazi Germany. However, his opinion was that if such meetings had taken place with confirmation of the facts, it would still be difficult for the British government to do anything about stopping the killings at this stage in the war. As an example, the only way that they could put an end to it would be by targeted aerial bombing and how would they achieve this? Even if they were in possession of the exact locations of the camps, they had neither the extra planes, nor crews to sacrifice for these dangerous missions. Also, we would very likely, be playing into the Nazis' hands, for in our efforts to destroy the killing factories, we would also be killing hundreds of innocent Jews in the process. Finally, of the three Allies, only Russia would eventually be in a position to be the first to reach those camps as it did appear from what I was telling him that most of them were situated in the East.

He continued, "If it's any consolation, Gunther and I'm sure it isn't, there are signs now that the war is turning in the Allies favour, so we will just have to tough it out until Nazi Germany is defeated and meanwhile, hope and pray that these rumours will be proved baseless.

Back to my private life and as I had expected, Hedda Hopper, the Hollywood columnist for the Randolph Hearst newspaper empire had been making sly insinuations in her column that Trixie and I had formed a romantic dalliance whilst on a war bond tour. As per usual, the by-line went something like this, 'Which married star has strayed from the marital nest?' Or 'Which two stars have been seen having a cosy get-together over dinner?' Fortunately, in the face of the united front that Marlene and I put up and the pressure put on Hedda by Trixie's studio, Hedda dropped the story and instead, did an interview with Marlene, who began by saying how happy we were now that we had the twins and how their birth had made life truly blessed. On and on she went, whilst Hedda scribbled frantically away, recording every piece of nonsense that came into Marlene's head. Hedda Hopper wielded a considerable amount of power in Hollywood. One sentence in her weekly column could either make or break the box office returns on a studio's film or likewise, do the same to an actor's career and that is what I admired and loved about Marlene. She wasn't afraid to take the rise out of anybody who she thought to be either pompous or arrogant and Hedda Hopper possessed both those qualities in full. By the way, I forgot to mention that prior to the media frenzy, anticipating the fact that there are no secrets in Hollywood, I had already briefed Marlene on the events occurring with Trixie on the bond drive. After listening to my account, Marlene had looked me straight in the eye and made the following observations.

"You do know, Gunther, I wasn't born yesterday. I have been anticipating the likelihood of this occurring for some time and for what little I know of her, my only observation of Trixie Montano, perhaps unfairly, is that what Trixie wants, she makes every effort to get. There is something else you may not know, Gunther, that this is a familiar theme amongst the Hollywood wives for when they get together and the general consensus amongst us is that you either trust your man or you don't. In my case, Gunther, I trust you implicitly and I hope that is mutual between us. The only thing to do with this incident is to put it in the trash bin where it firmly belongs and one other thing, don't let that head of yours get any bigger than it already is. You might think that you are catnip to all the unattached women out there but really, you are just a pawn in the battle of the sexes. In other words, you are mine Buster and don't you forget it." We both had a laugh over the stupidity of it all, but the back of my mind was a niggling thought that perhaps the satirist, James Thurber was right and that we males were pawns, in the game of life.

It was towards the end of October that a script landed on my doorstep that had all the markings of being a great movie and once I started reading it, I couldn't put it down. The plot concerned the lives of a captain and his crew serving aboard a newly commissioned destroyer destined to be stationed in the Pacific. The script adaptation was to tell the individual stories of some of the crew from the captain down and a lot of the story would be shown in flashback so that the cinema audiences could be involved with their home lives. The script was one of the best that I had read in a long time. It was taut with well-drawn characters and apart from myself, the proposed cast was impressive with leading actors such as, John Garfield, William Bendix, Hume Cronin, Donald Crisp and Raymond Massey. The proposed female contingent would be led by Claudette Colbert playing the captain's wife supported by a pool of studio actresses such as Jane Wyman, Ida Lupino and Priscilla Lane. The film was to be directed by none other than Michael Curtiz, who by now, was becoming my regular director. I phoned Hal Wallace, the producer at Warners with my acceptance.

As the film was not slated to start production for some time, it gave me the opportunity to catch up on some quality time with the family as well as to spend some time down at the Hollywood canteen helping Marlene out with the other volunteers to give our lads from the fighting services some time in which to relax. It certainly wasn't a Hollywood publicity stunt, for whenever I have attended there, it was not unusual to see either waiting on tables or working in the kitchen, the likes of Sidney Greenstreet, Warners' popular heavy, Reginald Gardner, who specialised in playing eccentric Englishman, Cuddles Z. Zakall, the studio's lovable character actor and Thomas Mitchell, the great Irish actor forever to be remembered for his role as Scarlett's father in the film *Gone with the Wind*. On reflection, I think it was the girls who made the greatest contribution to the canteen, supplying glamour and companionship to thousands of lonely servicemen cut off from their families facing an uncertain future. As the months had gone by, we all noticed the increase in servicemen in transit to all points of the compass, servicemen of all nationalities and religions. That is why it was important to give the men of the fighting forces our time so that at least we could contribute to their present lives some happiness and glamour, for God knows what the tomorrow would have in store for many of them.

As 1942 came to an end, I took the time to reflect the events of the last year. Time is a commodity that you have plenty of whilst you are waiting around between takes on a film set, endless hours are wasted every week sitting around waiting to film no more than two minutes of screen time as camera angles are set up and sets rearranged. Despite German and Japanese victories over the last two years, there were signs now beginning to emerge that the tide was turning in favour of the Allies. Hitler had bitten off more than he could chew with his invasion of Russia and his vision of a quick victory now lay in ruins. The German Army's invincibility was gradually being eroded particularly as it slugged it out with the Russians for possession of the city of Stalingrad, for the German army there was now in danger of becoming encircled by fresh Russian forces. As for the home front, most of the able-bodied male stars had already enlisted in the armed services leaving a shortage of leading men. Putting it bluntly, quite a few of the actors remaining, were over the hill physically and it certainly showed when they were paired up with the glamorous Hollywood actresses, not that it mattered, as the majority of the male audience only had eyes for the opposite sex.

There had been one major casualty of the war so far this year and that had been the actress Carole Lombard, wife of Clark Gable, who had been killed in a plane crash whilst on a nationwide tour selling war bonds, Carole's death had a profound effect on Clark to the extent that he had enlisted in the air force despite his age and was training as a rear gunner. I had a lot to be grateful for. The film that I was presently involved in had a feel of something special about it, even though a mock-up of some parts of the destroyer had been built on one of the studio sound stages and a large water tank was available in another to represent the Pacific sequences to be filmed towards the end of the movie. A considerable amount of exterior footage had been filmed on location in San Francisco and had involved a large portion of the cast, me included, being filmed in the natural surroundings of the docks. The norm was for the film studios to shoot their movies on the back lot but in this instance, the decision for Warners to film on location was an exception to the rule and it certainly added a feeling of authenticity.

The script was beautifully written by a young writer called Dalton Trumbo which brilliantly conveyed the emotional highs and lows of wartime servicemen and their families, as well as the strain of command placed on officers who had to make life and death decisions. Because of the strong bond that was beginning to emerge within the cast, the actors were bringing out some of the best performances from within themselves, never more so than between myself and Claudette Colbert, who played my wife in the movie. Because so many Americans were involved in theatres of war so far away from home, both Thanksgiving and Christmas intended to be bitter-sweet affairs. Both Marlene and I invited a selection of overseas servicemen to spend both holidays as our guests. On Thanksgiving day, we had a young British pilot officer serving in the RAF and a petty officer from the Royal Navy plus two Australian lads serving in the Australian army. I would like to think that we gave them a feeling of home, even though they were so far away from their own.

Even in our household, there was an absence of family members. Hansi and Lothar, Marlene's brothers, had managed to spend Thanksgiving day with us but they had to return to Los Alamos to work over the Christmas holiday. I had also managed to book time slots for transatlantic phone calls to Britain so that Marlene could wish the season greetings to her parents and likewise for Mary the children's nanny, whose parents lived in Scotland. The sombre mood carried through to New Year's Eve 1942. I suppose it was because we all realised that sacrifices would have to be made before the Allies achieved victory and that far too many families would experience the loss of a loved one, which possibly included our own. I fully understood the anguish that Marlene experienced, as she kept hidden the fact that she did not know the fate that had befallen her family in Europe and particularly her sister Greta and her family, whose whereabouts in Holland was completely unknown to us. I had made a point to support Marlene in her religious faith as well as to accompany her visits to the Bel-Air synagogue where she would find the spiritual support of the Jewish community, many of whom had family and friends living in Europe whose whereabouts were unknown to them. The thing that preyed on my mind the most was the knowledge that it was beyond my capabilities to chase her worries away knowing as I did now, the dreadful fate that could befall them.

It was towards the end of February 1943 when we received the news that the German Sixth Army trapped and encircled in the ruins of Stalingrad had finally surrendered to the Russian Army. From the information that was released to the public, we learnt that the German Field Marshal, Frederick von Paulus had led ninety odd thousand German soldiers into captivity. In excess of eight-hundred and fifty-thousand Axis soldiers had been killed or were missing in combat. To say that the Allies were jubilant was an understatement as this surely did signify the beginning of the end for Nazi Germany. The loss of prestige, manpower and material had revealed a massive decline in Hitler's invincibility.

The second event that occurred in early March was the fifteenth annual event of the Oscars which was held in the Coconut Grove at the Ambassadors Hotel in downtown Los Angeles, where the great and the good of the film industry would gather to give themselves a pat on the back. It was also an opportunity for the nation to temporarily take its mind off the grim realities of war. The Academy, in its wisdom, had invited me this year to present the Oscar for Best Actor, partly I would suspect, because I had not only been a presenter at the founding ceremony in 1929 but that I was still a prominent name in the film industry. It didn't hurt either that my most recent movie, *Conquest of the Sun*, was breaking box office records. To celebrate that particular milestone in my life, I had decided not only to take Marlene but Livy as well, knowing that despite her protestations, Livy enjoyed the glamour of Hollywood. Also, she would be good company for Marlene whilst I was involved in the Oscar ceremony.

On the night of the Oscars, I had hired a limousine to take us to the venue and despite the wartime austerity, which meant no glamorous evening wear, both of my womenfolk had done themselves proud, with Marlene wearing a simple black cocktail dress accessorised by silver shoes and purse, finished off with a white fur stole, whilst Livy had decided to wear a blue two-piece suit and pillbox hat. By the time we had arrived and been deposited onto the red carpet leading to the entrance to the hotel, the place was heaving with people and it took me some time to work the fans on both sides of the carpet, signing autographs or having a few words with the CBS radio announcer.

Once we had finally got into the Coconut Grove and found our located seats at table one, we were then able to find time to congratulate the honourees and to wish them luck before settling down to the proverbial steak dinner and a marathon catch up on Hollywood gossip. Once again, Marlene was the centre of attraction at our end of the table, despite the presence of Oscar nominees, Greer Garson and Jimmy Cagney, it never ceased to amaze me how people from all walks of life were drawn to her. She asserted her calming influence on many of the nominees seated at the table. Once the meal had been finished, the dirty crockery cleared away and the last order for drinks had been delivered so that staff could be withdrawn, the band started with a fanfare of *Hooray for Hollywood* with Bob Hope then walking on stage to the sound of his signature tune, *Thanks For The Memory*, whilst officially opening the ceremony.

It was easy to see why Bob had become very much, part of the Oscars. Not only had he become America's favourite film comedian, but he seemed tailor-made to be the master of ceremonies for the Oscars with his talent for delivering topical one-liners. After an hour, I left Marlene and Livy temporarily whilst I went backstage to prepare for my cue to go on and announce the recipient of the Oscar for Best Actor. What the ceremony lacked in razzmatazz and glamour, it more than made up for in the sheer quality and talent of the nominees. It was my duty to read out the names of the nominees for Best Actor and as it was usually the last but one award of the night, I had the opportunity to see the Oscars for the other categories being presented to the lucky recipients. First to be awarded was for the category of Best Supporting Actor and Actress which went to a young actress by the name of Teresa Wright for her role in *Mrs Miniver* and Van Heflin the young actor who Marlene and I had become acquainted with backstage in the Broadway production of *The Philadelphia Story*, for his performance in the gangster melodrama, *Johnny Eager*. The surprise of the night for me was the award of Best Actress which was won by Greer Garson for her role of Mrs Miniver in the movie of the same name, successfully beating the two favourites, Bette Davis and Katherine Hepburn.

It was time for the award for Best Actor. As soon as Bob Hope had introduced me, I walked on accompanied by a musical introduction of Bizet's *Bolero* which was part of the soundtrack from my latest movie, *Conquest of the Sun*. As I reached the microphone, clutching the golden envelope in my hand, I was met with warm applause which was extremely gratifying for my ego. Then, after nervously mouthing a few silly inanities, I slowly opened the envelope and proceeded to read out the names of the nominees. They were James Cagney in *Yankee Doodle Dandy*, Gary Cooper for *Pride of the Yankees*, Walter Pidgeon and Monty Woolley for *Mrs Miniver* and *The Pied Piper*, respectively. The winner was James Cagney for his portrayal of George M. Cohan in *Yankee Doodle Dandy*. Accompanied by a standing ovation, Jimmy bounced onto the stage to the sounds of *I'm a Yankee Doodle Dandy*. There was no doubt that it was a popular win for the audience as it was for the country. It was also nice to see that Irving Berlin received an Oscar for Best Song, *White Christmas*, which he had composed for the Fred Astaire and Bing Crosby movie, *Holiday Inn*, a song which I'm quite sure would still be played every Christmas for another fifty years or more.

Once I had completed my job as a presenter, I re-joined Marlene and Livy at our table. Not long after that, the ceremony came to a close, giving us the opportunity to table hop and to catch up with old acquaintances from the Hollywood community, especially those who we would not see often socially but would spend a lot of time with at the workplace such as scriptwriters, fashion designers and makeup artists. I particularly enjoyed spending some time reminiscing with the kings of studio makeup, the fabulous Westmore brothers, Perc, Wally and Bud. It so happened that all three brothers were departmental heads of makeup at different studios. I knew Perc Westmore very well, as most of my working mornings started with him in the makeup department at Warners and similarly his brother Wally, did the same at Paramount with the older brother Bud doing likewise at Universal. It was when we stopped at the writers' table that Marlene came across her friend, the actress-playwright, Ruth Gordon and her husband, Garson Kanin, both of whom worked as a scriptwriting team at MGM. One of their assignments had been

Woman of the Year, a recent release which had been warmly received by the moviegoing public.

I left Marlene happily chatting away while I had a word with Julius and Philip Epstein, another team of scriptwriters with whom I frequently lunched with in the Warners commissary. They too, had recently been the writers for a movie called *Casablanca*, directed by my old friend, Mike Curtiz and produced yet again by Hal B. Wallace. The film had only just recently been released into the national cinemas and was already gathering a growing audience. I had seen a private screening of the movie at Wallace's home and in all honesty, had thought of it at the time as no more than a pot-boiler and no different than my previous effort in *Marrakesh*. However, having said that, it had been lifted out of its class by the sheer quality of the script and its cast of actors. The film's male lead, Humphrey Bogart, had become an overnight screen heart throb with his portrayal of a cynical world weary American ex-pat. He had previously been Warners workhorse in supporting roles playing bad guys before being catapulted into stardom with roles in two films, *The Maltese Falcon* and *The High Sierras,* after George Raft an actor specialising in playing romantic tough guys who had turned both roles down. As I mentioned previously, he went on to do the same a third time with *Casablanca*. I guess you could call that a case of an actor being his own worst enemy!

Certainly, as the year 1943 progressed, the Allies were beginning to see light at the end of the tunnel, even though Russia, our recently acquired Ally, was paying a very high price in driving back the German invaders from their country and the United States, despite its massive industrial strength, was meeting with fanatical and stubborn resistance from the Japanese on land. Japan's once-powerful navy had been destroyed beyond recovery by the American naval task forces and was now no longer a threat to America in the Pacific. The United States' Air Force was also mounting an increasingly successful aerial war on Japan. As for the European theatre of war, the Allies were beginning to gain the upper hand. After successfully defeating and marching into captivity the remnants of Rommel's Afrika Korps and Mussolini's Italian divisions, the Allies had landed in Sicily from where they had successfully launched an invasion of mainland Italy by occupying the port of Salerno. By July, Mussolini had not only been deposed but was also under arrest. However, by September, Hitler has launched a daring rescue plan and brought him back to Germany where he successfully restored him as the leader of a fascist rump government.

I still operated covertly with David Hislop at the British legation in Los Angeles and even, at one point, was seriously considering joining an organisation called Friends of Russia, as I had a lot of sympathy at that time for the sacrifices that Russia was making, but David Hislop advised me against it as he believed that once the Allies had proved victorious over the Axis powers, it would not take long for Russia to attempt to destabilise the Balkan states in its efforts to spread communism throughout Europe. This would inevitably place a strain on the relationship between the Western governments and Russia and knowing America's ideological mistrust of communism, it could lead to a witch-hunt against citizens or aliens who were perceived to be fellow travellers.

True to form, Warners continued to keep my nose to the grindstone. No sooner had I completed the film *Pacific,* I was put to work on a film to be titled *Watch on the Rhine,* a film in which I agreed to take second billing to Bette Davies, Hollywood's reigning drama Queen. She had a fearsome reputation as a diva and had very little patience for those who did not see things her way. However, I found no difficulty in working with her and thought of her as a true professional. Maybe it was because despite my relatively young age, I was a respected screen veteran who had worked in both silent and sound films well before Bette had started her climb to fame in Hollywood. Whether we had a mutual respect for each other or just naturally bonded, I don't know, but the film schedule just sailed along. It was unfortunate that Bette and I both agreed on completion of the movie that it was all too sombre and theatrical for its own good, an opinion that was affirmed by the box office returns. I suppose you can't win them all.

Also, I was kept very busy on radio doing a radio adaptation of *Gaslight* for Lux theatre of the stars on NBC and *Jane Eyre* for Maxwell House but also was being kept pretty busy with guest appearances on the top variety shows of 1943 such as the Kate Smith hour, the Jimmy Durante extravaganzas and the Bob Hope and the Jack Benny comedy specials. As a consequence of doing these radio guest appearances, I was persuaded by Jimmy

Durante, to accompany him on a USO tour for the front-line troops in Italy with a stopover first in Britain. However, the tour wasn't scheduled until late August 1944 and the itinerary could be changed due to the fortunes of war. It would involve being away from home for about seven weeks. Because the start date was that far ahead, it would give Jimmy and myself time to rehearse some comedy sketches, more than likely they would be parodies of some of my more dramatic moments in recent movies. When I broke the news to Marlene and Livy, they expressed concern for my safety but as I pointed out, if it was good enough for our boys out there doing the fighting, it was good enough for me.

Life continued to bestow its blessings upon us despite the hardships and the absence of fathers and sons fighting overseas that were part of the everyday lives of most British and American families. We seemed, along with most of Hollywood, to be living in a pampered world. I think it was just as much the sense of guilt at our privileged position, as that of patriotism and the moral sense of duty that drove us both to contribute more. My girls Inger and Kim were growing fast and were rapidly approaching their third birthdays. Not only were they fully mobile but extremely talkative having discovered the power of speech. Consequently, they were forever chattering all day long, apart from the hours that they spent sleeping, of course! They were also full of mischief and many a time, the dogs were only just rescued from the effrontery of either being painted from head to toe in assorted colours or being dressed in an assortment of clothes.

With the arrival of the girls, our lives now had an added dimension. Instead of Marlene and I being the centre of attention for each other, we now had the girls as the centre of our universe. There was nothing quite like the feeling of joy to be able to enter one's home after a day's shooting at the studios to feel two small pairs of arms hugging your legs and two little faces lit up with happiness; the hugs weren't too bad either. That silly encounter with Trixie whilst on the fundraising tour last year had only confirmed the strength of the bond between Marlene and me. When I explained to her what had happened that night, she never doubted my version of having turned Trixie down but nevertheless, would add the incident to her arsenal of put-downs if I ever became in danger of becoming too big headed and finally, there was no way that she was going to give the two she-cats of

Hollywood, Louella Parsons and Hedda Hopper any satisfaction in their mischief-making.

Going over my business diary with Livy, I found that my work schedule for 1944 was looking pretty heavy. Not only that, although Jack Warner had agreed to my going on a USO tour in late 1944, he was still determined to get his pound of flesh out of me by lining up three movie projects. As yet, no movie scripts had been submitted to me, but I knew that sooner or later, that they would be arriving on my doorstep by courier and that Jack Warner would be expecting my approval with the minimum of delay. There was no doubt that my contractual arrangements with Warners regarding script and director approval plus daily finishing time was a privilege offered to very few actors and because of my experiences in Nazi Germany, I had developed an instinctive resentment to being pushed around. That is why within months of settling back in Hollywood for the second time, I had quickly become a member of the Screen Actors Guild, otherwise known as the SAG.

It so happened that in July, I had been elected to serve as one of three vice presidents of the organisation. Normally, elections were held every two years, but in this instance, a vacancy had arisen and after my name was put forward, I was duly elected. Jimmy Cagney, it so happens was halfway through his term as president which was convenient as we both worked out of Warners, Jimmy having come straight from Broadway to the studio and had been with them ever since 1931, along with fellow luminaries, Edward G. Robinson, Paul Muni and Pat O'Brien, so it was only natural that we began to spend some free time together discussing SAG business which was a pleasure, as I admired him both as an actor and human being. It was a shame that so far, we had never worked together on a movie which was a pity really but understandable as we both possessed two different screen personalities and also, Warners had a policy of never putting two major male stars together in one movie which simply did not make economic sense to them when they could get two movies for the price of one. In the old days of the depression, when movie customers were scarce, they thought nothing of cramming five or six major stars into one movie to lure the customers in. Come to think of it, two examples come to mind, *Grand Hotel* and *Dinner at Eight*. Another industrial event for me was that the recently released movie, *The Pacific* had been nominated for Best Picture along with Best Actor and Actress nominations for myself and Claudette Colbert for performances in the same film, the winners to be announced at the 1944 Oscar ceremonies.

To celebrate Marlene's birthday, towards the end of September, I took her away to Florida to a place called Key Largo on the Florida keys to enjoy some deep-sea fishing for a couple of weeks, even though it was officially the hurricane season. Thankfully, it remained calm but hot. There had been a hurricane in early September but that had been on the Western side striking land at St. Petersburg and had finally blown itself out on the Gulf before it had time to reach New Orleans. It was a vacation to treasure with just our own company, nothing fancy, just a basic but clean, family-owned Waterside Inn. The proprietor who went by the name of Jed Lebowski, was wheelchair-bound, suffering with acute arthritic hips, a wife whose name was Louise and two daughters who went by the names of Betty and June, who helped their parents run the Inn. They also had a son, Mark, who was at present, serving somewhere overseas in the United States Marine Corps of whom the old man was justifiably proud. I had also rented a boat complete with skipper and deckhand so that Marlene and myself would spend all day out on the water. Sometimes, we'd come back at night with catfish and on the odd occasion, some Marlin. Inevitably, after a day fishing, we would finish off by spending the evening in the snug of the Inn, listening to Jed at the piano, playing a repertoire of standards and requests, whilst Louise would work behind the bar and either Betty or June would wait on tables. It was the perfect environment in which to relax and enjoy a carefree vacation in the company of people who were not the slightest bit interested in who we were and even if they had some inclination of our identities, they kept it to themselves.

Whilst for us, it was a chance for us to take time out from the ugliness of the world with its persecution and brutality and recharge our vows to each other, it was also an opportunity to renew our faith in mankind so that when the war was eventually won, with the defeat of the Axis powers, the nations of the world would strive for greater diversity amongst ethnic minorities and grant equal rights to all its citizens. That is what Marlene and I hoped for, but in our heart of hearts, we both realised that all too often, the road to hell was paved with good intentions and that there would be no peace for mankind in our lifetime and probably not in our children's either. Oh yes, one other thing, on returning from our vacation, I drove Marlene to downtown Los Angeles and as a birthday gift, presented her with a painting of her choice which in this case, happened to be an early Monet, titled, *Beach in Pourville*, which had only just recently come onto the market. It had cost me an arm and a leg but was well worth it just to see the joy on Marlene's face. I remember reflecting as we both stood admiring it, how quickly our collection had grown and that if we ever fell on hard times in our old age, the paintings would represent quite a considerable nest egg, well anyway, that's what I hoped.

Just before Thanksgiving day, I received a phone call from Myron Selznick inviting me to lunch at the Brown Derby, the occasion being that he had recently acquired a great script tailor-made for my talents and if I was interested in it, we could take the package to Warners for their backing. Of course, I was interested and arranged to meet him the following day. You didn't hang about when it came to being a jump ahead of your competitors where a good script was concerned, hence my immediate reaction. When I walked into restaurant the following day, Myron had arrived before me and was comfortably ensconced in a booth. Having ordered our drinks, he immediately got down to business. Reaching down to his briefcase, he pulled out a bulky brown envelope which he pushed towards me whilst launching into a detailed synopsis.

Myron began, "What I have got here, Gunther, is a red-hot script. I acquired it when I bumped into the writer, Dalton Trumbo at a party last week and whilst we were exchanging shop talk, he mentioned that he had just finished a script which he felt I might be interested in. It concerned the career of Emiliano Zapata, the Mexican revolutionary, who rose to national prominence in the early part of the twentieth century and who was eventually betrayed and assassinated. Gunther, I would like you to do me a favour: take the script away and read it and if you like it, we'll take it over to Warners and persuade Hal Wallace to produce it."

"It certainly sounds interesting, Myron." I responded. "I'll take it home with me and read it over the weekend and phone you first thing Monday morning with my opinion. Though I can't complain about the quality of the movies that I have made so far at Warners, you would be surprised at the amount of rubbish that I have turned down and you know as well as I do, Myron, that if you have one successful role in Hollywood, you are forever typecast in the same role until the public gets sick of you."

"I couldn't agree with you more, Gunther!" Myron continued. "That is why want you to take the script away. I think that you will find the part of Zapata is tailor-made for you. Incidentally, I want to congratulate you yet again for your Oscar nomination as Best Actor in the movie *Pacific* which is also up for Best Picture. It appears to me that Wallace is proving to be a goldmine for Warners. He has three films in contention best film, *Pacific, Casablanca* and *Watch On The Rhine*. I think yours is the favourite and I can't see much opposition to you getting Best Actor either."

We spent the rest of the lunch chatting on various subjects including his brother David's latest opus which he was in the final stages of completing titled, *Since You Went Away*, starring Claudette Colbert and Jennifer Jones. The theme of the movie was a salute to the bravery and stoicism of the American families and Myron really believed that he could have another box office hit on his hands. As we parted company that afternoon, I couldn't help thinking how tired and drawn he looked and that he should be taking better care of himself.

Chapter 22

Liberation

The Friday after Thanksgiving, I took the opportunity of hiding myself away to read Dalton Trumbo's script. I had to agree with Myron's opinion, the plot more than compelling with the main characters well drawn. I was compelled to finish reading it in one sitting. The part of Zapata was the role of a lifetime. What I also liked about the script was the relationship between Zapata and his brother and it would require a strong actor to fill that role. In my opinion, the chemistry between the two men, if cast correctly, would enhance the movie considerably. I already had in my mind's eye the two actors that I would like to see play the brother, Eufemio, either Anthony Quinn or Pedro Armendariz, both of whom I had worked with on the film, *Conquest of the Sun*. Once I had read the script, I was too excited to wait until Monday to let Myron know of my enthusiasm and instead, rang him Saturday telling him to move heaven and earth to get Warners to make the movie.

I had to wait for three days in high anxiety and when Myron did finally call back, it wasn't good news. The project had been turned down by Jack Warner himself even though Hal Wallace had supported enthusiastically the whole concept and wanted to start shooting as soon as possible. Jack Warner refused to green light it on the grounds that the present political climate wasn't appropriate for that type of movie to be made bearing in mind that Mexico was part of the Pan American block of countries supporting the United States. In effect, Mexico was allied with America in the war against the Axis powers and the last thing he would want to do was to produce a movie about the overthrow of a Mexican government. Jack Warner also went on to say that he still had nightmares about how the good relationship between America and Mexico nearly came apart during the mid-thirties when MGM was filming on location in Mexico for the film *Villa Rides* and one of the movie's leading actors, Lee Tracey, supposedly stood on his hotel balcony slightly the worst for drink and relieved himself on a military parade marching beneath him.

That little episode nearly cost Hollywood the South American market, thereby losing ticket sales for its movies.

I made no bones about telling Myron how angry I was at Jack Warner's decision and went on for some time hooting and hollering until Myron interrupted me.

"Calm down, Gunther. Let me just remind you of the terms of your contract. You have the right of reasonable approval on any script that Warners offer you, but you don't have the legal right to enforce your choice of script on the studio. I know that you are angry and frustrated but just be patient. As an agent, I sense a wind of change beginning to blow through Tinseltown. Bette Davis had the courage to face Jack Warner down over the draconian terms of her contract and though she lost the legal fight, Jack Warner accepted her back on far better terms. Furthermore, as you well know, Jimmy Cagney has also stood up to Jack Warner and walked away from the studio. Eventually, he did return but Warners still continued with its old tricks, so he has walked again. I have also heard a whisper that Olivia de Havilland is far from happy by the legal chains that bind her to Warners and it is more than likely that sometime in the future, she too will challenge her contract. You know, Gunther, the signs are pretty clear that this war is going to come to an end soon and when it does, the major stars who are in uniform will be returning to civilian life and expecting more personal control over their careers. In other words, I predict that they will be looking for independence in the form of a distribution-production deal with the studios."

"I understand what you are saying Myron and wholeheartedly agree with you, but what about now? I am being denied an opportunity of a lifetime. This part could define my career but instead, I will be churning out mediocre rubbish for Jack Warner until my career burns out. I have just received by studio courier yet another romantic pot-boiler: this time the tragic love story of Crown Prince Rupert of Austria with a provisional title of *Mayerling*. Believe you me Myron, I can understand why Charles Boyer is so fed up being labelled the great lover. The whole experience is like being in a factory on an assembly line churning out the same old, same old."

"Just be patient, Gunther," Myron replied, intervening in my flow of bile. "Your time will come and incidentally, the quality and variation of your pictures can't be that bad considering you're up for a second Oscar nomination. I repeat, Gunther, keep your head down for the time being and keep taking the money."

That is how the best opportunity of my career slipped through my fingers leaving me brooding on it for many weeks. It also awoke within me the question of which route my future should take and from that moment on, I began planning the severance from my long-term studio contract.

The family finished 1943 celebrating the spirit of Christmas and started 1944 throwing a birthday party for Kim and Inger followed by celebrating New Year's Eve. It was the first time in five years that we could celebrate the arrival of a new year with confidence in the future. Even though there would be more sacrifices to come, most people knew that it was only a matter of time before Hitler and his gang would be finished. As for Japan, that was another story. Because of their ideology, the Japanese would fight to the last man. Not only would it take longer to beat them but that our casualties would be three times as high as in the European theatre of conflict.

Once again, on the evening of the second of March 1944, Marlene, Livy and I were sitting on the back seat of a limousine on our way to Grauman's Chinese Theatre in downtown Los Angeles to attend the sixteenth annual Academy Awards ceremony. The Academy was to be congratulated this year for holding the ceremony in a theatre, the main reason being that because it was wartime it, would be better to drop the banquet as it would hardly be in keeping with the present mood of the public during wartime. The other great idea that came out of the change of venue was that any servicemen or women turning up at the box office on that day wearing uniform would receive free passes to attend the presentations. The fans were certainly out in force when we finally pulled up outside Grauman's. I have to admit that a small dose of adulation from the fans worked wonders on the ego and as I worked my way along the red carpet, signing the autographs, shaking hands and listening to the cries of good luck, I couldn't help but notice that the fans were predominantly female, emphasising the fact that most males of military age had been drafted.

Even when we had entered the foyer, there was no escaping the bedlam of popping flashlights and the gauntlet of ABC, NBC and local radio stations and affiliates all vying for a few words from me and my fellow actors for their listeners. After posing, signing programmes for a couple of marine sergeants and several star-struck army nurses, we managed to get into the auditorium where we were guided to our seats on the fourth row of the stalls. Seated in the row behind me was fellow nominee, Paul Lucas and his wife, Daisy with whom we passed a few pleasantries including wishing him good luck. As I turned back in my seat, I noticed Gary Cooper, another nominee for Best Actor and his wife, Rocky. I had no sooner waved to them and wished him good luck when Humphrey Bogart and his wife, Mayo Methot, arrived and took their places in the row in front of us. There was also a rumour doing the rounds at Warners that there was some chemistry developing between Bogart and a young actress by the name of Lauren Bacall recently arrived from the east coast and making her first appearance in a new movie that Bogart was shooting on the sound stages there.

The theatre settled down very quickly with the introduction of a musical fanfare accompanied by the host of the evening, Jack Benny, striding onto the stage carrying his trademark violin, after which the evening passed very quickly with the winners of the various categories receiving their Oscars. Finally, towards the end of the ceremony, the winners of the last three categories, Best Actress, Best Actor and Best Picture, were announced. We began to feel optimistic when our movie received an Oscar in the Best Sound Recording category, but it was to be short lived. Marlene clenched my hand tightly in support as the winners of the three categories were announced. The first disappointment was when Jennifer Jones denied Claudette Colbert her victory by winning Best Actress award for her performance as Bernadette Soubirous in *The Song of Bernadette*, richly deserved I may add, for like most young people starting out in our profession, she had learnt her craft the hard way, surviving on any job that came her way, including small parts in 'B' Westerns. Like my co-star, Claudette Colbert who played my wife in *Pacific*, I fared no better when the winner of last year's Best Actor Oscar, Jimmy Cagney came out to announce this year's winner. I had lost out to Paul Lucas who received the Oscar for Best Actor for his performance in *Watch On The Rhine*. Paul and I were of the same generation of actors but after the demise of the silent film, where I had been fortunate to maintain my star status in Europe, Paul had continued his career as a star character actor in both theatre and films. As I sat there watching Paul receive his Oscar trying to look as nonchalant as possible to hide my disappointment, I couldn't help thinking to myself that I was beginning to fall into that category of always a bridesmaid but never the bride. Finally, the Oscar for Best Picture went to my home studio for the film *Casablanca* even then when the rightful recipient for the Best Picture Oscar, Hal Wallace, who as producer of the film was halfway out of his seat to collect the award, Jack Warner had raced ahead to the stage to grab the Oscar and the glory.

It was only after at a post Oscar party later that evening, that whilst Marlene and I were congratulating Hal on his film winning Best Oscar, he made it plain to me how humiliated he had been made to feel by Jack Warner's actions that evening and that in the very near future, he would be moving his production unit to another studio. In my opinion, this would represent a serious artistic loss to Warners as Hal had made some enormously successful films for the studio, films that included *The Adventures of Robin Hood, The Maltese Falcon, Sergeant York* and *Now Voyager.* All these films had cemented the reputation of huge international stars such as Errol Flynn, Humphrey Bogart, Gary Cooper and Bette Davis. It crossed my mind at the time that I only wished Hal would offer me the opportunity to star in one of his future productions.

It was towards the end of March that I suffered a serious loss from amongst my closest friends and colleagues. My friend and agent, Myron Selznick suddenly passed away with the cardiac condition, thrombosis, leaving Hollywood stunned by his death. Although as an agent, he had become the scourge of the studios by achieving top dollar for his clients, he was still considered part of Hollywood royalty, with his father Lewis, having been a founder member of the Hollywood studio system in the beginning of the twentieth century and his brother David, having built up a formidable reputation as a film producer, culminating in his masterpiece, *Gone with the Wind*. His passing came as a shock to me as it was only at the beginning of March that we'd had a meeting to discuss my leaving Warners and forming my own independent production company. It was a big step for me to contemplate considering the stranglehold that the big six studios had on film production in Hollywood. However, we had left the matter on the table for our next meeting and I can remember thinking at the time how unwell Myron was looking. Nevertheless, his death came as a great shock to me as his passing, at the early age of forty-five, reminded me of how fragile our mortality was and that we should live each day to its maximum. I had ample time in which to dwell upon these thoughts as I had been asked to act as a pallbearer at Myron's funeral, along with other close friends of the deceased. William Powell, who was a fellow pallbearer, also delivered the eulogy. I had known Bill since the silent days of cinema and whilst I had been away in Europe, he had re-established himself in the talkies playing debonair leading men in such films as *The Thin Man* series in which he played an urbane but heavy drinking private eye married to a society heiress. Consequently, he had become an extremely popular leading man with the moviegoing public and in doing so, he became the MGM answer to Cary Grant.

The passing of Myron Selznick had left me without an agent at a time when I most needed one. Not only had I become dissatisfied with Warners because of the poor choice of scripts being offered to me but I had got the idea into my head that I needed to contribute more to the war effort. It seemed obscene to me that whilst men of my own age and younger were not only fighting but dying as well in far-flung theatres of combat, I was enjoying all the trimmings of a privileged lifestyle. It was Jimmy Durante who came up with a solution. I had been chatting with him at a social gathering about what more I could do for the war effort when he had a suggestion for me.

"Gunther, don't you remember that we have already discussed this a long time ago and you promised me then that you would commit yourself to joining me in a tribute to our servicemen. So, if you are still willing, would you like to join me on a USO tour that I am putting together in the very near future? Our boys out there are crying out for some familiar faces from home and nothing would give them a greater thrill than to see some pretty girls and a few famous movie stars bringing a touch of home to them. The war department consider the tours a great morale booster and can't get enough of them. The only thing is, you must understand that it ain't going to be no picnic. You will be away from your family and Hollywood for at least two months and though you will be performing at rest camps in the rear, it will be pretty basic and you will even be in some danger but no more so than opening-night on Broadway!"

I replied enthusiastically, "That sounds just as good as it did last year, Jimmy and one that I would be more than happy to volunteer for. There does seem one obstacle and that is what would I do? Unlike your good self who just happens to be one of America's great vaudevillians, I am lost without a script and cameras."

"Don't you worry about that, kiddo," Jimmy replied, "We'll do a stand-up comic routine with 'youse' as the straight man. Just don't forget that though the GIs will be glad to see you and me. It will be the gals and their gams that they will appreciate the most."

Later that night, I had a long discussion with Marlene about the merits of doing a USO tour and she finally agreed that it was the right thing to do but if I went and got myself killed, she'd never forgive me.

With the passing of Myron Selznick, it was imperative that I acquired an agent to represent me. I had heard some good reports on an up-and-coming talent agency by the name of William Morris way back in the early thirties and decided that I would take a look at them. As it turned out, it was a fortuitous and wise decision, as it gave me the opportunity to meet up with its most senior partner, Abe Lastfogel, to whom I took an instant liking. Not only did he have a reputation as a skilled and pugnacious negotiator, but he was also, laid-back in his attitude to life and lacked any sign of pretension which was rather unusual amongst the denizens of Hollywood. I was also gratified to know that he was president of the USO camp shows and when I told him that I would like to volunteer for a USO tour with an idea for pairing up with Jimmy Durante in a double act, he thought it was a great idea and as Jimmy was already booked for a tour, he would arrange for me to join his company and just to add icing to the cake, he would negotiate with Jack Warner for me to take a three month leave of absence to contribute to the war effort.

The war had swung very much in the favour of the Allies since May 1943. The German Afrika Korps and been beaten and had surrendered in North Africa, the Italian dictator Benito Mussolini had been deposed by his own fascist counsel and the Allies had landed successfully at Salerno on the boot of mainland Italy after their invasion of Sicily. As for the Far East, Japan was proving a far harder nut to crack. Despite the defeat of the Japanese fleet at the Battle of Midway leading to the total collapse of Japan's Navy as a sea-power, her land forces were proving to be very resilient. Also, there were rumours that America intended to island hop its way to Tokyo, but that there was already evidence that Japan intended to defend fanatically every inch of ground to the last man.

As to my career, I could sense a feeling of stagnation. My last movie had not done as well as was expected at the box office and I desperately needed a good script and possibly a change in my screen persona, neither of which was forthcoming from Warners. As far as they were concerned, they had a huge captive wartime audience and a stable of actors under contract which they could rely on to appear in the same old rubbish to satisfy that demand. Now that circumstances had given me a new agent and my existing contract would be coming up for re-negotiation in the near future, I sensed that this would be the time for me to pursue my dream of having my own production company and make the films that I could be proud of. I had briefly brought this matter up with Abe Lastfogel and he was totally supportive of the idea, believing that once the war had ended, the studio system as we knew it now, would begin to crumble. He also thought that the studio chiefs were oblivious to the dangers of a more deadly rival, which at the moment, was lying dormant because of the war. He was referring to a new creation called television which he envisioned would eventually become the number one medium in the entertainment industry.

Because of the poverty that I endured during the early years of my life, I had always been a great believer in putting the majority of my earnings away for a rainy day and apart from my insurance policies, I had always favoured investing in real estate. I really couldn't have a better opportunity than right now. You could say that I was in the right place at the right time. Los Angeles was at a stage where in several years, it would be ready for a massive redevelopment, especially once the war was over. As well as blocks of existing real estate, there were vast tracts of undeveloped acres waiting to be snapped up at bargain prices. An opportunity had recently arisen to purchase a block of real estate on West Pico Boulevard near the old Eden Dale studios. It consisted of domestic apartments and duplexes plus a restaurant and some stores and as this block was already bringing in a steady revenue, I had already put in a successful bid to purchase it. It was whilst I was negotiating for the Plaza and its surrounding properties that I noticed a swathe of scrubland comprising some fifty acres that was looking for new owners and despite needing to take out a mortgage on it, I bought that as well. Following the advice of my business team and my own gut instincts, I was prepared to let it lie dormant until the right time came along, for I was pretty sure that it would prove to be a very nice nest egg for Marlene to rely on in her senior years.

By the end of August, I had completed a film entitled *Come the Dawn* which was a popular genre at the moment. Brought about by the war and the absence of men from the home front, it was known as a woman's picture. In it, I played the character of a refugee professor trying to enter the United States from Mexico and in the process of using a female American tourist to marry me so that I could obtain a visa, ended up falling in love with her. Once again, another dish of overheated dramatics in which I played second fiddle to another reigning drama queen at the studio, in this instance, Olivia de Havilland. The movie proved a big hit at the box office and de Havilland gave a great performance. It made me even more determined to be the master of my own destiny before the public grew tired of my portrayal of on-screen cardboard lovers.

Our home life was proving hectic for us. In many ways, this was a good thing for Marlene, for she was not only heavily committed to the Hollywood canteen but was also serving on various committees dealing with refugee and charity issues. Add to that, her determination to remain a full-time mother to our daughters kept her from dwelling too much on the fate of her relatives in Europe. Thank God her parents and brothers were safe and doing well both in Britain and America. What little time we had left during the day to spend time together was usually late in the evening when we would relax with a glass of wine to discuss the day's events. It was on one of these occasions that we decided that we would like to try for another child before it became too late for Marlene. I made no secret of the fact that I would be hoping for a boy but whatever the baby's sex turned out to be, he or she would no doubt be spoiled rotten by Kim and Inger. Livy was also blossoming out in the California sunshine living her own

American dream and though she was adept at keeping her private life close to her chest, Marlene had whispered a few discrete hints in my ear that Livy was stepping out with an eminent university professor! I would certainly have to find out a bit more on that one.

It was the second Tuesday in September, when the reality I had wished for finally materialised. Prior to that moment, I had been rehearsing a routine with Jimmy whenever we had time to spare and thanks to Jimmy's expertise and professionalism, I had achieved a reasonable standard of comedic timing which would hopefully create a few laughs from a hardened audience of GIs. That early Tuesday morning Marlene, Livy, our two daughters and the rest of the household staff had waited with me for the army bus to arrive. Marlene had fussed around me, making sure that I had packed enough clean socks and underwear! Just before we left the bedroom, we spent a few minutes together saying our farewells for we both shared that unspoken feeling that the tour would not be without its dangers and that is why those thoughts were very much on my mind as I waited aboard the Douglas C54 sky master awaiting take off from Salinas army air base. I was one of thirty-five passengers on board and alongside Jimmy Durante there was the singer, Ginny Deana, a film and radio singing star, a backing group called *The Doucets* and four dancers who would certainly be providing enough sex appeal and glamour for our soldiers. Finally, to round off our small troupe was a pianist and three musicians. The remainder of the passengers consisted of officers and diplomats being seconded to various posts overseas.

All that our troupe knew was that we were heading for Britain where we would have a stopover. We would then head over the channel for a destination unknown. All of us were hoping that it would be Paris for after the successful invasion of Europe on the beaches of Normandy, France, on the sixth of June and later, after a series of heavily contested battles across northern France, Paris had finally fallen to the Allied armies on the eighteenth of August. This particular C54 sky master was primarily used, according to my informant, to ferry the Allied leaders such as Winston Churchill and Franklin D. Roosevelt across the Atlantic, plus high-ranking military leaders and senior civil servants travelling backwards and forwards between London and Washington. Although we had a United States Air Force sergeant and two female corporals to attend to our needs, it was still a laborious journey across the Atlantic, especially whenever we hit air turbulence. Our final stopover, before we left the north American continent was at Gander, Newfoundland so that the aircraft could be refuelled.

After that, it was a long flight across the Atlantic until we landed at Shannon in Ireland. Once we were airborne again and had crossed the Irish sea, we learnt that our destination was to be the USAF air base situated at Great Ellingham in Norfolk. As we reached our destination and began to descend, I noticed how flat and green the countryside was beneath us. When we finally landed, we all made a hurried exit from the aircraft so that we could stretch our aching limbs caused by the long flight. After we had collected our baggage, we briefly stood huddled together protecting ourselves from a cooler breeze than we were acclimatised too. Eventually, we spied a line of vehicles speeding over the tarmac which finally came to a screeching halt in front of us. The leading jeep disgorged several officers. We were then introduced to an air force captain who after cordially welcoming us to Britain, shepherded our troupe into several jeeps. We were then ferried over to the officers mess where we were met by the camp adjutant, Major Lawrence and a group of other officers, including a WAC captain who was there to look after the welfare of our female group. Also, there was a representative of the USO by the name of Jack Gillingham, who told us what our schedule and military destinations were to be.

Our first show was scheduled for the afternoon of the following day at a USAF hospital just down the road at a place called Morley, near Wymondham. It was classified as a station hospital, that is, it received casualties directly from the battle zones. We would entertain casualties of high altitude flying most of whom were suffering from trauma to the upper and lower body extremities. We were told that the average age of the wounded airmen was between eighteen and twenty-five years-of-age with some recovering from the loss of one or two limbs. We were warned not to appear shocked when in their presence but to appear as cheerful as possible. Meanwhile, there was a breakfast buffet available in the mess hall after which we would be shown our quarters where we could catch up on some much-needed sleep. Later that evening, the camp commander, Colonel Wayne C. Staunton wondered if, due to the fact that our combat operations over Europe had been cancelled for the next twenty-four hours because of bad weather, we would be kind enough to spend some unofficial time with the station personnel bringing them news from home. The Colonel sent his apologies for not being there to welcome us but looked forward to meeting us that evening.

During breakfast, Captain Gillingham went over our itinerary yet again. Apparently, after we had finished our show tomorrow at 231 Station Hospital, we would continue to the Hendon airbase in London from where we would fly to France to entertain the combat troops and finally, he added, for own protection, could we pack away our civilian clothes and start wearing the army battledress assigned to us for the duration. He finished by saying that he hoped that we had a good breakfast and sleep and that he would meet us again at six o'clock in the evening.

Despite the change to our body clocks, I managed to sleep well and was suitably refreshed for whatever challenges the evening might bring. I did have some trepidations for I worried that once I was out of costume, how I would shape up, because like a lot of actors, I tended to be shy on a one-to-one basis in public. The last thing I wanted to appear to be was some condescending Hollywood star parroting phrases about me, me, me. I needn't have worried, for when we arrived at the assembly hall, we were met by a big turnout of station personnel and after being formally welcomed by the station commander, Colonel Staunton, I opened the proceedings by giving a short monologue about America being the land of the free and because it had become the melting pot for the downtrodden of other nations, it had become, alongside Britain, the bastion of defence against Nazism and Japanese imperialism and thanks to the sacrifices of our fighting forces, democracy was finally gaining the upper hand. At that point, I was interrupted, as previously rehearsed by Jimmy, striding onto the stage waving his hat in a greeting and profiling his famous proboscis, that as they say, brought the house down.

With the audience stamping their feet and cheering, once Jimmy had seated himself at the piano, there was no stopping him as he held them spellbound through his act of repartee and songs. Finally, I walked back on the stage and joined him in a duet of *Start Each Day With A Song* and we both finished by introducing Ginny Deana and her backing group *The Doucets* who willingly endured several minutes of gentle ribbing by Jimmy and a cacophony of wolf whistles from a very enthusiastic audience, climaxing with Jimmy and Ginny asking for a volunteer to come up on stage. There was no shortage of applicants who all waived their arms frantically and finally, a young airman was chosen and climbed on to the stage. After giving some messages home for his mother, father and sweetheart, it didn't take long to find out that he enjoyed dancing, so eventually, he was coerced into doing a boogie-woogie, number with Ginny, accompanied by a mass clapping of hands and foot stomping from the audience. The evening finally finished with a medley of songs performed by Ginny and *The Doucets* which included, *Beat Me Daddy, Boogie, That Old Black Magic* and *Dream A Little Dream Of Me.*

Before we were escorted back to the officers mess, we signed autographs which, in my opinion should have been the other way around. When I think that all these young lads would soon be flying out on bombing missions from which many would probably be wounded or not even return at all, I felt very humble, a feeling which I know was shared by all of us in our small troupe. Eventually, we were escorted back to the officer's mess where a buffet had been laid on for us as well as the bar being open for our refreshment. The girls in our troupe were soon surrounded by an adoring group of officers. The mess was also the proud owner of a Wurlitzer jukebox which provided the officers the opportunity of requesting a dance with Ginny and especially her singers who I felt some admiration for as I reckon that their feet would certainly be suffering at the end of the evening. Jimmy Durante and I did our best to hold court with the colonel and his senior officers plus a few WAC officers who were off duty at the time. It had not escaped me that most of the vaudevillians that I had met, particularly the great ones, had one thing in common. Once they had an audience, they were really switched on and Jimmy was no exception. It was thanks to him that the rest of the evening was a great success with his non-stop repartee making it a lot easier for the rest of us.

The following day, once we had consumed a hearty breakfast, we went for a brisk walk in the Norfolk air, accompanied by the camp recreational officer who took us on a brief tour of the base. Upon our return, we quickly packed up our gear and boarded a coach which, after a short drive, deposited us at 231 Station Hospital at Morley, near Wymondham. The hospital comprised of rows of brick buildings with an additional number of Nissan huts having been recently added. I learnt, as we were being driven there, that the term station hospital referred to the first medical unit that wounded air force personnel were sent to directly from a combat zone and from there, once stabilised, they were then sent on to a general military hospital for a full recovery. I also learnt that it had a capacity for fifteen-hundred patients. The whole troupe was reminded to try and keep their emotions under control for they would be seeing many patients recovering from some very severe injuries received in aerial combat, including amputations of both upper and lower regions. If we could manage to bring them news of home, entertainment and good cheer, we could all consider it a job well done.

Our musicians had unloaded their instruments and set them up on a stage situated in a large hall which obviously had not only been used as a cinema for the patients and staff but for other social occasion as well. Then, Ginny and *The Doucets,* plus the dancers, spent some time, fine-tuning their songs and dance routines. In the meantime, whilst that was all going on, I was able to spend some time rehearsing the routines between Jimmy and myself, after all said and done, I was somewhat of a novice when it came to this type of performance and I knew perfectly well that Jimmy could carry the whole show entirely on his own shoulders. He was the ultimate professional, but I still needed to pull my weight. To say that I was experiencing an attack of stage fright would be somewhat of an understatement. Although the show was still a few hours off, I was already suffering from sweaty palms, but Jimmy, sensing what I was going through, gave me some sound advice.

"Listen kid, you can't sing, you can't dance but you are an actor and a good one at that. Give them a speech from the heart and mean it and leave the rest to me. I'll guide you through the routine and you will be surprised how quickly you will adapt. Just remember, the boys out there will admire your courage if they sense that you are genuine and just remember kid, whatever reaction you get just keep going."

It was just after midday when the rehearsals were interrupted by the arrival of Captain Gillingham and a party of officers. Once again, we were welcomed by the officer commanding which in this case happened to be Lieutenant-

Colonel Bob Satterwhite MD and then we were introduced to the senior members of his staff. Knowing that we were on a tight schedule, he decided to leave us to finish our rehearsal and meet up again for lunch in thirty minutes time. Once they had left, Jack Gillingham quickly briefed us on our programme for the day. After lunch, we were to return to the hall and get ready to start the show. When our performance had concluded, we would visit the wards, meeting those airmen who were not ambulatory or fit enough to see the show, after which we would be rushed back to Great Ellingham in time to be flown down to Hendon, where we would be quartered for the next forty-eight hours. We would be pleased to know that we would be granted some recreational time to be used for us to do a little sightseeing of London, during which we would stop off at the House of Commons for a guided tour and take lunch with the Leader of the House. From there, we would return to Hendon and be flown over to Normandy to commence our USO tour, from where we were due to go on to Paris to join forces with Glenn Miller and his Orchestra to celebrate the liberation of Paris in a gala show. The granting of a forty-eight-hour pass was good news to me, for it meant that I could arrange to meet up with Marlene's parents in London.

By the time Jimmy Durante walked onto the stage to introduce the show, the hall was filled to capacity with the front row reserved for wheelchair patients with the rest of the audience made up of the majority of walking wounded, many of which were attired in dressing gowns and night clothes. It was also nice to see many off-duty nurses attending and I sincerely hoped that just for a few hours, we could help them to escape the horrors of war. There was no doubt that the stars of the show that afternoon were Jimmy Durante and Ginny Deana who with their natural warmth and genuineness, gave the show their all and the audience loved every moment of it. Even I received a warm welcome and was gratified with the spontaneous applause that I received after doing a humorous sketch with Jimmy. As soon as the curtain had fallen and we had given ourselves a quick wash and brush up, we were off to visit the wards and very quickly in the process, there developed an ever-growing entourage consisting of doctors, ward sisters and military photographers from *Air Force* magazine and *Stars & Stripes*.

I am glad that we had been for warned about what we might encounter on our tour of the wards. One poor devil was completely swathed in bandages, suffering from third-degree burns after being trapped in a flaming gun turret and another patient had recently had both legs amputated. Another had lost both hands and so the list went on and on. It just beggared belief the horror that the human race can bestow upon itself! I felt very humble in the presence of these lads and I am sure that went for the rest of the party, especially the girls, who maintained a happy face throughout the visit, successfully hiding their true emotions. Despite the horrific injuries and pain that these lads had endured, they all maintained an attitude of good cheer. One, a navigator by the name of Sergeant Harrison, who had been blinded in both eyes, was able to maintain a happy-go-lucky air of optimism and with the encouragement of Jimmy Durante was even flirting outrageously with Ginny Deana. What we were able to give to these lads paled into insignificance to the sacrifices that they had made for their country, but they did seem to be genuinely grateful for our visit and whatever ward we visited, we were always inundated with requests for personally signed photographs and especially autographs for those with limbs encased in plaster of paris.

Finally, we wrapped up our visit by posing with the doctors and young nurses in group photographs before we were rushed away to board a British Avro-Anson which promptly took off and flew us down south to Hendon airfield on the outskirts of north London. We would spend the next thirty hours or so there on a short sightseeing tour of the capital which was also to include a private lunch with the Leader of the House of Commons, Sir Bernard Dawson at the mother of all Parliaments in Westminster. The schedule was tight but did leave me just enough time for me to meet with Marlene's parents at the Savoy Hotel for morning coffee.

Though London had now ceased to be a daily target for bombing by the Luftwaffe due to their heavy losses in crews and aircraft on the Russian front, the amount of damage the city had received from the blitz was plain to see with a considerable number of bomb sites, shop windows blasted in and boarded up. Despite it all, the British public went about their everyday lives in a spirit of optimism. I was made aware that away from central

London, there had been a considerable destruction of private dwellings and the loss of many lives but still the average citizen was determined to lead a normal life with movie theatres, dance halls and variety shows all playing to capacity audiences. The only threat to the capital was Hitler's wonder weapon, the V2 rocket or the doodlebug, as it was known by the British. But even that was ceasing to be a serious threat for as the Allied armies advanced across France, the Germans were gradually losing their V2 launching sites, the weapon becoming more of a nuisance rather than a deadly danger. Both Jimmy Durante and Ginny Deana were enthralled by the pomp and history of the Houses of Parliament and although I had visited before, I was still overcome by the majesty of the occasion and without doubt, having lunch with the Leader of the Commons and several MPs from both sides of the dispatch box was certainly a privilege to be remembered.

The other great moment of our visit was standing in the central hall with Sir Bernard Dawson whilst he narrated the history of the British Parliament. It was during this moment that we witnessed an historical tradition being played out in front of us. Suddenly, with a steady beat of footsteps, there was a procession of men comprising three formally dressed in morning coats, knee breeches and buckled shoes closely followed by two men also formally dressed, wearing wigs and black silk robes. One of the three men who was apparently known as Black Rod, led the procession, carrying a black staff and following behind him were two sergeants-at-arms and as they marched past, we were discreetly told by Sir Bernard to stand still and remain silent. Unbeknown to me, it happened to be the state opening of Parliament and the occasion for this particular ceremony was the summoning of all party MPs from the House of Commons to the House of Lords where they would hear the King present the government's new legislation. Apparently, this could not commence until Black Rod had ceremoniously knocked three times on the doors to the House of Commons to inform the MPs within that the King was waiting. Though the ceremony was short, its aura was so laden with history that as a spectator, it would become one of life's memories. I completed the remainder of the day by making a dash to the Savoy Hotel which was situated in the Strand so that I could keep my appointment with Marlene's parents bringing Jimmy and Ginny with me rather than leaving them to kick their heels.

Thank goodness I arrived on time as both Hiram and Miriam were waiting for me in the foyer. Neither of them looked any older than when I last saw them and after many hugs and kisses, we adjourned to the Riverside restaurant for afternoon tea where we spent several hours catching up on news. I gave them a photo album of Marlene and the children telling them that it wouldn't be long now before the war ended and we could all meet up together as one family. I was pleased to hear that they were both leading busy lives with Miriam heavily involved in propaganda work and her singing engagements both on the radio and theatre, whilst Hiram was spending long days in the operating theatre, repairing the injured bodies of both military and civilian casualties. Apparently, he was also part of a committee of doctors working to produce a white paper on the effects which he called post-traumatic stress inflicted on military casualties, caused by the delayed after-effects which many servicemen experienced after having been involved in severe stressful conditions whilst under fire in combat fighting.

I was pleased to hear that Bill and Lucy plus John and Mary were all well. Hiram assured me that there was nothing to worry about as they were being well taken care of for their loyalty and hard work and were waiting for the day when we could all meet up again. Despite the severe bombing and shortages, the average British person was receiving higher wages and with little to spend the money on, was considerably better off and as Hiram pointed out, they too were experiencing some of the financial benefits. Because the air force had sequestered the big house, all the local council taxes plus energy bills and maintenance were being paid for by the government. This had meant that Hiram and Miriam's joint income after the everyday expenses and wages had been paid, had a surplus which enabled them to be able to put money aside for their twilight years. In the short time that I had been able to spend in London, I had learnt through various sources how admired and respected they had become and I knew how proud Marlene would be of them when I arrived back home and told her.

Once again, we were airborne, this time over the English Channel and after a short trip, were soon touching down at a military airfield somewhere in Normandy where on landing, we were met by a convoy of Jeeps at the landing strip. Not only were we now wearing battle fatigues full-time, but the troupe had also been issued with standard army steel helmets which had taken a little time to get adjusted too, particularly for the girls, who not only had to wear them in the correct way but also that they appeared suitably fashionable! By now, we were becoming familiar with the embarking and disembarking at destinations and in this instance, we had been met by a young army captain in charge of our security and venues, as well as the mandatory army photographer from the magazine *Stars & Stripes*. Shortly after that, we were on the move, bowling along the French highways to our first engagement which had been designated as an 'R and R' camp for our troops. It was situated on the outskirts of the city of Bayeux. According to the young captain who was escorting us, the city was also the home of the Bayeux tapestry, depicting the Battle of Hastings in 1066, otherwise known as the Norman conquest of Britain. It also had the distinction of being the first French city to be liberated by the Allies after the Normandy landings. Fortunately, Hitler had thrown the bulk of his forces into the defence of Caen leaving the city of Bayeux to be abandoned by the German forces who had fled, leaving the city virtually unscathed.

It was there in late June that General de Gaul made the first of two speeches proclaiming a free French national government from a French city. Because northern France was largely agriculture, away from the areas where the battle of Normandy had actually been fought in the parts of the countryside that the roundabout route that was imposed upon us for our own security, there didn't appear to be as much collateral damage on the civilian population as had occurred in the Normandy battle zone nor as we had seen inflicted on London. From time to time though, we did drive past destroyed farmhouse's and torn up fields caused by artillery bombardments. Fortunately, they were few and far between as there had been little resistance in this area as the German army caught completely by surprise by the speed of the Allied advance were fleeing back towards the German border to escape the trap of encirclement.

What we had observed, as we made our way towards Bayeux, was the continuous convoys of army trucks being driven by African American GIs in the opposite direction. We were told that they were known as the Red Ball Express, named after the fast-track delivery service operated by the American railways at the beginning of the century and that they operated twenty-four hours a day, transporting supplies and materials to the advancing American armies direct from the Normandy beaches because of the absence of any available port. It had been at that moment of time, a vitally important part of the European war effort, for without them, the Allied advancement would have ground to a halt. It was only just recently that the first major port to be recaptured by the Allies was Cherbourg, which in turn, coupled with the partial repair of the French railway system, was beginning to take the pressure off the convoys.

There were many delays caused by roadblocks set up by the military police. We later found out that this was because there were several groups of German fifth columnists dressed in American uniforms attempting to create havoc amongst the advancing Allies by sabotage and misdirection of the leading Allied units. However, we did eventually arrive at a large military camp, comprising of a huge château as its centrepiece, surrounded by a mixture of tents and prefabricated buildings. This camp was the first to be designated as an 'R and R' facility for battle-weary troops from the Normandy landings where they could spend a few days resting and relaxing and enjoying a few comforts from home such as going to the PX store, playing baseball, catching up on movies and writing home to loved ones. Previously, we had only experienced bringing comfort to the wounded but now, we were dealing with an army of young men fresh from the battlefield, being re-energised before their return to combat to fight an enemy although clearly in retreat but determined to make the Allied soldiers pay for every inch of ground that they took.

Once we had freshened up, we were taken to a newly erected stage laid out in the style of an outdoor amphitheatre, where we ran through a rehearsal for an anticipated late afternoon show. Because of the size of the theatre, the army technicians had set up some large sound boxes so that the volume could be increased for the benefit of those standing or sitting on the grass at the back. All of us in the troupe were gratified to see such a big turnout for the show. It was a bonus that we were only still in mid-autumn and that the weather had been relatively dry, for the fact was that the few chairs that were available, had been designated for the top brass and walking wounded. There was, by my own calculation, an audience of at least one thousand and in the true spirit of make and mend, every blade of grass was occupied by GIs who, in many instances, were placing their ponchos on the ground for the benefit of the nurses. Within minutes of opening the show, Jimmy had the audience in the palm of his hand and milking every drop of comedy and introducing a raunchy burlesque routine filled with innuendos involving the dancers as his stooges. The middle section of our show was where I came in, presenting a comedy version of the hit movie *Casablanca* with Jimmy playing the Humphrey Bogart role, with myself playing the Claude Rains character, Captain Renault and Ginny Deana playing Ingrid Bergman's role of Ilsa Lund and finally, for the last part of the show, Jimmy, Ginny and *The Doucets* went through a repertoire of songs including *Don't Fence Me In, Victory Polka* and *Don't Sit Under The Apple*, with a finale involving all of us singing, *I'll See You In My Dreams.*

When we had finished the show, we sat on the edge of the stage signing autographs whilst enquiring where all the boys' hometowns where located. The memory of this occasion will remain with me for the rest of my life for as I swapped conversation with the constant flow of young GIs from all parts of the United States about their families, wives or girlfriends, I couldn't help but feel humble in their presence. As far as they were concerned, they had been called upon by their country to defend the principles of freedom and democracy and even if it meant the ultimate sacrifice, they would give it their best shot! Hitler's dreams of world conquest ruled by a master race now lay in ruins with his armies in full retreat. In some quarters, it was even suggested that the war would be over with by Christmas. But deep down, I knew that once the Allied armies reached the borders of Germany, they would have to fight every inch of the way to Berlin overcoming the fanatical resistance of a German nation heavily indoctrinated by Nazi propaganda and a leader who was determined to destroy the country completely, as it was no longer worthy of his leadership.

By the time we reached Paris, the troupe was feeling exhausted and was looking forward to a few days of rest before returning to America. One of the high spots of our visit was for our troupe to be taking part in an Allied victory concert with Glenn Miller, Edith Piaf and Maurice Chevalier. Unfortunately, the horrors of war were brought home to us on a more personal level as the show had to be cancelled due to the tragic news that Major Glenn Miller had disappeared whilst flying over the channel from Britain to France and so far, no trace of wreckage from the plane had been found and no distress call had been received from it during its flight. Regrettably, it bestowed upon Glenn Miller the distinction of being the first major American entertainer to be killed in the line of fire whilst on active service.

Even after all that she had endured during the past four years whilst under the jackboot of Nazi Germany and even in the last few weeks, when she was finally liberated by the Allied forces, Paris was still the city that exuded so much glamour and romanticism, particularly right now in the fall. We were fortunate in obtaining another forty-eight-hour pass before returning to the United States via London and had been billeted in a hotel situated just off the Bois de Boulogne, overlooking the Lac Inferieur, the largest lake in the park. As we had been unloading our bags outside the hotel, we had been able to take in the magnificent view of the park which, we were informed by the hotel staff, had been built by Napoleon III way back in 1852 and even in the autumn sunshine, the falling leaves were laying upon the promenade like a carpet of gold. Once we had entered the hotel and been given our rooms, I enjoyed the luxury of a hot bath and a change of clothes and as previously arranged, met my fellow artists in the bar.

I had also learned that the hotel has been commandeered for war correspondents and USO artists, a fact which I had discovered after bumping into Ernest Hemingway as I entered the bar. I had first met Ernie at a weekend gathering at the house of Gary Cooper and his wife Rocky and had taken an immediate liking to him. Hemingway was physically a big man and larger-than-life in personality and he was very much a child of the twenties and thirties or what we are now beginning to call, the lost generation. Having spent his formative years as a writer and journalist in such localities as Paris, Spain and Africa, he had emerged as an international author of such novels as *The Sun Also Rises, A Farewell to Arms* and an African trilogy consisting of *The Snows of Kilimanjaro* and *The Short Happy Life of Francis Mocamber*. He had completed his most famous work, *For Whom the Bell Tolls,* set in Spain with the Spanish Civil War as its main theme. Anyway, I had no further time for contemplation as he placed an arm around my shoulder and propelled me into the bar area where he proceeded to introduce me to a group of men including a war photographer by the name of Robert Capa, as well as a middle-aged war correspondent, Ernie Pyle who I immediately identified as the Foxhole war reporter known as such for his habit of writing his dispatches whilst accompanying the infantry during their everyday combat experiences from their landings on the Normandy beaches to the liberation of Paris. It would be very amiss of me not to mention the solitary female amongst this group of men because Marlene had been very much part of the fashion world, I instantly recognised the young lady as being Lee Miller the fashion photographer of *Vogue* magazine who was obviously covering the Allied invasion of France as a war correspondent-photographer.

The evening turned into a marathon of heavy drinking whilst visiting the nightlife of Paris, including the Moulin Rouge and Montmartre and I had certainly picked a bunch of hard drinkers to do it with. I am afraid it was very much a case of the last man standing which certainly wasn't going to be me. The following day, I spent recovering from the previous night excesses, by drinking endless cups of coffee at a pavement café on the Avenue Champs Elysée. Apart from anything else, it gave me the opportunity to observe first-hand a city gradually recovering from its years of Nazi occupation. Since the Allied liberation of France in August, the interim government named the French Committee of National Liberation, was slowly beginning to restore French national pride by hunting down and arresting members of the Vichy government and leading French collaborators and abolishing agencies and laws created by the puppet government under Nazi Germany. Alongside the atmosphere of retribution aimed at those who had served their Nazi masters, was the beginnings of an awakening sense of Gallic pride amongst the average Parisian. Certainly, during my short stay, I could detect the re-emergence of the French fashion world as well as the world of literature, theatre and cinema, talking of which, it was very flattering to my ego that after four years of occupation, a Parisian couple approached my table and asked me for an autograph. They were overjoyed and surprised to see me so soon in the capital after its liberation. Naturally, I felt duty bound to do some liberation myself and ended up buying them coffees and donating them a packet of Lucky Strikes which they were extremely grateful for.

Once we had started our journey back to the United States, there was to be no let up, owing to the increased volume of one-way traffic to Europe in both materials and personnel. We had no sooner touched down in Britain when we had just two hours to have a hot meal before starting off across the Atlantic via Newfoundland. Despite the journey being long and cramped, we managed to keep ourselves entertained, swapping stories with the other passengers, who were mostly military personnel and a small percentage of civilians. Even with the noise of the aircraft engines forcing us to speak louder, Jimmy had no trouble entertaining everybody with his stories of showbiz, particularly with his memories of working in partnership with the great Buster Keaton during the early thirties. Eventually, with fatigue gradually overtaking most of us, we were soon grabbing the opportunity to catch up on some much-needed sleep. All too soon, we were awakened by the captain warning us that we were about to land at Botwood, Newfoundland, a place I knew from my journey back to America with Marlene and Livy. For those of us who hadn't been able to freshen up as much as we liked owing to the aircraft's limited facilities, we would be able to avail ourselves of the airfield's restrooms and as the estimated departure would be roughly in three hours, we would have the opportunity of a hot shower as well as a choice of meals in the station's mess hall. It was a welcome break and after freshening up, we all met up again at the mess hall where we treated ourselves to a huge breakfast of pancakes and syrup, eggs-over-easy, crispy bacon and sausages all washed down with copious amounts of fresh, hot coffee.

When the time came for us to board the aircraft, I can't say that I was sorry to be leaving, because at this time of year with winter settling in, Newfoundland could be a desolate place, with a combination of longer nights and cold and wet days. However, that didn't apply to the inhabitants most of whom were military personnel and who gave us nothing but a warm welcome especially for the girls in uniform who bought a touch of glamour to the airbase. There was a lot of autograph signing, particularly for Jimmy Durante who was an extremely popular entertainer, but I too, had my fair share of requests, which was pleasing to my ego and it also gave us the opportunity to collect some personal messages for loved ones which we would broadcast on the forces network when we returned to the States.

It just goes to show what a soft life we civilians had been leading, for by the time we touched down at Washington, we were all pretty exhausted and barely had time to pull ourselves together before we were put on a transport plane that would deliver us to Travis Air Force Base in Oakland, California which was only thirty-five miles, as the crow flies, from Los Angeles where on our arrival, the air force had kindly laid on a bus which would deposit us at Warners where our loved ones would be able to collect us. On receiving that information, it caused a minor stampede for the phones so that we could make the final arrangements for being picked up once we reached Los Angeles. I must admit an emotional moment, when I finally got connected through to Marlene and it was just as well that I finally ran out of nickels and quarters otherwise we would still be talking.

It was just after six o'clock the following morning when we finally touched down in Oakland and once again, the military revived our flagging spirits with a hearty breakfast and wash and brush up. But before placing us on the bus for the final stage of our journey home, we had the opportunity to phone our families and confirm our estimated time of arrival at Warners. Also, there was time for a photo shoot for *Stars & Stripes* magazine with the girls supplying some cheesecake shots with the air force training crews. There was an air of excitement within the bus as we rode through downtown Los Angeles and out towards the main gates at Warners for although it had only been under just two months since we started out on our tour, it had seemed as if it had been far longer and as well, the constant travelling and living out of a suitcase had left us all feeling pretty exhausted. There was an immense sense of pride amongst us for having undertaken the tour. We also felt that from the reactions from the troops we had met that they too were impressed and grateful for our efforts.

When we finally disembarked from the bus outside Warners main office, Marlene was standing on the steps with other relatives of the troupe. Jack Warner, never one for missing out on a publicity opportunity, had also gathered a small group of executives to welcome us. Marlene, of course, played the game to the hilt, going through all the motions of welcoming me home for the benefit of the studio cameramen before we made a run for the car and drove off the studio lot.

The last few weeks of 1944 were spent winding down from a hectic year to the point, I'm afraid to say, that I became quite indolent having no desire other than to spend as much time with my family as possible. Any decisions regarding my film career such as future film projects were put on hold and my business associates fobbed off with petty excuses. For the first time since we left Britain, Marlene and I spent the last weeks of 1944 enjoying each other's company and interacting with our two daughters. We also made the spontaneous decision to spend the Christmas holiday by renting a chalet at Aspen, Colorado, where we spent a heavenly three weeks, skiing, introducing Kim and Inger to the joys of building a snowman, snowball fights and tobogganing. Christmas Day and New Year's Eve were spent in a quietly reflective but happy mood, particularly New Year's Eve, where with the help of some of Marlene's girlfriends including Ann Sheridan, Alice Faye and Jane Wyman, we enjoyed the benefits of a large open log fire while toasting marshmallows.

Unfortunately, the forthcoming conclusion to the end of the Second World War and the defeat of Germany and Japan was still ahead of us which just goes to show you should never take anything for granted in this world. For in December, Hitler had launched one last counter-offensive against the Allies which became known as the Battle of the Bulge. Initially, it had been successful, catching the American armies by surprise but by the end of January, it had ground to a halt due to lack of air power and gasoline. Hitler had used up his last reserves and with the Allies now poised to cross the Rhine into Germany and the Russians racing through Poland with Berlin in their sights as their main objective, it now became clear that the European war was nearly over and now it was just a question of when that would be.

Chapter 23

Victory

I remember the moment well. It was a perfect Californian afternoon for that time of year. There had been no showers that day and the whole family, Marlene, me and Livy, with Mary McConachie supervising the girls, were just hanging out enjoying an afternoon around the pool, whilst over at the pond on the far side of the lawns, our Filipino gardener, Max, was attending to the waterlilies. Suddenly, Livy decided to make an announcement.

"I just wanted to let you know that I had developed a friendship with an American gentleman which has now turned into something more. To be quite honest with you, the gentlemen has asked me for my hand in marriage which, after much soul-searching, I have accepted. In truth, he is about as close that an American could get to being an English gentleman with all the appropriate attributes and more important, I have become extremely fond of him which is, I suppose, the nearest that an elderly spinster such as myself can get to being in love. Now, for goodness sakes, don't just sit there with your mouths hanging open, say something."

"Well," I finally replied, somewhat stunned by Livy's announcement, "You have certainly taken the wind out of our sails Livy. I don't think that Marlene or I ever thought that the day would arrive when you would contemplate becoming a married lady."

After hugs and congratulations, plus the excitement caused by the announcement, Marlene then proceeded to bombard Livy with a shower of questions.

"You certainly kept that quiet, Livy! And who is this lucky fellow? Where did you meet him?"

Livy straightened her skirt and addressed us with patience as a teacher would in a classroom filled with reluctant pupils.

"The last thing that I would be looking for at my time of life would be romance! However, it seems that instead, it came looking for me in the shape of a very distinguished gentleman by the name of Willard Pirelli, whom I was introduced to one night at a neighbour's housewarming party. It turned out to be a mutual attraction at first sight. On my part, it was the glorious mane of silver hair that crowned his head and that deep Midwestern accent that he possessed and finally the clincher, the bright yellow canary bow tie that he wore. I went on the assumption that any man that was brave enough to wear a tie like that had to be both dependable and have an interesting personality. On his part, I am convinced that it was my British accent that seduced him! As it turned out, my instincts were right, for in the process of getting to know each other better, I discovered that he was the Department Chair of National Science at UCLA, providing leadership towards the highest possible level of excellence. How rarefied was that! And what a catch for any woman, especially an old biddy like me. It did not take more than a few weeks for both of us to realise that we had found our lifetime partners in each other, so when Willard proposed to me, I found myself in a 'win, win,' situation. One, I was in love and two, although I was gradually becoming as old as Methuselah, I certainly recognised a chance in a lifetime for happiness when it came along."

"When are we going to be introduced to this lucky fellow Livy?" Marlene quickly interjected. "Also, have you both thought of a date to be married and where? I know that I speak for both Gunther and I when I say we would like to throw an engagement party for you and I know a lot of girls in this town who will want to celebrate your forthcoming marriage with a great send off by giving you a hen party that you will never forget."

"No!" Livy quickly replied. "Willard and I are getting much too old for that sort of rigmarole. I would be far more comfortable introducing him to you both at a private dinner party just for the four of us at my little cottage on the steps. As for the wedding, Willard and I have decided to get married out-of-town without any fuss at an obscure little place in the state of Nevada called Las Vegas, in a local desert hotel called the Last Outpost which also happens to be a gambling casino with a wedding chapel on the site."

To say that I was surprised was somewhat of an understatement, not because she had chosen to have a small intimate wedding without any fuss but the venue she had chosen to hold it in, an out-of-state casino-hotel in a small obscure desert town that I had never heard of before. I am afraid curiosity got the better of me compelling me to ask.

"Livy, I am intrigued at your choice of venue for your wedding. As far as we are concerned, if we are invited, it would not matter if you held it at the North Pole, but I am intrigued enough to ask, why Nevada?"

"In answer to the first part of your question, Gunther, there is no question of you not being invited. In fact, I am rather hoping that you will give me away and that Marlene would be my matron of honour. As to the second part, I am afraid that it is a case of pragmatism over romanticism. I haven't had time to mention that Willard's family are prominent investment bankers on Wall Street and although he broke with family tradition by pursuing his own career as an academic, he still is, however, an active board member of the company and to cut a long story short, the family are seeking to invest a considerable amount of money in buying real estate in Las Vegas as they believe that in the next few years, it could become one of the most important cities in America. Willard also has a nephew who happens to be vice president of the family company and who also believes passionately that Las Vegas could become the entertainment capital of the world. Well, the upshot of all this is that Willard's family have decided to back their nephew's hunch all the way and are despatching a management team to Las Vegas to explore all options. Willard and I have already decided, that as he is a serving member of the board that we will combine marriage with business by travelling to Las Vegas with the company reconnaissance party and have our wedding at the Last Outpost Hotel. I must admit that I have a historical sense of that great British spirit of empire building and feel that I will soon be setting off up the African Limpopo River to find the lost city of gold."

I had to hand it to Livy that her tally-ho spirit had me full of admiration. Here was a lady in the Indian summer of her years preparing to embark on a late marriage and at the same time, go prospecting for fortune in a desert mining town in Nevada that nobody has ever heard of. All that was left was for me to respond weakly.

"Livy, all I can say to you whilst I digest all this amazing information is to ask, when are you going to throw your engagement party so that Marlene and I can get to meet the lucky guy."

"How about next Tuesday evening at five o'clock in the afternoon?" Livy offered. "Nothing fancy, no hired help, just the four of us, with Willard and myself doing the cooking whilst the two of you open the wine."

That old expression, 'cometh the hour, cometh the man', certainly didn't apply to me when it came to finding Livy's bungalow. Because of never having had the opportunity due to other commitments at the time, I had been unable to visit Livy in her new home. It so happened that when we set out on that Tuesday evening, I was relying entirely upon Marlene's recollections from previous visits to help me in navigating the car to Livy's address. Unfortunately, they did not prove to be of much help. What should have only been a thirty-minute drive, turned out to just over an hour and a half. By the time I had retraced my steps and taken many wrong turns, the atmosphere in the car between Marlene and I had become decidedly frosty to say the least. Eventually, having located Silver Lake district, I quickly found N. Vendome Street and the steps which were nestled between numbers 923 to 925 that led up to Livy's bungalow. The next shock to my system was when we arrived at the foot of the stairs laden with gifts, only to discover that they appeared to go on forever into the heavens. As we were already running late, it was a case of biting the bullet and to start climbing. By the time we had reached the top, I had countered one-hundred and thirty-three steps. As for poor Marlene, she had started the evening the epitome of glamour but now looked slightly the worse for wear, especially as she had broken the stiletto heel on one of her shoes. We must have looked a sorry sight walking, whoops! I should say, limping, up the bungalow path, but more was to come.

Once inside, Livy had quickly offered us a glass of chilled wine whilst introducing us to Willard, who turned out to be quite a handsome devil in his early sixties, I would think, with a head of steel grey hair and a devilish smile, finished off with a deep California tan. It was while Livy had whisked Marlene away to the bedroom to restore her makeup that I mentioned to Willard our journey and the climbing of the stairs. It was whilst I was explaining to him about stairs that he suddenly burst out laughing.

"Why Gunther," he said, "Did you not realise that you could have saved your legs a long climb by just driving up to the front door? Next time you visit, just drive to number 1127 Walnut

Avenue which is just outside, instead of Vendome Street, which is at the bottom of the steps. Talk about life imitating art as way back in 1931, the steps and this area of Walnut Avenue were used as a location for a Laurel and Hardy movie called *The Music Box* in which they were required to move an upright piano all the way up the steps. The basis of the comedy lay in the fact that they made many attempts to climb the stairs whilst suffering many mishaps with the piano during the process and finally, the punchline to the comedy was that they did not have to climb the steps at all. Had they questioned the local mailman more closely at the start of the movie, they could have delivered the piano directly to the front door of this very bungalow in their truck."

It was at that point that Marlene and Livy emerged from the bedroom and upon hearing our laughter, were intrigued enough to ask for the reason. It soon became evident as Willard was repeating the story, that Livy had already told Marlene the reason for her unnecessary suffering which only resulted in a further burst of laughter. The rest of the evening was spent in getting to know Willard and forming the opinion that he was, borrowing an American expression, a solid guy. It was also apparent to both Marlene and I that it was to be a match made in heaven such was the compatibility between Livy and Willard. As the evening had progressed, it quickly became obvious that Willard was an extremely erudite person which was to be expected in view of his scholastic achievements. However, he didn't live in an ivory tower. His views on life, in general, were very much down to earth, sensible and forthright. I was certainly interested in his family's visions regarding the state of Nevada and would certainly be keeping an eye on its future development, particularly as a possible investment. As for their marriage, they both felt that the wedding was best held towards the end of the year, though the venue for it would still be in Las Vegas. By the end of the evening, that very intimate engagement party became a most treasured memory. At the end of the evening, to save our legs, Willard drove us back to our parked car.

With the help of my new agent, I had finally reached the conclusion of my existing contract with Warners. In return for one final commitment for a movie, I would be able to walk free and clear of any further obligations to the studio. It was during the final negotiations that I sensed a wind of change beginning to form in the corridors of power in Tinseltown. Though they had offered me a new contract, it had been for less money and according to Abe Lastfogel, this was becoming standard practice with the other studios when negotiating with my fellow stars. It may well be, Abe went on to inform me, that the rumours that he had heard of an Anti-Trust Bill floating around Capitol Hill in Washington may well be true, for if such a bill came to be passed, it would mean that all the major film studios would be forced to divest themselves of the chains of cinemas that they possessed, thereby losing control of a vital outlet for their product and a monopoly in the marketplace. There was one other danger that the studio moguls appeared to be oblivious too and that was television, for once the war was over, that industry would more than likely roar back into life threatening the very existence of the motion picture industry.

I remember the moment very well when I decided that I would follow my gut instincts and form my own company to make my films and at the end of January 1945, I formally activated the company with my new partners, calling it New Frontier Films. It would not be officially launched until I had completed my contract at Warners but in the meantime, I had hired a literary agent to keep abreast of the current book market and theatre world.

By the end of February, I was soon back in harness at Warners, completing my last movie for them. True to form, it was yet another romantic drama with me being asked to play yet another flawed romantic hero. I swore to God, if I played another one of these one-dimensional characters, my career as a movie actor would well and truly be in the trash can. It didn't help either that when I rehearsed my lines with Marlene in the evening that she vamped the parts to the point where I would inevitably end up in hysterics of laughter. With the European war now coming to an end, came the knowledge that thousands of us with relatives in Europe were now going to face the unpleasant task of finding out what had happened to them. Already, as early as November 1944, the Russians had liberated a concentration camp in Kraków, Poland where the sole purpose had been the elimination of the Jews. Now, the Allies had liberated camps at Belsen and Dachau, which had also been used as part of the Nazi's plan to remove forever, the Jewish population from every country that became part of the greater Reich. Just when I was at the point of being at my wits end on finding out how to trace the whereabouts of

Marlene's family, I received a summons from David Hislop to meet him as soon as possible at the British Consulate in downtown Los Angeles. All that he would tell me was that he had received a letter from Commander Burton in London thanking me for my contribution towards the war effort.

As luck would have it, I had a free day that week, the reason being that the Screen Actors Guild was beginning to flex its muscles within the industry. In this instance, the organisation was in dispute with Jack Warner over his heavy-handed firing of a character actor on the film that I was making at that time. There were still traces of the notorious Los Angeles smog hanging around as I entered the British Consulate that Tuesday morning, but as with the improving weather outside, even the mandatory photograph of the King hanging in the reception area seemed less stern. I also sensed an undercurrent of excitement from the members of consulate staff that I encountered as I waited for David Hislop, a fact borne out by his own demeanour when he finally arrived and commenced to briskly walk me to his office where once inside, he immediately got down to business after we had exchanged the usual pleasantries.

"Well, Gunther, the good news is, that this time, the European conflict will truly come to an end. The Russians appear to have won the race to Berlin and you will be pleased to know, have, at this very moment, arrived at the perimeters of the city and are starting a major offensive to fight their way to the very heart of the capital where Hitler remains trapped in his chancellery. Strictly between us, I will stick my neck out and tell you that the city will fall and Hitler will be finished before the end of this month. My job is nearly finished here in Los Angeles and I anticipate that I will be recalled back to London in a few months, so in case there will not be another opportunity, I would like to thank you for working with me on the assignment that we were given. As to the original purpose of this meeting I would like to hand you Commander Burton's letter. It arrived here in the diplomatic bag to be delivered to you personally. However, I have been instructed to give you background on some of the contents of the letter. To get to the point, Commander Burton is asking whether you would be prepared to undertake one final mission for British intelligence?"

"Exactly as before, David. You have whetted my curiosity," I answered cautiously.

"As we know, Gunther," he went on, "The war in Europe is finally drawing to its conclusion. However, as well as the Allies determination to bring to justice the war criminals responsible for the catastrophe of the Second World War, they also feel that it is only right and proper that it is now their responsibility to record for posterity on film their crimes against humanity, so that future generations may never forget. Commander Burton is asking if you would you be prepared to take a few months out from your career to travel to Europe for the purpose of supplying a commentary for a documentary concentrating on the evils of Nazi Germany especially with regard to their state sponsored programme of ethnic cleansing through the apparatus of the concentration camps?"

"David, I would jump at the opportunity of exposing the evils of Nazism and I can tell you now that I would be more than happy to work on that project for as long as it takes. It is almost as if fate has decreed that I must become part of this enterprise. For the first time in my working life, I am no longer dependent on studio contracts and hopefully, will be in a position where I am free to choose my own scripts and through the film company that I have formed, will be able to produce them as well as direct or act in them as I choose. So, you see, David, before I start the second phase of my life, I am in a position to take a sabbatical from my career to spend some time in bringing closure to the torment that my wife and her family have suffered for the last twelve years. Are you able to fill me in a little more as to what will be required of me?"

"I can certainly fill in the main outlines of the project, Gunther. The documentary will be made under the auspices of the British Crown Film Unit, a government run agency and a young British director, who I am sure you are aware of, by the name of Carol Reed, will both direct and be responsible for the overall making of the documentary. The Prime Minister has expressed a personal interest in the project and has specifically asked if you would provide the commentary knowing as he does, your pre-war contacts and personal recollections of many of the Nazi bigwigs plus the harrowing experience that both you and your wife suffered with the persecution of her family from the Nazis. Speaking as wartime comrades, Gunther, it is only a matter of days now before Hitler is defeated and peace restored to Europe. It is also general knowledge that the Allies number one priority is to seek justice for all the victims of the Second World War whether that means putting all the leaders of Nazi Germany up against a wall and shooting them or indicting them for crimes against humanity and placing them on trial. I would imagine that it will be the latter. Common sense dictates that it will take time in the immediate aftermath of the war to round up all those responsible for the war crimes that were carried out, who will more than likely, be scurrying around in all directions looking for a rat hole in which to hide. Far better, when they are caught, to place them all in one detention centre and to prepare a legal case against them and put them on trial in an international court of justice." At that point, I interrupted him with the question.

"Hold on a minute, David, that sounds more like a year or more rather than a few months and if so, that could be damaging to both my career and family life. I certainly don't wish to appear selfish, but my family may well be about to lose an employee, my long-time and highly valued assistant who not only was a trusted and loyal friend but was considered by us as to be a close member of the family as well. I certainly don't want to be away too long from my baby daughters and neither do I want to leave my wife alone during a most vulnerable period for her."

"I fear that I have explained myself rather badly, Gunther. In fact, your services would not be required until Carol Reed has finished shooting the film which I believe will either be at Bergen-Belsen which is situated in northern Germany or at Auschwitz in southern Poland. In case you are not aware, Gunther, those are the sites of two of the most notorious concentration camps and in the case of Auschwitz, operated for the express purpose of the murder of Jews on an industrial scale. Once the principal photography has been completed and a script prepared, it is only then that you will be called in to provide the narration. Hopefully, by that time, many of the leading Nazi politicians will have been apprehended and will have been incarcerated waiting for trial. At that point, you would be asked to stay on in Germany and as part of an official delegation, you will be asked to visit and record your conversations with many of those that you have known pre-war in the hope that mankind may be able to understand how a civilised nation could participate in such monstrous crimes against humanity. As I have already said, Gunther, I think it best that you take the letter from Commander Burton away with you and discuss its contents with your wife, after which, hopefully, you will let us know whether you will accept the assignment."

Eventually, after further discussions with David Hislop, mainly reminiscing about the previous four years, it was time to wind our meeting up. Tucking Commander Burton's letter into the inside of my jacket pocket, I bade David goodbye. Though he had not been a frontline soldier due to health issues, David had nevertheless, whilst in America, worked diligently on behalf of king and country to safeguard the interests of his nation.

As soon as I had left the legation, I stopped off at a coffee shop on my way out of town and after ordering coffee with a side order of a cream cheese and Lox Bagel, I settled down in an empty booth and started to read Commander Burton's letter. It was, as David had already explained to me, an invitation to narrate a documentary on the liberation of the Nazi concentration camps and to disclose to the world the appalling suffering and genocide that was carried out within their confines. And it was as David had said, to be made by the government Crown Film Unit and to be directed by Carol Reed with the script provided by a young, serving soldier by the name of Peter Ustinov. The second part of the letter was the most intriguing section for me, as in it, Commander Burton asked how I felt about carrying out a series of recorded interviews with various high-profile members of Hitler's government, many of which, after the war was over, would be tried for war crimes and crimes against humanity. He had raised this proposal with me, based on my pre-war association with many of the personalities of that period who possibly would let their guard down with somebody they knew and disclose more of their motivations for their actions. It would mean that I would be in Europe for at least three months and that I would have to put my film career on hold. However, when he concluded his letter by stating that I would be able to bring my wife and family to Britain to keep me company, I knew then that I wouldn't be able to refuse, for it would be a perfect opportunity for Miriam and Hiram to see their daughter and granddaughters after so long an absence and that I also would be in a better position to locate, if possible, any surviving members of their family, including Marlene's sister Greta and Miriam's mother and father. That evening, I put Commander Burton's proposition to Marlene and immediately, she fully supported my decision to accept. She seemed to realise that by my confronting these persecutors of her race, it would ultimately bring closure for her and her family. There was no stopping Marlene from that moment on. She insisted that immediately, I send an acceptance letter to Commander Burton and then, she began planning for our departure to Europe on the immediate cessation of the European conflict when it would inevitably occur.

On the twelfth of April, America received tragic and unexpected news that President Roosevelt had died. To say that it was a huge loss to the nation as well as the free world would be an understatement for it was he alone, who had stepped up to the plate to support Winston Churchill, the British Prime Minister, who with the British people, had defiantly stood up against Hitler when the rest of Europe was going down in flames. After that great loss for the American people, events followed thick and fast. On the thirtieth of April, according to the German propaganda machine, Hitler died fighting at the head of his troops in Berlin. Personally, I didn't believe a word of it. My suspicions, after seeing what had happened to his ally Mussolini's corpse, were that he chose to commit suicide. Finally, the greatest joy of all, after nearly six long years and the cost of God knows how many millions of lives, Germany finally surrendered on the fourth of May 1945. What a day of celebration and reflection that was. Los Angeles burst into a cacophony of blaring horns and spontaneous acts of dancing in the streets. I had just completed my final film for Warners and on that day, had returned to Warners' studio to view the final cut. When the news was announced, Jack Warner had immediately shut the studio down and called a day of celebration for the studio personnel.

After phoning the house to tell Marlene and Livy to come on down to join the celebration, picking up Willard on the way, all of us on the set organised a kitty for the supply of booze. By five o'clock that day, the sound stage was packed with people in all stages of inebriation. Marlene and I had even partaken in a giant conga line earlier that afternoon that had snaked-out into the lot and wound around another three sound stages growing longer as other people rushed out to join us. As the day turned into the evening, the revellers started to thin out, many going home happily to family and loved ones, whilst others were too inebriated or had to be helped into the back of cabs or deposited on various dressing room sofas. Most of the emigre actors of which I was one, finished up in their own group discussing the possibilities of their return to Europe. There certainly were many diverse opinions on the subject with some desperate to return to their homeland, of which many in this group had struggled to make a living in Hollywood often being reduced to walk on parts in 'B' films. There were also others, me included, who would continue to use Hollywood as their main base but would return to Europe when opportunities arose. Amongst those in that category attending that day was the great German actor, Albert Basserman and he and I had a lot in common. Although in his late seventies, he had enjoyed a long and distinguished career in the theatre until he had fallen foul, as I had, of Hitler's master race theories. He too had been given the choice of divorcing his Jewish wife, Elsa or leaving Germany and like me, he had chosen to leave. Amongst the others that we celebrated that eventful day with were, Charles Boyer, Marcel Dalio, Helmut Dantine and the great Russian actress, Maria Ouspenskaya.

Finally, as that eventful day drew to a close, the four of us decided to go for one late night stroll through the Warners lot and as we walked, we realised that the first part of our lives was coming to an end. At the age of forty-three, I stood on the edge of a new era and in the past twenty years had achieved great success both as a stage and screen actor and I had encompassed both silent films and the transition to sound, successfully. In the process, I had become part of cinema history although as far as I was concerned, I had plenty more to contribute. For once I had repaid my gratitude to my adopted country and discovered the fate of Marlene's family, I would seek my artistic independence from the studio system and make the films that I wanted to make. Meanwhile, whilst all this was to be achieved, the world would be changing. Whether it would be for better or for worse would be something which we would all have to wait and see. There was something else to look forward to, namely Livy's and Willard's forthcoming wedding. It was while Livy and Willard were standing away from us, conversing in their own private world that Marlene let her own small bombshell to drop.

"I know, Gunty, that you have set yourself goals for our future, but you may have forgotten one little thing."

"Oh, and what may that be?" I replied.

"Well, it is my intention to contribute a little something to our future too. You may be pleased to know that somewhere around Christmas you should be expecting a new addition to our family."

With that she threw her arms around my neck planted a big kiss on my lips and as she sauntered away from me leaving me with my mouth hanging open, she stopped and turned and looking very provocatively said.

"In the immortal words of Scarlet O'Hara, 'Tomorrow is another day,' so, you big lug, are you coming home with me? Or are you three, just going to stand there looking like refugees from the Marx Brothers."

I really couldn't let Marlene have the last word with the quote from *Gone with the Wind*. But on reflection, I realised that it was the most appropriate quote to finish the night on. Perhaps I could go one better and finish the evening by quoting one of my many favourite film characters but I decided against it and let Marlene have the last word.

The war was over, the peace was about to begin and life was already moving on to new and better things for all of us including, hopefully, a positive conclusion to the fate of Marlene's family in war-torn Europe.